THE DICK FRANCIS
COMPLETE TREASURY OF
GREAT RACING STORIES

The

DICK FRANCIS
Complete Treasury of
GREAT RACING
S T O R I E S

EDITED AND INTRODUCED BY
DICK FRANCIS AND JOHN WELCOME

BARNES
& NOBLE
BOOKS
NEW YORK

CONTENTS

The First Collection

The Second Collection

The

DICK FRANCIS
Complete Treasury of
GREAT RACING
STORIES

The First Collection

Acknowledgements

Grateful acknowledgement is made to Mrs R. Findlay for permission to reprint the story *The Dream*; to the authors and Messrs John Johnson Ltd for the stories *A Glass of Port with the Proctor* and *A Carrot for a Chestnut*; to the author and Mr Murray Pollinger for the story *Prime Rogues* from *Conversation Piece*, published in Virago Modern Classics in the Commonwealth and in the same series distributed by Penguin in the USA; to Mary Lovell for the story *The Splendid Outcast*; to Messrs Harold Ober Associates, acting on behalf of the Sherwood Anderson Estate, for the story *I'm a Fool* (copyright 1922 by Dial Publishing Co. Inc., copyright renewed 1949 by Eleanor Copenhaver Anderson); to the author and Messrs Faber & Faber Ltd for the story *The Major* from the *Faber Anthology*; to the Estate of J. P. Marquand for the story *What's It Get You?*; to Messrs Curtis Brown Ltd, acting on behalf of the William Fain Estate, for the story *Harmony* (copyright © 1955, 83 by Nicholas Fain); and to Messrs John Farquharson Ltd, acting on behalf of the Somerville and Ross Estate, for the story *The Bagman's Pony*.

INTRODUCTION

THE late D. W. E. Brock, a charming and authoritative sporting writer and anthologist who wrote between the wars, stated in one of his prefaces that racing literature was neither so plentiful nor of such a high standard as that of fox-hunting. He was incorrect on both counts, as we trust we have been able to show in this collection. A sport which can command the pens and claim the attention of such writers as George Moore, Siegfried Sassoon and John Galsworthy has little need to apologize for its lack of literary quality, and as to the plenitude of its material, the collection will, we trust, speak for itself.

Moore and Sassoon produced no short stories so the races and racing of which they wrote cannot, alas, be included here, but Galsworthy did. Patrician that he was, it might have seemed more likely that Galsworthy would, when writing of racing, have turned his attention to the pillars of society and the Establishment to whose exclusive circles his birth and education (Harrow and New College, Oxford) gave him entrée. But his sympathies, as displayed in all his writings, were always with the outsider, the little man, the human being against whom the odds are stacked, and he has written of him perceptively in *Had A Horse*, his tale of the timid and exploited man who for once turns the tables on his oppressors.

Kings, as we know from the oft-repeated saying, once made the sport their own. Charles II rode the Rowley Mile at Newmarket and gave it his name; more recently the Duke of Windsor, when he was Prince of Wales and the Prince Charming of the world, rode the best against the best in steeplechases and point-to-points, until a nervous court put a stop to his race-riding; in the present day The Princess Royal carries on the race-riding tradition, while Her Majesty

The Queen maintains her string and her stud, and The Queen Mother is the best-loved patron of steeplechasing. These notables are a far cry from some of the owners, trainers and riders depicted in this collection, but all are bound by the same threads that have captured hearts and minds from time immemorial – the thrill of the race and the roar of the ring. Romance and ruin, they say, stalk in double harness beside all who tread the Turf, but that only adds to its excitement and appeal. Whether, even in this egalitarian age, it remains true that all men are equal on the Turf, or under it, is open to doubt. Certainly Edgar Wallace's little cockney tipster, Educated Evans, had small reason to think so.

Wallace gained his knowledge of racing and experience of the Turf by the simple method of paying for it, since he maintained at enormous expense a large string of useless horses. 'Hair trunks' his friend Jack Leach, trainer, jockey and journalist, called them. Against all advice Wallace believed each and every one of them to be a potential classic winner, and he backed them accordingly. 'He fought,' Jack Leach went on to say, 'a continual battle against the bookmakers and scarcely won a round.' At least his experiences gave him the material to write several racing thrillers, of which *The Flying Fifty Five* is probably the best, and a racing play, *The Calendar*, which even Jack Leach, who liked him at the same time as he laughed at him, conceded to be the only good racing play he ever saw.

The idea of writing about the exploits of Educated Evans came to Wallace from a chance acquaintanceship struck up on the racecourse with an engaging rogue called Peter Christian Barrie, who had already done time – three years hard labour – as a result of running 'ringers' (horses running under false names and identities at various racecourses). This proved to be a profitable enterprise until over-confidence betrayed him and allowed the fraud to be discovered. Barrie's speciality was painting the lookalike so as to resemble more closely the switched horse, but on one occasion the paint came off at an inconvenient moment and alerted the authorities.

Though he was easily the most audacious, Barrie was far from the first to employ this ruse. Conan Doyle heard of a case in the eighties and used it as part of the plot in *Silver Blaze*. However, not all aspects of this famous story will commend themselves to purists in racing. It is unlikely, for instance, that Colonel Ross, who had been in racing and concerned with horses all his life, would have failed to recognize

Silver Blaze, however camouflaged. But the story is redeemed for all time by what is probably the most famous of all Holmesian pronouncements when he expounds to Watson the significance of the curious incident of the dog in the night-time.

Barrie, for his part, coined a phrase which deserves, even if it has not received, almost equal fame. When asked by the judge at his trial what he considered to be a good thing in racing, 'a useful three-year-old in a moderate two-year-old race, my lord,' was his reply. After his release from prison, Barrie, henceforth known on the racecourse and elsewhere as 'Ringer Barrie', went into the tipping business, circulating his selections to a wide range of clients from every walk of life, from parsons to peers of the realm. Wallace, captivated by Barrie's cheek and charm, first wrote his life story for *John Bull*, a tabloid of the time, and then adapted him as a character for his prolific pen. Not only that, but, still bemused by his self-assessed abilities as a tipster and expert on form, Wallace invested in the business, became a partner, and took over the tipping. Inevitably it failed. To quote Jack Leach again: 'I believe he did tip a winner once when the office boy got fed up with all the losers and changed the selection.'

The losses incurred by this failure and his own gambling must to some extent at least have been offset for Wallace by the royalties earned by the Educated Evans stories which throw a lively and humorous light on one of the gamier aspects of the racing scene.

Wallace himself never rode a race in his life, nor for that matter did Richard Findlay, who wrote *The Dream*, concerned as it is with the pre-race nerves and anticipations of an amateur jockey. Findlay was a serving officer in the R.A.F. when he wrote the story, and it must have been his understanding of what went on in the minds of men in action that enabled him to enter into the hopes and fears of his protagonist Bobby Coplow.

Colin Davy, one of the few who rode and wrote fiction, is, unfairly, all but forgotten now. He was an amateur soldier-rider in the great days of soldier-riding between the wars, though his career in the saddle was dogged by ill-luck and injury which may have prevented him from reaching the very top. He saw, as many did in those days of wine and roses (in fact, it was mostly champagne – the great racing drink held by its apologists to be so because it does not put on weight), the humour and the fun of it all, and he recorded it with a light touch which concealed the insider's knowledge that came from his experiences in riding and running a stable, both at home and in India and Egypt. Some of those experiences in the latter countries, when in partnership with a present pillar of the Turf, did not exactly commend themselves to the colonel of the exclusive regiment in which they were then young officers, but to the reader they certainly add to the enjoyment and serve to spice the brew — even if the battle cry 'twenty to one and not a pal on' was scarcely designed to attract favourable comment from their seniors. In *Ups and Downs* Davy wrote one of the best of all racing autobiographies, which he published when his career in the saddle was coming to a close. Unfortunately it came out in 1939 and was overshadowed by the outbreak of the war and it has not been reprinted. It remains a fascinating record of the true spirit of steeplechasing in its time, written by one who had lived it and loved it, and who knew and had experienced its many set-backs and the few triumphs that make it all worthwhile.

After the war, Davy continued to write novels and short stories. All of them, but especially the short stories, are full of life, fun and enjoyment. His characters, however, and the milieu in which they mixed, looked back to a vanished world. Fun, enjoyment and the copious consumption of champagne had little in common with the post-war austerities of the Attlee-Cripps regime. As he had not been a lucky rider so he was not a lucky writer and, as anyone who has had experience of both knows only too well, luck has a major part to play in both racing and writing; as a matter of fact, Davy called his first racing novel *Luck's Pendulum*. But he was felt to be out of touch with his times, his sales fell off and he put away his pen. However, at his best, Davy was splendid and his best is probably seen in his short humorous stories, an example of which we have included here.

The Americans J. P. Marquand and Sherwood Anderson came from very different backgrounds, both of them light years away from that of Colin Davy and the British cavalry. Marquand had impeccable New England ancestry which he put to good use in his slyly humorous social studies and conversation pieces, such as *The Late George Apley* and *Wickford Point* which, with others like them, became best-sellers making his name universally known and critically appreciated. Blessed with unflagging invention and a wide range of interests, Marquand was one of the most prolific of American writers, both before and just after the last war. Detective novels, historical and American civil war serials, *Saturday Evening Post* short stories, all flowed unceasingly from his pen. Many of the latter concerned racing and its characters, for racing and the racetrack and the raffish types who gathered there never ceased to fascinate him.

Although he earned a substantial income from writing, once he became established, Marquand's inbred New England caution precluded him from ever venturing into ownership, but he was delighted when a friend named a racehorse after him. The horse proved a dismal failure and disappeared from the track. Shortly afterwards Marquand was dining with the horse's owner at their Boston club when the waiter placed before them two steaks which proved uncommonly tough. 'I wonder,' Marquand said, sadly contemplating his plate, 'if by any chance this could be J. P. Marquand?'

Anderson, unlike Marquand, was the boy from the wrong side of the tracks. He began his restless and roving career at the age of fourteen, drifting into occupations and out of them, gathering material which he was later to transmute into some of the earliest, small town, realistic American writing. It was this drifting which led him into racing and it was of the drifters and the under-privileged that he wrote, having been one himself. 'His characters,' one critic said of him, 'are puzzled, groping, baffled', as indeed is the 'big, lumbering fellow of nineteen' who 'promised mother I'd give up racing for good.' Like many another he failed to keep that promise with the results shown in *I'm a Fool.*

Anderson's big lumbering fellow has little in common with the neat and stylish John Stephens of whom William Fain writes in *Harmony*, his sensitive study of an ageing top jockey with an appreciation of his own abilities and an independent cast of mind. This story is a little gem which first appeared in the pages of *The New York Magazine*. It provides not only a background glance at Lamorlaye and Longchamp, but also brief sketches of owners, trainers, the occasional bitchiness of the weighing room and the riding of the race, which anyone acquainted with them will immediately recognize as authentic.

John Stephens, remote, reserved, determined to preserve his own inner integrity, would nevertheless have felt an affinity with Somerville and Ross's reluctant owner of *The Bagman's Pony*, who let himself in for rather more than he bargained for after a mess dinner, and with Molly Keane's innocent Englishman exposed in *Prime Rogues* to the wiles and machinations of upper class Irish ladies with a taste for devilment.

Much has been written about Somerville and Ross for in sporting literature they stand second only to Surtees, who, incidentally, hated racing, especially steeplechasing, and had some hard words to say about those who took part in it. But no one, not even Surtees, has written better of the secret that exists between the sympathetic hands of the horseman and his mount than these two marvellous ladies.

The Bagman's Pony, the story we have included here, is less well known than those concerning that 'stable boy among gentlemen and gentleman among stable boys', Flurry Knox M.F.H., and his chronicler and frequent victim, Major Sinclair Yeates R.M., but it is nevertheless well qualified in its own right to stand alongside the earlier and more famous 'Experiences' of those two worthies, telling us as it does of a different type of racing, and revealing a glimpse of a long vanished India in the middle years of the Raj. It stems, as Miss Somerville candidly admits in her reminiscences, from a tale told by her uncle Colonel Kendall Coghill, a hero of the Mutiny and a veteran of Tel-El-kebir and 'one of the most delightful raconteurs in the world with a memory of steel for names and events'.

Molly Keane, a member of an illustrious Irish sporting family, commenced her writing career not long after the First World War. It was then considered not quite the thing for a young lady such as she to produce slightly racy sporting novels and, at a loss for a *nom de plume*, she adopted the pseudonym M. J. Farrell from a name glimpsed on a public house on the way home from hunting. Several novels set in the hunting country of County Wexford, which was lovingly described, followed in quick succession, of which *Mad Puppetstown* is outstanding.

This portrait of Irish country-house living in the troubled times and after is a magical evocation of the Irish sporting scene when, as she recalls, hunting and racing were almost a religion to those living there. To quote one of her own phrases, 'the blood and bones' of both sports were bred in her, for her father and brothers were brilliant across country and between the flags, and she, though she does not say it, was not far behind. That she put that inheritance to good use can be seen in the story *Prime Rogues*, taken from a collection called *Conversation Piece* can well

stand beside *Mad Puppetstown* and indeed *The Irish R.M.* not only as a
record of another age but as a landmark in sporting literature.

The use of the word 'landmark', though deserved, is perhaps to
predicate a heavy hand and a solemn approach which is far from the
case. These were young books full of life and fire, full of a passion for
houses and horses and for that 'fierce beauty', as she once so well
described it, of the Irish countryside.

Beryl Markham knew all about the hardships that a life with horses
can bring. A singularly beautiful woman brought up in the wilds, she
achieved worldwide fame in the thirties when she became the first
person to fly solo from England to America. But, brilliant aviatrix
though she was, it was with horses that her real genius lay. Not only
did she train them successfully in England and South Africa, but
from girlhood she knew, understood and loved them. She could also
write, when she put her mind and her pen to it, although there is still
argument whether she or her third husband, Raoul Schumacher,
wrote her now best-selling memoirs *West With The Night*. There
can be little doubt, however, that it was she who wrote *The Splendid
Outcast*, the story which we have included here, since it came from
her own experience.

A colt, cast out as unmanageable from a powerful English stable,
came into the ring at Tattersalls when she was there. In real life she
was able, her biographer tells us, to buy him cheaply. She renamed
him 'Messenger Boy' took him to Kenya and won races with him.
But the sight of him in the sales ring, handsome, splendid and in
chains, and the longing look of a little ex-jockey standing nearby
inspired the story.

All these writers in their very differing ways understood racing
people and what motivated them – be they punters, owners, riders
or those who just come for the spectacle and the thrill. John
Taintor Foote, whose story *The Look of Eagles* is a minor classic
of the genre, also understood them and, what is even more
important and a fact that is sometimes overlooked, he understood
those on whom the entire lifeblood of the sport depends – the
horses. Born in Leadville, Colorado, in 1891 he was a racing man
through and through, having haunted the local tracks – and all
others if he could get to them – from his early youth. He had
grown up with racing in his blood. He died in 1950, at the
comparatively early age of fifty-nine, leaving behind him a body

of stories on racing and his other love, fishing, all of which bear the stamp of insight, authority and affection.

The phrase 'The Look of Eagles' has now passed into current usage to describe that commanding presence which denotes a true champion and which only true champions have. But it was John Taintor Foote who coined the phrase and put it into print. He placed the making of the phrase into the mind and mouth of Old Man Sanford who, with his unfailing courtesy, old-world manners and all-seeing eye, is well worthy of taking his place amongst the finest delineations of real racing men, and the other characters in the story also ring true. The story first saw light in 1915, and, although its trappings may have dated somewhat, its main core and its characters remain ageless.

'Any damned fool knows that one horse can run faster than another,' is the dismissive comment said to have been made to him by his father when Paul Mellon, one of the most successful of modern owners, bought his first racehorse. But there is rather more to it than that, as we hope these stories show. If that were all, why is it that so many, from peers, prime ministers, priests and parsons to newly enriched entrepreneurs and the man on the Clapham omnibus, whoever he may be, have all sought solace and success on the racecourse, and why have so many differing authors made it their subject?

It is, after all, a matter of many delights, at the same time a spectacle containing the thrill of seeing in action and on the stretch one of the most beautiful of creatures, the thoroughbred racehorse; a medium for the heightened excitement of the wager, of the pitting of wits against the imponderables; a matter of endless discussion of the merits and faults of man and horse. It is even an opportunity for the upwardly mobile to acquire prestige and social advancement, for was it not the Duke of Windsor in his riding days who advised those anxious for social preferment: 'If you can't get in by the front door, try the stable door'.

There we leave it in the hope that our selection will at least have provided a few hours of what, after all, despite its ups and downs, racing aims to be all about – entertainment and enjoyment.

THE DREAM

Richard Findlay

USUALLY when Bobby Coplow awoke he got out of bed at once and began to shave, feeling pleased with the prospect of the day's work. But on this cold February morning he lay for several minutes without moving. He was queerly perturbed, and could not at first discover the cause. And then he remembered his dream. It was a dream which he had had once before in the same week, down to the tiniest detail. He was riding his horse October Miracle in the Covertcoat Steeplechase at Lutterton. It was raining hard, and the going was very heavy. On both occasions his dream had commenced as they were approaching the worst fence on the course, and Bobby could remember nothing of the earlier part of the race, nor did he know whether they were on the first or second circuit. October Miracle was striding out easily, running well within himself, and Bobby was holding him on a tight rein, keeping him three lengths behind the two leaders. One of the two leading horses was Grey Marvel, with the stocky, broad-shouldered figure of Billy Sprott up. The other horse, who was almost level with Grey Marvel, but on the extreme outside of the course, was Battleaxe, a notoriously uncertain jumper. The fence they were approaching was a plain fence, but it was four feet nine inches high, and was set on a sharp bend in such a way that one came at it at an awkward angle. The ground rose slightly towards it, and then fell away so that there was a seven-foot drop on the landing side. And like all the fences on the Lutterton course, it was as stiff as timber.

Bobby was thinking that Battleaxe might be a nuisance at this fence. You never knew what that horse was going to do. He would have to watch him very closely, he thought. He glanced quickly backwards over his left shoulder to see how much he was leading the nearest horse. He disliked looking back in a race because the action was apt to make one's horse unbalanced, but in this case the knowledge thus gained would make a difference to the way in which he would jump the fence. He was a good three lengths ahead of the field. He moved his hands forward a little on his horse's neck. October Miracle pricked his intelligent ears, and lengthened his stride appreciably to gain on the two leaders. Bobby kept him in the middle of the course as they began to round the bend. Twenty yards from the fence he pulled him in slightly to meet it squarely close to the inner wing. He moved his hands still farther forward, and sat very still. He saw Grey Marvel's forehand rise as he rose at the fence. A moment later he saw something else which made his heart leap sickeningly in his chest. Battleaxe had refused, and had swerved towards the inside of the fence. His jockey was fighting him desperately, but seemed unable to pull him up. October Miracle had seen what was happening, too, and made a gigantic effort to avert disaster. A full fifteen feet from the fence he took off with a tremendous spring. As he left the ground Battleaxe's shoulder struck him hard in the quarters, causing him to twist in the air so that he went over the fence back-first, on his side. God! thought Bobby. This is going to be a *hell* of a fall! Instinctively he withdrew his feet from the stirrup-irons and tried to push himself away from the falling horse, who otherwise must crush him beneath his weight. As the ground rushed up to meet him he tucked his head into his chest and raised his arms to shield his face, bracing himself for the impact. But the impact never came. Instead he found himself standing beside the fence, looking down at a figure which lay face downwards on the sodden turf, inert and still where it had fallen. He saw the black cap, the black woollen jersey with the saxe-blue chevrons, and knew that it was himself. A few feet away October Miracle lay on his side, his mud-streaked flanks heaving spasmodically. Bobby felt strangely light and detached. Suddenly, with a shock that was both pain and fear, he knew that he was dead. And then, almost in the same moment, it seemed, he found himself wide awake in his own bed. The sequence of events was exactly the same as on that other night when he had dreamed this dream.

As Bobby lay in his bed now he was thinking that the Lutterton Meeting was to be held this afternoon. He was riding his horse October Miracle in the Covertcoat Steeplechase at three o'clock. And underneath the emotions which those thoughts engendered was the odd excitement which he always felt on the day of a race. This excitement, which was partly fear and partly joy, invariably increased as the time of the race drew nearer. But as soon as he had the reins in his hand to mount, it vanished completely. Suddenly, as he stared through the window at the bleak daylight of the winter day, he remembered that recurring dreams of this sort were believed to be an omen of disaster. Oh, what the hell, he thought.

There was a knock at the door, and his servant came in carrying a tray. On the tray were a cup and saucer, a teapot, a milk-jug, a sugar-bowl and a plate containing two digestive biscuits. The man looked surprised to find Bobby still in bed. 'Good morning, sir,' he said. 'It's seven o'clock.'

'I know, Renton,' said Bobby. 'I've been thinking about the race this afternoon. The going'll be pretty heavy.'

Renton put the tray down on the table by the bedside. 'It will that, sir,' he replied. ''Ock deep, as the saying is. But the Miracle won't mind,' he added confidently. He poured out a cup of tea, and began to lay out some clothes on an armchair near the window.

Sipping his tea, and watching Renton's neat, methodical movements, Bobby thought what an excellent fellow he was, and wondered, with a sudden pang, if this was the last morning when he would do these things for him. The idea persisted, in spite of all his efforts to drive it from his mind. He got out of bed, and looked out of the window across the rolling grassland of the Leicestershire Wolds. Even under the dull grey sky, with the leafless trees dripping in the still, damp air, it seemed to him the loveliest countryside in all the world. Bobby thought again that the going would be very deep today. But, as Renton had said, October Miracle would not mind. Whether the ground was a rolling bog, or iron hard, it was all one to him. He was a hell of a horse.

Bobby crossed the room, and looked into the mirror above the wash-basin in the corner. The mirror reflected a narrow brown face, tousled dark hair, and a pair of large and rather wide-apart blue eyes. It was a strong face, but the expression just now, as always in repose, was a little sad. It was the face of a sensitive man who spent much time alone.

He shaved and washed quickly, pulled on a pair of jodhpurs and a dark-blue polo jersey, and went downstairs. In the hall he put on a cap, picked up his whip and gloves, and went out into the stable-yard. It was a little after half-past seven. Three racehorses, saddled and bridled, and with rugs under their saddles, were being led up and down the gravelled yard. Two of them were 'chasers, good performers up to three miles over park courses. The third was a hunter who, after a regular season's hunting, was now in training for point-to-point races. The stable-lads who were leading the three horses touched their caps as Bobby approached. He was smiling, but rather sadly, they thought. 'Good morning,' he said. 'A rotten day. How's October Miracle?' he went on to Hogan, the head-lad.

'Oh, he's fine, sir,' answered Hogan, who was leading one of the fencers, a chestnut mare. 'Always quiet, never fusses at all. I never did see the likes,' he added, with a puzzled expression on his weather-beaten face.

'Go on up to Throxton Park with this lot, Tom,' said Bobby, patting the mare's sleek neck. 'I want you and Arthur to take Annabel Lee and The Bowman a mile over fences. Jack,' he said to the lad who was holding the point-to-point horse, 'walk Torchlight about until I come up. If I'm not there by eight o'clock, canter him seven furlongs and bring him home.' He waited until the three horses had passed up the drive into the road, until the dip in the road hid them from view. Then he crossed the stable-yard, passed through an opening on its farther side, and reached a post and rails enclosing a small paddock. He rested his foot upon the lowest rail, and, his arms upon the topmost, gazed across the paddock at the horse who was being led round the gravel path encircling it. October Miracle was a bay, with black points and tail. He was nine years old. Little could be seen of him at the moment because of the rug which protected him from the cold, damp air, but Bobby well knew what he would see if the rug was removed. The horse was sixteen hands two inches high, but his make and shape were so nearly perfect that he looked smaller at first glance. His shoulders were strong and well placed, and he had great depth of girth. The line from hip to hock was long and straight, and his second thighs were wide and fully developed. When you stood behind him and watched him move, you realized the immense power of his hind-limbs and quarters. He had a lot of bone and stood over a lot of ground. But perhaps the thing which struck you most about him was his proud and honest outlook. He was a beautiful horse.

When he saw Bobby, October Miracle pricked his ears and whinnied softly. Bobby climbed the fence and made much of the horse, whose cool dark muzzle was thrust into his hand. As he looked at those large brown eyes, October Miracle seemed to him the very embodiment of loyalty and splendid courage, of a woman's tenderness and a lion's heart. Neither as a hunter, nor in point-to-point races, nor in his two victorious seasons under Rules, had this beloved horse of his ever given him a fall. He seemed always to feel a deep responsibility for the man upon his back, and in the old hunting days, even when he had been tired at the end of a long run, he had jumped his fences carefully without rush or blunder. Watching him now as the stable-lad led him on around the paddock, Bobby thought of the wonderful ride he had given him at Liverpool in the previous November, when, gaining yards on his opponents with every leap over 'those rasping five-foot fences', he had won the Grand Sefton Steeplechase in a canter. But the climax of his brilliant career lay still in the future, he thought. He would win the Grand National next month, if class meant anything at all. Thus would he join the ranks of the immortals. It was his due, the inalienable right of his great quality. He was a superhorse.

As he stood there, hearing once more the thunderous music of hoofs on grass, rapt in his dreams of glory, the shadow of that other, vivid dream, a dream of disaster, fell again across Bobby Coplow's mind. It made the dull day duller, changed the tenor of his thoughts to a minor key. But it could not quench the glory.

At eight o'clock the stable-lad brought October Miracle back to his box and gave him his morning feed. Bobby watched him with loving eyes as he fed, finding in the horse's quiet unconcern a sort of peace and comfort. After a few minutes he went back into the house. As he was having his bath he heard the other horses returning. 'How did they go, Tom?' he called out of the window.

'Annabel Lee went very well, sir,' Hogan called back. 'The Bowman stopped at the ditch again,' he added after a moment's pause, with a melancholy shake of his head.

'Oh, hell, he seems to be making a regular habit of that,' said Bobby. 'We must get him out of it somehow before Sandown next week. We'll give him a good school tomorrow.' No doubt about it, he thought as he dressed, The Bowman had completely lost confidence in himself since he had had that nasty fall at the second open ditch at Leicester in January. He would have to nurse him along very carefully, or he would never recover his old form. Whatever happened, he should have a good school tomorrow.

After breakfast Bobby went out to the stable-yard and watched October Miracle being boxed for his forty-mile journey to Lutterton. The horse walked up the ramp at the back of the box with a quick, springy step, like a conqueror eager for fresh victories. Bobby followed him into the box. 'See you soon, old man,' he said. The horse nuzzled his cheek. Bobby walked down the ramp, and round to the front of the box. 'Take it easy, Knocker,' he said to the chauffeur, who was sitting at the wheel with Hogan at his side. 'You've got plenty of time.'

The man touched his cap. 'Yes, sir,' he said. He was very fond of horses, and particularly of October Miracle, and would never in any circumstances have driven in such a way as to endanger his safety, or even to cause him discomfort. Moreover, he knew that Bobby was quite aware of these facts. But he always expected some such remark as Bobby had just made, and would have been disappointed if it had not been forthcoming. It was an essential part of the ritual. He let in the clutch, and the horse-box moved slowly up the drive. 'Bring Simon round to the front door at half-past ten.' Bobby said to one of the stable-lads. He went into the house, and looked in the paper at the list of runners in the Covertcoat Steeplechase at Lutterton. It was a four-mile steeplechase, and was worth four hundred pounds to the winner. There were fifteen probable starters, with several National candidates amongst them. But October Miracle would win all right. Grey Marvel, and Ramadan, who had been second in the National in the previous year, and who, like October Miracle, was set to carry twelve stone, were the two horses most to be feared. But, barring accidents, October Miracle would certainly win all right. He was invincible.

When Simon was brought round to the door Bobby got up on him and rode out through the village to Throxton Park. Between the village and the first gate into the park he met Tom Green, the trainer, coming back from exercising his second string. He was on his old brown hack, leading the string of about twenty horses. He trained Grey Marvel

'Hullo, squire,' he said. 'How's the champion this morning?'

'Fine,' said Bobby.

'Grey Marvel's all right, too,' said Tom Green. 'Never been better.

You won't see him this afternoon,' he added with absolute conviction. He was always optimistic, and usually with good reason. He was a good trainer, and had good horses to train.

'No, I'll be in front,' Bobby answered.

'Oh, yeah, wisecracker?' Tom Green said. He was a great cinema fan, and was always full of Americanisms. He was grinning. Oh, hell, do we have to go on talking bilge? thought Bobby. He could not help feeling depressed, and wanted to be alone. 'So long, Tom,' he said. 'See you at Lutterton.' He rode on. Eleven o'clock was striking from the church clock in the village as he passed through the last of the four gates and came out into the park. He shortened the reins, and dug his heels into Simon's flanks. The old horse started off in a fast gallop, his feet squelching on the sodden ground. On the far side of the park Bobby reined him in. Looking over the boundary wall, he saw the wide grass country stretching out to the misty horizon. It looked desolate under the lowering sky, but he knew every inch of it, and loved it all. Every detail seemed to stand out very clear. A mile away the bare trees of Sandon Spinney made a black smudge against the surrounding greyness. The whole world seemed drained of colour, lifeless. Bobby turned in his saddle and gazed back across the park. He saw the schooling gallops, the brush fences stretching away to the gate by which he had come in. Nearer to him were the remains of the old grandstand, relic of the days when Throxton Park had been a racecourse. In his imagination he saw it in its hey-day, women in crinolines, heavily whiskered men in swallow-tailed coats, moving leisurely in the sunshine of long ago. The jockeys were whiskered too, and rode with very long leathers horses with very long necks and very small heads, like the ones in the old sporting prints. Bobby knew, of course, that the horses were not really like that, but he always pictured them so. He had often laughed at himself for being so foolish. Departed glories! he thought. Those lovely yesterdays! he said to himself. And suddenly he realized that the world around him was not lifeless. It was alive with the lives of the men and women, yes by God, and horses too, who had passed that way once or twice or many times and now had gone. He could hear echoes of their laughter and of their sorrow and of the thud of horses' hoofs. Many of them had had their dreams of glory and they had all had to go from this place and no doubt most of them had gone bravely and gallantly. Horses in the main were brave and splendid animals and there was this to be said for the men and women who loved and rode them that, though they might have many faults, most of them were brave and some were splendid. They had built up a tradition that if they had to die it was a fine thing to die on horseback, perhaps in battle, perhaps with the music of hounds or the rattle of guard-rails in their ears. Horsemen and warriors! he thought with a sudden fierce joy. That was their tradition, and if he had to die and to go from this place, he would be loyal to it. But he hoped that he would not have to go yet, to leave all this beauty. He did not want to go yet. Dear God, he prayed, let me go on staying here for a bit. Please dear God don't make me go from here yet. He looked at his watch. 'Heavens!' he exclaimed. It was half-past eleven. 'Come up, Simon,' he said. The old hunter raised his head from the short, wet, brown grass. They did not take very long to get back to the house.

On the way to Lutterton, a solitary magpie flew quite low along the road in front of Bobby Coplow's car. It stayed there for so long that he thought it would never go away. It was very unlucky to see a single magpie. In the past it had always meant serious trouble of one sort or another. The bird would not go away. 'Get to hell out of here,' Bobby said. Eventually the magpie flew over a hedge and disappeared. Bobby was glad when it had gone. But he was worried, too. It was a bad omen, like his dream. He drove fast all the way, but the road was not very good. It was ten minutes past one when he arrived at the course. The first race, a two-mile selling hurdle race, was over, and the bookmakers were starting to pay out. The indefinable racecourse atmosphere stirred Bobby Coplow's blood. He looked through his glasses at the board by the judge's box, then at his card. Assurance had won by a head from Sussex Melody, with Kremlin third. There was a large crowd round the totalizator stand. Bobby saw several people whom he knew, but he did not want to talk to them. He walked round the back of the stand towards the stables. Tom Hogan was talking to Lord and Lady Cairngorm outside one of the boxes. Bobby took off his hat and shook hands with them both. 'How are you, Bobby?' old Lord Cairngorm murmured. He always spoke very quietly, and when his wife was with him he hardly spoke at all. It was not necessary, and in fact was almost impossible. Bobby liked him very much, and was rather sorry for him, too. But Lady Cairngorm had a lot of money.

'I'm so glad to see you, Bobby,' she said. 'Hogan tells me you've only got one ride this afternoon. October Miracle *is* a lovely horse, isn't he? I wish he were mine. Will you ride Bright Angel for me in the third race?' she asked.

'Why, what's happened to Croppy?' said Bobby.

'Didn't you see the first race?' asked Lady Cairngorm. 'Oh, you've only just arrived. That brute Stevedore fell three hurdles from home, and poor Croppy hurt his back rather badly. I've just come from the hospital. He won't be able to ride any more today, the doctor says. Such bad luck for the poor man. But there it is. You will ride Bright Angel, won't you?' she asked anxiously.

'Thanks very much, but I won't if you don't mind. I'm not feeling too good, and I think one ride will be enough for me today,' Bobby answered. 'You'll get a jockey all right, I expect,' he added after a moment's pause.

'Oh, how beastly of you!' said Lady Cairngorm plaintively. 'Bright Angel is just your affair. You couldn't look better, either. Still, I suppose you know best. But I do think it's beastly of you. Well, I must go and find somebody else, that's all. Come along, Angus,' she said, moving off with long strides towards the weighing-room.

'The best of luck, Bobby,' said old Lord Cairngorm, as he started to follow his wife. Most of his time was spent in following his wife. But that is neither here nor there, as they say.

Bobby and Hogan went into October Miracle's box. The horse rubbed his lean head against Bobby's shoulder, expelling air noisily through his expanded nostrils. Bobby did not want to watch the second race, and stayed looking at October Miracle and talking to Hogan for about twenty minutes. Then he went out, crossed the course by the gate above the grandstand, and walked along to the water jump. Reggie Hope was there with two of the Valentine girls and several other people. They were all very gay.

'I'm going to win a packet today, Bobby. I've got my camisole on you at threes,' Anne Valentine said.

'Listen, Anne, you're a damn fool,' said Bobby, 'Anything can happen in a 'chase, and I don't believe I'm going to win today. Go and hedge like hell on Grey Marvel; you'll get fours, I should think,' he said. He was very serious.

Anne Valentine looked at him 'All right, I will after this race,' she said. She took Bobby by the arm and led him away a few yards from the others. 'What's the matter, old boy?' she asked.

'Oh, nothing much; I don't think I shall win, that's all,' Bobby answered.

Anne Valentine looked at him very hard. She had grey eyes with long black lashes, set in a small, rather pointed face. Her skin was a pale golden colour, and her hair was thick and tawny. 'Oh, don't ride,' she said. Bobby smiled at her. Anne Valentine thought that she had never seen anything so sad as the smile on Bobby Coplow's face.

'I've got to ride,' he said.

The twelve runners were coming out for the third race, a three-mile steeplechase. They watched them through their glasses as they went down to the start. Gerry Gilson was riding Bright Angel.

'I've got a bit on him each way,' Anne Valentine told Bobby.

'He's no good. He'll blow up in the third mile; he always does,' Reggie Hope said.

'He'd have won a lot of races if they hadn't always used him too much at the start. He runs himself out when he's in front,' said Bobby. 'Gerry Gilson'll wait on him all right,' he went on.

'They're off now!' exclaimed Reggie Hope.

Bobby watched the race without much interest. But he hoped that Bright Angel would win, because Anne Valentine had backed him. She was a fine girl. The field had been reduced to ten by the time the water was reached. Bright Angel was lying fifth. All the jockeys were already spattered from head to foot with mud. Several of the horses slithered badly on landing, but none fell. 'Blooming awful going,' Reggie Hope exclaimed. He did not like swearing in front of women, although they often swore in front of him. He was very old-fashioned. The second ditch brought down another of the runners. The next fence was the fence of Bobby's dreams. Prioress, who was in the lead, fell heavily, bringing down Bombardier, and leaving Gorcock to go on from Bright Angel, with the rest of the field some lengths behind. Coplow felt quite sick when he saw the two horses fall. Both of them were on their feet again in a few moments, and one of the jockeys too. Bobby could not see what had happened to the other jockey, but he saw two ambulance men running across in front of the fence. He lowered his glasses, and took his cigarette-case out of his pocket. He saw that Anne Valentine was looking at him intently, her enormous grey eyes very wide. She was rather pale, he noticed. He held out his case, and she took a cigarette. But she did not say anything. Just before the last ditch Bright Angel began to go up. Two fences from home he was level with Gorcock's girths, and coming over the last fence he had his head in front. Gerry Gilson had his whip out, but he did not need to use it. Bright Angel held off Gorcock's challenge on the flat and went away to win the race by a length, running on strongly at the finish. 'Well, that's that,' said Reggie Hope.

The whole party began to move along towards the gate opposite the paddock. Bobby and Anne Valentine walked side by side a few yards in front of the others, not saying anything. The 'All Right' went up as they reached the paddock.

'I don't want to stay here; let's go and look at October Miracle,' Anne Valentine said.

On the way to the stables they met several people whom they knew, and had to stop and talk to them for a few minutes. It was nearly half-past two when they reached October Miracle's box. Tom Hogan was watching the lad sponging out his nostrils. He threw back his rug, so that Anne Valentine could see him properly.

'I've never seen him look fitter; he'll walk that race,' she said.

They did not stay very long in the box. When they got back to the gate which led to the dressing-room they stopped.

'I'll have to go in here now. You'd better hurry or you won't see the next race,' said Bobby.

'I don't want to see it,' Anne Valentine said.

'Yes, you'd better go and watch it,' said Bobby. 'You won't forget to back Grey Marvel, will you?' he asked anxiously.

Anne Valentine did not say anything for a moment or two. Her eyes were very bright. 'No, I won't forget,' she answered. She gripped his arm suddenly. 'All the luck in the world,' she said.

'That's sweet of you, Anne; you're a grand girl,' Bobby told her.

'I'll see you after the race,' said Anne Valentine.

Bobby watched her as she walked away towards the paddock. She was small and straight and very slender. At the corner of the stand she turned and waved her hand to him and he waved back. The next moment she was out of sight.

Bobby went into the dressing-room and started to change his clothes. The valet who always looked after him brought him the small bag containing his kit. His name was Sullivan and he was about sixty years old. Many years before he had been a successful steeplechase jockey and had made a lot of money. But unfortunately, like a good many jockeys before and since, he had spent it all as he earned it, so that instead of being able to set up as a trainer or perhaps retire altogether from racing he had had to go on working. Actually the drink was his trouble and when he got jobs with horses after he gave up riding races he lost them all through the drink. Now he was a jockeys' valet and on the whole he seemed quite happy. But sometimes he was silent for days at a time and his blue eyes were sombre and melancholy. He was never tired of talking about his racing days and he began now to tell Bobby of an experience that he had once had in Ireland. It appeared that he was riding in a hurdle race a horse who was inclined to be difficult at the post. So he arranged with the starter, who was a friend of his, that he should wait in the paddock until all the other runners were lined up, and that as soon as he was level with them the race should be started. None of the other jockeys knew of this arrangement and when they saw him cantering down behind them they naturally expected him to get into line in the ordinary way. Some of them were not even facing in the right direction. But when he was almost abreast of them the starter dropped his flag. 'Begob, I was over the first hurdle before they had the reins in their hands!' he said.

When Bobby laughed at this story it made the hollow feeling in his stomach seem more hollow. So he did not laugh very much. He pulled on his boots and put on his cap and picked up his whip and saddle, weight-cloth and number-cloth, and went along to weigh out. There was a lot of noise in the weighing-room and he had to wait for some time while the jockeys from the previous race weighed in. When he got off the scales he gave the saddle and weight-cloth and number-cloth to Hogan, and put on his overcoat, He went out to the parade ring. The numbers went up almost immediately. Bobby looked all round for Anne Valentine. He could not see her anywhere. Hogan and the lad came into the ring with October Miracle and the lad began to lead him round in the parade with the other horses. Hogan came over to the corner where Bobby was and stood beside him. 'Three to one bar one! Two to one the field!' shouted the bookmakers. There was no sign of Anne Valentine. It was a hell of a lonely business waiting about like this. At last the bell went. The lad brought October Miracle over and stripped off his rug and held his head while Hogan took Bobby's coat and gave him a leg up. 'Good luck, sir,' they said. The lad slipped off the leading strings and Bobby touched October Miracle with his heels and they walked out of the enclosure and through the gate on to the course. He touched him again and they cantered down to the start, Bobby feeling better than he had felt all day with October Miracle snorting and tossing his lovely head and moving under him with his beautiful easy action. It began to rain before they reached the post.

There was a certain amount of delay at the starting-gate because Battleaxe as usual gave a lot of trouble. He was a liver chestnut with one white stocking, and he was a proper handful. He fought his bit and nearly bucked Denton off and lashed out with his heels so that all the other horses were cannoning into one another to keep out of his way. There was a good deal of cursing, particularly from Captain FitzGerald, the starter, but at last Battleaxe gave up and moved into the centre of the line next to Idolatry. 'Come up there on Ramadan and Valiant Dust. Back on the grey; up on Starlight,' Captain FitzGerald called out. 'Steady now; easy,' he said. The line of horses moved forward slowly. The gate went up.

The fifteen runners thundered down at the black line of fence in a bunched mass. Bobby let October Miracle go and the horse took hold of his bit and a hundred yards from the start he was clear of the field. Fifty yards from the fence he began as usual to measure his take-off. He jumped perfectly, and went away after landing without checking at all. It was raining hard now, and Bobby lowered his head so that the visor of his cap should keep the rain out of his eyes. Half-way to the second fence he took a pull at the reins. After a moment October Miracle came back to him like a well-trained show-ring hack. He was mad keen to race, but he had perfect confidence in Bobby and was quite content to go at the pace he wanted. Grey Marvel, Battleaxe and Ramadan shot out in front. Bobby watched Battleaxe carefully over the next two fences. He over-jumped at the first, and pitched badly on landing, but he recovered all right. At the second, an open ditch, Denton had to use his whip on him. It looked as though he might fall or run out before very long. But Bobby knew, somehow, that he would not. They were approaching that sinister fence now. As they started to round the sharp bend towards it Bobby had a fleeting moment's fear. It passed at once and he felt quite normal again. Valiant Dust was close up on his inside, so he could not jump the fence as he wanted to. He let October Miracle increase his pace a little. Two lengths ahead of him Battleaxe was showing signs of wanting to run out. But Denton kept him at it and he got over safely. Bobby sat well forward as October Miracle took off and the fence fairly whistled under and then he lay back because of the big drop and slipped the reins and they landed yards out. He got forward again in a couple of strides, hearing a crash and a thud behind him and knowing that Valiant Dust was down. He pulled October Miracle back to his original pace and they galloped on behind the leaders. Well, he thought, we're over that fence all right and perhaps after all there was nothing in that dream. But then he thought: we've got to jump it again you fool and what about that? 'I'll go on watching Battleaxe,' he said, 'and forget the dream.' He went on watching Battleaxe. Three of the fifteen starters had fallen now. The remainder galloped on, through the rain and mud. Battleaxe was running in his usual uncertain manner. At one fence he was over-jumping and pitching and at the next he was trying to run out. And then he would hit one hard and Bobby would feel certain that he was going to fall, but he never did. Denton was having a hell of a ride, and it was amazing how he kept his seat at some of the fences. Grey Marvel was making all the running, and setting a hot pace, too. Going into the water jump he was a length in front of Battleaxe, with Ramadan two lengths behind. October Miracle shortened his stride a little as they approached the water. He took off half a length behind Ramadan and landed a length in front, a colossal leap. He did not mind the rain or the heavy going or anything else. He was only half-extended and jumping like a stag and pulling double. By God, thought Bobby, there never was such a horse as October Miracle.

They were going out into the country again for the second circuit. There were three plain fences now and then the third open ditch, and then the fence of dreams and nightmares. After the ditch, Bobby glanced quickly backwards over his left shoulder. He was a good three lengths in front of Ramadan, with the rest of the field some distance away. He moved his hands forward a little and October Miracle pricked his intelligent ears and lengthened his stride and began to go up to the two leaders. Bobby kept him in the middle of the course as they started to round the bend. He was very afraid. He had done all this twice before that week and something had happened both times and it was going to happen now. He clenched his teeth and twenty yards from the fence he pulled October Miracle in slightly to meet it squarely close to the inner wing. He moved his hands still farther forward, and sat very still. He saw Grey Marvel's forehand rise as he rose at the fence. A moment later he saw something else which made his heart leap sickeningly in his chest. Battleaxe had refused, and had swerved towards the inside of the fence. Denton was fighting him desperately, but seemed unable to pull him up. October Miracle had seen what was happening, too, and made a gigantic effort to avert disaster. A full fifteen feet from the fence he took off with a tremendous spring. As he left the ground Battleaxe's shoulder struck him hard in the quarters, causing him to twist in the air so that he went over the fence back-first, on his side. God, thought Bobby, it's happened all right! Instinctively he withdrew his feet from the stirrup irons and tried to push himself away from the falling horse, who otherwise must crush him beneath his weight. As the ground rushed up to meet him, he tucked his head into his chest and raised his arms to shield his face, bracing himself for the impact. He felt his body strike the ground with numbing force. There was a roaring in his ears and a sudden sharp pain in his head and then a great darkness enveloped him. But almost at once the darkness cleared and the pain and the roaring ceased and he found himself standing beside the fence, looking down at a figure which lay face downwards on the sodden turf, inert and still where it had fallen. He saw the black cap, the black woollen jersey with the saxe-blue chevrons, and knew that it was himself. A few feet away October Miracle lay on his side, his mud-streaked flanks heaving spasmodically. Bobby felt strangely light and detached. Suddenly, with a shock that was both pain and fear, he knew that he was dead. He felt himself falling endlessly through outer space. And then he was wide awake. But he was not in his own bed. He was lying on his back in the open air, with the rain beating in his face. Denton and two ambulance men were bending over him, looking strained and anxious. Denton's lips were trembling, and he was very white.

'Lie still; the ambulance will be here in a minute,' one of the Red Cross men said.

'Help me up; I must get up,' said Bobby.

'No, you lie still, sir,' the other Red Cross man said.

Bobby struggled to his knees. Something warm was trickling down his forehead. He put up his hand, and brought it away covered with blood. There was a deep cut in his forehead. He felt very sick and giddy, and he could not think clearly. One of the Red Cross men was unrolling a lint bandage. 'You must lie still, sir,' he said. He took Bobby by the arm. 'Help me up,' said Bobby. The man helped him up. A few feet from the fence October Miracle lay on his side, muddy, glistening with wet, unnaturally huddled. He would never win the Grand National now. His back was broken. Everything dropped inside Bobby. 'Oh, God, so it was you!' he said. He stumbled forward, and knelt down beside his horse. He put out his hand and touched the soft muzzle. October Miracle neighed feebly, and his muzzle stirred faintly in Bobby's hand. Suddenly he quivered, stretched his limbs, and was still. Bobby knelt beside him. The rain poured down. He felt a hand on his shoulder, and looked up. It was Denton.

'I don't know what to say, Mister Coplow,' he said. He was nearly crying.

'You mustn't worry; it wasn't your fault,' said Bobby. Blood and tears mingled in his mouth with a salty tang. He knelt beside his dead horse, in the rain.

SILVER BLAZE

A. Conan Doyle

'I AM afraid, Watson, that I shall have to go,' said Holmes, as we sat down together to our breakfast one morning.

'Go! Where to?'

'To Dartmoor – to King's Pyland.'

I was not surprised. Indeed, my only wonder was that he had not already been mixed up in this extraordinary case, which was the one topic of conversation through the length and breadth of England. For a whole day my companion had rambled about the room with his chin upon his chest and his brows knitted, charging and re-charging his pipe with the strongest black tobacco, and absolutely deaf to any of my questions or remarks. Fresh editions of every paper had been sent up by our newsagent only to be glanced over and tossed down into a corner. Yet, silent as he was, I knew perfectly well what it was over which he was brooding. There was but one problem before the public which could challenge his powers of analysis, and that was the singular disappearance of the favourite for the Wessex Cup, and the tragic murder of its trainer. When, therefore, he suddenly announced his intention of setting out for the scene of the drama, it was only what I had both expected and hoped for.

'I should be most happy to go down with you if I should not be in the way,' said I.

'My dear Watson, you would confer a great favour upon me by coming. And I think that your time will not be misspent, for there are points about this case which promise to make it an absolutely unique one. We have, I think, just time to catch our train at Paddington, and I will go further into the matter upon our journey. You would oblige me by bringing with you your very excellent field-glass.'

And so it happened that an hour or so later I found myself in the corner of a first-class carriage, flying along, *en route* for Exeter, while Sherlock Holmes, with his sharp, eager face framed in his ear-flapped travelling-cap, dipped rapidly into the bundle of fresh papers which he had procured at Paddington. We had left Reading far behind us before he thrust the last of them under the seat, and offered me his cigar-case.

'We are going well,' said he, looking out of the window, and glancing at his watch. 'Our rate at present is fifty-three and a half miles an hour.'

'I have not observed the quarter-mile posts,' said I.

'Nor have I. But the telegraph posts upon this line are sixty yards apart, and the calculation is a simple one. I presume that you have already looked into this matter of the murder of John Straker and the disappearance of Silver Blaze?'

'I have seen what the *Telegraph* and the *Chronicle* have to say.'

'It is one of those cases where the art of the reasoner should be used rather for the sifting of details than for the acquiring of fresh evidence. The tragedy has been so uncommon, so complete, and of such personal importance to so many people that we are suffering from a plethora of surmise, conjecture, and hypothesis. The difficulty is to detach the framework of fact – of absolute, undeniable fact – from the embellishments of theorists and reporters. Then, having established ourselves upon this sound basis, it is our duty to see what inferences may be drawn, and which are the special points upon which the whole mystery turns. On Tuesday evening I received telegrams, both from Colonel Ross, the owner of the horse, and from Inspector Gregory, who is looking after the case, inviting my co-operation.'

'Tuesday evening!' I exclaimed. 'And this is Thursday morning. Why did you not go down yesterday?'

'Because I made a blunder, my dear Watson – which is, I am afraid, a more common occurrence than anyone would think who only knew me through your memoirs. The fact is that I could not believe it possible that the most remarkable horse in England could long remain concealed, especially in so sparsely inhabited a place as the north of Dartmoor. From hour to hour yesterday I expected to hear that he had been found, and that his abductor was the murderer of John Straker. When, however, another morning had come and

I found that, beyond the arrest of young Fitzroy Simpson, nothing had been done, I felt that it was time for me to take action. Yet in some ways I feel that yesterday has not been wasted.'

'You have formed a theory then?'

'At least I have a grip of the essential facts of the case. I shall enumerate them to you, for nothing clears up a case so much as stating it to another person, and I can hardly expect your co-operation if I do not show you the position from which we start.'

I lay back against the cushions, puffing at my cigar, while Holmes, leaning forward, with his long thin forefinger checking off the points upon the palm of his left hand, gave me a sketch of the events which had led to our journey.

'Silver Blaze,' said he, 'is from the Isonomy stock, and holds as brilliant a record as his famous ancestor. He is now in his fifth year, and has brought in turn each of the prizes of the turf to Colonel Ross, his fortunate owner. Up to the time of the catastrophe he was first favourite for the Wessex Cup, the betting being three to one on. He has always, however, been a prime favourite with the racing public, and has never yet disappointed them, so that even at short odds enormous sums of money have been laid upon him. It is obvious, therefore, that there were many people who had the strongest interest in preventing Silver Blaze from being there at the fall of the flag next Tuesday.

'This fact was, of course, appreciated at King's Pyland, where the Colonel's training stable is situated. Every precaution was taken to guard the favourite. The trainer, John Straker, is a retired jockey, who rode in Colonel Ross's colours before he became too heavy for the weighing-chair. He has served the Colonel for five years as jockey, and for seven as trainer, and has always shown himself to be a zealous and honest servant. Under him were three lads, for the establishment was a small one, containing only four horses in all. One of these lads sat up each night in the stable, while the others slept in the loft. All three bore excellent characters. John Straker, who is a married man, lived in a small villa about two hundred yards from the stables. He has no children, keeps one maid-servant, and is comfortably off. The country round is very lonely, but about half a mile to the north there is a small cluster of villas which have been built by a Tavistock contractor for the use of invalids and others who may wish to enjoy the pure Dartmoor air. Tavistock itself lies two miles to the west, while across the moor, also about two miles distant, is the larger training establishment of Capleton, which belongs to Lord Backwater, and is managed by Silas Brown. In every other direction the moor is a complete wilderness, inhabited only by a few roaming gipsies. Such was the general situation last Monday night, when the catastrophe occurred.

'On that evening the horses had been exercised and watered as usual, and the stables were locked up at nine o'clock. Two of the lads walked up to the trainer's house, where they had supper in the kitchen, while the third, Ned Hunter, remained on guard. At a few minutes after nine the maid, Edith Baxter, carried down to the stables his supper, which consisted of a dish of curried mutton. She took no liquid, as there was a water-tap in the stables, and it was the rule that the lad on duty should drink nothing else. The maid carried a lantern with her, as it was very dark, and the path ran across the open moor.

'Edith Baxter was within thirty yards of the stables when a man appeared out of the darkness and called to her to stop. As he stepped into the circle of yellow light thrown by the lantern she saw that he was a person of gentlemanly bearing, dressed in a grey suit of tweed with a cloth cap. He wore gaiters, and carried a heavy stick with a knob to it. She was most impressed, however, by the extreme pallor of his face and by the nervousness of his manner. His age, she thought, would be rather over thirty than under it.

'"Can you tell me where I am?" he asked. "I had almost made up my mind to sleep on the moor when I saw the light of your lantern."

'"You are close to the King's Pyland training stables," she said.

'"Oh, indeed! What a stroke of luck!" he cried. "I understand that a stable-boy sleeps there alone every night. Perhaps that is his supper which you are carrying to him. Now I am sure that you would not be too proud to earn the price of a new dress, would you?" He took a piece of white paper folded up out of his waistcoat pocket. "See that the boy has this tonight, and you shall have the prettiest frock that money can buy."

'She was frightened by the earnestness of his manner, and ran past him to the window through which she was accustomed to hand the meals. It was already open, and Hunter was seated at the small table inside. She began to tell him of what had happened, when the stranger came up again.

'"Good evening," said he, looking through the window, "I

wanted to have a word with you." The girl has sworn that as he spoke she noticed the corner of the little paper packet protruding from his closed hand.

'"What business have you here?" asked the lad.

'"It's business that may put something into your pocket," said the other. "You've two horses in for the Wessex Cup – Silver Blaze and Bayard. Let me have the straight tip, and you won't be a loser. Is it a fact that at the weights Bayard could give the other a hundred yards in five furlongs, and that the stable have put their money on him?"

'"So you're one of those damned touts," cried the lad. "I'll show you how we serve them in King's Pyland." He sprang up and rushed across the stable to unloose the dog. The girl fled away to the house, but as she ran she looked back, and saw that the stranger was leaning through the window. A minute later, however, when Hunter rushed out with the hound he was gone, and though the lad ran all round the buildings he failed to find any trace of him.'

'One moment!' I asked. 'Did the stable-boy, when he ran out with the dog, leave the door unlocked behind him?'

'Excellent, Watson; excellent!' murmured my companion. 'The importance of the point struck me so forcibly, that I sent a special wire to Dartmoor yesterday to clear the matter up. The boy locked the door before he left it. The window, I may add, was not large enough for a man to get through.

'Hunter waited until his fellow grooms had returned, when he sent a message up to the trainer and told him what had occurred. Straker was excited at hearing the account, although he does not seem to have quite realized its true significance. It left him, however, vaguely uneasy, and Mrs Straker, waking at one in the morning, found that he was dressing. In reply to her inquiries, he said that he could not sleep on account of his anxiety about the horses, and that he intended to walk down to the stables to see that all was well. She begged him to remain at home, as she could hear the rain pattering against the windows, but in spite of her entreaties he pulled on his large mackintosh and left the house.

'Mrs Straker awoke at seven in the morning, to find that her husband had not yet returned. She dressed herself hastily, called the maid, and set off for the stables. The door was open; inside, huddled together upon a chair, Hunter was sunk in a state of absolute stupor, the favourite's stall was empty, and there were no signs of his trainer.

'The two lads who slept in the chaff-cutting loft above the harness-room were quickly roused. They had heard nothing during the night, for they are both sound sleepers. Hunter was obviously under the influence of some powerful drug; and, as no sense could be got out of him, he was left to sleep it off while the two lads and the two women ran out in search of the absentees. They still had hopes that the trainer had for some reason taken out the horse for early exercise, but on ascending the knoll near the house, from which all the neighbouring moors were visible, they not only could see no signs of the favourite, but they perceived something which warned them that they were in the presence of a tragedy.

'About a quarter of a mile from the stables, John Straker's overcoat was flapping from a furze bush. Immediately beyond there was a bowl-shaped depression in the moor, and at the bottom of this was found the dead body of the unfortunate trainer. His head had been shattered by a savage blow from some heavy weapon, and he was wounded in the thigh, where there was a long, clean cut, inflicted evidently by some very sharp instrument. It was clear, however, that Straker had defended himself vigorously against his assailants, for in his right hand he held a small knife, which was clotted with blood up to the handle, while in his left he grasped a red and black silk cravat, which was recognized by the maid as having been worn on the preceding evening by the stranger who had visited the stables.

'Hunter, on recovering from his stupor, was also quite positive as to the ownership of the cravat. He was equally certain that the same stranger had, while standing at the window, drugged his curried mutton, and so deprived the stables of their watchman.

'As to the missing horse, there were abundant proofs in the mud which lay at the bottom of the fatal hollow, that he had been there at the time of the struggle. But from that morning he has disappeared; and although a large reward has been offered, and all the gipsies of Dartmoor are on the alert, no news has come of him. Finally an analysis has shown that the remains of his supper, left by the stable lad, contain an appreciable quantity of powdered opium, while the people of the house partook of the same dish on the same night without any ill effect.

'Those are the main facts of the case stripped of all surmise and stated as baldly as possible. I shall now recapitulate what the police have done in the matter.

'Inspector Gregory, to whom the case has been committed, is an extremely competent officer. Were he but gifted with imagination he might rise to great heights in his profession. On his arrival he promptly found and arrested the man upon whom suspicion naturally rested. There was little difficulty in finding him, for he was thoroughly well known in the neighbourhood. His name, it appears, was Fitzroy Simpson. He was a man of excellent birth and education, who had squandered a fortune upon the turf, and who lived now by doing a little quiet and genteel bookmaking in the sporting clubs of London. An examination of his betting-book shows that bets to the amount of five thousand pounds had been registered by him against the favourite.

'On being arrested he volunteered the statement that he had come down to Dartmoor in the hope of getting some information about the King's Pyland horses, and also about Desborough, the second favourite, which was in the charge of Silas Brown, at the Capleton stables. He did not attempt to deny that he had acted as ascribed upon the evening before, but declared that he had no sinister designs, and had simply wished to obtain first-hand information. When confronted with the cravat he turned very pale, and was utterly unable to account for its presence in the hand of the murdered man. His wet clothing showed that he had been out in the storm of the night before, and his stick, which was a Penang lawyer, weighed with lead, was just such a weapon as might, by repeated blows, have inflicted the terrible injuries to which the trainer had succumbed.

'On the other hand, there was no wound upon his person, while the state of Straker's knife would show that one, at least, of his assailants must bear his mark upon him. There you have it all in a nutshell, Watson, and if you can give me any light I shall be infinitely obliged to you.'

I had listened with the greatest interest to the statement which Holmes, with characteristic clearness, had laid before me. Though most of the facts were familiar to me, I had not sufficiently appreciated their relative importance, nor their connection with each other.

'Is it not possible,' I suggested, 'that the incised wound upon Straker may have been caused by his own knife in the convulsive struggles which follow any brain injury?'

'It is more than possible; it is probable,' said Holmes. 'In that case, one of the main points in favour of the accused disappears.'

'And yet,' said I, 'even now I fail to understand what the theory of the police can be.'

'I am afraid that whatever theory we state has very grave objections to it,' returned my companion. 'The police imagine, I take it, that this Fitzroy Simpson, having drugged the lad, and having in some way obtained a duplicate key, opened the stable door, and took out the horse, with the intention, apparently, of kidnapping him altogether. His bridle is missing, so that Simpson must have put it on. Then, having left the door open behind him, he was leading the horse away over the moor, when he was either met or overtaken by the trainer. A row naturally ensued, Simpson beat out the trainer's brains with his heavy stick without receiving any injury from the small knife which Straker used in self-defence, and then the thief either led the horse on to some secret hiding-place, or else it may have bolted during the struggle, and be now wandering out on the moors. That is the case as it appears to the police, and improbable as it is, all other explanations are more improbable still. However, I shall very quickly test the matter when I am once upon the spot, and until then I really cannot see how we can get much further than our present position.'

It was evening before we reached the little town of Tavistock, which lies, like the boss of a shield, in the middle of the huge circle of Dartmoor. Two gentlemen were awaiting us at the station; the one a tall fair man with lion-like hair and beard, and curiously penetrating light blue eyes, the other a small alert person, very neat and dapper, in a frock-coat and gaiters, with trim little side-whiskers and an eyeglass. The latter was Colonel Ross, the well-known sportsman, the other Inspector Gregory, a man who was rapidly making his name in the English detective service.

'I am delighted that you have come down, Mr Holmes,' said the Colonel. 'The Inspector here has done all that could possibly be suggested; but I wish to leave no stone unturned in trying to avenge poor Straker, and in recovering my horse.'

'Have there been any fresh developments?' asked Holmes.

'I am sorry to say that we have made very little progress,' said the Inspector. 'We have an open carriage outside, and as you would no doubt like to see the place before the light fails, we might talk it over as we drive.'

A minute later we were all seated in a comfortable landau and were rattling through the quaint old Devonshire town. Inspector

Gregory was full of his case, and poured out a stream of remarks, while Holmes threw in an occasional question or interjection. Colonel Ross leaned back with his arms folded and his hat tilted over his eyes, while I listened with interest to the dialogue of the two detectives. Gregory was formulating his theory, which was almost exactly what Holmes had foretold in the train.

'The net is drawn pretty close round Fitzroy Simpson,' he remarked, 'and I believe myself that he is our man. At the same time, I recognize that the evidence is purely circumstantial, and that some new development may upset it?'

'How about Straker's knife?'

'We have quite come to the conclusion that he wounded himself in his fall.'

'My friend Dr Watson made that suggestion to me as we came down. If so, it would tell against this man Simpson.'

'Undoubtedly. He has neither a knife nor any sign of a wound. The evidence against him is certainly very strong. He had a great interest in the disappearance of the favourite, he lies under the suspicion of having poisoned the stable-boy, he was undoubtedly out in the storm, he was armed with a heavy stick, and his cravat was found in the dead man's hand. I really think we have enough to go before a jury.'

Holmes shook his head. 'A clever counsel would tear it all to rags,' said he. 'Why should he take the horse out of the stable? If he wished to injure it, why could he not do it there? Has a duplicate key been found in his possession? What chemist sold him the powdered opium? Above all, where could he, a stranger to the district, hide a horse, and such a horse as this? What is his own explanation as to the paper which he wished the maid to give to the stable-boy?'

'He says that it was a ten-pound note. One was found in his purse. But your other difficulties are not so formidable as they seem. He is not a stranger to the district. He has twice lodged at Tavistock in the summer. The opium was probably brought from London. The key, having served its purpose, would be hurled away. The horse may lie at the bottom of one of the pits or old mines upon the moor.'

'What does he says about the cravat?'

'He acknowledges that it is his, and declares that he had lost it. But a new element has been introduced into the case which may account for his leading the horse from the stable.'

Holmes pricked up his ears.

'We have found traces which show that a party of gipsies encamped on Monday night within a mile of the spot where the murder took place. On Tuesday they were gone. Now, presuming that there was some understanding between Simpson and these gipsies, might he not have been leading the horse to them when he was overtaken, and may they not have him now?'

'It is certainly possible.'

'The moor is being scoured for these gipsies. I have also examined every stable and outhouse in Tavistock, and for a radius of ten miles.'

'There is another training stable quite close, I understand?'

'Yes, and that is a factor which we must certainly not neglect. As Desborough, their horse, was second in the betting, they had an interest in the disappearance of the favourite. Silas Brown, the trainer, is known to have had large bets upon the event, and he was no friend to poor Straker. We have, however, examined the stables, and there is nothing to connect him with the affair.'

'And nothing to connect this man Simpson with the interests of the Capleton stable?'

'Nothing at all.'

Holmes leaned back in the carriage and the conversation ceased. A few minutes later our driver pulled up at a neat little red-brick villa with overhanging eaves, which stood by the road. Some distance off, across a paddock, lay a long grey-tiled outbuilding. In every other direction the low curves of the moor, bronze-coloured from the fading ferns, stretched away to the skyline, broken only by the steeples of Tavistock, and by a cluster of houses away to the westward, which marked the Capleton stables. We all sprang out with the exception of Holmes, who continued to lean back with his eyes fixed upon the sky in front of him, entirely absorbed in his own thoughts. It was only when I touched his arm that he roused himself with a violent start and stepped out of the carriage.

'Excuse me,' said he, turning to Colonel Ross, who had looked at him in some surprise. 'I was day-dreaming.' There was a gleam in his eyes and a suppressed excitement in his manner which convinced me, used as I was to his ways, that his hand was upon a clue, though I could not imagine where he had found it.

'Perhaps you would prefer at once to go on to the scene of the crime, Mr Holmes?' said Gregory.

'I think that I should prefer to stay here a little and go into one or two questions of detail. Straker was brought back here, I presume?'

'Yes, he lies upstairs. The inquest is tomorrow.'

'He has been in your service some years, Colonel Ross?'

'I have always found him an excellent servant.'

'I presume that you made an inventory of what he had in his pockets at the time of his death, Inspector?'

'I have the things themselves in the sitting-room, if you would care to see them.'

'I should be very glad.'

We all filed into the front room, and sat round the central table, where the Inspector unlocked a square tin box and laid a small heap of things before us. There was a box of vestas, two inches of tallow candle, an A.D.P. briar-root pipe, a pouch of sealskin with half an ounce of long-cut cavendish, a silver watch with a gold chain, five sovereigns in gold, an aluminium pencil-case, a few papers, and an ivory-handle knife with a very delicate inflexible blade marked Weiss & Co., London.

'This is a very singular knife,' said Holmes, lifting it up and examining it minutely. 'I presume, as I see bloodstains upon it, that it is the one which was found in the dead man's grasp. Watson, this knife is surely in your line.'

'It is what we call a cataract knife,' said I.

'I thought so. A very delicate blade devised for very delicate work. A strange thing for a man to carry with him upon a rough expedition, especially as it would not shut in his pocket.'

'The tip was guarded by a disc of cork which we found beside his body,' said the Inspector. 'His wife tells us that the knife had lain for some days upon the dressing-table, and that he had picked it up as he left the room. It was a poor weapon, but perhaps the best that he could lay his hand on at the moment.'

'Very possible. How about these papers?'

'Three of them are receipted hay-dealers' accounts. One of them is a letter of instructions from Colonel Ross. This other is a milliner's account for thirty-seven pounds fifteen, made out by Madame Lesurier, of Bond Street, to William Darbyshire. Mrs Straker tells us that Darbyshire was a friend of her husband's, and that occasionally his letters were addressed here.'

'Madame Darbyshire had somewhat expensive tastes,' remarked

Holmes, glancing down the account. 'Twenty-two guineas is rather heavy for a single costume. However, there appears to be nothing more to learn, and we may now go down to the scene of the crime.'

As we emerged from the sitting-room a woman who had been waiting in the passage took a step forward and laid her hand upon the Inspector's sleeve. Her face was haggard, and thin, and eager; stamped with the print of a recent horror.

'Have you got them? Have you found them?' she panted.

'No, Mrs Straker; but Mr Holmes, here, has come from London to help us, and we shall do all that is possible.'

'Surely I met you in Plymouth, at a garden-party, some little time ago, Mrs Straker,' said Holmes.

'No, sir; you are mistaken.'

'Dear me; why, I could have sworn to it. You wore a costume of dove-coloured silk with ostrich feather trimming.'

'I never had such a dress, sir,' answered the lady.

'Ah; that quite settles it,' said Holmes; and, with an apology, he followed the Inspector outside. A short walk across the moor took us to the hollow in which the body had been found. At the brink of it was the furze bush upon which the coat had been hung.

'There was no wind that night, I understand,' said Holmes.

'None; but very heavy rain.'

'In that case the overcoat was not blown against the furze bushes, but placed there.'

'Yes, it was laid across the bush.'

'You fill me with interest. I perceive that the ground has been trampled up a good deal. No doubt many feet have been there since Monday night.'

'A piece of matting has been laid here at the side, and we have all stood upon that.'

'Excellent.'

'In this bag I have one of the boots which Straker wore, one of Fitzroy Simpson's shoes, and a cast horseshoe of Silver Blaze.'

'My dear Inspector, you surpass yourself!'

Holmes took the bag, and descending into the hollow he pushed the matting into a more central position. Then stretching himself upon his face and leaning his chin upon his hands he made a careful study of the trampled mud in front of him.

'Halloa!' said he, suddenly, 'what's this?'

It was a wax vesta, half burned, which was so coated with mud that it looked at first like a little chip of wood.

'I cannot think how I came to overlook it,' said the Inspector, with an expression of annoyance.

'It was invisible, buried in the mud. I only saw it because I was looking for it.'

'What! You expected to find it?'

'I thought it not unlikely.' He took the boots from the bag and compared the impressions of each of them with marks upon the ground. Then he clambered up to the rim of the hollow and crawled about among the ferns and bushes.

'I am afraid that there are no more tracks,' said the Inspector. 'I have examined the ground very carefully for a hundred yards in each direction.'

'Indeed!' said Holmes, rising, 'I should not have the impertinence to do it again after what you say. But I should like to take a little walk over the moors before it grows dark, that I may know my ground tomorrow, and I think that I shall put this horseshoe into my pocket for luck.'

Colonel Ross, who had shown some signs of impatience at my companion's quiet and systematic method of work, glanced at his watch.

'I wish you would come back with me, Inspector,' said he. 'There are several points on which I should like your advice, and especially as to whether we do not owe it to the public to remove our horse's name from the entries for the Cup.'

'Certainly not,' cried Holmes, with decision; 'I should let the name stand.'

The Colonel bowed. 'I am very glad to have had your opinion, sir,' said he. 'You will find us at poor Straker's house when you have finished your walk, and we can drive together into Tavistock.'

He turned back with the Inspector, while Holmes and I walked slowly across the moor. The sun was beginning to sink behind the stables of Capleton, and the long sloping plain in front of us was tinged with gold, deepening into rich, ruddy brown where the faded ferns and brambles caught the evening light. But the glories of the landscape were all wasted upon my companion, who was sunk in the deepest thought.

'It's this way, Watson,' he said, at last. 'We may leave the question of who killed John Straker for the instant, and confine ourselves to finding out what has become of the horse. Now, supposing that he broke away during or after the tragedy, where could he have gone to? The horse is a very gregarious creature. If left to himself, his instincts would have been either to return to King's Pyland or go over to Capleton. Why should he run wild upon the moor? He would surely have been seen by now. And why should gipsies kidnap him? These people always clear out when they hear of trouble, for they do not wish to be pestered by the police. They could not hope to sell such a horse. They would run a great risk and gain nothing by taking him. Surely that is clear.'

'Where is he, then?'

'I have already said that he must have gone to King's Pyland or to Capleton. He is not at King's Pyland, therefore he is at Capleton. Let us take that as a working hypothesis, and see what it leads us to. This part of the moor, as the Inspector remarked, is very hard and dry. But it falls away towards Capleton, and you can see from here that there is a long hollow over yonder, which must have been very wet on Monday night. If our supposition is correct, then the horse must have crossed that, and there is the point where we should look for his tracks.'

We had been walking briskly during this conversation, and a few more minutes brought us to the hollow in question. At Holmes' request I walked down the bank to the right, and he to the left, but I had not taken fifty paces before I heard him give a shout, and saw him waving his hand to me. The track of a horse was plainly outlined in the soft earth in front of him, and the shoe which he took from his pocket exactly fitted the impression.

'See the value of imagination,' said Holmes. 'It is the one quality which Gregory lacks. We imagined what might have happened, acted upon the supposition, and find ourselves justified. Let us proceed.'

We crossed the marshy bottom and passed over a quarter of a mile of dry, hard turf. Again the ground sloped and again we came on the tracks. Then we lost them for half a mile, but only to pick them up once more quite close to Capleton. It was Holmes who saw them first, and he stood pointing with a look of triumph upon his face. A man's track was visible beside the horse's.

'The horse was alone before,' I cried.

'Quite so. It was alone before. Halloa! what is this?'

The double track turned sharp off and took the direction of King's Pyland. Holmes whistled, and we both followed along after it. His eyes were on the trail, but I happened to look a little to one side, and saw to my surprise the same tracks coming back again in the opposite direction.

'One for you, Watson,' said Holmes, when I pointed it out; 'you have saved us a long walk which would have brought us back on our own traces. Let us follow the return track.'

We had not to go far. It ended at the paving of asphalt which led up to the gates of the Capleton stables. As we approached a groom ran out from them.

'We don't want any loiterers about here,' said he.

'I only wished to ask a question,' said Holmes, with his finger and thumb in his waistcoat pocket. 'Should I be too early to see your master, Mr Silas Brown, if I were to call at five o'clock tomorrow morning?'

'Bless you, sir, if anyone is about he will be, for he is always the first stirring. But here he is, sir, to answer your questions for himself. No, sir, no; it's as much as my place is worth to let him see me touch your money. Afterwards, if you like.'

As Sherlock Holmes replaced the half-crown which he had drawn from his pocket, a fierce-looking elderly man strode out from the gate with a hunting-crop swinging in his hand.

'What's this, Dawson?' he cried. 'No gossiping! Go about your business! And you – what the devil do you want here?'

'Ten minutes' talk with you, my good sir,' said Holmes, in the sweetest of voices.

'I've no time to talk to every gadabout. We want no strangers here. Be off, or you may find a dog at your heels.'

Holmes leaned forward and whispered something in the trainer's ear. He started violently and flushed to the temples.

'It's a lie!' he shouted. 'An infernal lie!'

'Very good! Shall we argue about it here in public, or talk it over in your parlour?'

'Oh, come in if you wish to.'

Holmes smiled. 'I shall not keep you more than a few minutes, Watson,' he said. 'Now, Mr Brown, I am quite at your disposal.'

It was quite twenty minutes, and the reds had all faded into greys before Holmes and the trainer reappeared. Never have I seen such a change as had been brought about in Silas Brown in that short time. His face was ashy pale, beads of perspiration shone upon his brow, and his hands shook until the hunting-crop wagged like a branch in the wind. His bullying, overbearing manner was all gone too, and he cringed along at my companion's side like a dog with its master.

'Your instructions will be done. It shall be done,' said he.

'There must be no mistake,' said Holmes, looking round at him. The other winced as he read the menace in his eyes.

'Oh, no, there shall be no mistake. It shall be there. Should I change it first or not?'

Holmes thought a little and then burst out laughing. 'No, don't,' said he. 'I shall write to you about it. No tricks now or —'

'Oh, you can trust me, you can trust me!'

'You must see to it on the day as if it were your own.'

'You can rely upon me.'

'Yes, I think I can. Well, you shall hear from me tomorrow.' He turned upon his heel, disregarding the trembling hand which the other held out to him, and we set off for King's Pyland.

'A more perfect compound of the bully, coward and sneak than Master Silas Brown I have seldom met with,' remarked Holmes, as we trudged along together.

'He has the horse, then?'

'He tried to bluster out of it, but I described to him so exactly what his actions had been upon that morning, that he is convinced that I was watching him. Of course, you observed the peculiarly square toes in the impressions, and that his own boots exactly corresponded to them. Again, of course, no subordinate would have dared to have done such a thing. I described to him how when, according to his custom, he was the first down, he perceived a strange horse wandering over the moor; how he went out to it, and his astonishment at recognizing from the white forehead which has given the favourite its name that chance had put in his power the only horse which could beat the one upon which he had put his money. Then I described how his first impulse had been to lead him back to King's Pyland, and how the devil had shown him how he could hide the horse until the race was over, and how he had led it back and concealed it at Capleton. When I told him every detail he gave it up, and thought only of saving his own skin.'

'But his stables had been searched.'

'Oh, an old horse-faker like him has many a dodge.'

'But are you not afraid to leave the horse in his power now, since he has every interest in injuring it?'

'My dear fellow, he will guard it as the apple of his eye. He knows that his only hope of mercy is to produce it safe.'

'Colonel Ross did not impress me as a man who would be likely to show much mercy in any case.'

'The matter does not rest with Colonel Ross. I follow my own methods, and tell as much or as little as I choose. That is the advantage of being unofficial. I don't know whether you observed it, Watson, but the Colonel's manner has been just a trifle cavalier to me. I am inclined now to have a little amusement at his expense. Say nothing to him about the horse.'

'Certainly not, without your permission.'

'And, of course, this is all quite a minor case compared with the question of who killed John Straker.'

'And you will devote yourself to that?'

'On the contrary, we both go back to London by the night train.'

I was thunderstruck by my friend's words. We had only been a few hours in Devonshire, and that he should give up an investigation which he had begun so brilliantly was quite incomprehensible to me. Not a word more could I draw from him until we were back at the trainer's house. The Colonel and the Inspector were awaiting us in the parlour.

'My friend and I return to town by the midnight express,' said Holmes. 'We have had a charming little breath of your beautiful Dartmoor air.'

The Inspector opened his eyes, and the Colonel's lips curled in a sneer.

'So you despair of arresting the murderer of poor Straker,' said he.

Holmes shrugged his shoulders. 'There are certainly grave difficulties in the way,' said he. 'I have every hope, however, that your horse will start upon Tuesday, and I beg that you will have your jockey in readiness. Might I ask for a photograph of Mr John Straker?'

The Inspector took one from an envelope in his pocket and handed it to him.

'My dear Gregory, you anticipate all my wants. If I might ask you to wait here for an instant, I have a question which I should like to put to the maid.'

'I must say that I am rather disappointed in our London consultant,' said Colonel Ross, bluntly, as my friend left the room. 'I do not see that we are any further than when he came.'

'At least, you have his assurance that your horse will run,' said I.

'Yes, I have his assurance,' said the Colonel, with a shrug of his shoulders. 'I should prefer to have the horse.'

I was about to make some reply in defence of my friend, when he entered the room again.

'Now, gentlemen,' said he, 'I am quite ready for Tavistock.'

As we stepped into the carriage one of the stable-lads held the door open for us. A sudden idea seemed to occur to Holmes, for he leaned forward and touched the lad upon the sleeve.

'You have a few sheep in the paddock,' he said. 'Who attends to them?'

'I do, sir.'

'Have you noticed anything amiss with them of late?'

'Well, sir, not of much account; but three of them have gone lame, sir.'

I could see that Holmes was extremely pleased, for he chuckled and rubbed his hands together.

'A long shot, Watson; a very long shot!' said he, pinching my arm. 'Gregory, let me recommend to your attention this singular epidemic among the sheep. Drive on, coachman!'

Colonel Ross still wore an expression which showed the poor opinion which he had formed of my companion's ability, but I saw by the Inspector's face that his attention had been keenly aroused.

'You consider that to be important?' he asked.

'Exceedingly so.'

'Is there any other point to which you would wish to draw my attention?'

'To the curious incident of the dog in the night-time.'

'The dog did nothing in the night-time.'

'That was the curious incident,' remarked Sherlock Holmes.

Four days later Holmes and I were again in the train bound for Winchester, to see the race for the Wessex Cup. Colonel Ross met us, by appointment, outside the station, and we drove in his drag to the course beyond the town. His face was grave and his manner was cold in the extreme.

'I have seen nothing of my horse,' said he.

'I suppose that you would know him when you saw him?' asked Holmes.

The Colonel was very angry. 'I have been on the turf for twenty years, and never was asked such a question as that before,' said he. 'A child would know Silver Blaze with his white forehead and his mottled off foreleg.'

'How is the betting?'

'Well, that is the curious part of it. You could have got fifteen to one yesterday, but the price has become shorter and shorter, until you can hardly get three to one now.'

'Hum!' said Holmes. 'Somebody knows something, that is clear!'

As the drag drew up in the enclosure near the grandstand, I glanced at the card to see the entries. It ran:

Wessex Plate. 50 sovs. each, h ft, with 1,000 sovs. added, for four- and five-years olds. Second £300. Third £200. New course (one mile and five furlongs).

1. Mr Heath Newton's The Negro (red cap, cinnamon jacket).
2. Colonel Wardlaw's Pugilist (pink cap, blue and black jacket).
3. Lord Backwater's Desborough (yellow cap and sleeves).
4. Colonel Ross's Silver Blaze (black cap, red jacket).
5. Duke of Balmoral's Iris (yellow and black stripes).
6. Lord Singleford's Rasper (purple cap, black sleeves).

'We scratched our other one and put all hopes on your word,' said the Colonel. 'Why, what is that? Silver Blaze favourite?'

'Five to four against Silver Blaze!' roared the ring. 'Five to four against Silver Blaze! Fifteen to five against Desborough! Five to four on the field!'

'There are the numbers up,' I cried. 'They are all six there.'

'All six there! Then my horse is running,' cried the Colonel, in great agitation. 'But I don't see him. My colours have not passed.'

'Only five have passed. This must be he.'

As I spoke a powerful bay horse swept out from the weighing enclosure and cantered past us, bearing on its back the well-known black and red of the Colonel.

'That's not my horse,' cried the owner. 'That beast has not a white hair upon its body. What is this that you have done, Mr Holmes?'

'Well, well, let us see how he gets on,' said my friend, imperturbably. For a few minutes he gazed through my field-glass. 'Capital! An excellent start!' he cried suddenly. 'There they are, coming round the curve!'

From our drag we had a superb view as they came up the straight. The six horses were so close together that a carpet could have covered them, but half-way up the yellow of the Capleton stable showed to the front. Before they reached us, however, Desborough's bolt was shot, and the Colonel's horse, coming away with a rush, passed the post a good six lengths before its rival, the Duke of Balmoral's Iris making a bad third.

'It's my race anyhow,' gasped the Colonel, passing his hand over his eyes. 'I confess that I can make neither head nor tail of it. Don't you think that you have kept up your mystery long enough, Mr Holmes?'

'Certainly, Colonel. You shall know everything. Let us all go round and have a look at the horse together. Here he is,' he continued, as we made our way into the weighing enclosure where only owners and their friends find admittance. 'You have only to wash his face and his leg in spirits of wine and you will find that he is the same old Silver Blaze as ever.'

'You take my breath away!'

'I found him in the hands of a faker, and took the liberty of running him just as he was sent over.'

'My dear sir, you have done wonders. The horse looks very fit and well. It never went better in its life. I owe you a thousand apologies for having doubted your ability. You have done me a great service by recovering my horse. You would do me a greater still if you could lay your hands on the murderer of John Straker.'

'I have done so,' said Holmes, quietly.

The Colonel and I stared at him in amazement. 'You have got him! Where is he, then?'

'He is here.'

'Here! Where?'

'In my company at the present moment.'

The Colonel flushed angrily. 'I quite recognize that I am under obligations to you, Mr Holmes,' said he, 'but I must regard what you have just said as either a very bad joke or an insult.'

Sherlock Holmes laughed. 'I assure you that I have not associated you with the crime, Colonel,' said he; 'the real murderer is standing immediately behind you!'

He stepped past and laid his hand upon the glossy neck of the thoroughbred.

'The horse!' cried both the Colonel and myself.

'Yes, the horse. And it may lessen his guilt if I say that it was done in self-defence, and that John Straker was a man who was entirely unworthy of your confidence. But there goes the bell; and as I stand to win a little on this next race, I shall defer a more lengthy explanation until a more fitting time.'

We had the corner of the Pullman car to ourselves that evening as we whirled back to London, and I fancy that the journey was a short one to Colonel Ross as well as to myself, as we listened to our companion's narrative of the events which had occurred at the Dartmoor training stables upon that Monday night, and the means by which he had unravelled them.

'I confess,' said he, 'that any theories which I had formed from the newspaper reports were entirely erroneous. And yet there were indications there, had they not been overlaid by other details which concealed their true import. I went to Devonshire with the conviction that Fitzroy Simpson was the true culprit, although, of course, I saw that the evidence against him was by no means complete.

'It was while I was in the carriage, just as we reached the trainer's house, that the immense significance of the curried mutton occurred to me. You may remember that I was distrait, and remained sitting after you had all alighted. I was marvelling in my own mind how I could possibly have overlooked so obvious a clue.'

'I confess,' said the Colonel, 'that even now I cannot see how it helps us.'

'It was the first link in my chain of reasoning. Powdered opium is by no means tasteless. The flavour is not disagreeable, but it is perceptible. Were it mixed with any ordinary dish, the eater would undoubtedly detect it, and would probably eat no more. A curry was exactly the medium which would disguise this taste. By no possible supposition could this stranger, Fitzroy Simpson, have caused curry to be served in the trainer's family that night, and it is surely too monstrous a coincidence to suppose that he happened to come along with powdered opium upon the very night when a dish happened to be served which would disguise the flavour. That is unthinkable. Therefore Simpson becomes eliminated from the case, and our attention centres upon Straker and his wife, the only two people who could have chosen curried mutton for supper that night. The opium was added after the dish was set aside for the stable-boy, for the others had the same for supper with no ill effects. Which of them, then, had access to that dish without the maid seeing them?

'Before deciding that question I had grasped the significance of the silence of the dog, for one true inference invariably suggests others. The Simpson incident had shown me that a dog was kept in the stables, and yet, though someone had been in and had fetched out a horse, he had not barked enough to arouse the two lads in the loft. Obviously the midnight visitor was someone whom the dog knew well.

'I was already convinced, or almost convinced, that John Straker went down to the stables in the dead of the night and took out Silver Blaze. For what purpose? For a dishonest one, obviously, or why should he drug his own stable-boy? And yet I was at a loss to know why. There have been cases before now where trainers have made sure of great sums of money by laying against their own horses, through agents, and then prevented them from winning by fraud. Sometimes it is a pulling jockey. Sometimes it is some surer and subtler means. What was it here? I hoped that the contents of his pocket might help me to form a conclusion.

'And they did so. You cannot have forgotten the singular knife which was found in the dead man's hand, a knife which certainly no sane man would choose for a weapon. It was, as Dr Watson told us, a form of knife which is used for the most delicate operations known in surgery. And it was to be used for a delicate operation that night. You must know, with your wide experience of turf matters, Colonel Ross, that it is possible to make a slight nick upon the tendons of a horse's ham, and to do it subcutaneously so as to leave absolutely no trace. A horse so treated would develop a slight lameness which would be put down to a strain in exercise or a touch of rheumatism, but never to foul play.'

'Villain! Scoundrel!' cried the Colonel.

'We have here the explanation of why John Straker wished to take the horse out on to the moor. So spirited a creature would have certainly roused the soundest of sleepers when it felt the prick of the knife. It was absolutely necessary to do it in the open air.'

'I have been blind!' cried the Colonel. 'Of course, that was why he needed the candle, and struck the match.'

'Undoubtedly: But in examining his belongings, I was fortunate enough to discover, not only the method of the crime, but even its motives. As a man of the world, Colonel, you know that men do not carry other people's bills about in their pockets. We have most of us quite enough to do to settle our own. I at once concluded that Straker was leading a double life, and keeping a second establishment. The nature of the bill showed that there was a lady in the case, and one who had expensive tastes: liberal as you are with your servants, one hardly expects that they can buy twenty-guinea walking dresses for their women. I questioned Mrs Straker as to the dress without her knowing it, and having satisfied myself that it had never reached her, I made a note of the milliner's address, and felt that by calling there with Straker's photograph, I could easily dispose of the mythical Darbyshire.

'From that time on all was plain. Straker had led out the horse to a hollow where his light would be invisible. Simpson, in his flight, had dropped his cravat, and Straker had picked it up with some idea, perhaps, that he might use it in securing the horse's leg. Once in the hollow he had got behind the horse, and had struck a light, but the creature, frightened at the sudden glare, and with the strange instinct of animals feeling that some mischief was intended, had lashed out, and the steel shoe had struck Straker full on the forehead. He had already, in spite of the rain, taken off his overcoat in order to do his delicate task, and so, as he fell, his knife gashed his thigh. Do I make it clear?'

'Wonderful!' cried the Colonel. 'Wonderful! You might have been there.'

'My final shot was, I confess, a very long one. It struck me that so astute a man as Straker would not undertake this delicate tendon-nicking without a little practice. What could he practise on? My eyes fell upon the sheep, and I asked a question which, rather to my surprise, showed that my surmise was correct.'

'You have made it perfectly clear, Mr Holmes.'

'When I returned to London I called upon the milliner, who at once recognized Straker as an excellent customer, of the name of

Darbyshire, who had a very dashing wife with a strong partiality for expensive dresses. I have no doubt that this woman had plunged him over head and ears in debt, and so led him into this miserable plot.'

'You have explained all but one thing,' cried the Colonel. 'Where was the horse?'

'Ah, it bolted and was cared for by one of your neighbours. We must have an amnesty in that direction, I think. This is Clapham Junction, if I am not mistaken, and we shall be in Victoria in less than ten minutes. If you care to smoke a cigar in our rooms, Colonel, I shall be happy to give you any other details which might interest you.'

A GLASS OF PORT
WITH THE PROCTOR

John Welcome

By the time my third year at the long-ago Oxford of the 1930s had come round, I had acquired some small – very small – proficiency in the business of sitting a horse at racing pace over fences and making a pretence of staying on him if things went wrong. This had not been achieved without a considerable amount of bruising and breaking, hard work, dedication, disappointment, toil and sweat but as a result I had been permitted to become a sort of associate member in the unholy alliance between my best friend, Brian Manson, and his trainer Mr Alfred Kerrell who ran a racing stable of sorts out Headington way.

Brian was a tough, hard-bitten, rich young man with no interests in life beyond hunting and racing; Mr Kerrell was middle-aged – at least we thought he was; I imagine he was about forty – impecunious and every bit as tough and hard-bitten as Brian with the added cunning and experience which the years had given him. When the two of them were not combining to defeat a third party, they waged between themselves a bitter and unremitting battle of wits. In this power-game I acted as a pawn pushed hither and thither, now the ally of one, then of the other in their schemes, connivances, disasters and occasional triumphs.

It was, however, an accolade of sorts to be allowed to act as a most minor member of what was then a triumvirate and I had recently shared in a lucky touch when Brian and Kerrell brought one up at a long price in a hurdle at Stratford. This had enabled me to buy a point-to-point horse or, rather, Kerrell to buy one for me. He was a big rangy bay who had been given at some stage of his career the extraordinary name of The Circus probably because on his near side he bore a large circular white mark rather like an aircraft roundel. As his markings were individual so was his character. He liked his own way and I was only too anxious to give it to him.

Kerrell, as happens with some exceptional dealers and trainers, had the gift of matching horse and man. He knew that so far as I was concerned all that I could do in a race was to sit still and try to stay on, and that this was exactly the sort of rider the old horse needed to get the best out of him. Once you left him alone he was a superb conveyance only needing a hiss and a squeeze to change into top gear at the end of a race and display, as we all discovered to our astonishment, a surprising turn of foot.

Brian spoke scathingly about passengers on horseback as he watched us in action and when he was told by Kerrell to sit up on The Circus and ride him in a school he caught hold of his head and sent him along in real racing fashion. As a result he was promptly deposited into the bottom of the first fence they met, and I noticed that he did not appear unduly anxious to ride him again.

Anyway I won three open point-to-points on the trot with him and then began to get ideas above my station. After consultation with Kerrell I entered him in a Hunters' Chase at a meeting in Kent.

Brian just then had been having a run of bad luck but he had a point-to-pointer that could go more than a bit and which he had been saving up for something. Never anything other than contemptuous of my abilities, he entered this horse called, as far as I can remember, Jack Go Nimble, in the same Hunters' Chase. Having done so, he made open fun at my temerity in taking him on and Kerrell's foolishness in allowing me to do so. But as The Circus began to go better and better on the gallops he could be seen to be wearing a slightly pensive look. This was an expression that I knew well and had reason to fear for it invariably meant he was searching in his mind, in order, to use his own phrase, 'to think something up'.

Kerrell noticed it too. A day or two before the race he took me aside. 'You'll be all right, sir, you'll find,' he said. 'I haven't told him but yours is a stone better than his. I think we'll have a bet.'

'I wish I knew what was going on inside his head,' I said.

'Nobody, unless it's the Archangel Gabriel, knows that,' Kerrell said, 'and even he isn't going to help him much.'

'I don't suppose he'll call him in anyway,' I said. 'He'd be a bit conspicuous on a racecourse with all those wings. It'd more likely be Lucifer.'

'Ha,' said Kerrell, 'They'd be well-matched those two.' He spoke feelingly. A bloodlike brown horse with all the stamp of a Leicestershire hunter on him had recently passed from his ownership to Brian's. I didn't know the details of the transaction but from what I had gathered the sale or transfer had not been an entirely willing one and it was evident that its circumstances still rankled.

Brian and I had arranged to meet in the Mitre tavern for a drink the evening before the race. I was walking along The Turl when he caught me up. He appeared to have been running and was slightly out of breath. 'Go on in and order,' he said. 'I've got to see a man in B.N.C. I'll be along in a minute or two.'

I was sitting on a bench with a glass of beer on the table in front of me, waiting for him, when I felt my shoulder touched. Turning round I saw a large man in a bowler hat and a blue suit looking down at me. He was a proctor's bulldog. The proctorial procession was formed by a member of the disciplinary staff of the University attended by an escort of ex-N.C.O.s who were called bulldogs or, more familiarly 'bullers'. This procession wound its solemn way around the public houses of the city summoning undergraduates found on their premises to appear before the proctors and suffer a fine, since drinking in a public house was, by some absurd survival of the old days of town and gown violence, forbidden to undergraduates by University decree. I believe this ridiculous ban has been long since abolished.

'Excuse me, sir, are you a member of the University?' the bulldog enquired courteously.

'Yes,' I said. 'I am.'

'Ah,' said the proctor. 'Your name and college then, please.'

When I had given these to him he wrote them down in a little book. 'Kindly attend at the proctor's office at ten thirty tomorrow morning,' he said. The procession then left the public house and, a minute or two later, Brian came in. The full enormity of what had happened was only just beginning to become clear to me when he sat down opposite me.

'I've been progged,' I said.

'Bad luck, I saw them coming out.'

'Yes, but look, that means I won't be able to ride in the Hunters' Chase tomorrow. What time are you leaving?'

'Nine o'clock. It's a long way. No, you won't will you? We're all going on with the horses. Drink's an evil, isn't it? Have another?'

'Wait a bit,' I said, as something struck me. 'There's no rule against undergraduates riding in steeplechases, at least I don't think there is.'

'Isn't there? Of course there is. There must be.'

'I don't care. I'm going after him to see if he'll change the date. They're supposed to send a note around anyway.'

'Don't be a fool. He'll gate you for a month and then where'll you be?'

But I was already out of the door and running up the slope to the Turl. I caught up with the proctorial procession just as it was turning into the High.

'Excuse me, sir,' I said to the proctor.

He turned round and I noticed that he was rather older than the usual run of young dons who performed these duties. I was also aware of a pair of very bright, sardonic eyes which regarded me steadily. 'Yes, well, what is it? And speak up Mr – Er —. I'm a little deaf from a —'

'I wonder, sir, could you change the time of that appointment tomorrow morning?' I blurted out. 'You see I'm riding in a Hunters' Chase tomorrow and I won't be able to if —'

'God bless my soul. *What* did you say?'

'I'm riding in a Hunters' Chase tomorrow,' I shouted desperately at him.

'There is no need to raise the dead. I am not quite stone deaf. Mr – er – Welcome, I think it is, are you aware that this University is supposedly a seat of learning? Might I be informed what school you grace with your studies?'

'I'm reading law, sir.'

'Jurisprudence and steeplechasing. A strange juxtaposition.'

The conversation was rapidly taking on a sort of Alice in Wonderland quality. I think that was what made me say next: 'F. E. Smith used to ride in point-to-points, sir.'

'Scarcely a recommendation for a steady career at the bar. He also earned the name of "Galloper" as I recall. Am I to understand you wish to follow in his footsteps? Perhaps in one respect you may in view of where we have just met.'

'But its awfully important to me,' I said, miserably. 'It's my first chase and I think I have a chance.'

'Indeed. Mr Welcome, don't you think a racing stable would be a more suitable home for your talents?'

'Well, no, sir. It's difficult to explain if you sort of don't know about it, but I don't think I could go on as an amateur if I went to a racing stable and anyway I doubt if any racing stable would have me!'

'So this University which, may I remind you, was originally started as a home for poor scholars has to house you instead. But not, I fancy for very long.'

'But you see, sir,' I said desperately, 'it is usual, I think, to send a note around. It's such short notice and it means so much to me —'

He looked at me sternly. Then a quirk appeared at the corners of his mouth. 'Mr Welcome,' he said. 'You have at least one essential of successful advocacy which you appear to share with that great man you have just mentioned – audacity. On this occasion it has served you well. I accept your arguments and I hold in your favour though with the greatest reluctance. Very well then. Call on me at ten-thirty on Monday instead.' He turned to go. Then suddenly he stopped. 'Mr Welcome!'

'Yes, sir.'

'At what time do you propose to return from this field of battle to-morrow?'

'I'm going to dine in hall, sir.'

'I see. Then perhaps you'd do me the pleasure of having a glass of port with me after dinner in my rooms. I have long wanted to know the exact meaning and derivation of those strange racing animals a pony and a monkey. Perhaps you can explain these and other arcane mysteries to me.'

'Yes, sir, I'll try, sir. And, I say, sir, thank you, sir.'

'My pleasure, Mr Welcome. And, Mr Welcome, may I also wish you good luck?' With a swirl of his gown he was gone down the High and I was left to try to collect my scattered wits.

As they came back to me, I began to see one or two things very clearly. Brian had been in a hurry when he met me in the Turl, in fact he had been running. When we had arranged to meet he had said nothing about seeing someone in B.N.C. I doubted very much if he knew anyone in that College which was then crammed to bursting with bruisers who played Rugby Football. However much he decried my abilities, it was obviously to his advantage if The Circus and I should not compete tomorrow. Might it not very well be that he had encountered the progs on their way and then made sure that I was in the Mitre and he was not when they came along the Turl? I resolved to say nothing at all to him about my success with the proctor.

Back in the pub my suspicions were more or less confirmed. Brian had an evening paper open at the racing page in front of him, but he was not reading it. He was sipping his beer with the expression on his face of a cat who has just stolen a jug of cream and got away with it. I had seen him looking like that before when he had just taken advantage of an unexpected stroke of luck. 'Well, how did that go?' he said.

'More or less what you thought. He threatened to fine me double tomorrow for impertinence.'

'Well, what did you expect? You took the hell of a chance.' He picked up the paper. 'I see,' he said, 'that I am quoted at 10–1 tomorrow. That's quite a nice price.'

'Just as a matter of interest what is The Circus?'

'50–1 others. Let's have the other half. Don't look so glum. At least you won't fall off and break your neck.'

When we had finished our drinks I made my way back to my College and went into the telephone booth in the porter's lodge. There I rang up Kerrell and told him what had happened and my suspicions.

'I knew he'd be up to something,' Kerrell observed with satisfaction. 'Don't worry, sir, we'll do him properly this time. I'll send the horse on and tell him I advised you to get a race into him. I won't go with them at all. I can say I have something urgent to do in Oxford. Then I'll pick you up outside your digs in my car and bring you on myself.'

'That sounds just the job,' I said. 'Thanks, Mr Kerrell.'

'Wait till he sees us turn up together at the meeting. He'll have something to think about then, I shouldn't wonder.'

Kerrell drove an Essex coupé with an English fabric body which he had bought somewhere for twenty-five pounds or had taken in a partial swop for a horse, I forget which. Punctually to the minute he was there waiting for me the following morning parked at the pavement outside my digs. I put my bag containing my racing clothes in the back and away we went along the empty roads of that forgotten time on our long cold drive to the races.

When we approached the course, Kerrell pulled the car to the side of the road and stopped. He opened the door and got out. 'No need to tell Mr Manson we've arrived, until we have to,' he said, 'We can walk the course from here.'

After crossing a couple of fields, we climbed a very insecure boundary fence and were on the track. It was roughly circular in shape and beyond the winning post the ground sloped down to a dip and climbed fairly steeply on the far side. It was, as Kerrell said, rather like 'a bloomin' bicycle track' and we had to go three times round it to complete the three miles two furlongs of the Hunters' Chase. The turf, however, was firm and sound and the fences were well made. Kerrell, like most of his kind, was not a believer in tying down a rider with a great deal of advice and instructions. As we tramped around, he confined himself to saying it was not a track on which to give away distance, not to make up ground going up the hill, and to be there or thereabouts after the third last.

I was in my usual state of jelly-like cowardice by this time but I did absorb something of what he said. When we returned to the Essex, he muttered something about having a bet. 'A fiver, I think,' he said. 'That'll do nicely at the price.'

I put my hand into my trouser pocket and pulled out five single pound notes. That left about fifteen shillings in cash between me and my bank manager if The Circus did not oblige. I handed them over silently. After all, Kerrell's training bills would be the first casualty if we failed to touch.

Outside the weighing-room we met Brian. When he saw me a heavy scowl appeared on his face. 'What the devil are you doing here?' he asked.

'I cut the progs,' I said.

'Did you then. You'll be sent down.'

'Change of plan. There's been a change of plan, sir,' Kerrell said.

'So I gather. I asked Bill Johnson to ride The Circus. Now I'll have to tell him he's not wanted.'

'That's right, sir. Lucky, isn't it? You know the old horse goes better for Mr Welcome than anyone else.'

Somehow, as usual, I got through the preliminaries without being sick. In the parade ring Kerrell materialized beside me. 'I've got the money on,' he said.

'What price are we?' I asked him. Though just at this moment it didn't seem to matter much. I was far too busy wondering if I'd fall off at the first and thinking it was highly likely.

'100–8,' Kerrell said.

That did wake some response in me. I thought I'd risked my fiver at fifties and said so.

'You never get these prices in a Hunters' Chase here,' was the answer. 'It's a small market. Even a tenner knocks it down.'

'What's Brian at?'

'Fives. Now, watch him, sir. He wants to win this one and he'll be up to something, mark my words. Not that it matters,' he added hastily, to cheer me up. 'You'll be all right, you'll find. Remember, you've a stone in hand.' Then his hand was under my leg and I was whisked into the saddle.

The start was to the left of the stands just at the beginning of the dip. I remembered to go up past the judge's box and then turned round to canter down. There were seven other runners most of them inexperienced bumpers like myself who were cheerfully or glumly apprehensive. Brian and, I think, one other, were the only hard-faced toughs who had lost the right to claim and who knew exactly what they were about.

At first all went well. I left The Circus severely alone and he swung along, pulling himself to the front at the beginning of the second circuit. He was jumping the fences easily and effortlessly out of his stride. There had been one or two fallers to thin the field and just after what would be the second last fence Brian joined me. He was sitting tight and looking grim. About half way between the two fences to my astonishment I saw him appear to begin to shake up his horse. Then he looked at me. 'What the hell are you doing sitting there like a traffic policeman?' he called across to me. 'Don't you know we finish this time?'

Up till then I'd been relaxed and comfortable on the old horse, delighted we were going on so well and not, I fear, concentrating very much on anything. When I heard those words all sorts of thoughts and fears sprang alive in my mind. Could Kerrell have made a mistake in his instructions to me? I hadn't read the article carefully. Maybe they'd changed it and altered the distance. Brian, after all, had forgotten more about racing than I'd ever learn. This was my first chase and here I was making a mess of it.

'Come on, you fool,' Brian shouted again. 'Don't hang about or you'll be in trouble.'

God! I would, too, if I didn't make some show of riding my horse at the finish and was up before the stewards for not trying. That decided me. I squeezed The Circus with my legs and went after Brian.

The Circus took the next fence like a rocket. I shook the reins at him. Away we went down the straight with myself giving the best imitation I could of riding a finish. No challenge came. The judge's box flashed. It all seemed too easy. It was.

As I commenced to pull up the first doubts came to me. The noises from the crowd on my left did not exactly sound like cheering. Soon I realized they were the very opposite. Boos, catcalls jeers and lurid remarks about my ancestry were coming from the cheaper rings. At that moment Brian came past me with a satisfied grin on his face. I knew then just what had happened. I had fallen right into his trap. I had won my race a mile too soon.

By this time he was four lengths in front and going away from me. Two of the other runners came and caught me, their riders' faces adorned with wide grins.

Then I did what I should have done some time ago. I began to concentrate. I remembered that Kerrell had said I had a stone in hand. Steadying the old horse, I set off down the hill trying to give him what time I could to get his breath back.

The Circus was by now of course thoroughly unsettled. He got too near the fence at the bottom of the hill and nearly jumped me off. When I had climbed back into the saddle, I saw the two in front going hell for leather after Brian. I thought to myself that they were doing exactly what I had been warned not to and might soon run out of steam. I let Circus lope along. He jumped the ditch at the top of the hill perfectly. By now he seemed to be settled once more into his stride, and to my delight, I saw that the others were beginning to come back to me. At the third last he jumped past them, and then there was only Brian to beat.

I was alongside him at the next and when we landed I knew I was going the better. Brian began to kick and scrub. He gave me a sideways glance and then shouted. 'You don't want to make a damn fool of yourself again, do you? Don't you know we go round again?'

Despite myself I hesitated. Could he be right? At that moment a stentorian voice rang out from the rails beside me: 'Take no notice, sir! I heard him! He's up to his games again. Go on! Go on!' It was Kerrell come to the rescue once more.

I wondered how much The Circus had left in him. I was beginning to roll about a bit myself. It was all up to him now. I squeezed at him as best I could and he answered like the gallant old devil he was.

Jack Go Nimble was visibly tiring. Brian got out his whip. I couldn't do anything about that. I couldn't use a whip. The Circus stood back at the last and leaped. So did Jack Go Nimble, but the crash I heard as I landed told me that at least he had hit the top and gone through it. For the second time in five minutes, I sat down to try to ride a finish. This time it was all right. We came home alone and as I pulled up I saw Brian, who had sat on like a leech, passing the post in second place.

It was all even more dreamlike after that. I had actually won a steeplechase. I sat on a bench in the changing room in a happy trance with Brian glowering and muttering beside me. Then a man in a tweed suit came in. 'The stewards want a word with you, Mr Welcome,' he said.

'Me?' I said. 'Why me?'

'They want you to explain why you won your race half-way round,' Brian said with a crow of laughter. 'They'll probably take it away from you.'

'They want you, too, Mr Manson,' the man said.

'I can't think what they want me for,' Brian said as we stood outside the stewards' room.

'Probably they think you can tell them what happened,' I said to him sourly. I was feeling much the same as I had felt outside my headmaster's study not so long ago. 'You bloody well know, anyway.'

'Me? You must be mad or dreaming. And they're not likely to believe any cock and bull story from you, let me tell you.'

The door opened and we were ushered inside. The stewards' room at that meeting was as primitive as the rest of the appointments. It was draughty and bare and its walls were of unsheeted corrugated iron. Behind a plain deal table, the three of them were sitting. Another man, who had a heavy military moustache, was at the end of the table slightly away from them. The man in the middle was, I supposed, the senior steward. He had a long humorous face. I recognized him. He was a chap called Hugh Clumber, a well-known amateur from a year or two back who had won the National on his own horse as a serving cavalryman. We were in good hands anyway. He'd know what he was about.

'Now, then, Welcome,' he said. 'Can you give any explanation of that interesting display you gave and why you rode a finish a mile from home?'

'No, sir. I can't.'

'None at all?' His tone was more friendly than frightening.

'No, sir, except I think I must have lost my head.'

'Did you walk the course?'

'Yes, I did.'

'Well,' Clumber said slowly. 'You lost your head, you say. Not a very sensible thing to do in a steeplechase. You were beside him, Manson. Can you give us any help?'

'No, sir, I'm afraid I can't.' Brian stared ahead of him, po-faced as they say nowadays.

'Are you *quite* sure, Manson?'

'Yes, sir. Quite, sure.' Brian, who was no fool, shuffled his feet slightly. Something was afoot and both of us knew it.

'Major Warburton, I wonder if you would mind telling us what you saw – and heard,' Clumber said to the man at the end of the table. 'Major Warburton,' he explained to us, 'is the stewards' secretary.'

The man with the moustache leaned forward and spoke. 'I was standing down the course between the last two fences the second time round,' he said.

'Yes. And did you hear anything?'

'I heard Manson call across to Welcome to get on – that they finished this time.'

'I see. Manson has ridden quite a bit, hasn't he?'

'Yes. He lost the allowance six months ago.'

'Do you want to ask Major Warburton any questions, Manson?'

'No, sir.'

'I don't think I'll ask you any questions, either,' Clumber said aimably to him. 'I don't want to make you out a bigger liar than you've already made yourself.'

The three of them then put their heads together. After a minute or two, Clumber took a piece of paper from the table in front of him and wrote on it. He showed it to the others who nodded their heads. Then he looked at us. 'We've now considered the matter,' he said. 'As for you, Welcome, we've heard your explanation and we caution you against being such a bloody fool as to listen to what someone shouts at you in a race about where you finish. And we advise you not to do it again. That will be put into rather more Parliamentary language by the time it appears in the Calendar. Now, then, Manson —'

For the first time in our acquaintanceship, I thought Brian appeared apprehensive. He couldn't guess what was coming. Neither could I.

'The stewards,' Clumber went on and I noticed his lips twitching slightly, 'find you guilty of conduct unbecoming a gentleman rider. That won't appear in the Calendar, either, but this will.' He picked up the piece of paper and read from it: "The stewards enquired into the riding of Mr B. Manson in The Tallyho Hunters' Steeplechase, and not being satisfied with his explanation, they fined him ten sovereigns!" You can both go now, and don't let me see either of you in here again – ever.'

'Ten pounds! Ten bloomin' pounds! You bloody man!' Brian said, turning on me when we got outside.

'Sovereigns,' I said, savouring the word. 'Sovereigns. But why blame me. You tried it on once too often, that's all.'

'If you hadn't cut the progs —'

'Oh, but I didn't cut them at all. I only told you that. As a matter of fact, I'm going to have a glass of port with the prog and tell him something about racing. An arcane mystery, he called it. He may be right.'

Just then Kerrell came up with a bundle of notes in his hand. 'Your winnings, sir,' he said, holding them out to me. Then, turning to Brian: 'You'll be taking the horses home, sir. Mr Welcome is coming with me in the car. He has an appointment, I understand.'

The expression on Brian's face at that moment is one of the racing recollections I shall treasure to the end of my life.

Kerrell and I stopped on the way home to split a bottle of champagne. 'I knew he was up to something, sir,' Kerrell said as he buried his big nose in a pewter tankard brimming with bubbles. 'And when I saw what had happened first time, I thought he might try it again. Never gives up, does Mr Manson.'

'I wish I could ride like him,' I said, remembering how he had driven a tired horse, whip swinging, into the last and sat on him when he blundered.

'Ah,' said Mr Kerrell. 'They don't make 'em that way every day and that's a fact.'

I had time for a bath before dinner. Afterwards I walked towards the proctor's college through the mellow Oxford night. The stars were out, the old walls gleamed almost white in the pale light of the moon. I was tired and happy but a little apprehensive as to what I would find when I arrived and what sort of a don this would turn out to be.

I climbed his staircase and knocked on the door. A voice told me to come in. It was a long room running from window to window, panelled in dark oak and softly lighted. A large and ruby-red decanter with two glasses beside it stood on a salver. My host rose from his chair and reached out a hand towards it.

'Come in, Welcome,' he said. 'I expect you're tired. This should do you good.'

But I was looking past him to a portrait over the mantelpiece. It showed a man in racing colours sitting a big bay horse with a background of stands and paddock. Below it in a long glass case was a racing whip.

'You must speak up to me when you recount the events of the day,' he said. 'As I was about to mention to you last night when you so rudely interrupted me, I'm a little deaf from a fall at Cheltenham ten years ago. After that I'm afraid I couldn't resist having some amusement at your expense. Well, what happened?'

'I hacked it,' I said happily. 'At a hundred to eight.'

'Indeed. Then you will be able to pay your fine at all events. Now tell me about it.'

So I did. And we finished the port.

CARROT
FOR A CHESTNUT

Dick Francis

CHICK stood and sweated with the carrot in his hand. His head seemed to be floating and he couldn't feel his feet on the ground, and the pulse thudded massively in his ear. A clammy green pain shivered in his gut.

Treachery was making him sick.

The time: fifty minutes before sunrise. The morning: cold. The raw swirling wind was clearing its throat for a fiercer blow, and a heavy layer of nimbostratus was fighting every inch of the way against the hint of light. In the neat box stalls round the stable-yard the dozing horses struck a random hoof against a wooden wall, rattled a tethering chain, sneezed the hay dust out of a moist black nostril.

Chick was late. Two hours late. He'd been told to give the carrot to the lanky chestnut at four o'clock in the morning, but at four o'clock in the morning it had been pouring with rain – hard, slanting rain that soaked a man to the skin in one minute flat, and Chick had reckoned it would be too difficult explaining away a soaking at four o'clock in the morning. Chick had reckoned it would be better to wait until the rain stopped, it couldn't make any difference. Four o'clock, six o'clock, what the hell, Chick always knew better than anyone else.

Chick was a thin, disgruntled nineteen-year-old who always felt the world owed him more than he got. He had been a bad-tempered, argumentative child and an aggressively rebellious adolescent. The resulting snarling habit of mind was precisely what was now hindering his success as an adult. Not that Chick would have agreed, of course. Chick never agreed with anyone if he could help it. Always knew better, did Chick.

He was unprepared for the severity of the physical symptoms of fear. His usual attitude toward any form of authority was scorn (and authority had not so far actually belted him one across his sulky mouth). Horses had never scared him because he had been born to the saddle and had grown up mastering everything on four legs with contemptuous ease. He believed in his heart that no one could really ride better than he could. He was wrong.

He looked apprehensively over his shoulder, and the shifting pain in his stomach sharply intensified. That simply couldn't happen, he thought wildly. He'd heard about people getting sick with fear. He hadn't believed it. It couldn't happen. Now, all of a sudden, he feared it could. He tightened all his muscles desperately, and the spasm slowly passed. It left fresh sweat standing out all over his skin and no saliva in his mouth.

The house was dark. Upstairs, behind the black open window with the pale curtain flapping in the spartan air, slept Arthur Morrison, trainer of the forty-three racehorses in the stables below. Morrison habitually slept lightly. His ears were sharper than half a dozen guard dogs', his stable-hands said.

Chick forced himself to turn his head away, to walk in view of that window, to take the ten exposed steps down to the chestnut's stall.

If the guvernor woke up and saw him. . . . Gawd, he thought furiously, he hadn't expected it to be like this. Just a lousy walk down the yard to give a carrot to the gangly chestnut. Guilt and fear and treachery. They bypassed his sneering mind and erupted through his nerves instead.

He couldn't see anything wrong with the carrot. It hadn't been cut in half and hollowed out and packed with drugs and tied together again. He'd tried pulling the thick end out like a plug, and that hadn't worked either. The carrot just looked like any old carrot, any old carrot you'd watch your ma chop up to put in a stew. Any old carrot you'd give to any old horse. Not a very young, succulent carrot or a very aged carrot, knotted and woody. Just any old ordinary *carrot*.

But strangers didn't proposition you to give any old carrot to one special horse in the middle of the night. They didn't give you more than you earned in half a year when you said you'd do it. Any old carrot didn't come wrapped carefully alone in a polythene bag inside an empty cheese-cracker packet, given to you by a stranger in a car park after dark in a town six miles from the stables. You didn't give any old carrot in the middle of the night to a chestnut who was due to start favourite in a high-class steeplechase eleven hours later.

Chick was getting dizzy with holding his breath by the time he'd completed the ten tiptoed steps to the chestnut's stall. Trying not to cough, not to groan, not to let out the strangling tension in a sob, he curled his sweating fingers around the bolt and began the job of easing it out, inch by frightening inch, from its socket.

By day he slammed the bolts open and shut with a smart practiced flick. His body shook in the darkness with the strain of moving by fractions.

The bolt came free with the tiniest of grating noises, and the top half of the split door swung slowly outward. No squeaks from the hinges, only the whisper of metal on metal. Chick drew in a long breath like a painful, trickling, smothered gasp and let it out between his clenched teeth. His stomach lurched again, threateningly. He took another quick, appalled grip on himself and thrust his arm in a panic through the dark, open space.

Inside the stall, the chestnut was asleep, dozing on his feet. The changing swirl of air from the opening door moved the sensitive hairs around his muzzle and raised his mental state from semi-consciousness to inquisitiveness. He could smell the carrot. He could also smell the man: smell the fear in the man's sweat.

'Come on,' Chick whispered desperately. 'Come on, then, boy.'

The horse moved his nose around toward the carrot and finally, reluctantly, his feet. He took it indifferently from the man's trembling palm, whiffling it in with his black mobile lips, scrunching it languidly with large rotations of his jaw. When he had swallowed all the pulped-up bits he poked his muzzle forward for more. But there was no more, just the lighter square of sky darkening again as the door swung shut, just the faint sounds of the bolt going back, just the fading smell of the man and the passing taste of carrot. Presently he forgot about it and turned slowly round again so that his hindquarters were toward the door, because he usually stood that way, and after a minute or two he blinked slowly, rested his near hind leg lazily on the point of the hoof and lapsed back into twilight mindlessness.

Down in his stomach the liquid narcotic compound with which the carrot had been injected to saturation gradually filtered out of the digesting carrot cells and began to be absorbed into the bloodstream. The process was slow and progressive. And it had started two hours late.

Arthur Morrison stood in his stable-yard watching his men load the chestnut into the motor horse-box that was to take him to the races. He was eyeing the proceedings with an expression that was critical from habit and bore little relation to the satisfaction in his mind. The chestnut was the best horse in his stable: a frequent winner, popular with the public, a source of prestige as well as revenue. The big steeplechase at Cheltenham had been tailor-made for him from the day its conditions had been published, and Morrison was adept at producing a horse in peak condition for a particular race. No one seriously considered that the chestnut would be beaten. The newspapers had tipped it to a man and the bookmakers were fighting shy at 6–4 on. Morrison allowed himself a glimmer of warmth in the eyes and a twitch of smile to the lips as the men clipped shut the heavy doors of the horse van and drove it out of the yard.

These physical signs were unusual. The face he normally wore was a compound of concentration and disapproval in roughly equal proportions. Both qualities contributed considerably to his success as a racehorse trainer and to his unpopularity as a person, a fact Morrison himself was well aware of. He didn't in the least care that almost no one liked him. He valued success and respect much more highly than love and held in incredulous contempt all those who did not.

Across the yard Chick was watching the horse van drive away, his usual scowl in place. Morrison frowned irritably. The boy was a pest, he thought. Always grousing, always impertinent, always trying to scrounge up more money. Morrison didn't believe in boys having life made too easy: a little hardship was good for the soul. Where Morrison and Chick radically differed was the point at which each thought hardship began.

Chick spotted the frown and watched Morrison fearfully, his guilt pressing on him like a rock. He couldn't know, he thought frantically. He couldn't even suspect there was anything wrong with the horse or he wouldn't have let him go off to the races. The horse had looked all right, too. Absolutely his normal self. Perhaps there had been nothing wrong with the carrot. . . . Perhaps it had been the wrong carrot, even. . . . Chick glanced around uneasily and knew very well he was fooling himself. The horse might look all right but he wasn't.

Arthur Morrison saddled up his horse at the races, and Chick watched him from ten nervous paces away, trying to hide in the eager crowd that pushed forward for a close view of the favourite. There was a larger admiring crowd outside the chestnut's saddling stall than for any of the other seven runners, and the bookmakers had shortened their odds. Behind Morrison's concentrated expression an itch of worry was growing insistent. He pulled the girth tight and adjusted the buckles automatically, acknowledging to himself that his former satisfaction had changed to anxiety. The horse was not himself. There were no lively stamping feet, no playful nips from the teeth, no response to the crowd; this was a horse that usually played to the public like a film star. He couldn't be feeling well, and if he wasn't feeling well he wouldn't win. Morrison tightened his mouth. If the horse were not well enough to win, he would prefer him not to run at all. To be beaten at odds-on would be a disgrace. A defeat on too large a scale. A loss of face. Particularly as Morrison's own eldest son Toddy was to be the jockey. The newspapers would tear them both to pieces.

Morrison came to a decision and sent for the vet.

The rules of jump racing in England stated quite clearly that if a horse had been declared a runner in a race, only the say-so of a veterinarian was sufficient grounds for withdrawing him during the last three-quarters of an hour before post time. The Cheltenham racecourse veterinarian came and looked at the chestnut and, after consulting with Morrison, led it off to a more private stall and took its temperature.

'His temperature's normal,' the veterinarian assured Morrison.

'I don't like the look of him.'

'I can't find anything wrong.'

'He's not well,' Morrison insisted.

The veterinarian pursed his lips and shook his head. There was nothing obviously wrong with the horse, and he knew he would be in trouble himself if he allowed Morrison to withdraw so hot a favourite on such slender grounds. Not only that, this was the third application for withdrawal he'd had to consider that afternoon. He had refused both the others, and the chestnut was certainly in no worse a state.

'He'll have to run,' the veterinarian said positively, making up his mind.

Morrison was furious and went raging off to find a steward, who came and looked at the chestnut and listened to the vet and confirmed that the horse would have to run whether Morrison liked it or not. Unless, that was, Morrison cared to involve the horse's absent owner in paying a heavy fine?

With the face of granite Morrison resaddled the chestnut, and a stable-lad led him out into the parade ring, where most of the waiting public cheered and a few wiser ones looked closely and hurried off to hedge their bets.

With a shiver of dismay, Chick saw the horse reappear and for the first time regretted what he'd done. That stupid vet, he thought violently. He can't see what's under his bloody nose, he couldn't see a barn at ten paces. Anything that happened from then on was the vet's fault, Chick thought. The vet's responsibility, absolutely. The man was a criminal menace, letting a horse run in a steeplechase with dope coming out of its eyeballs.

Toddy Morrison had joined his father in the parade ring and together they were watching with worried expressions as the chestnut plodded lethargically around the oval walking track. Toddy was a strong, stock professional jockey in his late twenties with an infectious grin and a generous view of life that represented a direct rejection of his father's. He had inherited the same strength of mind but had used it to leave home at eighteen to ride races for other trainers, and had only consented to ride for his father when he could dictate his own terms. Arthur Morrison, in consequence, respected him deeply. Between them they had won a lot of races.

Chick didn't actually dislike Toddy Morrison, even though, as he saw it, Toddy stood in his way. Occasionally Arthur let Chick ride a race if Toddy had something better or couldn't make the weight. Chick had to share these scraps from Toddy's table with two or three other lads in the yard who were, though he didn't believe it, as good as he was in the saddle. But though the envy curdled around inside him and the snide remarks came out sharp and sour as vinegar, he had never actually come to hate Toddy. There was something about Toddy that you couldn't hate, however good the reason. Chick hadn't given a thought to the fact that it would be Toddy who would have to deal with the effects of the carrot. He had seen no further than his own pocket. He wished now that it had been some other jockey. Anyone but Toddy.

The conviction suddenly crystalized in Chick's mind as he looked at Toddy and Morrison standing there worried in the parade ring that he had never believed the chestnut would actually start in the race. The stranger, Chick said to himself, had distinctly told him the horse would be too sick to start. I wouldn't have done it, else, Chick thought virtuously. I wouldn't have done it. It's bloody dangerous, riding a doped steeplechaser. I wouldn't have done that to Toddy. It's not my fault he's going to ride a doped steeplechaser, it's that vet's fault for not seeing. It's that stranger's fault, he told me distinctly the horse wouldn't be fit to start. . . .

Chick remembered with an unpleasant jerk that he'd been two hours late with the carrot. Maybe if he'd been on time the drug would have come out more and the vet would have seen. . . .

Chick jettisoned this unbearable theory instantly on the grounds that no one can tell how seriously any particular horse will react to a drug or how quickly it will work, and he repeated to himself the comforting self-delusion that the stranger had promised him the horse wouldn't ever start — though the stranger had not in fact said any such thing. The stranger, who was at the races, was entirely satisfied with the way things were going and was on the point of making a great deal of money.

The bell rang for the jockeys to mount. Chick clenched his hands in his pockets and tried not to visualize what could happen to a rider going over jumps at thirty miles an hour on a doped horse. Chick's body began playing him tricks again: he could feel the sweat trickling down his back and the pulse had come back in his ears.

Supposing he told them, he thought. Supposing he just ran out there into the ring and told Toddy not to ride the horse, it hadn't a chance of jumping properly, it was certain to fall, it could kill him bloody easily because its reactions would be all shot to bits.

Supposing he did. The way they'd look at him. His imagination blew a fuse and blanked out on that picture because such a blast of contempt didn't fit in with his overgrown self-esteem. He could not, could *not* face the fury they would feel. And it might not end there. Even if he told them and saved Toddy's life, they might tell the police. He wouldn't put it past them. And he could end up in the dock. Even in jail. They weren't going to do that to him, not to *him*. He wasn't going to give them the chance. He should have been paid more. Paid more because he was worth more. If he'd been paid more, he wouldn't have needed to take the stranger's money. Arthur Morrison had only himself to blame.

Toddy would have to risk it. After all, the horse didn't look too bad, and the vet had passed it, hadn't he, and maybe the carrot being two hours late was all to the good and it wouldn't have done its work properly yet, and in fact it was really thanks to Chick if it hadn't; only thanks to him that the drug was two hours late and that nothing much would happen, really, anyway. Nothing much would happen. Maybe the chestnut wouldn't actually *win*, but Toddy would come through all right. Of course he would.

The jockeys swung up into their saddles, Toddy among them. He saw Chick in the crowd, watching, and sketched an acknowledging wave. The urge to tell and the fear of telling tore Chick apart like the Chinese trees.

Toddy gathered up the reins and clicked his tongue and steered the chestnut indecisively out on to the track. He was disappointed that the horse wasn't feeling well but not in the least apprehensive. It hadn't occurred to him, or to Arthur Morrison, that the horse might be doped. He cantered down to the post standing in his stirrups, replanning his tactics mentally now that he couldn't rely on reserves in his mount. It would be a difficult race now to win. Pity.

Chick watched him go. He hadn't come to his decision, to tell or not to tell. The moment simply passed him by. When Toddy had gone he unstuck his leaden feet and plodded off to the stands to watch the race, and in every corner of his mind little self-justifications sprang up like nettles. A feeling of shame tried to creep in round the edges, but he kicked it out smartly. They should have paid him more. It was their fault, not his.

He thought about the wad of notes the stranger had given him with the carrot. Money in advance. The stranger had trusted him, which was more than most people seemed to. He'd locked himself into the bathroom and counted the notes, counted them twice, and they were all there, £300 just as the stranger had promised. He had never had so much money all at once in his life before. . . . Perhaps he never would again, he thought. And if he'd told Arthur Morrison and Toddy about the dope, he would have to give up that money, give up the money and more. . . .

Finding somewhere to hide the money had given him difficulty. Three hundred used £1 notes had turned out to be quite bulky, and he didn't want to risk his ma poking around among his things, like she did, and coming across them. He'd solved the problem temporarily by rolling them up and putting them in a brightly coloured round tin which once held toffees but which he used for years for storing brushes and polish for cleaning his shoes. He had covered the money with a duster and jammed the brushes back on the shelf in his bedroom where it always stood. He thought he would probably have to find somewhere safer, in the end. And he'd have to be careful how he spent the money – there would be too many questions asked if he just went out and bought a car. He'd always wanted a car . . . and now he had the money for one . . . and he still couldn't get the car. It wasn't fair. Not fair at all. If they'd paid him more. . . . Enough for a car. . . .

Up on the well-positioned area of stands set aside for trainers and jockeys, a small man with hot dark eyes put his hand on Chick's arm and spoke to him, though it was several seconds before Chick started to listen.

'. . . I see you are here, and you're free, will you ride it?'

'What?' said Chick vaguely.

'My horse in the Novice Hurdle,' said the little man impatiently. 'Of course, if you don't want to. . . .'

'Didn't say that,' Chick mumbled. 'Ask the guvnor. If he says I can, well, I can.'

The small trainer walked across the stand to where Arthur Morrison was watching the chestnut intently through the race glasses and asked the same question he'd put to Chick.

'Chick? Yes, he can ride it for you, if you want him.' Morrison gave the other trainer two full seconds of his attention and glued himself back on his race glasses.

'My jockey was hurt in a fall in the first race,' explained the small man. 'There are so many runners in the Novice Hurdle that there's a shortage of jockeys. I just saw that boy of yours, so I asked him on the spur of the moment, see?'

'Yes, yes,' said Morrison, ninety per cent uninterested. 'He's moderately capable, but don't expect too much of him.' There was no spring in the chestnut's stride. Morrison wondered in depression if he was sickening for the cough.

'My horse won't win. Just out for experience you might say.'

'Yes. Well, fix it with Chick.' Several other stables had the coughing epidemic, Morrison thought. The chestnut couldn't have picked a worse day to catch it.

Chick, who would normally have welcomed the offer of a ride with condescending complacency, was so preoccupied that the small trainer regretted having asked him. Chick's whole attention was riveted on the chestnut, who seemed to be lining up satisfactorily at the starting tape. Nothing wrong, Chick assured himself. Everything was going to be all right. Of course it was. Stupid getting into such a state.

The start was down the track to the left, with two fences to be jumped before the horses came past the stands and swung away again on the left-hand circuit. As it was a jumping race, they were using tapes instead of stalls, and as there was no draw either, Toddy had lined up against the inside rails, ready to take the shortest way home.

Down in the bookmakers' enclosure they were offering more generous odds now and some had gone boldly to evens. The chestnut had cantered past them on his way to the start looking not his brightest and best. The bookmakers in consequence were feeling more hopeful. They had expected a bad day, but if the chestnut lost, they would profit. One of them would profit terrifically – just as he would lose terrifically if the chestnut won.

Alexander McGrant (Est. 1898), real name Harry Buskins, had done this sort of thing once or twice before. He spread out his fingers and looked at them admiringly. Not a tremble in sight. And there was always a risk in these things that the boy he'd bribed would get cold feet at the last minute and not go through with the job. Always a gamble, it was. But this time, this boy, he was pretty sure of. You couldn't go wrong if you sorted out a vain little so-and-so with a big grudge. Knockovers, that sort were. Every time.

Harry Buskins was a shrewd middle-aged East End Londoner for whom there had never been any clear demarcation between right and wrong and a man who thought that if you could rig a nice little swindle now and then, well, why not? The turnover tax was killing betting . . . you had to make a quick buck where you could . . . and there was nothing quite so sure or quick as raking in the dough on a red-hot favourite and knowing for certain that you weren't going to have to pay out.

Down at the post the starter put his hand on the lever and the tapes went up with a rush. Toddy kicked his chestnut smartly in the ribs. From his aerie on top of the stand the commentator moved smartly into his spiel, 'They're off, and the first to show is the grey. . . .' Arthur Morrison and Chick watched with hearts thumping from different sorts of anxiety, and Harry Buskins shut his eyes and prayed.

Toddy drove forward at once into the first three, the chestnut beneath him galloping strongly, pulling at the bit, thudding his hoofs into the ground. He seemed to be going well enough, Toddy thought. Strong. Like a train.

The first fence lay only one hundred yards ahead now, coming nearer. With a practiced eye Toddy measured the distance, knew the chestnut's stride would meet it right, collected himself for the spring and gave the horse the signal to take off. There was no response. Nothing. The chestnut made no attempt to bunch his muscles, no attempt to gather himself on to his haunches, no attempt to waver or slow down or take any avoiding action whatsoever. For one incredulous second Toddy knew he was facing complete and imminent disaster.

The chestnut galloped straight into the three-foot-thick, chest-high solid birch fence with an impact that brought a groan of horror from the stands. He turned a somersault over the fence with a flurry of thrashing legs, threw Toddy off in front of him and fell down on top and rolled over him.

Chick felt as if the world were turning grey. The colours drained out of everything and he was halfway to fainting. Oh God, he thought. Oh God. *Toddy.*

The chestnut scrambled to his feet and galloped away. He followed the other horses toward the second fence, stretching out into a relentless stride, into a full-fledged thundering racing pace.

He hit the second fence as straight and hard as the first. The crowd gasped and cried out. Again the somersault, the spread-eagled legs, the crashing fall, the instant recovery. The chestnut surged up again and galloped on.

He came up past the stands, moving inexorably, the stirrups swinging out from the empty saddle, flecks of foam flying back now from his mouth, great dark patches of sweat staining his flanks. Where the track curved round to the left, the chestnut raced straight on. Straight on across the curve, to crash into the rail around the outside of the track. He took the solid timber across the chest and broke it in two. Again he fell in a thrashing heap and again he rocketed to his feet. But this time not to gallop away. This time he took three painful limping steps and stood still.

Back at the fence Toddy lay on the ground with first-aid men bending over him anxiously. Arthur Morrison ran down from the stands toward the track and didn't know which way to turn first, to his son or his horse. Chick's legs gave way and he sagged down in a daze on to the concrete steps. And down in the bookmakers' enclosure Harry Buskins' first reaction of delight was soured by wondering whether, if Toddy Morrison were badly injured, that stupid boy Chick would be scared enough to keep his mouth shut.

Arthur Morrison turned toward his son. Toddy had been knocked unconscious by the fall and had had all the breath squeezed out of him by the chestnut's weight, but by the time his father was within 100 yards he was beginning to come round. As soon as Arthur saw the supine figure move, he turned brusquely round and hurried off toward the horse: it would never do to show Toddy the concern he felt. Toddy would not respect him for it, he thought.

The chestnut stood patiently by the smashed rail, only dimly aware of the dull discomfort in the foreleg that wouldn't take his weight. Arthur Morrison and the veterinarian arrived beside him at the same time, and Arthur Morrison glared at the vet.

'You said he was fit to run. The owner is going to hit the roof when he hears about it.' Morrison tried to keep a grip on a growing internal fury at the injustice of fate. The chestnut wasn't just any horse – it was the best he'd ever trained, had hoisted him higher up the stakes-won list than he was ever likely to go again.

'Well, he seemed all right,' said the vet defensively.

'I want a dope test done,' Morrison said truculently.

'He's broken his shoulder. He'll have to be put down.'

'I know. I've got eyes. All the same, I want a dope test first. Just being ill wouldn't have made him act like that.'

The veterinarian reluctantly agreed to take a blood sample, and after that he fitted the bolt into the humane killer and shot it into the chestnut's drug-crazed brain. The best horse in Arthur Morrison's stable became only a name in the record books. The digested carrot was dragged away with the carcass but its damage was by no means spent.

It took Chick fifteen minutes to realize that it was Toddy who was alive and the horse that was dead, during which time he felt physically ill and mentally pulverized. It had seemed so small a thing, in the beginning, to give a carrot to the chestnut. He hadn't thought of it affecting him much. He'd never dreamed anything like that could make you really sick.

Once he found that Toddy had broken no bones, had recovered consciousness and would be on his feet in an hour or two, the bulk of his physical symptoms receded. When the small trainer appeared at his elbow to remind him sharply that he should be inside changing into colours to ride in the Novice Hurdle race, he felt fit enough to go and do it, though he wished in a way that he hadn't said he would.

In the changing room he forgot to tell his valet he needed a lightweight saddle and that the trainer had asked for a breast girth. He forgot to tie the stock round his neck and would have gone out to ride with the ends flapping. He forgot to take his watch off. His valet pointed out everything and thought that the jockey looked drunk.

The novice hurdler Chick was to ride wouldn't have finished within a mile of the chestnut if he'd started the day before. Young, green, sketchily schooled he hadn't even the virtue of a gold streak waiting to be mined: this was one destined to run in the ruck until the owner tired of trying. Chick hadn't bothered to find out. He'd been much too preoccupied to look in the form book, where a consistent row of noughts might have made him cautious. As it was, he mounted the horse without attention and didn't listen to the riding orders the small trainer insistently gave him. As usual, he thought he knew better. Play it off the cuff, he thought scrappily. Play it off the cuff. How could he listen to fussy little instructions with all that he had on his mind?

On his way out from the weighing-room he passed Arthur Morrison, who cast an inattentive eye over his racing colours and said, 'Oh yes . . . well, don't make too much of a mess of it. . . .'

Morrison was still thinking about the difference the chestnut's death was going to make to his fortunes and he didn't notice the spasm of irritation that twisted Chick's petulant face.

There he goes, Chick thought. That's typical. *Typical.* Never thinks I can do a bloody thing. If he'd given me more chances . . . and more money . . . I wouldn't have given. . . . Well, I wouldn't have. He cantered down to the post, concentrating on resenting that remark, 'don't make too much of a mess of it', because it made him feel justified, obscurely, for having done what he'd done. The abyss of remorse opening beneath him was too painful. He clutched at every lie to keep himself out.

Harry Buskins had noticed that Chick had an unexpected mount in the Novice Hurdle and concluded that he himself was safe, the boy wasn't going to crack. All the same, he had shut his bag over its swollen takings and left his pitch for the day and gone home, explaining to his colleagues that he didn't feel well. And in truth he didn't. He couldn't get out of his mind the sight of the chestnut charging at those fences as if he couldn't see. Blind, the horse had been. A great racer who knew he was on a racetrack starting a race. Didn't understand there was anything wrong with him. Galloped because he was asked to gallop, because he knew it was the right place for it. A great horse, with a great racing heart.

Harry Buskins mopped the sweat off his forehead. They were bound to have tested the horse for dope, he thought, after something like that. None of the others he'd done in the past had reacted that way. Maybe he'd got the dose wrong or the timing wrong. You never knew how individual horses would be affected. Doping was always a bit unpredictable.

He poured himself half a tumbler of whisky with fingers that were shaking after all, and when he felt calmer he decided that if he got away with it this time he would be satisfied with the cleanup he'd made, and he wouldn't fool around with any more carrots. He just wouldn't risk it again.

Chick lined up at the starting post in the centre of the field, even though the trainer had advised him to start on the outside to give the inexperienced horse an easy passage over the first few hurdles. Chick didn't remember this instruction because he hadn't listened, and even if he had listened he would have done the same, driven by his habitual compulsion to disagree. He was thinking about Toddy lining up on this spot an hour ago, not knowing that his horse wouldn't see the jumps. Chick hadn't known dope could make a horse blind. How could anyone expect that? It didn't make sense. Perhaps it was just that the dope had confused the chestnut so much that, although its eyes saw the fence, the message didn't get through that he was supposed to jump over it. The chestnut couldn't have been really blind.

Chick sweated at the thought and forgot to check that the girths were still tight after cantering down to the post. His mind was still on the inward horror when the starter let the tapes up, so that he was caught unawares and flat-footed and got away slowly. The small trainer on the stand clicked his mouth in annoyance, and Arthur Morrison raised his eyes to heaven.

The first hurdle lay side-by-side with the first fence, and all the way to it Chick was illogically scared that his horse wouldn't rise to it. He spent the attention he should have given to setting his horse right in desperately trying to convince himself that no one could have given it a carrot. He couldn't be riding a doped horse himself . . . it wouldn't be fair. Why wouldn't it be fair? Because . . . because . . .

The hurdler scrambled over the jump, knocked himself hard on the timber frame, and landed almost at a standstill. The small trainer began to curse.

Chick tightened one loose rein and the other, and the hurdler swung to and fro in wavering indecision. He needed to be ridden with care and confidence and to be taught balance and rhythm. He needed to be set right before the jumps and to be quickly collected afterwards. He lacked experience, he lacked judgment and he badly needed a jockey who could contribute both.

Chick could have made a reasonable job of it if he'd been trying. Instead, with nausea and mental exhaustion draining what skill he had out of his muscles, he was busy proving that he'd never be much good.

At the second fence he saw in his mind's eye the chestnut somersaulting through the air, and going round the bend his gaze wavered across to the broken rail and the scuffed-up patches of turf in front of it. The chestnut had died there. Everyone in the stable would be poorer for it. He had killed the chestnut, there was no avoiding it anymore, he'd killed it with that carrot as surely as if he'd shot the bolt himself. Chick sobbed suddenly, and his eyes filled with tears.

He didn't see the next two hurdles. They passed beneath him in a flying blurr. He stayed on his horse by instinct, and the tears ran down and were swept away as they trickled under the edge of his jockey's goggles.

The green hurdler was frightened and rudderless. Another jump lay close ahead, and the horses in front went clattering through it, knocking one section half over and leaving it there at an angle. The hurdler waited until the last minute for help or instructions from the man on his back and then in a muddled way dived for the leaning section, which looked lower to him and easier to jump than the other end.

From the stands it was clear to both the small trainer and Arthur Morrison that Chick had made no attempt to keep straight or to tell the horse when to take off. It landed with its forefeet tangled up in the sloping hurdle and catapulted Chick off over its head.

The instinct of self-preservation which should have made Chick curl into a rolling ball wasn't working. He fell through the air flat and straight, and his last thought before he hit was that that stupid little sod of a trainer hadn't schooled his horse properly. The animal hadn't a clue how to jump.

He woke up a long time later in a high bed in a small room. There was a dim light burning somewhere. He could feel no pain. He could feel nothing at all. His mind seemed to be floating in his head and his head was floating in space.

After a long time he began to believe that he was dead. He took the thought calmly and was proud of himself for his calm. A long time after that he began to realize that he wasn't dead. There was some sort of casing round his head, holding it cushioned. He couldn't move.

He blinked his eyes consciously and licked his lips to make sure that they at least were working. He couldn't think what had happened. His thoughts were a confused but peaceful fog.

Finally he remembered the carrot, and the whole complicated agony washed back into his consciousness. He cried out in protest and tried to move, to get up and away, to escape the impossible, unbearable guilt. People heard his voice and came into the room and stood around him. He looked at them uncomprehendingly. They were dressed in white.

'You're all right, now,' they said. 'Don't worry, young man, you're going to be all right.'

'I can't move,' he protested.

'You will,' they said soothingly.

'I can't feel . . . anything. I can't feel my feet.' The panic rose suddenly in his voice. 'I can't feel my hands. I can't . . . move . . . my hands.' He was shouting, frightened, his eyes wide and stretched.

'Don't worry,' they said. 'You will in time. You're going to be all right. You're going to be all right.'

He didn't believe them, and they pumped a sedative into his arm to quiet him. He couldn't feel the prick of the needle. He heard himself screaming because he could feel no pain.

When he woke up again he knew for certain that he'd broken his neck.

After four days Arthur Morrison came to see him, bringing six new-laid eggs and a bottle of fresh orange juice. He stood looking down at the immobile body with the plaster cast round its shoulders and head.

'Well, Chick,' he said awkwardly. 'It's not as bad as it could have been, eh?'

Chick said rudely, 'I'm glad you think so.'

'They say your spinal cord isn't severed, it's just crushed. They say in a year or so you'll get a lot of movement back. And they say you'll begin to feel things any day now.'

'They say,' said Chick sneeringly. 'I don't believe them.'

'You'll have to, in time,' said Morrison impatiently.

Chick didn't answer, and Arthur Morrison cast uncomfortably around in his mind for something to say to pass away the minutes until he could decently leave. He couldn't visit the boy and just stand there in silence. He had to say *something*. So he began to talk about what was uppermost in his mind.

'We had the result of the dope test this morning. Did you know we had the chestnut tested? Well, you know we had to have it put down anyway. The results came in this morning. They were positive. . . . *Positive*. The chestnut was full of some sort of narcotic drug, some long name. The owner is kicking up hell about it and so is the insurance company. They're trying to say it's my fault. My security arrangements aren't tight enough. It's ridiculous. And all this on top of losing the horse itself, losing that really great horse. I questioned everyone in the stable this morning as soon as I knew about the dope, but of course no one knew anything. God, if I knew who did it I'd strangle him myself.' His voice shook with the fury which had been consuming him all day.

It occurred to him at this point that Chick being Chick, he would be exclusively concerned with his own state and wouldn't care a damn for anyone else's troubles. Arthur Morrison sighed deeply. Chick did have his own troubles now, right enough. He couldn't be expected to care all that much about the chestnut. And he was looking very weak, very pale.

The doctor who checked on Chick's condition ten times a day came quietly into the small room and shook hands with Morrison.

'He's doing well,' he said. 'Getting on splendidly.'

'Nuts,' Chick said.

The doctor twisted his lips. He didn't say he had found Chick the worst-tempered patient in the hospital. He said, 'Of course, it's hard on him. But it could have been worse. It'll take time, he'll need to learn everything again, you see. It'll take time.'

'Like a bloody baby,' Chick said violently.

Arthur Morrison thought, a baby again. Well, perhaps second time around they could make a better job of him.

'He's lucky he's got good parents to look after him once he goes home,' the doctor said.

Chick thought of his mother, forever chopping up carrots to put in the stew. He'd have to eat them. His throat closed convulsively. He knew he couldn't.

And then there was the money, rolled up in the shoe-cleaning tin on the shelf in his bedroom. He would be able to see the tin all the time when he was lying in his own bed. He would never be able to forget. Never. And there was always the danger his ma would look inside it. He couldn't face going home. He couldn't face it. And he knew he would have to. He had no choice. He wished he were dead.

Arthur Morrison sighed heavily and shouldered his new burden with his accustomed strength of mind. 'Yes, he can come home to his mother and me as soon as he's well enough. He'll always have us to rely on.'

Chick Morrison winced with despair and shut his eyes. His father tried to stifle a surge of irritation, and the doctor thought the boy an ungrateful little beast.

THE LOOK OF EAGLES

John Taintor Foote

I HAD waited ten minutes on that corner. At last I ventured out
from the curb and peered down the street, hoping for the sight
of a red and white sign that read: THIS CAR FOR THE RACES. Then a
motor horn bellowed, too close for comfort. I stepped back hastily in
favour of the purring giant that bore it, and looked up into the
smiling eyes of the master of Thistle Ridge. The big car slid its
length and stopped. Its flanks were white with dust. Its little stint that
morning had been to sweep away the miles between Lexington and
Louisville.

'Early, aren't you?' asked Judge Dillon as I settled back contentedly
at his side.

'Thought I'd spend a few hours with our mutual friend,' I explained.

I felt an amused glance.

'Diverting and – er – profitable, eh? What does the victim say
about it?'

'He never reads them,' I confessed; and Judge Dillon chuckled.

'I've come over to see our Derby candidate in particular,' he
informed me. 'I haven't heard from him for a month. Your friend is
a poor correspondent.'

The gateman at Churchill Downs shouted directions at us a few
moments later and the car swung to the left, past a city of stables. As
we wheeled through a gap in a line of whitewashed stalls we heard
the raised voice of Blister Jones. He was confronting the hapless
Chick and a steaming bucket.

'Fur the brown stud, eh?' we heard. 'Let's look at it.'

Chick presented the bucket in silence. Blister peered at its contents.

'Soup!' he sniffed. 'I thought so. Go rub it in your hair.'

'You tells me to throw the wet feed into him, didn't you?' Chick inquired defensively.

'Last week – yes,' said Blister. 'Not all summer. Someday a thought'll get in your nut 'n' bust it!' His eyes caught the motor and his frown was instantly blotted out.

'Why, how-de-do, Judge!' he said. 'I didn't see you.'

'Don't mind us,' Judge Dillon told him as we alighted. 'How's the colt?'

Blister turned and glanced at a shining bay head protruding from an upper door.

'Well, I'll tell you,' he said deliberately. 'He ain't such a bad sort of a colt in some ways. Fur a while I liked him; but here lately I get to thinkin' he won't do. He's got a lot of step. He shows me a couple o' nice works; but if he makes a stake hoss I'm fooled bad.'

'Huh!' grunted Judge Dillon. 'What's the matter? Is he sluggish?'

'That wouldn't worry me so much if he was,' said Blister. 'They don't have to go speed crazy all at once.' He hesitated for a moment, looking up into the owner's face. Then, as one breaking terrible news: 'Judge,' he said, 'he ain't got the class.'

There followed a silence. In it I became aware that the blue and gold of Thistle Ridge would not flash from the barrier on Derby Day.

'Well, ship him home,' said Judge Dillon at last as he sat down rather heavily on a bale of hay. He glanced once at the slim bay head, then turned to us with a smile. 'Better luck next year,' he said.

I was tongue-tied before that smile, but Blister came to the rescue.

'You still like that Fire Fly cross don't you?' he asked with a challenge in his voice.

'I do,' asserted Judge Dillon firmly. 'It gives 'em bone like nothing else.'

'Yep,' agreed Blister, ''n' a lot of it goes to the head. None of that Fire Fly blood fur mine. Nine out of ten of 'em sprawl. They don't gather up like they meant it. Now you take ole Torch Bearer—'

I found a chair and became busy with my own thoughts. I wondered if, after all, the breeding of speed horses was not too cruelly disappointing to those whose heart and soul were in it. The moments of triumph were wonderful, of course. The thrill of any other game was feeble in comparison; but oh, the many and bitter disappointments!

At last I became conscious of a little old man approaching down the line of stalls. His clothes were quite shabby; but he walked with crisp erectness, with something of an air. He carried his soft hat in his hand and his silky hair glistened like silver in the sunshine. As he stopped and addressed a stable boy, a dozen stalls from where we sat, the courteous tilt of his head was vaguely familiar.

'Who's that old man down there?' I asked. 'I think I've seen him before.'

Blister followed my eyes and sat up in his chair with a jerk. He looked about him as though contemplating flight.

'Oh, Lord!' he said. 'Now I'll get mine!'

'Who is it?' I repeated.

'Ole Man Sanford,' answered Blister. 'I ain't seen him fur a year. I hopped a hoss fur him once. I guess I told you.'

I nodded.

'What's he talking about?' asked Judge Dillon.

And I explained how Old Man Sanford, a big breeder in his day, was now in reduced circumstances; how he had, with a small legacy, purchased a horse and placed him in Blister's hands; how Blister had given the horse stimulants before a race, contrary to racing rules; and how Mr Sanford had discovered it and had torn up his tickets when the horse won.

'Tore up his tickets!' exclaimed Judge Dillon. 'How much?'

'Fifteen hundred dollars,' I replied. 'All he had in the world.'

Judge Dillon whistled.

'I've met him,' he said. 'He won a Derby thirty years ago.' He bent forward and examined the straight, white-haired little figure. 'Tore up his tickets, eh?' he repeated. Then softly: 'Blood will tell!'

'Here he comes,' said Blister uneasily. 'He'll give me the once-over 'n' brush by, I guess.'

But Old Man Sanford did nothing of the sort. A radiant smile and two extended hands greeted Blister's awkward advance.

'My deah young friend, how is the world treatin' you these days?'

'Pretty good, Mr Sanford,' answered Blister and hesitated. 'I kinda thought you'd be sore at me,' he confessed. 'While I didn't mean it that way, I give you a raw deal, didn't I?'

A hand rested on Blister's sleeve for an instant.

'When yoh hair,' said Old Man Sanford, 'has taken its colour from the many wintuhs whose stohms have bowed yoh head, you will have learned this: We act accohdin' to our lights. Some are brighter, some are dimmer, than others; but who shall be the judge?'

Whether or not Blister got the finer shadings of this, the sense of it was plain.

'I might have knowed you wouldn't be sore,' he said relievedly. 'Here's Chick. You remember Chick, Mr Sanford.'

Chick was greeted radiantly. Likewise 'Petah.'

'And the hawses? How are the hawses? Have you a nice string?' Blister turned and 'made us acquainted' with Old Man Sanford.

'Chick,' he called, 'get a chair fur Mr Sanford. Pete – you boys start in with the sorrel hoss 'n' bring 'em all out, one at a time!'

'Why, now,' said Mr Sanford, 'I mustn't make a nuisance of myself. It would be a great pleasuh, suh, to see yoh hawses; but I do not wish to bothah you. Suppose I just walk from stall to stall?'

He tried to advance toward the stalls, but was confronted by Blister, who took him by the arms, smiled down into his face, and gave him a gentle shake.

'Now listen!' said Blister. 'As long as we're here you treat this string like it's yours. They'll come out 'n' stand on their ears if you want to see it. You got me?'

I saw a dull red mount slowly to the wrinkled cheeks. The little figure became straighter, if possible, in its threadbare black suit. I saw an enormous silk handkerchief, embroidered and yellow with age, appear suddenly as Old Man Sanford blew his nose. He started to speak, faltered, and again was obliged to resort to the handkerchief.

'I thank you, suh,' he said at last, and found a chair as Judge Dillon's eyes sought mine.

We left him out of our conversation for a time; but as the string was led before him one by one the horseman in Mr Sanford triumphed. He passed loving judgment on one and all, his face keen and lighted. Of the colt I had just heard doomed he said:

'A well-made youngsteh, gentlemen; his blood speaks in every line of him. But as I look him oveh I have a feeling – it is, of cohse, no moh than that – that he lacks a certain quality essential to a great hawse.'

'What quality?' asked Judge Dillon quickly.

'A racin' heart, suh,' came the prompt reply.

'Oh, that's it, is it?' said Judge Dillon, and added dryly: 'I own him.'

Mr Sanford gave one reproachful glance at Blister.

'I beg yoh pahdon, suh,' he said earnestly to Judge Dillon. 'A snap judgment in mattehs of this sawt is, of cohse, wo'thless. Do not give my words a thought, suh. They were spoken hastily, without due deliberation, with no real knowledge on which to base them. I sincerely hope I have not pained you, suh.'

Judge Dillon's big hand swung over and covered one of the thin knees encased in shiny broadcloth.

'No sportsman,' he said, 'is hurt by the truth. That's just exactly what's the matter with him. But how did you know it?'

Mr Sanford hesitated.

'I'm quite likely to be mistaken, suh,' he said; 'but if it would interest you I may say that I missed a certain look about his head, and moh pahticularly in his eyes, that is the hallmark – this is merely my opinion, suh – of a really great hawse.'

'What kind of a look?' I asked.

Again Mr Sanford hesitated.

'It is hard to define, suh,' he explained. 'It is not a matteh of skull structure – of confohmation. It is—' He sought for words. 'Well, suh, about the head of a truly great hawse there is an air of freedom unconquerable. The eyes seem to look on heights beyond our gaze. It is the look of a spirit that can soar. It is not confined to hawses; even in his pictures you can see it in the eyes of the Bonaparte. It is the birthright of eagles. They all have it— But I express myself badly.' He turned to Judge Dillon. 'Yoh great mayeh has it, suh, to a marked degree.'

'Très Jolie?' inquired Judge Dillon, and Mr Sanford nodded.

I had heard of a power – psychic, perhaps – which comes to a few, a very few, who give their lives and their hearts to horses. I looked curiously at the little old man beside me. Did those faded watery eyes see something hidden from the rest of us? I wondered.

Blister interrupted my thoughts.

'Say, Mr Sanford,' he asked suddenly, 'what did you ever do with Trampfast?'

'I disposed of him, suh, foh nine hundred dollahs.'

Blister considered this for a moment.

'Look-a-here!' he said. 'You don't like the way I handled that hoss fur you, 'n' I'd like a chance to make good. I know where I can buy a right good plater fur nine hundred dollars. I'll make him pay his way or no charge. What do you say?'

Mr Sanford shook his head. 'As a matteh of fact,' he stated, 'I have only six hundred dollahs now in hand. Aside from having learned that my racing methods are not those of today, I would not care to see the pu'ple and white on a six-hundred-dollah hawse.'

'Why, look-a-here!' urged Blister. 'All the big stables race platers. There's good money in it when it's handled right. Let a goat chew dust a few times till you can drop him in soft somewheres, 'n' then put a piece of change on him at nice juicy odds. The boy kicks a win out of him, maybe; 'n' right there he don't owe you nothin'.'

Once more I saw a dull red flare up in Mr Sanford's face; but now he favoured Blister with a bristling stare.

'I have difficulty in following you at times, suh,' he said. 'Am I justified in believing that the word "goat" is applied to a thorough-bred race hawse?'

'Why, yes, Mr Sanford,' said Blister, 'that's what I mean, I expect.'

The old gentleman seemed to spend a moment in dismissing his wrath. When he spoke at last no trace of it was in his voice.

'I am fond of you, my young friend,' he said. 'Under a cynical exterior I have found you courteous, loyal, tender-hearted; but I deplore in you the shallow flippancy of this age. It is the fashion to sneer at the finer things; and so you call a racin' thoroughbred a goat. He is not of stake quality perhaps.' Here the voice became quite gentle: 'Are you?'

'I guess not, Mr Sanford,' admitted Blister.

'Never mind, my boy. If man breeds one genius to a decade it is enough. And so it goes with hawses. Foh thirty years, with love, with reverence, I tried to breed great hawses – hawses that would be a joy, an honoh to my state. In those days ninety colts were foaled each spring at Sanfo'd Hall. I have spent twenty thousand dollahs foh a single matron. How many hawses – truly great hawses – did such brood mayehs as that produce? How many do you think?'

Judge Dillon gave Mr Sanford the warm look of a brother.

'Not many,' he murmured.

'Why, I dunno, Mr Sanford,' said Blister. 'You tells me about one – the filly that copped the Derby fur you.'

'Yes; she was one. And one moh, suh. Two in all.'

'I never hear you mention but the one,' said Blister.

'The other never raced,' explained Mr Sanford. 'I'll tell you why.'

He lapsed into silence, into a sort of reverie, while we waited.

When he spoke it was totally without emotion. His voice was dull. It seemed somehow as though speech had been given to the dead past.

'It has been a long time,' he said, more to himself than to us. 'A long time!' he repeated, nodding thoughtfully, and again became silent.

'In those days,' he began at last, 'it was the custom of their mistress to go to the no'th pastuh with sugah, and call to the weanlin's. In flytime the youngstehs preferred the willow trees by the creek, and there was a qua'tah of a mile of level bluegrass from those willows to the pastuh gate. She would stand at the gate and call. As they heard her voice the colts would come oveh the creek bank as though it were a barrier − a fair start and no favohs asked. The rascals like sugah, to be sure; but an excuse to fight it out foh a qua'tah was the main point of the game.

'One year a blood bay colt, black to the hocks and knees, was foaled in January. In June he got his sugah fuhst by two open lengths. In August he made them hang their heads foh shame − five, six, seven lengths he beat them; and their siahs watchin' from the paddocks.

'In the spring of his two-year-old fohm he suffered with an attack of distempah. He had been galloped on the fahm track by then, and we knew just what he was. We nuhsed him through it, and by the following spring he was ready to go out and meet them all foh the honoh of the pu'ple and white.

'Then, one night, I was wakened to be told that a doctoh must be fetched and that each moment was precious. I sent my body sehvant to the bahns with the message that I wished a saddle on the best hawse in stable. When pahtially dressed I followed him, and was thrown up by a stable man. . . .

'There was a moon − a gracious moon, I remembah − the white road to Gawgetown, and a great fear at my heart. I did not know what was under me until I gave him his head on that white, straight road. Then I knew. I cannot say in what time we did those four miles; but this I can tell you − the colt ran the last mile as stanchly as the first, and one hour later he could barely walk. His terrific pace oveh that flinty road destroyed his tendons and broke the small bones in his legs. He gave his racin' life foh his lady, like the honest gentleman he was. His sacrifice, howeveh, was in vain. . . . Death had the heels of him that night. Death had the heels of him!'

In a tense silence I seemed to hear a bell tolling. 'Death had the heels of him!' it boomed over and over again.

Blister's eyes were starting from their sockets, but he did not hear the bell. He wet his parted lips.

'What become of him?' he breathed.

'When the place was sold he went with the rest. You have seen his descendants race on until his name has become a glory. The colt I rode that night was – Torch Bearer.'

Blister drew in his breath with a whistling sound.

'Torch Bearer!' he gasped. 'Did you own Torch Bearer?'

'I did, suh,' came the quiet answer. 'I bred and raised him. His blood flows in the veins of many – er – goats, I believe you call them.'

'Man, oh, man!' said Blister, and became speechless.

I, too, was silent of necessity. There was something wrong with my throat.

And now Judge Dillon spoke, and it was apparent that he was afflicted like myself. Once more the big hand covered the thin knee.

'Mr Sanford,' I heard, 'you can do me a favour if you will.'

'My deah suh, name it!'

'Go to Lexington. Look over the colts at Thistle Ridge. If you find one good enough for the purple and white, bring him back here. . . . He's yours!'

I went along. Oh, yes; I went along. I should miss two days of racing; but I would have missed more than that quite willingly. I was to see Old Man Sanford pick out one from a hundred colts – and all 'bred clear to the clouds', as Blister explained to us on the train. I wondered whether any one of them would have that look – 'the birthright of eagles' – and hoped, I almost prayed, that we should find it.

That the colt was to be a purchase, not a gift, had made our journey possible. Five hundred dollars cash and 'my note, suh, for a like amount'.

Judge Dillon had broken the deadlock by accepting; then offered his car for the trip to Lexington. At this a grin had appeared on Blister's face.

'No chance, Judge,' he said.

'I thank you, suh, foh youh generosity,' apologized Mr Sanford. 'It gives me the deepest pleasuh, the deepest gratification, suh; but, if you will pahdon me, I shall feel moh at home on the train.'

'You couldn't get him in one of them things on a bet,' Blister explained; and so a locomotive pulled us safely into Lexington.

We spent the night at the hotel and drove to Thistle Ridge early next morning behind a plodding pair. Even in Kentucky, livery horses are – livery horses.

A letter from Judge Dillon opened the big gates wide and placed us in charge of one Wesley Washington – as I live by bread, that was his name – suspicious by nature and black as a buzzard. I reminded him of my previous visit to Thistle Ridge. He acknowledged it with no sign of enthusiasm.

'What kinda colt you want?' he asked Blister.

'A good one!' answered Blister briefly.

Wesley rolled the whites of his eyes at him and sniffed.

'You ain' said nothin',' he stated. 'Dat's all we got.'

'You're lucky,' Blister told him. 'Well, trot 'em out.'

Then Wesley waved his wand – it chanced to be a black paw with a pinkish palm – and they were trotted out; or, rather, they came rearing through the doorway of the biggest of the big stables. Bays, browns, blacks, sorrels, chestnuts, roans – they bubbled out at us in an endless stream. Attached precariously to each of them – this was especially true when they reared – was a coloured boy. These Wesley addressed in sparkling and figurative speech. His remarks, as a rule, were prefaced by the word 'Niggah.'

At last Blister shouted through the dust.

'Say,' he said, 'this ain't gettin' us nowhere. Holy fright! How many you got?'

'Dat ain' half,' said Wesley ominously.

'Cut it out!' directed Blister. 'You'll have me popeyed in a minute. We'll go through the stalls 'n' pick out the live ones. This stuff's too young anyway. We want a two-year-old broke to the barrier. Have you got any?'

I turned to Mr Sanford. He was standing hat in hand, as was his custom, his face ablaze.

'The grandest spectacle I have witnessed in thirty yeahs, suh!' he informed me.

'Has we got a two-year-old broke to de barrieh?' I heard from Wesley. 'Hush! Jus' ambulate oveh disaway.' He led us to a smaller stable. It contained two rows of box stalls with a wide alley down the middle. Through the iron gratings in each stall I could see a snakelike head. The door at the opposite end of the stable looked out on the tawny oval of the farm track, and suddenly something flashed across the doorway so quickly that I only guessed it to be a thoroughbred with a boy crouching along his neck.

Wesley's eye swept up and down the two lines of box stalls. He looked at Blister with a prideful gleam.

'All two-yeah-olds,' he said, 'an' ready to race.'

If this statement made any impression it was concealed. Blister yawned and sauntered to the first stall on the right.

'Well, there might be a plater among 'em,' he said. 'This all you got?'

'Ain' dat enough?' inquired Wesley with a snort.

'Not if they're the culls,' said Blister. 'You read that letter, didn't you? We're to see 'em all. Don't forget that.'

'Hyar dey is,' said Wesley. 'Jus' use yoh eyes an' yoh han's.'

'All right,' said Blister as he opened the stall door – 'but don't hold nothin' out on us. Mr Sanford here is an old friend of the Judge.'

Wesley rolled an inspecting eye over Mr Sanford.

'I ain' neveh seen him roun' hyar,' he stated, and honours were easy.

The battle was on in earnest a moment later. The colt in the first stall was haltered and led out into the runway. He was jet black with one white star, and wonderful to see.

'Nothing' finah on fo' laigs,' said Wesley, and I mentally agreed with him; but Blister walked once round that glorious creature and waved him back into his stall.

'Yep,' he said; 'he's right good on four legs, but he'll be on three when that curb begins to talk to him.'

'Shuh!' said Wesley in deep disgust. 'You ain' goin' to call dat little fullness in de tendon a curb, is you? He'll die of ole aige an' neveh know he's got it.'

'He dies of old age before I own him,' said Blister, and walked to the second stall.

And so it went for an hour. Mr Sanford was strangely silent. When he ventured an opinion at all it was to agree with Wesley, and I was disappointed. I had hoped for delightful dissertations, for superhuman judgments. I had expected to see a master at work with his chosen medium. Instead, he seemed a child in the hands of the skillful Wesley; and I felt that Blister was our only hope.

This opinion had become settled when the unexpected happened. After a more than careful inspection of a chestnut colt, Blister turned to Wesley.

'What's this colt done?' he asked.

'Half in fifty,' Wesley stated. 'Jus' play foh him.'

'Put a boy on him 'n' let's see him move,' said Blister.

Then Mr Sanford spoke.

'It will be unnecessary,' he said quietly. 'I do not like him.'

A puzzled expression spread itself over Blister's face.

'All right,' he said with a shade of annoyance in his voice. 'You're the doctor.'

And then I noticed Wesley – Wesley, the adroit – and a look of amazement, almost of terror, was in his eyes as he stared at Mr Sanford.

'Yessuh,' he said with a gulp. 'Yessuh.' Then he pulled himself together. 'Put him up, black boy,' he directed magnificently, and moved to the next stall.

I stayed behind and displayed a quarter cautiously.

'Do you like this colt?' I asked, looking the boy straight in the face.

For a moment he hesitated. Then:

'No, suh,' he whispered.

'Why not?' I inquired.

There was a flicker of contempt in the white eyeballs.

'He's a houn',' I barely heard as the quarter changed owners.

It was a well-spent quarter; it had purchased knowledge. I knew now that among our party was a pair of eyes that could look deep into the heart of things. Old they were and faded, those eyes; but I felt assured that a glistening flank could not deceive them.

We worked down one side of the stable and up the other. We had seen twenty colts when we arrived at the last stall. It contained a long-legged sorrel and Blister damned him with a grunt when he was led out.

'If he ever gets tangled up,' was his comment, 'you don't get his legs untied that year. This all you got?'

Wesley assured him it was. We seemed to have reached an *impasse*. Then, as Blister frowned absently at the sorrel colt, a voice began singing just outside the stable. It was a rich treble and it chanted in a minor key. I saw the absent look wiped slowly from Blister's face. It was supplanted by a dawning alertness as he listened intently.

Suddenly he disappeared through the doorway and there came to me a regular scuff-scuff on the gravel outside, in time to the words of the song, which were these:

> '*Bay colt wuck in fo'ty-eight,*
>   *Goin' to de races – goin' to de races;*
> *Bay colt wuck in fo'ty-eight,*
>   *Goin' to de races now.*'

I felt my jaw begin to drop, for Blister's voice had joined the unknown singer's.

> '*Bay colt wuck in fo'ty-eight,*'

sang the voice; and then a bellow from Blister:

> '*Goin' to the races – goin' to the races.*'

The voice repeated:

> '*Bay colt wuck in fo'ty-eight,*'

and resigned to Blister's:

> '*Goin' to the races now!*'

I went hastily through that doorway and arrived at the following phenomena:

Exhibit A – One chocolate-coloured boy, not more than three feet high. His shoes (I mention them first because they constituted one-half of the whole exhibit) were— But words are feeble – *prodigious*, *Gargantuan*, are only mildly suggestive of those shoes. His stockings – and now I cross my heart and hope to die – were of the variety described commercially as ladies' hose, and they were pink and they were silk. Somewhere beneath their many folds two licorice sticks performed the miracle of moving those unbelievable shoes through an intricate clog dance.

Exhibit B – One Blister Jones, patting with feet and hands an accompaniment to the wonders being performed by the marvellous shoes.

Both exhibits were entirely in earnest and completely absorbed. As has been already told, they were joined in song.

As I assured myself that the phenomena were real and not imaginary, the words of the song changed.

> *'Bay colt wuck in fo'ty-eight,'*

came steadfastly from the smaller singer; but Blister, instead of 'Going to the races', sang:

> *'Where's he at? Where's he at?'*
> *'Bay colt wuck in fo'ty-eight,'*

insisted Exhibit A; and Exhibit B sang:

> *'Where's that bay colt now?'*

They learn early, in Kentucky, that track and farm secrets are sacred. A suspicion of all outsiders, though dulled by the excitement of white folks' appreciation, still flickered somewhere in the kinky dome of Exhibit A. The song was twice repeated without variation, and the 'Where's he at?' became tragic in its pleading tone.

At last Exhibit A must have decided that his partner in song was a kindred spirit and worthy of trust. At any rate,

> *'Oveh in de coolin' shed – oveh in de coolin' shed,'*

I heard; and Blister brought the duet to a triumphant close with:

> *'Over in the coolin' shed now!'*

He swung round and grinned at Wesley, who was standing stupefied in the doorway.

'Why, Wes!' he said reproachfully. 'I'm surprised at you!'

Wesley glowered at Exhibit A.

'You ramble!' he said and the marvellous shoes bore their owner swiftly from our sight.

So, through song, was the wily Wesley brought to confusion. We found four two-year-olds in the long, squatty cooling shed, and Wesley admitted, under pressure, that they were the pick of their year, kept for special training.

Three of them stood in straw to their knees, confined in three tremendous box stalls. One was being led under blankets up and down the runway. His sides lifted their covering regularly. His clean-cut velvet nostrils widened and contracted as he took his breath. His eyes were blazing jewels. To him went Blister, like iron filings to a magnet.

'Peel him fur a minute,' he said, and the still dazed and somewhat chastened Wesley nodded his permission.

Then appeared the most perfect living creature I had ever seen. He was a rich bay – now dark mahogany because of a recent bath – and the sheer beauty of him produced in me a feeling of awe, almost of worship. I was moved as though I listened to the Seventh Symphony or viewed the Winged Victory; and this was fit and proper, for my eyes were drinking in a piece by the greatest of all masters.

Blister was cursing softly, reverently, as though he were at prayer.

'If he's only half as good as he looks!' he sighed at last. 'How about *him*, Mr Sanford?'

I had forgotten Old Man Sanford. I now discovered him standing before a stall and gazing raptly at what was within. At Blister's words he turned and surveyed the bay colt.

'The most superb piece of hawseflesh,' he said, 'I have eveh had the pleasuh of observing. I could not fault him with a microscope. He is nothing shawt of perfection, suh – nothing shawt of perfection.' His eyes lingered for an instant on the wet flanks of the uncovered colt. 'He's too wahm to be without his clothing,' he suggested, and turned again to the stall before him.

Blister covered the colt with one dexterous swing. He glanced at the name embroidered on the blankets.

'Postman,' he read aloud. 'He'll be by Messenger, won't he?' The boy at the colt's head nodded. 'Worked in forty-eight just now, eh?' said Blister to no one in particular. Again the boy nodded. 'Well,' decided Blister, 'we'll take a chance on him. Train fur Looeyville at four o'clock – ain't they, Wes?'

Wesley gave a moan of anguish.

'My Gawd!' he said.

'What's bitin' you?' demanded Blister. 'We're payin' fur him, ain't we?'

'Lemme have dat letter one moh time,' said Wesley. He absorbed the letter's contents as though it were poison, and came at last to the fatal 'John C. Dillon' at the end. This he read aloud and slowly shook his head. 'He's los' his min',' he stated, and glared at Mr Sanford. 'What you payin' fo' dis hyar colt?' he demanded.

Mr Sanford glanced in our direction. His eyes had a far-away look.

'Were you addressing me?' he asked.

'Yessuh,' replied Wesley. 'I was inquirin' de price you aim to pay foh dis colt.'

'That is a matteh,' said Old Man Sanford, 'that concerns only yoh mas – employeh and myself. Howeveh, I am not going to pu'chase the colt to which you refeh.' He glanced dreamily into the stall before which he seemed rooted. 'I have taken a fancy to my little friend in hyar. . . . Could you oblige me with a piece of sugah?'

As one man, Blister and I made a rush for that stall. We peered through the bars for a moment and our amazed eyes met. In Blister's an angry despair was dawning. He turned savagely on Mr Sanford.

'You goin' to buy that shrimp?' he demanded.

'Yes, suh,' said Old Man Sanford mildly. 'I expect to pu'chase him. . . . Ah, here's the sugah!' He took some lumps of sugar from the now beaming Wesley and opened the stall door.

Blister stepped inside the stall and devoted some moments to vain pleadings. Mr Sanford was unmoved by them.

Then the storm broke. Blister became a madman who raved. He cursed not only the small black two-year-old, standing knee-deep in golden straw, but the small, white-haired old gentleman who was placidly feeding him sugar. The storm raged on, but Mr Sanford gave no sign.

At last I saw a hand that was extended to the colt's muzzle begin to tremble, and I took Blister by the arm and drew him forcefully away.

'Stop!' I said in an undertone. 'You're doing no good and he's an old man.'

Blister tore his arm from mine.

'He's an old fool!' he cried. 'He's chuckin' away the chance of a lifetime!' Then his eye fell on the bay colt and his voice became a wail. 'Ain't it hell?' he inquired of high heaven. 'Ain't it just hell?'

At this point Wesley saw fit to emit a loud guffaw. Blister advanced on him like a tiger.

'Laugh, you black boob!' he shot out, and Wesley's joyous expression vanished.

I saw that I was doing no good and joined Mr Sanford in the stall.

'Rather small, isn't he?' I suggested.

'He could be a little larger,' Mr Sanford admitted. 'He could stand half a han' and fifty pounds moh at his aige; but then, he'll grow. He'll make a hawse some day.'

And now came Blister, rather sheepish, and stood beside us.

'I got sore, Mr Sanford,' he said. 'I oughta be kicked!'

Old Man Sanford proffered a lump of sugar to the slim black muzzle. It was accepted so eagerly that the sugar was knocked from the extended hand. Mr Sanford pointed a reproving finger at the colt.

'Not quite so fast, young man!' he admonished. Then he turned to Blister with a gentle smile. 'Youth is hasty,' he said, 'and sometimes – mistaken.'

I returned to Cincinnati and work that night, filled with speculations about a small black colt and his new owner. The latter, I felt, had reached a stubborn dotage.

Two months rolled by; they crawled for me. . . . The powers above decreed that the paper should fight the Bull Moose to the death. I trained the guns of the editorial page on a dauntless smile and adored its dynamic owner in secret.

Those were full days, but I found time somehow for a daily glance at the racing news. One morning I read the following:

Postman, a bay colt, bred and owned by John C. Dillon, captured the two-year-old event without apparent effort. It was the winner's first appearance under colors. He is a big, rangy youngster, as handsome as a picture. He appears to be a very high-class colt and should be heard from.

'Poor Blister!' I thought; and later, as I read again and again of smashing victories by a great and still greater Postman, I became quite venomous when I thought of Old Man Sanford. I referred to him mentally as 'That old fool!' and imagined Blister in horrid depths of despair.

Then the bugle called for the last time that year at Lexington, and the thoroughbreds came to my very door to listen for it.

For days thereafter, as luck would have it, I was forced to pound my typewriter viciously, everlastingly, and was too tired when night came to do more than stagger to bed. At last there came a lull, and I fled incontinently to Latonia and the world of horse.

I approached Blister's stalls as one draws near a sepulchre. I felt that my voice, when I addressed him, should be pitched as though in the presence of a casket. I was shocked, therefore, at his lightness of mien.

'Hello, Four Eyes!' he said cheerfully. 'How's the ole scout?'

I assured him that my scouting days were not yet over. And then: 'I've been reading about Postman,' I said.

'Some colt!' said Blister. 'He's bowed 'em home five times now. They've made him favourite fur the Hammond against all them Eastern babies.'

There was genuine enthusiasm in his voice and I was filled with admiration for a spirit that could take a blow so jauntily. His attitude was undoubtedly the correct one, but I could not accomplish it. I thought of the five thousand dollars that went, with the floral horseshoe, to the winner of the Hammond stake. I thought of a gentle, fine, threadbare old man who needed that five thousand – Oh, so desperately – and I was filled with bitter regrets, with malice and bad words.

'Of course he'll win it!' I burst out spitefully.

'Why, I dunno,' drawled Blister, and added: 'I thought Judge Dillon was a friend of yours.'

'Oh, damn!' I said.

'Why, Four Eyes!' said Blister. ''N' Chick listenin' to you too!'

Chick grinned appreciatively. 'Don't let him kid ya,' he advised. 'He wasn't so gay hisself till—'

'Take a shot of grape juice,' interrupted Blister, ''n' hire a hall.'

Chick's voice trailed off into unintelligible mutterings as he turned away.

'How about Mr Sanford's colt?' I asked. 'Have you still got him?'

To my astonishment Blister broke into one of his rare fits of laughter. He all but doubled up with unaccountable mirth.

'Say, Chick,' he called when he could control his voice, 'he wants to know if we still got the Sanford colt!'

Chick had turned a rather glum face our way; but at the words his expression became instantly joyous.

'Oh, say!' he said.

Then began a series of hilarious exchanges, entirely without meaning to me.

'He's hangin' round somewhere, ain't he, Chick?'

'Why, maybe he is,' said Chick.

'You still throw a little rough feed into him occasionally, don't you, Chick?'

'When I got the time,' said Chick; and the two imbeciles roared with laughter.

At last Blister began beating me between the shoulder blades.

'We got him, Four Eyes,' he told me between thumps. 'Yep – we got him.'

'Stop!' I shouted. 'What the devil's the matter with you?'

Blister became serious.

'Come here!' he said, and dragged me to a stall. He threw back the upper door and a shaft of sunlight streamed into the stall's interior, bathing a slim black head and neck until they glistened like a vein of coal. 'Know him?' asked Blister.

'Yes,' I said. 'He's bigger though.'

'Look at him good!' ordered Blister.

I peered at the relaxed inmate of the stall, who blinked sleepily at me through the shaft of sunlight. Blister pulled me back, closed the stall door, and tightened his grip on my arm.

'Now listen!' he said. 'You just looked at the best two-year-old God ever put breath in!'

I took in this incredible information slowly. I exulted in it for a moment, and then came doubts.

'How do you know?' I demanded.

'How do I know!' exclaimed Blister. 'It 'ud take me a week to tell you. Man, he can fly! He makes his first start tomorrow – in the Hammond. Old Man Sanford'll get in tonight. Come out 'n' see a real colt run.'

My brain was whirling.

'In the Hammond?' I gasped. 'Does Mr Sanford know all this?'

Blister gave me a slow, a thoughtful look.

'It sounds nutty,' he said; 'but I can't figger it no other way. As sure as you 'n' me are standin' here – he knowed it from the very first!'

Until I closed my eyes that night I wondered whether Blister's words were true. If so, what sort of judgment, instinct, intuition had been used that day at Thistle Ridge? I gave it up at last and slept, to dream of a colt that suddenly grew raven wings and soared over the grandstand while I nodded wisely and said: 'Of course – the birthright of eagles!'

I got to Blister's stalls at one o'clock next day, and found Mr Sanford clothed in a new dignity hard to describe. Perhaps he had donned it with the remarkable flowered waistcoat he wore – or was it due to his flowing double-breasted coat, a sprightly blue in colour and suggesting inevitably a leather trunk, dusty, attic-bound, which had yawned and spat it forth?

'Welcome, suh; thrice welcome!' he said to me. 'I take the liberty of presuming that the pu'ple and white is honoured with yoh best wishes today.'

I assured him that from the bottom of my heart this was so. He wrung my hand again and took out a gold watch the size of a bun.

'Three hours moh,' he said, 'before our hopes are realized or shattered.'

'You think the colt will win?' I inquired.

Mr Sanford turned to the southwest. I followed his eyes and saw a bank of evil-looking clouds creeping slowly up the sky.

'I like our chances, suh,' he told me; 'but it will depend on those clouds yondeh. We want a fast track foh the little chap. He is a swallow. Mud would break his heart.'

'She's fast enough now,' said Blister, who had joined us; and Mr Sanford nodded.

So for three hours I watched the sky prayerfully and saw it become more and more ominous. When the bugle called for the Hammond at last, Latonia was shut off from the rest of the world by an inverted inky cup, its sides shot now and then with lightning flashes. We seemed to be in a great vacuum. I found my lungs snatching for each breath, while my racing card grew limp as I clutched it spasmodically in a sweating hand.

I had seen fit to take a vital interest in the next few moments; but I glanced at faces all about me in the grandstand and found them strained and unnatural. Perhaps in the gloom they seemed whiter than they really were; perhaps my own nerves pricked my imagination until this packed humanity became one beating heart.

I do not think that this was so. The dramatic moment goes straight to the soul of a crowd, and this crowd was to see the Hammond staged in a breathless dark, with the lightning's flicker for an uncertain spotlight.

No rain would spoil our chances that day, for now, across the centre field at the half-mile post, a mass of colours boiled at the barrier. The purple and white was somewhere in the shifting, surging line, borne by a swallow, so I had been told. Well, even so, the blue and gold was there likewise – and carried by what? Perhaps an eagle!

Suddenly a sigh – not the customary roar, but a deep intaking of the grandstand's breath — told me they were on the wing. I strained my eyes at the blurred mass of them, which seemed to move slowly in the distance as it reached the far turn of the back stretch. Then a flash of lightning came and my heart skipped a beat and sank.

They were divided into two unequal parts. One was a crowded, indistinguishable mass. The other, far ahead in unassailable isolation, was a single spot of bay with a splash of colour clinging above.

A roar of 'Postman!' shattered the quiet like a bombshell, for that splash of colour was blue and gold. The favourite was making a runaway race of it. He was coming home to twenty thousand joyful backers, who screamed and screamed his name.

Until that moment I had been the victim of a dream. I had come to believe that the little old man, standing silent at my side, possessed an insight more than human. Now I had wakened. He was an old fool in a preposterous coat and waistcoat, and I looked at him and laughed a mirthless laugh. He was squinting slightly as he peered with his washed-out eyes into the distance. His face was placid; and as I noticed this I told myself that he was positively witless. Then he spoke.

'The bay colt is better than I thought,' he said.

'True,' I agreed bitterly and noted, as the lightning flashed again, that the blue and gold was an amazing distance ahead of those struggling mediocre others.

'A pretty race,' murmured Old Man Sanford; and now I thought him more than doddering — he was insane.

Some seconds passed in darkness, while the grandstand gave off a contented murmur. Then suddenly the murmur rose to a new note. It held fear and consternation in it. My eyes leaped up the track. The bay colt had rounded the curve into the stretch. He was coming down the straight like a bullet; but — miracle of miracles! — it was plain that he was not alone. . . .

In a flash it came to me: stride for stride, on the far side of him, one other had maintained a flight equal to his own. And then I went mad; for this other, unsuspected in the darkness until now, commenced to creep slowly, surely, into the lead. Above his stretching neck his colours nestled proudly. He was bringing the purple and white safe home to gold and glory.

Nearer and nearer he came, this small demon whose coat matched the heavens, and so shot past us, with the great Postman — under the whip — two lengths behind him!

I remember executing a sort of bear dance, with Mr Sanford enfolded in my embrace. I desisted when a smothered voice informed me that my conduct was 'unseemly, suh – most unseemly!'

A rush to the track followed, where we found Blister, quite pale, waiting with a blanket. Suddenly the grandstand, which had groaned once and become silent, broke into a roar that grew and grew.

'What is it?' I asked.

Blister whirled and stared at the figures on the timing board. I saw a look of awe come into his face.

'What is it?' I repeated. 'Why are they cheering? Is it the time?'

'Oh, no!' said Blister with scornful sarcasm and a look of pity at my ignorance. 'It ain't the time!' He nodded at the figures. 'That's only the world's record fur the age 'n' distance.'

And now there came, mincing back to us on slender, nervous legs, something wet and black and wonderful. It pawed and danced wildly in a growing ring of curious eyes.

Then, just above the grandstand, the inky cup of the sky was broken and there appeared the light of an unseen sun. It turned the piled white clouds in the break to marvels of rose and gold. They seemed like the ramparts of heaven, set there to guard from earthly eyes the abode of the immortals.

'Whoa, man! Whoa, hon!' said Blister, and covered the heaving sides.

As he heard Blister's voice and felt the touch of the blanket the colt grew quiet. His eyes became less fiery wild. He raised his head, with its dilated blood-red nostrils, and stared – not at the mortals standing reverently about him, but far beyond our gaze – through the lurid gap in the sky, straight into Valhalla.

I felt a hand on my arm.

'The look of eagles, suh!' said Old Man Sanford.

PRIME ROGUES

Molly Keane

'You've walked the course, I suppose,' Lady Honour asked me, and I nodded. Indeed, Dick and I had but just completed the three miles in time for me to meet her in the throng that seethed (quite irrespective of owner or jockeyship) in the saddling enclosure before the horses went out for the second race.

We had been late in starting from Pullinstown that morning. James, who was staying behind to minister to the wants of a bed-ridden and sulking Willow, had not, I think, quite put the spur on his underlings in the matter of lunch, or at any rate not to the extent he would have done had he himself been in a fever to see the start of the first race on the card.

'Ah, what matter the first race,' he said in answer to Dick's protests, 'that confined race is no race. And for walking the course, Master Dick, that'll hardly delay ye any length, for it's a course needs very little improvement.'

I was still pondering on the true inwardness of this statement when the car, mercifully driven by Dick, got under way. We had not, however, proceeded very far down the avenue before our attention was attracted by a rook-like squawking from James and steam-whistle yells from a young member of Pullinstown's domestic staff, who at the same time pursued the car at a pace that did equal credit to her legs and lungs.

Dick reversed impatiently to meet her, wondering voluably as he did so what dire necessity of the day James had forgotten to pack into the car.

'A limon, Master Dick,' she breathed in his ear, thrusting her empurpled face in at the window, 'would ye bring a limon from the town, if ye please, and a couple o' round o' Beckett's Blue; and would ye leave the bets in with Miss Doyle.' She handed several mysterious little packages through the window.

'If Bridgie Hogan,' said Dick swiftly, 'hadn't broken down the bicycle with the weight she is from taking no exercise, I'd say she could ride it into town herself for her lemons and put on her own bets. As it is, she can go in on Shank's mare and out again. You may tell her that from me.'

'Oh great and merciful God—' The young messenger clapped a hand to her mouth and subsided in giggles, so we drove on and left her.

'Those divils,' Sir Richard observed negligently; 'how much work will they do today, I wonder.'

'Drinking tea and passing rude remarks with the stable-boys,' Dick commented. 'By the way, father, did ye tell Johnny to put that blister on Goldenrod?'

'I did, I think. I think I did. I wonder, Dick, would it have been wiser to have had him fired?'

'I wonder, would it?' Dick was never very committal with his father, I had noticed.

'I have had nothing but worry with that horse since he came into the place,' Sir Richard pondered grievously. 'I was really *hurt* when Lady Duncannon sent him back to me. You know she's a suspicious sort of woman – *very*. She wouldn't believe my word it was only splints he was lame on – all the same I'll never buy a horse again that's back of his knees, they always go on their tendons. Mrs Pheelan is out pretty smart to open the gate this morning, I notice. I think she kept Oliver and me waiting half an hour last night.'

'I suppose she thought you and Oliver were stopping out the night at Templeshambo – I know we did.' Dick shot a look at his father in which was as much censure as he dared combine with raillery.

'Ah,' said Sir Richard, 'we walked the soles off our boots looking for those young horses of your cousin Honour's. They might be anywhere in that place.'

'So they might. It's a great range for young horses. I hear she has a very nice two-year-old – out of the old mare. Is that true, father?'

'She has a very nice foal there, and not a bad sort of a yearling at all. I didn't think much of the two-year-old – she's a leggy divil, but, of course, the old ladies are cracked about her.'

'Out of their minds, I suppose.' Dick let the subject drop. He had no more curiosity in it. At this, indeed, I did not wonder, for I had myself unfolded to him and Willow every circumstance of our doings at Templeshambo, not omitting Sir Richard's secret visit to Mycross Station.

'I don't know what he's at,' Willow had commented. 'He has me puzzled.' And neither could Dick throw any light on Sir Richard's perplexing behaviour. 'It might be nothing at all,' Willow had said, 'or it might be *a bit of a plan*'; and there was as much dark secrecy in the way she said this as to fill my mind with a hundred suppositions of possible roguery.

But today I could not think why anything should be wrong. I was glad to be having a ride round, and very glad that the ride should be Lady Honour's horse. Unlikely, I knew, that I would beat Dick on Romance, even though he was giving me a lot of weight. Still, they say Dick is worth a stone to any horse he rides. There were other good things in the race besides Romance, for this was the end of the point-to-pointing season, which meant a fairly hot class of horses in an open light-weight race. The possible stars that had crowded the fields earlier in the season had now waned in their owners' estimation. They ran them no longer. Lady Honour being, I suppose, an exception to this, as to most other rules.

'Tootle around and enjoy yourself,' had been Willow's parting advice to me. 'Try not to take a fall, because falls hurt. Barring accidents, Dick should win it, though I'm a bit frightened of that horse of old Colonel Power's. I think he'd have beaten me at Lisgarry if he hadn't fallen, and he's receiving 7 lb from us today.'

'Ah, he'll tip up again—' Dick had been optimistic.

'Well, if he doesn't, Dick? It rained a lot last night and the going will be deep. Romance isn't too fond of the mud, and the 7 lb might just beat her. D'you remember that awful day at Kylemore? Ah, that race went *through* the mare; absolutely went through her.' Her voice was frail and vibrant at this suffering memory.

'I don't know. I'd be more afraid of something unknown in the field, such as Oliver's ride, for instance. D'you know, I think I'm giving him 21 lb - it's a divil of a penalty.'

'That, my dear? A four-year-old and I never liked her lack of guts. She was a good lepper, though, for a young horse. All Honour's horses lep like dogs. She has them following her round the country on strings like dogs - that's why. Well, I hope you enjoy yourself, Oliver, and collect all the chat for me.' Willow had said.

And we had walked the course, Dick and I – three miles over a very fair country it was. Banks with ditches mostly to you, a few stone walls, and not a twisty course either. 'All the same, mind you, this course walks a lot nicer than it rides, I always think,' Dick told me. 'I don't know what it is about these banks. They'd all meet you right if you were going the other way round. As it is there's always a lot of clouting and falling here.'

In the shelter of a gorse-blown bank we lit our cigarettes, the loud, small flutter of a white flag in our ears. Far and away blue shadows were painted wet and heavy on the mountains, and nearer fields of young oats were square-cut tourmalines in the flowing bright air – thickened to honey and burdened by almonds this loving air. But beyond any loving, far and unto itself, the little flame of a lark's song burned against the sky.

Dick took a walk out across the field and came back to me. 'I wonder how much ground you'd save if you did that,' he said, and stood considering the matter, his head sunk, his hands in his breeches pockets. 'You could jump the wall there instead of the bank, and not miss a flag at all. I do think that'd be the shortest course to go, Oliver. We'd better go back to the car and eat a sandwich now, I suppose. And you have to meet your owner.' He grinned unkindly: 'I'd rather ride for the devil himself,' said he, 'than ride a horse for Cousin Honour.'

But I found her still enchanting. When we had struggled out of the throng in the enclosure and through the mob that surged about the bookies' stand, she went straight as a bird to the spot where her car was parked, and this was a position which had (in addition to being not too far away from the weighing tent) the advantages of combining an excellent view of the course and an easy exit from the car park; this she told me on our way thither. 'And,' she said, unfolding her shooting stick, spearing it into the ground and seating her person thereon immediately before the dirtiest and most demure of the old, blunt-nosed Morris cars, 'Let me introduce you, Oliver, to Mr Billy Morgan; Captain Pulleyns – Mr Morgan.'

'Very pleased to meet you,' a preposterously good-looking young man shook me by the hand. He gave me his left hand because his right arm was in a sling, and he gave me three parts of a glance out of his navy-blue eyes that surprised me. He was tall, Mr Morgan. Yes, and dark, and handsome. Only his legs were vulgar, although he

had taken some pains about them, for his brown field boots were by
an excellent maker. His voice, too, was as preposterous as his looks,
and there hung about it the same rich comeliness. My cousins, Dick
and Willow, frequently speak in a strange brogue, and indeed express
their meaning more coarsely than did this young man; nevertheless
their voices cannot be compared. Theirs never lack a certain quality.
His never attained that certain quality.

'What bad luck about your collar bone,' I said.

'Wasn't it – rotten! Lady Honour's very cross with me,' there was a
certain charm about him, 'and Lady Eveleen won't speak to me at all.'

It was only now that I perceived Lady Eveleen seated in the car –
on the seat beside her was a vast blue roll of cotton wool, neatly
rolled white bandages, a saddle and a weight cloth. She looked as
important as any priestess at any other altar.

'Good morning,' I said, taking off my hat. 'Good morning,' said
she, and that was all. I could not help disliking her still evident
displeasure in the prospect of my riding. After all, how did she know
I would not give the horse a real good ride? Lady Honour, though
very sweet, was a little strained, perhaps a little silent. I wondered if
they could really be having a good bet on their horse, but thought it
unlikely. Mr Morgan only was happy, confident and friendly. He
stood upon the step of the car, his glasses to his eyes, and kept up a
running commentary on the horses going down to the start.

'God, that's a common divil of Hanlon's. Do you like that mare of
Johnny Kehoe's, Lady Honour? You know she's bred fit to win
races. I like the way she goes, too – near the ground and doesn't take
too much out of herself, She would stay. Look at young O'Brien
now, having a preliminary. What's that – black and a cerise cap – a
chestnut horse. Is it Bonny Judy? They're all down there now, I
think; twelve starters, that's not a bad field at all to go out in a
Farmer's race. Johnny Kehoe can't get a pull on that mare; look at
her shaking her head, she'll gallop into the bog-hole if he doesn't
watch himself – that's a shocking soft bog there on your left, mind,
as you go down to the start. Keep in beside the fence— They're off –
they're not; false start. God, he could have let them go, this isn't five
furlongs. Now they're off – there's some wicked riding the first mile
in this race, I tell you. That thing of Johnny Kehoe's is jumping very
ignorant – Johnny went out between her two ears. I thought he'd
never meet the saddle again. Wait now, this is a straight one they're

coming to. A horse very rarely meets it really right. I think there's not a big enough ditch to you for the height of it. They get under it somehow. Furlong's down! Well, the *welt* he hit it. Bonny Judy's down and there's another down. I can't see who it is. Johnny Kehoe's taking them a good gallop. He may quieten himself now – this is a real soft field and so is the next. That thing of Hartigan's is going very easily – he's jumping well; I wouldn't wonder if he beat Johnny.'

'What's leading, Major?' An incredibly old man, balancing on the fence beside the car, grasped my hand to pull me up beside him.

'I'll tell you in a minute.' I had found them again now. 'Kehoe's horse is leading still; Vain Lady second; and a chestnut horse third.'

'A chaistnut horse? Is it Tommy Hartigan is on him?'

'I couldn't tell you.'

'It must be them spy-glasses is not great good so. God knows ye'd nearly see that much with the sight o' yer eyes.'

I ventured after this to read the race aloud no more, and indeed the horses were but four fences from home, so we could see them plainly. The chestnut horse had gone up to the leaders now, and something of a contest was in progress.

'Come on, Hartigan! *Come* on, Hartigan!' The old man clung to me for his balance, and we swayed together on the bank in an ecstasy of excitement. 'Aha! Aha! He have John Kehoe bestered. Look at he sweepin' home. *God, he's off* —' as the chestnut horse, in landing over the last fence, made a bad mistake and a grand recovery. 'He's off! He's not! He's not, b'god! Only for he to be so great a jock and so constant he was gone —'

Tears streaming from his eyes, and the wind blowing his long hair and beard upwards and backwards, this ancient votary of sport clasped both my hands and would for very little, I think, have kissed me as a salute to speed and young courage, and to the emotion of dangerous endeavour.

'Bedam, he was as wise as a dog,' he said, 'I'd have to cry to see the poor bastard so courageous. 'Tis for a passion o' love I'd cry, or for the like of a horse race I'd rain tears from me two eyes. Did ye remark the way Hartigan did was to foster Johnny Kehoe always. Did he go nigh him at all till he come to win his race? He did not. Did he ever let him more than a couple o' perches out before him? He did not. Ah, Johnny Kehoe puts great conceit out of himself to be a real up-to-date jock, but – be the Holy Seaman – young Hartigan have him bewitched, bothered and bewildered.' He whipped round on a dreary young friend who up to the moment had simmered unnoticed beside him, and recommenced his masterly analysis of the race. But the time now being more than come when I should struggle again towards the weighing tent, I picked up saddle and weight cloth and accompanied by Lady Honour (her hand-bag full of spare lead), regretfully parted from my old companion.

'See here, Oliver,' said she to me as we clove our way through a party of young girls who had chosen the only gap in the fence as a suitable spot in which to drink pink lemonade and sport with their loves. 'Don't pay *any* attention to *anything* Beauty says to you about riding the mare.' I looked down to see two deep triangles of carnation in her cheeks, and tears, I think, excited her eyes. 'I don't like to say any one is a fool,' said she, and the tears snapped back from her eyes, 'but I think poor Beauty's *dull*.'

'She's not far out in thinking me a very inexperienced jockey over banks,' I put in guardedly.

'My dear boy,' Lady Honour was indeed in earnest, 'provided you don't actually fall off the mare the race is a gift to us. The mare's fit, she won't fall down and she has the legs of the lot of them; what more do you want?'

After which encomium of confidence I felt that any blame for defeat would more than certainly be laid at my door, which, since my mount was a four-year-old and this her first time out, I felt would be manifestly unfair. In fact, Lady Honour's unbridled expression of confidence in her horse depressed rather than cheered me. Almost I found myself at one with Lady Eveleen in wishing Mr Billy Morgan and not myself had the honour of the ride.

But that was before I had seen Surprise, for such was the name of Lady Honour Dermot's brown mare, four years old, to whom almost every other horse in the field of ten was giving a stone and some so much as 21 lb. I think only two of the entries on the card were at level weights with us, and I knew one of these did not run. In my opinion Surprise looked like giving weight and a beating to any horse in the race, although as a four-year-old she was so justly entitled to receive both. That she was indeed, but four off I found it difficult to believe, such muscle and such condition are not often carried by a young horse. I have seldom seen anything fitter run in a point-to-point, or look more like winning one.

Lady Honour and Lady Eveleen quarrelled outrageously over the saddling of their horse, a task with which Mr Billy Morgan and an astute-looking lad in a purple coat and trousers proceeded undeterred by the commands and suggestions of either lady.

'Put a pad under the saddle,' Lady Eveleen insisted. 'Can't any fool see it will cut the withers out of the mare the way it's down on her back?'

'Do no such thing; leave the saddle the way it is. Take up that girth, Jim. Willy, you put those bandages on beautifully in spite of your arm. I never saw bandages better put on, even by you.'

Mr Morgan, very quick and certain in his way of saddling a horse, accepted the compliment in silence.

'All the same,' Lady Eveleen was almost in tears, 'I can't bear the mare to go out with the saddle like that on her.'

'It's not down on her, Lady Eveleen. Really, it's not,' Mr Morgan found patience to tell her.

'Are you sure? Oh, did you *see* that poor horse that came in after the first race. Did you *see* it's back?'

'No, but Beauty, did you see the jockey's boots?' Lady Honour included even the lad in her exasperated witticism, 'they were oozing blood!'

'Now get mounted, please. Get mounted, please. Come on now, jockeys, get mounted, please.' An impatient steward made his first effort to get the horses out of the saddling enclosure and down to the start.

'*Oliver*,' Lady Eveleen hissed in my ear, 'you go up to the front and stay there. You'll keep out of trouble and interference.'

'*Do no such thing*.' Lady Honour's angrier hiss overrode her sister's whisper in my other ear. 'Let young Dick make the pace. That mare of his won't stay two miles in this going. Goodness me, she's tied to the ground with that penalty on her. Come away from him the last mile, and don't go winning the race before that, mind.'

All Mr Morgan said, as the boy led my mount out of the enclosure and clove for us a path through the mob outside was: 'You can fall and win the race. So don't let her go from you if you do fall.' And with such instructions I set out on my lone (lone at last) adventure.

'Thanks, thanks very much. *Would* you mind letting us through? We *rather* want to ride our horses —' It was Dick in the crowd behind me; Dick sitting on top of a packet of lead and Romance shaking her game little head and laying the ears back at the crowd. And there were others; the lad with the ankle-length boots and spurs two inches long and his breeches worn over his stockings, riding a savage of a brown horse that had killed one man and frightened several so badly that they never wanted to ride again; an M.F.H. with a face like one of his own dog hounds and a very pretty sort of hunting seat on a horse. An old man of a curious brave fragility. 'Many happy returns, Colonel Power,' Dick said to him. He told me afterwards that this was a sixty-fourth birthday party.

But we were out of the crowd now and riding our horses down a series of three small, bare fields, their grass eaten low by sheep and geese, and through a gap where a wall had been summarily knocked down to let us out into a lane and back into the country again through another gap of the same nature. The mare fidgeted and pulled me as we went, her head carried low, her back up under the saddle, she was, I have no doubt, switching her tail in a way that would have frightened me worse could I have seen it. As it was I felt miserably nervous. A cold wind turned knifishly on my cheek and made fun of the jersey (royal blue and a yellow sash, Lady Honour's colours) which I wore. I was the strange victim of that unhappy lack of feeling, in which state one belongs neither to one-self nor to one's horse, but to a chill blankness in which habit and instinct take the place of reasoned action.

Dick, riding up beside me, looked as strained and as paper-thin and as anxious as he always does look when going out to ride a race; keyed to the moment so that should one but gently touch him one might think he would thrum like a fiddle-string. He looked at me now and at the mare. 'Oliver,' he said, 'I'd say you'd beat me if you stand up. I never saw anything come on like that mare. I don't know her at all.' He looked puzzled for a moment instead of strained. It was then, I think, that my feeling of blankness and nerves fell from me. I was warm again and knew what I was about. I felt the mare's mouth and sat forward to canter down to the start, and it was when she felt me take hold of her that she jumped off after a fashion which might have told a sillier man even than I am that she had been ridden in work at least. I wondered; and I dropped my hands to her, and she stopped like an old chaser who has had plenty of it might do. And then I think, had I been wise, was the moment for me to decide on a soft fall out in the country or such palpable missing of a flag as could not but be objected to. But I am seldom wise though often lucky. Besides I had felt the mare's low, powerful stride, and the strange lust that comes on men to ride a race was on me now. Which is an emotional way of stating that when the starter let us go I was quite as mad to win my race as though no feelings of doubt had ever plucked at my reason as to whether or no my horse was qualified to run at all, much less to win.

This course doesn't ride as nice as it walks, Dick had said. Neither, he had said, did the fences meet you kindly. But if the fences did not meet us right, we met them so well that I would not have faulted them in any respect.

Never shall I describe my ride on Surprise that day. I may say that in the matter of riding to instructions I obeyed Lady Eveleen's to the letter, for after we had jumped the first fence blinded, and saved a fall how I knew not – I thought there was something in keeping out of trouble, and sent the mare on with the first three. Before we had gone a mile I knew without any doubt that I had the legs of the lot of them and a couple of stone in hand. The course rode heavy enough, and a field of plough followed by two with pretty deep going, brought Dick and Romance back to us all right. It was then that I sent Surprise into the lead, for, I thought, Dick won't want to lose me altogether, and the going and the weight between them will beat him here. Four banks in a nice straight line from us, the last one jumped on the down-hill and I went on at them. Dick stuck to me; I think he was right, for he knew now my mount was unlikely to tip up, and he could see she was going very easily; it would be difficult for him to make up ground later. The course turned pretty sharp left after the fourth of these nice banks, and Dick as he landed in the field beyond fairly cut the nose off me. '*There's* a rudeness,' I said to him as his sister Willow might have done, and terrified lest no nicer considerations should prevent his either pushing me off or tripping my horse up, I took a frightened look over my shoulder and went away from him like a scalded cat. We were less than a mile from home now, and I think Romance was stone-cold. How Dick sat still on her and held her together I do not know, but game and honest little bit that she is, Romance was giving us more weight than she could have done, even on top of the ground. We won very easily. Dick was not going to kill the mare when he saw he could not win. He finished third. The gentleman who was celebrating his sixty-

fourth birthday second, and not a feather out of him. He was very
fit.

It was Lady Eveleen (surprisingly enough) who detached herself
from the crowd and beat her sister by a short head only for the
honour of leading their horse in to unsaddle.

'My dear,' she said, 'you gave her a great ride and I'm so *delighted*
we've beaten Richard.' She was looking back at me and talking, her
face very gently radiant, not minding at all where she was going or
leading the horse. But I thought it unkind of Lady Honour to snatch
the rein from her sister with a biting comment. But Lady Eveleen
refused to be shaken off, and so conducted by them both I
dismounted at last and departed with my saddle towards the scales,
while they alternately assisted the boy to scrape lather off the mare,
and turned from their task to receive the congratulations of their
friends.

Any man who wins a race, whether point-to-point, steeplechase, or
on the flat is, for that brief moment, a hero and a good jockey. Let
him be beaten by a better horse and a short head when riding the
race of his life, and his stock is down at once. No one but can put a
finger then on some gross error in judgement on his part and there
are few among the commentators unconvinced that they (or almost
any one, indeed) could have ridden the race better. Today I was in
the former and more enviable position, and enjoyed it to the full as I
sat on the step of Lady Honour's car eating salmon sandwiches
(Dick's salmon was all right in sandwiches, anyhow) with a whisky
and soda, half a horn tumbler full of port and a rapidly cooling cup
of coffee ranged on the grass beside me. The arrival of Mr Billy
Morgan interrupted the praises and the questions of my two owners,
which I was enjoying almost as much as their food and drink.

'Well, didn't I tell you you'd enjoy yourself?' he said to me by
way, I suppose, of congratulation. 'But isn't she a great mare? A
different class from the ordinary point-to-point horse, isn't she? I
think indeed it's a pity for Lady Honour to knock her about in point-
to-points at all. That mare should be winning chases this minute.'

'Will you have a bun, Mr Morgan?' Lady Eveleen asked him, and
her manner was more than repressive.

'Thank you, but I don't care about sweet cakes.' Mr Morgan accepted
a salmon sandwich and a cup of tea, and we all ate comfortably, our
anxieties so happily over and the glow of success so close about us.

'Do you know anything, Lady Honour,' Mr Morgan inquired suddenly, 'is good for the nerves?'

'Goodness knows you're not troubled with nerves, Billy,' Lady Honour was both surprised and amused.

'Ah no, not in regard o' horses I wouldn't be,' Mr Morgan reassured us. 'But,' he went on seriously, 'when I'd be readin' a book – when I'd get to the excitin' part I'd have to t'row it down. I'd accuse it,' he added thoughtfully, 'on drinkin' tea.' And swilling the dregs of his cup three times round he aimed them with great precision at the nearest gorse bush.

'Has the mare started for home?' Lady Honour asked, fitting the lid on to a sandwich box with quick dexterity.

'Yes. I sent the boy off with her at once.' Mr Morgan put his cup away in a basket and rose to his feet; whether or not he had seen Dick and Sir Richard's approach, he took his departure without undue delay.

'Well, Oliver, you brat, that was a noble victory,' Dick smiled at me. 'Wait till Willow hears you defeated the mare – she'll tear you. I must congratulate Cousin Honour,' he said, and did so with all politeness. Sir Richard, too, expressed himself delighted that the race if not his should then be hers. 'Were you satisfied with Oliver's riding, Beauty?' he asked Lady Eveleen, but did not embarrass her by requiring an answer. 'I'm coming over to you tomorrow to look at that filly again,' he said to Lady Honour. 'I must get the car out now before the last race. Some of these cars will be here tomorrow morning.' He gathered Dick and myself to him with a glance in which appeal and authority balanced each other, and so we left the ladies of Templeshambo. But before we had gone Lady Eveleen caught awkwardly at the elbow of my coat and 'come tomorrow with Richard, Oliver,' she said. She was earnest and without charm, but there was a steadfastness behind her nervous face like a light beyond lanternglass. When Lady Honour laughed and told me not to waste my time visiting two old women, I said that I would like to come, but would not trouble her since Lady Eveleen had promised to look after me.

'You'll have Honour and Beauty at one another's throats,' Sir Richard said to me a little later as we seated ourselves in the car and proceeded to repulse the army of mendicant guardians of its safety who swarmed for alms about our departure.

' 'Twas I minded the car, sir —'

'No, 'twas I, yer honour – any looked near it I belted hell out o' them, and the young lad of a son I have pasted them also.'

I gave the young lad two shillings. Sir Richard disposed himself in the car beside Dick. 'Be off, now, the lot of you.'

'Sure, that's not my son, your honour – the lad with the locks is my son.' But Sir Richard wound up his window, immovable to further petition.

In the back of the car I turned up the collar of my coat, an even simplicity of delight about me, the limber glow that succeeds striven effort, the level mind that follows on success were mine. I lit two cigarettes, one for Dick and one for myself, and handed him his when we had lurched, our engine racing, out of the field and down the rutted lane towards the main road.

'Thank you, Oliver.' Dick leaned forward to set the windscreen wiper working, for a shower of rain lashed bitterly towards us from the mountains. The day was turned suddenly to indigo and silver, darkly changing behind the sloped spears of rain. I thought of the fire in Willow's room where Dick and I would sit making toast and telling of our doings. I thought of little rivers rushing low and dark beneath blackthorns and hazel, and the hewn wings of a gull brought a pale greyhound bitch to my mind, I had called her Sally. But Dick was talking:

'Twenty-one pounds was a cruel penalty to put on that little mare. She was tied to the floor. I couldn't stop you coming up on the inside, could I, Oliver? Ah, she was stone-cold going up the hill. I knew I couldn't do it, so I thought I'd finish without a fall. Would I have done it if we'd been on top of the ground, Father. I wouldn't?'

'You would not,' said Sir Richard suddenly. 'You did what five steeplechase jockeys out of ten can't do, and nine point-to-point jockeys out of ten can't do – you sat still on her and you kept hold of her head. And I'll tell you another thing, Dick, you wouldn't have beaten Oliver today at level weights either.'

'What? And that mare only four years old – well, five now. Oh, Sir Richard!'

'Four years old?' said Sir Richard. 'A four-year-old — *She is?*'

'What d'you mean, father?' Dick asked him, but he would not tell us, switching into another topic with the disconcerting independence of mind that was particularly his own.

'That lad,' he said, 'that Honour had with the mare – do you know where I saw him last? In Tommy Redmond's stables. And as tough a place as Tommy's is – they didn't keep that beauty long in it.'

'Who is Tommy Redmond?' I asked.

'Tommy? Oh, he trains horses. He's a sort of relation of Honour's and Beauty's. Well, in a kind of a way, he's one of the old Lords. And a horrible fellow. There's no villainy or trickery or roguery he's not up to it and he runs his horses about as straight as a ram's horn.'

'Oh,' I said, and a lonely blankness settled now on my spirit. Coldly and slowly the pieces of a difficult and sorry business fitted their places in my mind. The memory of my ride was distant from me now, apart from its heat and effort it would seem to have been but a nasty ramp. But I had not known. How could I even now be sure? I must wait and see what would follow. There was no cohesion in this villainy. Any key there might be to the matter was in Sir Richard's canny grasp. Somehow I felt that there would be suffering yet over this, and it was not Honour who would suffer most for it but that poor Beauty, poor stricken goose.

And the weight of this doubt stayed with me heavily, disallowing Willow's generous congratulations and Dick's assurances that the Sir was never without a bee in his bonnet over any horse that was good enough to beat one of his own. I would have liked, I think, to talk the matter over with James, but since the neuralgia he said was stitching in and out through his poll like the devil's needle, I could not think the evening opportune for the discussion of my own trivial affairs.

The afternoon of the following day a strangely solemn and silent Sir Richard drove me over to Templeshambo. Sometimes, as we drove, I saw his lips move, and I knew he was rehearsing to himself the speeches of his part in whatever piece this was which presently he would stage. I wondered how my part was cast and I felt, indeed, a soured and unwilling puppet. The more so when I saw the airy nonchalance of manner which could not quite disguise the shifting anxiety in Lady Honour's eyes as she greeted us.

'To see you three days running, Richard, it makes us feel quite young and silly,' Lady Honour was naughty, not sentimental, 'and *Oliver*, my dear, Beauty will be mad with excitement' – here was malice.

She went on before us down the long narrow dark hall, her little head poised back, her narrow shoulder blades knife-sharp under her coat. She had a peculiar way of walking, sliding her feet very evenly past each other like a little fox. When she turned her head to smile round at us, I thought I saw again in her the vixen and forgot how yesterday her bird-like charm had ravished me.

'We are sitting in here today,' she said, opening a door at the end of the hall, 'because one of Beauty's puppies has the yellows and as she insisted on lighting a fire for it I thought we might as well have the good of it too.'

'Well, after your win yesterday,' Sir Richard said swiftly, 'I should think you might light fires all over the house and hang the expense, eh, Honour?'

'Indeed, if we had only backed the mare we were right,' Lady Honour answered regretfully. 'But poor Beauty has no courage. She wouldn't let me do it. Well, I suppose she was right, really. What did we know about the mare except that she could lep and we *thought* she could gallop? But a four-year-old and running in such good company – wouldn't we have been very silly, Richard? Don't you think so? We would have been, wouldn't we?'

'Well,' said Sir Richard, with undue weightiness, 'circumstances, of course, alter cases.' He sat himself down on a minor inquisition in the shape of a sofa and added, 'My dear Honour.' I sat down on a chair near the sick puppy's basket, wishing very much that I might be bidden to take myself off for a little walk in the garden, rain it never so hard; failing this I could only look about the room and pretend I was not there. And such a room, as different as it could be from that room of fragile adventure where yesterday we had drunk our tea in the glamour of a Perhaps that Never Was. Here was Time Past; and rightly so, I thought, my mind petrifying in its contemplation of case upon glass case of stuffed birds, gulls of every variety, their beauty betrayed forever to clumsiness: hawks primly hovering, jays and magpies perched for ever; two white owls, in all the sulkiness of their unspread wings, squinted forbiddingly down their crooked parrot beaks. A stuffed fox was curled woodenly in a chair, and a badger lay for a footstool beneath a distant writing-table – his back was worn nearly bare by the feet that had rested on it so often. And there was (this startled me) a little monkey stuffed, and for more ghastly realism chained to the corner of a bookcase. The curtains in the high windows and all the chair covers were dark red and every inch of woodwork had been painted dark brown. The rain lashed forbiddingly against the windows and the sick puppy rose waveringly from its basket. I wished very much that Lady Eveleen would come in.

'And so you see, Richard,' Lady Honour was saying, 'as the filly's really as much Beauty's as mine, I have very little say in the matter. And you know Beauty is wickedly obstinate.'

'I see. And I suppose Tommy Redmond has a share in her too?'

'What do you mean?' Poor sorry little fox! A thin, frightened shadow passed, it seemed, right through her. Now she was indeed beset.

'Well, the fact is, Honour,' Sir Richard said, 'there's been a certain amount of talk about the running of your mare yesterday, which puts me in a very difficult position as a steward, because I happen to know what I would a lot rather I didn't know, and that is, the mare is not yours at all but Tommy Redmond's, and what's more, she's a winner under rules, and she's unqualified to run at any point-to-point meeting.'

'And may one ask how you came to that interesting conclusion?' Lady Honour was game.

'Well, there *are* such things as consignments of the boxing of horses to be seen at railway stations, if a person has the wit to go and look for them, eh, Honour? That was a silly mistake you made, you know. She should have gone in your name from Killanna Station instead of being booked in Tommy's from Myross. It was only six miles farther to walk her to Killanna, that's where you should have ordered the box. No, if there is any fuss about it, I'm afraid —'

'If there is any fuss about it, the best thing *you* could do, Richard, would be to keep your mouth shut.' Such complete and sudden acceptance of the matter on Lady Honour's part fairly surprised me, nor was I less taken aback by Sir Richard's answer.

'Now, Honour, if there is any inquiry, I don't see how I can help saying what I know. Some one might know I knew it, you never can tell.'

'You can't do that, Richard – a nice mess you'd get Oliver into. However satisfactory the explanation of his part of the business is, you know yourself that any one mixed up with Tommy must put up with the reputation of being fairly hot.'

'Too hot to touch.' Sir Richard looked over at me sourly. I could feel that in his imagination he already saw me in the part of a willing accomplice to the ramp. 'What a lucky thing for you Billy Morgan laid himself up,' he said. 'It looked a lot better for Oliver to have the ride. I suppose you thought I'd keep quiet about it all rather than see him in a scrape. B'God, Honour, you very nearly brought the thing off nicely. I'm sorry about Oliver; I wish now I'd never allowed you to give him the ride. I encouraged the idea in my innocence.' He looked sadly from one to the other of us. 'Poor Beauty,' he said, 'will be very upset,' and as he said it I saw her going past the windows in a mackintosh, carrying a bucket of dogs' food and leaning towards its weight and into the rain.

'If you won't mind,' I said, 'I think I'll go out and help Lady Eveleen feed the dogs while you and Cousin Richard think of some way out of this difficulty. I really feel so shaken by all this —'

She was not with the dogs, Lady Eveleen, but I found her in the tower-foot room regulating the incubator. 'I hope these eggs are all right,' she said. 'We forgot about them yesterday in our excitement over the point-to-point. I hope they'll be all right. Honour and I never seem to have any success with things like chickens. By the way, Oliver, I had a fiver on the mare for you yesterday.' She said this so sadly as she pushed in a drawer of eggs that I wondered whether she knew what had brought Sir Richard here today. She would not look at me at all and then I saw why. She was crying, poor Beauty in distress – I saw her tears – they were helpless and foolish and how they grieved and shocked me I never can tell. Back and forth went her awkward hands over the tidy drawers of eggs. The light in the little room was almost none, the white sprouting of potatoes in a corner illuminated the darkness. Her pale, stooped neck another moony thing.

'What is it?' I was saying. I took her arm and sat her down on a dishevelled chair. I put my handkerchief in her hand, for hers, I observed, she had used to wipe tears from her eyes and from the eggs with indiscriminate carefulness for the latter's welfare.

'Honour and Richard are so *unkind*,' she whimpered at last. 'Honour is such a dreadful tease. She goes on and on and on, until – oh, *please* don't mind me, I'm a silly disgusting old woman to cry like this. It is very shameful.'

'Why do they tease you?'

'Oh, for no reason – it's just my stupidity.' She was incoherent; a

cruel colour blazed down her long neck. And when I turned and saw
Lady Honour laughing in the doorway and Sir Richard, blue and
beaky in the rain behind her, I was almost staggered by the strength
of my pity for my poor goose.

'Come in, Richard; come in out of the rain.' Lady Honour would
suckle him still to her with sweet, twisty ways, I thought. A turn in
her voice and a light in her eye, alike they said, 'Escape me, never!'

'See, Beauty,' she addressed her poor sister, 'Richard has bid me
within twenty-five pounds of the price you put on the filly. Will you
deal?'

'I will not,' said Lady Eveleen. She was calm now and passionately
determined. 'I won't sell that mare for one penny less than I said I
would.'

Sir Richard from the doorway gave her a very dark look and said
he: 'Well, indeed, my dear Beauty, I came her today on a very
different matter, but as Honour seemed anxious, and rightly so, to
get out of the mare, I made her my outside bid for her, and neither
will I go one penny beyond it.'

'And what did you come for then?' Lady Eveleen held on to the
seat of her chair and faced them both with the unanswerable
gallantry of a goose at bay.

'Oh.' Sir Richard jerked his head, the fine tilted bones of his face
were drawn with sudden impressionistic beauty against the dreary
light. 'Honour has persuaded me to say no more about the matter I
came for, and though I hate to tell a lie' – his hands on his stick
before him crossed and knotted, Sir Richard appeared for the
moment the very epitome of aristocratic impeccability – 'though it
really *hurts* me to tell a lie I think, b'God, it would put you all in a
very uncomfortable position if I told the truth. And when I think of
poor Oliver. You know I loved his father' – here he waited for a
moment and I could feel that indeed he spoke the truth, without a
doubt he had loved my father, and while that love would never
straiten him in any present convenient betrayal, nevertheless it was a
truthful emotion – 'and more for his sake than any of your sakes I've
agreed to keep quiet about this matter, do you see, Beauty?'

'*Well*, Beauty?' Lady Honour's voice slipped exasperatedly into the
silence that fell when Sir Richard, having said his say, waited for
some answer.

But Beauty made no answer. Her pale unfocused eyes sought

blindly from one to the other of them. One saw her mind groping helpless in its stupidity for some telling weapon wherewith to strike at them, and finding none, I feared she would weep again. I was angry because they had made of me and of her sad memory of my father a twice-knotted stick with which to beat her to submission, angry and ashamed for their unkindness.

'I leave it entirely to you, Honour,' she said at last, 'whatever you think best —' She gave us all a queer, stricken look, grotesque in its youthfulness, and slipped out into the rain to feed her dogs.

'I'm too kindhearted,' Sir Richard said, as down the avenue to Pullinstown young horses advanced swooping and stopping, upon us. 'That's the worse of me. You know, Oliver, I should *never* have bought that mare from the old ladies. This place is rotten with horses as it is. And I'm not really fond of the mare, you know. There are several things I don't like about her.'

'Then why did you buy her, Cousin Richard?' I asked curiously.

'Ah well, it's not a bad thing for Honour to have a good fright now and again. That was a shocking thing she did, you know – running that mare yesterday. I must say I was surprised at her. And she thought she had me nicely cornered if she gave you the ride; I couldn't say a word about anything then – she must think I have very little regard for the truth – that's what hurt me. That's what shocked me.'

'Anyhow,' I said, with the graven and crude condemnation of my age, 'between you, you twisted poor Beauty's tail till you got the filly out of her for your own price.'

'Oh, I gave Beauty her price in the end,' Sir Richard's excellent manners entirely ignored my rather rude speech. 'You see, I had a tenner on the mare when you won yesterday – I could afford to give her another twenty-five quid. But I gave Honour a good fright too.' And he added, with almost sentimental satisfaction, 'The prime little rogue!'

THE COOP

Edgar Wallace

SOMETIMES they referred to Mr Yardley in the newspapers as 'the Wizard of Stotford', sometimes his credit was diffused as the 'Yardley Confederation'; occasionally he was spoken of as plain 'Bert Yardley' but invariably his entries for any important handicaps were described as 'The Stotford Mystery'. For nobody quite knew what Mr Yardley's intentions were until the day of the race. Usually after the race, for it is a distressing fact that the favourite from his stable was usually unplaced, and the winner – also from his stable – started amongst the '100 to 7 others'.

After the event was all over and the 'weighed in' had been called, people used to gather in the paddock in little groups and ask one another what this horse was doing at Nottingham, and where were the stewards, and why Mr Yardley was not jolly well warned off. And they didn't say 'jolly' either.

For it is an understood thing in racing that, if an outsider wins, its trainer ought to be warned off. Yet neither Bert Yardley, nor Colonel Rogersman, nor Mr Lewis Feltham – the two principal owners for whom he trained – were so much as asked by the stewards to explain the running of their horses. Thus proving that the Turf needed reform, and that the stipendiary steward was an absolute necessity.

Mr Bert Yardley was a youngish man of thirty-five, who spoke very little and did his betting by telegram. He had a suite at the Midland Hotel, and was a member of a sedate and respectable club in Pall Mall. He read extensively, mostly such classics as *Races to Come*, and the umpteenth volume of the Stud Book, and he leavened his studies with such lighter reading as the training reports from the daily sporting newspapers – he liked a good laugh.

His worst enemy could not complain of him that he refused information to anybody.

'I think mine have some sort of chance, and I'm backing them both. Tinpot? Well, of course, he may win; miracles happen, and I shouldn't be surprised if he made a good show. But I've had to ease him in his work and when I galloped him on Monday he simply wouldn't have it – couldn't get him to take hold of his bit. Possibly he runs better when he's a little above himself, but he's a horse of moods. If he'd only give his running, he'd trot in! Lampholder, on the other hand, is as game a horse as ever looked through a bridle. A battler! He'll be there or thereabouts.'

What would you back on that perfectly candid, perfectly honest information straight, as it were, from the horse's mouth?

Lampholder, of course; and Tinpot would win. Even stipendiary stewards couldn't make Lampholder win, not if they got behind and shoved him. And that, of course, is no part of a stipendiary steward's duties.

Mr Bert Yardley was dressing for dinner one March evening when he discovered that a gold watch had disappeared. He called his valet, who could offer no other information than that it had been there when they left Stotford for Sandown Park.

'Send for the police,' said Mr Yardley, and there came to him Detective-Sergeant Challoner.

Mr Challoner listened, made a few notes, asked a few, a very few, questions of the valet and closed his book.

'I think I know the person,' he said, and to the valet: 'A big nose – you're sure of the big nose?'

The valet was emphatic.

'Very good,' said The Miller. 'I'll do my best, Mr Yardley. I hope I shall be as successful as Amboy will be in the Lincoln Handicap.'

Mr Yardley smiled faintly.

'We'll talk about that later,' he said.

The Miller made one or two inquiries and that night pulled in Nosey Boldin, whose hobby it was to pose as an inspector of telephones and who, in this capacity, had made many successful experiments. On the way to the station, Nosey, so-called because of a certain abnormality in that organ, delivered himself with great force and venom.

'This comes of betting on horse races and follering Educated

Evans's perishin' five-pounds specials! Let this be a warning to you, Miller!'

'Not so much lip,' said The Miller.

'He gave me one winner in ten shots, and *that* started at 11 to 10 on,' ruminated Nosey. 'Men like that drive men to crime. There ought to be a law so's to make the fifth loser a *felony*! And after the eighth loser he ought to 'ang! That'd stop 'em.'

The Miller saw his friend charged and lodged for the night and went home to bed. And in the morning, when he left his rooms to go to breakfast, the first person he saw was Educated Evans, and there was on that learned man's unhappy face a look of pain and anxiety.

'Good morning, Mr Challoner. Excuse me if I'm taking a liberty, but I understand that a client of mine is in trouble?'

'If you mean Nosey, he is,' agreed The Miller. 'And what's more, he attributes his shame and downfall to following your tips. I sympathize with him.'

Educated Evans made an impatient clicking sound, raised his eyebrows and spread out his hand.

'Bolsho,' he said simply.

'Eh?' The Miller frowned suspiciously. 'You didn't give Bolsho?'

'Every guaranteed client received "Bolsho: fear nothing,"' said Evans even more simply: 'following Mothegg (ten to one, beaten a neck, hard lines), Toffeetown (third, hundred to eight, very unlucky), Onesided (won, seven to two, what a beauty!), followin' Curds and Whey (won, eleven to ten – can't help the price). Is that fair?'

'The question is,' said The Miller deliberately, 'Did Nosey subscribe to your guarantee wire, your five pounds special, or your Overnight nap?'

'That,' said Educated Evans diplomatically, 'I can't tell till I've seen me books. The point is this: if Nosey wants bail, am I all right? I don't want any scandal, and you know Nosey. He ought to have been in advertisin'.'

The advertising propensities of Nosey were, indeed, well known to The Miller. He had the knack of introducing some startling feature into the very simplest case, and attracting to himself the amount of newspaper space usually given to scenes in the House and important murders.

It was Nosey who, by his startling statement that pickles were a greater incentive to crime than beer, initiated a press correspondence which lasted for months. It was Nosey who, when charged with hotel larceny – his favourite aberration – made the pronouncement that buses were a cause of insanity. Upon the peg of his frequent misfortunes, it was his practice to hang a showing up for somebody.

The case of Nosey was dealt with summarily. Long before the prosecutor had completed his evidence he realized that his doom was sealed.

'Anything known about this man?' asked the magistrate.

A jailer stepped briskly into the box and gave a brief sketch of Nosey's life, and Nosey, who knew it all before, looked bored.

'Anything to say?' asked the magistrate.

Nosey cleared his throat.

'I can only say, your worship that I've fell into thieving ways owing to falling in the hands of unscrupulous racing tipsters. I'm ruined by tips, and if the law was just, there's a certain party who ought to be standing here by my side.'

Educated Evans, standing at the back of the court, squirmed.

'I've got a wife, as true a woman as ever drew the breath of life,' Nosey went on. 'I've got two dear little children, and I ask your worship to consider me temptation owing to horse-racing, and betting and this here tipster.'

'Six months,' said the magistrate, without looking up.

Outside the court Mr Evans waited patiently for the appearance of The Miller.

'Nosey never had more than a shilling on a horse in his life,' he said bitterly, 'and he *owes*! Here's the bread being took out of my mouth by slander and misrepresentation; do you think they'll put it in the papers, Mr Challoner?'

'Certain,' said The Miller cheerfully, and Educated Evans groaned.

'That man's worse than Lucreature Burgia, the celebrated poisoner,' he said, 'that Shakespeare wrote a play about. He's a snake in the grass and viper in the bosom. And to think I gave him Penwiper for the Manchester November, and he never so much as asked me if I was thirsty! Mr Challoner.'

Challoner, turning away, stopped.

'Was that Yardley? I mean the trainer?'

The Miller looked at him reproachfully.

'Maybe I'm getting old and my memory is becoming defective,' he said, 'but I seem to remember that when you gave me Tellmark the other day, you said that you were a personal friend of Mr Yardley's, and that the way he insisted on your coming down to spend the weekends was getting a public nuisance.'

Educated Evans did not bat a lid.

'That was his brother,' he said.

'He must have lied when he told me he had no brothers,' said The Miller.

'They've quarrelled,' replied Educated Evans frankly. 'In fact, they never mention one another's names. It's tragic when brothers quarrel, Mr Challoner. I've done my best to reconcile 'em – but what's the use? He didn't say anything about Amboy, did he?'

'He said nothing that I can tell you,' was his unsatisfactory reply, and he left Mr Evans to consider means and methods by which he might bring himself into closer contact with the Wizard of Stotford.

All that he feared in the matters of publicity was realized to the full. One evening paper said:

RUINED BY TIPSTERS

Once prosperous merchant goes to prison for theft.

And in the morning press one newspaper may be quoted as typical of the rest:

TIPSTER TO BLAME

Pest of the Turf wrecks a home.

Detective-Sergeant Challoner called by appointment at the Midland Hotel, and Mr Yardley saw him.

'No, thank you, sir,' The Miller was firm.

Mr Yardley put back the fiver he had taken from his pocket.

'I'll put you a tenner on anything I fancy,' he said. 'Who's this tipster, by the way ? – the man who was referred to by the prisoner?'

The Miller smiled.

'Educated Evans,' he said, and when he had finished describing him Mr Yardley nodded.

He was staying overnight in London *en route* for Lincoln and he was inclined to be bored. He had read the *Racing Calendar* from the list of the year's races to the last description of the last selling hurdle race on the back page. He had digested the surprising qualities of stallions and he could have almost recited the forfeit list from Aaron to Znosberg. And he was aching for diversion when the bell boy brought a card.

It was a large card, tastefully bordered with pink and green roses: Its edge was golden and in the centre were the words:

J. T. EVANS
(better known as 'Educated Evans'!!)
The World's Foremost and Leading Turf
Adviser and Racing Cricit
c/o Jockey Club, Newmarket or direct:
92 Bayham Mews, N.W.1
'The Man Who Gave Braxted!!
What a beauty!' – *vide* Press.

Mr Yardley read, lingering over the printer's errors.

'Show this gentleman up, page,' he said.

Into his presence came Educated Evans, a solemn purposeful man.

'I hope the intrusion will be amply excused by the important nature or character of my business,' he said. This was the opening he had planned.

'Sit down, Mr Evans,' said Yardley, and Educated Evans put his hat under the chair and sat.

'I've been thinking matters over in the privacy of my den —' began Evans, after a preliminary cough.

'You're a lion tamer as well?' asked the Wizard of Stotford, interested.

'By "den" I mean "study",' said Evans, gravely. 'To come to the point without beating about the bush – to use a well-known expression -- I've heard of a coop.'

'A what?'

'A coop,' said Evans.

'A chicken coop?' asked the puzzled Wizard.

'It's a French word, meaning "ramp",' said Evans.

'Oh yes, I see. "Coup" – it's pronounced "coo," Mr Evans.'

Educated Evans frowned.

'It's years since I was in Paris,' he said; 'and I suppose they've altered it. It used to be "coop" but these French people are always messing and mucking about with words.'

'And who is working this coop?' asked the trainer, politely adopting the old French version.

'Higgson.'

Educated Evans pronounced the word with great emphasis. Higgson was another mystery trainer. His horses also won when least expected. And after they won, little knots of men gathered in the paddock and asked one another if the Stewards had eyes, and why wasn't Higgson warned off?

'You interest me,' said the trainer of Amboy. 'Do you mean that he's winning with St Kats?'

Evans nodded more gravely still.

'I think it's me duty to tell you,' he said. 'My information' – he lowered his voice and glanced round to the door to be sure that it was shut – 'comes from the boy who does this horse!'

'Dear me!' said Mr Yardley.

'I've got correspondents everywhere,' said Educated Evans mysteriously. 'My man at Stockbridge sent me a letter this morning – I daren't show it to you – about a horse in that two-year-old race that will win with his ears pricked.'

Mr Yardley was looking at him through half-closed eyes.

'With his ears pricked?' he repeated, impressed. 'Have they trained his ears too? Extraordinary! But why have you come to tell me about Mr Higgson's horse?'

Educated Evans bent forward confidentially.

'Because you've done me many a turn, sir,' he said; 'and I'd like to do you one. I've got the information. I could shut my mouth an' make millions. I've got nine thousand clients who'd pay me the odds to a pound – but what's money?'

'True,' murmured Mr Yardley, nodding. 'Thank you, Mr Evans. St Kats, I think you said? Now, in return for your kindness, I'll give you a tip.'

Educated Evans held his breath. His amazingly bold plan had succeeded.

'Change your printer,' said Mr Yardley, rising. 'He can't spell. Good night.'

Evans went forth with his heart turned to stone and his soul seared with bitter animosity.

Mr Yardley came down after him and watched the shabby figure as it turned the corner, and his heart was touched. In two minutes he had overtaken the educated man.

'You're a bluff and a fake,' he said, good humouredly, 'but you can have a little, a very little, on Amboy.'

Before Educated Evans could prostrate himself at the benefactor's feet Mr Yardley was gone.

The next day was a busy one for Educated Evans. All day Miss Higgs, the famous typist of Great College Street, turned her duplicator, and every revolution of the cylinder threw forth, with a rustle and a click, the passionate appeal which Educated Evans addressed to all clients, old and new. He was not above borrowing the terminology of other advertisement writers.

> You want the best winners – I've got them.
> Bet in Evans' way! Eventually, why not now?
> I've got the winner of the Lincoln!
>> What a beauty!
>> What a beauty!
>> What a beauty!
> Confidentially! From the trainer! This is the coop
> of the season! Help yourself! Defeat ignored!

To eight hundred and forty clients this moving appeal went forth.

On the afternoon of the race Educated Evans strolled with confidence to the end of the Tottenham Court Road to wait for the *Star*. And when it came he opened the paper with a quiet smile. He was still smiling, when he read:

> Tenpenny, 1
> St Kats, 2
> Ella Glass, 3
> All probables ran.

'Tenpenny? – never heard of it,' he repeated, dazed, and produced his noon edition. Tenpenny was starred as a doubtful runner.

It was trained by – Yardley.

For a moment his emotions almost mastered him.

'That man ought to be warned off,' he said hollowly, and dragged his weary feet back to the stable-yard.

In the morning came a letter dated from Lincoln.

> Dear Mr Evans, – What do you think of my coop? –
> Yours, H. YARDLEY

There was a P.S. which ran:

> I put a fiver on for you. Your enterprise deserved it.

Evans opened the cheque tenderly and shook his head.

'After all,' he said subsequently to the quietly jubilant Miller, 'clients can't expect to win *every* time – a Turf Adviser is entitled to his own coops'

Tenpenny started at 25 to 1.

THE
SPLENDID OUTCAST

Beryl Markham

THE stallion was named after a star, and when he fell from his particular heaven, it was easy enough for people to say that he had been named too well. People like to see stars fall, but in the case of Rigel, it was of greater importance to me. To me and to one other – to a little man with shabby cuffs and a wilted cap that rested over eyes made mild by something more than time.

It was at Newmarket, in England, where, since Charles I instituted the first cup race, a kind of court has been held for the royalty of the turf. Men of all classes come to Newmarket for the races and for the December sales. They come from everywhere – some to bet, some to buy or sell, and some merely to offer homage to the resplendent peers of the Stud Book, for the sport of kings may, after all, be the pleasure of every man.

December can be bitterly cold in England, and this December was. There was frozen sleet on buildings and on trees, and I remember that the huge Newmarket track lay on the downs below the village like a noose of diamonds on a tarnished mat. There was a festive spirit everywhere, but it was somehow lost on me. I had come to buy new blood for my stable in Kenya, and since my stable was my living, I came as serious buyers do, with figures in my mind and caution in my heart. Horses are hard to judge at best, and the thought of putting your hoarded pounds behind that judgement makes it harder still.

I sat close on the edge of the auction ring and held my breath from time to time as the bidding soared. I held it because the casual mention of ten thousand guineas in payment for a horse or for anything else seemed to me wildly beyond the realm of probable things. For myself, I had five hundred pounds to spend and, as I waited for Rigel to be shown, I remember that I felt uncommonly maternal about each pound. I waited for Rigel because I had come six thousand miles to buy him, nor was I apprehensive lest anyone should take him from me; he was an outcast.

Rigel had a pedigree that looked backward and beyond the pedigrees of many Englishmen – and Rigel had a brilliant record. By all odds, he should have brought ten thousand guineas at the sale, but I knew he wouldn't, for he had killed a man.

He had killed a man – not fallen upon him, nor thrown him in a playful moment from the saddle, but killed him dead with his hoofs and with his teeth in a stable. And that was not all, though it was the greatest thing. Rigel had crippled other men and, so the story went, would cripple or kill still more, so long as he lived. He was savage, people said, and while he could not be hanged for his crimes, like a man, he could be shunned as criminals are. He could be offered for sale. And yet, under the implacable rules of racing, he had been warned off the turf for life – so who would buy?

Well, I for one – and I had supposed there would not be two. I would buy if the price were low enough, because I had youth then, and a corresponding contempt for failure. It seemed probable that in time and with luck and with skill, the stallion might be made manageable again, if only for breeding – especially for breeding. He could be gentled, I thought. But I found it hard to believe what I saw that day. I had not known that the mere touch of a hand, could in an instant, extinguish the long-burning anger of an angry heart.

I first noticed the little man when the sale was already well on its way, and he caught my attention at once, because he was incongruous there. He sat a few benches from me and held his lean, interwoven fingers upon his knees. He stared down upon the arena as each horse was led into it, and he listened to the dignified encomiums of the auctioneer with the humble attention of a parishioner at mass. He never moved. He was surrounded by men and women who, by their impeccable clothes and by their somewhat bored familiarity with pounds and guineas, made him conspicuous. He was like a stone of granite in a jeweller's window, motionless and grey against the glitter.

You could see in his face that he loved horses – just as you could see, in some of the faces of those around him, that they loved the idea of horses. They were the cultists, he the votary, and there were, in fact, about his grey eyes and his slender lips, the deep, tense lines so often etched in the faces of zealots and of lonely men. It was the cast of his shoulders, I think, the devotion of his manner that told me he had once been a jockey.

A yearling came into the ring and was bought, and then another, while the pages of catalogues were quietly turned. The auctioneer's voice, clear but scarcely lifted, intoned the virtues of his magnificent merchandise as other voices, responding to this magic, spoke reservedly of figures. 'A thousand guineas . . . two thousand . . . three . . . four . . .'

The scene at the aution comes to me clearly now, as if once again it was happening before my eyes.

'Five, perhaps?' The auctioneer scans the audience expectantly as a groom parades a dancing colt around the arena. There is a moment of near silence, a burly voice calls, 'Five!' and the colt is sold while a murmur of polite approval swells and dies.

And so they go, one after another, until the list is small, the audience thins and my finger traces the name, Rigel, on the last page of the catalogue. I straighten on my bench and hold my breath a little, forgetting the crowd, the little man, and a part of myself. I know this horse. I know he is by Hurry On out of Bounty – the sire unbeaten, the dam a great steeplechaser – and there is no better blood than that. Killer or not, Rigel has won races, and won them clean. If God and Barclays Bank stay with me, he will return to Africa when I do.

And there, at last, he stands. In the broad entrance to the ring, two powerful men appear with the stallion between them. The men are not grooms of ordinary size; they have been picked for strength, and in the clenched fist of each is the end of a chain. Between the chain and the bit there is on the near side a short rod of steel, close to the stallion's mouth – a rod of steel, easy to grasp, easy to use. Clenched around the great girth of the horse, and fitted with metal rings, there is a strap of thick leather that brings to mind the restraining harness of a madman.

Together, the two men edge the stallion forward. Tall as they are, they move like midgets beside his massive shoulders. He is the biggest thoroughbred I have ever seen. He is the most beautiful. His coat is chestnut, flecked with white, and his mane and tail are close to gold. There is a blaze on his face – wide and straight and forthright, as if by this marking he proclaims that he is none other than Rigel, for all his sins, for all the hush that falls over the crowd.

He is Rigel and he looks upon the men who hold his chains as a captured king may look upon his captors. He is not tamed. Nothing about him promises that he will be tamed. Stiffly, on reluctant hoofs, he enters the ring and flares his crimson nostrils at the crowd, and the crowd is still. The crowd whose pleasure is the docile beast of pretty paddocks, the gainly horse of cherished prints that hang upon the finest walls, the willing winner of the race – upon the rebel this crowd stares, and the rebel stares back.

His eyes are lit with anger or with hate. His head is held disdainfully and high, his neck an arc of arrogance. He prances now – impatience in the thudding of his hoofs upon the tanbark, defiance in his manner – and the chains jerk tight. The long stallion reins are tightly held – apprehensively held – and the men who hold them glance at the auctioneer, an urgent question in their eyes.

The auctioneer raises his arm for silence, but there is silence. No one speaks. The story of Rigel is known – his breeding, his brilliant victories, and finally his insurgence and his crimes. Who will buy the outcast? The auctioneer shakes his head as if to say that this is a trick beyond his magic. But he will try. He is an imposing man, an experienced man, and now he clears his throat and confronts the crowd, a kind of pleading in his face.

'This splendid animal —' he begins – and does not finish. He cannot finish.

Rigel has scanned the silent audience and smelled the unmoving air, and he – a creature of the wind – knows the indignity of this skyless temple. He seems aware at last of the chains that hold him, of the men who cling forlornly to the heavy reins. He rears from the tanbark, higher and higher still, until his golden mane is lifted like a flag unfurled and defiant. He beats the air. He trembles in his rising anger, and the crowd leans forward.

A groom clings like a monkey to the tightened chain. He is swept from his feet while his partner, a less tenacious man, sprawls ignobly below, and men – a dozen men – rush to the ring, some shouting, some waving their arms. They run and swear in lowered voices; they grasp reins, chains, rings, and swarm upon their towering Gulliver. And he subsides.

With something like contempt for this hysteria, Rigel touches his forehoofs to the tanbark once more. He has killed no one, hurt no one, but they are jabbing at his mouth now, they are surrounding him, adding fuel to his fiery reputation, and the auctioneer is a wilted man.

He sighs, and you can almost hear it. He raises both arms and forgoes his speech. 'What,' he asks with weariness, 'am I offered?' And there is a ripple of laughter from the crowd. Smug in its wisdom, it offers nothing.

But I do, and my voice is like an echo in a cave. Still there is triumph in it. I will have what I have come so far to get – I will have Rigel.

'A hundred guineas!' I stand as I call my price, and the auctioneer is plainly shocked – not by the meagreness of the offer, but by the offer itself. He stares upward from the ring, incredulity in his eyes.

He lifts a hand and slowly repeats the price. 'I am offered,' he says, 'one hundred guineas.'

There is a hush, and I feel the eyes of the crowd and watch the hand of the auctioneer. When it goes down, the stallion will be mine.

But it does not go down. It is still poised in mid-air, white, expectant, compelling, when the soft voice, the gently challenging voice is lifted. 'Two hundred!' the voice says, and I do not have to turn to know that the little jockey has bid against me. But I do turn.

He has not risen from the bench, and he does not look at me. In his hand he holds a sheaf of bank notes. I can tell by their colour that they are of small denomination, by their rumpled condition that they have been hoarded long. People near him are staring – horrified, I think – at the vulgar spectacle of cash at a Newmarket auction.

I am not horrified, nor sympathetic. Suddenly I am aware that I have a competitor, and I am cautious. I am here for a purpose that has little to do with sentiment, and I will not be beaten. I think of my stable in Kenya, of the feed bills to come, of the syces to be paid, of the races that are yet to be won if I am to survive in this unpredictable business. No, I cannot now yield an inch. I have little money, but so has he. No more, I think, but perhaps as much.

I hesitate a moment and glance at the little man, and he returns my glance. We are like two gamblers bidding each against the other's unseen cards. Our eyes meet for a sharp instant – a cold instant.

I straighten and my catalogue is crumpled in my hand. I moisten my lips and call, 'Three hundred!' I call it firmly, steadily, hoping to undo my opponent at a stroke. It is a wishful thought.

He looks directly at me now, but does not smile. He looks at me as a man might look at one who bears false witness against him, then soundlessly he counts his money and bids again, 'Three fifty!'

The interest of the crowd is suddenly aroused. All these people are at once conscious of being witnesses, not only before an auction, but before a contest, a rivalry of wills. They shift in their seats and stare as they might stare at a pair of duelists, rapiers in hand.

But money is the weapon, Rigel the prize. And prize enough, I think, as does my adversary.

I ponder and think hard, then decide to bid a hundred more. Not twenty, not fifty, but a hundred. Perhaps by that I can take him in my stride. He need not know there is little more to follow. He may assume that I am one of the casual ones, impatient of small figures. He may hesitate, he may withdraw. He may be cowed.

Still standing, I utter, as indifferently as I can, the words, 'Four fifty!' and the auctioneer, at ease in his element of contention, brightens visibly.

I am aware that the gathered people are now fascinated by this battle of pounds and shillings over a stallion that not one of them would care to own. I only hope that in the heat of it some third person does not begin to bid. But I need not worry; Rigel takes care of that.

The little jockey has listened to my last offer, and I can see that he is already beaten — or almost, at least. He has counted his money a dozen times, but now he counts it again, swiftly, with agile fingers, as if hoping his previous counts had been wrong.

I feel a momentary surge of sympathy, then smother it. Horse training is not my hobby. It is my living. I wait for what I am sure will be his last bid, and it comes. For the first time, he rises from his bench. He is small and alone in spirit, for the glances of the well-dressed people about him lend him nothing. He does not care. His eyes are on the stallion and I can see that there is a kind of passion in them. I have seen that expression before — in the eyes of sailors appraising a comely ship, in the eyes of pilots sweeping the clean, sweet contours of a plane. There is reverence in it, desire — and even hope.

The little man turns slightly to face the expectant autioneer, then clears his throat and makes his bid. 'Four eighty!' he calls, and the slight note of desperation in his voice is unmistakable, but I force myself to ignore it. Now, at last, I tell myself, the prize is mine.

The auctioneer receives the bid and looks at me, as do a hundred people. Some of them, no doubt, think I am quite mad or wholly inexperienced, but they watch while the words 'Five hundred' form upon my lips. They are never uttered.

Throughout the bidding for Rigel, Rigel has been ignored. He has stood quietly enough after his first brief effort at freedom, he has scarcely moved. But now, at the climax of the sale, his impatience overflows, his spirit flares like fire, his anger bursts through the circle of men who guard him. Suddenly there are cries, shouts of warning, the ringing of chains and the cracking of leather, and the crowd leaps to its feet. Rigel is loose. Rigel has hurled his captors from him and he stands alone.

It is a beautiful thing to see, but there is terror in it. A thoroughbred stallion with anger in his eye is not a sight to entrance anyone but a novice. If you are aware of the power and the speed and the intelligence in that towering symmetrical body, you will hold your breath as you watch it. You will know that the teeth of a horse can crush a bone, that hoofs can crush a man. And Rigel's hoofs have crushed a man.

He stands alone, his neck curved, his golden tail a battle plume, and he turns, slowly, deliberately, and faces the men he has flung away. They are not without courage, but they are without resource. Horses are not tamed by whips or by blows. The strength of ten men is not so strong as a single stroke of a hoof; the experience of ten men is not enough, for this is the unexpected, the unpredictable. No one is prepared. No one is ready.

The words 'Five hundred' die upon my lips as I watch, as I listen. For the stallion is not voiceless now. His challenging scream is shrill as the cry of winter wind. It is bleak and heartless. His forehoofs stir the tanbark. The auction is forgotten.

A man stands before him — a man braver than most. He holds nothing in his hands save an exercise bat; it looks a feeble thing, and is. It is a thin stick bound with leather — enough only to enrage Rigel, for he has seen such things in men's hands before. He knows their meaning. Such a thing as this bat, slight as it is, enrages him because it is a symbol that stands for other things. It stands, perhaps, for the confining walls of a darkened stable, for the bit of steel, foreign, but almost everpresent in his mouth, for the tightened girth, the command to gallop, to walk, to stop, to parade before the swelling crowd of gathered people, to accept the measured food gleaned from forbidden fields. It stands for life no closer to the earth than the sterile smell of satin on a jockey's back or the dead wreath hung upon a winner. It stands for servitude. And Rigel has broken with his overlords.

He lunges quickly, and the man with a bat is not so quick. He lifts the pathetic stick and waves it in desperation. He cries out, and the voice of the crowd drowns his cry. Rigel's neck is outstretched and straight as a sabre. There is dust and the shouting of men and the screaming of women, for the stallion's teeth have closed on the shoulder of his forlorn enemy.

The man struggles and drops his bat, and his eyes are sharp with terror, perhaps with pain. Blood leaves the flesh of his face, and it is a face grey and pleading, as must be the faces of those to whom retribution is unexpected and swift. He beats against the golden head while the excitement of the crowd mounts against the fury of Rigel. Then reason vanishes. Clubs, whips, and chains appear like magic in the ring, and a regiment of men advance upon the stallion. They are angry men, brave in their anger, righteous and justified in it. They advance, and the stallion drops the man he has attacked, and the man runs for cover, clutching his shoulder.

I am standing, as is everyone. It is a strange and unreal thing to see this trapped and frustrated creature, magnificent and alone, away from his kind, remote from the things he understands, face the punishment of his minuscule masters. He is, of course, terrified, and the terror is a mounting madness. If he could run, he would leave this place, abandoning his fear and his hatred to do it. But he cannot run. The walls of the arena are high. The doors are shut, and the trap makes him blind with anger. He will fight, and the blows will fall with heaviness upon his spirit, for his body is a rock before these petty weapons.

The men edge closer, ropes and chains and whips in determined hands. The whips are lifted, the chains are ready; the battle line is formed, and Rigel does not retreat. He comes forward, the whites of his eyes exposed and rimmed with carnelian fire, his nostrils crimson.

There is a breathless silence, and the little jockey slips like a ghost into the ring. His eyes are fixed on the embattled stallion. He begins to run across the tanbark and breaks through the circle of advancing men and does not stop. Someone clutches at his coat, but he breaks loose without turning, then slows to an almost casual walk and approaches Rigel alone. The men do not follow him. He waves them back. He goes forward, steadily, easily and happily, without caution, without fear, and Rigel whirls angrily to face him.

Rigel stands close to the wall of the arena. He cannot retreat. He does not propose to. Now he can focus his fury on this insignificant David who has come to meet him, and he does. He lunges at once as only a stallion can – swiftly, invincibly, as if escape and freedom can be found only in the destruction of all that is human, all that smells human, and all that humans have made.

He lunges and the jockey stops. He does not turn or lift a hand or otherwise move. He stops, he stands, and there is silence everywhere. No one speaks; no one seems to breathe. Only Rigel is motion. No special hypnotic power emanates from the jockey's eyes; he has no magic. The stallion's teeth are bared and close, his hoofs are a swelling sound when the jockey turns. Like a matador of nerveless skill and studied insolence, the jockey turns his back on Rigel and does not walk away, and the stallion pauses.

Rigel rears high at the back of the little man, screaming his defiant scream, but he does not strike. His hoofs are close to the jockey's head, but do not touch him. His teeth are sheathed. He hesitates, trembles, roars wind from his massive lungs. He shakes his head, his golden mane, and beats the ground. It is frustration – but of a new kind. It is a thing he does not know – a man who neither cringes in fear nor threatens with whips or chains. It is a thing beyond his memory perhaps – as far beyond it as the understanding of the mare that bore him.

Rigel is suddenly motionless, rigid, suspicious. He waits, and the grey-eyed jockey turns to face him. The little man is calm and smiling. We hear him speak, but cannot understand his words. They are low and they are lost to us – an incantation. But the stallion seems to understand at least the spirit if not the sense of them. He snorts, but does not move. And now the jockey's hand goes forward to the golden mane – neither hurriedly nor with hesitance, but unconcernedly, as if it had rested there a thousand times. And there it stays.

There is a murmur from the crowd, then silence. People look at one another and stir in their seats – a strange self-consciousness in their stirring, for people are uneasy before the proved worth of their inferiors, unbelieving of the virtue of simplicity. They watch with open mouths as the giant Rigel, the killer Rigel, with no harness save a head collar, follows his Lilliputian master, his new friend, across the ring.

All has happened in so little time – in moments. The audience begins to stand, to leave. But they pause at the lift of the auctioneer's hand. He waves it and they pause. It is all very well, his gestures say, but business is, after all, business, and Rigel has not been sold. He looks up at me, knowing that I have a bid to make – the last bid. And I look down into the ring at the stallion I have come so far to buy. His head is low and close to the shoulder of the man who would take him from me. He is not prancing now, not moving. For this hour, at least, he is changed.

I straighten, and then shake my head. I need only say, 'Five hundred,' but the words won't come. I can't get them out. I am angry with myself – a sentimental fool – and I am disappointed. But I cannot bid. It is too easy – twenty pounds too little, and yet too great an advantage.

No. I shake my head again, the auctioneer shrugs and turns to seal his bargain with the jockey.

On the way out, an old friend jostles me. 'You didn't really want him then,' he says.

'Want him? No. No, I didn't really want him.'

'It was wise,' he said. 'What good is a horse that's warned off every course in the Empire? You wouldn't want a horse like that.'

'That's right. I wouldn't want a horse like that.'

We move to the exit, and when we are out in the bright cold air of Newmarket, I turn to my friend and mention the little jockey. 'But he wanted Rigel,' I say.

And my old friend laughs. 'He would,' he says. 'That man has himself been barred from racing for fifteen years. Why, I can't remember. But it's two of a kind, you see – Rigel and Sparrow. Outlaws, both. He loves and knows horses as no man does, but that's what we call him around the tracks – the Fallen Sparrow.'

I'M A FOOL

Sherwood Anderson

IT was a hard jolt for me, one of the bitterest I ever had to face. And it all came about through my own foolishness, too. Even yet sometimes, when I think of it, I want to cry or swear or kick myself. Perhaps, even now, after all this time, there will be a kind of satisfaction in making myself look cheap by telling of it.

It began at three o'clock one October afternoon as I sat in the grandstand at the fall trotting-and-pacing meet at Sandusky, Ohio.

To tell the truth, I felt a little foolish that I should be sitting in the grandstand at all. During the summer before I had left my home-town with Harry Whitehead and, with a nigger named Burt, had taken a job as swipe with one of the two horses Harry was campaigning through the fall race-meets that year. Mother cried and my sister Mildred, who wanted to get a job as a schoolteacher in our town that fall, stormed and scolded about the house all during the week before I left. They both thought it something disgraceful that one of our family should take a place as a swipe with racehorses. I've an idea Mildred thought my taking the place would stand in the way of her getting the job she'd been working so long for.

But after all I had to work, and there was no other work to be got. A big lumbering fellow of nineteen couldn't just hang around the house and I had got too big to mow people's lawns and sell newspapers. Little chaps who could get next to people's sympathies by their sizes were always getting jobs away from me. There was one fellow who kept saying to everyone who wanted a lawn mowed or a cistern cleaned, that he was saving money to work his way through college, and I used to lay awake nights thinking up ways to injure him without being found out. I kept thinking of wagons running over him and bricks falling on his head as he walked along the street. But never mind him.

I got the place with Harry and I liked Burt fine. We got along splendid together. He was a big nigger with a lazy sprawling body and soft, kind eyes, and when it came to a fight he could hit like Jack Johnson. He had Bucephalus, a big black pacing stallion that could do 2.09 or 2.10, if he had to, and I had a little gelding named Doctor Fritz that never lost a race all fall when Harry wanted him to win.

We set out from home late in July in a box car with the two horses, and after that, until late November, we kept moving along to the race-meets and the fairs. It was a peachy time for me, I'll say that. Sometimes now I think that boys who are raised regular in houses, and never have a fine nigger like Burt for best friend, and go to high schools and college, and never steal anything, or get drunk a little, or learn to swear from fellows who know how, or come walking up in front of a grandstand in their shirt sleeves and with dirty horsy pants on when the races are going on and the grandstand is full of people all dressed up – What's the use of talking about it? Such fellows don't know nothing at all. They've never had no opportunity.

But I did. Burt taught me how to rub down a horse and put the bandages on after a race and steam a horse out and a lot of valuable things for any man to know. He could wrap a bandage on a horse's leg so smooth that if it had been the same colour you would think it was his skin, and I guess he'd have been a big driver, too, and got to the top like Murphy and Walter Cox and the others if he hadn't been black.

Gee whizz! it was fun. You got to a county seat town, maybe say on a Saturday or Sunday, and the fair began the next Tuesday and lasted until Friday afternoon. Doctor Fritz would be, say in the 2.25 trot on Tuesday afternoon, and on Thursday afternoon Bucephalus would knock 'em cold in the 'free-for-all' pace. It left you a lot of time to hang around and listen to horse talk, and see Burt knock some yap cold that got too gay, and you'd find out about horses and men and pick up a lot of stuff you could use all the rest of your life, if you had some sense and salted down what you heard and felt and saw.

And then at the end of the week when the race-meet was over, and Harry had run home to tend up to his livery-stable business, you and Burt hitched the two horses to carts and drove slow and steady cross country, to the place for the next meeting, so as to not overheat the horses, etc., etc., you know.

Gee whizz! Gosh a'mighty! the nice hickory-nut and beech-nut and oaks and other kinds of trees along the roads, all brown and red, and the good smells, and Burt singing a song that was called Deep River, and the country girls at the windows of houses and everything. You can stick your colleges up your nose for all me. I guess I know where I got my education.

Why, one of those little burgs of towns you come to on the way, say now on a Saturday afternoon, and Burt says, 'Let's lay up here'. And you did.

And you took the horses to a livery stable and fed them, and you got your good clothes out of a box and put them on.

And the town was full of farmers gaping, because they could see you were racehorse people, and the kids maybe never see a nigger before and was afraid and run away when the two of us walked down their main street.

And that was before prohibition and all that foolishness, and so you went into a saloon, the two of you, and all the yaps come and stood around, and there was always someone pretended he was horsy and knew things and spoke up and began asking questions, and all you did was to lie and lie all you could about what horses you had, and I said I owned them, and then some fellow said, 'Will you have a drink of whisky?' and Burt knocked his eye out the way he could say, off-hand like, 'Oh well, all right, I'm agreeable to a little nip. I'll split a quart with you.' Gee whizz!

But that isn't what I want to tell my story about. We got home late in November and I promised mother I'd quit the racehorses for good. There's a lot of things you've got to promise a mother because she don't know any better.

And so, there not being any work in our town any more than when I left there to go to the races, I went off to Sandusky and got a pretty good place taking care of horses for a man who owned a teaming and delivery and storage and coal and real-estate business there. It was a pretty good place with good eats, and a day off each week, and sleeping on a cot in a big barn, and mostly just shovelling in hay and oats to a lot of big good-enough skates of horses, that couldn't have trotted a race with a toad. I wasn't dissatisfied and I could send money home.

And then, as I started to tell you, the fall races came to Sandusky and I got the day off and I went. I left the job at noon and had on my good clothes and my new brown derby hat, I'd just bought the Saturday before, and a stand-up collar.

First of all I went down-town and walked about with the dudes. I've always thought to myself, 'Put up a good front', and so I did it. I had forty dollars in my pocket, and so I went into the West House, a big hotel, and walked up to the cigar-stand. 'Give me three twenty-five-cent cigars,' I said. There was a lot of horsemen and strangers and dressed-up people from other towns standing around in the lobby and in the bar, and I mingled amongst them. In the bar there was a fellow with a cane and a Windsor tie on, that it made me sick to look at him. I like a man to be a man and dress up, but not to go put on that kind of airs. So I pushed him aside, kind of rough, and had me a drink of whisky. And then he looked at me, as though he thought maybe he'd get gay, but he changed his mind and didn't say anything. And then I had another drink of whisky, just to show him something, and went out and had a hack out to the races, all to myself, and when I got there I bought myself the best seat I could get up in the grandstand, but didn't go in for any of these boxes. That's putting on too many airs.

And so there I was, sitting up in the grandstand as gay as you please and looking down on the swipes coming out with their horses, and with their dirty horsy pants on and the horse blankets swung over their shoulders, same as I had been doing all the year before. I liked one thing about the same as the other, sitting up there and feeling grand and being down there and looking up at the yaps and feeling grander and more important, too. One thing's about as good as another, if you take it just right. I've often said that.

Well, right in front of me, in the grandstand that day, there was a fellow with a couple of girls and they was about my age. The young fellow was a nice guy all right. He was the kind maybe that goes to college and then comes to be a lawyer or maybe a newspaper editor or something like that, but he wasn't stuck on himself. There are some of that kind are all right and he was one of the ones.

He had his sister with him and another girl and the sister looked around over his shoulder, accidental at first, not intending to start anything – she wasn't that kind – and her eyes and mine happened to meet.

You know how it is. Gee, she was a peach! She had on a soft dress, kind of blue stuff and it looked carelessly made, but was well sewed and made and everything. I knew that much. I blushed when she looked right at me and so did she. She was the nicest girl I've ever seen in my life. She wasn't stuck on herself and she could talk proper grammar without being like a schoolteacher or something like that. What I mean is, she was O.K. I think maybe her father was well-to-do, but not rich enough to make her chesty because she was his daughter, as some are. Maybe he owned a drugstore or a dry-goods store in their home town, or something like that. She never told me and I never asked.

My own people are all O.K., too, when you come to that. My grandfather was Welsh and over in the old country, in Wales he was — But never mind that.

The first heat of the first race come off and the young fellow sitting there with the two girls left them and went down to make a bet. I knew what he was up to, but he didn't talk big and noisy and let everyone around know he was a sport, as some do. He wasn't that kind. Well, he come back and I heard him tell the two girls what horse he'd bet on, and when the heat was trotted they all half got to their feet and acted in the excited, sweaty way people do when they've got money down on a race, and the horse they bet on is up there pretty close at the end, and they think maybe he'll come on with a rush, but he never does because he hasn't got the old juice in him, come right down to it.

And then, pretty soon, the horses came out for the 2.18 pace and there was a horse in it I knew. He was a horse Bob French had in his string, but Bob didn't own him. He was a horse owned by a Mr Mathers down at Marietta, Ohio.

This Mr Mathers had a lot of money and owned some coal mines or something, and he had a swell place out in the country, and he was stuck on racehorses, but was a Presbyterian or something, and I think more than likely his wife was one, too, maybe a stiffer one than himself. So he never raced his horses hisself, and the story round the Ohio race-tracks was that when one of his horses got ready to go to the races he turned him over to Bob French and pretended to his wife he was sold.

So Bob had the horses and he did pretty much as he pleased and you can't blame Bob, at least, I never did. Sometimes he was out to

win and sometimes he wasn't. I never cared much about that when I
was swiping a horse. What I did want to know was that my horse
had the speed and could go out in front, if you wanted him to.

And, as I'm telling you, there was Bob in this race with one of Mr
Mathers' horses, which was named 'About Ben Ahem' or something
like that, and was fast as a streak. He was a gelding and had a mark of
2.21, but could step in .08 or .09.

Because when Burt and I were out, as I've told you, the year
before there was a nigger, Burt knew, worked for Mr Mathers and
we went out there one day when we didn't have no race on at the
Marietta Fair and our boss Harry was gone home.

And so everyone was gone to the fair but just this one nigger and
he took us all through Mr Mathers' swell house and he and Burt
tapped a bottle of wine Mr Mathers had hid in his bedroom, back in
a closet, without his wife knowing, and he showed us this Ahem
horse. Burt was always stuck on being a driver but didn't have much
chance to get to the top, being a nigger; and he and the other nigger
gulped that whole bottle of wine and Burt got a little lit up.

So the nigger let Burt take this About Ben Ahem and step him a mile
in a track Mr Mathers had all to himself, right there on the farm.
And Mr Mathers had one child, a daughter, kinda sick and not very
good looking, and she came home and we had to hustle and get
About Ben Ahem stuck back in the barn.

I'm only telling you to get everything straight. At Sandusky, that
afternoon I was at the fair, this young fellow with the two girls was
fussed, being with the girls and losing his bet. You know how a
fellow is that way. One of them was his girl and the other his sister. I
had figured that out.

'Gee whizz!' I says to myself, 'I'm going to give him the dope.'

He was mighty nice when I touched him on the shoulder. He and
the girls were nice to me right from the start and clear to the end.
I'm not blaming them.

And so he leaned back and I give him the dope on About Ben
Ahem. 'Don't bet a cent on this first heat because he'll go like an
oxen hitched to a plough, but when the first heat is over go right
down and lay on your pile.' That's what I told him.

Well, I never saw a fellow treat anyone sweller. There was a fat
man sitting beside the little girl, that had looked at me twice by this

time, and I at her, and both blushing, and what did he do but have the nerve to turn and ask the fat man to get up and change places with me so I could sit with his crowd.

Gee whizz, craps a'mighty! There I was. What a chump I was to go and get gay up there in the West House bar, and just because that dude was standing there with a cane and that kind of a necktie on, to go and get all balled up and drink that whisky, just to show off.

Of course she would know, me sitting right beside her and letting her smell of my breath. I could have kicked myself right down out of that grandstand and all around that race-track and made a faster record than most of the skates of horses they had there that year.

Because that girl wasn't any mutt of a girl. What wouldn't I have given right then for a stick of chewing-gum to chew, or a lozenger, or some liquorice, or most anything. I was glad I had those twenty-five-cent cigars in my pocket and right away I gave that fellow one and lit one myself. Then that fat man got up and we changed places and there I was, plunked right down beside her.

They introduced themselves and the fellow's best girl, he had with him, was named Miss Elinor Woodbury, and her father was a manufacturer of barrels from a placed called Tiffin, Ohio. And the fellow himself was named Wilbur Wessen and his sister was Miss Lucy Wessen.

I suppose it was their having such swell names got me off my trolly. A fellow, just because he has been a swipe with a racehorse, and works taking care of horses for a man in the teaming, delivery, and storage business, isn't any better or worse than anyone else. I've often thought that, and said it, too.

But you know how a fellow is. There's something in that kind of nice clothes, and the kind of nice eyes she had, and the way she had looked at me, awhile before, over her brother's shoulder, and me looking back at her, and both of us blushing.

I couldn't show her up for a boob, could I?

I made a fool of myself, that's what I did. I said my name was Walter Mathers from Marietta, Ohio, and then I told all three of them the smashingest lie you ever heard. What I said was that my father owned the horse About Ben Ahem and that he had let him out to this Bob French for racing purposes, because our family was proud and had never gone into racing that way, in our own name, I mean. Then I had got started and they were all leaning over and listening, and Miss Lucy Wessen's eyes were shining, and I went the whole hog.

I told about our place down at Marietta, and about the big stables and the grand brick house we had on a hill, up above the Ohio River, but I knew enough not to do it in no bragging way. What I did was to start things and then let them drag the rest out of me. I acted just as reluctant to tell as I could. Our family hasn't got any barrel factory, and, since I've known us, we've always been pretty poor, but not asking anything of anyone at that, and my grandfather, over in Wales – but never mind that.

We sat there talking like we had known each other for years and years, and I went and told them that my father had been expecting maybe this Bob French wasn't on the square, and had sent me up to Sandusky on the sly to find out what I could.

And I bluffed it through I had found out all about the 2.18 pace, in which About Ben Ahem was to start.

I said he would lose the first heat by pacing like a lame cow and then he would come back and skin 'em alive after that. And to back up what I said I took thirty dollars out of my pocket and handed it to Mr Wilbur Wessen and asked him, would he mind, after the first heat, to go down and place it on About Ben Ahem for whatever odds he could get. What I said was that I didn't want Bob French to see me and none of the swipes.

Sure enough the first heat come off and About Ben Ahem went off his stride, up the back stretch, and looked like a wooden horse or a sick one, and come in to be last. Then this Wilbur Wessen went down to the betting-place under the grandstand and there I was with the two girls, and when that Miss Woodbury was looking the other way once, Lucy Wessen kinda, with her shoulder you know, kinda touched me. Not just tucking down, I don't mean. You know how a woman can do. They get close, but not getting gay either. You know what they do. Gee whizz!

And then they give me a jolt. What they had done, when I didn't know, was to get together, and they had decided Wilbur Wessen would bet fifty dollars, and the two girls had gone and put in ten dollars each, of their own money, too. I was sick then, but I was sicker later.

About the gelding, About Ben Ahem, and their winning their

money, I wasn't worried a lot about that. It come out O.K. Ahem stepped the next three heats like a bushel of spoiled eggs going to market before they could be found out, and Wilbur Wessen had got nine to two for the money. There was something else eating at me.

Because Wilbur come back, after he had bet the money, and after that he spent most of his time talking to that Miss Woodbury, and Lucy Wessen and I was left alone together like on a desert island. Gee, if I'd only been on the square, or if there had been any way of getting myself on the square. There ain't any Walter Mathers, like I said to her and them, and their hasn't ever been one, but if there was, I bet I'd go to Marietta, Ohio, and shoot him tomorrow.

There I was, big boob that I am. Pretty soon the race was over, and Wilbur had gone down and collected our money, and we had a hack down-town, and he stood us a swell supper at the West House, and a bottle of champagne beside.

And I was with that girl and she wasn't saying much, and I wasn't saying much either. One thing I know. She wasn't stuck on me because of the lie about my father being rich and all that. There's a way you know. . . . Craps a'mighty! There's a kind of girl, you see just once in your life, and if you don't get busy and make hay, then you're gone for good and all, and might as well go jump off a bridge. They give you a look from inside of them somewhere, and it ain't no vamping, and what it means is – you want that girl to be your wife, and you want nice things around her like flowers and swell clothes, and you want her to have the kids you're going to have, and you want good music played and no ragtime. Gee whizz!

There's a place over near Sandusky, across a kind of bay, and it's called Cedar Point. And after we had supper we went over to it in a launch, all by ourselves. Wilbur and Miss Lucy and that Miss Woodbury had to catch a ten o'clock train back to Tiffin, Ohio, because, when you're out with girls like that you can't get careless and miss any trains and stay out all night, like you can with some kinds of Janes.

And Wilbur blowed himself to the launch, and it cost him fifteen cold plunks, but I wouldn't never have knew if I hadn't listened. He wasn't no tin-horn kind of a sport.

Over at the Cedar Point place, we didn't stay around where there was a gang of common kind of cattle at all.

There was big dance-halls and dining-places for yaps, and there was a beach you could walk along and get where it was dark, and we went there.

She didn't talk hardly at all and neither did I, and I was thinking how glad I was my mother was all right, and always made us kids learn to eat with a fork at table, and not swell soup, and be noisy and rough like a gang you see around a race-track that way.

Then Wilbur and his girl went away up the beach and Lucy and I sat down in a dark place, where there was some roots of old trees the water had washed up, and after that the time, till we had to go back in the launch and they had to catch their trains, wasn't nothing at all. It went like winking your eye.

Here's how it was. The place we were sitting in was dark, like I said, and there was the roots from that old stump sticking up like arms, and there was a watery smell, and the night was like – as if you could put your hand out and feel it – so warm and soft and dark and sweet like an orange.

I 'most cried and I 'most swore and I 'most jumped up and danced, I was so mad and happy and sad.

When Wilbur come back from being alone with his girl, and she saw him coming, Lucy she said, 'We got to go to the train now,' and she was 'most crying too, but she never knew nothing I knew, and she couldn't be so all busted up. And then, before Wilbur and Miss Woodbury got up to where we was, she put her face up and kissed me quick and put her head up against me and she was all quivering and – Gee whizz!

Sometimes I hope I have cancer and die. I guess you know what I mean. We went in the launch across the bay to the train like that, and it was dark, too. She whispered and said it was like she and I could get out of the boat and walk on the water, and it sounded foolish, but I knew what she meant.

And then quick we were right at the depot, and there was a big gang of yaps, the kind that goes to the fairs, and crowded and milling around like cattle, and how could I tell her? 'It won't be long because you'll write and I'll write to you.' That's all she said.

I got a chance like a hay-barn afire. A swell chance I got.

And maybe she would write me, down at Marietta that way, and the letter would come back, and stamped on the front of it by the U.S.A., 'There ain't any such guy,' or something like that, whatever they stamp on a letter that way.

And me trying to pass myself off for a big bug and a swell – to her, as decent a little body as God ever made. Craps a'mighty – a swell chance I got!

And then the train come in, and she got on it, and Wilbur Wessen he come and shook hands with me, and that Miss Woodbury was nice, too, and bowed to me, and I at her, and the train went and I busted out and cried like a kid.

Gee, I could have run after that train and made Dan Patch look like a freight train after a wreck but, sock a'mighty, what was the use? Did you ever see such a fool?

'I'll bet you what – if I had an arm broke right now or a train had run over my foot – I wouldn't go to no doctor at all. I'd go sit down and let her hurt and hurt – that's what I'd do.

I'll bet you what – if I hadn't a drunk that booze I'd a never been such a boob as to go tell such a lie – that couldn't never be made straight to a lady like her.

I wish I had that fellow right here that had on a Windsor tie and carried a cane. I'd smash him for fair. Gosh darn his eyes. He's a big fool – that's what he is.

And if I'm not another you just go find me one and I'll quit working and be a bum and give him my job. I don't care nothing for working, and earning money, and saving it for no such boob as myself.

HAD A HORSE

John Galsworthy

SOME quarter of a century ago, there abode in Oxford a small bookmaker called James Shrewin – or more usually 'Jimmy,' a run-about and damped-down little man, who made a precarious living out of the effect of horses on undergraduates. He had a so-called office just off the 'Corn,' where he was always open to the patronage of the young bloods of Bullingdon, and other horse-loving coteries, who bestowed on him sufficient money to enable him to live. It was through the conspicuous smash of one of them – young Gardon Colquhoun – that he became the owner of a horse. He had been far from wanting what was in the nature of a white elephant to one of his underground habits, but had taken it in discharge of betting debts, to which, of course, in the event of bankruptcy, he would have no legal claim. She was a three-year-old chestnut filly, by Lopez out of Calendar, bore the name Calliope, and was trained out on the Downs near Wantage. On a Sunday afternoon, then, in late July Jimmy got his friend, George Pulcher, the publican, to drive him out there in his sort of dog-cart.

'Must 'ave a look at the bilkin' mare,' he had said; 'that young "Cocoon" told me she was a corker; but what's third to Referee at Sandown, and never ran as a two-year-old? All I know is, she's eatin' 'er 'ead off!'

Beside the plethoric bulk of Pulcher, clad in a light-coloured box cloth coat with enormous whitish buttons and a full-blown rose in the lapel, Jimmy's little, thin, dark-clothed form, withered by anxiety and gin, was, as it were, invisible; and compared with Pulcher's setting sun, his face, with shaven cheeks sucked-in, and smudged-in eyes, was like a ghost's under a grey bowler. He spoke off-handedly about his animal, but he was impressed, in a sense abashed, by his ownership. What the 'ell? was his constant thought. Was he going to race her, sell her – what? How, indeed, to get back out of her the sum he had been fool enough to let 'young Cocoon' owe him, to say nothing of her trainer's bill? The notion, too, of having to confront that trainer with his ownership was oppressive to one whose whole life was passed in keeping out of the foreground of the picture. Owner! He had never owned even a white mouse, let alone a white elephant. And an 'orse would ruin him in no time if he didn't look alive about it!

The son of a small London baker, devoted to errandry at the age of fourteen, Jimmy Shrewin owed his profession to a certain smartness at sums, a dislike of baking, and an early habit of hanging about street corners with other boys, who had their daily pennies on an 'orse. He had a narrow calculating head, which pushed him towards street corner books before he was eighteen. From that time on he had been a surreptitious nomad, till he had silted up at Oxford, where, owing to Vice-Chancellors, an expert in underground life had greater scope than elsewhere. When he sat solitary at his narrow table in the back room near the 'Corn' – for he had no clerk or associate – eyeing the door, with his lists in a drawer before him, and his black shiny betting book ready for young 'bloods,' he had a sharp, cold, furtive air, and but for a certain imitated tightness of trouser, and a collar standing up all round, gave no impression of ever having heard of the quadruped called horse. Indeed, for Jimmy 'horse' was a newspaper quantity with figures against its various names. Even when, for a short spell, hanger-on to a firm of cheap-ring book-makers, he had seen almost nothing of horse; his racecourse hours were spent ferreting among a bawling, perspiring crowd, or hanging round within earshot of tight-lipped nobs, trainers, jockeys, anyone who looked like having 'information'. Nowadays he never went near a race-meeting – his business, of betting on races, giving him no chance – yet his conversation seldom deviated for more than a minute at a time from that physically unknown animal the horse. The ways of making money out of it, infinite, intricate, variegated, occupied the mind in all his haunts, to the accompaniment of liquid and tobacco. Gin and bitters was Jimmy's drink; for choice he smoked cheroots; and he would cherish in his mouth the cold stump of one long after it had gone out, for the homely feeling it gave him, while he talked, or listened to talk on horses. He was of that vast number, town bred, who, like crows round a carcase, feed on that which to them is not alive. And now he had a horse!

The dog-cart travelled at a clinking pace behind Pulcher's bob-tail. Jimmy's cheroot burned well in the warm July air; the dust powdered his dark clothes and pinched, sallow face. He thought with malicious pleasure of that young spark 'Cocoon's' collapse – high-'anded lot of young fools, thinking themselves so knowing; many were the grins, and not few the grittings of his blackened teeth he had to smother at their swagger. 'Jimmy, you robber!' 'Jimmy, you little blackguard!' Young sparks – gay and languid – well, one of 'em had gone out!

He looked round with his screwed-up eyes at his friend George Pulcher, who, man and licensed victualler, had his bally independence; lived remote from 'the Quality' in his Paradise, The Green Dragon; had not to kow-tow to anyone; went to Newbury, Gatwick, Stockbridge, here and there, at will. Ah! George Pulcher had the ideal life – and looked it: crimson, square, full-bodied. Judge of a horse, too, in his own estimation; a leery bird – for whose judgement Jimmy had respect – who got 'the office' of any clever work as quick as most men! And he said:

'What am I going to do with this blinkin' 'orse, George?'

Without moving its head the oracle spoke, in a voice rich and raw: 'Let's 'ave a look at her first, Jimmy! Don't like her name – Calliope; but you can't change what's in the Stud-book. This Jenning that trains 'er is a crusty chap.'

Jimmy nervously sucked-in his lips. The cart was mounting through the hedgeless fields which fringed the Downs; larks were singing, the wheat was very green, and patches of charlock brightened everything; it was lonely, few trees, few houses, no people, extreme peace, just a few rooks crossing under a blue sky.

'Wonder if he'll offer us a drink?' said Jimmy.

'Not he; but help yourself, my son.'

Jimmy helped himself from a large wicker-covered flask.

'Good for you, George – here's how!'

The large man shifted the reins and drank, in turn, tilting up a face whose jaw still struggled to assert itself against chins and neck.

'Well, here's your bloomin' horse,' he said. 'She can't win the Derby now, but she may do us a bit of good yet.'

★

The trainer, Jenning, coming from his Sunday afternoon round of the boxes, heard the sound of wheels. He was a thin man, neat in clothes and boots, medium in height, with a slight limp, narrow grey whiskers, thin shaven lips, eyes sharp and grey.

A dog-cart stopping at his yard-gate and a rum-looking couple of customers!

'Well, gentlemen?'

'Mr Jenning? My name's Pulcher – George Pulcher. Brought a client of yours over to see his new mare. Mr James Shrewin, Oxford city.'

Jimmy got down and stood before his trainer's uncompromising stare.

'What mare's that?' said Jenning.

'Calliope.'

'Calliope – Mr Colquhoun's?'

Jimmy held out a letter.

'DEAR JENNING,

'I have sold Calliope to Jimmy Shrewin, the Oxford bookie. He takes her with all engagements and liabilities, including your training bill. I'm frightfully sick at having to part with her, but needs must when the devil drives.

'GARDON COLQUHOUN.'

The trainer folded the letter.

'Got proof of registration?'

Jimmy drew out another paper.

The trainer inspected it, and called out; 'Ben, bring out Calliope. Excuse me a minute,' and he walked into his house.

Jimmy stood, shifting from leg to leg. Mortification had set in; the dry abruptness of the trainer had injured even a self-esteem starved from youth.

The voice of Pulcher boomed. 'Told you he was a crusty devil. 'And 'im a bit of his own.'

The trainer was coming back.

'My bill,' he said. 'When you've paid it you can have the mare. I train for gentlemen.'

'The hell you do!' said Pulcher.

Jimmy said nothing, staring at the bill – seventy-eight pounds three shillings! A buzzing fly settled in the hollow of his cheek, and he did not even brush it off. Seventy-eight pounds!

The sound of hoofs roused him. Here came his horse, throwing up her head as if enquiring why she was being disturbed a second time on Sunday! In the movement of that small head and satin neck was something free and beyond present company.

'There she is,' said the trainer. 'That'll do, Ben. Stand, girl!'

Answering to a jerk or two of the halter, the mare stood kicking slightly with a white hind foot and whisking her tail. Her bright coat shone in the sunlight, and little shivers and wrinklings passed up and down its satin because of the flies. Then, for a moment, she stood still, ears pricked, eyes on the distance.

Jimmy approached her. She had resumed her twitchings, swishings, and slight kicking, and at a respectful distance he circled, bending as if looking at crucial points. He knew what her sire and dam had done, and all the horses that had beaten, or been beaten by them; could have retailed by the half-hour the peculiar hearsay of their careers; and here was their offspring in flesh and blood, and he was dumb! He didn't know a thing about what she ought to look like, and he knew it; but he felt obscurely moved. She seemed to him 'a picture'.

Completing his circle, he approached her head, white-blazed, thrown up again in listening, or scenting, and gingerly he laid his hand on her neck, warm and smooth as a woman's shoulder. She paid no attention to his touch, and he took his hand away. Ought he to look at her teeth or feel her legs? No, he was not buying her, she was his already; but he must say something. He looked round. The trainer was watching him with a little smile. For almost the first time in his life the worm turned in Jimmy Shrewin; he spoke no word and walked back to the cart.

'Take her in,' said Jenning.

From his seat beside Pulcher, Jimmy watched the mare returning to her box.

'When I've cashed your cheque,' said the trainer, 'you can send for her'; and, turning on his heel, he went towards his house. The voice of Pulcher followed him.

'Blast your impudence! Git on, bob-tail, we'll shake the dust off 'ere.'

Among the fringing fields the dog-cart hurried away. The sun slanted, the heat grew less, the colour of young wheat and of the charlock brightened.

'The tyke! By Gawd, Jimmy, I'd 'ave hit him on the mug! But you've got one there. She's a bit o' blood, my boy, and I know the trainer for her, Polman – no blasted airs about 'im.'

Jimmy sucked at his cheroot.

'I ain't had your advantages, George, and that's a fact. I got into it too young, and I'm a little chap. But I'll send the . . . my cheque tomorrow. I got my pride, I 'ope!' It was the first time that thought had ever come to him.

Though not quite the centre of the Turf, The Green Dragon had nursed a *coup* in its day, nor was it without a sense of veneration. The ownership of Calliope invested Jimmy Shrewin with the importance of those out of whom something can be had. It took time for one so long accustomed to beck and call, to mole-like procedure, and the demeanour of young bloods to realize that he had it. But slowly, with the marked increase of his unpaid-for cheroots, with the way in which glasses hung suspended when he came in, with the edgings up to him, and a certain tendency to accompany him along the street, it dawned on him that he was not only an out-of-bounds bookie, but a man. So long as he had remained unconscious of his double nature he had been content with laying the odds, as best he might, and getting what he could out of every situation, straight or crooked. Now that he was also a man, his complacency was ruffled. He suffered from a growing headiness connected with his horse. She was trained, now, by Polman, further along the Downs, too far for Pulcher's bob-tail; and though her public life was carried on at The Green Dragon, her private life required a train journey over night. Jimmy took it twice a week – touting his own horse in the August mornings up on the Downs, without drink or talk, or even cheroots. Early morning, larks singing, and the sound of galloping hoofs! In a moment of expansion he confided to Pulcher that it was 'bally 'olesome'.

There had been the slight difficulty of being mistaken for a tout by his new trainer Polman, a stoutish man with the look of one of those large sandy Cornish cats, not precisely furtive because reticence and craft are their nature. But, that once over, his personality swelled slowly. This month of August was one of those interludes, in fact, when nothing happens, but which shape the future by secret ripening.

An error to suppose that men conduct finance, high or low, from greed, or love of gambling; they do it out of self-esteem, out of an itch to prove their judgement superior to their neighbours', out of a longing for importance. George Pulcher did not despise the turning of a penny, but he valued much more the consciousness that men were saying: 'Old George, what 'e says goes – knows a thing or two – George Pulcher!'

To pull the strings of Jimmy Shrewin's horse was a rich and subtle opportunity, absorbingly improvable. But first one had to study the animal's engagements, and, secondly, to gauge that unknown quantity, her 'form'. To make anything of her this year they must 'get about it'. That young 'toff', her previous owner, had of course flown high, entering her for classic races, high-class handicaps, neglecting the rich chances of lesser occasions.

Third to Reference in the three-year-old race at Sandown Spring – two heads – was all that was known of her, and now they had given her seven two in the Cambridgeshire. She might have a chance, and again she might not. He sat two long evenings with Jimmy in the little private room off the bar, deliberating this grave question.

Jimmy inclined to the bold course. He kept saying: 'The mare's a flyer, George – she's the 'ell of a flyer!'

'Wait till she's been tried,' said the oracle.

Had Polman anything that would give them a line?

Yes, he had The Shirker (named with that irony which appeals to the English), and one of the most honest four-year-olds that ever looked through bridle, who had run up against almost every animal of mark – the one horse that Polman never interfered with, for if interrupted in his training, he ran all the better; who seldom won, but was almost always placed – the sort of horse that handicappers pivot on.

'But,' said Pulcher, 'try her with The Shirker, and the first stable money will send her up to tens. That 'orse is so darned regular. We've got to throw a bit of dust first, Jimmy. I'll go over and see Polman.'

In Jimmy's withered chest a faint resentment rose – it wasn't George's horse, but it sank again beneath his friend's bulk and reputation.

The 'bit of dust' was thrown at the ordinary hour of exercise over the Long Mile on the last day of August – the five-year-old Hangman carrying eight stone seven, the three-year-old Parrot seven stone five; what Calliope was carrying nobody but Polman knew. The forethought of George Pulcher had secured the unofficial presence of the Press. The instructions to the boy on Calliope were to be there at the finish if he could, but on no account to win. Jimmy and George Pulcher had come out over night. They sat together in the dog-cart by the clump of bushes which marked the winning-post, with Polman on his cob on the far side.

By a fine, warm light the three horses were visible to the naked eye in the slight dip down by the start. And, through the glasses, invested in now that he had a horse, Jimmy could see every movement of his mare with her blazed face – rather on her toes, like the bright chestnut and 'bit o' blood' she was. He had a pit-patting in his heart, and his lips were tight pressed. Suppose she was no good after all, and that young 'Cocoon' had palmed him off a pup! But mixed in with his financial fear was an anxiety more intimate, as if his own value were at stake.

From George Pulcher came an almost excited gurgle.

'See the tout! See 'im behind that bush. Thinks we don't know 'e's there, wot oh!'

Jimmy bit into his cheroot. 'They're running,' he said.

Rather wide, the black Hangman on the far side, Calliope in the middle, they came sweeping up the long mile. Jimmy held his tobaccoed breath. The mare was going freely – a length or two behind – making up her ground! Now for it! —

Ah! she 'ad the 'Angman beat, and ding-dong with this Parrot! It was all he could do to keep from calling out. With a rush and cludding of hoofs they passed – the blazed nose just behind the Parrot's bay nose – dead heat all but, with the Hangman beat a good length!

'There 'e goes, Jimmy! See the blank scuttlin' down the 'ill like a blinkin' rabbit. That'll be in tomorrow's paper, that trial will. Ah! but 'ow to read it – that's the point.'

The horses had been wheeled and were sidling back; Polman was going forward on his cob.

Jimmy jumped down. Whatever that fellow had to say, he meant to hear. It was his horse! Narrowly avoiding the hoofs of his hot, fidgeting mare, he said sharply:

'What about it?'

Polman never looked you in the face; his speech came as if not intended to be heard by anyone:

'Tell Mr Shrewin how she went.'

'Had a bit up my sleeve. If I'd hit her a smart one, I could ha' landed by a length or more.'

'That so?' said Jimmy with a hiss. 'Well, *don't* you hit her; she don't want hittin'. You remember that.'

The boy said sulkily: 'All right!'

'Take her home,' said Polman. Then, with that reflective averted air of his, he added: 'She was carrying eight stone, Mr Shrewin; you've got a good one there. She's the Hangman at level weights.'

Something wild leaped up in Jimmy – the Hangman's form unrolled itself before him in the air – he had a horse – he dam' well had a horse!

But how delicate is the process of backing your fancy! The planting of a commission – what tender and efficient work before it will flower! That sixth sense of the racing man, which, like the senses of savages in great forests, seizes telepathically on what is not there, must be dulled, duped, deluded.

George Pulcher had the thing in hand. One might have thought the gross man incapable of such a fairy touch, such power of sowing with one hand and reaping with the other. He intimated rather than asserted that Calliope and the Parrot were one and the same thing. 'The Parrot,' he said, 'couldn't win with seven stone – no use thinkin' of this Calliope.'

Local opinion was the rock on which, like a great tactician, he built. So long as local opinion was adverse, he could dribble money on in London; the natural jump-up from every long shot taken was dragged back by the careful radiation of disparagement from the seat of knowledge.

Jimmy was the fly in his ointment of those balmy early weeks while snapping up every penny of long odds, before suspicion could begin to work from the persistence of enquiry. Half-a-dozen times he found the 'little cuss within an ace of blowing the gaff on his own blinkin' mare'; seemed unable to run his horse down; the little beggar's head was swellin'! Once Jimmy had even got up and gone out, leaving a gin and bitters untasted on the bar. Pulcher improved on his absence in the presence of a London tout.

'Saw the trial meself! Jimmy don't like to think he's got a stiff 'un.'

And next morning his London agent snapped up some thirty-threes again.

According to the trial the mare was the Hangman at seven stone two, and really hot stuff – a seven-to-one chance. It was none the less with a sense of outrage that, opening the *Sporting Life* on the last day of September, he found her quoted at 100–8. Whose work was this?

He reviewed the altered situation in disgust. He had invested about half the stable commission of three hundred pounds at an average of thirty-to-one, but, now that she had 'come' in the betting, he would hardly average tens with the rest. What fool had put his oar in?

He learned the explanation two days later. The rash, the unknown backer, was Jimmy! He had acted, it appeared, from jealousy; a bookmaker – it took one's breath away!

'Backed her on your own just because that young "Cocoon" told you he fancied her!'

Jimmy looked up from the table in his 'office', where he was sitting in wait for the scanty custom of the Long Vacation.

'She's not *his* horse,' he said sullenly. 'I wasn't going to have *him* get the cream.'

'What did you put on?' growled Pulcher.

'Took five hundred to thirty, and fifteen twenties.'

'An' see what it's done – knocked the bottom out of the commission. Am I to take that fifty as part of it?'

Jimmy nodded.

'That leaves an 'undred to invest,' said Pulcher, somewhat mollified. He stood, with his mind twisting in his thick still body. 'It's no good waitin' now,' he said; 'I'll work the rest of the money on today. If I can average tens on the balance, we'll 'ave six thousand three hundred to play with and the stakes. They tell me Jenning fancies this Diamond Stud of his. *He* ought to know the form with Calliope, blast him! We got to watch that.'

They had! Diamond Stud, a four-year-old with eight stone two, was being backed as if the Cambridgeshire were over. From fifteens he advanced to sevens, thence to favouritism at fives. Pulcher bit on it. Jenning *must* know where he stood with Calliope! It meant – it meant she couldn't win! The tactician wasted no time in vain regret. Establish Calliope in the betting and lay off. The time had come to utilize The Shirker.

It was misty on the Downs – fine-weather mist of a bright

October. The three horses became spectral on their way to the starting-point. Polman had thrown the Parrot in again, but this time he made no secret of the weights. The Shirker was carrying eight seven, Calliope eight, the Parrot seven stone.

Once more, in the cart, with his glasses sweeping the bright mist, Jimmy had that pit-patting in his heart. Here they came! His mare leading – all riding hard – a genuine finish! They passed – The Shirker beaten, a clear length, with the Parrot at his girth. Beside him in the cart, George Pulcher mumbled;

'She's The Shirker at eight stone four, Jimmy!'

A silent drive, big with thought, back to a river inn; a silent breakfast. Over a tankard at the close the Oracle spoke.

'The Shirker, at eight stone-four, is a good 'ot chance, but no cert, Jimmy. We'll let 'em know this trial quite open, weights and all. That'll bring her in the betting. And we'll watch Diamond Stud. If he drops back we'll know Jenning thinks he can't beat us now. If Diamond Stud stands up, we'll know Jenning thinks he's still got our mare safe. Then our line'll be clear: we lay off the lot, pick up a thousand or so, and 'ave the mare in at a nice weight at Liverpool.'

Jimmy's smudged-in eyes stared hungrily.

'How's that?' he said. 'Suppose she wins!'

'Wins! If we lay off the lot, she *won't* win.'

'Pull her!'

George Pulcher's voice sank half an octave with disgust.

'Pull her! Who's talked of pullin'? She'll run a bye, that's all. We shan't ever know whether she could 'a won or not.'

Jimmy sat silent; the situation was such as his life during sixteen years had waited for. They stood to win both ways with a bit of hand-ling.

'Who's to ride?' he said.

'Polman's got a call on Docker. He can just ride the weight. Either way he's good for us – strong finisher, and a rare judge of distance; knows how to time things to a T. Win or not, he's our man.'

Jimmy was deep in figures. Laying-off at sevens, they would still win four thousand and the stakes.

'I'd like a win,' he said.

'Ah!' said Pulcher. 'But there'll be twenty in the field, my son; no more uncertain race than that bally Cambridgeshire. We could pick up a thou – as easy as I pick up this pot. Bird in the 'and, Jimmy, and a good 'andicap in the bush. If she wins, she's finished. Well, we'll put this trial about and see 'ow Jenning pops.'

Jenning popped amazingly. Diamond Stud receded a point, then re-established himself at nine to two. Jenning was clearly not dismayed.

George Pulcher shook his head, and waited, uncertain still which way to jump. Ironical circumstances decided him.

Term had begun; Jimmy was busy at his seat of custom. By some miracle of guardianly intervention, young Colquhoun had not gone broke. He was 'up' again, eager to retrieve his reputation, and that little brute Jimmy would not lay against his horse! He merely sucked in his cheeks, and answered: 'I'm not layin' my own 'orse.' It was felt that he was not the man he had been; assertion had come into his manner, he was better dressed. Someone had seen him at the station looking quite a 'toff' in a blue box-cloth coat standing well out from his wisp of a figure, and with a pair of brown race-glasses slung over the shoulder. Altogether the 'little brute was getting too big for his boots'.

And this strange improvement hardened the feeling that his horse was a real good thing. Patriotism began to burn in Oxford. Here was a 'snip' that belonged to them, as it were, and the money in support of it, finding no outlet, began to ball.

A week before the race – with Calliope at nine to one, and very little doing – young Colquhoun went up to town, taking with him the accumulated support of betting Oxford. That evening she stood at sixes. Next day the public followed on.

George Pulcher took advantage. In this crisis of the proceedings he acted on his own initiative. The mare went back to eights, but the deed was done. He had laid off the whole bally lot, including the stake money. He put it to Jimmy that evening in a nutshell.

'We pick up a thousand, and the Liverpool as good as in our pocket. I've done worse.'

'Jimmy grunted out: 'She could 'a won.'

'Not she. Jenning knows – and there's others in the race. This Wasp is goin' to take a lot of catchin', and Deerstalker's not out of it. He's a hell of a horse, even with that weight.'

Again Jimmy grunted, slowly sucking down his gin and bitters. Sullenly he said:

'Well, I don't want to put money in the pocket of young

"Cocoon" and his crowd. Like his impudence, backin' my horse as if
it was his own.'

'We'll 'ave to go and see her run, Jimmy.'

'Not me,' said Jimmy.

'What! First time she runs! It won't look natural.'

'No,' repeated Jimmy. 'I don't want to see 'er beat.'

George Pulcher laid his hand on a skinny shoulder.

'Nonsense, Jimmy. You've got to, for the sake of your reputation.
You'll enjoy seein' your mare saddled. We'll go up over night. I
shall 'ave a few pound on Deerstalker. I believe he can beat this
Diamond Stud. And you leave Docker to me; I'll 'ave a word with
him at Gatwick tomorrow. I've known 'im since he was that 'igh;
an' 'e ain't much more now.'

'All right!' growled Jimmy.

The longer you can bet on a race the greater its fascination.
Handicappers can properly enjoy the beauty of their work; clubmen
and oracles of the course have due scope for reminiscence and
prophecy; bookmakers in lovely leisure can indulge a little their own
calculated preferences, instead of being hurried to soulless conclusions
by a half-hour's market on the course; the professional backer has the
longer in which to dream of his fortune made at last by some hell of
a horse – spotted somewhere as interfered with, left at the post,
running green, too fat, not fancied, backward – now bound to win
this hell of a race. And the general public has the chance to read the
horses' names in the betting news for days and days; and what a
comfort that is!

Jimmy Shrewin was not one of those philosophers who justify the
great and growing game of betting on the ground that it improves
the breed of an animal less and less in use. He justified it much more
simply – he lived by it. And in the whole of his career of nearly
twenty years since he made hole-and-corner books among the boys
of London, he had never stood so utterly on velvet as that morning
when his horse must win him five hundred pounds by merely losing.
He had spent the night in London anticipating a fraction of his gains
with George Pulcher at a music-hall. And, in a first-class carriage, as
became an owner, he travelled down to Newmarket by an early
special. An early special key turned in the lock of the carriage door,
preserved their numbers at six, all professionals, with blank, rather

rolling eyes, mouths shut or slightly fishy, ears to the ground; and the only natural talker, a red-faced man, who had 'been at it thirty years'. Intoning the pasts and futures of this hell of a horse or that, even he was silent on the race in hand; and the journey was half over before the beauty of their own judgements loosened tongues thereon. George Pulcher started it.

'I fancy Deerstalker,' he said; 'he's a hell of a horse.'

'Too much weight,' said the red-faced man. 'What about this Calliope?'

'Ah!' said Pulcher. 'D'you fancy your mare, Jimmy?'

With all eyes turned on him, lost in his blue box-cloth coat, brown bowler, and cheroot smoke, Jimmy experienced a subtle thrill. Addressing the space between the red-raced man and Pulcher, he said:

'If she runs up to 'er looks.'

'Ah!' said Pulcher, 'she's dark – nice mare, but a bit light and shelly.'

'Lopez out o' Calendar,' muttered the red-faced man. 'Lopez didn't stay, but he was the hell of horse over seven furlongs. The Shirker ought to 'ave told you a bit.'

Jimmy did not answer. It gave him pleasure to see the red-faced man's eye trying to get past, and failing.

'Nice race to pick up. Don't fancy the favourite meself; he'd nothin' to beat at Ascot.'

'Jenning knows what he's about,' said Pulcher.

Jenning! Before Jimmy's mind passed again that first sight of his horse, and the trainer's smile, as if he – Jimmy Shrewin, who owned her – had been dirt. Tyke! To have the mare beaten by one of his! A deep, subtle vexation had oppressed him at times all these last days since George Pulcher had decided in favour of the mare's running a bye. D—n George Pulcher! He took too much on himself! Thought he had Jimmy Shrewin in his pocket! He looked at the block of crimson opposite. Aunt Sally! If George Pulcher could tell what was passing in his mind!

But driving up to the Course he was not above sharing a sandwich and a flask. In fact, his feelings were unstable and gusty – sometimes resentment, sometimes the old respect for his friend's independent bulk. The dignity of ownership takes long to establish itself in those who have been kicked about.

'All right with Docker,' murmured Pulcher, sucking at the wicker flask. 'I gave him the office at Gatwick.'

'She could 'a won,' muttered Jimmy.

'Not she, my boy; there's two at least can beat 'er.'

Like all oracles, George Pulcher could believe what he wanted to.

Arriving, they entered the grandstand enclosure, and over the dividing railings Jimmy gazed at the Cheap Ring, already filling up with its usual customers. Faces and umbrellas – the same old crowd. How often had he been in that Cheap Ring, with hardly room to move, seeing nothing, hearing nothing but 'Two to one on the field!' 'Two to one on the field!' 'Threes Swordfish!' 'Fives Alabaster!' 'Two to one on the field!' Nothing but a sea of men like himself, and a sky overhead. He was not exactly conscious of criticism, only of a dull 'Glad I'm shut of that lot' feeling.

Leaving George Pulcher deep in conversation with a crony, he lighted a cheroot and slipped out on to the Course. He passed the Jockey Club enclosure. Some early 'toffs' were there in twos and threes, exchanging wisdom. He looked at them without envy or malice. He was an owner himself now, almost one of them in a manner of thinking. With a sort of relish he thought of how his past life had circled round those 'toffs', slippery, shadowlike, kicked about; and now he could get up on the Downs away from 'toffs', George Pulcher, all that crowd, and smell the grass, and hear the bally larks, and watch his own mare gallop!

They were putting the numbers up for the first race. Queer not to be betting, not to be touting round; queer to be giving it a rest! Utterly familiar with those names on the board, he was utterly unfamiliar with the shapes they stood for.

I'll go and see 'em come out of the paddock, he thought, and moved on, skimpy in his bell-shaped coat and billycock with flattened brim. The clamour of the Rings rose behind him while he was entering the paddock.

Very green, very peaceful, there; not many people, yet! Three horses in the second race were being led slowly in a sort of winding ring; and men were clustering round the further gate where the horses would come out. Jimmy joined them, sucking at his cheroot. They were a picture! Damn it! he didn't know but that 'orses laid over men! Pretty creatures!

One by one they passed out of the gate, a round dozen. Selling platers, but pictures for all that!'

He turned back towards the horses being led about; and the old instinct to listen took him close to little groups. Talk was all of the big race. From a tall 'toff' he caught the word Calliope.

'Belongs to a bookie, they say.'

Bookie! Why not? Wasn't a bookie as good as any other? Ah! and sometimes better than these young snobs with everything to their hand! A bookie – well, what chance had he ever had?

A big brown horse came by.

'That's Deerstalker,' he heard the 'toff' say.

Jimmy gazed at George Pulcher's fancy with a sort of hostility. Here came another – Wasp, six stone ten, and Deerstalker nine stone – top and bottom of the race!

My 'orse'd beat either o' them, he thought stubbornly. Don't like that Wasp.

The distant roar was hushed. They were running in the first race! He moved back to the gate. The quick clamour rose and dropped, and here they came – back into the paddock, darkened with sweat, flanks heaving a little!

Jimmy followed the winner, saw the jockey weigh in.

'What jockey's that?' he asked.

'That? Why, Docker!'

Jimmy stared. A short, square, bow-legged figure, with a hard-wood face! Waiting his chance, he went up to him and said:

'Docker, you ride my 'orse in the big race.'

'Mr Shrewin?'

'The same,' said Jimmy. The jockey's left eyelid drooped a little. Nothing responded in Jimmy's face. 'I'll see you before the race,' he said.

Again the jockey's eyelid wavered, he nodded and passed on.

Jimmy stared at his own boots; they struck him suddenly as too yellow and not at the right angle. But why, he couldn't say.

More horses now – those of the first race being unsaddled, clothed, and led away. More men – three familiar figures: young 'Cocoon' and two others of his Oxford customers.

Jimmy turned sharply from them. Stand their airs? – not he! He had a sudden sickish feeling. With a win, he'd have been a made man – on his own! Blast George Pulcher and his caution! To think of being back in Oxford with those young bloods jeering at his beaten horse! He bit deep into the stump of his cheroot, and suddenly came on Jenning standing by a horse with a star on its bay forehead. The trainer gave him no sign of recognition, but signed to the boy to lead the horse into a stall, and followed, shutting the door. It was exactly as if he had said: 'Vermin about!'

An evil little smile curled Jimmy's lips. The tyke!

The horses for the second race passed out of the paddock gate, and he turned to find his own. His ferreting eyes soon sighted Polman. What the cat-faced fellow knew, or was thinking, Jimmy could not tell. Nobody could tell.

'Where's the mare?' he said.

'Just coming round.'

No mistaking her; fine as a star; shiny-coated, sinuous, her blazed face held rather high! Who said she was 'shelly'? She was a picture! He walked a few paces close to the boy.

'That's Calliope. . . . H'm! . . . Nice filly! . . . Looks fit. . . . Who's this James Shrewin? . . . What's she at? . . . I like her looks.'

His horse! Not a prettier filly in the world!

He followed Polman into her stall to see her saddled. In the twilight there he watched her toilet; the rub-over; the exact adjustments; the bottle of water to the mouth; the buckling of the bridle – watched her head high above the boy keeping her steady with gentle pulls of a rein in each hand held out a little wide, and now and then stroking her blazed nose; watched her pretence of nipping at his hand: he watched the beauty of her exaggerated in this half-lit isolation away from the others, the life and litheness in her satin body, the wilful expectancy in her bright soft eyes.

Run a bye! This bit o' blood – this bit o' fire! This horse of his! Deep within that shell of blue box-cloth against the stall partition a thought declared itself: I'm — if she shall! She can beat the lot! And she's — well going to!

The door was thrown open, and she led out. He moved alongside. They were staring at her, following her. No wonder! She was a picture, his horse – his! She had gone to Jimmy's head.

They passed Jenning with Diamond Stud waiting to be mounted. Jimmy shot him a look. Let the — wait!

His mare reached the palings and was halted. Jimmy saw the short square figure of her jockey, in the new magenta cap and jacket – *his* cap, *his* jacket! Beautiful they looked, and no mistake!

'A word with you,' he said.

The jockey halted, looked quickly round.

'All right, Mr Shrewin. I know.'

Jimmy's eyes smouldered at him; hardly moving his lips, he said, intently: 'You — well don't! You'll — well ride her to win. Never mind *him*! If you don't, I'll have you off the turf. Understand me! You'll — well ride 'er to win.'

The jockey's jaw dropped.

'All right, Mr Shrewin.'

'See it is,' said Jimmy with a hiss . . .

'Mount jockeys!'

He saw magenta swing into the saddle. And suddenly, as if smitten with the plague, he scuttled away.

He scuttled to where he could see them going down – seventeen. No need to search for his colours; they blazed, like George Pulcher's countenance, or a rhododendron bush in sunlight, above that bright chestnut with the white nose, curveting a little as she was led past.

Now they came cantering – Deerstalker in the lead.

'He's a hell of a horse, Deerstalker,' said someone behind.

Jimmy cast a nervous glance around. No sign of George Pulcher!

One by one they cantered past, and he watched them with a cold feeling in his stomach. Still unused to sight of the creatures out of which he made his living, they *all* seemed to him hells of horses.

The same voice said:

'New colours! Well, you can see 'em, and the mare too. She's a showy one. Calliope? She's goin' back in the bettin', though.'

Jimmy moved up through the Ring.

'Four to one on the field!' 'Six Deerstalker!' 'Sevens Magistrate!' 'Ten to one Wasp!' 'Ten to one Calliope!' 'Four to one Diamond Stud!' 'Four to one on the field!'

Steady as a rock, that horse of Jenning, and his own going back.

'Twelves Calliope!' he heard, just as he reached the stand. The telepathic genius of the Ring missed nothing – almost!

A cold shiver went through him. What had he done by his words to Docker? Spoiled the golden egg laid so carefully? But perhaps she couldn't win even if they let her! He began to mount the stand, his mind in the most acute confusion.

'A voice said: 'Hullo, Jimmy! Is she going to win?'

One of his young Oxford sparks was jammed against him on the stairway!

He raised his lip in a sort of snarl, and, huddling himself, slipped through and up ahead. He came out and edged in close to the stairs where he could get play for his glasses. Behind him one of those who improve the shining hour among backers cut off from opportunity, was intoning the odds a point shorter than below. 'Three to one on the field.' 'Fives Deerstalker.' 'Eight to one Wasp.'

'What price Calliope?' said Jimmy, sharply.

'Hundred to eight.'

'Done!' Handing him the eight, he took the ticket. Behind him the man's eyes moved fishily, and he resumed his incantation.

'Three to one on the field . . . three to one on the field. Six to one Magistrate.'

On the wheeling bunch of colours at the start Jimmy trained his glasses. Something had broken clean away and come half the course – something in yellow.

'Eights Magistrate. Eight to one Magistrate,' drifted up.

So they had spotted that! Precious little they didn't spot!

Magistrate was round again, and being ridden back. Jimmy rested his glasses a moment, and looked down. Swarms in the Cheap Ring, Tattersalls, the stands – a crowd so great you could lose George Pulcher in it. Just below a little man was making silent, frantic signals with his arms across to someone in the Cheap Ring. Jimmy raised his glasses. In line now – magenta third from the rails!

'They're off!' The hush, you could cut it with a knife! Something in green away on the right – Wasp! What a bat they were going! And a sort of numbness in Jimmy's mind cracked suddenly; his glasses shook; his thin, weasely face became suffused and quivered. Magenta – magenta – two from the rails! He could make no story of the race such as he would read in tomorrow's paper – he could see nothing but magenta.

Out of the dip now, and coming fast – green still leading – something in violet, something in tartan, closing.

'Wasp's beat!' 'The favourite – the favourite wins!' 'Deerstalker – Deerstalker wins!' 'What's that in pink on the rails?'

It was *his* in pink on the rails! Behind him a man went suddenly mad.

'Deerstalker – Come on with 'im, Stee! Deerstalker'll win – Deerstalker'll win!'

Jimmy sputtered venomously: 'Will 'e? Will 'e?'

Deerstalker and his own out from the rest – opposite the Cheap Ring – neck and neck – Docker riding like a demon.

'Deerstalker! Deerstalker!' 'Calliope wins! She wins!'

Gawd! His horse! They flashed past – fifty yards to go, and not a head between 'em!

'Deerstalker! Deerstalker!' 'Calliope!'

He saw his mare shoot out – she'd won!

With a little queer sound he squirmed and wriggled on to the stairs. No thoughts while he squeezed, and slid, and hurried – only emotion – out of the Ring, away to the paddock. His horse!

Docker had weighed in when he reached the mare. All right! He passed with a grin. Jimmy turned almost into the body of Polman standing like an image.

'Well, Mr Shrewin,' he said to nobody, 'she's won.'

Damn you! thought Jimmy. Damn the lot of you! And he went up to his mare. Quivering, streaked with sweat, impatient of the gathering crowd, she showed the whites of her eyes when he put his hand up to her nose.

'Good girl!' he said, and watched her led away.

Gawd! I want a drink! he thought.

Gingerly, keeping a sharp lookout for Pulcher, he returned to the stand to get it, and to draw his hundred. But up there by the stairs the discreet fellow was no more. On the ticket was the name O. H. Jones, and nothing else. Jimmy Shrewin had been welshed! He went down at last in bad temper. At the bottom of the staircase stood George Pulcher. The big man's face was crimson, his eyes ominous. He blocked Jimmy into a corner.

'Ah!' he said; 'you little crow! What the 'ell made you speak to Docker?'

Jimmy grinned. Some new body within him stood there defiant. 'She's my 'orse,' he said.

'You – Gawd-forsaken rat! If I 'ad you in a quiet spot I'd shake the life out of you!'

Jimmy stared up, his little spindle legs apart, like a cock-sparrow confronting an offended pigeon.

'Go 'ome,' he said, 'George Pulcher; and get your mother to mend your socks. You don't know 'ow! Thought I wasn't a man, did you? Well, now you — well know I am. Keep off my 'orse in future.'

Crimson rushed up on crimson in Pulcher's face; he raised his heavy fists. Jimmy stood, unmoving, his little hands in his bell-coat pockets, his withered face upraised. The big man gulped as if swallowing back the tide of blood; his fists edged forward and then – dropped.

'That's better,' said Jimmy, 'hit one of your own size.'

Emitting a deep growl, George Pulcher walked away.

'Two to one on the field – I'll back the field – Two to one on the field.' 'Threes Snowdrift – Fours Iron Dook.'

Jimmy stood a moment mechanically listening to the music of his life, then edging out, he took a fly and was driven to the station.

All the way up to town he sat chewing his cheroot with the glow of drink inside him, thinking of that finish, and of how he had stood up to George Pulcher. For a whole day he was lost in London, but Friday saw him once more at his seat of custom in the 'Corn'. Not having laid against his horse, he had had a good race in spite of everything; yet, the following week, uncertain into what quagmires of quixotry she might lead him, he sold Calliope.

But for years betting upon horses that he never saw, underground like a rat, yet never again so accessible to the kicks of fortune, or so prone before the shafts of superiority, he would think of the Downs with the blinkin' larks singin', and talk of how once he – had a horse.

THE MAJOR

Colin Davy

M Y attention to the conversation flagged, and I found
myself thinking how well the name Jonathan Pluck
suited the man. There was a Quakerish simplicity and
good will in his smooth, round face which would have charmed the
stingiest old maid of her last penny, a guileless candour which invited
trust.

It was only when he smiled and his small eyes twinkled and
screwed up that one sensed the mischief and adventure within
bidding one beware. And as Pluck was a contradiction of Jonathan,
his smart clothes and almost swashbuckling manner were a contradiction of this bucolic simplicity of expression.

Jonathan Pluck: half quaker, half laughing cavalier. A man unread,
uneducated, who could hardly write his name, yet capable of
devising the most intricate racing 'ramp', shy and diffident with
strangers, yet full of confidence in himself in his own metier; ready to
give a sovereign to the most undeserving tramp, or a hundred
pounds to the first 'confidence man', yet a hard and implacable rival
in the business of racing.

And above all, a man of indomitable courage who, on a score of
occasions in a score of different countries, had seen his last penny lost
in some gigantic gamble, and laughing, had battled on. . . .

My thoughts were disturbed by our companion rising.

'Looks a proper old sport,' remarked Jonathan Pluck, as the
stranger bade us good night and left the smoking saloon.

'He certainly is that,' said I. 'He was owning and riding horses
when you and I were in our cradles. He rode in his last 'chase on his
sixtieth birthday. He was one of the "heads" in Roddy Owen's day.'

'Was he now? And did he always wear glasses?'

'Yes, and it can't have been much fun. It was before Triplex was invented. I can't think how fellows do it. Think of a wet day with your glasses all misted over, to say nothing of the mud sticking on them. You need some guts to smack one into the last fence when you're three parts blind,' said I.

'I've smacked 'em into the last when I was *more* then three parts blind,' said Johnnie, with a laugh, and added, 'but not blind the way you mean.

'I had an owner once wot rode in glasses,' he went on. 'And he was a proper sport, too. He'd ride anything, and he never knew when he was beat. He was a major in the Marines. Can you beat that, Cap? He's the only officer of Marines I've ever heard who rode anything 'cept in a cab. He was a good rider, too, and as I sez, 'e never knew when he was beat.

'Determination, that's what it was. It didn't matter whether the other jocks had knocked him rotten (and some of them were rough in those days), he'd never stop trying. He won no end of races when everyone else thought he was beat. He was a devil to scrap, too. If one of the jocks gave him any sauce or had done anything a bit tough in a race, he'd come into the jocks' room and call the feller out for a scrap, no matter who he was. I remember once down in the Isle of Wight . . .' Johnny broke off. 'But you want to go to bed, Cap.'

'Not until I've had one more drink,' I protested. 'Go on, Johnnie.'

As the barman replenished our glasses Johnnie began.

'It was six or seven years ago, when I had a few jumpers at Fittleton on Salisbury Plain. Two of 'em was owned by this major of Marines. Slapstoke-Keene his name was, and his friends called him "Slapper". None of the horses was muchers: a selling hurdler or two, two selling 'chasers and an odd one qualified to run in hunt 'chases. I'd have been tickled to death if anyone had offered me six hundred quid for the lot. None of me owners were rich. We were all pretty much in the same boat -- scratching ourselves for the next tenner.

'Sometimes the bills were paid, and more often they weren't. If one of the horses fluked a race I got the stakes to put against the training bill, and the forage merchant got a bit to be goin' on with. Often enough it was difficult to find the dibs to pay the rail fare to a meeting, and many a time I couldn't find enough for a return ticket. If the horse didn't win he had to stay on at the nearest stable to the racecourse until we scraped enough to get him back. Once I had to leave one at Tenby from Easter until the Whitsuntide meeting came round, because we couldn't find his fare back.

'Quite frequently we had to put the major up because we couldn't find the fee for a professional, and, though he was a good rider for an amateur, he was by no means first class. Well, from that you can imagine we didn't often send a horse to a meeting unless we thought he had a fair chance of winning. There wasn't any question of keeping a horse and getting his weight down for a certain race. There was usually sixty or seventy quid at the winning-post which we wanted bad, and probably five or six quid gone on the rail fair; so it wasn't often we could afford to have one stopped to have a bet another day. No. No one could have hardly said we were a betting stable in those days.

'You know, Cap, people talk a lot of nonsense about 'chasing in England being crooked. How often do you hear people talk about a horse having been kept on ice for months for a certain race? If they knew that it costs about twenty quid every time you run a horse, and if they did a bit of calculating they'd see that what they were saying was all foolishness. Say one is stopped three times. Well, there's sixty quid gone. The 'oss may be dropped in the weights, but everyone else knows that as well as you.

'You find he starts at six to four or even money, and you've got to risk a hell of a lot to get even that sixty back. And say you do, you're still only left with the stake to come. Your bet has only covered out-of-pocket expenses. So you'd be just as well off if you'd won the stake the first time. No. Keeping horses in order to have a bet is no job for a poor man.

'Well, I must get on with me story. One Easter I set off for the meeting at the Isle of Wight with two 'osses. One chestnut plater called Solvent belonged to the major, and the other, an awful squib of a mare called Elsie B, belonged to me. She'd been owned by a grocer in Andover, but he hadn't been able to pay his bill and I'd took the mare in payment.

'Now Solvent was the best horse we had in the stable, a real old battler, a fine old jumper and honest as the day. He'd been a hell of a good horse in his day, but had got a bit slow. He was still a good horse for a three-mile seller or a small handicap. There was a three-mile handicap on the first day of the meeting in which there was nothing much good entered, and I thought he must have a good chance of winning it. The major had wired that he couldn't get away to ride, and we had decided we could afford to put up a good pro. I'd actually engaged Hawkey Stud to ride him. Hawkey was a real good lad and was always glad to ride as good a jumper as old Solvent.

'Well, crossing over from Southampton on the boat there was all the racin' crowd and Hawkey among them. He comes up to me in the bar and asks me about the 'osses and particular about old Solvent.

'"'E's top hole," I tells Hawkey. "If Strumper don't go, 'e's the cat's pyjamas for the three-mile chase."

'"Strumper *don't* go," sez Hawkey. "Billy told me Tuesday. He goes at Torquay."

'"Then you've nothing to bother about," sez I. "It's a moral. That's the only one I was afraid of. If only things had gone a bit better I'd have a tenner on him."

' "Been goin' bad?" asks Hawkey.

'"I been scrubbing me brains out to get the rail fare for these two 'osses," I sez.

'Hawkey looks very thoughtful for a few minutes, and then he sez, "I know of a job what's being worked at this meeting. I might get you into it, if you had a mind."

'"I wish you would," sez I. "I'd be more than grateful."

'"It's a bit difficult," sez Hawkey, scratching his head, "but I'll go and have a talk with Bert."

'Now by Bert he meant Bert Scoop, a big West Country bookmaker who had a finger in every pie. There was a time when he had as many as twenty horses in training, and had S.P. offices all over the country into the bargain. It was almost impossible to work anything big in the West without him.

'When he mentioned Bert I thought to meself that the job he was talking about must be a big one. Bert wouldn't be coming to a little meeting like the Isle of Wight just for the sake of his health.

'A few minutes later Hawkey comes up with Bert, and we stroll to the back end of the ship to get a bit of fresh air and find a place where we won't be interrupted.

'"Hawkey tells me you wouldn't mind bein' in on a job we've been thinking of," said Bert.

'"You've got it right there, Mr Scoop," I said. "If you can let me in on it, I'd be more than obliged."

'"Well, it's like this," said Scoop. "There's an animal in one race which we're thinking of backing in an S.P. job, but we're not quite sure of the opposition. If it's done properly it ought to be returned at 100 to 6. If I can be sure of the opposition we can get five hundred on."

'"Five hundred," sez I. "Can you get all that lot on and not affect the price?"

'"All the wires are written out now. They're Dublin, if you want to know. I've only to telegraph one word and they'll be sent off five minutes before the race. There's not a chance of the price being spoiled. And the animal *will* start at a 100 to 6. It's got no form at all and I shall be laying it at that price on me own books. You leave it to me. But it's no good talking of that yet since I haven't yet arranged about the opposition. Now, Pluck, *say you had a runner in the race*, how much would you like put on for you? What would you consider fair?"

'"A fiver each way," sez I, laughing. "So long as the price was 100 to 6."

'"Well, you're on a fiver, each way, price guaranteed," says he.

'"But which race is it?" I asks, suddenly feeling that I'd spoken out of my turn.

'"The three-mile handicap," sez Scoop.

'"But I've got Solvent in that," said I. "'E's a moral to win it, now that Strumper don't go. Hawkey's booked to ride. I couldn't crook *him*. What would the major say? Why the stake's worth eighty quid."

'"Thought you said you'd be satisfied with a fiver each way," said Scoop; "but perhaps I'm getting hard of hearing."

'"I didn't think you were talking of that race," I said. "What about the others? What are they on?"

'"Never mind the others. They're my affair. It's you and your Major Slapper we're talkin' of now," sez Scoop. "What do you think he'd want out of it? Would the stake be enough?"

'I thought for a bit then, Cap, and did some calculating. I knew if the major was here he wouldn't consider the thing for a moment. He'd have seen himself dead before he stopped one. He was funny that way. But if I could give him a cheque equal to the stake, and tell him his horse hadn't got a winner's penalty, I thought I could square things somehow. What the eye doesn't see the heart doesn't grieve about, and anyhow, beggars can't be choosers. In the end we settled that I should have seven quid each way at 100 to 6, and the stakes to give to the major.

'It was then Scoop told me he'd squared all the others. He didn't tell me which horse was going to win, but it was to go out in front, all the others was to lie well back, and those that hadn't fallen off was to run out at the ditch on the far side of the course the second time round. You can't see that fence from the stands: it's behind a hill, and hidden by trees and gorse bushes. Nothing was to be left to chance. Even though this job horse fell at one of the last three fences the jock must be able to remount and win. All the others had to be definitely out of the race.

'As you may imagine, Cap, I didn't sleep much. I was doing multiplication sums all night.'

'Well, it never rains but it snows, Cap. Next day damned if I didn't have a hunch that that squib of mine, Elsie B, might do her stuff, and I has thirty bob on her at eights in the selling hurdle. Up she comes to win by half a length, and I'm sittin' pretty with the price of me return journey *and* a bottle o' wine.

'Then we comes to the three-mile handicap. I sees Bert Scoop just before I go to weigh out Hawkey, and he whispers "All serene. I've sent the wire to Dublin." Well, just as Hawkey was getting on the scale, I feels a tap on my back and looks round. And who do you think it is? With his boots and breeches and colours on, and a saddle on his arm. The major!

'I nearly dropped.

'"Hulloa, major," sez I. "Where have you sprung from?"

'"I found I could just do it," he says with a smile. "I got away earlier than I expected. Got a fellow to motor me to Southampton, got a motor-launch from there, and here I am. Good work, what?"

'"Good 'evvings!" says I.

'"I'm still in time to weigh out for Solvent," he goes on. "I came here because I wanted to ride. I've a hunch he's going to do the trick."

'"Do the trick," says I, feeling as if someone had kicked me in the belly. "I should think 'e is!"

'"I'm sorry, Studd," he says to Hawkey. "Sorry to take you off. Of course you'll get your fee, and your present, too, if he wins."

'Hawkey looks at me, and I looks at Hawkey. "Major, you can't hardly do that," says I.

'"Of coure I can. Can't I?" says he, turning to the clerk of the scales.

'"It's quite in order as long as you weigh out now, major," comes the reply. "I'll send out a man to alter the board."

'You see, Cap, it was before the days of starting declarations.

'Well, before we could think of anything to say, he's on the scales and has passed, and 'e's off to saddle the old horse. I left Hawkey standing by the scales with his mouth wide open as if he'd seen a ghost.

'I followed the major with his saddle, and I'm thinking of a million things at once. I knew it was hopeless suggesting to him that he shouldn't have a go on the old horse. I'd tried it once before and he'd been that wild I thought he was going to knock me down. Then I thinks, I know what I can do. I'll slip enough leads out of his cloth so that even if he does win he can't draw the weight. That cheered me up a bit. We're not goosed after all, I thinks.

'So when we got to the box I says: "I'll fix him up, major. You go and borrow a pair of spurs. It might make all the difference."

'"Right," says he, and off he goes.

'And then I looks at his gear, and he's got one of those damned heavy saddles and no weight cloth at all. There was nothing I could pinch which he wouldn't notice.

'When we got into the paddock I daren't look off the ground; I'm so afraid of what Bert Scoop will be looking like – and all the others too. I tries to spin the yarn to the major that the 'oss has been off his feed and perhaps it would be better if he didn't give him too hard a race, but while I'm saying it, the old devil gives out a squeal and three kicks to show what a liar I am. Then I suggests that he should lie well back in the race, which was no way to ride the horse at all.

'The major gives me a funny look and says that he knows how to ride the horse better than anyone else, which is quite true. I couldn't think of anything else, and a minute later the bell rang and he was up in the saddle and off. I didn't know which way to turn. I couldn't think of anything but 500 quid each way, seven of which was mine, all up the spout because of a major of Marines what wouldn't see reason. Such folks never ought to be allowed on a course, Cap.

'As soon as the race started it was quite obvious which runner was the job. It was a little horse called Scollops, belonging to Percy Edward who trained down in Sussex.

'He nicked off in front straight away. Another thing was pretty plain too. I hadn't been the only one doing some thinking since the major's name was put in the frame in place of Hawkey's. The other jocks was round the major like bees round a hive, and Whip Wilson gives 'im a proper duffy-up at the second fence, in spite of the fact that it was right in front of the stands.

'At the third fence Billy Twist has a go at him. Cuts right across him, trying to put him over the wing. But the major slips him, and Billy goes over the wing instead.

'At the fourth two more have a go, but old Solvent is so clever he props and twists and gets himself out of trouble, although he damn near lost the major. Both his stirrups were gone, but the luggage was still on board. After that the major nicks off after Scollops and gets clear, but the other jocks is after him like hounds running to view.

'Cap, you never see such a race. A three-mile 'chase and they hadn't yet gone a mile. . . . Jack Trudge on Scollops going a hell of a gallop in front, then the major, and hard on his heels the rest of them, half of them with their whips out. It was so funny there were times when I forgot all the money at stake.

'Well, passing the stands the second time the order was the same. Scollops in front, the major two lengths behind, and the rest hunting the major. Going over the water they began to close up on him, and as they went out of sight down the hill by the gorse bushes I thought, this is where they'll get him.

'Poor old major, I thought. You'll get what's comin' to you now. I couldn't help but feel sorry for him, Cap.

'Well, when they come into view out of the gorse bushes there's only two in it. There's Scollops still in the lead and – well, I hadn't to use me glasses. It could only be one person. The major! He'd slipped 'em somehow.

'Three fences from home Trudge looks over his shoulder, and what he sees he doesn't like, for he draws his bat. Scollops meets the next all wrong and is down as near as a toucher. The major lands level with him.

'Then it was plain to see that Scollops was beat and that Solvent was going strong. A little fellow with a squeaky voice on the top of the stand shouts out: "Scollops wins nothing. Fifty to one bar Solvent!"

'He wasn't far wrong.

'Now when Scollops had made that blunder he had let Solvent up on his inside, and that was how they were running as they came to the last. Trudge is riding for his life, but he glances over his left shoulder to see where the major is. Then, in the last two strides he smacks his horse straight into the left wing, right across the major. The major sees what he's after, but sets his teeth and won't pull out. They hit in mid-air with a smack you could hear right down the course.

'I can see those two chestnut horses now, and in my dreams I can hear the smack. It was the worst bump I've ever seen.

'Well, there was only one thing that could happen; they both come head over heels. It was the most horrible fall you ever did see.

'There's the crowd roaring 'emselves silly and two chestnut horses sitting up on their hunkers wondering where they was, and two jocks on their knees with their heads in their hands.

'Jack Trudge gives a kick or two, stumbles to his feet, and then falls flat on his face and stays there. The major gets up slowly, staggers about for a second, then, seeing no one coming, grabs the reins. A copper standing there gives him a leg up, and he trots down the straight to win the race. Lord, Cap, you should have heard the people cheer! I never heard anything like it, not even on Derby Day.

'Well, I runs down to meet him, and for the moment I've forgotten all about the starting price job. But as I'm leading him in I remember. And then I sees Bert Scoop, the tears running down his face and laughing fit to die.

'"What the hell is there to laugh about?" I said to him.

'"Your governor," he said, "'e got on the wrong 'oss."

'And then I looked. And Cap, if I die today, it's the truth. The 'oss I was leading in was Scollops. The major had won on him!'

WHAT'S
IT GET YOU?

J. P. Marquand

THE day had been a hard one at the Seven Oaks track. Following a custom which was invariable with him when he possessed the capital, Jack White had been betting on a series of long shots. He had not been betting blindly; instead, he had drawn upon his encyclopaedic knowledge of past performances, and of sires and dams through the equine generations. For Jack White lived from an accurate digest of facts and from the reservoir of his own personal experience derived from thirty years at the track. In speaking of the financial difficulties besetting the nation, Jack White often said that if the bankers and the brokers had known as much about their securities as he did about four-legged-prospects, there would have been no need for a New Deal.

'Furthermore,' he said, 'they don't take distress like gentlemen, and distress is good for the soul. That's why I've got a beautiful nature, and I have got a beautiful, even, tolerant, forgiving disposition, haven't I boys? All because I know distress.'

He was right, in a way. He was a magnificent object of fortitude in his bedroom in the Hotel Dixie that evening, tilted back in his chair, his shoes off, his vest unbuttoned. He had played five of his selections to win that afternoon and had watched them good-naturedly through his nickel-rimmed spectacles as they had faded; and now he seemed oblivious of nervous strain, only gently, hospitably weary.

'It was a nice day, boys,' he said; 'it always is, with sun and seven good honest races. Set down on the bed, boys, and help yourselves to cigars and whisky; it's all on me.' His partner, Henry Bledsoe, stirred a spoonful of bicarbonate of soda into a glass of water. It was evident that Mr Bledsoe did not agree with Mr White.

'Honest hell!' he said. 'This track is packed with operators who ought to be in stripes. The stewards and the paddock judges are blind, and what's more' – Mr Bledsoe groaned – 'the sport is gone,' he said; 'there ain't no gentlemen anymore.'

Jack White looked at him in mild rebuke. 'Henry,' he said, 'don't get passionate. Henry, you've been saying the same thing for thirty years.'

Mr Bledsoe's lean jaws clamped together and he slapped a bony hand on his knee. 'Well, it's true,' he said. 'Ain't it?'

Jack White answered with another question: 'You and I've been honest, haven't we? And yet we've made a living.'

'Well, it ain't your fault we have,' snapped Henry.

Jack White blew a cloud of cigar smoke before him. 'No, not anybody's fault,' he answered. 'I may be romantic, but I do like to have ideals. I like to think that the average race is straight, and I believe it is. Maybe a race is straight because a horse is straight if he has a proper family tree. He's there to run because his kind have run. He's there to run because he's honest. If he has the heart to go, he goes; and no ninety-pound boy on him is going to stop him much and no electric shocks and dope will make him go much faster. If he has the heart, he goes; if he hasn't, he fades out. No, sir, it's the horse who wins the race.'

'Gentlemen,' said Henry Bledsoe, 'ain't it amazing that he never learns a thing?'

Jack White stared into another cloud of smoke without giving any signs of having heard. His mind was clearly back at the track again, moving pleasantly through a gallery of memories. 'Henry,' he said, 'Honeyboy in the fifth race, did he remind you of anything? He did me, Henry.'

Mr Bledsoe scratched his chin, and the room was silent, as he thought, respectfully silent.

At any moment, in such company, a piece of information might be dropped that was as sound as a Coolidge dollar. Henry Bledsoe's slightly haggard face had brightened with understanding.

'You can't fool me on horses, Jack,' he said. 'I seen it in the paddock. He was like Mr Cavanaugh's Fighting Bob, but I could tell the difference in the dark.' Mr Bledsoe glanced around the room and smiled bitterly. 'And what's more, gentlemen,' he said, 'I can tell you just what's coming. My dear old friend, Mr White, who would lose his shirt each meeting if it weren't for me, is going to tell you a story to back up his own convictions. He's going to tell you about Daisy Cavanaugh, who handled horses down in the state of Maryland last year; and he's going to tell you about Mr Cavanaugh's Fighting Bob, an unlikely three-year-old, if there ever was one, in order to prove that there are still gentlemen on the track; and when he's finished, it won't mean a damn thing, that's all . . . Jack, do I have to listen? If I do, I want more soda.'

Jack White blew another cloud of smoke. 'Give him more soda, boys,' he said. 'But there's one thing, Henry: the old man was a gentleman.'

Henry Bledsoe seemed refreshed by his second spoonful of bicarbonate. 'Yes,' he said, 'old Mr Cavanaugh, he certainly was a gentleman, and what did it get him, White?'

Gentlemen [said Jack White], I don't need to tell you about the track at Langleyville, that Mecca where sportsmen have gathered each spring and autumn to follow the vicissitudes of the running horse for over a generation. Losing or winning, I can be happy at Langleyville. The officials, right down to the gate keepers, are capital fellows, and the restaurant proprietor is very apt to trust you, if you look him in the eye. I love to look across that fine oval of green out to the rolling country beyond it. It all speaks to me of horse-flesh. Yes, and educated money, and best of all I like the air, the spring air of the Chesapeake that is half rich land and half salt water. . . . All right, Henry, I won't go on, but I love artistic places.

That is why I always stop at Mrs Griscom's boarding house when I am down at Langleyville. The exterior of that boarding house, two miles out of town, may not be superficially attractive, but, believe me, it has ever been a sanctuary of the harassed racing men. Mrs Griscom, you may recall, is the widow of Sam Griscom, one of the most passionate plungers in the history of the track, who shot himself at New Orleans the day when Lightning Joe ran fourth in the Creole Handicap. Though I do not approve personally of such heights of feeling, that accident of Sam's, who was essentially a capital fellow, did much for Mrs Griscom's charity. Yes, gentlemen, you can take it from me, go to Mrs Griscom when you are in distress. Her features may be stern, but in her heart she knows the accidents of chance.

Accurately speaking, Henry and I were not in great throes of distress when a kindly motorist set us down at Langleyville one early April morning three days before the meet opened. Personally, I should have preferred taking the train, but Henry was holding the toll, and Henry is kind of mean with money. Henry's got a Yankee streak that way. It was a beautiful, early April morning, and the sun was shining on the dewy streets of Langleyville. As we stood on the sidewalk with our suitcases, near the courthouse, it was like coming home. We hadn't been in front of the courthouse half a minute before a party I had seen near the paddock in Miami came up to us.

'Hey, Mr White,' he said, 'hey, Mr Bledsoe, will you join me at breakfast at the Langley House?'

I did not like his looks. He was the kind who wouldn't do something for nothing; he was youngish – which wasn't against him – and well dressed – and that wasn't against him, either. It was his face a pinky face with sandy eyebrows and a round button of a nose and rosebud lips. I did not like his face.

'That's kind of you, mister,' I began.

'Greenway,' he said – 'Joe Greenway, to you, Mr White. You're here early, aren't you? So am I.'

Then Henry spoke up. 'Thank you, Mr Greenway,' he said. 'Mr White and I have had a very hearty breakfast. We're waiting for a bus. Good morning, Mr Greenway.'

I don't know what it is about Henry, but he has no sentiment and gentle manners. 'Henry,' I said, 'I was hungry and you took away my breakfast.'

Henry only snapped his jaws together. 'I'd rather go hungry,' he said, 'and keep my reputation. Won't you never learn to be careful who you're seen with? That boy is one of the Maxey crowd.'

Now, everybody at the track has heard of Maxey. Personally, I have found him a capital fellow within limits, but everybody didn't. Jake Maxey had got into trouble at Miami, and there was a little shooting trouble in Hamilton last summer where his name was mentioned. I could see Henry's point in not wanting to be seen with one of Maxey's boys.

'What's he doing here?' I asked.

Henry clicked his teeth again. 'We'll find out soon enough,' he said. 'You keep away from Maxey, White. Thank God I've got the roll.'

'If you won't eat with Maxey's boy,' I said, 'let's you and me go to the hotel ourselves.'

'I said,' said Henry, 'thank God I've got the roll. You and me are conserving capital, White, and we'll keep on conserving until we find an investment. We'll get breakfast at Mrs Griscom's.'

'Then let's hire a cab. I'm getting faint,' I said.

'Hire a cab, nothing,' said Henry. 'We'll wait here till we get a free ride. We've only got three hundred dollars, and we don't break in until we get an investment.'

It took us two hours to get to Mrs Griscom's, but Henry was right, for we finally got set down there in front of her place for nothing. It was like being at home, once we got to Mrs Griscom's. She took us into the parlour right away.

'You're early, boys,' she said. 'You wouldn't be here early, if you wasn't in distress. Well, all the rooms are taken.'

'Mrs Griscom,' I said, 'you come out on the front porch with me. . . . Henry, you stay here.' I knew that Mrs Griscom would be all right when we were alone. 'Did you take a good look at Henry?' I asked her. 'He looks just the way Sam did at New Orleans, Mrs Griscom. You don't want Henry on your conscience, do you?'

'He's got money, and he's holding out,' she said. 'I know Henry.'

'Yes, Mrs Griscom, you're right,' I told her. 'But you know how Henry is when he gets moods. Just now he wants to feel he's getting something for nothing. When he gets it, Henry will pay for it all right.'

'All right,' said Mrs Griscom, 'you can have the two back rooms, and you better go into the dining room. They're having a late breakfast.'

'Who?' I asked.

'The Cavanaughs,' she told me. 'Old Mr Cavanaugh and his daughter Daisy.'

'Not old Hendrick Cavanaugh, the owner?' I asked her. 'I thought old Cavanaugh was through.'

'Well, he's here,' she said. 'They've brought down six horses they've been boarding at Oak Hill, and the girl, she's conditioning them. She's a dear, sweet girl, too, even if she dresses like a jockey. She's going to turn the horses over to Shiny Denny.'

The name made me remember Mr Greenway by the courthouse. You have to be quick in my business in putting facts together. 'I want to know,' I said. 'Shiny Denny was Maxey's trainer, wasn't he, back in '32?'

Mrs Griscom understood me, and we exchanged a meaning glance. Life on the track moves as fast as the horses. I could recall the time just as well as she could when the Cavanaugh stables were known up and down the coast and when you could see the Cavanaugh colours – maroon and white and yellow – on almost any track.

'Mr Cavanaugh needs money,' she said.

'Does he own anything?' I asked.

And Mrs Griscom sighed. 'One three-year-old,' she said, 'that Fighting Bob. Out of his old Daisy Dimple by Bob Bender. Maxey's trainer will saddle him in part payment for conditioning his string.'

Names, as everyone must know, have a way of bobbing up and down. Horse breeding and horse sense don't often go hand in hand. In the minute, as I stood on the front porch, I was fitting together in my mind everything I had heard about old man Cavanaugh. The word was that the depression had cleaned him out. His place, Oak Hill, with its five hundred acres, its thirty-room house, its stables and its private track, had been on sale for the past five years, while the paint was peeling off it and the roofs were beginning to leak. His racing string had been sold off five years back, with the exception of two colts and his old mare, Daisy Dimple. Then he had gone in for boarding for friends and others. It was none of my business, but just the same it hurt me to think of an operator like Maxey, whose money was made from half a dozen rackets, boarding horses at Oak Hill. As I say, I was piecing the facts together, even down to this three-year-old, Fighting Bob, that was Cavanaugh's own property. Fighting Bob had performed once the previous year on the track in one of the maiden races. He had been so wild then that they couldn't get him in the starting stall. The Daisy Dimple colts were either brilliant or very wild. I looked at Mrs Griscom and asked her a single question, purely out of curiosity:

'How does it happen Cavanaugh's staying with you?'

'Same reason as you,' she said. 'He was a friend of my husband's. He was awful kind to Sam.' Then she looked me up and down and made a remark which I do not care to interpret:

'Mr Cavanaugh's a real gentleman.'

I sighed. 'I don't like it,' I said; 'it don't fit right.'

'What don't fit right?' she asked.

'Maxey's trainer boarding horses with a gentleman!'

I had never met Mr Cavanaugh socially until that morning in Mrs Griscom's dining room. He was the kind who had the same manners for everyone – elegant, fine manners. He stood up when Mrs Griscom introduced us, a thin old man, slightly sprung in the knees. He wore a suit with small black-and-white checks that might have been smart fifteen years ago, and a pearl-grey Ascot tie. His face was lean and clean-bred like his hands. He had a snow-white moustache, waxed at the ends, and white curly hair.

'Gentlemen,' he said, 'I'm very greatly honoured. Though our paths have, unfortunately, never met, reputation travels far. Everyone who knows the sport of kings has seen Mr Bledsoe at the track in the mists of early morning, and, Mr White, I have heard you highly spoken of in many, many places. It is an honour to have you both complete our company. I look forward to happy evenings during the meeting, gentlemen. . . . Daisy, my dear, may I present Mr Bledsoe and Mr White?'

At first I thought it was all make-believe, but it wasn't. It was only the way he talked. His eyes were kind and steady, like his voice. He was bowing to a girl in boots and breeches standing beside him, his daughter, Daisy. Ready to ride, she would not have tipped the scales at ninety pounds. She had a figure like a boy's in the paddock; she even had that jockey slouch. She had short yellow, curly hair and her face was as pretty as a movie queen's. Her eyes were steady like the old man's and she had a rider's mouth, firm, but not hard enough to be cruel. Daisy Cavanaugh was a lady, pants and boots and all.

'You've got nice hands, miss,' I said. 'I can always tell a rider as soon as I shake hands.'

'Thank you,' she said, 'I have to have them. We've brought down Mr Denny's horses from the farm, six of them – they're quite a handful – and one of our own, Fighting Bob.'

Henry didn't say anything. Henry is never much at talking.

'Perhaps Mr Bledsoe is surprised,' Daisy Cavanaugh said. 'I suppose I'm about the only girl in this business.'

'Daisy,' said Mr Cavanaugh, 'now, Daisy!'

'I'm sure that Shiny Denny will be very pleased when he gets here,' I said. 'May I ask when he arrives?'

'Sometime tomorrow morning,' she told me. 'He has Stable No. 2. He's trucking down Mr Maxey's Lighthouse. Lighthouse is entered in the South Cove Handicap next week.'

'Yes,' I said. 'And he will be the favourite. It's kind of hard on Mr Maxey to run a favourite, even for a big purse.' She looked at me for a second before she answered, and I looked back.

'Well,' she said, 'what of it?'

'Nothing of it,' I said, 'nothing, miss. I'm acquainted with Mr Maxey. Lighthouse is very fast.'

'And may I venture to add,' Mr Cavanaugh broke in, 'that I, for one, have found Mr Maxey strictly honourable in all his dealings.'

'I'm glad, sir,' I said.

Daisy was still looking at me. 'You know a great deal, don't you, Mr White?' she remarked. 'You follow the races, don't you?'

'Daisy,' said Mr Cavanaugh, 'Daisy.'

'Yes, miss,' I told her. 'Racing is all I know. I'm just an ordinary gambler, miss.'

The hard look left her eyes. 'Call me "Daisy"; don't call me "miss". I'm just a common horse conditioner myself.'

'Call me "Jack",' I said. 'Every morning I'm at the track to see the exercising, I'll look forward to seeing you.'

'Thanks, Jack,' she said. 'I'm going to breeze Fighting Bob tomorrow. We're entering him in the third race, Monday – an allowance race for three-year-olds. Will you clock him for me? I think he's ready.'

'And believe me, sir,' said Mr Cavanaugh, 'I should be delighted to receive your opinion as a friend and an expert.'

Then Henry Bledsoe spoke up. 'Mrs Griscom,' he called, 'I'll trouble you for a glass of water and a spoon. I'm taking my bicarbonate now.'

I liked Daisy and Mr Cavanaugh. We had a capital time all day. We spent a long while together, running over old races and talking of this and that, and to hear him was like the fresh air from the bay. There was no hard words from Mr Cavanaugh about anything or anybody.

'If I wager on an animal of mine, sir,' he said, 'I wager on him to win, and so I will do with Fighting Bob. He has the makings of a great horse, sir, and his dam's courage to run a fine race. I hope you'll agree with me, sir, when we work him out tomorrow.'

Toward evening, after supper, Henry and I walked down the road a piece alone. 'Old fool,' Henry kept saying beneath his breath, 'old fool and a tenth-rate horse.'

'But, Henry,' I told him, 'Mr Cavanaugh's a gentleman.'

'Yes,' said Henry, 'and that's why he's a fool, ain't it? There's something isn't right, White; there's something isn't right.'

It disturbed me to hear Henry say it, because Henry is quick that way. I knew myself that something wasn't right, but I would have bet my bottom dollar that neither Mr Cavanaugh nor Daisy was in it.

It has been my custom for many years to rise at dawn and to proceed to the track to see the horses train. At such times, Henry would hold the watch, while I would simply sit and look and maybe walk around the stables and talk to friends. That is the time, in those early sessions, when one can learn all sorts of useful things, if one has ears and eyes. It is always a beautiful sight to me to see the horses jogging around the track, past the deserted grandstand, more beautiful than any picture.

'Believe me, sir,' said Mr Cavanaugh, 'there is no Turner in the National Gallery to equal it. May I tempt you with a touch of my flask, sir? The world may change, but good horse-flesh is the same, thank God.'

He said it as we stood leaning on the rail of the deserted judges' stand at the Langleyville track that next morning. Mr Cavanaugh was wrapped in an old coaching coat that made him look like a faded sporting print on some tack-room wall. He was peering through an antiquated pair of field glasses. The sun was coming up, driving away the mist.

'Ah!' he said. 'Daisy is bringing out Fighting Bob!'

Now, what I'm trying to tell you is right dramatic in its way. Take people alone, and they may have no interest, but take them in their relations to others and you can have anything from tragedy to comedy. Down by the stable then, I saw Daisy, with the sun streaking that gold hair of hers, riding a rangy bay out to the track. He was stepping soft, as though he had eggs under him.

'You like him, sir?' asked Cavanaugh, and he twisted the corner of his moustache. He was pleased to see his own horse on the track. Before I had time to think of a truthful answer – the horse's looks were good enough, but I didn't like his action – a young fellow in a leather windbreak jacket came bounding up the steps.

'Good morning, Mr Cavanaugh,' he said. 'I'm glad to see you here.' Mr Cavanaugh twisted the end of his moustache again. I had known the boy since he was a kid exercising for the Whitlers. His name was Tommy Cole. As long as I had known him, he had been sober and well-behaved, and now he was training for the Huntley stables and worth all the money that they paid him.

'Morning, Mr Bledsoe,' Tom Cole said. 'Miss Cavanaugh asked will you please clock Fighting Bob? She's going to turn him loose out of the six-furlong chute.'

I was pleased to see that Fighting Bob had improved. He went into the stall like he was used to it, and then he came out a-roaring to a clean, fast start. Daisy Cavanaugh was riding him like a man. She was saving him till she got around the turn, and then I saw her hands move, and Fighting Bob moved with them, and then I forgot about Daisy's riding.

Tom Cole nudged me with his elbow. 'Did you ever see anything so beautiful?' he asked. He was thinking of Daisy, but I was thinking of the horse. There was something in Fighting Bob's conformation that reminded me of an animal that had paid me money once. Daisy gave him his head, and he went across the line in style. Daisy eased him up and came walking back, rubbing her eyes on her sleeve, but I hardly looked at her, I was looking at the horse.

'What's the time?' she called, and Henry Bledsoe called it back.

'Mr White, sir,' said Mr Cavanaugh, 'I trust you agree with me that Fighting Bob's is a credit to the Oak Hill stock.'

'He'll have mighty fine odds Monday, sir,' I said. I might have added, it is one thing for a horse running by himself and another as to how he behaves in a crowd.

'Pa,' called Daisy, 'come on down to the stables! Shiny Denny's here. . . . And won't you gentlemen come too?'

We walked behind them slowly toward Stable No. 2, and Henry and I exchanged a glance. Henry and I may be different in some ways, but we understand each other.

'Henry,' I said, 'I'd kind of like to get up close to Fighting Bob. Does he remind you of anything?' There isn't much that Henry doesn't remember. He has the clocker's gift for spotting a horse in the twilight under wraps, if he has seen him as much as once.

'White,' he said in my ear, 'you're a born fool with money, but you're not a fool about everything. As far as my facts go, Fighting Bob might as well be Maxey's Lighthouse. Comical, ain't it, that Fighting Bob and Maxey's Lighthouse should be in the same stable?

White stocking on the near foreleg, star the size of a half dollar on the forehead.'

'That's the difference,' I said; 'Fighting Bob's forehead is plain.'

'Yes,' said Henry Bledsoe softly, 'the difference of a white half dollar.'

Then I mentioned another thought to Henry which was running in my mind: 'The odds are going to be almighty heavy on Fighting Bob, third race, Monday, Henry. If ever there was a rank outsider who might start at 60 to 1, it's Fighting Bob.' Henry coughed behind his hand.

'White,' he asked me, 'do you reckon Maxey's thought of that?'

The door to Stable No. 2 was closed. Mr Cavanaugh and Daisy and Tom Cole were out in front of it and with them was that button-nosed Greenway and Shiny Denny. Shiny Denny was in his store clothes, polishing his nails. He was a little, leather-faced, black-eyed man, who had been a jockey when I had known him first.

'How's Lighthouse, Shiny?' I asked him. 'Did he van down nice?' Shiny laughed, showing a set of yellow teeth, and jerked his thumb toward the closed door.

'Lighthouse is resting comfortably inside,' he said. 'Honest, boys, I wish I could take you in to see him, but now that Miss Cavanaugh's turned over to me, the stable is closed. No offence intended. Mr Maxey's orders.'

'Why, Shiny,' I told him, 'I always believed in quiet stables. How is Maxey? When's he coming down?'

'Mr Maxey's coming down on Monday,' Shiny said; 'not that he's got anything running, you understand.' Then he polished his nails again and turned to Daisy Cavanaugh. 'You done a swell job on those horses, Miss,' he added, 'and I've got a piece of news for you that makes me kind of sick. I've got to leave for New York tonight. My old mother's dying up in the Bronx. It hurts me, because I know you're counting on me for Monday. I can't be here, I simply can't, to saddle Fighting Bob.'

I saw Mr Cavanaugh twitch his moustache and I saw Daisy's lips come tight together, and I knew the only thing they cared about was seeing Fighting Bob in that Monday's race. Furthermore in all the years I'd known him, I'd never heard Shiny speak of his mother in Bronx. I knew one thing just as sure as shooting. There was something going to happen that Monday, and Maxey was getting out from under.

'I'm very sorry, sir,' I heard Mr Cavanaugh saying. 'This is a bitter blow to me, but we'll forget it. Fighting Bob can't start without a trainer.'

Then I saw Daisy and young Tom Cole looking at each other, and then Tom Cole cleared his throat. 'If you'll let me, Mr Cavanaugh,' he said, 'I'll be proud to saddle Fighting Bob the third race Monday, and Mr Huntley will be proud to have me. None of our own are entered. You know and I know that no horse can enter a race unless a licensed trainer saddles him.'

'Why,' Mr Cavanaugh began, 'that's a great kindness, Mr Cole.' And they looked at each other for a second or two, and then Tom Cole said: 'I'd do a sight more than that, you know.'

Then I looked at Denny, because he interested me more than anybody else just then. It seemed to me that he was pleased – too pleased.

'That's fine,' he said; 'then everything's all right. You've got a great horse, Mr Cavanaugh.'

Henry Bledsoe did not have much to say that day. There wasn't much need to talk, because Henry and I understood each other. About an hour before supper, he spoke to Mrs Griscom.

'Jack and I won't be in to supper,' he said; 'we're walking up to town.'

It was the first I had heard that we were going into town, but I understood what Henry meant. Henry was thinking of the roll. Henry was on to something, and I knew what.

There is only one drugstore in Langleyville, and Henry and I walked in. First Henry bought a packet of cigarettes and some matches. This surprised me, because Henry thinks cigarette smoking is a sin, and he doesn't spend money without reason. Then Henry began to talk to the clerk, and talking is not in Henry's line. On the back counter of the store was a row of patent medicines, sarsaparilla, and Indian remedies. Henry is good on patent medicines, since he's tried them all, and right away the clerk knew he was talking to a master.

'Are you a salesman, mister?' the clerk said.

'No,' said Henry. 'Bless you, no, I've never sold the stuff. It's only I'm interested in my own insides. How's your line of hair dye?' said Henry. 'Do you move much hair dye, friend?'

'Well, no, sir,' the clerk said; 'hair dye goes mighty slow hereabouts.'

'I want to know,' Henry said. 'You'd think somebody would buy it.'

'Well,' the clerk said, 'now you speak of it, I did sell a bottle this afternoon.'

'I want to know,' said Henry. 'Who bought it? An oldish man?'

The boy in the white coat grinned. 'Why, no,' he said. 'That's why I remember it. The party didn't look as though he needed hair dye for himself. He was a youngish fellow with a round button nose and a kind of rosebud mouth. One of the racing crowd, a stranger here like you, sir.'

'Well,' said Henry, 'would you give me a glass of water and a spoonful of bicarbonate? They tell me soda puts colour in the hair.'

Once we were outside the store, Henry tapped my arm. He did not need to comment on what we had heard, because I had ears. Greenway had bought a bottle of brown hair dye, and Maxey's horse named Lighthouse had a white star on his forehead.

'Come on,' said Henry; 'we're going to the track.'

It was pitch dark at the track by then. A light wind was blowing, sighing through the emptiness of the grandstand, and you could swear that horses' ghosts were running on the wind. There were lights in the superintendent's house; and lights in the stable tack rooms were just small dots of light in a bare black carpet. Henry tapped my arm again.

'White,' he whispered, 'I'm going into Stable 2. I want to look at them two horses close. Take these cigarettes. There's a pile of straw outside of Stable 3. You walk by it, light a cigarette and drop a match in the straw. And when it takes, you holler "Fire!" That'll fetch 'em out, and all I want is half a minute.'

Now, everybody knows there's nothing more serious around a track than fire. I wanted to argue with Henry, but he is hard to argue with, and I did exactly what he said. I walked over to the rubbish pie and dropped three matches in it. The straw took fire like tinder, and then I started running, shouting:

'Fire in Stable No. 3!'

The sight of the blaze brought the boys out of the stables like bees out of hives. Even when it was out, a crowd still stood around the straw pile, talking, and then Henry was back, tapping on my arm.

'All right, let's blow,' he said. 'Them two are alike as two peas. You go back to Griscom's, White. I want to watch that Greenway party. He'll be calling in the bank tomorrow morning or else I miss my bet.'

I was tired when I got back to Griscom's, but somehow I couldn't sleep, and maybe you can't blame me, now that you see the picture as I saw it. In a sense, we were on to something good, but I was troubled by conscience just the same. The trouble was that Mr Cavanaugh was a gentleman.

Next morning was Saturday, a bright clear day. Around noon Henry came back and we walked down the road a piece. Henry was looking pretty pleased.

'Greenway cashed a telegraph order for seventy-five hundred dollars,' he said. 'I guess we know where it's going, White – on Fighting Bob, third race, Monday afternoon – and our roll is going with it.'

But somehow I couldn't do it quite like that.

'No, Henry,' I said, 'no, we don't. I'm going to tell Mr Cavanaugh about this, Henry.'

Henry's mouth fell open. Sometimes Henry is mighty ugly when he is mad. 'You mind your own business,' he snapped. 'What are these Cavanaughs and these crooks to you and me?' I could see his point; but still, I have a conscience.

'No,' I said, 'Mr Cavanaugh's a friend of mine. Mr Cavanaugh must decide for himself.' Then Henry began to swear. He turned the air sky-blue, but I knew that I was right.

'The trouble is, Henry,' I said, 'Mr Cavanaugh's a gentleman.'

'Well, we ain't, are we?' Henry shouted.

'No,' I said, 'but we've got instincts. No, Henry you leave this to me. We ought to tell Mr Cavanaugh on Monday. It's up to him, not us.'

Maybe I was a fool. I'm never wholly sure. It isn't easy, in my position, to see a sure thing tossed away, but when I think of the race track at Langleyville that Monday, maybe I was right.

We had a touch of bourbon whisky before we left for the track.

'I admire your abstemiousness, Mr White,' Mr Cavanaugh told me, 'and I honour it, but I must beg of you for once to break your invariable rule. It isn't often these days that a horse of mine is running. Maybe this will be the last time I see my colours on a track. I must beg of you, sir, to touch glasses with me. To my three-year-old, sir, Fighting Bob!'

'To Fighting Bob, sir,' I said.

'Daisy,' he said, 'fill up my flask in case these gentlemen or I should need encouragement. . . . And, gentlemen, we take our places in the clubhouse today. The admission is on me. . . . No, sir, I insist. You must gratify an old man's whim.'

Once he was inside the club, Mr Cavanaugh was bowing, smiling, taking. He knew everybody who was worth while there at the club. He went into one of the upper rooms and ordered a round of drinks, though I took lemonade.

'Yes, gentlemen,' he kept saying, 'keep your eyes on my Fighting Bob in the third race. His dam was Daisy Dimple – you remember Daisy Dimple, gentlemen.'

When the horses were going to the post for the first race, Henry and I got up. 'If you'll excuse us,' I said, 'we're going down to the stands.' And then I lowered my voice and added, 'Mr Cavanaugh, I admire you very greatly; that's why I have a request to make. There's a man I want you to see in private. Could you arrange to see us in this room, alone? I want to see him before the horses are led out to the paddock for the third.'

Mr Cavanaugh's head went back. 'This is most unusual,' he said. 'Are you insinuating that there is something wrong? If there is, I'll ask for you to kindly tell me now.'

'You'll know why when I get back,' I told him. 'I can only say right now, I think you'll thank me, sir.'

Money was going down on Fighting Bob – so much that he had dropped from 50 to 1 to 20 on the probable-odds board.

'Jack,' said Henry, 'there's still time. Will you be a born fool all your life?' I knew by the odds that Maxey had placed his money, and Henry knew it too.

'No,' I said, 'after Mr Cavanaugh's seen Maxey, maybe we'll bet then.'

When Maxey is at the track, he always stands between races at the hotdog stand near Entrance No. 6, in case anyone should want to see him. Maxey was standing there smoking a cigarette, a broad-shouldered little man with smooth black hair and a face the colour of unbaked clay. It was the sort of face that would not change at anything. When I came up, he turned a pair of eyes on me, icy cold.

'Howdy, Jack,' he said. 'What's on your mind?'

And I put my arm through his and whispered in his ear:

'Maxey, you and I are walking over to the clubhouse to see Mr Cavanaugh, unless you want for me to holler for the track detective.'

I felt Maxey's arm grow stiff.

'What's your game, pal?' he asked.

'It's not my game,' I said; 'it's yours. We're going up to the clubhouse to talk about Fighting Bob.' Maxey's eyelids fluttered, but that was the only sign he gave.

Daisy and Mr Cavanaugh were waiting for us in the room upstairs, alone, when Henry and Maxey and I came in. I closed the door and put my back against it.

'Mr Cavanaugh,' I said, 'there's something I think you ought to know. And what you do is your business, not mine. I'll never say a word, and Mr Maxey here will tell you whether I'm right or wrong. It's my opinion that Mr Maxey has been making use of you, Mr Cavanaugh. Right this minute Lighthouse is in Fighting Bob's stall, with the star on his forehead painted out. He's ready to run for Fighting Bob in the third race, and I thought you ought to know.'

Maxey smiled and lighted a cigarette.

'That's baloney,' he said.

I looked at Daisy and Mr Cavanaugh. Both their faces had grown white. Mr Cavanaugh started to speak, and stopped. 'Now wait, Mr Cavanaugh,' I went on. 'I'm not blaming this on you, and generally I don't go in for reform. Maxey is betting seventy-five hundred on Fighting Bob, because Lighthouse is ringing for him. If you want my opinion, Maxey has done a first-rate job. It's my honest belief that if Lighthouse runs, no one will know it. I believe that Lighthouse is a sure winner if he runs. Henry, here, is ready to go down and bet. I thought I ought to tell you first, that's all.'

'Hey,' said Maxey, and his voice was no longer cool,' 'if you know so damn much why didn't you play along and keep your mouth shut?'

'Because I've got a conscience, Maxey,' I told him. 'And Mr Cavanaugh's a gentleman. I suggest we walk down to the stable right now, quick, before they lead 'em out, and see if I'm right or wrong; or maybe, Maxey, you'd like me to call for the detective. You can take your choice.'

Mr Cavanaugh stood up very straight and spoke very slowly. There was no great change in his voice, but somehow his voice was terrible.

'We'll go to the stables,' he said.

Maxey licked his lips.

'Now wait a minute,' he said, 'wait a minute. Let's talk sense. We're all sensible here, ain't we? Sure, I had the thought two weeks ago. Lighthouse is a ringer for that dog, Fighting Bob. Listen, folks, I know when I'm licked, and now I got a business proposition. We all sit down and take it easy. We don't say a word until this race is over. I've got seventy-five hundred up on Bob and we ought to get 20 to 1. Now, come, you don't want to bust up a sure thing. Seventy-five hundred, and fifteen minutes from now it's a hundred and fifty grand.' Maxey licked his lips again. 'I'm being straight. I'm telling you clean truth, and here's my proposition, folks: a fifty-fifty cut, just as soon as we cash in. I'm no piker; I've never been a piker. Fifty grand for you and the little lady, Mr Cavanaugh, and twenty-five grand split between White and Bledsoe, and that's more money than any of you folks'll see again. What do you say? Let's sit down and be sociable.'

Maxey's voice stopped, and when it did you could hear the noise from the crowd outside, a restless sound like the ocean against the rocks. It was a good quarter of a minute before anyone said a word. Mr Cavanaugh took a cigar from his pocket, cut off the end and lighted it, but his fingers were trembling when he held the match.

'Mr White,' he said, 'this is very shocking, both to me and to my daughter. I hope sincerely you feel we are in no wise connected with this, and I am very deeply grateful to you, sir. Neither my daughter nor I would have permitted a friend of hers to saddle a horse which we did not own. As for me, I want you to know that I've always raced clean. My money's down on Fighting Bob and I owe it to the public to put him on the track.'

He bowed to me and turned toward Maxey. It was like a show to see it. 'And as for you, you rascal,' said the colonel, 'I could hand you to the law, but I'm going to be the law. We're going to the stables now and my eye will be on you, Mr Maxey. You've put your money on Fighting Bob, and if I were you, Mr Maxey, I'd yell for Fighting Bob to win. We'll start walking to the stables, now. Mr Maxey, you'll walk between Mr White and me, please.'

I was proud to be walking with Mr Cavanaugh. There are not so many things that I can be proud of, but I was proud of that. He walked to Stable No. 2 not too fast, and not too slow, just as the

horses were moving out from the paddock for the second race. Mr
Cavanaugh chatted to us just as though nothing were wrong. 'It's a
very fine day for racing, Mr White,' he said, 'and the crowd is in a
betting mood. Do you remember the old days at Saratoga? This is
like a Saratoga day.... Mr Maxey, tell your men to get outside; we
shall want the stable to ourselves.' We blinked, once the stable door
was closed behind us, and then we were used to the fainter light. A
horse was standing in the third stall on the right. His bridle was on
already. I could have sworn he was Fighting Bob. Mr Cavanaugh
stood in front of him.

'White,' he said, 'I declare, I think you're wrong.'

'Take the flask out of your pocket, Mr Cavanaugh,' I said; 'wash
his face for him. Whisky will take out the dye.'

Mr Cavanaugh's motions were deliberate. He drew out his flask
and sopped his handkerchief with the whisky.

'Steady, boy,' he said, and rubbed hard between the horse's eyes.
There was a small white star between the eyes when he took his
handkerchief away. Holding the handkerchief between his thumb
and forefinger, he offered it to Mr Maxey. 'Take it as a souvenir,' he
said, 'and I should keep it carefully if I were you. Where's Fighting
Bob?'

'There,' Daisy said, 'down there on the left.'

'Daisy,' said Mr Cavanaugh, 'lead him out.... Help me to shift
those horses, Maxey, if you don't want to go to prison. Then call a
boy to lead my entry to the paddock.'

Then, just as though nothing had happened, we walked back to
the clubhouse again and stood on the terrace waiting for the start.
'Yes,' said Mr Cavanaugh, 'it's a nice day for a race.' Maxey did not
say a word.

'If you'll excuse me,' said Henry, 'I think I'll place a bet.'

'By all means,' said Mr Cavanaugh, 'and if you'll take a tip from
me, I'd bet on Fighting Bob.'

Then a voice shouted from the loudspeakers like a voice of doom:
'The horses are now going to the post.'

Maxey cleared his throat. 'The betting windows are closed now,'
he said; 'if you'll excuse me, this company is too holy. I never seen
fifty grand tossed away like that. Maybe you're a gentleman, but
what's it get you, Cavanaugh?'

'My dear fellow,' said Mr Cavanaugh, 'it's never got me anything.

It's always been a minus quality. Must you be going really? Then don't come back again.' Maxey drew a deep breath that was almost like a sigh.

'Mister,' he said, 'you're damn well right, I won't.'

Then Daisy took my hand. 'Thank you,' she whispered, 'thank you, Mr White.'

Mr Cavanaugh was looking through his battered glasses. 'He's standing nicely, my dear,' he said; 'he'll start this time.' And then there was a sound like waves, that sound that will make me roll over when I'm dead, a soft sound, too hushed to be a shout, and our own voices joined in it as we said, 'They're off!'

Now, believe me, that first second when they're off is always just pure gold. The colour and the motion is like the sun through a stained-glass window, I sometimes think. It's a brave sight, a fine sight.

'Daisy,' said Mr Cavanaugh, 'we've got a good boy up. Take the glasses, my dear. He's fourth; he's on the rail.'

Then Daisy's voice was shaking. 'Yes,' she said, 'he's going well! He's coming up! He's coming up!' I did not like to be there to see it. The boy was Jerry Hoberg, a good rider. There was a black from the Nixon stables that I had always fancied; at the halfway mark this black came out of the bunch easily. At the last turn he took second place and then he moved out ahead. Mr Cavanaugh looked away from the track.

'A very pretty race. The Nixon black wins,' he said.

'Wait a minute,' I said to him – wait a minute. Bob is coming up.' The crowd saw it a second later. Fighting Bob was moving as though he were pushed upon a wave. He was in third, he was in second before the boy on the black horse looked behind him. Just for an instant I thought the rush might pull him through, but the boy in front looked soon enough. Down came his whip, and the black drew off. Fighting Bob was gaining, but not enough, not enough. Daisy was holding my hand, and I saw that she was crying, and then Mr Cavanaugh saw it too.

'Don't cry, my dear,' he said. 'That was a pretty challenge. He hasn't got his dam's courage, but how could we tell that?'

'Father,' Daisy was sobbing, 'it's my fault. I thought he was better. It was my fault to make you put up your bottom dollar.' Mr Cavanaugh patted her shoulder very gently. 'My dear,' he said, 'others have lost with us. After all, what's racing for? It was a very pretty race.'

'Yes, sir,' I said, and then I saw that Henry Bledsoe was back. Henry was beckoning to me. 'White,' he said, 'come over here. I don't want the old man to know.'

'Know what?' I asked him, and Henry looked embarrassed. 'White,' said Henry, 'he ain't our kind. We got to keep away from sports like him. I kind of got to liking him, White, down there in the stable, and you know what I found myself doing? I found myself putting our roll on Fighting Bob to win.'

I felt a little cold inside, but Henry and I have been broke before. 'We're in good company,' I said.

'No, we ain't,' said Henry, 'and that's why I'm ashamed. I been a piker, White. The last minute I put down on Fighting Bob to run second, and now he's paying 12 to 1, but don't tell the old man, will you, please? Just tell him we bet on Fighting Bob?'

HARMONY

William Fain

JOHN Stephens nodded while Auslander, the American, gave him instructions about how to ride the race. They were at St Cloud, walking to the paddock. Stephens wished Auslander would not put his arm around his shoulder. Why did people think that because a jockey was a small man it was all right to touch him all the time? He did not much like owners, anyway. It would be a grand sport without them, he thought, and smiled; he had no sense of humour, and for him this was a pretty fair joke. Stephens did not like riding instructions much, either. Did Auslander have any idea of all the things that could happen during a race? Still, he half listened, and nodded.

'I've never run him in the mud, but I don't think he'll mind it,' Auslander was saying.

When they got to the paddock, and to the horse Stephens was to ride, Auslander's trainer, Garnier, gave the jockey a leg up. Stephens didn't have much use for Garnier, but at least he offered no instructions.

The race was nothing special – a handicap at a mile and a quarter for four-year-olds and up. Stephens was on a seven-year-old bay called Pantagruel that was top weight although he had no chance of winning. He had won a couple of races the year before but would not do much that spring, even in cheap company; he was nearly burned out and had never had much heart anyway. Without thinking about it, Stephens knew what to do.

He got a good hold on Pantagruel as the tapes flew up, and took him to the rail. At the Fouilleuse, the horse had moved up on his own initiative to be about ten lengths off the leaders. Coming into the stretch, Stephens began to ride him. That is, he started scrubbing, moving with the horse, encouraging him with hands and heels but not whipping him. The horse responded pretty well; Stephens had been patient, and Pantagruel had a little run in him. He moved up to third, halfway down the stretch, and Stephens began to think the old horse might get there. He was gaining, but not fast; he could make only a little run. Then suddenly, the horse running second, an aged chestnut mare of Archer's, stopped, and Pantagruel passed her. Stephens saw it was no use whipping; the horse in front, which Dumesnil was riding, was making it all right and should win by a good four lengths. Stephens eased Pantagruel and held on to second by half a length. That was better than he had expected. Second money was seventy thousand francs; ten per cent of that was seven thousand.

Riding back to the scales, Stephens picked mud off his face. He was used to it. The waiting race was his speciality.

A man and a woman watched him ride back and talked about him; of course he didn't hear them.

'In his old age, Stephens is making combinations,' the man said angrily.

'He looks terrible,' the woman said. 'His face looks like death. It's almost black.'

'That's only mud, from being behind all the time,' the man said. 'The Englishman has just lost an unlosable race.'

'No, under the mud he looks awful. His face looks a hundred years old.'

'He must be almost fifty,' the man said. 'Perhaps he is senile. Really, his way of riding becomes ridiculous. He should retire. He has plenty of money. He never spends any.'

Stephens was not very tired. Every race is somewhat tiring, especially at the beginning of the season, but this one had been easy. Pantagruel was a steady old horse – no good, but easy to ride.

Stephens went to the jockeys' room. Pantagruel was his only mount of the day. He was bringing himself along slowly, as he had done every spring in recent years, riding only a horse or two a day and gradually bringing his weight down and getting into form. Besides, at forty-nine, and after being fired (everyone believed) by Perrault the fall before, he was not being offered many mounts.

He didn't speak to anyone in the jockeys' room. He rarely did. He washed and dressed carefully, cleaning the mud out from under his nails and combing his heavy black hair neatly, using plenty of brilliantine. He put on clean white riding breeches, a tweed sports jacket, and well-shined black boots. If the woman who had pitied him as he rode back with mud on his face had seen him walking out of the jockeys' room, she would have been surprised. Cleaned up and dressed in fresh clothes, his binocular case slung over his shoulder, stopping to take a cigarette from his case and light it with his gold lighter, furrowing his brow as he lit it, then drawing in a good lungful of smoke with enjoyment, then letting the smoke out as the wrinkles in his brow smoothed out, he looked only about thirty-five, and quite chipper. Though he had little interest in women, he liked to be neatly dressed. He got a haircut and a manicure once a week. He was careful about money, but he liked good things – well-cut breeches, boots that cost forty thousand francs a pair, a good wristwatch, a good cigarette-case, a good lighter, Charvet Eau de Cologne on his face after a shower. Having the best of things like that cost very little more in the long run, he reasoned. Cheap boots wore out quickly, for example.

Auslander came up as Stephens was lighting his cigarette. He was a fat man with grey hair. His face was flushed. 'Nice kid, very nice,' Auslander said. Stephens figured he had had a place bet. 'Next time we'll do better.'

'I expect that's the best he'll do,' Stephens said.

'He needed a race, that's all. Don't you think?'

'He runs good when he's fresh, Mr Auslander. That's about the best he'll do. He's getting to be an old horse.'

'I liked the way you rode him, Jack,' Auslander said. 'You didn't take too much out of him. He'll be all the better for it. We'll win a race with him, and I'm going to put you up again, too.'

Stephens looked at the tote board. Pantagruel had paid forty-three francs for a ten-franc place bet.

'Did you back him for the place, Mr Auslander?' he asked.

'Just five hundred each way, to encourage him,' Auslander said.

The stingy liar, Stephens thought. 'You were lucky,' he said.

'Jack, I'm going to give you a good many mounts this spring, and see how we do,' Auslander said.

'What do you want with me?' Stephens said. 'Garnier's got young Luzzi on contract.'

'Oh, there can't be any contract,' Auslander said quickly. 'I don't care about the Perrault business, but —'

'I don't want a contract just now,' Stephens said, just as quickly. 'I'm better off on my own.'

'Sure,' Auslander said. 'Well, I expect to use you often.'

'Much obliged,' Stephens said.

Stephens did not stay for the rest of the races. There was nothing of interest. As he left the racecourse, he stepped on a piece of chewing gum. Scraping the sticky pink stuff from his boot with his little gold penknife, he thought, automatically, Americans.

He went to the parking lot reserved for trainers and jockeys, unlocked his Renault *quatre-chevaux*, and drove home to Paris. He and his wife had an apartment near the Parc Monceau. During his dinner – a steak, salad without dressing, two hard, dry *biscottes* – his wife asked him, 'Did it go well today?'

'Not bad,' he said. 'We were second.'

Stephens' wife was a Frenchwoman not much younger than he, whom he had married right after he first came out from England. She took no interest in racing. She did not think much of it as an occupation for a man to be in, and she did not realize that her husband was quite a famous man in France. Although a good deal of money came into the house, she did not believe this would continue; she never had believed so. She saved money, and hoped (without ever saying anything about it) that eventually they would buy a shop – an *épicerie*, a *charcuterie*, or a bakery. There was nothing like food, she knew; no matter what happened, people ate. Her father had been a baker in Argenteuil. She considered it a little discreditable that her husband was English, and she never brought the matter up, to him or anyone else. They spoke French to each other, though Stephens had never learned the language thoroughly.

A little later, Stephens said, 'Auslander, the American, is going to give me some mounts. It was his horse I was second on today. I hear he's got a pretty fair three-year-old.'

'There will be a contract?'

'No.'

'Ah! Naturally! He is very glad, I'm sure, to make use of you without a contract. You should have insisted. Why do you permit this American to take advantage of you?'

'He already has a contract jockey,' Stephens said. 'His trainer has this young Italian, this Luzzi.'

'That is to say, the American uses you when he wishes, and then puts you to the door,' said his wife. 'I'm sure it's very interesting for him.'

Her voice was high-pitched and irascible, not because of real ill nature but because she had been brought up to believe that life was a struggle in which you must ever be on guard against being tricked. Stephens was used to her piercing voice, laden with suspicion, and it did not bother him. She was his wife, and he assumed that that was the way wives were. He and she got along well; as a matter of fact, he never thought much about whether they got along or not, though sometimes he wished he had someone to talk to about horses.

After dinner, Stephens went out to buy a *Sport Complet*. He sat in a café and read it for half an hour, with a quarter litre of vichy in front of him. The waiter knew him but acted as if he had never seen him before; he considered Stephens a cheapskate. Stephens believed that only fools gave large tips.

When he went home, his wife told him that Garnier had called from Chantilly. She said he wanted Stephens out there at seven the next morning for the workouts. 'If I were in your place, I shouldn't go,' she said. 'You are not under contract. He's taking advantage of you.'

Stephens didn't answer.

'Well, will you go?' she asked.

'I'll decide in the morning,' Stephens said.

Stephens did not go to Chantilly in the morning. He wanted to; he liked morning workouts almost more than anything else in racing. But a full-fledged jockey does not exercise horses except for the man who holds his contract, or in preparation for a classic race in which he is to ride. He could not go.

He saw Auslander at the races that afternoon, at Le Tremblay Auslander said he wanted to talk to him, and they walked through the gardens by the paddock, where flowers were planted all along the paths. Le Tremblay was so pretty that Stephens could hardly take it seriously as a racecourse.

'I was hoping you'd be out this morning,' Auslander said.

'I'm not available in the mornings, Mr Auslander,' Stephens said.

'We might work out a contract later.'

'I don't want a contract,' Stephens told him. 'How many horses have you? Ten? You don't need me.'

Auslander was a man who hated to lose at anything. 'I need your help, Jack,' he said. 'I need your advice. Why don't you come out and take a look tomorrow? I'd like your opinion on what I've got.'

'No harm in that, I suppose,' Stephens said.

'I've got to be getting along,' Auslander said. 'My sister-in-law is in the stands. You wouldn't have a winner, would you, Jack? I'd like to give her one. What do you like in the Prix Matchem? Domrémy should be able to take it, don't you think?'

'I've no idea at all, Mr Auslander,' Stephens said.

Auslander went back to the stands and told his sister-in-law Stephens had given him a strong tip on Domrémy. The horse finished third. 'Next time,' Auslander said.

Stephens rode only once that day, in the last race. It was a cheap handicap at a mile and three-quarters for three-year-olds. In England, they would have thought it a long way to send three-year-olds early in the year. But these were horses of no quality, anyway.

Stephens rode a Norseman colt belonging to Médlizélatis, the Greek. As usual, Stephens waited, going along in last place for a mile. Coming into the final turn, he was next to last, and he felt then that the colt was ready to move. He had no class but he could run all day. Stephens took the colt to the far outside to make his run, but the field of twenty horses swung very wide, and the colt was carried wider still, losing half a dozen lengths.

Seeing that he was beaten, Stephens did not persevere. He galloped past the winning post in seventh or eighth position, beaten a good ten lengths. The Greek's trainer, Barsant, stopped him as he went to dress.

'Why did you go to the outside?' he asked angrily. 'There was room for a regiment of cavalry on the rail.'

'Where were you watching from?' Stephens asked him.

'From the top of the stands,' Barsant said. 'There was a veritable *autostrade* on the rail for you. It appears you are too old to take chances now.'

'The race is over,' Stephens said. He walked away from Barsant and went to the dressing-room.

It was a little race of no importance, but it annoyed him that he had made a mistake. Every jockey makes mistakes, and they do not ordinarily upset him, and no one holds them against him as long as he gets his share of winners. An apprentice that everybody's talking about may make three in one day, but if he is getting good mounts and also rides a couple of winners that day, the mistakes are forgotten. When a jockey is going down, people remember his mistakes, and he remembers them; there are not enough good mounts to blot them out. Of course, Stephens didn't think he was going down, but things were not going well at the moment.

The worst of the race just over was that it reminded him of his last ride for Perrault. Octave Perrault, the automobile man, was the biggest owner in Europe. Stephens, his contract rider, had ridden Astolat, the best three-year-old in Europe, in all his races, Astolat was second in the Guineas (the mile was too short for him) and won the Jockey-Club and the Grand Prix de Paris. In the big fall race at a mile and a half, the Prix de l'Arc de Triomphe, Stephens waited and kept Astolat far back under a tight hold as they climbed the long green hill at Longchamp, and then began moving him up as they came down the hill and into the turn. He swung Astolat to the outside on the turn, the field drifted out, and Stephens had to take him wider and wider, losing ground all the time.

Astolat was a good colt, the best in the race, a long-striding colt with stamina, and he lost no momentum in making the turn − no rhythm of his stride − but he was too far back, and as he passed the winning post, he was second, beaten a neck. He passed the winner in the next few strides, and the crowd booed Stephens back to the scales.

Perrault had been in racing a long time, and yet he believed that if you have the best bloodstock, the best trainer, the best jockey, the best lads, the best stud farm with the best grass in Normandy, one of the best biologists in France as an adviser on breeding, and the best equipment, right down to the leather in the saddles, you should never lose a race. Perrault's secretary telephoned Stephens that night and told him to come to the great man's office. Stephens went. Perrault had a whole building in the Faubourg St Denis − a big modern thing, with lots of glass. The building was dark when Stephens arrived. A silent elevator operator took him up in a silent elevator, and he walked down the bare modern hall to Perrault's office. Perrault, a heavy, frowning man with black-rimmed glasses, sat behind his desk.

'Well, what happened, Stephens?' he asked.

On the way there, Stephens had thought he might tell Perrault that Astolat was a long-striding colt who liked to run by himself, away from other horses, and that he wouldn't have kept his stride if Stephens had squeezed him through on the rail. There was some truth in it; the horse did like to run along on the outside. Stephens liked riding the Perrault horses. He liked being first jockey for the greatest stable in Europe. Perrault had, over the past twenty years, developed a breed of horses of his own – long-striding horses that never tired, that were always going on at the end. They did not have a great deal of what the French call, in racehorses, *brio*, but they had an everlasting sturdiness and gameness. Stephens liked to ride them. He believed no one suited them as he did. He could tell Perrault none of this. 'I'm taking myself off all your horses, Mr Perrault,' he said.

Since then, things had gone badly. He had not had many good mounts, and he had lost some races that he might have won. The Auslander connection might help. He had had a little luck with Pantagruel. But Stephens had got the mount on Pantagruel only because Luzzi was riding another horse for Garnier. Stephens had no use for Luzzi, but the kid was riding well just now. He had had a lot of luck the past year.

At dinner, Stephens' wife said, 'It went well today?'

'No luck today,' Stephens said.

At six the next morning, Stephens got up and drove to Chantilly. There were no cars on the road. It had rained during the night, and everything was fresh and clean. It would be a fine day. The leaves were a little behind the leaves in Paris, but they were all coming out. He drove along slowly.

Garnier had a big place out at Chantilly, opposite the Piste de Lamorlaye, where he had Auslander's horses and those of four or five other owners. The stables were stone, forming a big square with green clipped lawn in the centre. Stephens parked his car and walked into the big courtyard. Auslander and Garnier were standing there on the grass with Jim Craye, Garnier's head lad. Stephens walked across the grass and shook hands with them.

'Mr Auslander wants me to put you on Tekel, the Admiral Drake colt,' Garnier said. 'We've got him eligible for everything at Longchamp, but I don't know if he'll do anything.'

Garnier spoke in English. Around a French stable, everybody can speak English; even the French grooms usually talk English to the horses. There is a theory that horses find English more soothing.

' 'E's a nice little 'orse,' Jim Craye said. He was a little Cockney with bright-blue eyes and a jutting chin and no teeth, who had come from England fifty years before. He was one of the handful of Englishmen left around the stables at Chantilly. Although they were all getting to be old men, they were in great demand. Even French trainers believe that an Englishman is better than anybody else with a horse. Jim had been a good jockey, years ago.

'I could've sold him last week for two million, and bought Dupré's colt,' Auslander said. 'Maybe I should've done it.'

'He didn't do anything last year, did he?' Stephens asked.

'I only ran him twice,' Garnier said. 'I didn't expect him to do anything. I'm against two-year-olds racing, on principle.'

Garnier was a short, stout, sallow man with a little black moustache. He had become a trainer because his father had been one. He never expected his horses to win; he was always against racing them. And yet, because he was patient and careful, he won a lot of races for his clients.

'Tekel hasn't grown much during the winter,' Auslander said. 'I should've sold him and bought something else.'

' 'E's a nice little 'orse,' Jim Craye said. ' 'E'll win 'is race.'

'Bring him out, Jim,' Garnier said. 'Let's have a look at him.'

Jim Craye went and led Tekel, a rather small, almost black colt, out of his box.

'What do you think, Jack?' Auslander asked anxiously.

'I've no idea at all, Mr Auslander,' Stephens said. 'He looks all right. Bit small, but that doesn't matter.'

There was the sound of a car stopping quickly, and Luzzi, the Italian jockey, came into the courtyard. He shook hands with everybody, Stephens last.

'So you going to help me, eh, old man?' Luzzi said to Stephens, smiling. Luzzi was a dark-haired kid of nineteen, with sharp dark eyes in a face still soft and without the lines and angles a jockey's face eventually gets. He looked almost girlish.

'That's right,' Stephens said.

The first lot of horses was brought out of the stalls, fifteen of them, and jockeys and lads mounted them. Stephens got on Tekel's back. Jim Craye said, 'Don't 'urry 'im and don't bother 'im. 'E's not mean, but 'e's got a mind of 'is own, as you might say.'

The fifteen of them rode out in a long line, Luzzi first on a chestnut five-year-old, Stephens next on Tekel, and Jim Craye third, on a three-year-old bay colt. They rode to the grassy training course, the Piste de Lamorlaye, across the road. The horses walked slowly, dancing a little and stretching their necks. They were all feeling good. So were the lads. They whistled tunelessly as they rode along in the early-morning light. The sound of many birds was loud on the training course.

Garnier and Auslander walked across, and Garnier asked Stephens to work Tekel a mile. 'Start off at the château,' Garnier said. 'Jim will get away ahead of you. Pass him after half a mile, and finish out a mile here. Let him run the last half mile, understand, but don't *ride* him.'

Jim Craye started off, going ahead fifteen lengths. Stephens rode behind, taking his time. They went along that way for a while, Tekel galloping nicely. Stephens watched old Craye, riding far forward in the saddle, light and spry as a boy, coaxing the best out of a horse that would never be worth anything. Jim was closer to seventy than to sixty. It was a pleasure to watch him. After half a mile, Stephens let Tekel run a little and passed the other horse easily. Tekel had a nice run in him, Stephens found, although he had a rather short stride and Stephens could not tell whether the run would last long under pressure. At the end of the mile, he pulled Tekel up by Garnier and Auslander and slid off.

'What do you think?' Auslander asked.

'He's a very nice colt, Mr Auslander,' Stephens said, patting Tekel's muzzle. 'I should think he'd do.'

'Do you think he's a Poule d'Essai colt?' Auslander asked. The Poule d'Essai des Poulains is the French Two Thousand Guineas, a classic mile for three-year-olds.

'Hard to tell. I shouldn't sell him if I were you, though.'

'I've got him in a mile race at Longchamp in a week,' Garnier said. 'I'm not sure he's ready for it.'

'He's ready,' Stephens said.

'You think he can win?' Auslander said. 'It's the Prix St James. There's not much in it.'

'He's ready to run a good race, that's all I know,' Stephens said.

'Well, anyway, one thing sure, I'm not going to sell him,' Auslander said happily. Then he added, 'Not right away, anyhow.'

Stephens went back to the stables. He had hung his sports jacket in the tack room. He got it and put it over the grey turtleneck sweater he was wearing. As he went out again, he passed Tekel's stall. Jim Craye was standing beside it, and the colt was kicking the wooden wall. 'Know what 'e wants?' Craye said. ' 'E wants 'is breakfast. 'E'll kick down the barn if 'e don't get it.'

Stephens had known Jim Craye for thirty-five years, off and on. In the days when Stephens was an apprentice at Newmarket, Craye was a jockey living in France but sometimes riding in England for a French stable.

'You've a nice berth here, Jim,' Stephens said.

'Can't complain,' Jim said.

'Do you ever go to the races these days?'

'I've not been on a racecourse in ten years,' Jim said. 'Too busy out 'ere.'

Things went along pretty quietly for a while. Stephens rode better as the season wore on, but he did not win often. He won the Prix St James – a trial for the Poule d'Essai – on Tekel, by a neck. Auslander complained that Stephens had made it too close. Stephens began to find Auslander more and more tiresome; like all owners, he was obsessed with winning.

Every morning now, Stephens went out to Chantilly to work horses for Garnier. He was happy doing this. He began to wonder if he enjoyed only practice races on the training course, where the result was decided in advance. He did not care as much as he had about winning on the racecourse. He lost some races that he could have won. Sometimes he lost because, without thinking it out, he felt that he could not win smoothly and easily, that there would be something forced and strained about winning, which was distasteful to him. He could not explain these feelings to himself, and of course he could not explain them to owners and trainers, so he did not get many good mounts. He did not mind, except for the money, he told himself, and he reminded himself now and then that he had plenty of money.

He had enjoyed being one of the great jockeys of Europe. It did not seriously occur to him now that he was ceasing to be that. His self-esteem was high still. He knew that he was as strong as ever, and that his sense of pace, his knowledge of when to move, and his understanding of a horse were as fine as ever. He told himself that he would like to ride a really great horse, like Astolat, again, one for whom everything was easy and smooth, one of those long-striding, irresistible Perrault horses. If he had a great horse, he would give him a great ride.

Stephens rode Tekel in all his workouts and became fond of the little colt. Tekel had a neat, extremely pure action, although his stride was perhaps too short for him to get a distance in good company. He was courageous; if, in training, Stephens permitted another horse to come up to him at the end of a workout, Tekel would draw away on his own courage, without urging. He had some temperament; in the morning, walking to the training course, he would shy in pretended fright at every shadow. But it was all good-natured and innocent. Stephens found that once he had called on Tekel for an effort, that was enough. The horse did not like to be reminded of what he was supposed to do when he was already doing it. Once he had begun to run, the best thing was to sit absolutely still on him. ' 'E knows what 'e was put on earth for,' Jim Craye said. Stephens never whipped him and did not intend to. He and Tekel went well together. He thought Tekel was good, and might be very good.

Auslander and Garnier decided to run Tekel in the Poule d'Essai, and Stephens won with him fairly easily, letting him go to the front after half a mile. Tekel was improving all the time. In Chantilly, he began to be mentioned as a horse that might be one of the good ones. Auslander got very enthusiastic and talked of the Jockey-Club and the Grand Prix.

Luzzi, Garnier's contract jockey, heard this talk and complained that Garnier should have let him ride Tekel. Garnier told him that Stephens happened to fit the colt, and that besides, it was a whim of Mr Auslander's to have Stephens ride him. Luzzi couldn't do anything, for though Garnier had first call on Luzzi he was not obliged to use him. Still, Luzzi was resentful and talked against Stephens in the jockeys' rooms at the racecourses and in the bars of Chantilly.

One day, in a little race at St Cloud, Stephens and Luzzi were both riding. Stephens brought his horse through on the rail and won handily, but in slipping through to take the lead near the last turn, his horse brushed against Luzzi's. After the race, walking to the jockeys' room, Luzzi said to him. 'You think you're pretty hot, old man, don't you?'

'I didn't bother you,' Stephens said. 'You weren't going anywhere.'

'You think you're hot,' Luzzi said. 'Sometime someone will slam you so hard you'll go down and you won't get up.'

'Never mind about me,' Stephens said, and walked away.

From then on, Luzzi said something unpleasant to Stephens every time he saw him. The other jockeys encouraged him and hoped that something would happen between him and Stephens. There was a feeling that because Stephens did not drink and talk with the others at the Derby, the Jockey-Club, or any of the other Chantilly bars, he was too pleased with himself. '*M. Stephens, c'est un* gentleman,' they said, using the English word derisively.

Stephens paid no attention to Luzzi. He had always gone his own way. He had never been liked.

Luzzi was not popular, either. He was a foreigner. He had ridden only one other season in France. He was young and successful. Feeling unpopular and unsure of himself, Luzzi believed he could make himself liked by quarrelling with Stephens. This was only a little successful. Some of the others even resented it, feeling that, after all, they had disliked Stephens first.

Auslander decided to run Tekel in the Prix Lupin, one of the big spring tests for three-year-olds. The Lupin is at a mile and five-sixteenths. Stephens and Garnier told him this was too far.

'You mean he can't win?' Auslander asked.

'Oh, he might win,' Stephens said.

'It's not his distance,' Garnier said. 'A mile is about his limit. He might go farther in the fall, when he's grown a little.'

'God damn it,' Auslander said. 'I think I've got a classic colt here. I want to run him in the Jockey-Club.' The Jockey-Club, at a mile and a half, is the French Derby.

'I'd much rather wait, Mr Auslander,' Garnier said. 'If you give this little horse some time, he'll win plenty of nice races for you. You don't want to run him in the Jockey-Club.'

'That's just what I do want,' Auslander said. So it was decided to try him first in the Lupin.

The race was run on a Sunday, at Longchamp. It rained during the night and morning, but the sun came out before noon. Longchamp is the loveliest racecourse in the world, with the long sweeping green turns of the course, the speckled shade of the walking ring under the chestnut trees, and the calm, cheerful trees themselves. Fresh from the rain, the chestnut trees slick and wet, the sky a fresh light blue, and all the green a richer green, it was more beautiful than usual that day. A racecourse is at its best and happiest, Stephens thought, before the first race on an important day when the weather is fine. Then everything is clean and everything is before you. The lawns have not been littered with torn-up pari-mutuel tickets. No one has been saddened or angered by losing.

Stephens and Garnier went out on the course to see how the going was. It was heavy. Tekel had never run in the mud, and Stephens had a feeling he was too fragile to relish it. The heavy going and the distance would combine to stop him. 'It's asking too much of him,' Stephens said to Garnier.

'Just see that he does the best he can,' Garnier said.

'He'll do that,' Stephens said.

'If we can win this, it will do you a lot of good,' Garnier said. 'You'll be getting mounts from a lot of people.'

'I'll win if I can,' Stephens said. 'I've won the better part of the classics in Europe. What's it matter if I win this or not?'

'They forget those other races,' Garnier said.

Stephens rode in one race besides the Prix Lupin that day – a mile for three-year-old maidens that came just before the Lupin. He had taken the mount, on a big, nervous, unmanageable gelding of the Vicomtesse de Rantigny-Lazarches, because he wanted to find out ahead of the main race what the course was like. He had worked the horse once or twice at Chantilly, and did not believe he could do anything.

The field was big – twenty-five runners – and Stephens' number was 23. Luzzi, No. 24, was to start next to him on a colt of the Nawab of Bhopal. As the horses circled around behind the barrier, Stephens knew he would have trouble. His mount was in a lather, trembling and rearing, the way the ones that amount to nothing so often do. At the start, when the tapes flew up, he swerved to the left and slammed into Luzzi's colt, knocking him almost to his knees. After that, there was no chance for either of them. They just galloped along behind the field.

After the race, Luzzi came up to Stephens outside the jockeys' room and said, 'I don't let anybody do that to me.' His lips were white and compressed, because he had decided he must hit Stephens.

'It was an accident,' Stephens said.

'I don't allow that,' Luzzi said, uncertain of the right words and trying to work himself into the state of fury he wished to be in.

Luzzi knew a little about boxing. He feinted low with his left hand, and then hit Stephens between the eyes with his right, knocking him down.

Stephens knew nothing of boxing. He had not been in a fight since childhood. But he had imagined being in fights, and it had never occurred to him that he could be beaten in one. He jumped up after a second and awkwardly pushed his right fist at Luzzi. Luzzi stuck his left in Stephens' face before Stephens' fist could land. The punch hit Stephens' nose, and he went down again, caught off balance. He got up quickly, and Luzzi struck him again between the eyes. As he was getting up the third time, some people grabbed Luzzi and pulled him away.

The fight had lasted only a few seconds. Not many of the big crowd had seen it, but gossip travels as quickly as tips around a racecourse, and soon everyone knew that Luzzi had beaten up the Englishman. Many people who really did not care one way or the other, but who had heard that Stephens thought he was better than anyone else, or who had at some time lost a bet on a mount of Stephens', said it was about time.

Stephens walked into the jockeys' room in a fury. He was furious partly because his nose was bleeding and the blood was dripping down over the Vicomtesse de Rantigny-Lazarches's yellow-and-white silks, which seemed to him a dirty, disgusting, and ridiculous thing to have to happen. He felt sick at his stomach. He washed and changed into Auslander's silks – grey, with red hoops on the sleeves, and black 'A's on the back and on the black cap – and as he was combing his hair, Garnier came in. The bleeding had stopped, but Stephens still felt sick. His face ached, and he would soon have two black eyes.

Garnier's pudgy, sallow, unhappy face had a look of embarrassment. 'This is terrible,' he said. 'You understand, you don't need to ride.'

Stephens, concentrating on combing his thick black hair, didn't look around. 'Who will you put up?' he asked. 'Luzzi?'

'Of course not,' Garnier said. 'I can get Kemp.'

'Kemp's nearly as old as I am,' Stephens said. 'Do you think your horse'll do better with him?'

'You're not well,' Garnier said.

'Don't be a bloody fool,' Stephens said. 'I'm riding him unless you order me off.'

'I'm not doing that,' Garnier said.

'Does Auslander order me off him? Is that it?'

'No, but he's worried. That's natural.'

'Tell him to stop worrying,' Stephens said. 'He can buy his tickets. I expect to win this race.'

Garnier walked out to the paddock with Stephens and gave him a leg up on Tekel. Everyone there looked at Stephens' battered face. He had been ready to hear them laugh, but no one did. His face hurt, though, and he felt old and sick. Auslander came up beside Garnier, smiling worriedly. He said nothing.

There was a field of eleven for the Lupin, and Stephens believed only three could trouble him: Mohilal, a good colt of the Aga Khan's that had finished well in his two races of the year; Djérama, a Boussac colt that had won his three starts; and Heronwood, a Rothschild horse that had chased Tekel in the Prix St James and the Poule d'Essai. Boussac also had entered another three-year-old, called Phactaris, that would be sacrificed to make the pace.

The race started. The Boussac pacemaker went to the front at the signal. Stephens took up Tekel and held him in fourth position. Mohilal was second and Djérama third. They continued that way up the hill. Tekel was full of run in spite of the heavy going, and Stephens' arms ached from holding him. As they entered the little wood just below the crest of the hill, Stephens sensed that Phactaris, the Boussac flier, was having it too easy. There was not enough pace. He let out a wrap on Tekel, who bounded forward to draw even with Djérama, and an instant later the two of them went after Mohilal almost together. Tekel was running willingly, and after he and Djérama had moved past Mohilal, he gradually drew away from Djérama, and Stephens sent him after Phactaris, still four lengths in front and holding on courageously. Coming down the hill, Stephens let Tekel all the way out and clucked to him, and he moved right past Phactaris in a few bounds to take the lead. Phactaris dropped out of the race, Djérama and Mohilal stayed fairly close in second and third, and Heronwood, the Rothschild colt, began to move up.

At the bottom of the hill, Tekel faltered for an instant and seemed to flounder in the sticky mud. Stephens sat absolutely still on him, and Tekel regained his stride. Stephens knew the colt was terribly tired, though he was still going well.

Taking the last turn, Stephens sat like a rock on Tekel, not moving his hands, not looking back for fear the movement might throw Tekel off stride, though he knew the Rothschild colt would be coming at him. There was no change in Tekel's neat, flawless stride. The race was too long for him, it was beyond his powers and he was exhausted, but his heart was fine, so he kept right on, running smoothly and cleanly, with no choppiness, through the holding mud. Stephens continued to sit still. It was not his way of riding – his race was the waiting race and then the drive in the last half-mile – but this was the way to ride Tekel. The horse must do it all; Stephens' job was to make it as easy for him as possible.

At the beginning of the stretch, Heronwood came at Tekel, not with a rush but with a steady, plodding attack. Three hundred yards from the end, Heronwood's head was even with Stephens' left boot. When Heronwood was a neck behind Tekel, Tekel felt the challenge and began to fight it off, drawing away a little from the colt. Then he faltered again, and slid a little; his legs would not quite obey his heart. Heronwood gained a head on him.

Stephens had the whip in his left hand. He put it between his teeth, took the reins in his left hand without easing the slight pressure he always kept on the bit, took the whip in his right hand, and started whipping. Heronwood was so close Stephens could not whip left-handed.

Tekel floundered under the whip as if shocked. Then he straight-ened out and moved again. Stephens flogged him as hard as he could all the way, raising the bat high and bringing it down with a crack on Tekel's crupper again and again, even after they had passed the finish line a neck in front of Heronwood.

It was a popular win; the crowd had made Tekel the favourite, and they cheered Stephens back to the scales.

'You see,' a man in the crowd said, 'he can win when he wants to.'

When Stephens had weighed in, he saw Auslander hurrying through the enclosure toward him. Stephens avoided him and went to the jockeys' room. He changed quickly, and got his car and drove home.

'My God, what has happened to you?' his wife said when she saw him. 'Look at your face!'

Stephens looked at himself in an oak-framed mirror that hung in the dark hall. Both his eyes were black, and a band of purple-black spread across the bridge of his nose.

'Not pretty, I admit,' he said.

'You've fallen off a horse!' his wife screamed.

'I have not!' Stephens said angrily. '*Ne parle pas comme une idiote.*' His French tended to be a literal translation of English.

'You've fallen off a horse,' his wife said. 'Riding horseback may be all right for rich men. For a man in your station, it's ridiculous.'

'Perhaps you're right,' he said.

'Come into the kitchen and let me take care of your face,' she said. 'A man who is almost fifty! It's idiotic.'

Like an irascible, loving mother, she took care of his face.

For a week, Stephens stayed at home. Garnier telephoned and said he would like to see him. Stephens said he wanted to rest. Garnier told him the commissioners had set down Luzzi for a month. Stephens asked him how Tekel was, and Garnier told him that the horse had limped when he was cooled out after the race, and that he had not been worked since. 'His ankles look bad.' Garnier said. 'There may be a bowed tendon. The vet will tell me in a day or two.' Garnier's voice sounded uncomfortable, as though he were trying to keep anger out of it.

'Well, I'm sorry to hear that,' Stephens said.

Stephens was sure Tekel would never run with good horses again, and he believed it was his fault. He didn't blame Auslander, who was only the owner.

There is nothing wrong with whipping a horse. It doesn't hurt him much, and many won't run without it. But Stephens knew he had done something ugly when he laid the whip on Tekel. He had asked the colt for more than he could give, and Tekel, with wild generosity, had given it. Tekel had given Stephens everything he might have had in every other race he might run in his life.

Stephens stayed indoors that week, drinking coffee and reading *Sport Complet* – he sent his wife out to get it – and she began saying, 'Perfect! You are in retirement, then. Do you wish me to go into service?'

But after a week, when his face looked all right, he said to her, 'I'm going out to Chantilly in the morning.'

'Why?'

'To ride some of Garnier's horses for him.'

'The races!' she said. 'I hoped you were finished with that.'

'Oh, I'm through with racing,' Stephens said. 'Sick of it.'

'So much the better. What will you do?'

'Exercise horses for Garnier.'

'He'll pay you?' she asked.

'Of course.'

'How much?'

'About forty thousand a month, I think lad's get,' Stephens said.

'That's very good. A regular salary, even though it's smaller, is better than depending on the generosity of foreigners.' She had always believed that all racehorse owners were foreigners and that jockeys were paid in tips, like waiters.

'We'd better leave Paris,' Stephens said. 'Too expensive. How would you like to live in Chantilly?'

'We could buy a little store there,' she said. 'I've always wanted a little business.'

'Have you?' Stephens asked, smiling. 'Well, I suppose we might. Have to look about a bit first, and go into it carefully.'

'Of course,' his wife said happily.

In the morning, Stephens drove out to Chantilly. It was green all along the way, now. At the village of Lamorlaye, where he turned off for Garnier's, he passed le Derby. Mme Bernard, the lean, muscular owner, was flinging water from a bucket out over the stone terrace. He thought that perhaps he'd stop and have a glass of white wine there, after the morning's work. Because he had been so serious about his profession, he had drunk almost nothing for thirty years, but now he thought with pleasure of drinking cold white wine when the workouts were over. He'd drink it out on the terrace there.

In the courtyard at Garnier's, he met Jim Craye. Garnier wasn't up. Jim showed Stephens around, talking about the horses in the slow, steady, gentle way that men have who have worked around horses all their lives. Tekel was not in his stall, and Jim explained that Auslander was selling him. Tekel had not bowed a tendon after all, Jim said, but he was finished just the same.

'You'll be out 'ere regular now?' Jim asked Stephens.

'Yes, I'm going to live out here,' Stephens said.

'It's a good place. The boss is all right.'

Garnier came down from his house, which was in front of the stables, facing the road. He had not shaved, and was wearing carpet slippers.

'I want you to gallop a little two-year-old for me, Jack,' Garnier said. He walked with Stephens to the two-year-old's box. 'Take him out,' Garnier said.

Stephens led the colt out.

'He's not ready for anything,' Garnier said. 'Maybe he never will be. Mme de Ratigny-Lazarches wants to run him at Deauville, but I'm against it. Today we'll just give him a nice gallop.'

The other lads were bringing their horses out and mounting. Stephens mounted, and they all rode out across the road to the Piste de Lamorlaye and walked the horses out onto the grass.

The dewy grass, bent from being ridden over, looked blue and purple with the long morning shadows on it. The horses felt fine; they were snorting and shying. The lads felt fine, all whistling their monotonous, tuneless little tunes. Stephens, on a fresh two-year-old that had never been on a racecourse, felt fine, too. In the thickets along the sides of the training course, the birds were just tearing into their songs, as if they knew that the world had been made new that morning – a fresh, new, morning world. Stephens heard them and thought, it's all nonsense about birds singing. They don't really sing songs, they chirp. And yet – although surely no bird listened to the others – it all went fine together when they set to it early in the morning.

THE
BAGMAN'S PONY

Somerville & Ross

WHEN the regiment was at Delphi, a T.G. was sent to us from the 105th Lancers, a bagman, as they call that sort of globe-trotting fellow that knocks about from one place to another, and takes all the fun he can out of it at other people's expense. Scott in the 105th gave this bagman a letter of introduction to me, told me that he was bringing down a horse to run at the Delhi races; so, as a matter of course, I asked him to stop with me for the week. It was a regular understood thing in India then, this passing on the T.G. from one place to another; sometimes he was all right, and sometimes he was a good deal the reverse – in any case, you were bound to be hospitable, and afterwards you could, if you liked, tell the man that sent him that you didn't want any more from him.

The bagman arrived in due course, with a rum-looking roan horse, called the 'Doctor'; a very good horse, too, but not quite so good as the bagman gave out that he was. He brought along his own grass-cutter with him, as one generally does in India, and the grass-cutter's pony, a sort of animal people get because he can carry two or three more of these beastly clods of grass they dig up for horses than a man can, and without much regard to other qualities. The bagman seemed a decentish sort of chap in his way, but, my word! he did put his foot in it the first night at mess; by George, he did! There was somehow an idea that he belonged to a wine merchant business in England, and the Colonel thought we'd better open our best cellar for the occasion, and so we did; even got out the old Madeira, and told the usual story about the number of times it had been round the Cape. The bagman took everything that came his way, and held his tongue about it, which was rather damping. At last, when it came to dessert and the Madeira, Carew, one of our fellows, couldn't stand it any longer – after all, it *is* aggravating if a man won't praise your best wine, no matter how little you care about his opinion, and the bagman was supposed to be a *connoisseur*.

'Not a bad glass of wine that,' says Carew to him; 'what do you think of it?'

'Not bad,' says the bagman, sipping it, 'I think I'll show you something better in this line if you'll come and dine with me in London when you're home next.'

'Thanks,' says Carew, getting as red as his own jacket, and beginning to splutter – he always did when he got angry – 'this is good enough for me, and for most people here —'

'Oh, but nobody up here has got a palate left,' says the bagman, laughing in a very superior sort of way.

'What do you mean, sir?' shouted Carew, jumping up. 'I'll not have any d—d bagmen coming here to insult me!'

By George, if you'll believe me, Carew had a false palate, with a little bit of sponge in the middle, and we all knew it, *except the bagman*. There was a frightful shindy, Carew wanting to have his blood, and all the rest of us trying to prevent a row. We succeeded somehow in the end, I don't quite know how we managed it, as the bagman was very warlike too; but, anyhow, when I was going to bed that night I saw them both in the billiard room, very tight, leaning up against opposite ends of the billiard table, and making shoves at the balls – with the wrong ends of their cues, fortunately.

'He called me a d—d bagman,' says one, nearly tumbling down with laughter.

'Told me I'd no palate,' says the other, putting his head down on the table and giggling away there, 'best thing I ever heard in my life.'

Every one was as good friends as possible next day at the races, and for the whole week as well. Unfortunately for the bagman his horse didn't pull off things in the way he expected, in fact he hadn't a look in – we just killed him from first to last. As things went on the bagman began to look queer, and by the end of the week he stood to lose a pretty considerable lot of money, nearly all of it to me. The way we arranged these matters then was a general settling-up day after the races were over; every one squared up his books and planked ready money down on the nail, or if he hadn't got it he went and borrowed from someone else to do it with. The bagman paid up what he owed the others, and I began to feel a bit sorry for the fellow when he came to me that night to finish up. He hummed and hawed a bit, and then asked if I should mind taking an I.O.U. from him, as he was run out of the ready.

Of course I said, 'All right, old man, certainly, just the same to me,' though it's usual in such cases to put down the hard cash, but still – fellow staying in my house, you know – sent on by this pal of mine in the 11th – absolutely nothing else to be done.

Next morning I was up and out on parade as usual, and in the natural course of events began to look about for my bagman. By George, not a sign of him in his room, not a sign of him anywhere. I thought to myself, this is peculiar, and I went over to the stable to try whether there was anything to be heard of him.

The first thing I saw was that the 'Doctor's' stall was empty.

'How's this?' I said to the groom; 'where's Mr Leggett's horse?'

'The sahib has taken him away this morning.'

I began to have some notion then of what my I.O.U. was worth.

'The sahib has left his grass-cutter and his pony,' said the *sais*, who probably had as good a notion of what was up as I had.

'All right, send for the grass-cutter,' I said.

The fellow came up, in a blue funk evidently, and I couldn't make anything of him. Sahib this, and sahib that, and salaaming and general idiocy – or shamming – I couldn't tell which.

This is a very fishy business, I thought to myself, and I think it's well on the cards the grass-cutter will be out of this tonight on his pony. No, by Jove, I'll see what the pony's good for before he does that. 'Is the grass-cutter's pony there?' I said to the *sais*.

'He is there, sahib, but he is only *akattiawa tattoo*,' which is the name for a common kind of mountain pony.

I had him out, and he certainly was a wretched-looking little brute, dun with a black stripe down his back, like all that breed, and all bony and ragged and starved.

'Indeed, he is a *gareeb kuch kam ki nahin*,' said the *sais*, meaning thereby a miserable beast, in the most intensified form, 'and not fit to stand in the sahib's stable.'

All the same, just for the fun of the thing, I put the grass-cutter up on him, and told him to trot him up and down. By George! the pony went like a flash of lightning! I had him galloped next; same thing – fellow could hardly hold him. I opened my eyes, I can tell you, but no matter what way I looked at him I couldn't see where on earth he got his pace from. It was there anyhow, there wasn't a doubt about that. 'That'll do,' I said, 'put him up. And you just stay here,' I said to the grass-cutter; 'till I hear from Mr Leggett where you're to go to. Don't leave Delhi till you get orders from me.'

It got about during the day that the bagman had disappeared, and had had a soft thing of it as far as I was concerned. The 112th were dining with us that night, and they all set to work to draw me after dinner about the business – thought themselves vastly witty over it.

'Hullo Paddy, so you're the girl he left behind him!' 'Hear he went off with two suits of your clothes, one over the other.' 'Cheer up, old man; he's left you the grass-cutter and the pony, and what *he* leaves must be worth having, I'll bet!' and so on.

I suppose I'd had a good deal more than my share of the champagne, but all of a sudden I began to feel pretty warm.

'You're all d—d funny,' I said, 'but I daresay you'll find he's left me something that *is* worth having.'

'Oh, yes!' 'Go on!' 'Paddy's a great man when he's drunk,' and a lot more of the same sort.

'I tell you what it is,' said I, 'I'll back the pony he's left here to trot his twelve miles an hour on the road.'

'Bosh!' says Barclay of the 112th. 'I've seen him, and I'll lay you a thousand rupees even he doesn't.'

'Done!' said I, whacking my hand down on the table.

'And I'll lay another thousand,' says another fellow.

'Done with you too,' said I.

Every one began to stare a bit then.

'Go to bed, Paddy,' says the Colonel, 'you're making an exhibition of yourself.'

'Thank you, sir; I know pretty well what I'm talking about,' said I; but, by George, I began privately to think I'd better pull myself together a bit, and I got out my book and began to hedge – laid three to one on the pony to do eleven miles in the hour, and four to one on him to do ten – all the fellows delighted to get their money on. I was to choose my own ground, and to have a fortnight to train the pony, and by the time I went to bed I stood to lose about £1,000.

Somehow in the morning I didn't feel quite so cheery about things – one doesn't after a big night – one gets nasty qualms, both mental and the other kind. I went out to look after the pony, and the first thing I saw by way of an appetiser was Biddy, with a face as long as my arm. Biddy, I should explain, was a chap called Biddulph, in the Artillery; they called him Biddy for short, and partly, too, because he kept a racing stable with me in those days, I being called Paddy by every one, because I was Irish – English idea of wit – Paddy and Biddy, you see.

'Well,' said he, 'I hear you've about gone and done it this time. The 112th are going about with trumpets and shawms, and looking round for ways to spend that thousand when they get it. There are to be new polo ponies, a big luncheon, and a piece of plate bought for the mess, in memory of that benefactor of the regiment, the departed bagman. Well, now, let's see the pony. That's what I've come down for.'

I'm hanged if the brute didn't look more vulgar and wretched than ever when he was brought out, and I began to feel that perhaps I was more parts of a fool than I thought I was. Biddy stood looking at him there with his underlip stuck out.

'I think you've lost your money,' he said. That was all, but the way he said it made me feel conscious of the shortcomings of every hair in the brute's ugly hide.

'Wait a bit,' I said, 'you haven't seen him going yet. I think he has the heels of any pony in the place.'

I got a boy on to him without any more ado, thinking to myself I was going to astonish Biddy. 'You just get out of his way, that's all,' says I, standing back to let him start.

If you'll believe it, he wouldn't budge a foot – not an inch – no amount of licking had any effect on him. He just humped his back, and tossed his head and grunted – he must have had a skin as thick as three donkeys! I got on to him myself and put the spurs in, and he went up on his hind legs and nearly came back with me – that was all the good I got of that.

'Where's the grass-cutter?' I shouted, jumping off him in about as great a fury as I ever was in. 'I suppose *he* knows how to make this devil go!'

'Grass-cutter went away last night, sahib. Me see him try to open stable door and go away. Me see him no more.'

I used pretty well all the bad language I knew in one blast. Biddy began to walk away, laughing, till I felt as if I could kick him.

'I'm going to have a front seat for this trotting match,' he said, stopping to get his wind. 'Spectators along the route requested to provide themselves with pitchforks and fireworks, I suppose, in case the champion pony should show any of his engaging little temper. Never mind, old man, I'll see you through this, there's no use in getting into a wax about it. I'm going shares with you, the way we always do.'

I can't say I responded graciously, I rather think I cursed him and everything else in heaps. When he was gone I began to think of what could be done.

'Get out the dog-cart,' I said, as a last chance. 'Perhaps he'll go in harness.'

We wheeled the cart up to him, got him harnessed to it, and in two minutes that pony was walking, trotting, anything I wanted – can't explain why – one of the mysteries of horseflesh. I drove him out through the Cashmere gate, passing Biddy on the way, and feeling a good deal the better for it, and as soon as I got on to the flat stretch of road outside the gate I tried what the pony could do. He went even better than I thought he could, very rough and uneven, of course, but still promising. I brought him home, and had him put into training at once, as carefully as if he was going for the Derby. I chose the course, took the six-mile stretch of road from the Cashmere gate to Sufter Jung's tomb, and drove him over it every day. It was a splendid course – level as a table, and dead straight for the most part – and after a few days he could do it in about forty minutes out and thirty-five back. People began to talk then, especially as the pony's look and shape were improving each day, and after a little time every one was planking his money on one way or another – Biddy putting on a thousand on his own account – still, I'm bound to say the odds were against the pony. The whole of Delhi got into a state of excitement about it, natives and all, and every day I got letters warning me to take care, as there might be foul play. The stable the pony was in was a big one, and I had a wall built across it, and put a man with a gun in the outer compartment. I bought all his corn myself, in feeds at a time, going here, there, and everywhere for it, never to the same place for two days together – I thought it was better to be sure than sorry.

The day of the match every soul in the place turned out, such crowds that I could scarcely get the dog-cart through when I drove to the Cashmere gate. I got down there, and was looking over the cart to see that everything was right, when a little half-caste *keranie*, a sort of low-class clerk, came up behind me and began talking to me in a mysterious kind of way, in that vile *chi-chi* accent one gets to hate so awfully.

'Look here, Sar,' he said, 'you take my car, Sar; it built for racing. I do much trot-racing myself' – mentioning his name – 'and you go much faster my car, Sar.'

I trusted nobody in those days, and thought a good deal of myself accordingly. I hadn't found out that it takes a much smarter man to know how to trust a few.

'Thank you,' I said, 'I think I'll keep my own, the pony's accustomed to it.'

I think he understood quite well what I felt, but he didn't show any resentment.

'Well, Sar, you no trust my car, you let me see your wheels?'

'Certainly,' I said, 'you may look at them,' determined in my own mind I should keep my eye on him while he did.

He got out a machine for propping the axle, and lifted the wheel off the ground.

'Make the wheel go round,' he said.

I didn't like it much, but I gave the wheel a turn. He looked at it till it stopped.

'You lose match if you take that car,' he said, 'you take my car, Sar.'

'What do you mean?' said I, pretty sharply.

'Look here,' he said, getting the wheel going again. 'You see here, Sar, it die, all in a minute, it jerk, doesn't die smooth. You see *my* wheel, Sar.'

He put the lift under his own, and started the wheel revolving. It took about three times as long to die as mine, going steady and silent and stopping imperceptibly, not so much as a tremor in it.

'Now, Sar!' he said, 'you see I speak true, Sar. I back you two hundred rupee, if I lose I'm ruin, and I beg you, Sar, take my car! Can no win with yours, mine match car.'

'All right!' said I with a sort of impulse, 'I'll take it.' And so I did.

I had to start just under the arch of the Cashmere gate, by a pistol shot, fired from overhead. I didn't quite care for the look of the pony's ears while I was waiting for it – the crowd had frightened him a bit, I think. By Jove, when the bang came he reared straight up, dropped down again and stuck his fore-legs out, reared again when I gave him the whip, every second of course telling against me.

'Here, let me help you,' shouted Biddy, jumping into the trap. His weight settled the business, down came the pony, and we went away like blazes.

The three umpires rode with us, one each side and one behind, at least that was the way at first, but I found the clattering of their hoofs made it next to impossible to hold the pony. I got them to keep back, and after that he went fairly steadily, but it was anxious work. The noise and excitement had told on him a lot, he had a tendency to break during all that six miles out, and he was in a lather before we got to Sufter Jung's tomb. There were a lot of people waiting for me out there, some ladies on horseback, too, and there was a coffee-shop going, with drinks of all kinds. As I got near they began to call out, 'You're done, Paddy, thirty-four minutes had gone already, you haven't the ghost of a chance. Come and have a drink and look pleasant over it.'

I turned the pony, and Biddy and I jumped out. I went up to the table, snatched up a glass of brandy and filled my mouth with it, then went back to the pony, took him by the head, and sent a squirt of brandy up each nostril; I squirted the rest down his throat, went back to the table, swallowed half a tumbler of Curaçoa or something, and was into the trap and off again, the whole thing not taking more than twenty seconds.

The business began to be pretty exciting after that. You can see four miles straight ahead of you on that road; and that day the police had special orders to keep it clear, so that it was a perfectly blank, white stretch as far as I could see. You know how one never seems to get any nearer to things on a road like that, and there was the clock hanging opposite to me on the splash board; I couldn't look at it, but I could hear its beastly click–click through the trotting of the pony, and that was nearly as bad as seeing the minute hand going from pip to pip. But, by George, I pretty soon heard a worse kind of noise than that. It was a case of preserve me from my friends. The people who had gone out to Sufter Jung's tomb on horseback to meet me thought it would be a capital plan to come along after me and see the fun, and encourage me a bit – so they told me afterwards. The way they encouraged me was by galloping till they picked me up, and then hammering along behind me like a troop of cavalry till it was all I could do to keep the pony from breaking.

'You've got to win, Paddy,' calls out Mrs Harry Le Bretton, galloping up alongside, 'you promised you would!'

Mrs Harry and I were great friends in those days – very sporting little woman, nearly as keen about the match as I was – but at that moment I couldn't pick my words.

'Keep back!' I shouted to her; 'keep back, for pity's sake!'

It was too late – the next instant the pony was galloping. The penalty is that you have to pull up, and make the wheels turn in the opposite direction, and I just threw the pony on his haunches. He nearly came back into the cart, but the tremendous jerk gave the backward turn to the wheels and I was off again. Not even that kept the people back. Mrs Le Bretton came alongside again to say something else to me, and I suddenly felt half mad from the clatter and the frightful strain of the pony on my arms.

'D—n it all! Le Bretton!' I yelled, as the pony broke for the second time, 'can't you keep your wife away!'

They did let me alone after that – turned off the road and took a scoop across the plain, so as to come up with me at the finish – and I pulled myself together to do the last couple of miles. I could see that Cashmere gate and the Delhi walls ahead of me; 'pon my soul I felt as if they were defying me and despising me, just standing waiting there under the blazing sky, and they never seemed to get any nearer. It was like the first night of a fever, the whizzing of the wheels, the ding–dong of the pony's hoofs, the silence all round, the feeling of stress and insane hurrying on, the throbbing of my head, and the scorching heat. I'll swear no fever I've ever had was worse than that last two miles.

As I reached the Delhi walls I took one look at the clock. There was barely a minute left.

'By Jove!' I gasped. 'I'm done!'

I shouted and yelled to the pony like a madman, to keep up what heart was left in the wretched little brute, holding on to him for bare life, with my arms and legs straight out in front of me. The grey wall and the blinding road rushed by me like a river – I scarcely knew what happened – I couldn't think of anything but the ticking of the clock that I was somehow trying to count, till there came the bang of a pistol over my head.

It was the Cashmere gate, and I had thirteen seconds in hand.

There was never anything more heard of the bagman. He can, if he likes, soothe his conscience with the reflection that he was worth a thousand pounds to me.

But Mrs Le Bretton never quite forgave me.

The
DICK FRANCIS
Complete Treasury of
GREAT RACING
S T O R I E S

The Second Collection

Acknowledgements

Grateful acknowledgement is made to the following for permisssion to reprint the material in this volume

The authors and Messrs John Johnson Ltd. for the stories *Spring Fever* and *My First Winner.*

American Entertaiment Rights Company, LLC, the copyright proprietor for the story *Pick The Winner* by Damon Runyon, copyright 1933 by P.F. Collier & Son Co.; copyright renewal © 1961 by Damon Runyon Jr. and Mary Runyon McCann. The copyright was assigned to American Entertainment Rights Company, LLC by the copyright proprietor in January 2000.

The Dead Cert by J.C. Squire is reprinted by permission of the Peters, Fraser & Dunlop Group, Ltd.

The author and Mr. Murray Pollinger for the story *Pullinstown* from *Conversation Piece*, published in Virago Modern Classics in the Commonwealth and the same series distributed by Penguin in the U.S.A.

The story of *Occasional Licenses*, copyright   E. CE. Sommerville & Martin Ross, reproduced by permission of John Farquharson, Ltd.

The author and David Higham Associates for the story *The Good Thing*.

The Richards Literary Agency for the story *The Losers* by Maurice Gee.

Whilst all reasonable attempts have been made to contact the original copyright holder, the Publishers would be happy to hear from those they have been unable to trace, and due acknowledgement will be made in future editions.

INTRODUCTION

THE lot of those who compile collections such as this, happy though it may be, is not without its hazards. The most obvious is, of course, the accusation of omission, the sin of leaving out fondly recalled favourites of whatever reader or critic happens to pick up the collection. Avoidance of the hackneyed is seldom accepted as an excuse; nevertheless it is suggested that freshness and rediscovery must play a major part, especially in a second selection. Perhaps, too, it may be pointed out that anthologies are of their very nature a matter of personal choice and for better or worse must stand or fall as such. It has to be said, however, that those who venture into the sphere of sporting anthologies are facing a further obstacle to be surmounted. What they select must be authentic. Nothing can be more damaging than to include a story which, however compelling its narrative, fails this test. One recalls how Ouida, beloved by the Victorians for her bestsellers of high society featuring dashing guardsmen and languorous ladies, made herself into a laughing-stock when she wrote of the boatrace that all the Oxford crew rowed hard but none rowed harder than stroke. This was almost as bad a gaffe as the writer, who shall be nameless, who made his hero own a colt who won the Derby in successive years!

That having been said, times they are a'changing in racing as in everything else and one or two of the stories included here, accurate when written, may appear to modern eyes to contain errors of plot and procedure. However, when that explanation is borne in mind, mistakes do nothing to derogate from the stories' strength and effectiveness. The jockey in C. C. L. Browne's splendid tale of the ups and downs of a run-of-the-mill steeplechase rider's day would have been unlikely in these softer times to have been passed by the doctor as fit to ride again. But in the sterner ethos of an earlier day the decision was his, he made it and got away with it. He would today also earn considerably more than £7 a ride.

Similarly in Donn Byrne's story, the rule in which nominations became void on death was abolished by the friendly test case of the Jockey Club versus Edgar Wallace decided in the late twenties, years after the time in which the story is set. And in *Occasional Licences* the race in which the immortal Flurry Knox with the connivance of the rascally Slipper cajoled the coachhorse, Sultan, to win at the gymkhana meeting would certainly nowadays rank as an illegal or flapping contest, bringing condign penalties down upon its participants. Only the pens of those two ladies could adequately have recorded Flurry's forceful comments on the same, had they done so.

Much has recently been written of Somerville and Ross and their position in literature, sporting and otherwise, and there is nothing further usefully to add to it here. Donn Byrne, however, immensely popular in his day but largely forgotten now, may be regarded as a rediscovery. Born in Brooklyn in 1899 of Irish-American parentage he was educated in Ireland and France. Later he roamed the continents in a variety of employments including that of a cowpuncher and, it is believed, a strapper in a racing stable, before he took to writing. Unashamedly romantic in his theme and outlook, as his novels and stories show, he struck a chord which matched the thinking of his time and enjoyed great success on both sides of the Atlantic. In 1928 at the age of thirty-nine he returned to Ireland, and purchased a castle in county Cork. Tragically he was killed in a motor accident soon after his arrival and just before the publication of his last collection, *Destiny Bay*, from which this story is taken.

Edgar Wallace was another romantic but of a very different sort. He fell in love with racing but, unfortunately for him, his enthusiasm, especially where his own horses were concerned, far outran his judgment. When he wrote of one of his characters, 'Sir Jacques was merely one of many racing people who harboured the illusion that they knew more than the bookmaker. It brought many a promising racing career to an untimely end', he might have been writing about himself.

He died suddenly in Hollywood in 1932 aged fifty-seven. Steve Donoghue, an old friend who was in America at the time, tells in his memoirs that it was he who made the arrangements for despatching the coffin back to England, and Wallace would have found it entirely appropriate that it was the greatest jockey of his time who was given this task. When the estate was marshalled by his executors it was found that there were precious few assets and debts amounting to £140,000, none of them, however, to the bookies with whom he had always settled promptly.

Wallace, although foolish in his betting and his ownership of bad horses he insisted on believing to be world-beaters, nevertheless knew racing. When he put his mind to it and was not dashing off bits and pieces in a hurry to keep the bookies quiet, he could write of it tellingly and well. The story which we have reproduced, improbable though it may appear at first sight, may well have been based on an actual incident in the Ascot Gold Cup some years before when the favourite, Tracery, nearly suffered the same fate. And Wallace did signal service to the sport he loved when he financed at his own expense the case we have mentioned above. We have already written about Wallace in our first collection and of several of the authors collected here, but a word needs to be said of certain of the others more especially the Americans, Damon Runyon, Gordon Grand and John Taintor Foote. With the exception of Runyon, little is known of them on this side of the Atlantic and even Runyon's popularity peaked over forty years ago. In their very diversity these three demonstrate the many facets of the sport's appeal.

Runyon was a newspaperman on the New York American who loved, above all, to write of racing and boxing. The genesis of the many stories he wrote of 'the bandits of Broadway', Harry the Horse, Sam the Gonoph, Dave the Dude and the rest is strange indeed. He was in despair, thinking he was written out, when suddenly the idea came to him of putting them all and their adventures into print as he saw them through the eyes of his comic genius. In so doing he invented and perfected a line of light literature as unique and original as that of Wodehouse. His end was tragic; he died of cancer in December 1946, having suffered terribly during the last two years of his life, but kept going only by his indomitable and buoyant spirit. To the end he never lost his love of racing. He was a versifier, too, of light verse and jingles, and the scribbled few lines sent across to a friend from the press box

of one of the last Kentucky Derbies he attended well describe how
he saw and loved it all:

> Say, have they turned the pages
> Back to the past once more?
> Back to the racin' ages
> An' a Derby out of the yore?
> Say, don't tell me I'm daffy,
> Ain't that the same ol' grin?
> Why, it's that handy
> Guy named Sande,
> Bootin' a winner in?

Earl Sande was the leading American jockey of the twenties.
Among a host of other winners he rode Zev in the famous Zev–Papyrus match at Belmont Park in October 1923. Papyrus had won
the Derby of that year and Zev was an American champion. The
match was made in an effort to start a series of international races
but it was long before its time and it failed dismally. The track
was dirt and saturated by a night's rain, and to handicap him
further Papyrus, who had had a hard season being narrowly
defeated in the St Leger the previous month, was wrongly plated.
He was beaten out of sight with Donoghue, who rode him, having
accepted the inevitable, virtually pulling him up. Runyon reported
the preliminaries and the race itself in his usual graphic style for
Sande was then and remained always one of his heroes.

Gordon Grand's background was very different. He was born
to a fox-hunting and racing family and saw his first day to hounds
in 1891 at the age of eight when he was warned by the Master to
'keep your pony where it belongs, in the Field, and not pretend
you can't hold him!' He later became president of that pack, the
Millbrook Hounds, and hunted, raced and bred horses all his life.
He was the amateur where Runyon was the professional. The story
of his which we include is from a collection called *The Silver Horn*.
Written to alleviate a long illness it only saw print almost as an
afterthought in America and later in England. Its success encouraged him to follow it up with more hunting and racing stories,
many featuring Colonel Weatherford. But when his editor at the
Derrydale Press, who had discovered and encouraged him, died,
'I put my pen away and employed the time formerly given over

to writing, to gardening, raising a colt or two on my farm, fox-hunting and business interests.'

Little appears to be known of John Taintor Foote save that he, too, truly loved racing and wrote of it with humour, understanding and knowledge of the American turf, its characters and characteristics. He was a playwright and screenwriter as well as novelist, several of his plays being produced on Broadway; his screen credits include *Kentucky* and *The Story of Sea Biscuit*. Born in Leadville, Colorado in 1891, he died in 1950 and will at least always be remembered for having coined the phrase, 'The look of eagles', which has been repeated all over the world as the hallmark of a true champion.

In contrast to the Americans, Sir John Squire was the quintessential Englishman. He is little thought of now for in himself and his life he was the exemplar of an all but vanished type, the literary cove with sporting tastes. As editor of *The London Mercury* he had at one time immense influence on the London literary scene, he founded and captained an eccentric touring cricket team called 'The Invalids', he produced a very bad blank verse epic about an intervarsity rugby match, and he wrote some of the best verse parodies in the language. He knew little or nothing about the nuts and bolts of racing and would have cared less, but in *The Dead Cert* he showed that he knew all about how they talk and tip in pubs – he was something of an expert on pubs – and what happens when the conversation takes an unusual turn. The story is yet another instance of the many sides to the racing game and the diversity of those who interest themselves in it, and has a typical Squireish twist at its end.

If Squire exemplified one type of Englishman then A. B. 'Banjo' Paterson did the same for Australia. He was, like Runyon, a newspaperman and a versifier, one of the band of Bush Balladeers who sang of racing and riding on the outback and on city tracks, whose numbers included Adam Lindsay Gordon, Will H. Ogilvie and the tragic 'Breaker' Morant. He is best known in England as the author of *Waltzing Matilda* which the Anzacs adopted as their marching song, though he wrote many other stirring rhymes of the racetrack and those who rode it, all of them laced with humour. His *Riders In The Stand* is a classic and as true today as the day he wrote it, which, to quote only one short verse, will show:

They'll say Chevalley lost his nerve, and Regan lost his head;
They'll tell how one was 'livened up' and something else was 'dead' –
In fact, the race was never run on sea, or sky, or land,
But what you'd get it better done by riders in the Stand.

As well as being one of the poets of the sport he was a prolific
writer of racing journalism, and editor for some ten years of a
racing paper. Also to his credit was a racing novel *The Shearer's
Colt* and a parody of Nat Gould, whom he disliked both as a man
and an author. When he died he left behind an unfinished history
of Australian racing and numerous racing short stories of which
The Oracle is as good a description of a racing pest still extant as
one is ever likely to get.

Paterson and indeed all the authors represented here, with the
possible exception of Maurice Gee, whose *The Losers* is included
to show that the sport has its darker side, would have echoed the
words of Reginald Herbert, who in the early days of steeplechasing
wrote one of the most lively of all racing reminiscences, *When
Diamonds Were Trumps*. Red and white diamonds were his racing
colours and the title gives some idea of the flavour of the book.
'I may be said to know something about it,' he wrote, and indeed
he did having ridden over fences with success for upwards of thirty
years, 'And I unhesitantly affirm that, "there's nowt like racing".'

It is the editors' hope that the stories here included bear out that
testimony.

SPRING FEVER

Dick Francis

LOOKING back, Mrs Angela Hart could identify the exact instant in which she fell irrationally in love with her jockey. Angela Hart, plump, motherly, and fifty-two, watched the twenty-four year old man walk into the parade ring at Cheltenham races in her gleaming pink and white colours, and she thought: how young he is, how fit, how lean . . . how *brave*.

He crossed the bright turf to join her for the usual few minutes of chit-chat before taking her horse away to its two-mile scurry over hurdles, and she looked at the way the weather-tanned flesh lay taut over the cheekbone and agreed automatically that yes, the spring sunshine was lovely, and that yes, the drier going should suit her Billyboy better than all the rains of the past few weeks.

It was a day like many another. Two racehorses having satisfactorily replaced the late and moderately lamented Edward Hart in Angela's affections, she contentedly spent her time in going to steeplechase meetings to see her darlings run, and in clipping out mentions of them from '*The Sporting Life*', and in ringing up her trainer, Clement Scott, to enquire after their health. She was a woman of kindness and good humour, but suffered from a dangerous belief that everyone was basically as well-intentioned as herself. Like children who pat tigers, she expected a purr of appreciation in return for her offered friendship, not to have her arm bitten off.

Derek Roberts, jockey, saw Mrs Angela Hart prosaically as the middle-aged owner of Billyboy and Hamlet. A woman to whom he spoke habitually with a politeness born of needing the fees he was paid for riding her horses. His job, he reckoned, involved pleasing the customers before and after each race as well as doing his best for them in the event, and as he had long years ago discovered that most owners were pathetically pleased when a jockey praised their horses, he had slid almost without cynicism into a way of conveying optimism even when not believing a word of it.

When he walked into the parade ring at Cheltenham, looking for Mrs Hart and spotting her across the grass in her green tweed coat and brown fur hat, he was thinking that as Billyboy hadn't much chance in today's company he had better prepare the old duck for the coming disappointment and at the same time insure himself against being blamed for it.

'Lovely day,' he said, shaking her hand. 'Real spring sunshine.'

'Lovely.'

After a short silence, when she said nothing more, he tried again. 'Much better for Billyboy, now all that rain's drying out.'

'Yes, I'm sure you're right.'

She wasn't as talkative as usual, he thought. Not the normal excited chatter. He watched Billyboy plod round the ring and said encouragingly, 'He should run well today . . . though the opposition's pretty hot, of course.'

Mrs Hart, looking slightly vague, merely nodded. Derek Roberts, shrugging his mental shoulders, gave her a practised half-genuine smile and reckoned (mistakenly) that if she had something on her mind, and didn't want to talk, it was nothing to do with him.

A step away from them, also with his eyes on the horse, stood Billyboy's trainer, Clement Scott. Strong, approaching sixty, a charmer all his life, he had achieved success more through personality than any deep skill with horses. He wore good clothes. He could talk.

Underneath the attractive skin there was a coldness which was apparent to his self-effacing wife, and to his grown and married children, and eventually to anyone who knew him well. He was good company, but lacked compassion. All bonhomie on top; ruthlessly self-seeking below.

Clement Scott was old in the ways of jockeys and owners, and professionally he thought highly of the pair before him: of Derek because he kept the owners happy and rode well enough besides, and of Angela because her first interest was in the horses themselves and not in the prize-money they might fail to win. Motherly sentimental ladies, in his opinion, were the least critical and most forgiving of owners, and he put up gladly with their gushing telephone calls because they also tended to pay his bills on receipt. Towards Angela, nicely endowed with a house on the edge of Wentworth golf course, he behaved with the avuncular roguishness that had kept many a widow faithful to his stable in spite of persistent rumours that he would probably cheat them if given half a chance.

Angela, like many another lady, didn't believe the rumours. Clement, dear naughty Clement who made owning a racehorse such satisfying fun, would never in any case cheat *her*.

She stood beside Clement on the stands to watch the race, and felt an extra dimension of anxiety: not simply, as always, for the safe return of darling Billyboy, but also, acutely, for the man on his back. Such risks he takes, she thought, watching him through her binoculars; and before that day she had thought only of whether he'd judged the pace right, or taken an available opening, or ridden a vigorous finish. During that race her response to him crossed conclusively from objectivity to emotion, a change which at the time she only dimly perceived.

Derek Roberts, by dint of not resting the horse when it was beaten, urged Billyboy forwards into fourth place close to the winning post, knowing that Angela would like fourth better than fifth or sixth or seventh. Clement Scott smiled to himself as he watched. Fourth or seventh, the horse had won no prize-money; but that lad Derek, with his good looks and crafty ways, he sure knew how to keep the owners sweet.

Her raceglasses clutched tightly to her chest, Angela Hart breathed deeply from the release of pulse-raising tensions. She thought gratefully that fourth place wasn't bad in view of the hot opposition, and Billyboy had been running on at the end, which was a good sign . . . and Derek Roberts had come back safely.

With her trainer she hastened down to meet the returning pair, and watched Billyboy blow through his nostrils in his usual post-race sweating state, and listened to Derek talking over his shoulder to her while he undid the girth buckles on the saddle.

' . . . Made a bit of a mistake landing over the third last, but it didn't stop him . . . He should win a race pretty soon, I'd say . . . '

He gave her the special smile and a sketchy salute and hurried to weigh-in and change for the next race, looping the girths round the saddle as he went. Angela watched until he was out of sight and asked Clement when her horses were running next.

'Hamlet had a bit of heat in one leg this morning,' he said. 'And Billyboy needs a fortnight at least between races.' He screwed up his eyes at her, teasing. 'If you can't wait that long to see them again, why don't you come over one morning and watch their training gallops?'

She was pleased. 'Does Derek ride the gallops?'

'Sometimes,' he said.

It was on the following day that Angela, dreamily drifting around her house, thought of buying another horse.

She looked up Derek Roberts's number and telephoned.

'Find you another horse?' he said. 'Yeah . . . sure . . . I think another horse is a grand idea, but you should ask Mr Scott . . . '

'If Clement finds me a horse,' Angela said, 'Will you come with me to see it? I'd really like your opinion, before I buy.'

'Well . . . ' He hesitated, not relishing such a use of his spare time but realising that another horse for Angela meant more fees for himself.

' . . . All right, certainly I'll come, Mrs Hart, if I can be of use.'

'That's fine,' she said. 'I'll ring Clement straight away.'

'Another horse?' Clement said, surprised. 'Yes, if you like, though it's a bit late in the season. Why not wait . . . ?'

'No,' Angela interrupted. 'Dear Clement, I want him now.'

Clement Scott heard but couldn't understand the urgency in her voice. Four days later, however, when she came to see her existing two horses work, having made sure beforehand that Derek would be there to ride them, he understood completely.

Angela, fiftyish matronly Angela, couldn't keep her eyes off Derek Roberts. She intently watched him come and go, on horse and on foot, and scanned his face uninterruptedly while he spoke. She asked him questions to keep him near, and lost a good deal of animation when he finally went home.

Clement Scott, who had seen that sort of thing often enough before, behaved to her more flirtatiously than ever and kept his sardonic smile to himself. He had luckily heard of a third horse for her he said and he would take her to see it.

'Actually,' Angela said diffidently, 'I've already asked Derek to come with me . . . and he said he would.'

Clement, that evening, telephoned to Derek.

'Besotted with me?' said Derek astounded. 'That's bloody non-

sense. I've been riding for her for more than a year. You can't tell
me I wouldn't have noticed.'

'Keep your eyes open, lad,' Clement said. 'I reckon she wants
this other horse just to give her an excuse to see you oftener, and
that being so, lad, I've a little proposition for you.'

He outlined the little proposition at some length, and Derek
discovered that his consideration of Mrs Hart's best interests came
a poor second to the prospect of a tax-free instant gain equal to
half his annual earnings.

He drove to her house at Wentworth a few days later, and they
went on together in her car, a Rover, with Derek driving. The
horse belonged to a man in Yorkshire, which meant, Angela
thought contentedly, that the trip would take all day. She had
rationalised her desire to own another horse as just an increase in
her interest in racing, and also she had rationalised her eagerness
for the Yorkshire journey as merely impatience to see what Clement had described as 'an exciting bargain, at sixteen thousand. A
real smasher. One to do you justice, my dear Angela.'

She could just afford it, she thought, if she didn't go on a cruise
this summer, and if she spent less on theatre tickets and clothes.
She did not at any point admit to herself that what she was buying
at such cost was a few scattered hours out of Derek Roberts's life.

Going North from Watford, Derek said, 'Mrs Hart, did Mr
Scott tell you much about this horse?'

'He said you'd tell me. And call me Angela.'

'Er . . . ' He cleared his throat. 'Angela . . . ' He glanced at her
as she sat beside him, plump and relaxed and happy. It couldn't
be true, he thought. People like Mrs Hart didn't suffer from infatu-
ations. She was far too old. Fifty . . . an unimaginable age to him
at twenty-four. He shifted uncomfortably in his seat and felt
ashamed (but only slightly) at what he was about to do.

'Mr Scott thinks the horse has terrific potential. Only six years
old. Won a hurdle race last year . . . ' He went on with the sales
talk, skilfully weaving in the few actual facts which she could
verify from form books if she wanted to, and putting a delicately
rosy slant on everything else. 'Of course the frost and snow has
kept it off the racecourse during the winter . . . but I'll tell you,
just between ourselves . . . er . . . Angela . . . that Mr Scott thinks
he might even enter him for the Whitbread. He might even be in
that class.'

Angela listened entranced. The Whitbread Gold Cup, scheduled
for six weeks ahead, was the last big race of the season. To have
a horse fit to run in it, and to have Derek Roberts ride it, seemed
to her a pinnacle in her racing life that she had never envisaged.
Her horizons, her joy, expanded like flowers.

'Oh, how lovely,' she said ecstatically; and Derek Roberts
(almost) winced.

'Mr Scott wondered if you'd like me to do a bit of bargaining
for you,' he said. 'To get the price down a bit.'

'Dear Clement is so thoughtful.' She gave Derek a slightly anxious smile. 'Don't bargain so hard that I lose the horse, though,
will you?'

He promised not to.

'What is it called?' she said, and he told her 'Magic.'

Magic was stabled in the sort of yard which should have warned
Angela to beware, but she'd heard often enough that in Ireland
champions had been bought out of pigsties, and caution was
nowhere in her mind. Dear Clement would certainly not buy her
a bad horse, and with Derek himself with her to advise . . . She
looked trustingly at the nondescript bay gelding produced for her
inspection and saw only her dreams, not the mud underfoot, not
the rotten wood round the stable doors, not the dry cracked leather
of the horse's tack.

She saw Magic being walked up and down the weedy stable
yard and she saw him being trotted round a bit on a lunging rein
in a small dock-grown paddock; and she didn't see the dismay that
Derek couldn't altogether keep out of his face.

'What do you think?' she said, her eyes still shining in spite of
all.

'Good strong shoulder,' he said judiciously. 'Needs a bit of
feeding to improve his condition, perhaps.'

'But do you like him?'

'He nodded decisively. 'Just the job.'

'I'll have him then.' She said it without the slightest hesitation,
and he stamped on the qualms which pricked like teeth.

She waited in the car while Derek bargained with Magic's owner,
watching the two men who stood together in the stable yard
shaking their heads, spreading their arms, shrugging, and starting
again. Finally, to her relief, they touched hands on it, and Derek

came to tell her that she could have the horse for fifteen thousand, if she liked.

'Think it over,' he said, making it sound as if she needn't.

She shook her head. 'I've decided. I really have. Shall I give the man a cheque?'

'No,' he said. 'Mr Scott has to get a vet's report, and fix up transport and insurance and so on. He'll do all the paperwork and settle for the horse, and you can pay him for everything at once. Much simpler.'

'Darling Clement,' she said warmly. 'Always so sweet and thoughtful.'

Darling Clement entered Magic for the Whitbread Gold Cup at Sandown Park, and also for what he called a 'warm-up' race three weeks before the big event.

'That will be at Stratford-upon-Avon,' he told Angela. 'In the Pragnell Cup, first week of April.'

'How marvellous,' Angela said.

She telephoned several times to Derek for long cosy consultations about Magic's prospects and drank in his heady optimism like the word of God. Derek filled her thoughts from dawn to dusk. Dear Derek, who was so brave and charming and kind.

Clement and Derek took Magic out onto the gallops at home and found the 'exciting bargain' unwilling to keep up with any other horse in the stable. Magic waved his tail about and kicked up heels and gave every sign of extreme bad temper. Both Clement and Derek, however, reported to a delighted Angela that Magic was a perfect gentleman and going well.

When Angela turned up by arrangement at ten one morning to watch Magic work, he had been sent out by mistake with the first lot at seven, and was consequently resting. Her disappointment was mild, though, because Derek was there, not riding but accompanying her on foot, full of smiles and gaiety and friendship. She loved it. She trusted him absolutely, and she showed it.

'Well done, lad,' Clement said gratefully, as she drove away later. 'With you around our Angela wouldn't notice an earthquake.'

Derek, watching her go, felt remorse and regret. It was hardly fair, he thought. She was a nice old duck really. She'd done no one any harm. He belatedly began not to like himself.

They went to Stratford races all hoping for different things: Derek that Magic would at least get round, Angela that her horse would win, and Clement that he wouldn't stop dead in the first furlong.

Three miles. Fast track. Firm ground. Eighteen fences.

Angela's heart was beating with a throb she could feel as Magic, to the relief of both of the men, deigned to set off in the normal way from the start, and consented thereafter to gallop along steadily among the rear half of the field. After nearly two miles of this mediocrity both men relaxed and knew that when Magic ran out of puff and pulled up, as he was bound to do soon, they could explain to Angela that 'he had needed the race,' and 'he'll be tuned up nicely for the Whitbread'; and she would believe it.

A mile from home, from unconscious habit, Derek gave Magic the speeding-up signs of squeezing with his legs and clicking his tongue and flicking the reins. Magic unexpectedly plunged towards the next fence, misjudged his distance, took off too soon, hit the birch hard and landed in a heap on the ground.

The horse got to his feet and nonchalantly cantered away. The jockey lay still and flat.

'Derek,' cried Angela, agonised.

'Bloody fool,' Clement said furiously, bustling down from the stands, 'Got him unbalanced. What does he expect?'

Angela at first stayed where she was, in a turmoil of anxiety, watching through her binoculars as the motionless Derek was loaded slowly onto a stretcher and carried carefully to an ambulance; and then she walked jerkily round to the first aid room to await his return.

I should never have bought the horse, she thought in anguish. If I hadn't bought the horse, Derek wouldn't be . . . wouldn't be . . .

He was alive. She saw his hands move as soon as the blue-uniformed men opened the ambulance doors. Her relief was almost as shattering as her fear. She felt faint.

Derek Roberts had broken his leg and was in no mood to worry about Angela's feelings. He noticed she was there because she made little fluttery efforts to reach his side – efforts constantly thwarted by the stretcher-bearers easing him out – saying to him over and over, 'Derek, oh Derek, are you all right?'

Derek didn't answer. His attention was on his leg, which hurt, and on getting into the ambulance room without being bumped. There was always a ghoulish crowd round the door, pressing forward to look. He stared up at the faces peering down and hated their probing interest. It was a relief to him, as always on these occasions, when they carried him through the door and shut out the ranks of eyes.

Inside, waiting for the doctor and lying quietly on a bed, he reflected gloomily that his present spot of trouble served him right.

Angela, outside, wandered aimlessly about, not seeing anyone she knew and wondering whether to go for a drink on her own. Dear Clement, who would have sustained her, had been last seen hurrying down the course to help catch the riderless horse. She thought that she ought to worry about the horse, but she couldn't; she had room in her mind only for Derek.

'Never mind, missus,' a voice said cheerfully. 'Yon Magic is all right. Cantering round the middle there and giving them the devil's own job of catching him. Don't you fret none. He's all right.'

Startled, she looked at the sturdy man with the broad Yorkshire accent who stood confidently in her way.

'Came from my brother, did that horse,' he said, 'I'm down here special like, to see him run.'

'Oh,' said Angela vaguely.

'Is the lad all right? The one who rode him?'

'I think he's broken his leg.'

'Dear, oh dear. Bit of hard luck, that. He drove a hard bargain with my brother, did that lad.'

'Did he?'

'Aye. My brother said Magic was a flier but your lad, he wouldn't have it. Said the horse hadn't any form to speak of, and looked proper useless to him. My brother was asking seven thousand for it, but your lad beat him down to five. I came here, see, to learn which was right.' He beamed with goodwill. 'Tell you the truth, the horse didn't run up to much, did it? Reckon your lad was right. But don't you fret, missus, there'll be another day.'

He gave her a nod and a final beam, and moved away. Angela felt breathless, as if he had punched her.

Already near the exit gate, she turned blindly and walked out through it, her legs taking her automatically towards her car. Shaking, she sat in the driving seat, and with a feeling of unreality drove all the one hundred miles home.

The man must have got it wrong, she thought. Not seven and five thousand, but seventeen and fifteen. When she reached her house she looked up the address of Magic's previous owner, and telephoned.

'Aye,' he said. 'Five thousand, that's right.' The broad Yorkshire voice floated cheerfully across the counties. 'Charged you a bit more, did they?' He chuckled. 'Couple of hundred, maybe? You can't grudge them that missus. Got to have their commission, like. It's the way of the world.'

She put down the receiver, and sat on her lonely sofa, and stared into space. She understood for the first time that what she had felt for Derek was love. She understood that Clement and Derek must have seen it in her weeks ago, and because of it had exploited and manipulated her in a way that was almost as callous as rape.

All the affection she had poured out towards them . . . all the joy and fond thoughts and happiness . . . they had taken them and used them and hadn't cared for her a bit. They don't like me, she thought. Derek doesn't even like me.

The pain of his rejection filled her with a depth of misery she had never felt before. How could she, she wondered wretchedly, have been so stupid, so blind, so pathetically immature?

She walked after a while through the big house, which was so quiet now that Edward wasn't there to fuss, and went into the kitchen. She started to make herself a cup of tea: and wept.

Within a week she visited Derek in hospital. He lay halfway down a long ward with his leg in traction, and for an instant he looked like a stranger; a thin young man with his head back on the pillows and his eyes closed. A strong young man no longer, she thought. More like a sick child.

That too was an illusion. He heard her arrive at his bedside and opened his eyes, and because he was totally unprepared to find her there she saw quite clearly the embarrassment which flooded through him. He swallowed, and bit his lip; and then he smiled. It was the same smile as before, the outward face of treason. Angela felt slightly sick.

She drew up a chair and sat by his bed.

'Derek,' she said. 'I've come to congratulate you.'

He was bewildered. 'What for?'

'On your capital gain. The difference between five thousand pounds and fifteen.'

His smile vanished. He looked away from her. At anything but her. He felt trapped and angry and ashamed, and he wished above all things that she would go away.

'How much of it,' Angela said slowly, 'Was your share? And how much was Clement's?'

After a stretching silence of more than a minute, he said, 'Half and half.'

'Thank you,' Angela said. She got to her feet, pushing back the chair. 'That's all, then. I just wanted to hear you admit it.' And to find out for sure, she thought, that she was cured. That the fever no longer ran in her blood. That she could look at him and not care: and she could.

He still couldn't look at her, however. 'All?' he said.

She nodded. 'What you did wasn't illegal, just . . . horrid. I should have been more businesslike.' She took a step away. 'Goodbye, Derek.'

She had gone several more steps before he called after her, suddenly, 'Angela . . . Mrs Hart.'

She paused and came halfway back.

'Please,' he said. 'Please listen. Just for one moment.'

Angela returned slowly to his bedside.

'I don't suppose you'll believe me,' he said, 'But I've been lying here thinking about that race at Stratford . . . and I've a feeling that Magic may not be so useless after all.'

'No,' Angela said. 'No more lies. I've had enough.'

'I'm not . . . this isn't a lie. Not this.'

She shook her head.

'Listen,' he said. 'Magic made no show at Stratford because nobody asked him to, except right at the end, when I shook him up. And then he fell because I'd done it so close to the fence . . . and because when I gave him the signal he just shot forward as if he'd been galvanised.'

Angela listened, disbelieving.

'Some horses,' he said, 'won't gallop at home. Magic won't. So we thought . . . I thought . . . that he couldn't race either. And I'm not so sure, now. I'm not so sure.'

Angela shrugged. 'It doesn't change anything. But anyway, I'll find out when he runs in the Whitbread.'

'No.' He squirmed. 'We never meant to run him in the Whitbread.'

'But he's entered,' she said.

'Yes, but . . . well, Mr Scott will tell you, a day or two before the race, that Magic has a temperature, or has bruised his foot, or something, and can't run. He . . . we . . . planned it. We reckoned you wouldn't quibble about the price if you thought Magic was Whitbread class . . . that's all.'

Angela let out an 'Oh' like a deep sigh. She looked down at the young man who was pleating his sheets aimlessly in his fingers and not meeting her eyes. She saw shame and the tiredness and the echo of pain from his leg, and she thought that what she had felt for him had been as destructive to him as to herself.

At home, after thinking it over, Angela telephoned to Clement.

'Dear Clement, how is Magic?'

'None the worse, Angela, I'm glad to say.'

'How splendid,' she said warmly. 'And now there's the Whitbread to look forward to, isn't there?'

'Yes, indeed.' He chuckled. 'Better buy a new hat, my dear.'

'Clement,' Angela said sweetly, 'I am counting on you to keep Magic fit and well-fed and uninjured in every way. I'm counting on his turning up to start in the Whitbread, and on his showing us just exactly how bad he is.'

'*What?*'

'Because if he doesn't Clement dear, I might just find myself chattering to one or two people . . . you know, pressmen and even the taxman, and people like that . . . about you buying Magic for five thousand pounds one day and selling him to me for fifteen thousand the next.'

She listened to the silence travelling thunderously down the wire, and she smiled with healthy mischief. 'And Clement, dear, we'll both give his new jockey instructions to win if he can, won't we? Because it's got to be a fair test, don't you think? And just to encourage you, I'll promise you that if I'm satisfied that Magic has done his very best, win or lose, I won't mention to anyone what I paid for him. And that's a bargain, Clement dear, that you can trust.'

He put the receiver down with a crash and swore aloud. 'Bloody old bag. She must have checked up.' He telephoned to Yorkshire and found out that indeed she had. Damn and blast her, he thought. He was going to look a proper fool in the eyes of the racing world, running rubbish like Magic in one of the top races. It would do his reputation no damn good at all.

Clement Scott felt not the slightest twinge of guilt. He had, after all, cheated a whole succession of foolish ladies in the same way, though not perhaps to the same extent. If Angela talked – and she could talk for hours when she liked – he would find that the gullible widowed darlings were all suddenly suspicious and buying their horses from someone else.

Magic, he saw furiously, would have to be trained as thoroughly as possible, and ridden by the best jockey free.

On Whitbread morning, Angela persuaded a friend of hers to promise to back Magic for her: a hundred pounds each way on the Tote, just in case. 'Anything can happen in a handicap,' she said. 'All the good horses might fall – you never know.'

In the parade ring at Sandown Park Angela was entirely her old self, kind and gushing and bright-eyed.

She spoke to her new jockey, who was unlike Derek Roberts to a comfortable degree. 'I expect you've talked it over with darling Clement,' she said gaily. 'But I think it would be best, don't you, if you keep Magic just sort of back a bit among all the other runners for most of the way, and then about a mile from the winning post tell him it's time to start winning, if you see what I mean, and of course after that it's up to both of you to do what you can.'

The jockey glanced at the stony face of Clement Scott.

'Do what the lady wants,' Clement said.

The jockey, who knew his business, carried out the instructions to the letter. A mile from home he dug Magic sharply in the ribs and was astonished at the response. Magic, young, lightly-raced and carrying bottom weight, surged past several older, tireder contenders, and came towards the last fence lying fifth.

Clement could hardly believe his eyes. Angela could hardly breathe. Magic floated over the last fence and charged up the straight and finished third.

'There,' Angela said. 'Isn't that lovely?'

Since almost no one else had backed her horse, Angela collected a fortune in place money from the Tote; and a few days later, for exactly what she'd paid, she sold Magic to a scrap-metal merchant from Kent. He had offered her more, and couldn't understand why she wouldn't take it.

Angela sent Derek Roberts a get-well card. A week later she

sent him an impersonal case of champagne and a simple message, 'Thanks.'

I've learned a lot, she thought, because of him. A lot about greed and gullibility, about façades and consequences and the transience of love. And about racing . . . too much.

She sold Billyboy and Hamlet, and took up pottery instead.

MY FIRST WINNER

John Welcome

THE story I am about to relate happened in the far-off days of the nineteen-thirties when I was a member of the Oxford University Air Squadron. The aircraft in which we young men disported ourselves across the skies of southern England were called Avro Tutors. The Tutor was constructed of canvas stretched across metal ribs, had two open cockpits, a radial Armstrong-Siddeley air-cooled engine and a cruising speed of ninety m.p.h. It was a biplane with an exciting mass of rigging between the wings through which the winds sometimes sang, a fixed under-carriage, and slots in the leading edges of its upper wings to lower the stalling speed. It was also said to be indestructible, and that it was almost impossible to kill yourself flying one.

It had need of both of these qualities when it was in the hands of the young gentlemen from the dreaming spires. I can, myself, bear witness to the truth of its reputation. One sunny morning at Eastchurch, where we held our summer camp, I was coming in to land for the mid-morning break. The sky at that time was always, in the words of a Canadian member of the squadron, 'lousy with aircraft'. As I approached the fence, another cheerful aviator flew so close across my bows that I could have thrown a biscuit into his empty forward cockpit.

Instinctively and very foolishly I yanked back the stick. The nose came up, and the slots fell forward. The Tutor then gave that peculiar yawing motion which in any other aircraft betokened a stall, an instant spin and subsequent severe contact with the earth. Desperately I slammed the stick forward. As a result I flew straight into the ground. The wheels hit the earth with a resounding bang and I went up again. To stop stalling once more I pushed on the stick and the whole performance was repeated. We covered the length of the grass airfield at Eastchurch in what are called in Irish horsey circles 'standing leps'. At last, on the fourth bounce, I regained sufficient of my scattered senses to push the throttle forward. The engine fired and caught and I went round again. When I came in there was a reception committee of the top brass of the squadron and station waiting for me.

I prefer to gloss over the next few minutes. But an examination of the oleo legs of the aircraft found them to have suffered no damage. They must have been built like the Forth Bridge. No wonder we could not go fast.

All this, you may say, has little to do with riding winners but in my particular case it had, as I shall show. Because you were strapped into a Tutor, you could not fall out of it, unless you were to lose speed on the upward arc of a loop and hang on the top. Then you could have a fairly good try at falling out, and it was necessary to hope that your straps were secure.

Had it been possible I am sure that I would have fallen off, or out of, an aircraft. For, although I had lived with horses all my life, I seemed to be constitutionally incapable of sitting on one over a fence. This happens to a few unlucky people and I was one of them. In Ireland where I was born and brought up, it did not matter so much. You have an instant's grace on the top of a bank while the horse is changing legs. In that instant you can grab at something, the mane, the neckstrap, or even the front of the saddle. In England you go much faster, there is no moment's pause, and so the horse and I parted company.

My best friend at the University was a man called Brian Manson. His father was dead, and he had been left with more money than was good for him. In retrospect, undergraduates of those days appear to have been divided into two classes, those who had too much money, and those who had enough to buy drink but not enough to buy food. I belonged to the latter class and I sometimes wonder if my constitution has ever really recovered.

Brian kept a couple of hunters and a chaser or two with a man called Kerrell out Headington way. Kerrell ran a racing stable cum riding school cum livery establishment. The Warren Farm was its name and it was there that Brian spent most of his time instead of at his books. Not that his books would have made much difference to him, had he attended to them, for he was a member of what we called The Dung Club. In other words he read Agriculture, a school whose members did not expect to have to devote themselves to earning a living in later life.

Kerrell was a tall gaunt man with a long face and a look in his eyes in which roguery and humour were mixed. The years and a bad fall had stopped his riding career, so Brian used to ride his horses for him in amateur and sometimes professional races. They were as thick as thieves (and the analogy is not all that inapt) in getting the horses ready together, trying them, arguing and wrangling about placing them, and what to do with them when they ran. Frequently those arguments led to side bets between themselves and they kept some sort of running account in which Brian's livery and training fees, Kerrell's bets, their own side bets, entries, stakes and travelling expenses were all inextricably mixed. During the time I knew them, I do not believe one ever settled with the other.

Undergraduates who had too much money in those days ran sports cars. Brian's choice was an Aston Martin. This was not the gilded carriage of today, but a chunky, spartan vehicle with bicycle type mudguards and a snarl in its throat. Sometimes I was permitted to accompany Brian racing and, huddled in the tiny back seat, I would endure the rigours of winter wind and rain, for the spartan nature of his car extended to its lack of weather-proofing. Thus the three of us would storm along the all but empty roads, Brian hunched over the wheel and Kerrell's great nose jutting out over the vestigial windscreen like the prow of a pirate ship. Once on the racecourse I would be sent off on mysterious errands clutching bundles of pound notes which I invested, according to instructions, with the ready money bookmakers in Tatts.

One February afternoon, having finished flying at Abingdon, I returned to my rooms to find Brian in an armchair in front of the fire reading *Horse and Hound*.

'Well, Baron von Richthofen,' he said; 'How many did you shoot down today?'

'Ten before breakfast,' I answered, putting my flying helmet with the headphones attached (we rather fancied ourselves walking about with them) onto a chair and taking off my coat.

'Rather below average, Baron. Something wrong with the Spandaus?'

'I'm afraid so. Not spitting correctly.' (There was just then a fashion for flying magazines containing highly-coloured stories of the First World War, and a favourite cliché of their contributors was to describe the machine-guns of German aircraft as 'spitting Spandaus'.)

'I've been looking at *Horse and Hound*,' he said. 'There's an Air Squadron race at the Bullingdon Grind. You should go in for that. You could just about win it.'

'Nonsense. I'd be jumped off at the first fence.'

'Not this time, you won't. Kerrell's just bought a horse that could have been made for you. Even you won't be able to fall off him.'

'I could fall off a gym horse standing still.'

'Not this one. Anyway, come out tomorrow and try him. It can't do you any harm.'

'I still won't ride him in that race.'

'It isn't a race. The man who won it last year had only been riding for three weeks. No one else got round. He was jumped off twice and remounted.'

Of course I went. The horse was a big gentle chestnut called Friar Tuck. He looked like a high-class Leicestershire hunter but in those days you could still ride that type in point-to-points.

Kerrell had a series of schooling fences and I went over them at half-speed, in company with Brian. I only fell off once but, as I pointed out when we came in, once, in a race, is enough.

'Not in this sort of a race,' Brian said. 'What did I tell you about last year's winner?'

'You'll be all right, sir,' Kerrell said. 'Besides, the faster they go, the easier it is to sit on.'

Now it cannot be denied that somewhere inside me was the desire to ride in a race and, even more, to win one. I was getting tired of being a standing joke where horses and aeroplanes were concerned, and I knew that if ever I was to win a race, this presented the best possible chance. Here I had better explain that the conditions of those undergraduate races were so framed that you could enter and ride a horse you had hired from a livery stable provided you paid the entry money and insurance yourself.

'We'll do a fast school over the course tomorrow,' Kerrell said.

'The course' was a series of birch fences Kerrell had built into the existing fences round his farm. You made a circuit of, I suppose, a mile to a mile-and-a-half and jumped six fences in doing it.

The following morning saw us preparing to go out over these fences. Kerrell decided to come along too. He sat up on a big black horse on which Brian had won two 'chases; Brian was on some hot thing of his own that they were getting ready.

'Now, remember,' Kerrell counselled me. 'Don't hang on to his head going into the fences, or you'll get pulled off. You've lost your confidence. This fellow knows it all. Let him have his head and hold on by the neck-strap.'

'What are you two coffee-housing about?' Brian said sourly. 'Come on. I'm off.'

We seemed to go into the first fence very fast indeed. I remembered what I'd been told. The fence disappeared beneath me and I was still there. In fact I survived two circuits despite a bump and a curse from Brian towards the end.

'There now,' Kerrell said. 'You're all right now. You're home and dried.'

I thought Brian looked pensive, but as I was so jubilant, I put it down to his preoccupation over his own mount.

Two days later he said to me in his offhand way, 'Now you're sitting on like Billy Stott, you'd better get some experience riding upsides with a few others, just like a race. I've arranged to go round the course tomorrow. Tim Maitland and Mike Rashley will come along.'

Tim and Mike were horsey acquaintances of ours. Mike was a gay spark from the Pytchley. He had a couple of useful horses and often crossed swords with Brian. He was nothing like as good a rider as Brian but he had, I think, rather more money and resources. They were on good enough terms off the racecourse. On it they were at daggers drawn.

The school seemed a good idea until we got to the Warren Farm. There Brian flatly announced he was not going to allow Friar Tuck to risk getting hurt so soon before the race, and that we were to draw lots for our rides. He held the straws. I drew the hot thing he had been riding in the earlier school. Kerrell had gone off somewhere to look for oats.

'This is bloody silly,' I said.

'Nonsense. Now you've got your confidence you want a bit of experience on other horses.'

The hot thing kicked and sidled and played up as we went down to the start. It jumped the first fence so fast that I did not have time to fall off. At the second it went straight into the air and turned itself into a fair imitation of a corkscrew. I went sailing away. The ground came up to meet me with an almighty bang.

I got up slowly and observed the riderless horse pursuing the others. There was nothing to do but walk back to the yard. At the gate I met Kerrell who, it seemed, had returned sooner than expected. He was watching the finish of the school. 'Been down, sir? You're all right, sir?' he said with a heavy scowl.

They came back in, Brian leading the riderless horse which he had caught. Kerrell produced a bottle of whisky. The scowl had disappeared and had been replaced by the expression he wore when he was thinking furiously. Brian had a glint in his eye and seemed to be savouring some secret joke. Before we left I thought I heard them having words.

The following Saturday I drove to the course with Brian. I knew Mike Rashley had a horse in our race but Brian said he thought he was going in an earlier one. There were four other runners. Two of them I did not know at all. They were in different flights of the Squadron from mine. One was riding a horse of his own, the other something hired from a livery stable which, Brian assured me, could not gallop enough to warm itself. The others were a conceited chap who flew very well indeed but who had only recently taken to point-to-pointing, and a man in The House I knew slightly who assured me he was only having a bump around. Friar Tuck was fit enough and he could jump. If I could only stay on top I must have a chance, or so I told myself.

The college kitchen had put up a lavish lunch in a hamper for Brian – he was not himself riding at the meeting – and he pressed me to salmon mousse, tinned asparagus, cold pheasant, chicken, white wine, port and brandy. I nibbled a biscuit, and surreptitiously poured away behind the car the beakers of port and brandy which he handed to me. So many times did he ask me how I was feeling that I snapped at him. He looked into the middle distance and grinned.

Kerrell was bringing the horses over. Tim Maitland was riding one of his in another race. Somehow the time dragged by. I changed and passed through the scales as in a dream. My shaking fingers could not tie my cap properly and I had to get Brian to do it for me. Then I was standing in the ring with Brian beside me. Kerrell seemed to have disappeared. I wondered why everything had taken on a strange ethereal dimension as if there was a haze suspended between me and reality.

Then something happened to jerk me out of my trance. A smiling undergraduate walked past wearing a racing jersey and white breeches. He wished me luck. 'That's Mike,' I said. 'I thought he was going before.'

'He's changed his mind,' Brian said shortly. 'Says this is an easier one to win.'

A faint suspicion as to what might be going on crossed my mind for the first time. 'When did he tell you that?' I said.

'Oh, a little while ago.'

'You and Mike have got very confiding all of a sudden, haven't you?'

Somebody shouted, 'Riders, get up, please.' In the bustle and flurry I did not hear his answer, if he made one.

It would be idle to pretend that after a lapse of over thirty years I remember every detail of that race. I do, however, recall the first fence very vividly. It was approached down a fair slope and there was a small stream in front of it. Friar Tuck had become a bit excited and the thud of hooves round him as we went down to that fence set him going. He caught hold of his bit and went on. True to my instructions I slipped my reins and gripped the neck-strap. It was as well that I did. Friar Tuck, feeling his head free, shortened his stride, popped and jumped off his hocks with a fiendish upward thrust. I went straight into the air. But my hands on the neck-strap kept me, if not in contact, at least within reasonable flying distance of my mount. I came down into the saddle with a bang, having been airborne alone for what seemed like several long seconds. We were over in more or less one piece, and I had the satisfaction of seeing the conceited chap describing a graceful parabola beside me as a result of being well and truly jumped off.

Somehow we survived the next few fences and then approached the one where I felt sure I was bound to go. It was a small fence with a stiffish drop on landing from which the ground sloped sharply away. Friar Tuck was galloping on strongly now and appeared to be enjoying himself even if his rider was not.

At this fence his whole shoulder and front simply disappeared underneath me and I became airborne once more, but even the neck-strap could not save me this time. As I hit the ground I thought, 'Well, there it goes. I've done it again. It's all over.' I also remember using some exceedingly bad language about myself.

Then, suddenly, out of nowhere a familiar voice was saying: 'Get up, sir. You're all right. Nothing wrong with you, sir.' Kerrell was standing over me. In some miraculous way he had caught Friar Tuck. His hand went under my leg and I was shot into the saddle again. 'Go on, sir. Go on!' he adjured me. 'They're all stone cold in front of you. You'll catch them easy. You've got it won. Leave him alone. Let him stride on!'

With these stirring words in my ears I went off in pursuit. I had lost my crash helmet and my whip but it did not matter. Friar Tuck entered into the spirit of the race. He put his head down and slogged along as hard as he could go. He was moving so easily and meeting each fence so exactly that even I could hardly fall off him. I began to enjoy myself.

As we passed the hill where the spectators were, only Mike and the chap who was having a bump around were in front of me. The second circuit was a sort of inner one with only three fences in it. At the first of these, the 'bump around' ended with an inglorious refusal. And then only Mike and I were left in the race.

Fired with the lust of battle and the chase, I began to close the gap. At the last fence we were all but level. It had to be jumped out of plough, and my antics in the saddle must have taken more out of Friar Tuck than three ordinary races. He hit the top of the fence and burst his way through it. I went up his neck. Friar Tuck did not fall but he all but came to a standstill on the other side.

Mike Rashley should have won the race by five lengths. But he was not really a very good or experienced race-rider. Instead of sitting down to ride, he kept looking over his shoulder to see where I was and what was happening.

I was on the flat now with no more of these infernal obstacles to surmount. I had, after all, ridden horses all my life. I pulled Friar Tuck together and gave him a kick. He snorted, got himself going – I was precious little help to him – and began to gallop. He was a game old brute. I've never forgotten him.

Mike, startled at this capless, whipless apparition bearing down on him, pulled out his own whip and began to use it. That completed his undoing. Rolling round in the saddle, flailing about with his whip he succeeded in stopping his horse instead of driving him on.

Friar Tuck came at him and caught him. I knew Mike was stopping. I threw everything I had, heart, head, legs and lungs, into those last three strides. We got up by a neck.

'Where did you come from, damn you?' Mike said as we rode in. 'Brian said you were bound to fall off.' Then, being Mike, he slapped me on the back. 'Well done, anyway, you old devil,' he said.

The reception by my best friend was scarcely so happy. He was standing waiting for us with a look of thunder on his face.

'You idiot,' he said. 'I had fifty quid with Kerrell you wouldn't finish. And I had a pony on Mike to win. Why didn't you fall off?'

'Oh, but he did, sir,' came from Kerrell who had suddenly materialised beside us. 'At the drop fence. I thought he might. I put him on again.'

For a second Brian was speechless, a state to which he was very seldom reduced. 'Fancy losing that on someone who couldn't ride a donkey on Margate sands,' he said, looking at me in fury. But that night he stood me dinner – and a magnum of champagne – in The George.

THE MAN WHO SHOT THE 'FAVOURITE'

Edgar Wallace

'THERE always will be a certain percentage of mysteries turnin' up, that simply won't untwist themselves, but the mystery that I'm thinkin' of particularly is the Wexford Brothers' Industrial Syndicate, which unravelled itself in a curious fashion,' said PC Lee.

If you don't happen to know the Wexford Brothers, I can tell you that you haven't missed much. It was a sort of religious sect, only more so, because these chaps didn't smoke, an' didn't drink, or eat meat, or enjoy themselves like ordinary human bein's, an' they belonged to the anti-gamblin', anti-Imperial, anti-life-worth-livin' folks.

The chief chap was Brother Samsin, a white-faced gentleman with black whiskers. He was a sort of class leader, an' it was through him that The Duke started his Wexford Brothers' Industrial Society.

The Duke wasn't a bad character, in spite of his name, which was given to him by the lads of Nottin' Dale. He was a bright, talkative, an' plausible young feller, who'd spent a lot of time in the Colonies, an' had come back to London broke to the world owin' to speculation.

'Why I know so much about him is that he used to lodge in my house. He was a gentleman with very nice manners, an' when Brother Samsin called on me one afternoon an' met The Duke, the Brother was so impressed with the respect an' reverence with which the Duke treated him that he asked him home to tea.

* * *

'To cut a long story short, this bright young man came to know all the brothers and sisters of the society an' became quite a favourite.

'I thought at first he had thoughts of joinin' the Brotherhood, but he soon corrected that.

' "No, Lee," ses he, "that would spoil the whole thing. At present I'm attracted to them because I'm worldly and wicked. If I became a brother, I'd be like one of them. At present they've no standard to measure me by, an' so I'm unique.'

'What interested the brothers most was the Duke's stories of his speculations in the Colonies, of how you can make a thousand pounds in the morning, lose two thousand in the evening, an' wake up next mornin' to find that you've still got a chance of makin' all you've lost an' a thousand besides.

'Well, anyway, he got the brothers interested, an' after a lot of palaver an' all sorts of secret meetin's, it was decided to start the Industrial Society, an' make the Duke chief organiser an' secretary.

'The idea was to subscribe a big sum of money, an' allow the Duke to use it to the best of his ability "on legitimate enterprises" – those were the words in the contract.

'The Duke took a little office over a barber's shop near the Nottin' Hill Gate Station, an' started work. Nothin' happened for a month. There were directors' meetin's an' money was voted, but in the second week of April, two months after the society was formed, the Duke said the society was now flourishin' an' declared a dividend of twenty per cent. What is more, the money was paid, an' you may be sure the brothers were delighted.

'A fortnight later, he declared another dividend of 30 per cent, an' the next week a dividend of 50 per cent, an' the brothers had a solemn meetin' an' raised his salary. Throughout that year hardly a week passed without a dividend bein' declared and paid.

'Accordin' to his agreement the Duke didn't have to state where the money came from. On the books of the society were two assets:

Gold mine . . . £1,000
Silver mine . . . £500

an' from one or the other the dividends came.

'All went well to the beginning of this year. You would think that the brothers, havin' got their capital back three times over, would be satisfied to sit down an' take their "divvies," but of all true sayin's in this world the truest is that "the more you get, the more you want".'

'From what I hear, the Duke paid no more dividends at all from the end of November to the end of February, an' only a beggarly ten per cent in March. So the directors had a meetin' an' passed a vote of censure on the secretary.

'He wasn't the kind of man to get worried over a little affair like that, but he was annoyed.

' "What these perishers don't understand," he ses to me, "is that the gold mine doesn't work in the winter."

' "Where is it?" I asked.

'He thought a bit. "In the Klondike," he ses, thoughtful.

' "An' where's the silver mine?"

' "In the never-never land," he ses, very glib.

'He got the brothers quiet again by the end of March, for he declared a dividend of twenty per cent, but somehow or other all those weeks of non-payment got their backs up, an' they wasn't so friendly with him as they used to be.

'Mr Samsin asked me to call round an' see him, an' I went.

'When I got to his house, I was shown into the parlour, an' to my surprise, I found about a dozen of the brothers all sittin' round a table very solemn an' stern.

' "We've asked you to come, Mr Lee," ses Samsin, "because bein' a constable, an' acquainted with law, an' moreover," he ses with a cough, "acquainted with our dear young friend who's actin' as secretary to our society, you may be able to give us advice."

' "You must know," he ses, mysteriously, "that for three months no dividends have been forthcomin' to our society."

'I nodded.

' "We have wondered why," he ses, "but have never suspected one whom we thought was above suspicion."

' "Meanin', the Duke?" I ses.

' "Meanin' Mr Tiptree," ses Brother Samsin. Tiptree was the Duke's private name.

' "We have made a discovery," ses Samsin, impressively, "an' when I say 'we' I mean our dear Brother Lawley."

'A very pale gent in spectacles nodded his head.

' "Brother Lawley," ses Samsin, "was addressin' a meetin' on

Lincoln racecourse – he bein' the vice-president of the Anti-Race-course League – an' whilst runnin' away from a number of mis-guided sinners, who pursued him with contumely – "

' "An' bricks," ses Brother Lawley.

' "An' bricks," Samsin went on, "he saw Tiptree!"

'He paused, and there was a hushed silence.

' "He was bettin'!" ses Brother Samsin.

' "Now," he adds, "I don't want to be uncharitable, but I've got an idea where our dividends have gone to."

' "Stolen," ses I.

' "Stolen an' betted," ses the brother, solemnly.

' "Well," ses I, "if you report the matter to me, an' you've got proof, an' you'll lay information, I'll take it to my superior, but if you ask me anythin' I'll tell you that you haven't much of a case. It's no offence to bet – "

' "It's an offence against our sacred principles," ses Brother Samsin.

The upshot of this conversation was – they asked me to watch the Duke an' report any suspicious movement, an' this I flatly refused to do.

'An' with that I left 'em. I don't know what they would have done, only suddenly the society began to pay dividends. Especially the Gold Mine, which paid a bigger dividend every week.

'So the brothers decided to overlook the Duke's disgraceful con-duct, especially in view of the fact that Brother Lawley was prepa-rin' for one of the most terrible attacks on horse-racin' that had ever been known.

'I got to hear about it afterwards. Brother Lawley was all for bein' a martyr to the cause. He said he wanted to draw attention to the horrible gamblin' habits of the nation, but there were lots of people who said that the main idea was to call attention to Brother Lawley.

'Be that as it may, he thought out a great plan, an' he put it into execution on the day before Derby Day.

'A number of our fellows were drafted down for the races and I went with them.

'On the Monday as I went down on the Tuesday, I saw the Duke. He still lodged in my house, although he was fairly prosper-ous, an' happenin' to want to borrow the evenin' paper to see what young Harry Bigge got for a larceny I was interested in, I went to his room.

'He was sittin' in front of a table, an' was polishin' up the lenses of a pair of race-glasses, an' I stopped dead when I remembered my conversation with the brothers.

' "Hullo!" I ses, "you an' me are apparently goin' to the same place."

' "Epsom? Yes," ses he, coolly. "An' if you take my tip you'll back Belle of Maida Vale in the second race."

' "I never bet," I ses, "an' I take no interest in horse-racing' an', moreover," I ses, "she can't give Bountiful Boy seven pounds over a mile an' a quarter."

'When I got downstairs I went over her "form". She was a consistent winner. The year before she'd won eight races at nice prices, an' I decided to overcome my aversion to bettin' an' back her, although I'd made up my mind to have my week's salary on Bountiful Boy.

'There was the usual Tuesday crowd at Epsom, an' I got a glimpse of Brother Lawley holdin' his little meetin'. He was on his own. It wasn't like the racecourse Mission, that does its work without offence, but Lawley's mission was all brimstone an' heat.

'We cleared the course for the first race, an' after it was over I casually mentioned to Big Joe France, the Bookmaker, that if Belle of Maida Vale was 20 to 1 I'd back her.

' "I'm very sorry, Mr Lee," he ses, "but you'll have to take a shorter price – I'll lay you sixes."

'I took the odds to 30s and laid half of it off with Issy Jacobs a few minutes later at threes.

'The course was cleared again for the second race, an' it was whilst the horses were at the post that I saw Brother Lawley leanin' over the rails near the winnin' post. He looked very white an' excited, but I didn't take much notice of him, because that was his natural condition.

'In the rings the bookies were shoutin' "Even money on Belle of Maida Vale," an' it looked as if somebody was havin' a rare gamble on her.

'The bell rang, an' there was a yell. "They're off!" '

'I was on the course, near the judge's box, an' could see nothin' of the race till the field came round Tattenham Corner with one horse leadin' – and that one the Belle.

'Well out by herself she was, an' there she kept right along the straight to the distance. There was no chance of the others catchin' her, an' they were easin' up when suddenly from the rails came a report like the snap of a whip, an' the Belle staggered, swerved, an' went down all of a heap.

'For a moment there was a dead silence, an' then such a yell as I've never heard before.

'They would have lynched Brother Lawley, with his smokin' pistol in his hand, but the police were round him in a minute.

' "I've done it!" he yelled. "I've drawn attention to the curse – "

' "Shut up!" I said, "an' come along before the people get you."

'Next day there was a special meetin' of the Wexford Brothers' Industrial Society, an' the Duke attended by request.

'Brother Samsin was in the chair.

' "We are gathered," he ses, "to consider what can be done for the defence of our sainted Brother Lawley, who's in the hands of the myrmidons of the law. I propose that we vote a sum out of the society – "

' "Hold hard," ses the Duke, roughly, "you can't vote any money – because there ain't any."

' "Explain yourself," ses Brother Samsin. "What of the gold mine?"

' "The gold mine," ses the Duke sadly, "was a horse called Belle of Maida Vale, that I bought out of the society's funds – she's dead."

' "An' the silver mine?" faltered Samsin.

' "That was the Belle of Maida Vale, too," ses the Duke. "A good filly, she was. She won regularly every month at a nice price – but she won't win any more dividends." '

PICK THE WINNER

Damon Runyon

WHAT am I doing in Miami associating with such a character as Hot Horse Herbie is really quite a long story, and it goes back to one cold night when I am sitting in Mindy's restaurant on Broadway thinking what a cruel world it is, to be sure, when in comes Hot Horse Herbie and his ever-loving fiancée, Miss Cutie Singleton.

This Hot Horse Herbie is a tall, skinny guy with a most depressing kisser, and he is called Hot Horse Herbie because he can always tell you about a horse that is so hot it is practically on fire, a hot horse being a horse that is all readied up to win a race, although sometimes Herbie's hot horses turn out to be so cold they freeze everybody within fifty miles of them.

He is following the races almost since infancy, to hear him tell it. In fact, old Captain Duhaine, who has charge of the Pinkertons around the race tracks, says he remembers Hot Horse Herbie as a little child, and that even then Herbie is a hustler, but of course Captain Duhaine does not care for Hot Horse Herbie, because he claims Herbie is nothing but a tout, and a tout is something that is most repulsive to Captain Duhaine and all other Pinkertons.

A tout is a guy who goes around a race track giving out tips on the races, if he can find anybody who will listen to his tips, especially suckers, and a tout is nearly always broke. If he is not broke, he is by no means a tout, but a handicapper, and is respected by one and all, including the Pinkertons, for knowing so much about the races.

Well, personally, I have nothing much against Hot Horse Herbie, no matter what Captain Duhaine says he is, and I certainly have nothing against Herbie's ever-loving fiancée, Miss Cutie Singleton. In fact, I am rather in favour of Miss Cutie Singleton, because in all the years I know her, I wish to say I never catch Miss Cutie Singleton out of line, which is more than I can say of many other dolls I know.

She is a little, good-natured blonde doll, and by no means a crow, if you care for blondes, and some people say that Miss Cutie Singleton is pretty smart, although I never can see how this can be, as I figure a smart doll will never have any truck with a guy like Hot Horse Herbie, for Herbie is by no means a provider.

But for going on ten years, Miss Cutie Singleton and Hot Horse Herbie are engaged, and it is well known to one and all that they are to be married as soon as Herbie makes a scratch. In fact, they are almost married in New Orleans in 1928, when Hot Horse Herbie beats a good thing for eleven C's, but the tough part of it is the good thing is in the first race, and naturally Herbie bets the eleven C's right back on another good thing in the next race, and this good thing blows, so Herbie winds up with nothing but the morning line and is unable to marry Miss Cutie Singleton at this time.

Then again in 1929 at Churchill Downs, Hot Horse Herbie has a nice bet on Naishapur to win the Kentucky Derby, and he is so sure Naishapur cannot miss that the morning of the race he sends Miss Cutie Singleton out to pick a wedding ring. But Naishapur finishes second, so naturally Hot Horse Herbie is unable to buy the ring, and of course Miss Cutie Singleton does not wish to be married without a wedding ring.

They have another close call in 1931 at Baltimore when Hot Horse Herbie figures Twenty Grand a standout in the Preakness, and in fact is so sure of his figures that he has Miss Cutie Singleton go down to the city hall to find out what a marriage licence costs. But of course Twenty Grand does not win the Preakness, so the information Miss Cutie Singleton obtains is of no use to them, and anyway Hot Horse Herbie says he can beat the price on marriage licences in New York.

However, there is no doubt but what Hot Horse Herbie and Miss Cutie Singleton are greatly in love, although I hear rumours that for a couple of years past Miss Cutie Singleton is getting somewhat impatient about Hot Horse Herbie not making a scratch as soon as he claims he is going to when he first meets up with her in Hot Springs in 1923.

In fact, Miss Cutie Singleton says if she knows Hot Horse Herbie is going to be so long delayed in making his scratch she will never consider becoming engaged to him, but will keep her job as a manicurist at the Arlington Hotel, where she is not doing bad, at that.

It seems that the past couple of years Miss Cutie Singleton is taking to looking longingly at the little houses in the towns they pass through going from one race track to another, and especially at little white houses with green shutters and yards and vines all around and about, and saying it must be nice to be able to live in such places instead of in a suitcase.

But of course Hot Horse Herbie does not put in with her on these ideas, because Herbie knows very well if he is placed in a little white house for more than fifteen minutes the chances are he will lose his mind, even if the house has green shutters.

Personally, I consider Miss Cutie Singleton somewhat ungrateful for thinking of such matters after all the scenery Hot Horse Herbie lets her see in the past ten years. In fact, Herbie lets her see practically all the scenery there is in this country, and some in Canada, and all she has to do in return for all this courtesy is to occasionally get out a little crystal ball and deck of cards and let on she is a fortune teller when things are going especially tough for Herbie.

Of course Miss Cutie Singleton cannot really tell fortunes, or she will be telling Hot Horse Herbie's fortune, and maybe her own, too, but I hear she is better than a raw hand at making people believe she is telling their fortunes, especially old maids who think they are in love, or widows who are looking to snare another husband and other such characters.

Well, anyway, when Hot Horse Herbie and his ever-loving fiancée come into Mindy's, he gives me a large hello, and so does Miss Cutie Singleton, so I hello them right back, and Hot Horse Herbie speaks to me as follows:

'Well,' Herbie says, 'we have some wonderful news for you. We are going to Miami,' he says, 'and soon we will be among the waving palms, and revelling in the warm waters of the Gulf Stream.'

Now of course this is a lie, because while Hot Horse Herbie is in Miami many times, he never revels in the warm waters of the Gulf Stream, because he never has time for such a thing, what with hustling around the race tracks in the daytime, and around the dog tracks and the gambling joints at night, and in fact I will lay plenty of six to five Hot Horse Herbie cannot even point in the direction of the Gulf Stream when he is in Miami, and I will give him three points, at that.

But naturally what he says gets me to thinking how pleasant it is in Miami in the winter, especially when it is snowing up north, and a guy does not have a flogger to keep himself warm, and I am commencing to feel very envious of Hot Horse Herbie and his ever-loving fiancée when he says like this:

'But,' Herbie says, 'our wonderful news for you is not about us going. It is about you going,' he says. 'We already have our railroad tickets,' he says, 'as Miss Cutie Singleton, my ever-loving fiancée here, saves up three C's for her hope chest the past summer, but when it comes to deciding between a hope chest and Miami, naturally she chooses Miami, because,' Herbie says, 'she claims she does not have enough hope left to fill a chest. Miss Cutie Singleton is always kidding,' he says.

'Well, now,' Herbie goes on, 'I just run into Mr Edward Donlin, the undertaker, and it seems that he is sending a citizen of Miami back home tomorrow night, and of course you know,' he says, 'that Mr Donlin must purchase two railroad tickets for this journey, and as the citizen has no one else to accompany him, I got to thinking of you. He is a very old and respected citizen of Miami,' Herbie says, 'although of course,' he says, 'he is no longer with us, except maybe in spirit.'

Of course such an idea is most obnoxious to me, and I am very indignant that Hot Horse Herbie can even think I will travel in this manner, but he gets to telling me that the old and respected citizen of Miami that Mr Donlin is sending back home is a great old guy in his day, and that for all anybody knows he will appreciate having company on the trip, and about this time Big Nig, the crap shooter, comes into Mindy's leaving the door open behind him so that a blast of cold air hits me, and makes me think more than somewhat of the waving palms and the warm waters of the Gulf Stream.

So the next thing I know, there I am in Miami with Hot Horse Herbie, and it is the winter of 1931, and everybody now knows that this is the winter when the suffering among the horse players in Miami is practically horrible. In fact, it is worse than it is in the winter of 1930. In fact, the suffering is so intense that many citizens are wondering if it will do any good to appeal to Congress for relief for the horse players, but The Dancer says he hears Congress needs a little relief itself.

Hot Horse Herbie and his ever-loving fiancée, Miss Cutie Single-ton, and me have rooms in a little hotel on Flagler Street, and while it is nothing but a fleabag, and we are doing the landlord a favour by living there, it is surprising how much fuss he makes any time anybody happens to be a little short of the rent. In fact, the landlord hollers and yells so much any time anybody is a little short of the rent that he becomes a very great nuisance to me, and I have half a notion to move, only I cannot think of any place to move to. Furthermore, the landlord will not let me move unless I pay him all I owe him, and I am not in a position to take care of this matter at the moment.

Of course I am not very dirty when I first come in as far as having any potatoes is concerned, and I start off at once having a little bad luck. It goes this way a while, and then it gets worse, and sometimes I wonder if I will not be better off if I buy myself a rope and end it all on a palm tree in the park on Biscayne Boulevard. But the only trouble with the idea is I do not have the price of a rope, and anyway I hear most of the palm trees in the park are already spoken for by guys who have the same notion.

And bad off as I am, I am not half as bad off as Hot Horse Herbie, because he has his ever-loving fiancée, Miss Cutie Single-ton, to think of, especially as Miss Cutie Singleton is putting up quite a beef about not having any recreation, and saying if she only has the brains God gives geese she will break off their engage-ment at once and find some guy who can show her a little speed, and she seems to have no sympathy whatever for Hot Horse Herbie when he tells her how many tough snoots he gets beat at the track.

But Herbie is very patient with her, and tells her it will not be long now, because the law of averages is such that his luck is bound to change, and he suggests to Miss Cutie Singleton that she get the addresses of a few preachers in case they wish to locate one in a hurry. Furthermore, Hot Horse Herbie suggests to Miss Cutie Singleton that she get out the old crystal ball and her deck of cards, and hang out her sign as a fortune teller while they are waiting for the law of averages to start working for him, although personally I doubt if she will be able to get any business telling fortunes in Miami at this time because everybody in Miami seems to know what their fortune is already.

Now I wish to say that after we arrive in Miami I have very little truck with Hot Horse Herbie, because I do not approve of some of his business methods, and furthermore I do not wish Captain Duhaine and his Pinkertons at my hip all the time, as I never permit myself to get out of line in any respect, or anyway not much. But of course I see Hot Horse Herbie at the track every day, and one day I see him talking to the most innocent-looking guy I ever see in all my life.

He is a tall, spindling guy with a soft brown Vandyke beard, and soft brown hair, and no hat, and he is maybe forty-odd, and wears rumpled white flannel pants, and a rumpled sports coat, and big horn cheaters, and he is smoking a pipe that you can smell a block away. He is such a guy as looks as if he does not know what time it is, and furthermore he does not look as if he has a quarter, but I can see by the way Hot Horse Herbie is warming his ear that Herbie figures him to have a few potatoes.

Furthermore, I never know Hot Horse Herbie to make many bad guesses in this respect, so I am not surprised when I see the guy pull out a long flat leather from the inside pocket of his coat and weed Herbie a bank-note. Then I see Herbie start for the mutuels windows, but I am quite astonished when I see that he makes for a two-dollar window. So I follow Hot Horse Herbie to see what this is all about, because it is certainly not like Herbie to dig up a guy with a bank roll and then only promote him for a deuce.

When I get hold of Herbie and ask him what this means, he laughs, and says to me like this:

'Well,' he says, 'I am just taking a chance with the guy. He may be a prospect, at that,' Herbie says. 'You never can tell about people. This is the first bet he ever makes in his life, and furthermore,' Herbie says, 'he does not wish to bet. He says he knows one horse can beat another, and what of it? But,' Herbie says, 'I give him a good story, so he finally goes for the deuce. I think he is a college professor somewhere,' Herbie says, 'and he is only wandering around the track out of curiosity. He does not know a soul here. Well,' Herbie says, 'I put him on a real hot horse, and if he wins maybe he can be developed into something. You know,' Herbie says, 'they can never rule you off for trying.'

Well, it seems that the horse Herbie gives the guy wins all right and at a fair price, and Herbie lets it go at that for the time being, because he gets hold of a real good guy, and cannot be bothering with guys who only bet deuces. But every day the professor is at the track and I often see him wandering through the crowds, puffing at his old stinkaroo and looking somewhat bewildered.

I get somewhat interested in the guy myself, because he seems so much out of place, but I wish to say I never think of promoting him in any respect, because this is by no means my dodge, and finally one day I get to talking to him and he seems just as innocent as he looks. He is a professor at Princeton, which is a college in New Jersey, and his name is Woodhead, and he has been very sick, and is in Florida to get well, and he thinks the track mob is the greatest show he ever sees, and is sorry he does not study this business a little earlier in life.

Well, personally, I think he is a very nice guy, and he seems to have quite some knowledge of this and that and one thing and another, although he is so ignorant about racing that it is hard to believe he is a college guy.

Even if I am a hustler, I will just as soon try to hustle Santa Claus as Professor Woodhead, but by and by Hot Horse Herbie finds things getting very desperate indeed, so he picks up the professor again and starts working on him, and one day he gets him to go for another deuce, and then for a fin, and both times the horses Herbie gives him are winners, which Herbie says just goes to show you the luck he is playing in, because when he has a guy who is willing to make a bet for him, he cannot pick one to finish fifth.

You see, the idea is when Hot Horse Herbie gives a guy a horse he expects the guy to bet for him, too, or maybe give him a piece of what he wins, but of course Herbie does not mention this to Professor Woodhead as yet, because the professor does not bet enough to bother with, and anyway Herbie is building him up by degrees, although if you ask me, it is going to be slow work, and finally Herbie himself admits as much, and says to me like this:

'It looks as if I will have to blast,' Herbie says. 'The professor is a nice guy, but,' he says, 'he does not loosen so easy. Furthermore,' Herbie says, 'he is very dumb about horses. In fact,' he says, 'I never see a guy so hard to educate, and if I do not like him personally, I will have no part of him whatever. And besides liking him personally,' Herbie says, 'I get a gander into that leather he carries the other day, and what do I see,' he says, 'but some large, coarse notes in there back to back.'

Well, of course this is very interesting news, even to me, because large, coarse notes are so scarce in Miami at this time that if a guy runs into one he takes it to a bank to see if it is counterfeit before he changes it, and even then he will scarcely believe it.

I get to thinking that if a guy such as Professor Woodhead can be going around with large, coarse notes in his possession, I make a serious mistake in not becoming a college professor myself, and naturally after this I treat Professor Woodhead with great respect.

Now what happens one evening, but Hot Horse Herbie and his ever-loving fiancée, Miss Cutie Singleton, and me are in a little grease joint on Second Street putting on the old hot tripe à la Creole, which is a very pleasant dish, and by no means expensive, when who wanders in but Professor Woodhead.

Naturally Herbie calls him over to our table and introduces Professor Woodhead to Miss Cutie Singleton, and Professor Woodhead sits there with us looking at Miss Cutie Singleton with great interest, although Miss Cutie Singleton is at this time feeling somewhat peevish because it is the fourth evening hand running she has to eat tripe à la Creole, and Miss Cutie Singleton does not care for tripe under any circumstances.

She does not pay any attention whatever to Professor Woodhead, but finally Hot Horse Herbie happens to mention that the professor is from Princeton, and then Miss Cutie Singleton looks at the professor, and says to him like this:

'Where is this Princeton?' she says. 'Is it a little town?'

'Well,' Professor Woodhead says, 'Princeton is in New Jersey, and it is by no means a large town, but,' he says, 'it is thriving.'

'Are there any little white houses in this town?' Miss Cutie Singleton asks. 'Are there any little white houses with green shutters and vines all around and about?'

'Why,' Professor Woodhead says, looking at her with more interest than somewhat, 'you are speaking of my own house,' he says. 'I live in a little white house with green shutters and vines all around and about, and,' he says, 'it is a nice place to live in, at that, although it is sometimes a little lonesome, as I live there all by myself, unless,' he says, 'you wish to count old Mrs Bixby, who keeps house for me. I am a bachelor,' he says.

Well, Miss Cutie Singleton does not have much to say after this, although it is only fair to Miss Cutie Singleton to state that for a doll, and especially a blonde doll, she is never so very gabby, at that, but she watches Professor Woodhead rather closely, as Miss Cutie Singleton never before comes in contact with anybody who lives in a little white house with green shutters.

Finally we get through with the hot tripe à la Creole and walk around to the fleabag where Hot Horse Herbie and Miss Cutie Singleton and me are residing, and Professor Woodhead walks around with us. In fact, Professor Woodhead walks with Miss Cutie Singleton, while Hot Horse Herbie walks with me, and Hot Horse Herbie is telling me that he has the very best thing of his entire life in the final race at Hialeah the next day, and he is expressing great regret that he does not have any potatoes to bet on this thing, and does not know where he can get any potatoes.

It seems that he is speaking of a horse by the name of Breezing Along, which is owned by a guy by the name of Moose Tassell, who is a citizen of Chicago, and who tells Hot Horse Herbie that the only way Breezing Along can lose the race is to have somebody shoot him at the quarter pole, and of course nobody is shooting horses at the quarter pole at Hialeah, though many citizens often feel like shooting horses at the half.

Well, by this time we get to our fleabag, and we all stand there talking when Professor Woodhead speaks as follows:

'Miss Cutie Singleton informs me,' he says, 'that she dabbles somewhat in fortune telling. Well,' Professor Woodhead says, 'this is most interesting to me, because I am by no means sceptical of fortune telling. In fact,' he says, 'I make something of a study of the matter, and there is no doubt in my mind that certain human beings *do* have the faculty of foretelling future events with remarkable accuracy.'

Now I wish to say one thing for Hot Horse Herbie, and this is that he is a quick-thinking guy when you put him up against a situation that calls for quick thinking, for right away he speaks up and says like this:

'Why, Professor,' he says, 'I am certainly glad to hear you make this statement, because,' he says, 'I am a believer in fortune telling myself. As a matter of fact, I am just figuring on having Miss Cutie Singleton look into her crystal ball and see if she can make out anything on a race that is coming up tomorrow, and which has me greatly puzzled, what with being undecided between a couple of horses.'

Well, of course, up to this time Miss Cutie Singleton does not have any idea she is to look into any crystal ball for a horse, and furthermore, it is the first time in his life Hot Horse Herbie ever asks her to look into the crystal ball for anything whatever, except to make a few bobs for them to eat on, because Herbie by no means believes in matters of this nature.

But naturally Miss Cutie Singleton is not going to display any astonishment, and when she says she will be very glad to oblige, Professor Woodhead speaks up and says he will be glad to see this crystal gazing come off, which makes it perfect for Hot Horse Herbie.

So we all go upstairs to Miss Cutie Singleton's room, and the next thing anybody knows there she is with her crystal ball, gazing into it with both eyes.

Now Professor Woodhead is taking a deep interest in the proceedings, but of course Professor Woodhead does not hear what Hot Horse Herbie tells Miss Cutie Singleton in private, and as far as this is concerned neither do I, but Herbie tells me afterwards that he tells her to be sure and see a breeze blowing in the crystal ball. So by and by, after gazing into the ball a long time, Miss Cutie Singleton speaks in a low voice as follows:

'I seem to see trees bending to the ground under the force of a great wind,' Miss Cutie Singleton says. 'I see houses blown about by the wind,' she says. 'Yes,' Miss Cutie Singleton says, 'I see pedestrians struggling along and shivering in the face of this wind, and I see waves driven high on a beach and boats tossed about like paper cups. In fact,' Miss Singleton says, 'I seem to see quite a blow.'

Well, then, it seems that Miss Cutie Singleton can see no more, but Hot Horse Herbie is greatly excited by what she sees already, and he says like this:

'It means this horse Breezing Along,' he says. 'There can be no doubt about it. Professor,' he says, 'here is the chance of your lifetime. The horse will be not less than six to one,' he says. 'This is the spot to bet a gob, and,' he says, 'the place to bet it is downtown with a bookmaker at the opening price, because there will be a ton of money for the horse in the machines. Give me five C's,' Hot Horse Herbie says, 'and I will bet four for you, and one for me.'

Well, Professor Woodhead seems greatly impressed by what Miss Cutie Singleton sees in the crystal ball, but of course taking a guy from a finnif to five C's is carrying him along too fast, especially when Herbie explains that five C's is five hundred dollars, and naturally the professor does not care to bet any such money as this. In fact, the professor does not seem anxious to bet more than a sawbuck, tops, but Herbie finally moves him up to bet a yard, and of this yard twenty-five bobs is running for Hot Horse Herbie, as Herbie explains to the professor that a remittance he is expecting from his New York bankers fails him.

The next day Herbie takes the hundred bucks and bets in with Gloomy Gus downtown, for Herbie really has great confidence in the horse.

We are out to the track early in the afternoon and the first guy we run into is Professor Woodhead, who is very much excited. We speak to him, and then we do not see him again all day.

Well, I am not going to bother telling you the details of the race, but this horse Breezing Along is nowhere. In fact, he is so far back that I do not recollect seeing him finish, because by the time the third horse in the field crosses the line, Hot Horse Herbie and me are on our way back to town, as Herbie does not feel that he can face Professor Woodhead at such a time as this. In fact, Herbie does not feel that he can face anybody, so we go to a certain spot over on Miami Beach and remain there drinking beer until a late hour, when Herbie happens to think of his ever-loving fiancée, Miss Cutie Singleton, and how she must be suffering from lack of food, so we return to our fleabag so Herbie can take Miss Cutie Singleton to dinner.

But he does not find Miss Cutie Singleton. All he finds from her is a note, and in this note Miss Cutie Singleton says like this: 'Dear Herbie,' she says, 'I do not believe in long engagements any more, so Professor Woodhead and I are going to Palm Beach to be married tonight, and are leaving for Princeton, New Jersey, at once, where I am going to live in a little white house with green shutters and vines all around and about. Goodbye, Herbie,' the note says. 'Do not eat any bad fish. Respectfully, Mrs Professor Woodhead.'

Well, naturally this is most surprising to Hot Horse Herbie, but I never hear him mention Miss Cutie Singleton or Professor Woodhead again until a couple of weeks later when he shows me a letter from the professor.

It is quite a long letter, and it seems that Professor Woodhead wishes to apologise, and naturally Herbie has a right to think that the professor is going to apologise for marrying his ever-loving fiancée, Miss Cutie Singleton, as Herbie feels he has an apology coming on this account.

But what the professor seems to be apologising about is not being able to find Hot Horse Herbie just before the Breezing Along race to explain a certain matter that is on his mind.

'It does not seem to me,' the professor says, as near as I can remember the letter, 'that the name of your selection is wholly adequate as a description of the present Mrs Professor Woodhead's wonderful vision in the crystal ball, so,' he says, 'I examine the programme further, and finally discover what I believe to be the name of the horse meant by the vision, and I wager two hundred dollars on this horse, which turns out to be the winner at ten to one, as you may recall. It is in my mind,' the professor says, 'to send you some share of the proceeds, inasmuch as we are partners in the original arrangement, but the present Mrs Woodhead disagrees with my view, so all I can send you is an apology, and best wishes.'

Well, Hot Horse Herbie cannot possibly remember the name of the winner of any race as far back as this, and neither can I, but we go over to the Herald office and look at the files, and what is the name of the winner of the Breezing Along race but Mistral, and when I look in the dictionary to see what this word means, what does it mean but a violent, cold and dry northerly wind.

And of course I never mention to Hot Horse Herbie or anybody else that I am betting on another horse in this race myself, and the name of the horse I am betting on is Leg Show, for how do I know for certain that Miss Cutie Singleton is not really seeing in the crystal ball just such a blow as she describes?

A NIGHT AT THE OLD BERGEN COUNTY RACE-TRACK

Gordon Grand

I HAD arranged to meet Colonel Weatherford at his club at four o'clock, motor to the country with him and hunt in the morning. Upon reaching the club I found a note advising me that the Colonel would be detained, but telling me to take his car and that he would be up on the seven o'clock train. I was to give his man, Albert, whom I would find in the car, a message about having the Colonel met at the train, and regarding the horse he wished to hunt in the morning. I located the car and started for the country.

I had bought an afternoon paper, which I read while we were motoring through Central Park. The sporting page contained one of those disagreeable accounts from the race-track telling of a sponge having been found in a horse's nostril. This incident reminded me of something about which I rather wanted to learn. Albert was sitting in the back of the car with me, the front seat having been given over to a steamer trunk, so I said, 'Albert, an old friend of Colonel Weatherford whom I met the other day asked me if I had ever heard about a little run-in which the Colonel had years ago with some bookmakers over at the old Bergen County track in New Jersey. What was the story?' 'Well, Sir,' said Albert, 'it's not a thing I like to talk about, because it puts me in a very bad light, Sir, but it was so long ago I guess it doesn't matter now.' Albert then told me the story.

A few years after I took service with Colonel Weatherford, he became interested in flat racing. At the time you speak about, Sir, he had four horses in training over at the old Bergen County track in New Jersey. There were some very rough characters around that track in those days, and the gambling was pretty heavy.

One of the Colonel's horses was a brown colt he had imported from France called *Le Grand Chên* by the English horse, *White Oak.* You know how the Colonel is, Sir, about certain of his horses and hunting dogs. Every once in a while he takes a very particular liking to some animal, and when he does he puts great store by him. Well, *Le Grand Chên* was one of them, and you couldn't blame the Colonel for feeling the way he did about that colt. Of course, Sir, I'm not a horseman, but it didn't take a horseman to admire that horse. He was a big seal-brown three-year-old with white on three of his legs, a white star on his forehead, and the largest, finest eye I ever saw on any horse. When you opened his box he would turn his head, look you square in the eye like some people do, then walk up and visit and stand looking at you as long as ever you stayed with him. The boys who took care of the colt were very sweet on him because he seemed to be always trying to do just what you wanted him to do.

There was one big important stake to be run for at that meeting called the North Jersey Stakes, and the Colonel was a deal set on winning it with this colt. He had come down from Massachusetts and was staying a fortnight at the old Holland House in New York, and had brought me down with him. He thought a powerful lot of that hotel, and even now says there was never a hotel like it.

Well, it came along to a Friday morning. The stake was to be run the next day. The Colonel had spent Thursday at the track, and said to me when he came home that the colt was tight, should win in a canter, and that a pot of money had been wagered on him to win. The Colonel was in fine spirits about his chances. I had never seen him so enthusiastic about anything as he was about that colt that evening.

About eight o'clock Friday morning he sent for me. I bought a morning paper for him, went to his room, found what he wanted for breakfast, ordered it, and was laying out his clothes when he said, 'Albert, what is that on the floor over by the door.' I went over to the door, picked up a soiled, mussy-looking envelope, looked at it, saw the Colonel's name scrawled across it in lead pencil and handed it to him. I returned to the bureau and was starting to pull out a drawer, when I heard the Colonel jump out of bed. As he did so he said, 'I'm in a hurry. Telephone about breakfast,' and went in the bathroom where I heard a big commotion going on. All the spigots in the place must have been turned on at once. He was out in jig time and into his clothes. He paid little attention to his breakfast, and as soon as he had finished he gathered up his hat, gloves and stick, said he was going to the track, and started out of the door. Then he turned and told me to stay in the hotel and be where the telephone operator could reach me. I was a good deal troubled, Sir, for the Colonel had acted quite upset. While he was dressing he had walked over to the window and stood looking out over Fifth Avenue with his hands behind his back, and kept tapping the floor with his foot. They weren't just taps, Sir, for his foot came down hard and deliberate like. I put things to rights and went downstairs.

As I was passing the head porter's desk he called me over, took me into his back office, shut the door and said, 'Albert, what's gone wrong with your Governor's horse? I have a bet on him and all the boys in the house are on him. Come on now – be a good fellow – what's up?' I told him I hadn't heard a thing except that the Colonel was very sweet on the colt and had told me only the night before that he expected to win with him. Then it was my turn, so I said, 'Jim, now you come across.' He sort of fiddled about and then said, 'Well, Albert, all I know is that a pretty smart guy who doesn't often get burned, went out of his way to send word to me at six o'clock this morning to lay off, or if it was too late, then to hedge and take care of myself.'

I stayed in the hotel all day, but nothing happened. Then at four o'clock a call came, a voice I didn't recognise said I was to come to the track right away, meet the Colonel at his stable and get supper on the way.

Our four horses were in a small, detached stable at the end of a long line of boxes. When I arrived I found the Colonel entirely alone and sitting on a bale of hay which he had placed in front of the box where *Le Grand Chên* always stood. There was no one else in or around the stable. He asked me if I had had supper. I told him I had. Then he said, 'Albert, I want you to sit here and watch these four stalls and stay here until either Pat Dwyer or I come to relieve you. You are not to permit anyone to enter any

part of the stable or even approach the stall doors. I have telephoned Dwyer to catch the first train from Boston, and he will
be here in the morning. (Pat Dwyer was the Colonel's head groom
then as he is now.) I will rely on you not to fall asleep nor to
leave the place for an instant. I have discharged every one connected
with the stable.' He started to move away, but came back and,
handing me a pistol, said, 'Should you be molested, this may be
serviceable in summoning assistance. Do not use it for any other
purpose if you can avoid it, and Albert, I don't think I would turn
my back to that swamp. Good night.'

As I said, our stable was off by itself. In the rear a dreary-
looking field strewn with rocks and bushes stretched away to the
west. To the north and about three hundred feet away lay a patch
of woods with a lane running through it leading to some shanties
where they said a good deal of gambling and other things went
on. In front of the stable the ground sloped down to a swamp
with cat-tails and alder bushes growing in it. The nearest other
stable was three or four hundred feet to the south. It was close to
dusk when the Colonel left me, for it was the Fall Meeting and
the days were short. I made myself as comfortable as might be on
the bale of hay and sat there watching it grow dark. Pretty soon
lanterns began to show at the different stables and I could hear
box stalls and tack room doors being closed, and saw the lights
moving up and down the long rows of stables. Before long the
lanterns became fewer and fewer as the boys went away to their
suppers and for the night. It became very quiet. After about an
hour I saw a lantern coming down the long line of boxes. It
stopped at the stable next to ours and I knew from the sounds that
followed that some of the swipes had started a crap game in the
tack room. I was glad of it, for the place didn't seem so lonesome.
They played a long time. Once I heard a horse coughing, and one
of the boys took the lantern and went into the horse's box. The
game ended about midnight. The boys came out, closed the tack
room door, and the lantern slowly disappeared. I sat a few minutes
staring into the dark, then walked to the end of our stable and
looked over towards the track and the rest of the stabling. Everything was dark except for one light away off, maybe half a mile
away, and as I watched even it disappeared. I climbed back on the
bale of hay and sat there. Once I heard a horse in a distant stable
kicking the side of his box, and it sounded sort of good to me. I

kept wishing our horses would move about or do something. I took the pistol out of my pocket and turned it over in my hand the way you do.

Of a sudden I heard something moving in the swamp. The sound was so faint I could hardly hear it and couldn't have told anyone what kind of a sound it was, yet I knew something was moving. I slipped off the bale and tip-toed slowly towards the edge of the swamp. Sometimes I couldn't hear anything, then there would be the sound of feet moving in the soft ground. Once or twice I heard the dry stems of the cat-tails clicking against each other. I started to take a step backward, when a clump of cat-tails rustled so close to me that I instinctively raised the pistol. Something was coming straight towards me. I didn't know whether to stand steady or move back towards the stable, when a goat walked out of the swamp and went off towards one of the stables.

I returned to the stable and was laying the pistol down when I saw something white on the hay. Putting my hand on it I found it to be a piece of paper. I had had no paper in my pocket and I knew there had been nothing on the hay when I walked over to the edge of the swamp.

I don't know how it was, Sir, but that piece of paper gave me sort of a turn. I didn't like to strike a match, but it seemed like I just had to find out what the paper was, so I crept up to the far end of the stable, went maybe ten feet around the corner, turned my back on the swamp, unbuttoned my coat, ducked my head down like you see people trying to light a match in a wind, struck a match right close to me, looked at the paper and read, 'Get out of here while you can.' I blew out the match, listened a minute, then went back to the hay. A clock away off somewhere struck two o'clock. I heard the brown colt get up on his feet and walk around his box. The handle of the water pail rattled, so I knew he was taking a drink.

It's odd, Sir, isn't it, the sort of things that come into your head at times like those. I got to thinking of the games of cribbage I used to play every night at the Holland House with Jim the porter in his snug little office. I hadn't rightly thought much of that office before, but sitting out there in the dark it seemed a cosy, safe kind of place. Then I got to thinking of the Colonel's fine home away up in Massachusetts where he lived.

Of a sudden I felt a cold damp blast of air on my face. A fresh east wind had blown up and was driving big clouds of fog in from the sea. In less than a minute it turned dreadful cold. Mr Pendleton, Sir, I've been cold lots of times, but never anything like I was then. I didn't have any overcoat and only a light suit. I began to shake and my teeth to chatter. It didn't seem like I could stand it. I wanted to go in with one of the horses, but the Colonel had said he didn't want any of the boxes opened or the horses disturbed. I tried our tack room thinking maybe to find a blanket, but the door was locked. All of a sudden I remembered that before it had grown dark I had seen some blankets or coolers hanging on a line back of the stable next to ours, and hoped that maybe they had been left out all night. It was pitch dark, but I thought I could walk right to 'em even in the fog, so started. I walked with my hands out in front of me and had good luck, for pretty soon I touched a corner of the stable and knew that the line was about thirty feet to the rear of the building. It took a good deal of groping about to find the line, but I finally brushed up against the blankets, took two of them and started back. Mr Pendleton, Sir, I don't know whatever I did to get twisted about after that. I thought I was headed straight for our stable, but after walking a short way the ground started to slope down very steep like. I stopped a second, then took a couple of more steps, but the footing felt soft and slippery. I had gotten twisted around and had walked straight for the swamp. I stood and listened a spell, but there was no sound from our stable. Then I figured out that if I walked along the edge of the swamp about three hundred feet, then turned sharp to the left, and could walk a straight line, I would hit some part of the stable. I have never seen anything like the dark of that night. It seemed as though you had to shove the fog away before you could move. I started walking, feeling my way every step and trying to keep on the edge of the swamp.

It's an odd thing, Sir, how for no reason that you know about, you can tell when things aren't right. I had been pretty good up to then, but all of a sudden I began to feel jumpy. I had walked maybe half the distance along the swamp and had stopped to calculate about where I should be, when of a sudden I heard a footstep and someone crossed right in front of me. I froze where I stood and reached for the pistol. It was on the bale of hay. Whoever had been moving had stopped. A horse over at our stable struck the side of his box the way they do sometimes when getting to their feet in a hurry. It didn't seem like I could walk straight ahead knowing that someone was standing there waiting, so I made a quarter-turn to the left and trusted to luck to hit the stable. I raised my foot, took a step and was just raising the other foot when I heard a pistol being cocked. I stopped short. The ground was sticky, and pretty soon I heard someone shifting his weight from one foot to another. Then I heard a low whistle from somewhere out in the swamp. That settled it. I knew then that I had to get to our stable no matter what happened. I gulped and started. I walked maybe ten paces right smart then stopped short to listen. Someone was following close behind me. I dropped the blankets and stepped quickly to one side. Someone tripped over the blankets but went on. I couldn't stand the thing any longer. I knew where the stable ought to be, so I clenched my fists and ran for it as fast as ever I could run. I had gone maybe a hundred feet, when something struck me a blow on the head that knocked me to the ground. I tried to get to my feet but was sick and dizzy like. I knew I would be hit again and should get up but couldn't. Then I heard a noise near me and listened. It was a horse getting upon his feet. I had hit my head on one of the posts of our stable. I reached out my hand, took hold of the post, got to my feet and listened. There was not a sound to be heard. I walked over to the bale of hay, found it against the colt's box, and the pistol where I had left it. Everything seemed all right. I picked up the pistol, cocked it and sat bolt upright listening and staring into the fog.

The half-hours and hours tolled off but I never heard another sound from the swamp or any place else. Finally it commenced to grow light and I could see people moving about at the different stables, and saw a colt being led over to the track for an early trial. I was mighty glad, Sir, to see the end of that night.

At a quarter to eight the Colonel and Pat Dwyer drove up in a cab. Pat whipped off his coat and started feeding and watering, while the Colonel inspected the horses. I was lending Pat a hand when of a sudden I heard the Colonel call me. He was standing at *Le Grand Chên*'s box. He closed the box and walked over to meet me. Never before nor since, Sir, have I seen him look as he did that moment. He started to speak to me, but instead called to Dwyer and pointed to the colt's box, then turned his back on me and walked off a few paces. Finally he turned, came back and faced me. It's wonderful, Sir, how he can hide what he is feeling and thinking. His face had entirely changed from what it was when he stood at the colt's box. Then I heard Pat Dwyer come out of the colt's box and say, 'Good God a'mighty, Mr John.'

The Colonel looked at me for what seemed an age, then said in a quiet voice, 'Albert, did you leave the stable last night?' 'Yes, Sir,' I said, 'I walked over to that clothes line over there back of that stable. It was very cold, Sir, and I wanted a blanket. It was about three o'clock.' He turned and studied the clothes line. 'How long did it take you?' 'Well, Sir,' I said, 'I didn't think it would take more than three or four minutes, but it was very dark and I couldn't find the blankets right away, then when I did find them I got some mixed up and twisted around in trying to get back. It might have taken me ten minutes or maybe fifteen.'

He didn't say anything for perhaps half a minute, then continued more to himself than to me, 'Three or four minutes to get a horse blanket if you were cold. Who the devil wouldn't? They thought he had left for good. If he had come back sooner they would have got him. If he hadn't gone they might have got him. I had no right to leave him here alone.' He walked over to the edge of the swamp and stood a long time examining the ground, then he deliberately stepped into the soft clay at the fringe of the swamp with one foot, held his foot there a while, came back to the stable, sat down on the bale, and went to studying the muddy shoe. He called Dwyer to him and they had a serious talk about the colt. It struck me as wonderful the way the Colonel took the whole thing. Dwyer asked him for a piece of paper and wrote out a prescription. Then the Colonel again sat looking at the mud on his shoe as though he had nothing else in the world to think about. He handed me the prescription and told me to get it filled. I asked him if I might look at the colt, but he said he did not want him disturbed.

When I got back to the stable with the medicine Pat Dwyer was doing up the horses, while the Colonel sat on the bale reading the morning paper.

About half-past eleven I heard someone come up and speak to the Colonel. I turned around and saw it to be a man by the name of Jake Katz. This Katz was one of the best-known gamblers around the track in those days, but nobody half-way respectable would be seen speaking to him. I don't guess there are any of his kind around these days. He was the leader of a group of book-makers who had made a pile of money through being mixed up with a chain of pool rooms and in other ways. This Katz was the brains of the outfit. I was surprised to see him down at our stable talking to the Colonel. They were standing outside of the tack room where I was cleaning a bridle for Pat, and I heard Katz say, 'Well, Colonel, and how is that grand colt of yours? I declare he is the best-looking three-year-old I've seen out in ten years and he moves just as sweet as he looks. He is the kind of a horse I like to have a look at once in a while just to keep my eye in. Could I have a peek at him?'

The Colonel smiled at him as though he was his very best friend and said, 'I'd be delighted to have you look at him, Mr Katz. I appreciate the complimentary things you have said about the colt. We are a bit short-handed today but, of course, we will show him to you. Albert, slip the blanket off the brown colt.' I went to the colt's box, opened the door and removed his blanket. Mr Pendleton, Sir, I couldn't understand how the Colonel could ever do such a thing. That was the first time I had seen the colt that morning and there he was standing in one corner with his head down pretty near to his knees, his eyes glassy, and when I took the blanket off I could see that he was having a hard time to breathe. I wished I had never seen him.

The Colonel and Katz stood at the door looking into the box. Neither of them spoke. Then I suppose Katz felt that he ought to say something as long as he had asked to see the colt, so he said, 'That's one of the best-balanced colts that ever looked through a bridle,' and continued to look at him. Then I saw the Colonel do a very queer thing, Sir. On the excuse of lighting his pipe he stepped back of Katz, struck a match, but did not use it, then rejoined Katz. You see, Sir, I was looking at the Colonel because I was hoping he would signal me to put the blanket back, for never in my life had I seen such a sick animal. As soon as he had rejoined Katz he said, 'Mr Katz, I suppose I should have some sort of a wager on my horse for this afternoon's race. I understand the talent doesn't think as much of him as they did. They don't approve of my discharging my trainer just before an important race. I am told that the odds have lengthened very much on the colt this morning. I admit the horse does not look as fit as I would wish him, but still I am sentimental about him. What are you quoting on him, or rather what will you quote me on him?' Katz cleared his throat. This was not what he had expected. 'Well, Mr

Weatherford,' he said, 'I don't know. They say the colt has a turn of speed and can go the route. On the other hand it looks like there would be a big field. I could make it 6 to 1.' 'No,' said the Colonel. 'That would not interest me.' Katz turned and looked at the colt again and stood looking at him, then said, 'Mr Weatherford, I have never had the pleasure of doing any business with you. I would like to make a start. I will make it 10 to 1.' Without a second's hesitation the Colonel took out his wallet and handed Katz four five-hundred-dollar bills. There was no mistake about Katz being taken back by the size of the wager. He held the bills in his hand, turned around, looked closely at the colt, folded the bills, put them in his pocket, said, 'All right, Mr Weatherford, much obliged,' and went off. I had been putting the blanket back on the colt while they were talking, and came out of the box just as Katz started away. The Colonel was standing with his feet apart, swinging his walking-stick behind his back, and following Katz with his eye. I also looked and there on the back of each of Katz's heels was a dab of light yellow clay. When Katz was out of sight the Colonel put his stick in a corner of the stable, sat down on the bale of hay, asked me if I would get something which would take the clay off his heels, took a magazine out of his pocket, and started to read.

Mr Pendleton, Sir, it seemed like I had enough to worry about and feel bad about that morning without the Colonel making that $2000 bet. To be game was all right, but I couldn't see the use of fighting after you were licked. Next to being sore at myself, I was most sore at Pat Dwyer. I knew he must have told the Colonel that he could fix the colt up in an hour or two so he could run. It seemed to me just like one of those Irish superstitions. You know, Sir, one of those quack remedies he most likely got from a witch and all that. He was in the colt's box fussing with him every ten minutes. Why, I had brought enough stuff and paraphernalia from the drug store to start a horse hospital with. I couldn't see how a man like the Colonel could be fooled by such rubbish, because even if the colt did get all right before the race, he was bound to be right weak.

At noon time the Colonel told me I would not be needed until just before our race, so to go to lunch, and gave me some telegrams to send for him. As I was about to start he called me and handed me a hundred dollar bill saying, 'Albert, put this on our colt for

Pat and yourself, but mind you lay it only with one of these four bookmakers.' He handed me a corner torn from the morning newspaper with four names written on it. One of them was Katz.

I never spent three such bad hours in my life. The only thing I could think of was that fine colt over at our stable. How sick he looked, how bad he must feel. Then of the Colonel and Dwyer trying to cure him in time to race, of how much the Colonel thought of the colt, how his heart had been sure set on winning this big stake, but worst of all I was thinking of my going off in the fog to get those blankets. I didn't feel good when I was at the stable, but it seemed like I felt worse when I was away from it.

I went back to the stable just before it was time for the horses entered in the stake to start for the saddling paddock. As I approached the stable I saw Dwyer leading *Le Grand Chên* up and down all covered up with a cooler. Certainly Dwyer seemed to have done him some good, for he looked brighter in the eye and walked free, but even so I couldn't understand why the Colonel, who didn't need the money, would ever ask a horse he was fond of to run in that condition. He wasn't my horse, but it didn't seem like I could watch him strain and struggle the way they have to. I heard the Colonel tell Dwyer they would wait until the last minute because he didn't want the colt standing in the paddock any longer than he could help. When time was up we started, Dwyer leading the colt, the Colonel and I following. As we approached the paddock the Colonel called me over close to him and said, 'Albert, this horse may look a little better to some people when we take his cooler off than they are expecting. I am going to hold him and Dwyer saddle him. The instant the cooler comes off you look sharp. Stand back of me and keep your eyes open. I don't want anyone coming within arm's length of this colt. Don't worry about insulting anyone or getting arrested. I will take care of you.'

Dwyer found a corner in the paddock where we could be off by ourselves, slipped the cooler off and started to saddle. It wasn't half a minute before I saw a small group of people huddled together and looking our way. Four or five hard-looking customers were even pointing at the colt. Then one of them slipped under the rail and went up to two men who were saddling a horse and pretty soon they all began to edge up towards us. The Colonel had seen the whole thing and immediately led *Le Grand Chên* away. Then the bugle blew. On the way to the track the Colonel took one side of the colt's bridle and Dwyer the other. As soon as the colt was safe on the track I hurried off to get a seat.

I couldn't rightly make up my mind whether I wanted to watch the race or not, but anyway I went on with the crowd. There were twelve starters and the distance was a mile and a quarter. The field got off to a prompt start, but for the first quarter I couldn't find our colt, then the field commenced to string out and I found him. There were three horses out front, then came a horse called *St Anthony*, a good horse that won a lot of races after that. He was running alone right back of the leaders. A couple of lengths back of *St Anthony* were four horses bunched together. Then *Le Grand Chên* running by himself and three horses trailing him. I didn't know a lot about horses in those days, but it seemed to me we must have had the gamest colt in the world, for even in the condition he was in he was out-running three horses. At the end of the next quarter one of the leading horses had dropped back. *St Anthony* had moved up and there were now four horses back of our brown colt. They ran this way until the three-quarter pole, then our horse moved up a little closer to the horses right in front of him and they started around the turn. There was a man standing next to me with a pair of field-glasses. He must have seen that I was mighty interested in that race, for he said, 'Have a look,' so I took the glasses. As I was saying, Sir, they were rounding the turn. The horses in front of our colt ran wide. Then I could hardly believe what I saw through the glasses. Of a sudden the boy on *Le Grand Chên* took him close to the rail and shot him through. It was wonderful, Sir. I was returning the glasses to the man when I heard someone back of me say, 'What the h— is that brown colt doing?' and someone whispered, 'Shut up, it's all right, I tell you.' I couldn't help turning around. The first speaker was the man I had seen slip under the paddock fence when we were saddling. The horses had passed the mile and were well started on the last quarter. *St Anthony* in front by three lengths, then a chestnut colt and *Le Grand Chên* at the chestnut's quarters. Then something happened that made me so mad, Sir, that I could hardly look at the race, for the boy on our colt drew his whip and went to it, and he did go to it. It was terrible, for I was just thinking how fine and game the colt had been, and to see anyone hit him seemed more than I could stand. The boy hadn't more than touched the colt when he shot past the chestnut horse as though he had been tied. Why, Mr Pendleton, he overhauled *St Anthony* like he was standing still. But *St Anthony* had a lot in reserve. You see his jockey had been caught napping. Our colt caught him in a couple of strides, but then the race started. Both boys were at their bats. They fought it out inch by inch. The crowd was roaring and everywhere around me I kept hearing, 'Come on you, *Anthony*, come on you, *Anthony*.' Neither colt would give up. They were a couple of lions to take punishment and the boys knew it and kept sailing into them. When they were three strides from the finish you couldn't tell which was in front. Neither colt could gain, and they finished just that way. No one in the stand knew who had won. There were about 15,000 people at the race and they all stood up watching the board, then I saw our colt's number put up. Think of it, Sir.

I hurried as fast as ever I could to get to the Colonel and the colt and Pat Dwyer. I've heard, Sir, about people throwing their arms around horses' necks and all that. Well, I don't know but what if there had been nobody around maybe I would have done the same. I wanted to go back to our stable with them all, but the Colonel handed me a note he had written to one of the stewards and told me to find him and give it to him. I knew the gentleman well by sight but it took me half an hour to find him, then I went to the stable. I didn't walk, Sir, I ran. When I got there the colt's box was open, the Colonel was standing at the door looking in, and Pat Dwyer was in the box and down on his knees doing something to the colt's legs. Mr Pendleton, after seeing the way that horse ran, it was pitiful to see what the race had taken out of him. He was standing there absolutely exhausted, with his head way down, and you could see the blanket going up and down as he tried to breathe. It struck me that human beings didn't have any right to do such things with animals. As I said, Dwyer was working on the horse's legs. He had a can of something and a roll of cotton. He would wet the cotton and rub it up and down the leg. I stood beside the Colonel watching Dwyer, but not paying much attention to what he was doing. Of a sudden something happened that made me doubt whether I was in my right senses. As I stood watching Dwyer swabbing the colt's off front leg that was white half-way to the knee, it turned brown. I started to say something then checked myself. The Colonel and Dwyer never said a word. When Dwyer had finished with that leg, he dried it with a towel, then started on the two white hind legs. In no time at all some sticky substance began to come off and the colt had two brown hind legs. Then Dwyer stood up, took his can and cotton, walked in front of the horse and stood looking at him. He turned to the Colonel and said, 'Mr John, it's yourself is a grand animal painter. There is no more illigant star on any horse in County Limerick than yourself has painted on this one.' Then he removed the star. As he was drying the horse's forehead he said, 'Albert, would you be going up to the end box and bringing the winner of this here North Jersey stake down to his own box? He'll rest better the night.' I said nothing, but went up to the tack room, found a halter shank, went to the end box and brought a beautiful brown colt down to his own box that looked as fresh as a daisy and as though he had never run a mile and a quarter. As I was leading him in, the Colonel said, 'Albert, find me a cab. I am going back to the Holland House to a particularly good dinner.' Mr Pendleton, Sir, if I may say so, Sir, Jim the porter and I had a right smart snack of dinner that night and a game of cribbage. Thank you, Sir.

BLISTER

John Taintor Foote

How my old-young friend 'Blister' Jones acquired his remarkable nickname, I learned one cloudless morning late in June.

Our chairs were tipped against number 84 in the curving line of box stalls at Latonia. Down the sweep of white-washed stalls the upper doors were yawning wide, and from many of these openings, velvet black in the sunlight, sleek snaky heads protruded.

My head rested in the center of the lower door of 84. From time to time a warm moist breath, accompanied by a gigantic sigh, would play against the back of my neck; or my hat would be pushed a bit farther over my eyes by a wrinkling muzzle – for Tambourine, gazing out into the green of the center field, felt a vague longing and wished to tell me about it.

The track, a broad tawny ribbon with a lacework edging of white fence, was before us; the 'upper-turn' with its striped five-eighths pole, not fifty feet away. Some men came and stretched the starting device across the track at this red-and-white pole, and I asked Blister what it meant.

'Goin' to school two-year-olds at the barrier,' he explained. And presently – mincing, sidling, making futile leaps to get away, the boys on their backs standing clear above them in the short stirrups – a band of deerlike young thoroughbreds assembled, thirty feet or so from the barrier.

Then there was trouble. Those sweet young things performed, with the rapidity of thought, every lawless act known to the equine brain. They reared. They plunged. They bucked. They spun. They surged together. They scattered like startled quail. I heard squeals, and saw vicious shiny hoofs lash out in every direction; and the dust spun a yellow haze over it all.

'Those jockeys will be killed!' I gasped.

'Jockeys!' exclaimed Blister contemptuously. 'Them ain't jockeys – they're exercise boys. Do you think a jock would school a two-year-old?'

A man who Blister said was a trainer stood on the fence and acted as starter. Language came from this person in volcanic blasts, and the seething mass, where infant education was brewing, boiled and boiled again.

'That bay filly's a nice-lookin' trick, Four Eyes!' said Blister, pointing out a two-year-old standing somewhat apart from the rest. 'She's by Hamilton 'n' her dam's Alberta, by Seminole.'

The bay filly, I soon observed, had more than beauty – she was so obviously the outcome of a splendid and selected ancestry. Even her manners were aristocratic. She faced the barrier with quiet dignity and took no part in the whirling riot except to move disdainfully aside when it threatened to engulf her. I turned to Blister and found him gazing at the filly with a far-away look in his eyes.

'Ole Alberta was a grand mare,' he said presently. 'I see her get away last in the Crescent City Derby 'n' be ten len'ths back at the quarter. But she come from nowhere, collared ole Stonebrook in the stretch, looked him in the eye the last eighth 'n' outgamed him at the wire. She has a hundred 'n' thirty pounds up at that.

'Ole Alberta dies when she has this filly,' he went on after a pause. 'Judge Dillon, over near Lexington, owned her, 'n' Mrs Dillon brings the filly up on the bottle. See how nice that filly stands? Handled every day since she was foaled, 'n' never had a cross word. Sugar every mawnin' from Mrs Dillon. That's way to learn a colt somethin'.'

At last the colts were formed into a disorderly line.

'Now, boys, you've got a chance – come on with 'em!' bellowed the starter. 'Not too fast . . . ' he cautioned. 'Awl-r-r-right . . . let 'em go-o-!'

They were off like rockets as the barrier shot up, and the bay filly flashed into the lead. Her slender legs seemed to bear her as though on the breast of the wind. She did not run – she floated – yet the gap between herself and her struggling schoolmates grew ever wider.

'Oh, you Alberta!' breathed Blister. Then his tone changed.

'Most of these wise Ikes talk about the sire of a colt, but I'll take a good dam all the time for mine!'

Standing on my chair, I watched the colts finish their run, the filly well in front.

'She's a wonder!' I exclaimed, resuming my seat.

'She acts like she'll deliver the goods,' Blister conceded. 'She's got a lot of step, but it takes more'n that to make a race hoss. We'll know about *her* when she goes the route, carryin' weight against class.'

The colts were now being led to their quarters by stable boys. When the boy leading the winner passed, he threw us a triumphant smile.

'I guess she's bad!' he opined.

'Some baby,' Blister admitted. Then with disgust: 'They've hung a fierce name on her though.'

'Ain't it the truth!' agreed the boy.

'What *is* her name?' I asked, when the pair had gone by.

'They call her Trez Jolly,' said Blister. 'Now, ain't that a hell of a name? I like a name you can kinda warble.' He had pronounced the French phrase exactly as it is written, with an effort at the 'J' following the sibilant.

'Très Jolie – it's French,' I explained, and gave him the meaning and proper pronunciation.

'Traysyolee!' he repeated after me. 'Say, I'm a rube right. Tra-aysyole-e in the stretch byano-o-se!' he intoned with gusto. 'You can warble that!' he exclaimed.

'I don't think much of Blister – for beauty,' I said. 'Of course, that isn't your real name.'

'No; I had another once,' he replied evasively. 'But I never hears it much. The old woman calls me "thatdam-brat," 'n'the old man the same, only more so. I gets Blister handed to me by the bunch one winter at the New Awlin' meetin'.'

'How?' I inquired.

'Wait till I get the makin's 'n' I'll tell you,' he said, as he got up and entered a stall.

'One winter I'm swipin' fur Jameson,' he began, when he returned with tobacco and papers. 'We ships to New Awlins early that fall. We have twelve dogs – half of 'em hopheads 'n' the other half dinks.

'In them days I ain't much bigger 'n a peanut, but I sure thinks

I'm a clever guy. I figger they ain't a gazabo on the track can hand
it to me.

'One mawnin' there's a bunch of us ginnies settin' on the fence
at the wire, watchin' the workouts. Some trainers 'n' owners is
standin' on the track rag-chewin'.

'A bird owned by Cal Davis is finishin' a mile-'n'-a-quarter,
under wraps, in scan'lous fast time. Cal is standin' at the finish
with his clock in his hand lookin' real contented. All of a sudden
the bird makes a stagger, goes to his knees 'n' chucks the boy over
his head. His swipe runs out 'n' grabs the bird 'n' leads him in a-
limpin'.

'Say! That bird's right-front tendon is bowed like a barrel stave!

'This Cal Davis is a big owner. He's got all kinds of kale – 'n'
he don't fool with dinks. He gives one look at the bowed tendon.

' "Anybody that'll lead this hoss off the track, gets him 'n' a
month's feed," he says.

'Before you could spit I has that bird by the head. His swipe
ain't goin' to let go of him, but Cal says: "Turn him loose, boy!"
'N' I'm on my way with the bird.

'That's the first one I ever owns. Jameson loans me a stall fur
him. That night a ginnie comes over from Cal's barn with two
bags of oats in a wheelbarrow.

'A newspaper guy finds out about the deal, 'n' writes it up so
everybody is hep to me playin' owner. One day I see the starter
point me out to Colonel King, who's the main squeeze in the
judge's stand, 'n' they both laugh.

'I've got all winter before we has to ship, 'n' believe me I sweat
some over this bird. I done everythin' to that tendon, except make
a new one. In a month I has it in such shape he don't limp, 'n' I
begins to stick mile gallops 'n' short breezers into him. He has to
wear a stiff bandage on the dinky leg, 'n' I puts one on the left
fore, too – it looks better.

'It ain't so long till I has this bird cherry ripe. He'll take a-holt
awful strong right at the end of a stiff mile. One day I turns him
loose, fur three-eights, 'n' he runs it so fast he makes me dizzy.

'I know he's good, but I wants to know *how* good, before I
pays entrance on him. I don't want the clockers to get wise to
him, either!

'Joe Nickel's the star jock that year. I've seen many a good boy
on a hoss, but I think Joe's the best judge of pace I ever see. One

day he's comin' from the weighin' room, still in his silks. His valet's with him carryin' the saddle. I steps up 'n' says:

' "Kin I see you private a minute, Joe?"

' "Sure thing, kid," he says. 'N' the valet skidoos.

' "Joe," I says, "I've got a bird that's right. I don't know just how good he is, but he's awful good. I want to get wise to him before I crowds my dough on to the 'Sociation. Will you give him a work?"

'It takes an awful nerve to ask a jock like Nickel to work a hoss out, but he's the only one can judge pace good enough to put me wise, 'n' I'm desperate.

' "It's that Davis cripple, ain't it?" he asks.

' "That's him," I says.

'He studies a minute, lookin' steady at me.

' "I'm your huckleberry," he says at last. "When do you want me?"

' "Just as she gets light tomorrow mawnin'," I says quick, fur I hasn't believed he'd come through, 'n' I wants to stick the gaff into him 'fore he changes his mind.

'He give a sigh. I knowed he was no early riser.

' "All right," he says. "Where'll you be?"

' "At the half-mile post," I says. "I'll have him warmed up fur you."

' "All right," he says again – 'n' that night I don't sleep none.

'When it begins to get a little gray next mawnin' I takes the bird out 'n' gallops him a slow mile with a stiff breezer at the end. But durin' the night I gives up thinkin' Joe'll be there, 'n' I nearly falls off when I comes past the half-mile post, 'n' he's standin' by the fence in a classy overcoat 'n' kid gloves.

'He takes off his overcoat, 'n' comes up when I gets down, 'n' gives a look at the saddle.

' "I can't ride nothin' on that thing,' he says. 'Slip over to the jocks' room 'n' get mine. It's on number three peg – here's the key."

'It's gettin' light fast 'n' I'm afraid of the clockers.

' "The sharpshooters'll be out in a minute," I says.

' "I can't help it," says Joe. "I wouldn't ride a bull on that saddle!"

'I see there's no use to argue, so I beats it across the center field, cops the saddle 'n' comes back. I run all the way, but it's gettin' awful light.

' "Send him a mile in forty-five 'n' see what he's got left," I says, as I throws Joe up.

' "Right in the notch – if he's got the step," he says.

'I click Jameson's clock on them, as they went away – Joe whisperin' in the bird's ear. The backstretch was the stretch, startin' from the half. I seen the bird's mouth wide open as they come home, 'n' Joe has double wraps on him. "He won't beat fifty under that pull!" I says to myself. But when I stops the clock at the finish it was at forty-four-'n'-three-quarters. Joe ain't got a clock to go by neither – that's judgin' pace! – take it from me!

' "He's diseased with speed," says Joe, when he gets down. "He's oil in the can. Thirty-eight fur him – look at my hands!"

'I does a dance a-bowin' to the bird, 'n' Joe stands there laughin' at me, squeezin' the blood back into his mitts.

'We leads the hoss to the gate, 'n' there's a booky's clocker named Izzy Goldberg.

' "You an exercise boy now?' he asks Joe.

' "Not yet," says Joe. "M'cousin here owns this trick, 'n' I'm givin' him a work."

' "Up kinda early, ain't you? Say! He's good, ain't he, Joe?" says Izzy; 'n' looks at the bird close.

' "Naw, he's a mutt," says Joe.

' "What's he doin' with his mouth open at the end of that mile?" Izzy says, 'n' laughs.

' "He only runs it in fifty," says Joe, careless. "I takes hold of him 'cause he's bad in front, 'n' he's likely to do a flop when he gets tired. So long, Bud!" Joe says to me, 'n' I takes the bird to the barn.

'I'm not thinkin' Izzy ain't wise. It's a cinch Joe don't stall him. Every booky would hear about that workout by noon. Sure enough the *Item's* pink sheet has this among the tips the next day:

' "Count Noble" – that was the bird's name – "a mile in forty-four. Pulled to a walk at the end. Bet the works on him; his first time out, boys!"

'That was on a Saturday. On Monday I enters the bird among a bunch of dogs to start in a five-furlong sprint Thursday. I'm savin' every soomarkee I gets my hands on 'n' I pays the entrance to the secretary like it's a mere bag of shells. Joe Nickel can't ride fur me – he's under contract. I meets him the day before my race.

' "You're levelin' with your hoss, ain't you?" he says. "I'll send my valet in with you, 'n' after you get yours on, he'll bet two hundred fur me."

' "Nothin' doin', Joe!' I says. "Stay away from it. I'll tell you when I gets ready to level. You can't bet them bookies nothin' – they're wise to him."

' "Look-a-here, Bud!" says Joe. "That bird'll cakewalk among them crabs. No jock can make him lose, 'n' not get ruled off."

' "Leave that to me," I says.

'Just as I figgers – my hoss opens up eight-to-five in the books.

'I gives him all the water he'll drink afore he goes to the post, 'n' I has bandages on every leg. The paddock judge looks at them bandages, but he knows the bird's a cripple, 'n' he don't feel 'em.

' "Them's to hold his legs on, ain't they?" he says, 'n' grins.

' "Surest thing you know," I says. But I feels some easier when he's on his way – *there's seven pounds of lead in each of them bandages.*

'I don't want the bird whipped when he ain't got a chance.

' "This hoss backs up if you use the bat on him," I says to the jock, as he's tyin' his reins.

' "He backs up anyway, I guess," he says, as the parade starts.

'The bird gets away good, but I'd overdone the lead in his socks. He finished a nasty last – thirty len'ths back.

' "Roll over, kid!" says the jock, when I go up to slip him his feel. "Not fur ridin' that hippo. It'ud be buglary – he couldn't beat a piano!"

'I meets Colonel King comin' out of the judge's stand that evenin'.

' "An owner's life has its trials and tribulations – eh, my boy?" he says.

' "Yes, sir!" I says. That's the first time Colonel King ever speaks to me, 'n' I swells up like a toad. "I'm gettin' to be all the gravy 'round here," I says to myself.

'Two days after this they puts an overnight mile run fur maidens on the card, 'n' I slips the bird into it. I knowed it was takin' a chance so soon after his bad race, but it looks so soft I can't stay 'way from it. I goes to Cal Davis, 'n' tells him to put a bet down.

' "Oh, ho!" he says. "Lendin' me a helpin' hand, are you?" Then I tells him about Nickel.

' "Did Joe Nickel work him out for you?" he says. "The best is good enough fur you, ain't it? I'll see Joe, 'n' if it looks good to him I'll take a shot at it. Much obliged to you."

' "Don't never mention it," I says.

' "How do you mean that?" he says, grinnin'.

' "Both ways," says I.

'The mawnin' of the race, I'm givin' the bird's bad leg a steamin', when a black swipe named Duckfoot Johnson tells me I'm wanted on the phone over to the secretary's office, 'n' I gets Duckfoot to go on steamin' the leg while I'm gone.

'It's a feed man on the phone, wantin' to know when he gets sixteen bucks I owe him.

' "The bird'll bring home your coin at four o'clock this afternoon," I tells him.'

' "Well, that's lucky," he says. "I thought it was throwed to the birds, 'n' I didn't figure they'd bring it home again."

'When I gets back there's a crap game goin' on in front of the stall, 'n' Duckfoot's shootin'. There's a hot towel on the bird's leg, 'n' it's been there too long. I takes it off 'n' feel where small blisters has begun to raise under the hair – a little more 'n' it 'ud been clear to the bone. I cusses Duckfoot good, 'n' rubs vaseline into the leg.'

I interrupted Blister long enough to inquire:

'Don't they blister horses sometimes to cure them of lameness?'

'Sure,' he replied. 'But a hoss don't work none fur quite a spell afterwards. A blister, to do any good, fixes him so he can't hardly raise his leg fur two weeks.

'Well,' he went on, 'the race fur maidens was the last thing on the card. I'm in the betting-ring when they chalks up the first odds, 'n' my hoss opens at twenty-five-to-one. The two entrance moneys have about cleaned me. I'm only twenty green men strong. I peels off ten of 'em 'n' shoved up to a booky.

' "On the nose fur that one," I says, pointin' to the bird's name.

' "Quit your kiddin'," he says. "What'ud you do with all that money? This fur yours." 'N' he rubs to twelve-to-one.

' "Ain't you the liberal gink?" I says, as he hands me the ticket.

' "I starts fur the next book, but say! – the odds is just meltin' away. Joe's 'n' Cal's dough is comin' down the line, 'n' the gazabos, thinkin' it's wise money, trails. By post time the bird's a one-to-three shot.

'I've give the mount to Sweeney, 'n' like a nut I puts him hep to the bird, 'n' he tells his valet to bet a hundred fur him. The bird has on socks again, but this time they're empty, 'n' the race was a joke. He breaks fifth at the getaway, but he just mows them dogs down. Sweeney keeps thinkin' about that hundred, I guess, 'cause he rode the bird all the way, 'n' finished a million len'ths in front.

'I cashes my ticket, 'n' starts fur the barn to sleep with that bird, when here comes Joe Nickel.

' "He run a nice race," he says, grinnin', 'n' hands me six hundred bucks.

' "What's this fur?" I says. "You better be careful . . . I got a weak heart."

' "I win twelve hundred to the race," he says. "'N' we splits it two ways."

' "Nothin' doin'," I says, 'n' tries to hand him back the wad.

' "Go awn!" he says, "I'll give you a soak in the ear. I bet that money fur you, kiddo."

'I looks at the roll 'n' gets wobbly in the knees. I never see so much kale before – not at one time. Just then we hears the announcer sing out through a megaphone:

' "The o-o-owner of Count Nobul-l-l-l is wanted in the judge's stand!"

' "Oy, oy!" says Joe. "You'll need that kale – you're goin' to lose your happy home. It's Katy bar the door fur yours, Bud!"

' "Don't worry – watch me tell it to 'em," I says to Joe, as I stuffs the roll 'n' starts fur the stand. I was feelin' purty good.

' "Wait a minute," says Joe, runnin' after me. "You can't tell them people nothin'. You ain't wise to that bunch yet, Bud – why, they'll kid you silly before they hand it to you, 'n' then change the subject to somethin' interestin', like where to get pom-pono cooked to suit 'em. I've been up against it," he says, "'n' I'm tellin' you right. Just keep stallin' around when you get in the stand, 'n' act like you don't know the war's over."

' "Furget it," I says. "I'll show those big stiffs where to head in. I'll hypnotise the old owls. I'll give 'em a song 'n' dance that's right!"

'As I goes up the steps I see the judges settin' in their chairs, 'n' I takes off my hat. Colonel King ain't settin', he's standin' up with his hands in his pockets. Somehow, when I sees *him* I begins to

wilt – he looks so clean. He's got a white mustache, 'n' his face
is kinda brown 'n' pink. He looks at me a minute out of them
blue eyes of his.

' "Are you the owner of Count Noble, Mr – er – ?"

' "Jones, sir," I says.

' "Jones?" says the colonel.

' "Yes, sir," I says.

' "Mr Jones," says the colonel, "how do you account for the
fact that on Thursday Count Noble performs disgracefully, and on
Saturday runs like a stake horse? Have the days of the week anything to do with it?"

'I never says nothin'. I just stands there lookin' at him, foolin'
with my hat.

' "This is hell," I thinks.

' "The judges are interested in this phenomenon, Mr Jones, and
we have sent for you, thinking perhaps you can throw a little light
on the matter," says the colonel, 'n' waits fur me again.

' "Come on . . . get busy!" I says to myself. "You can kid along
with a bunch of bums, 'n' it sounds good – don't get cold feet the
first time some class opens his bazoo at you!" But I can't make a
noise like a word, on a bet.

' "The judges, upon looking over the betting sheets of the two
races in which your horse appeared, find them quite interesting,"
says the colonel. "The odds were short in the race he did *not* win;
they remained unchanged – in fact, rose – since only a small
amount was wagered on his changes. On the other hand, these
facts are reversed in today's race, which he *won*. It seems possible
that you and your friends who were pessimists on Thursday
became optimists today, and benefited by the change. Have you
done so?"

'I see I has to get some sorta language out of me.'

' "He was a better hoss today – that's all I knows about it," I
says.

' "The *first* part of your statement seems well within the facts,"
says the colonel. "He was, apparently, a much better horse today.
But these gentlemen and myself, having the welfare of the American thoroughbred at heart, would be glad to learn by what method
he was so greatly improved."

'I don't know why I ever does it, but it comes to me how

Duckfoot leaves the towel on the bird's leg, 'n' I don't stop to think.

' "I blistered him," I says.

'Of course any dope knows that after you blister a hoss fur a sore tendon he can't more 'n' walk around in his stall fur the next thirty days.

' "You – *what?*" says the colonel. I'd have give up the roll quick, sooner'n spit it out again, but I'm up against it.

' "I blisters him," I says.

'The colonel's face gets red. His eyes bung out 'n' he turns 'round 'n' starts to cough 'n' make noises. The rest of them judges does the same. They holds on to each other 'n' does it. I know they're givin' me the laugh fur that fierce break I makes.

' "You're outclassed, kid!" I says to myself. "They'll tie a can to you, sure. The gate fur yours!"

'Just then Colonel King turns round, 'n' I see I can't look at him no more. I looks at my hat, waitin' fur him to say I'm ruled off. I've got a lump in my throat, 'n' I think it's a bunch of bright conversation stuck there. But just then a chunk of water rolls out of my eye, 'n' hits my hat – pow! It looks bigger'n Lake Erie, 'n' 'fore I kin jerk the hat away – pow! – comes another one. I knows the colonel sees 'em, 'n' I hopes I croak.

' "Ahem – ," he says.

' "Now I get mine!" I says to myself.

' "Mr Jones," says the colonel, 'n' his voice is kinda cheerful. "The judges will accept your explanation. You may go if you wish."

Just as I'm goin' down the steps the colonel stops me.

' "I have a piece of advice for you, Mr Jones," he says. His voice ain't cheerful neither. It goes right into my gizzard. I turns and looks at him. "*Keep that horse blistered from now on!*" says the colonel.

'Some ginnies is in the weighin' room under the stand, 'n' hears it all. That's how I gets my name.'

THE DEAD CERT

J. C. Squire

EVERY Wednesday night, from eight o'clock until closing time, Mr William Pennyfeather was to be found sitting on a high stool at the counter in the Saloon Bar of The Asparagus Tree. He had other ports of call in various quarters of London. But gradually, almost without intention, over a period of years, he had drifted into the one methodical habit of his life: at the same hour on the same day he was almost always to be found in the same public-house. All his haunts had this much in common: they were none of them very riotous, and they were none of them frigidly quiet. Even those which were in the middle of the glaring West End were tucked away up side streets and depended more on regular frequenters than on casual droppers-in. Otherwise they differed, their customers ranging from the auctioneers, solicitors, doctors and prosperous tradesmen of his favourite resort at Ealing, to the dockers and draymen with whom he consorted in the Butchers' Arms near the southern end of the Rotherhithe Tunnel. Geographically and socially, The Asparagus Tree split the difference between these extremes: it was within five minutes of Waterloo Station, it had a Saloon Bar, and the tone of that aristocratic *enclave* was set by shabby-respectable members of the vaudeville and racing fraternities. The reader may have guessed by now that Mr Pennyfeather was a student of mankind. If so, the reader has guessed right. He was even a professional student of mankind. His novels did not sell very well, but they kept him in comfortable celibacy: as all the reviewers said in unison once a year: 'Whatever the changing fashions of the market, there is always room for the genuine novel of Cockney life, and no man knows his Londoners, with their irrepressible humour, indomitable courage, and racy idiom, better than the author of *Battersea Bill.*'

Things, at eight o'clock, were quiet. Two cadaverous, shaggy and grubby actors, at the other end of the bar, were earnestly discussing something in voices at once husky and subdued. Mr Pennyfeather, comfortably sheltered from the November night in stuffy warmth with a pipe and a pint, was talking to the landlord. The landlord had known him for two or three years, but probably did not know his name: this place was very unlike the 'hotel' at Ealing, where not merely his name but his profession were known, and where he frequently played billiards with certain cronies. Here people were incurious: willing to enjoy a talk with a stranger and ask no questions, to develop a gradual semi-intimacy and still refrain from inquiry. They might, he thought, when he had left the bar, sometimes say to each other, 'I wonder what that chap does: might be a lawyer's clerk, perhaps, or something to do with the railway.' He could even hear Mr Porter, the septuagenarian ex-bookmaker, shrewdly observing to his pals, 'Shouldn't be surprised if 'e 'ad a bit of money of 'is own.' Well, if he ever did achieve that desirable condition, it would be partly due to Mr Porter, who had already appeared in three of his books under three different names, with many of his conversations reported as nearly verbatim as might be – for Mr Pennyfeather was a realist, and could not invent conversations anything like as good as those which he overheard.

'Quiet, this evening!' remarked Mr Pennyfeather.

'Oh, I dessay some of 'em 'll be in presently,' replied the landlord.

At this moment he was called to the jug-and-bottle department by the tapping of a coin on wood; the swing door of the Saloon Bar groaned, and there entered Mr Porter himself, beaming and buttonholed, with a grey soft hat and a new suit of checks: he was the Croesus of The Asparagus Tree, and a man who had three prosperous sons in the old business. 'Took the Missus to the Zoo,' he said, explaining his especial grandeur: then, to the dark minx of a barmaid who had suddenly appeared, 'Guinness, me dear.'

No one else had come in, Mr Pennyfeather observed with satisfaction; there was a chance, therefore, that Mr Porter might become confidential, which usually meant that he divulged deeds of peculiar rascality, with a jolly Falstaffian frankness that made his worst swindles appear the innocent pranks of a child. Tonight, however, the sight of the two actors in the corner switched him in a more edifying direction. He jerked his thumb towards them, gave an upward fling of his head, and whispered: 'Pore devils, ruinin' theirselves.'

'How?' asked Pennyfeather.

'Bettin', o' course. Lot o' babies, that's what they are. Comes 'ere for tips – from each other! Hinside hinformation!'

'Stupid, isn't it?'

'Yes. But there, we're all of us mugs sometimes. W'y, on'y larst year I'll be jiggered if I didn't back a 'orse meself on a tip I got 'ere.'

'What made you do it?'

'Off me chump, I s'pose. Just like the rest of 'em, when it came to the point! Said to meself, 'Nah this one *is* all right.' Jockey it come from; at least, he used to be. Little Dicky 'Arris. Come in 'ere with 'is precious tip, an' I went an' believed 'im. 'Orse called Absalom. Down at the first 'urdle. Come in last!'

'But you've always been so funny about jockeys' tips.'

'Don't rub it in. I'm a mug, that's what I am. I thought this was different. You see, this little Dicky 'Arris – believe it or not – he's straight.'

The dramatic revelation of this eccentricity demanded another couple of drinks. The calamity was shelved, and Mr Porter entered on a long story of how he had suborned, and for some years virtually employed, several police constables, and finally a sergeant, to protect his street betting operations. With a sigh over the fallibility of human nature, he took a deep draught, then looked round the room, which had been filling up. 'Why, blimey!' he exclaimed, with pleasure on his face, 'if there isn't the very little chap that I was talkin' about!'

'D'you mean the sergeant?' inquired Pennyfeather.

'Garn, that old skunk?' frowned Mr Porter. 'No! it's Dicky 'Arris, the little boy from Epsom. Dicky!' he called; and there stepped towards them a minute horsy man, with very sharp features but an agreeable smile, a blue-eyed, sunburnt, wrinkled man with white eyelashes, like an unsophisticated and even kindly weasel.

''Allo, Dicky! 'aven't seen you for months!' Mr Porter cheerily greeted him. 'Pint, please, me dear.' Then, nudging each companion with an elbow, ''Ow's Absalom? Near broke me over that, you did, you villain!'

Little Harris threw back his head in mock weariness. Then he spoke, in a Cockney thick beyond phonetic rendering.

'Cheese it, Mr Porter! D'you know, sir, 'e's bin raggin' me about thet there 'orse for twelve munce.'

'Dead cert?' inquired Pennyfeather, with a knowing twinkle.

'Lumme! I can see you know all abaht it. All the sime, I give 'im some good 'uns in me time, and 'e knows it.'

'So you 'ave, Dicky, so you 'ave,' admitted Mr Porter. His eyes wandered; he caught sight of some friends, and with a hearty apology he left the novelist and the jockey together.

Mr Pennyfeather liked Dicky Harris's face, and before long he liked Dicky Harris himself, very much. It wasn't long before the little man pulled out of his inside coat pocket a picture of a trim wife and a healthy baby, and it wasn't much longer before he was pouring out, to the most sympathetic listener he had ever met, the story of his life. He was forty, and, until recently, had been a jockey – at one time particularly successful on the flat. Then, he said – and Pennyfeather looked down on a figure which was like the skeleton of a small rat – he had put on too much weight, and obtained a job around a training stable. 'A bit of 'ard luck; boss give up': for three months he had been out of work, though another job was now promised. Meanwhile he had got into debt: that he hadn't saved anything, he accounted for by the disarming explanation, 'But then, lumme, jockeys never do! Give a jockey the Benk of England, and it'll be gorn before you can wink.' It would be different now he'd got a missus and a kid. But here he was, work beginning next week, he hadn't been able to keep up the instalments on his furniture – including a pianner which his missus's sister Mabel sometimes come in and played – and the men were arriving to fetch it away tomorrow. 'Nice little 'ome it was, too!' He sighed.

Pennyfeather lit a fresh pipe, and looked around the bar. It had filled up: numerous picturesque characters were babbling in groups, Mr Porter laughing lustily in the middle of one of them; but their own corner was still their own. He looked at the profile of the ex-jockey, who was gazing sadly at his own reflection in his tankard. 'Poor plucky little sparrow!' he thought: then, clearing his throat awkwardly and trying to look nonchalant, he asked: 'How much are they dunning you for?'

'Might as well be a thousand,' was the gloomy and evasive reply.

'But what is it?'

'Ten pahnd, guv'nor.'

The tide of impulse was now running strong. It came to Penny-feather two or three times a year on odd occasions, and he had so regularly failed to regret his wanton generosities, that he could almost have budgeted so much a year for the purchase of happiness by absurd prodigality.

'Look here, I say,' he remarked, gazing earnestly into the little man's eyes, 'please don't take offence, but couldn't I lend it to you?'

Harris gaped at the prodigy; and he went on:

'I can't bear to see a chap done down by such rotten luck as this. It wouldn't in the least matter when you paid it back.'

'Thenks all the sime, mister,' Harris mumbled, 'but I caunt tike it.'

'But you simply must. Look here,' hurriedly fumbling under the counter, 'here it is. It's nothing at all to me. I've got tons.'

He had his way. 'My Gawd, sir, you're a peach!' stammered the little man. For half a minute he was on the verge of tears. Then he pulled himself together and grinned. He refused another drink, saying candidly, 'I'm goin' 'ome before it burns a nole in me pocket.'

He moved as to go, and then came back and put his face very close to the novelist's. 'Look 'ere, sir, do you ever 'ave anythink on a 'orse?'

'Not often,' replied Pennyfeather, with a gross understatement.

'Well, once in a way's enough,' said Harris. 'But Mangel-Wurzel for the 3.30 tomorrow. It's all right. Lad 'oo's ridin' 'er's a pal o' mine.'

'Thanks for the tip,' said Pennyfeather, 'and good night, if you must be going. Your wife can cheer up now. I'm always here on Wednesday evenings, and I hope we shall meet again.'

He resumed his original solitude. No, he did not bet 'often'. In youth he had tried four several infallible betting systems, and each one had left in his mind's eye a panorama of disastrous scenes, the last of which was himself receiving from a pawnbroker an inadequate sum for his grandfather's gold watch.

Conversation grew noisier, the passage of drinks was speeded up, friends began departing with affectionate salutations, there was a general welter of 'Just one more!' 'Well, goo' night, Tom !' 'Goo' night, Bill!' 'Till tomorrow, then!' 'Goo' night', and smashing clean through this tissue of sound the landlord's blaring 'Time now, gentlemen! Time, please, gentlemen! Long past time!'

He went out in the wet street, started out for his Tube station, and by the time he reached his lodgings in Paddington had completely forgotten, for he made no effort to remember, even the name of the horse for tomorrow, much less the time of the race.

Dicky Harris appeared in The Asparagus Tree the very next Wednesday night. He peered round the door, then rushed up, snatched Pennyfeather away from Mr Porter (who had been talking about horse-doping) and began chattering eagerly in an undertone. He had only a few minutes, he said, having a train to Epsom to catch, but he couldn't miss a chance of seeing his benefactor.

'I 'hope you were On, sir!' he whispered.

'On?' inquired the benefactor, rather stupidly.

'Why, the filly, sir! Mangel-Wurzel. The tip I give you. Fifteen to one.'

Pennyfeather blushed with shame, having now no option but to confess. He assumed an expression of exasperation at his own folly. 'Ass that I was,' he said. 'I searched the papers for all I was worth in the morning, and I simply couldn't remember the name of the damned horse.'

Harris was chapfallen to the point of misery.

'Fifteen to one!' he repeated. 'Why, with only a fiver that 'ud a' bin seventy-five quid. Look 'ere, sir,' he went on pathetically, 'I won't give you no duds, I promise you I won't. I can tell yer when they're bahnd to win, and when they're almost bahnd to win.' Pennyfeather, he said, could put his shirt on horses in the former category, and a modicum on the latter. 'Friday, nah,' said Harris, 'it ain't quite what yer'd call a cert, but next door to it. One of our own 'orses. Ten bob wouldn't do you no 'arm, would it?'

Assured on this point, he made Pennyfeather promise, honour being involved, to take a chance on 'Flibbertigibbet'. (This horse, as it happened, fell at the last hurdle when leading.) Harris's tip had not been bad; but there you were, that was racing; and Pennyfeather, who had not the slightest intention of ever backing another horse for the rest of his life, congratulated himself on saving his ten shillings.

Harris, the following week, was full of apologies; it had been miles the best horse running, but the jockey was a fool.

'That's all right,' observed Pennyfeather with easy sportsman-ship, 'one must take the rough with the smooth'; and he agreed to recoup his losses and a bit over by backing a runner in the four o'clock at Salisbury, twelve days later, this runner being in the cert class.

So it proved, and when he met his 'Epsom Correspondent', he admitted with bold mendacity to having made nine pounds on the race. A wild thought even crossed his mind to clinch conviction by offering to dock his winnings from the ten-pound loan; but he realised at once how such a suggestion would wound his little friend.

Harris went away happy: one good turn had not only deserved but received another; and if he did not make his noble helper's fortune, he was no stable lad but a Dutchman.

During the next three months Harris appeared seven times with seven tips – not to mention new photographs of his family, of his sister-in-law playing the piano, and of strings of cavalry galloping over the Downs. Of the seven horses five won and two lost; and Pennyfeather managed so to manipulate the amounts he alleged himself to have put on as to give the impression that he was winning very moderately. The only money that, so far as he was responsible, actually passed on these races was not his own.

One evening in February he happened to go, being engaged on a chapter in which a fast young clerk embezzled money, to one of his places, which was a billiard-saloon-cum-drinking-den at the back of Shaftesbury Avenue. Here, in his efforts to produce really free conversation from three young bucks, with whom he had made recent acquaintance, he consumed so many more whiskies than was his wont, that his own tongue became unloosed. Tempor-arily the experienced man-about-town, and speaking with the off-hand air of one who Knew the Owner (in this case a chilled meat baronet), he impressed upon his young friends the necessity, if they wished to make their futures safe, of putting all they possessed on the tip that Dicky Harris had given him for the next day. In the morning, as he held his head over the desk which bore the half-written chapter about the wastrel clerk, he remembered his indiscretion and cursed himself for it: in the afternoon, when the evening paper informed him that the disgusting animal had crawled in last, he felt quite sick: and for weeks afterwards he took circuitous routes round Shaftesbury Avenue.

Dicky's abject apologies after that occasion drew from him a wry smile which bewildered Dicky. But next week the run of success was resumed.

There came at last the week before the Grand National, and with it the visitor from Epsom, who had not been seen at The Asparagus Tree for three weeks. The tavern was very full: the names of at least twenty probable winners were excitedly handed about, whilst a procession of anxious-looking men sought a private word with Mr Porter and others who were supposed to be authorities.

Pennyfeather, watching the scene with amusement, and occasionally catching an augur's wink from Mr Porter, had been wondering which of the twenty dead certs would be Dicky's, when, with a hist-and-finger-to-lip air, the little figure stole in at the door, stealthily approached him, and took him to a plush-covered bench in a far corner, as one who had momentous tidings to communicate. He had.

Having fetched drinks, he opened, with an unprecedented solemnity of expression and a clenched right fist: 'Have you got twenty pounds to play with, mister?'

For an instant Pennyfeather was chilled by the thought that more borrowing was proposed, but the phraseology, as the sentence was repeated, made the situation clear. A mammoth bet was going to be suggested; and doubtless on the Grand National. Well, it didn't matter: it wouldn't go on, anyhow.

'Yes, yes; I think I have,' he said.

'That's the stuff!' resumed the Man on the Spot. 'It's for next week's big race. I've got *the* absolute cert. Can't lose!'

'But,' the novelist ventured, 'isn't the National always uncertain? Can anybody ever know the winner of it beforehand?'

'Yus, and no; once in a while the thing's a cert, and this 'orse next week's a cert.'

'What's its name?'

Harris looked around; then leaned forward, and putting his hand over his mouth hoarsely muttered 'Absalom'.

The name rang uneasily in Pennyfeather's head. Absalom? Absalom? Harris? Then he remembered, with amazement: it was the very tip the little man had given old Porter a year ago, and the esteemed Absalom had come in last. Fidelity was doubtless a fine quality, but Harris was, perhaps, carrying it too far.

'Didn't that horse,' he inquired in a tentative way, 'run last year?'

'Yus, boss, it did; come in nowhere. All the jockey's fault. Boss, you got to believe me. Took 'im hover the sticks meself larst week. 'E *cawn't* lose. 'E'll leave the rest standin'. S'welp me, bob, 'e's bahnd to! . . . An' nobody knows. Only the stible and the howner. Kep it dark – you'll get *any* price. Mister, never speak to me again if it's a wrong 'un this time.'

Pennyfeather did not hesitate long. After all, it would cost nothing to humour the grateful little expert. 'All right,' said he, 'I'll back him.'

'For the twenty pahnds wot you promised?'

'I'll take your word for it.'

'Boss, I'll put it on for you meself, if you like.'

Pennyfeather hastily disclaimed any desire to give Mr Harris trouble. As a matter of fact, he improvised; his few small commissions were always put through a West End firm of which a cousin was a director.

'Can you ring him up nah? persisted Harris, touchingly determined that the glorious good thing should not be missed.

'Sheep as a lamb!' shot through Pennyfeather's brain. 'I will,' he declared with resolution; 'there's always somebody there late.' Then went to the telephone box behind the curtains, carefully closed the door, got his club number, asked the porter whether there were any letters for him, and returned with a thoroughly plausible rubbing of the hands. 'So that's that,' he observed with hearty finality. 'What's yours?'

'Since it's tonight,' replied Dicky, 'I'll have a double Scotch . . . And here's to you, and here's,' in a gleeful undertone, 'to Absalom.'

On the homeward bus he made up his mind that this must be the end of his career of kindly hypocrisy. Fake telephone calls were really too elaborate. He should have to announce his intention, when he next saw Dicky, of resting on his laurels.

The week passed. Pennyfeather did a good deal of work, and

contrived to bring into his book what he thought a satisfactory picture of a thoroughly innocent jockey; he worked so well, indeed, that he 'cut out' most of his social life, and only once remembered the existence of the Grand National, then humorously thanking his stars that he was old enough not to risk his bank balance on anything with four legs. On the Wednesday, as he did once every six months or so, he took a train to Guildford to have tea with a comfortable aunt. They fell to playing cribbage, and he stayed to early supper: by the time he reached Waterloo it was half-past nine, and dark, and the station almost deserted. Turning over in his mind the scene of the country parlour, the old lady, the lamp, the woolwork, as possible material, he walked down the sloping roadway impatiently waving away a vaguely clamorous newsboy. Then he automatically turned left; and in five minutes reached the accustomed lights and din of The Asparagus Tree. Pushing open the door against pressure, he found himself in a dense mob, and with difficulty struggled through to his accustomed corner. He shouted for a drink, then felt a clutch at his sleeve and, turning, saw beside him Dicky Harris, whose eyes gleamed with unusual excitement from a face preternaturally white and drawn. The small man gulped and then stammered: 'Gawd forgive me, I thought you was off somewheres else and wasn't goin' to come to see me!' and then clutched at his hand and grasped it feverishly. 'If only I could explain how unnecessary his anguish is!' thought Pennyfeather.

'Nonsense, Dicky!' he said, 'we can none of us always win. I can afford to lose that twenty.'

'Stroike me pink!' gasped Harris incredulously. 'D'yer mean yer don't *know*!'

'What is it?' asked Pennyfeather weakly, the fear that he might have, hypothetically, won quite a large sum flashing across his mind.

'Why, you've won!' shouted Harris, forgetting his habitual secrecy so entirely that half the crowd turned round and craned its necks to see who had won what.

'By Gad, I'm grateful to you,' cried Pennyfeather, with fine aplomb, slapping the other on the shoulder. 'What was the price?'

'Well, I'm damned!' said Dicky slowly, his eyes blazing, his face wrinkled in a rigid smile. 'To be on a 'undred to one 'orse an' not know it! Yer've won two thousand bloomin' quid!'

The figure was staggering. Pennyfeather felt faint; then he was aghast as the clamour swelled around him and finally cheer after cheer broke out. Half those present knew him; the other half were resolved to be in on anything good that was going. 'Hip! Hip! Hip!' they yelled, and the nearest swarmed round him, cramming him painfully against the bar, and fought for the privilege of wringing him by the hand, forearm or biceps. He was completely dazed; and scarcely conscious of what was happening, when 'Silence! Silence!' rose above the tumult in the voice of Mr Porter, which had roared the odds on the Epsom Hill for forty years. Mr Porter had mounted a chair.

'Silence! Silence!' repeated Mr Porter. 'Give the gentleman a chance.'

Silence was secured. People from the street were gaping through every crevice and every unfrosted patch of glass; the landlord, the august landlady with her golden chignon, the little barmaid with a look in her eyes that offered Mr Pennyfeather a lifelong devotion, were clustered in front of the hero.

'We are all delighted,' proceeded the aged rascal, 'that our friend Mr – er – our old friend has had such a stroke of good luck, and 'as honoured us with 'is presence 'ere tonight.' (Loud cheers.) 'I know our old friend well enough to know that 'e's a real sportsman and one of the best.' (Loud cheers.) 'Sir,' as he raised his glass in the air, 'your 'ealth and many of 'em!'

The cheering was terrific. Great roars of it now came from even the remotest of the more plebeian compartments in the background. Then the ham-like hand of Mr Porter commanded silence again. There was a pause of agony. Mr Pennyfeather realised that he was expected to reply. No; there was no way out. He had to play the man. He set his jaw and stared at Mr Porter.

'Mr Porter,' he said, in a voice that sounded very remote to himself, 'I thank you all very much and I hope that everybody present will take a drink with me!'

There was a new outbreak of hurrahing, mingled with mild cat-calling. Somebody far away started the National Anthem on a mouth organ; the whole concourse took it up with great enthusiasm and in several keys. While the ovation was at its height, the landlord leant across the bar and took hold of his coat.

'Champagne, sir?' he asked hoarsely.

'Of course,' said Mr Pennyfeather, with patrician calm.

They didn't all drink champagne, but the gold-necked bottles arrived by the case, nevertheless. Feeling like a visitor from another planet, Mr Pennyfeather stood in the centre of the pandemonium and waited patiently for time, pretending to drink with dozens of men, and occasionally clasping the overjoyed Dicky by the hand. . . .

Time came, and with it a beckoning from the landlord. In a back parlour he was presented with a bill, written with a blunt pencil, for £57 10s 0d. He wrote a cheque, said good night, and passed, with a gruff greeting, through a crowd of his more proletarian admirers who still lingered around the darkened doorway.

Next day he rose gloomily and faced his loss. An idea came to him. He could recover some of it, at any rate, if he wrote the story down.

THE INSIDE VIEW

C. C. L. Browne

EW of the crowd that passes ceaselessly up and down the busy street ever notice the little alley that runs between the chemist's and the draper's shops. It is no more to them than a black gap, an absence of a shop-front and therefore a negation of attraction. Their gaze automatically skips it to fasten on the next window with its calculated, eye-trapping display. Concentrating on the plate-glass cages which hold so much that is covetable, they seldom see the faded sign over the mouth of the alley which reads:

J. BOSSINGTON
Turf Accountant

Mr Bossington would have to think twice before he recognised that such a mode of address referred to him. For thirty years he has made a reasonable living by catering for those who like to put something on a horse, and for as long as he can remember he has been known to all as 'Jem'. He has not visited a racecourse for a quarter of a century, for he is too busy as a shopkeeper, selling money. The reason why his trade makes him a living is that he charges more than the value of the money he offers; and that, in essence, is how a Starting-Price bookmaker flourishes.

His overheads are small. He has a large room for his clients with, for their greater comfort, a coal-stove and a dozen collapsible chairs ranged along one wall. Opposite is a huge blackboard ruled in lines, on which his man, Steve, lists the runners by races, marks the ever-fluctuating odds against each horse, and ultimately records which ones are placed, together with their official starting-prices. The third wall has two copies of the day's *Sporting Life* drawing-pinned to it so that punters can read up form and study the prophecies of the experts before plunging. The fourth wall is peculiarly Jem's own. Along it is built a narrow room, not unlike a railway station ticket-office, with one small *guichet* through which he both receives bets and pays out any winnings. There he lives from noon to five p.m. on every day when there is racing, ceaselessly receiving scraps of paper stating that someone (for initials only are used) is eager to wager 2s 6d on Blue Moon in the two-thirty p.m. race at Wye.

Finally, there is the most important feature of the room. High up on a shelf stands a dusty and old-fashioned loudspeaker, and from it at intervals comes a dispassionate and rather metallic female voice. It is the Blower, that means of racecourse communication by which are announced over hired telephone-lines such matters as the runners, changes in riders, moment-by-moment odds, the 'OFF', a brief commentary, the result and the starting-prices of the placed horses.

It is the link between the man on the course, ceaselessly recording how the money is being staked, and the little group in Jem's office wondering how best to place their shillings. That old loudspeaker is the very Voice of Racing.

Let us momentarily insert ourselves in spirit among the thirty or so of Jem's clients, some talking together, others brooding over the race-sheets, a few sitting silently on chairs. There is a click and the Voice speaks.

'Three-thirty race at Lingfield,' it says. 'Cross out numbers 2, 7, 11, 14, 17 and 20. Numbers 2, 7, 11, 14, 17 and 20. Thirteen runners in all.'

Steve picks up his rag and rubs out the names of the non-runners. What he had previously written on the board was the list of likely starters from the morning's paper, but seldom do they all come to the post. One has lamed himself in his horse-box, another has been withheld from an encounter with a rival who is thought to be too good for him at the weights, and a third is not going because he is known to be unable to act in the heavy going produced by the morning's rain.

The group study the reduced list with interest. They have now only to find the best horse among thirteen; not, as a few minutes ago, among nineteen. But the Voice interrupts them again. Two hundred miles away a frame has been hoisted opposite the stands and a pair of binoculars studies the list of runners and riders.

Click! 'No. 8 will be ridden by D. Garnham,' it announces,

'No. 13 by Mr R. Widnes.' Click! Steve chalks in the names against their mounts. There is a moment's pause and then the Voice of Racing speaks again.

'Kilbrennan – five to two, two and a half,' it says in its level monotone. 'Beggars' Roost – three to one, Sultan IV – five to one, Porphyry – eight to one.' Steve chalks the odds against the horses named. He stands no truck with arithmetical niceties, and when the price is a hundred to eight or a hundred to six he firmly writes up twelve or sixteen. After all, it is only a guide and will shortly be amended. A few minutes later the Voice announces fresh odds. The old ones are lightly crossed out and the onlookers study the new quotations.

All that the Voice is saying in several thousand bookies' offices scattered over the United Kingdom comes from a lynx-eyed gentleman with a flair for race-reading developed by years of practice. High in the stands he watches the busy scene below him. Little escapes his gaze, and his asides to the Lady of the Microphone are relayed nationwide. Thousands of pounds will be placed as a result of his commentary.

But even he cannot see everything.

At three-thirty-one p.m. on a certain dirty winter's day Ted Frisby was conscious only of gross discomfort. He was one of a dozen riders sitting their restless horses in front of the starting-gate. Normally, National Hunt horses are reasonably sedate at the post. They are not excitable two-year-olds, ready to swerve at the flap of an umbrella as they canter past the crowd. They are older and more experienced, and they know that their work does not begin until they form line and wait for the release that will send them off on the journey some of them will not complete. But this was a hurdle-race and the hurdler is usually a younger horse. He may be a cast-off from flat-racing or a would-be chaser being smartened up. Anyhow, the four-year-olds in this race were uneasy. They were being required to face into driving sleet, and they twisted and sidled to try to take the wind on a flank rather than straight into their eyes.

Ted Frisby had ridden in all the three previous races that afternoon, two steeplechases and another hurdle-race, and his luck had not been with him. In the first race a horse had jumped across him at the last but one fence and his mount had done well to get over with no more than a sprawl. He had lost two or three lengths by the incident and had never made them up in the run-in, so that when he rode his horse into the second pen in the unsaddling enclosure he was aware of a furious owner waiting to catch him on his way to the scales.

'Sorry, Mr Nicholls,' said Ted, 'I thought we had it, but that cow of a chestnut came right across me and we were as near as a touch down. If it hadn't been for that we'd have walked it.'

The fat, angry owner was in a difficult mood. 'None of your damned excuses,' he said. 'You're paid to ride and not to get boxed in. Why the hell can't you keep out of trouble? Anyone with the wit of a duck would have got himself a clear view instead of riding in another horse's pocket. Don't expect any more rides from me. In future I'll get me a jockey who can use his loaf.'

For a moment Ted was tempted to speak his mind and tell the owner that he ought to try it himself instead of always criticising what he could neither understand nor do. But he remembered in time that owners were few and riders a-plenty, and that he needed the £7 amount that he got. The trainer would see the owner later and would tell him that he ought to be grateful to his rider for getting him even-place money. In a week or two it would all be forgotten and he'd get another mount. Meanwhile he had to weigh-in and get ready for the next race. So he made as mollifying an answer as he could contrive and thanked his stars that there was no question of an objection. He hated them, and he knew that the circumstances in this case did not permit of one being lodged.

'I'm real sorry, Mr Nicholls,' he repeated, 'but I'd got the inside and he was crowding me. There was nothing I could do except try to get ahead, and he was keeping half a length in front of me all the time.'

He touched his cap and went to the changing-room. After he had weighed-in he took his new colours and warmed himself by the fire for a few precious moments. Then he presented himself at the scales, weighed-out and gave the saddle and weight-cloth to the trainer of his next horse. Five minutes later he was standing in the parade-ring, talking with forced confidence to the owner. The rain was lashing down with a cold, relentless fury that discouraged hope. It increased the hazards while diminishing the enthusiasm. On a day like this only the stout-hearted won races. They had to conquer their own feelings as well as their horses' before they could begin to think about besting the others. And even that was insufficient, for luck played a bigger part than on a dry day. A hoof-full of mud in your face or a slip-up on landing and where were you? Blinded or down!

As it turned out, that race was wasted effort. Ted kept his horse wide of the turns, where there was only torn turf, and brought him with a run between the last two hurdles. He was no more than a length behind the leaders when his horse suddenly faltered with that horrible little dip and lurch that tells of a tendon gone; and that was that. Ted pulled him up to a walk and they made their sad, limping progress back to the stables, Ted to get ready for the next race and the horse to pass out of the racing-scene, for a season if it was lucky and for ever if it was not.

He had had an undistinguished ride in the third race, a two-mile steeplechase for novices. His horse was just not good enough, and after driving him into fourth place as the last fence loomed ahead, he had eased him up the finishing straight when he saw that he had no hope of improving his position. He was a conscientious man like all his profession, with an intuitive feeling of what the horse might be thinking in its simple mind.

'No good pushing him,' he thought, as he eased the reins, 'only give him a rotten taste in his mouth for racing. Why they jump and why we ride them in filthy weather like this beats me! Some day this one will win but not today,' and he turned off the course up the cinder path that led back to the stables.

The same ritual was observed. Change silks, into clean breeches, weigh-out, keep under cover until the last possible moment and then out to talk to yet another owner. One had to give an owner a strong feeling of confidence in oneself if there were to be more rides. And so Ted talked with that cheerful ring in his voice that was so comforting to an owner who, having backed his horse too heavily, had begun to see with uneasy clarity that the vile conditions were upsetting form.

Ted did not know this horse. He had been offered the ride an hour before when the stable-jockey had broken a collar-bone. The trainer told him that it was running better and improving with every race. 'But keep him back,' he said; 'he takes a fair hold and burns himself out. He does best when held up for a late run.'

Ted nodded and glanced at the plaited reins. Privately he thought, 'Takes a fair hold, does he? Pulls your guts out, I suppose!

I would get a tearaway sort in weather like this!' Aloud, he said, 'What's he called?'

'Tornado,' said the other. 'Own brother to Four Winds,' and Ted recognised the latter name. It was that of an older horse that had won several two-mile chases.

The time came to mount and he was given his leg-up into the little saddle. Within thirty seconds he was soaked to the skin, his silks clinging to him. It was misery to face into the half-sleet, and when he turned right on to the course and started to canter, Tornado took such a hold that, with the wind behind him urging him on, he was near to being unstoppable. They were past the starting-gate before Ted could check him. He turned him eventually and took him back very steadily, circling him round at a trot and finally at a walk once they had rejoined the others. Tornado was upset, sidling and plunging and fretting until it was all Ted could do to get him to go up to the others. One rider was late, having delayed to tighten a breast-girth, and the moments of waiting seemed like hours.

Ted humoured his restless mount almost automatically. The conscious part of his mind was reviewing the financial future and was not best pleased with what it saw. By National Hunt rules he got £7 a ride, and if he won a race most owners gave him a present. He himself was not allowed to bet lest it affected the honesty of his riding, but it was an understood thing that the riders of winners were treated by owners as though they had put £5 on themselves. If, thought Ted, you got only one ride at a meeting you barely made money. Expenses and paying the valet for producing your kit ate into it. Two or more rides showed a good profit on the day, and there was also the regular wage that he got from his trainer for riding-work. But if you could get a win you were well up. Yet, how often could you? He'd had twenty-odd in the last six months and he'd been lucky. No damaging falls had come his way and no meetings had been lost through frost. These were the two ever-present hazards in his career, and there was nothing much he could do about them. And his riding-life was not long. Few National Hunt riders continued much after they were thirty. Flesh and blood could not take indefinitely the battering that came their way, and eventually, when you had broken a dozen bones and been concussed several times you lost the art of riding Berlin-or-Bust. Once that happened your winners became few and far between and then you were offered rides less often and people began to talk behind your back about your nerve, and once that occurred you'd had it.

No, if you were lucky you had twelve years of it, and you must make all you could in the time and hope for some long-priced winners. Only two months before, he'd taken the ride that had been refused by two better jockeys on a flashy brute that had fallen in the three previous races, and after nearly being on the floor twice had got him up in the last few strides to snatch a victory by a neck. Twenty to one he had started at and Lord Castlethorpe had put him a tenner on. But he was a real gentleman who had ridden a lot himself when younger and knew how hard was the life of a N.H. 'jock'. That was one reason why the professionals like himself never looked sideways at an amateur. He'd once been asked by a reporter if he did not resent G.R.'s taking the bread out of the mouths of the professionals, so to speak, but he'd never seen it that way. The more amateurs that rode and enjoyed it the more there would be who would keep horses in training when they grew too old to ride themselves, and that was where the likes of him would benefit.

The missing rider appeared and Ted had one last thought before he lined up with the others. He was chilled to the bone and tired, but if thrust would win a race he would not lose this one. He badly needed a win. He wanted the money for a TV set for his wife. Little he saw of her when the jumping-season was on. She lived in their cottage in the shadow of the Berkshire Downs and could not but be lonely. She was a good wife to him and he knew that her days were drab now that their boy was away at school morning and afternoon. With all his heart he longed for the win that would let him give her a television set. It had to be that way because she would have no truck with hire-purchase.

The Starter called over the names of the runners, his mackintosh collar turned up and rain dripping off the brim of his bowler on to the paper in his hand. He climbed up to the platform and watched them come forward. Tornado backed out of the line and the gap closed so that Ted had no option but to take him up on the outside. For an instant the shifting, wavering line was fairly straight and in that instant the Starter released the catch, the wire whipped upwards and they were off. He stood for a moment watching them thunder away before descending to ground level and getting back into his car. 'God help all jockeys!' said the Starter.

High in the Stand, the Blower's race-reader tried to make out the runners. He called the two leaders by name, then cursed and hurriedly wiped the object-glasses of his big binoculars. He swung on to them again, confirmed the two leaders and was then forced to say 'They're out of sight.' They were not, but their colours were indistinguishable in the driving rain while they were on the far side of the course. He waited for them to come nearer, and two hundred miles away the crowd in Jem's office waited also, silently eyeing the list of runners as though to will their chosen horses into the lead.

Tornado had not been mentioned; for he was deep in the bunch on the rails with horses all round him. Ted had taken him straight across to the inside of the course in order to prevent him from pulling into the van prematurely, and now he lay tucked in behind the leaders and boxed round by other runners. His position was much better than it looked. Shut in he might be, but presently gaps would occur and horses would make their way forward or drop back. Ted foresaw little difficulty in extricating himself when the moment came. For the time being all he had to do was to keep in touch with the leaders and try to restrain Tornado without fighting him too much. When they had gone a little farther he would be able to judge the pace and decide if the race was being truly run and when he should start turning on the tap.

The flights of hurdles came sliding towards him in quick succession. Tornado was taking them easily and Ted had a half-thought that at any rate he had been well schooled. There was no check, no measuring of distance unless it was to take off a stride earlier if in doubt. This was no place for the putting in of a short one as the clever chaser does when something goes wrong and he finds he is going to take off underneath the fence. Above all things the hurdler must not check. Gallop he must; jump he should. The rider's seat over hurdles showed that. Catch the horse short by the head, keep your seat on the plate and crouch so that your face is in your horse's mane. There must be no dwelling on landing. Your horse must be really galloping and you must be in that attitude which will best help him to keep up his momentum. And that means having your weight forward all the time.

They rounded the last bend and turned downwind. There were

only two more flights of hurdles and then the run-in to the finishing-post. Ted still sat quiet but he could see his plan clearly now. There were four or five horses ahead of him: before the last flight he would move out and give Tornado a clear view. He wanted to start his run before they reached the last hurdles. A horse could not quicken sharply on a day like this. He must work up gradually to the top-speed of his final burst.

The leaders were accelerating perceptibly as they came at the penultimate flight, and Ted felt his horse strong under him. And then, even as he dared to be hopeful, disaster struck.

A tired horse ahead of him failed to rise sufficiently and hit the hurdle hard. He got over with a lurch and a stagger but the hurdle sprang back and struck Tornado's fore-legs as he was in mid-air. Whether it was that they were knocked from under him or whether the pain of the blow dulled his mount's reactions Ted never knew, but the result was the same; for the pair of them were down in the mud even as other horses took off behind them. From as far away as the stands watchers could see the horrible impact of a following horse which, brought down by Tornado's struggles, struck Ted's body with such force as to turn him over and over like a doll pitched along a floor, a sprawl of arms and legs.

The ambulance, its engine already running, needed no signal to send it to the spot. It whirled down the course, and the doctor in the front jumped off even before it stopped and ran to the muddy, motionless figure. 'It could be anything,' he thought as he ran, 'legs, arms, ribs; even his neck if he's unlucky.' But, to his surprise, Ted slowly sat up. To the doctor's question he made no reply but sat, sobbing for breath as a badly winded man does, and pressing with shaking hands on his ribs. Rain poured down on them as the doctor made his first quick examination. Within thirty seconds he had satisfied himself that there were no major breaks and that Ted could be moved, and quickly the men had him on a stretcher and into the ambulance. They took him back and by the time the ambulance stopped Ted was able to walk out of it. The doctor led him into the little surgery and examined him. He found Ted shaken and slow to answer, but there were no fractures and no concussion, and in the end he said, 'You're lucky. You've no bones broken but you'll be very stiff tomorrow. Have you anyone to see you home?'

Ted did not really answer him. He stood up slowly, felt his

neck, moved his head about gingerly, retrieved his cap and whip from a chair, said 'Thank you, sir,' vaguely, and limped out of the door and down the passage to the changing-room. There he sat on a bench and rested his face in his hands, waiting for his head to clear. The others looked at him curiously but left him alone. They knew all too well the brain-loosening jar that a heavy fall can give and how that after such a shock a man craves solitude. They were anything but unsympathetic, but they knew from their own experience, even if they had never formulated it in words, that a man can grapple for and recover his fortitude only by himself. So they went about their own business and left him to his.

Two minutes later Ted felt a touch on his shoulder and looked up to find the trainer for whom he worked bending over him.

'Are you fit to ride, Ted?' he asked. 'If you're not, there's Tim Parks that'll take the mount. How do you feel?'

Ted considered it. It never occurred to him that he had heard the trainer the first time only because he was bending over him, but then it had equally never occurred to him that he had burst his right ear-drum in the concussion of the last fall.

'I'm all right, Mr Skipwith,' he answered. 'That was a dirty one I had, but it's passing,' and he put his hand up to feel his neck. Again, he was not aware that he had torn some of the muscles at the base of it. All he knew was that so long as people wanted him to ride he was ready to ride. His very living depended on it.

The valet helped him to change, saw him weigh-out and then started to clear up in the changing-room.

Luckily for Ted, the owner of the mount did not come into the parade-ring and he was spared the effort of making cheerful conversation. He stood in the centre, a small, undistinguished figure looking at the horses as they filed round. When the time came to mount, he watched the trainer draw off the rug and look to the girth before he himself slipped out of his big coat and took the leg-up. He knew the horse, which had been in training with them for some months. He was honest enough and a reasonable jumper, but he lacked that touch of class that would make him notable. There were lots like him about. If he was placed right and had a bit of luck he would win an occasional race, but he had not done so up to date. He had a depressing name, Mediocrity, and even the lad who 'did' him found it hard to enthuse over his charge.

The Voice of the Blower spoke to the crowd in Jem's room. 'Parson's Pleasure,' it said, 'two to one; Verification – seven to two, three and a half; Cosmopolis – four to one; Poisson d'Avril – six to one; The Firefly – seven to one; Sporting Sam – ten to one.' It did not mention Mediocrity or half a dozen of the other runners because there was little money being wagered on them. Individually, their chances of winning were perhaps one in twenty, though the layers would have been the first to admit that horses did not run true to form in such vile weather. They were not quoted simply because the public was not supporting them.

The hinged rail was lifted and the runners filed out on to the track that led down to the course. Ordinarily, there would have been crowds within a few feet of them out of which would have come cheery remarks from friends, but there were few today. The spectators had placed their bets and were back in the shelter of the stands. Ted missed the calls. They heartened a man with their implied suggestion that someone cared how he did. As it was, he could only mop his streaming face on his sleeve, and as he did so he winced. Nothing broken, the doctor had said, but all the same his neck was somewhat painful. Still, it was the last race of the day and in ten minutes it would be over, one way or another. He turned on to the course and shook his horse up. He would need to move smartly if he were to be warmed and loosened up by the time they reached the start.

He let Mediocrity stride out, conscious only at first of the relief of moving downwind. He did not try to check him until he was nearing the start, and when he did take a pull he nearly cried out with pain. He felt as if red-hot pincers had gripped the muscles low down on one side of his neck and it was agony to pull with his right arm. He overshot the start and careered on for two or three furlongs before he could turn his horse. The other riders had preceded him down to the start and so the whole field had to wait for him. He dared not go back too quickly, and with his left hand gripping both reins and taking most of the pull he made his way back at a steady trot. There were angry looks to meet as he rejoined the others, but no one said anything. All that everyone wanted was to get going. They were too cold to realise that Mediocrity was the only horse that was truly warmed-up. He had benefited by his overshoot while they were having to wait for him.

Back in Jem's office the Blower said unemotionally, 'the flag's up.' They had come under Starter's Orders.

The twelve horses came up in a rough line, broke dressing and were turned away. The Starter brought them up again and this time caught them in a reasonable line for an instant. The gate went up and they were gone.

('They're off!' said the Blower.)

Mediocrity went straight into the lead. It was no wish of Ted's but he just could not hold him back. He loathed waiting in front. You could not see where the danger would come from. Another horse could get the first run on you and by the time you had yours moving too you could be a few strides to the bad with inadequate time in which to catch up. Provided a race was truly run he preferred to lead only at the finish. But there was no option here. Ted's side hurt at every breath and he had not the power to take a real pull at Mediocrity. All he could do was to keep the steady tension on the reins that a horse requires if it is to lean on the bit.

('Mediocrity leading by four lengths from The Firefly, Cosmopolis and Poisson d'Avril.')

He took two plain fences in succession without incident, and the field entered the bend towards the far side of the course. They were travelling almost directly away from the stands and only the tail horses could be identified. All down the far side Mediocrity led the field, jumping freely and easily, and Ted wondered what was happening behind him. The wind was across them and no sound of hoofs reached him from behind as he crouched over his horse's withers. The Open Ditch came and went, two more plain fences followed and then they were going at the water. Ted wondered if the landing-side would be slippery. It was no more likely to be so than any other fence, but because it was different his mind concentrated on it and he felt a real relief when his horse took it immaculately. He wished he could see who were next behind him, but when he tried to turn his head as he rounded the next bend he experienced such a twinge as dismissed any further hopes of a quick squint backwards.

('Mediocrity leading by eight lengths from Poisson d'Avril, The

Firefly and Cosmopolis. The following have fallen – Sporting Sam, Dhargelis and Cuneo. Man of Mystery has been pulled up.')

He led the field past the stands and began the second circuit of the three-mile ordeal. He got a momentary relief as he travelled straight down wind, but it ceased as he bent left-handed and the wind became increasingly antagonistic. He was inside the wings of one fence when a hissing gust hit them with such force that he felt his horse check perceptibly, but Mediocrity was still fresh enough to jump big and he got over with no more than a burst through the top of the packed birch.

Though it was not severe enough to unsettle his horse the pace was slowing down. Judgment of it went by the board under such conditions. Any horse that finished would be a very tired one. Worse, Ted felt that he himself was tiring. His neck was hurting more and more and, though he strove to disregard it, the pull on his arms was aggravating it. It was just bearable when he was galloping on the flat, but the change of position as he took the fences caused him to wince, and in spite of his determination he felt himself getting slacker in the saddle. It was no longer easy to help his horse. He could only concentrate on staying on top and keeping his horse balanced, and that was becoming harder as he sensed that his horse was weakening, too. Yet there was nothing he could do but sit still and try to keep a reserve for a final effort. He wondered dully what was happening behind him. He had not seen another horse since he took the lead at the start.

('It's still Mediocrity by two lengths from Poisson d'Avril and The Firefly. Only four horses still racing.')

There were three fences left now and then the run-in. He was tempted to ease his horse off a trifle to give him a short breather before the final effort that would almost certainly be required of him. But he resisted the impulse. Whatever his lead, someone behind him was trying to cut it down and it would be silly to help him. There was a saying that a good horse could give away weight but that only a world-beater could give away distance. And the next behind him was giving away both, thanks to Mediocrity's early lead before the others had warmed up. He kept his horse going and rode at the fence ahead.

('Mediocrity leads by one length from Poisson d'Avril with The Firefly ten lengths behind.')

His horse took it normally and as he was getting away he heard another one landing just behind him. It needed no more than a slight turn of the head to see that Tommy Cullen was coming up outside him, challenging. But he kept Mediocrity plugging on and Tommy seemed to make no further gain on him; and in this order they came at the last fence but one. He took it a length ahead of the other, but though Mediocrity jumped normally he slipped on landing and pecked slightly, and in that instant Tommy on Poisson d'Avril drew level.

('Mediocrity and Poisson d'Avril running together.')

Glancing sideways, Ted could see that the other horse was as tired as his own. There was a labour to his action that showed how much the effort of making up the distance under a heavy weight had told on him. Yet even as Ted noted this he saw Tommy Cullen pick up his whip and give his horse a reminder and at once they began to draw ahead. It was no more than an inch at every stride, but slowly they began to pull clear, and as they did so a blackness of mind settled on Ted. He had done his best and no man could do more, and it was not good enough. There, a length ahead of him, went his hope of a long-priced winner and with it the money that would get the TV set for his wife, and at the thought the pain in his neck and his ribs seemed to double in intensity. But he neither felt panic nor threw his hand in. He and his horse were good, he reckoned, for one last, small additional effort and it would be useless to make it too early.

('One fence to go. Poisson d'Avril leads Mediocrity by a length.')

As he saw it, his only chance was a slim one – it was to speed up his horse before the last fence and ask him for a big stand-back. A fine jump could gain a length over a normal one, and the impetus of it could carry him past his rival. But it all depended on whether the horse had the necessary 'pop' left in him. The only way he could find out if Mediocrity had it was to ask him the question, and as the last fence grew larger and clearer through the rain he began to ride him hard. He drove him up to within half a length of Poisson d'Avril, gave him a smartener and went at the jump 'with his neck for sale'. All the high endeavour and calculated recklessness in his sober mind crystallised into that moment of time and focused like a burning spot of compulsion. His horse felt it even through his weariness. He responded to the call made on him, and as he got level with the wings he put all his available energy into one tremendous jump.

Ted felt what was coming, and even as his horse over-jumped he shifted his weight back, and as Mediocrity pitched on landing he was lying back so far that he had the reins by the buckle. He felt the horse overbalancing on his landing leg, and as though in slow motion he saw him reach desperately for support with the other, fail to get it completely and begin to peck badly. All the pain and urge in Ted's body and mind combined, like a drug, to make him extra-perceptive, able to break down the flowing sequence of actions by his horse into individual movements. Slowly, it seemed to him, the horse's head went down until it momentarily touched the ground and the white snip on his nose became muddied. But even while Ted sat and suffered, expecting to feel the hindquarters rise higher and higher behind him until he was flung ahead as they curved over in a fall, the momentary support of his nose gave Mediocrity that fractional chance to save himself. With a desperate clawing motion he got a foreleg free from under him and put it out ahead, and with a stagger and a slip he kept upright and lurched forward again.

Ted knew the effort that his horse had put into saving himself and the demand that it had made on his store of energy, and he knew, too, that there would now be nothing more to give. He felt no relief or pride at having survived so bad a peck. What use was it when his plan of out-jumping his rival had been neutralised by the check and delay of the landing slither? Numb with disappointment and his body one hotbed of pain, he looked for his rival. To his amazement nothing was to be seen, and he forced his neck round for a glance back. Only then did he understand. Poisson d'Avril had fallen while he himself was striving to keep his horse up, and Tommy Cullen was slowly getting to his feet.

('Mediocrity is over the last fence thirty lengths clear of The Firefly. Poisson d'Avril has fallen.')

Ted eased his tired horse into a canter and stood up in his stirrups. Once past the post he dropped to a walk and turned back up the cinder path to the unsaddling-ring. He rode Mediocrity into the winner's pen, slid off his back and took off the saddle and weightcloth. He was near to reeling with the fatigue that is the legacy of continued pain, but his mind was full of light and radiance and colour. In his inarticulate way he felt that no one could have spent himself more unstintedly than he had and, for once, it had paid. He was too tired, too drained of emotion to take it all in fully, but he knew that he was happy. Others in the changing-room congratulated him and he answered them as best he could, but only sometimes could he hear what they said.

Two hundred miles away the Voice spoke for the last time that day.

'Starting-prices,' it said in its flat voice, 'Mediocrity – a hundred to six, The Firefly – seven to one. Only two finishers. That is all. Goodbye.'

The little crowd in Jem's room filed out into the last of the after-noon light.

Jem swept the coins out of his change-bowl into a linen bag, dropped it into his old-fashioned Gladstone, followed it up with a thick wad of notes, locked the bag and padlocked it by its chain to the metal collar round his wrist.

Ted watched, dog-tired, as the valet packed his bag for him, took it out to a waiting taxi and handed it in after him. He wanted to get home. He had done his day's work and now he wanted nothing more than to rest.

In his box, Mediocrity cleaned up his feed, walked stiffly round twice and then lay down in the golden straw.

The day's racing was over.

THE TALE OF THE GYPSY HORSE

Donn Byrne

I THOUGHT first of the old lady's face, in the candlelight of the dinner table at Destiny Bay, as some fine precious coin, a spade guinea perhaps, well and truly minted. How old she was I could not venture to guess, but I knew well that when she was young men's heads must have turned as she passed. Age had boldened the features much, the proud nose and definite chin. Her hair was grey, vitally grey, like a grey wave curling in to crash on the sands of Destiny. And I knew that in another woman that hair would be white as scutched flax. When she spoke, the thought of the spade guinea came to me again, so rich and golden was her voice.

'Lady Clontarf,' said my uncle Valentine, 'this is Kerry, Hector's boy.'

'May I call you Kerry? I am so old a woman and you are so much a boy. Also I knew your father. He was of that great line of soldiers who read their Bibles in their tents, and go into battle with a prayer in their hearts. I always seem to have known,' she said, 'that he would fondle no grey beard.'

'Madame,' I said, 'what should I be but Kerry to my father's friends!'

It seemed to me that I must know her because of her proud high face, and her eyes of a great lady, but the title of Clontarf made little impress on my brain. Our Irish titles have become so hawked and shopworn that the most hallowed names in Ireland may be borne by a porter brewer or former soap boiler. O'Conor Don and MacCarthy More mean so much more to us than the Duke of This or the Marquis of There, now the politics have so

muddled chivalry. We may resent the presentation of this title or
that to a foreigner, but what can you do? The loyalty of the
Northern Irishman to the Crown is a loyalty of head and not of
heart. Out of our Northern country came the United Men, if you
remember. But for whom should our hearts beat faster? The Stuarts
were never fond of us, and the Prince of Orange came over to us,
talked a deal about liberty, was with us at a few battles, and went
off to grow asparagus in England. It is so long since O'Neill and
O'Donnel sailed for Spain!

Who Lady Clontarf was I did not know. My uncle Valentine is
so off-hand in his presentations. Were you to come on him closeted
with a heavenly visitant he would just say: 'Kerry, the Angel
Gabriel.' Though as to what his Angelicness was doing with my
uncle Valentine, you would be left to surmise. My uncle Valentine
will tell you just as much as he feels you ought to know and no
more – a quality that stood my uncle in good stead in the days
when he raced and bred horses for racing. I did know one thing:
Lady Clontarf was not Irish. There is a feeling of kindness between
all us Irish that we recognise without speaking. One felt courtesy,
gravity, dignity in her, but not that quality that makes your
troubles another Irish person's troubles, if only for the instant. Nor
was she English. One felt her spiritual roots went too deep for
that. Nor had she that brilliant armour of the Latin. Her speech
was the ordinary speech of a gentlewoman, unaccented. Yet that
remark about knowing my father would never fondle a grey beard!

Who she was and all about her I knew I would find out later
from my dear aunt Jenepher. But about the old drawing-room of
Destiny there was a strange air of formality. My uncle Valentine
is most courteous, but to-night he was courtly. He was like some
Hungarian or Russian noble welcoming an empress. There was an
air of deference about my dear aunt Jenepher that informed me
that Lady Clontarf was very great indeed. Whom my aunt Jenepher
likes is lovable, and whom she respects is clean and great. But the
most extraordinary part of the setting was our butler James Carabine. He looked as if royalty were present, and I began to say to
myself: 'By damn, but royalty is! Lady Clontarf is only a racing
name. I know that there's a queen or princess in Germany who's
held by the Jacobites to be Queen of England. Can it be herself
that's in it? It sounds impossible, but sure there's nothing impossible where my uncle Valentine's concerned.'

                              *   *   *

At dinner the talk turned on racing, and my uncle Valentine inveighed bitterly against the late innovations on the track; the starting gate, and the new seat introduced by certain American jockeys, the crouch now recognised as orthodox in flat-racing. As to the value of the starting gate my uncle was open to conviction. He recognised how unfairly the apprentice was treated by the crack jockey with the old method of the flag, but he dilated on his favourite theme: that machinery was the curse of man. All these innovations –

'But it isn't an innovation, sir. The Romans used it.'

'You're a liar!' said my uncle Valentine.

My uncle Valentine, or any other Irishman for the matter of that, only means that he doesn't believe you. There is a wide difference.

'I think I'm right, sir. The Romans used it for their chariot races. They dropped the barrier instead of raising it.' A tag of my classics came back to me, as tags will. '*Repagula submittuntur*, Pausanias writes.'

'Pausanias, begob!' My uncle Valentine was visibly impressed.

But as to the new seat he was adamant. I told him competent judges had placed it about seven pounds' advantage to the horse.

'There is only one place on a horse's back for a saddle,' said my uncle Valentine. 'The shorter your leathers, Kerry, the less you know about your mount. You are only aware whether or not he is winning. With the ordinary seat, you know whether he is lazy, and can make proper use of your spur. You can stick to his head and help him.'

'Races are won with that seat, sir.'

'Be damned to that!' said my uncle Valentine. 'If the horse is good enough, he'll win with the rider facing his tail.'

'But we are boring you, Madame,' I said, 'with our country talk of horses.'

'There are three things that are never boring to see: a swift swimmer swimming, a young girl dancing, and a young horse running. And three things that are never tiring to speak of: God, and love, and the racing of horses.'

'A *kushto jukel* is also *rinkeno, mi pen*,' suddenly spoke our butler, James Carabine.

'*Dabla*, James Carabine, you *roker* like a *didakai*. A *jukel* to catch *kanangre!*' And Lady Clontarf laughed. 'What in all the *tem* is as *dinkeno* as a *kushti-dikin grai?*'

'A *tatsheno jukel, mi pen*, like Rory Bosville's,' James Carabine evidently stood his ground, 'that *noshered* the Waterloo Cup through *wafro bok!*'

'*Avali!* You are right, James Carabine.' And then she must have seen my astonished face, for she laughed, that small golden laughter that was like the ringing of an acolyte's bell. 'Are you surprised to hear me speak the *tawlo lshib*, the black language, Kerry? I am a gypsy woman.'

'Lady Clontarf, Mister Kerry,' said James Carabine, 'is saying there is nothing in the world like a fine horse. I told her a fine greyhound is a good thing too. Like Rory Bosville's, that should have won the Waterloo Cup in Princess Dagmar's year.'

'Lady Clontarf wants to talk to you about a horse, Kerry,' said my uncle Valentine. 'So if you would like us to go into the gunroom, Jenepher, instead of the withdrawing room while you play – '

'May I not hear about the horse, too?' asked my aunt Jenepher.

'My very, very dear,' said the gypsy lady to my blind aunt Jenepher, 'I would wish you to, for where you are sitting, there a blessing will be.'

My uncle Valentine had given up race horses for as long as I can remember. Except with Limerick Pride, he had never had any luck, and so he had quitted racing as an owner, and gone in for harness ponies, of which, it is admitted, he bred and showed the finest of their class. My own two chasers, while winning many good good Irish races, were not quite up to Aintree form, but in the last year I happened to buy, for a couple of hundred guineas, a handicap horse that had failed signally as a three-year-old in classic races, and of which a fashionable stable wanted to get rid. It was Ducks and Drakes, by Drake's Drum out of Little Duck, a beautifully shaped, dark grey horse, rather short in the neck, but the English stable was convinced he was a hack. However, as often happens, with a change of trainers and jockeys, Ducks and Drakes became a different horse and won five good races, giving me so much in hand that I was able to purchase for a matter of nine hundred guineas a colt I was optimistic about, a son of Saint Simon. Both horses were in training with Robinson at the Curragh.

And now it occurred to me that the gypsy lady wanted to buy one or the other of them. I decided beforehand that it would be across my dead body.

'Would you be surprised,' asked my uncle Valentine, 'to hear that Lady Clontarf has a horse she expects to win the Derby with?'

'I should be delighted, sir, if she did,' I answered warily. There were a hundred people who had hopes of their nominations in the greatest of races.

'Kerry,' the gypsy lady said quietly, 'I think I will win.' She had a way of clearing the air with her voice, with her eyes. What was a vague hope now became an issue.

'What is the horse, Madame?'

'It is as yet unnamed, and has never run as a two-year-old. It is a son of Irlandais, who has sired many winners on the Continent, and who broke down sixteen years ago in preparation for the Derby, and was sold to one of the Festetics. Its dam is Iseult III, who won the Prix de Diane four years ago.'

'I know so little about Continental horses,' I explained.

'The strain is great-hearted and, with the dam, strong as an oak tree. I am a gypsy woman, and I know a horse, and I am an old, studious woman,' she said, and she looked at her beautiful, un-ringed golden hands, as if she were embarrassed, speaking of something we, not Romanies, could hardly understand, 'and I think I know propitious hours and days.'

'Where is he now, Madame?'

'He is at Dax, in the Basses-Pyrénées, with Romany folk.'

'Here's the whole thing in a nutshell, Kerry: Lady Clontarf wants her colt trained in Ireland. Do you think the old stables of your grandfather are still good?'

'The best in Ireland, sir, but sure there's no horse been trained there for forty years, barring jumpers.'

'Are the gallops good?'

'Sure, you know yourself, sir, how good they are. But you couldn't train without a trainer, and stable boys – '

'We'll come to that,' said my uncle Valentine. 'Tell me, what odds will you get against an unknown, untried horse in the winter books?'

I thought for an instant. It had been an exceptionally good year for two-year-olds, the big English breeders' stakes having been bitterly contested. Lord Shere had a good horse; Mr Paris a danger-

ous colt. I should say there were fifteen good colts, if they wintered
well, two with outstanding chances.

'I should say you could really write your own ticket. The ring
will be only too glad to get money. There's so much up on Sir
James and Toison d'Or.'

'To win a quarter-million pounds?' asked my uncle Valentine.

'It would have to be done very carefully, sir, here and there, in
ponies and fifties and hundreds, but I think between four and five
thousand pounds would do it.'

'Now if this horse of Lady Clontarf's wins the Two Thousand
and the Derby, and the Saint Leger – '

Something in my face must have shown a lively distaste for the
company of lunatics, for James Carabine spoke quietly from the
door by which he was standing.

'Will your young Honour be easy, and listen to your uncle and
my lady.'

My uncle Valentine is most grandiose, and though he has lived
in epic times, a giant among giants, his schemes are too big for
practical business days. And I was beginning to think that the
gypsy lady, for all her beauty and dignity, was but an old woman
crazed by gambling and tarot cards, but James Carabine is so wise,
so beautifully sane, facing all events, spiritual and material, four-
square to the wind.

' – what would he command in stud fees?' continued quietly my
uncle Valentine.

'If he did this tremendous triple thing, sir, five hundred guineas
would not be exorbitant.'

'I am not asking you out of idle curiosity, Kerry, or for information,' said my uncle Valentine. 'I merely wish to know if the
ordinary brain arrives at these conclusions of mine; if they are, to
use a word of Mr Thackeray's, apparent.'

'I quite understand, sir,' I said politely.

'And now,' said my uncle Valentine, 'whom would you suggest
to come to Destiny Bay as trainer?'

'None of the big trainers will leave their stables to come here,
sir. And the small ones I don't know sufficiently. If Sir Arthur
Pollexfen were still training, and not so old – '

'Sir Arthur Pollexfen is not old,' said my uncle Valentine. 'He
cannot be more than seventy-two or seventy-three.'

'But at that age you cannot expect a man to turn out at five in the morning and oversee gallops.'

'How little you know Mayo men,' said my uncle Valentine. 'And Sir Arthur with all his triumphs never won a Derby. He will come.'

'Even at that, sir, how are you going to get a crack jockey? Most big owners have first or second call on them. And the great free lances, you cannot engage one of those and ensure secrecy.'

'That,' said my uncle Valentine, 'is already arranged. Lady Clontarf has a Gitano, or Spanish gypsy, in whom her confidence is boundless. And now,' said my uncle Valentine, 'we come to the really diplomatic part of the proceeding. Trial horses are needed, so that I am commissioned to approach you with delicacy and ask you if you will bring up your two excellent horses Ducks and Drakes and the Saint Simon colt and help train Lady Clontarf's horse. I don't see why you should object.'

To bring up the two darlings of my heart, and put them under the care of a trainer who had won the Gold Cup at Ascot fifty years before, and hadn't run a horse for twelve years, and have them ridden by this Gitano or Spanish gypsy, as my uncle called him; to have them used as trial horses to this colt which might not be good enough for a starter's hack. Ah, no! Not damned likely. I hardened my heart against the pleading gaze of James Carabine.

'Will you or won't you?' roared my uncle diplomatically.

My aunt Jenepher laid down the lace she was making, and reaching across, her fingers caught my sleeve and ran down to my hand, and her hand caught mine.

'Kerry will,' she said.

So that was decided.

'Kerry,' said my uncle Valentine, 'will you see Lady Clontarf home?'

I was rather surprised. I had thought she was staying with us. And I was a bit bothered, for it is not hospitality to allow the visitor to Destiny to put up at the local pub. But James Carabine whispered: ''Tis on the downs she's staying, Master Kerry, in her own great van with four horses.' It was difficult to believe that the tall graceful lady in the golden and red Spanish shawl, with the quiet speech of our own people, was a roaming gypsy, with the whole world as her home.

'Good night, Jenepher. Good night, Valentine. *Boshto dok*, good luck, James Carabine!'

'*Boshto dok, mi pen.* Good luck, sister.'

We went out into the October night of the full moon – the hunter's moon – and away from the great fire of turf and bogwood in our drawing-room; the night was vital with an electric cold. One noted the film of ice in the bogs, and the drumming of snipes' wings, disturbed by some roving dog, came to our ears. So bright was the moon that each whitewashed apple tree stood out clear in the orchard, and as we took the road toward Grey River, we could see a barentine offshore, with sails of polished silver – some boat from Bilbao probably, making for the Clyde, in the daytime a scrubby ore carrier but to-night a ship out of some old sea story, as of Magellan or our own Saint Brendan:

'*Feach air muir lionadh gealach buidhe mar ór,*' she quoted in Gaelic, 'See on the filling sea the full moon yellow as gold. . . . It is full moon and full tide, Kerry; if you make a wish, it will come true.'

'I wish you success in the Derby, Madame.'

Ahead of us down the road moved a little group to the sound of fiddle and mouth organ. It was the Romany bodyguard ready to protect their chieftainess on her way home.

'You mean that, I know, but you dislike the idea. Why?'

'Madame,' I said, 'if you can read my thoughts as easily as that, it's no more impertinent to speak than think. I have heard a lot about a great colt to-night, and of his chance for the greatest race in the world, and that warms my heart. But I have heard more about money, and that chills me.'

'I am so old, Kerry, that the glory of winning the Derby means little to me. Do you know how old I am? I am six years short of an hundred old.'

'Then the less – ' I began, and stopped short, and could have chucked myself over the cliff for my unpardonable discourtesy.

'Then the less reason for my wanting money,' the old lady said. 'Is not that so?'

'Exactly, Madame.'

'Kerry,' she said, 'does my name mean anything to you?'

'It has bothered me all the evening. Lady Clontarf, I am so sorry my father's son should appear to you so rude and ignorant a lout.'

'Mifanwy, Countess Clontarf and Kincora.'

I gaped like an idiot. 'The line of great Brian Boru. But I thought – '

'Did you really ever think of it, Kerry?'

'Not really, Madame,' I said. 'It's so long ago, so wonderful. It's like that old city they speak of in the country tales, under Ownaglass, the grey river, with its spires and great squares. It seems to me to have vanished like that, in rolling clouds of thunder.'

'The last O'Neill has vanished, and the last Plantagenet. But great Brian's strain remains. When I married my lord,' she said quietly, 'it was in a troubled time. Our ears had not forgotten the musketry of Waterloo, and England was still shaken by fear of the Emperor, and poor Ireland was hurt and wounded. As you know, Kerry, no peer of the older faith sat in College Green. It is no new thing to ennoble, and steal an ancient name. Pitt and Napoleon passed their leisure hours at it. So that of O'Briens, Kerry, sirred and lorded, there are a score, but my lord was Earl of Clontarf and Kincora since before the English came.

'If my lord was of the great blood of Kincora, myself was not lacking in blood. We Romanies are old, Kerry, so old that no man knows our beginning, but that we came from the uplands of India centuries before history. We are a strong, vital race, and we remain with our language, our own customs, our own laws until this day. And to certain families of us, the Romanies all over the world do reverence, as to our own, the old Lovells. There are three Lovells, Kerry, the *dinelo* or foolish Lovells, the *gozvero* or cunning Lovells, and the *puro* Lovells, the old Lovells. I am of the old Lovells. My father was the great Mairik Lovell. So you see I am of great stock, too.'

'Dear Madame, one has only to see you to know that.'

'My lord had a small place left him near the Village of Swords, and it was near there I met him. He wished to buy a horse from my father Mairik, a stallion my father had brought all the way from the Nejd in Arabia. My lord could not buy that horse. But when I married my lord, it was part of my dowry, that and two handfuls of uncut Russian emeralds, and a chest of gold coins, Russian and Indian and Turkish coins, all gold. So I did not come empty-handed to my lord.'

'Madame, do you wish to tell me this?'

'I wish to tell it to you, Kerry, because I want you for a friend to my little people, the sons of my son's son. You must know everything about friends to understand them.

'My lord was rich only in himself and in his ancestry. But with the great Arab stallion and the emeralds and the gold coins we were well. We did a foolish thing, Kerry; we went to London. My lord wished it, and his wishes were my wishes, although something told me we should not have gone. In London I made my lord sell the great Arab. He did not wish to, because it came with me, nor did I wish to, because my father had loved it so, but I made him sell it. All the Selim horses of to-day are descended from him, Sheykh Selim.

'My lord loved horses, Kerry. He knew horses, but he had no luck. Newmarket Heath is a bad spot for those out of luck. And my lord grew worried. When one is worried, Kerry, the heart contracts a little – is it not so? Or don't you know yet? Also another thing bothered my lord. He was with English people, and English people have their codes and ordinances. They are good people, Kerry, very honest. They go to churches, and like sad songs, but whether they believe in God, or whether they have hearts or have no hearts, I do not know. Each thing they do by rote and custom, and they are curious in this: they will make excuses for a man who has done a great crime, but no excuses for a man who neglects a trivial thing. An eccentricity of dress is not forgiven. An eccentric is an outsider. So that English are not good for Irish folk.

'My own people,' she said proudly, 'are simple people, kindly and loyal as your family know. A marriage to them is a deep thing, not the selfish love of one person for another, but involving many factors. A man will say: Mifanwy Lovell's father saved my honour once. What can I do for Mifanwy Lovell and Mifanwy Lovell's man? And the Lovells said when we were married: Brothers, the *gawjo rai*, the foreign gentleman, may not understand the gypsy way, that our sorrows are his sorrows, and our joys his, but we understand that his fights are our fights, and his interests the interests of the Lovell Clan.

'My people were always about my lord, and my lord hated it. In our London house in the morning, there were always gypsies waiting to tell my lord of a great fight coming off quietly on Epsom Downs, which it might interest him to see, or of a good horse to be bought cheaply, or some news of a dog soon to run in a coursing match for a great stake, and of the dog's excellences or his defects. They wanted no money. They only wished to do him a kindness. But my lord was embarrassed, until he began to loathe the sight of a gypsy neckerchief. Also, on the racecourses, in the betting ring where my lord would be, a gypsy would pay hard-earned entrance money to tell my lord quietly of something they had noticed that morning in the gallops, or horses to be avoided in betting, or of neglected horses which would win. All kindnesses to my lord. But my lord was with fashionable English folk, who do not understand one's having a strange friend. Their uplifted eyebrows made my lord ashamed of the poor Romanies. These things are things you might laugh at, with laughter like sunshine, but there would be clouds in your heart.

'The end came at Ascot, Kerry, where the young queen was, and the Belgian king, and the great nobles of the court. Into the paddock came one of the greatest of gypsies, Tyso Herne, who had gone before my marriage with a great draft of Norman trotting horses to Mexico, and came back with a squadron of ponies, some of the best. Tyso was a vast man, a *pawni Romany*, a fair gypsy. His hair was red, and his moustache was long and curling, like a Hungarian pandour's. He had a flaunting *diklo* of fine yellow silk about his neck, and the buttons on his coat were gold Indian mohurs, and on his bell-shaped trousers were braids of silver bells, and the spurs on his Wellingtons were fine silver, and his hands were covered with rings, Kerry, with stones in them such as even the young queen did not have. It was not vulgar ostentation. It was just that Tyso felt rich and merry, and no stone on his hand was as fine as his heart.

'When he saw me he let a roar out of him that was like the roar of the ring when the horses are coming in to the stretch.

' "Before God," he shouted, "it's Mifanwy Lovell." And, though I am not a small woman, Kerry, he tossed me in the air, and caught me in the air. And he laughed and kissed me, and I laughed and kissed him, so happy was I to see great Tyso once more, safe from over the sea.

' "Go get your *rom, mi tshai*, your husband, my lass, and we'll go to the *kitshima* and have a jeroboam of Champagne wine."

'But I saw my lord walk off with thunder in his face, and all the English folk staring and some women laughing. So I said: "I will go with you alone, Tyso." For Tyso Herne had been my

father's best friend and my mother's cousin, and had held me as
a baby, and no matter how he looked, or who laughed, he was
well come for me.

'Of what my lord said, and of what I said in rebuttal we will
not speak. One says foolish things in anger, but, foolish or not,
they leave scars. For out of the mouth come things forgotten,
things one thinks dead. But before the end of the meeting, I went
to Tyso Herne's van. He was braiding a whip with fingers light
as a woman's, and when he saw me he spoke quietly.

' "Is all well with thee, Mifanwy?"

' "Nothing is well with me, father's friend."

'And so I went back to my people, and I never saw my lord
any more.'

We had gone along until in the distance I could see the gypsy
fire, and turning the headland we saw the light on Farewell Point.
A white flash; a second's rest; a red flash; three seconds' occultation;
then white and red again. There is something heartening and brave
in Farewell Light. Ireland keeps watch over her share of the Atlantic
sea.

'When I left my lord, I was with child, and when I was delivered
of him, and the child weaned and strong, I sent him to my lord,
for every man wants his man child, and every family its heir. But
when he was four and twenty he came back to me, for the roving
gypsy blood and the fighting Irish blood were too much for him.
He was never Earl of Clontarf. He died while my lord still lived.
He married a Herne, a grandchild of Tyso, a brave golden girl.
And he got killed charging in the Balkan Wars.

'Niall's wife – my son's name was Niall – understood, and when
young Niall was old enough, we sent him to my lord. My lord
was old at this time, older than his years, and very poor. But of
my share of money he would have nothing. My lord died when
Niall's Niall was at school, so the little lad became Earl of Clontarf
and Kincora. I saw to it he had sufficient money, but he married
no rich woman. He married a poor Irish girl, and by her had two
children, Niall and Alick. He was interested in horses, and rode
well, my English friends tell me. But mounted on a brute in the
Punchestown races, he made a mistake at the stone wall. He did
not know the horse very well. So he let it have its head at the
stone wall. It threw its head up, took the jump by the roots, and

so Niall's Niall was killed. His wife, the little Irish girl, turned her face away from life and died.

'The boys are fifteen and thirteen now, and soon they will go into the world. I want them to have a fair chance, and it is for this reason I wish them to have money. I have been rich and then poor, and then very rich and again poor, and rich again and now poor. But if this venture succeeds, the boys will be all right.'

'Ye-s,' I said.

'You don't seem very enthusiastic, Kerry.'

'We have a saying,' I told her, 'that money won from a book-maker is only lent.'

'If you were down on a race meeting and on the last race of the last day you won a little, what would you say?'

'I'd say I only got a little of my own back.'

'Then we only get a little of our own back over the losses of a thousand years.'

We had come now to the encampment. Around the great fire were tall swarthy men with coloured neckerchiefs, who seemed more reserved, cleaner than the English gypsy. They rose quietly as the gypsy lady came. The great spotted Dalmation dogs rose too. In the half light the picketed horses could be seen, quiet as trees.

'This is the Younger of Destiny Bay,' said the old lady, 'who is kind enough to be our friend.'

'*Sa shan, rai!*' they spoke with quiet courtesy. 'How are you, sir?'

Lady Clontarf's maid hurried forward with a wrap, scolding, and speaking English with beautiful courtesy. 'You are dreadful, sister. You go walking the roads at night like a courting girl in spring. Gentleman, you are wrong to keep the *rawnee* out, and she an old woman and not well.'

'Supplistia,' Lady Clontarf chided, 'you have no more manners than a growling dog.'

'I am the *rawnee's* watchdog,' the girl answered.

'Madame, your maid is right. I will go now.'

'Kerry,' she stopped me, 'will you be friends with my little people?'

'I will be their true friend,' I promised, and I kissed her hand.

'God bless you!' she said. And '*koshto bok, rai!*' the gypsies wished me. 'Good luck, sir!' And I left the camp for my people's

house. The hunter's moon was dropping toward the edge of the
world, and the light on Farewell Point flashed seaward its white
and red, and as I walked along, I noticed that a wind from Ireland
had sprung up, and the Bilbao boat was bowling along nor'east
on the starboard tack. It seemed to me an augury.

In those days before my aunt Jenepher's marriage to Patrick Herne,
the work of Destiny Bay was divided in this manner: My dear
aunt Jenepher was, as was right, supreme in the house. My uncle
Valentine planned and superintended the breeding of the harness
ponies, and sheep, and black Dexter cattle which made Destiny
Bay so feared at the Dublin Horse Show and at the Bath and West.
My own work was the farms. To me fell the task of preparing
the stables and training grounds for Lady Clontarf's and my own
horses. It was a relief and an adventure to give up thinking of
turnips, wheat, barley, and seeds, and to examine the downs for
training ground. In my great-grandfather's time, in pre-Union
days, many a winner at the Curragh had been bred and trained at
Destiny Bay. The soil of the downs is chalky, and the matted
roots of the woven herbage have a certain give in them in the
driest of weather. I found out my great-grandfather's mile and a
half, and two miles and a half with a turn and shorter gallops of
various gradients. My grandfather had used them as a young man,
but mainly for hunters, horses which he sold for the great Spanish
and Austrian regiments. But to my delight the stables were as
good as ever. Covered with reed thatch, they required few repairs.
The floors were of chalk, and the boxes beautifully ventilated.
There were also great tanks for rainwater, which is of all water
the best for horses in training. There were also a few stalls for
restless horses. I was worried a little about lighting, but my uncle
Valentine told me that Sir Arthur Pollexfen allowed no artificial
lights where he trained. Horses went to bed with the fowls and
got up at cockcrow.

My own horses I got from Robinson without hurting his feelings. 'It's this way, Robinson,' I told him. 'We're trying to do a
crazy thing at Destiny, and I'm not bringing them to another
trainer. I'm bringing another trainer there. I can tell you no more.'

'Not another word, Mr Kerry. Bring them back when you want
to. I'm sorry to say good-bye to the wee colt. But I wish you
luck.'

We bought three more horses, and a horse for Ann-Dolly. So that with the six we had a rattling good little stable. When I saw Sir Arthur Pollexfen, my heart sank a little, for he seemed so much out of a former century. Small, ruddy-cheeked, with the white hair of a bishop, and a bishop's courtesy, I never thought he could run a stable. I thought, perhaps, he had grown too old and had been thinking for a long time now of the Place whither he was going, and that we had brought him back from his thoughts and he had left his vitality behind. His own servant came with him to Destiny Bay, and though we wished to have him in the house with us, yet he preferred to stay in a cottage by the stables. I don't know what there was about his clothes, but they were all of an antique though a beautiful cut. He never wore riding breeches but trousers of a bluish cloth and strapped beneath his varnished boots. A flowered waistcoat with a satin stock, a short covert coat, a grey bowler hat and gloves. Always there was a freshly-cut flower in his buttonhole, which his servant got every evening from the greenhouses at Destiny Bay, and kept overnight in a glass of water into which the least drop of whiskey had been poured. I mention this as extraordinary, as most racing men will not wear flowers. They believe flowers bring bad luck, though how the superstition arose I cannot tell. His evening trousers also buckled under his shoes, or rather half Wellingtons, such as army men wear, and though there was never a crease in them there was never a wrinkle. He would never drink port after dinner when the ladies had left, but a little whiskey punch which James Carabine would compound for him. Compared to the hard shrewd-eyed trainers I knew, this bland, soft-spoken old gentleman filled me with misgiving.

I got a different idea of the old man the first morning I went out to the gallops. The sun had hardly risen when the old gentleman appeared, as beautifully turned out as though he were entering the Show Ring at Ballsbridge. His servant held his horse, a big grey, while he swung into the saddle as light as a boy. His hack was feeling good that morning, and he and I went off toward the training ground at a swinging canter, the old gentleman half standing in his stirrups, with a light firm grip of his knees, riding as Cossacks do, his red terrier galloping behind him. When we settled down to walk he told me the pedigree of his horse, descended through Matchem and Whalebone from Oliver Cromwell's great charger The White Turk, or Place's White Turk, as it was called from the Lord Protector's stud manager. To hear him follow the intricacies of breeding was a revelation. Then I understood what a great horseman he was. On the training ground he was like a marshal commanding an army, such respect did every one accord him. The lads perched on the horses' withers, his head man, the grooms, all watched the apple-ruddy face, while he said little or nothing. He must have had eyes in the back of his head, though. For when a colt we had brought from Mr Gubbins, a son of Galtee More, started lashing out and the lad up seemed like taking a toss, the old man's voice came low and sharp: 'Don't fall off, boy.' And the boy did not fall off. The red terrier watched the trials with a keen eye, and I believe honestly that he knew as much about horses as any one of us and certainly more than any of us about his owner. When my lovely Ducks and Drakes went out at the lad's call to beat the field by two lengths over five furlongs, the dog looked up at Sir Arthur and Sir Arthur looked back at the dog, and what they thought toward each other, God knoweth.

I expected when we rode away that the old gentleman would have some word to say about my horses, but coming home, his remarks were of the country. 'Your Derry is a beautiful country, young Mister Kerry,' he said, 'though it would be treason to say that in my own country of Mayo.' Of my horses not a syllable.

He could be the most silent man I have ever known, though giving the illusion of keeping up a conversation. You could talk to him, and he would smile, and nod at the proper times, as though he were devouring every word you said. In the end you thought you had a very interesting conversation. But as to whether he had even heard you, you were never sure. On the other hand when he wished to speak, he spoke to the point and beautifully. Our bishop, on one of his pastoral visitations, if that be the term, stayed at Destiny Bay, and because my uncle Cosimo is a bishop too, and because he felt he ought to do something for our souls he remonstrated with us for starting our stable. My uncle Valentine was livid, but said nothing, for no guest must be contradicted in Destiny Bay.

'For surely, Sir Valentine, no man of breeding can mingle with the rogues, cutpurses and their womenfolk who infest racecourses, drunkards, bawds and common gamblers, without lowering himself to some extent to their level,' his Lordship purred. 'Yourself, one of the wardens of Irish chivalry, must give an example to the common people.'

'Your Lordship,' broke in old Sir Arthur Pollexfen, 'is egregiously misinformed. In all periods of the world's history, eminent personages have concerned themselves with the racing of horses. We read of Philip of Macedon, that while campaigning in Asia Minor, a courier brought him news of two events, of the birth of his son Alexander and of the winning, by his favourite horse, of the chief race at Athens, and we may reasonably infer that his joy over the winning of the race was equal to if not greater than that over the birth of Alexander. In the life of Charles the Second, the traits which do most credit to that careless monarch are his notable and gentlemanly death and his affection for his great race horse Old Rowley. Your Lordship is, I am sure,' said Sir Arthur, more blandly than any ecclesiastic could, 'too sound a Greek scholar not to remember the epigrams of Maecius and Philodemus, which show what interest these antique poets took in the racing of horses. And coming to present times, your Lordship must have heard that his Majesty (whom God preserve!) has won two Derbies, once with the leased horse Minoru, and again with his own great Persimmon. The premier peer of Scotland, the Duke of Hamilton, Duke of Chastellerault in France, Duke of Brandon in England, hereditary prince of Baden, is prouder of his fine mare Eau de Vie than of all his titles. As to the Irish families, the Persses of Galway, the Dawsons of Dublin, and my own, the Pollexfens of Mayo, have always been interested in the breeding and racing of horses. And none of these – my punch, if you please, James Carabine! – are, as your Lordship puts it, drunkards, bawds, and common gamblers. I fear your Lordship has been reading' – and he cocked his eye, bright as a wren's, at the bishop, 'religious publications of the sensational and morbid type.'

It was all I could do to keep from leaping on the table and giving three loud cheers for the County of Mayo.

Now, on those occasions, none too rare, when my uncle Valentine and I differed on questions of agricultural economy, or of national polity, or of mere faith and morals, he poured torrents of invective over my head, which mattered little. But when he was really aroused to bitterness he called me 'modern.' And by modern my uncle Valentine meant the quality inherent in brown buttoned boots, in white waistcoats worn with dinner jackets, in nasty little motor cars – in fine, those things before which the angels of God recoil in horror. While I am not modern in that sense, I am modern in this, that I like to see folk getting on with things. Of Lady Clontarf and of Irlandais colt, I heard no more. On the morning after seeing her home I called over to the caravan but it was no longer there. There was hardly a trace of it. I found a broken fern and a slip of oaktree, the gypsy patteran. But what it betokened or whither it pointed I could not tell. I had gone to no end of trouble in getting the stables and training grounds ready, and Sir Arthur Pollexfen had been brought out of his retirement in the County of Mayo. But still no word of the horse. I could see my uncle Valentine and Sir Arthur taking their disappointment bravely, if it never arrived, and murmuring some courteous platitude, out of the reign of good Queen Victoria, that it was a lady's privilege to change her mind. That might console them in their philosophy, but it would only make me hot with rage. For to me there is no sex in people of standards. They do not let one another down.

Then one evening the horse arrived.

It arrived at sundown in a large van drawn by four horses, a van belonging evidently to some circus. It was yellow and covered with paintings of nymphs being wooed by swains, in clothes hardly fitted to agricultural pursuits: of lions of terrifying aspect being put through their paces by a trainer of an aspect still more terrifying: of an Indian gentleman with a vast turban and a small loincloth playing a penny whistle to a snake that would have put the heart crosswise in Saint Patrick himself; of a most adipose lady in tights swinging from a ring while the husband and seven sons hung on to her like bees in a swarm. Floridly painted over the van was 'Arsène Bombaudiac, Prop., Bayonne.' The whole added no dignity to Destiny Bay, and if some sorceress had disclosed to Mr Bombaudiac of Bayonne that he was about to lose a van by fire at low tide on the beach of Destiny in Ireland within forty-eight hours – the driver was a burly gypsy while two of the most utter scoundrels I have ever laid eyes on sat beside him on the wide seat.

'Do you speak English?' I asked the driver.

'Yes, sir,' he answered, 'I am a Petulengro.'

'Which of these two beauties beside you is the jockey?'

'Neither, sir. These two are just gypsy fighting men. The jockey is inside with the horse.'

My uncle Valentine came down stroking his great red beard. He seemed fascinated by the pictures on the van. 'What your poor aunt Jenepher, Kerry,' he said, 'misses by being blind!'

'What she is spared, sir! Boy,' I called one of the servants, 'go get Sir Arthus Pollexfen. Where do you come from?' I asked the driver.

'From Dax, sir, in the South of France.'

'You're a liar,' I said. 'Your horses are half-bred Clydesdale. There is no team like that in the South of France.'

'We came to Dieppe with an *attelage basque*, six yoked oxen. But I was told they would not be allowed in England, so I telegraphed our chief, Piramus Petulengro, to have a team at Newhaven. So I am not a liar, sir.'

'I am sorry.'

'Sir, that is all right.'

Sir Arthur Pollexfen came down from where he had been speaking to my aunt Jenepher. I could see he was tremendously excited, because he walked more slowly than was usual, spoke with more deliberation. He winced a little as he saw the van. But he was of the old heroic school. He said nothing.

'I think, Sir Valentine,' he said, 'we might have the horse out.'

'Ay, we might as well know the worst,' said my uncle Valentine.

A man jumped from the box, and swung the crossbar up. The door opened and into the road stepped a small man in dark clothes. Never on this green earth of God have I seen such dignity. He was dressed in dark clothes with a wide dark hat, and his face was brown as soil. White starched cuffs covered half of his hands. He took off his hat and bowed first to my uncle Valentine, then to Sir Arthur, and to myself last. His hair was plastered down on his forehead, and the impression you got was of an ugly rugged face, with piercing black eyes. He seemed to say: 'Laugh, if you dare!' But laughter was the farthest thing from us, such tremendous masculinity did the small man have. He looked at us searchingly, and I had the feeling that if he didn't like us, for two pins he would have the bar across the van door again and be off with the horse. Then he spoke gutturally to some one inside.

A boy as rugged as himself, in a Basque cap and with a Basque sash, led first a small donkey round as a barrel out of the outrageous van. One of the gypsies took it, and the next moment the boy led out the Irlandais colt.

He came out confidently, quietly, approaching gentlemen as a gentleman, a beautiful brown horse, small, standing perfectly. I had just one glance at the sound strong legs and the firm ribs, before his head caught my eye. The graceful neck, the beautiful small muzzle, the gallant eyes. In every inch of him you could see breeding. While Sir Arthur was examining his hocks, and my uncle Valentine was standing weightily considering strength of lungs and heart, my own heart went out to the lovely eyes that seemed to ask: 'Are these folk friends?'

Now I think you could parade the Queen of Sheba in the show ring before me without extracting more than an off-hand compliment out of me, but there is something about a gallant thoroughbred that makes me sing. I can quite understand the trainer who, pointing to Manifesto, said that if he ever found a woman with a shape like that, he'd marry her. So out of my heart through my lips came the cry: '*Och, asthore!*' which is, in our Gaelic, 'Oh, my dear!'

The Spanish jockey, whose brown face was rugged and impassive as a Pyrenee, looked at me, and broke into a wide, understanding smile.

'*Si, si, Señor,*' he uttered, '*si, si!*'

Never did a winter pass so merrily, so advantageously at Destiny Bay. Usually there is fun enough with the hunting, but with a racing stable in winter there is always anxiety. Is there a suspicion of a cough in the stables? Is the ground too hard for gallops? Will snow come and hold the gallops up for a week? Fortunately we are right on the edge of the great Atlantic drift, and you can catch at times the mild amazing atmosphere of the Caribbean. While Scotland sleeps beneath its coverlet of snow, and England shivers in its ghastly fog, we on the north-east seaboard of Ireland go through a winter that is short as a midsummer night in Lofoden. The trees have hardly put off their gold and brown before we perceive their cheeping green. And one soft day we say: 'Soon on that bank will be the fairy gold of the primrose.' And behold, while you are looking the primrose is there!

Each morning at sun-up, the first string of horses were out. Quietly as a general officer reviewing a parade old Sir Arthur sat on his grey horse, his red dog beside him, while Geraghty, his head man, galloped about with his instructions. Hares bolted from their forms in the grass. The sun rolled away the mists from the blue mountains of Donegal. At the starting gate, which Sir Arthur had set up, the red-faced Irish boys steered their mounts from a walk toward the tapes. A pull at the lever and they were off. The old man seemed to notice everything. 'Go easy, boy, don't force that horse!' His low voice would carry across the downs. 'Don't lag there, Murphy, ride him!' And when the gallop was done, he would trot across to the horses, his red dog trotting beside him, asking how Sarsfield went. Did Ducks and Drakes seem interested? Did Rustum go up to his bit? Then they were off at a slow walk toward their sand bath, where they rolled like dogs. Then the sponging and the rubbing, and the fresh hay in the mangers kept as clean as a hospital. At eleven the second string came out. At half-past three the lads were called to their horses, and a quarter of an hour's light walking was given to them. At four, Sir Arthur made his 'stables', questioning the lads in each detail as to how the horses had fed, running his hand over their legs to feel for any heat in the joints that might betoken trouble.

Small as our stable was, I doubt if there was one in Great Britain and Ireland to compare with it in each fitting and necessity for training a race horse. Sir Arthur pinned his faith to old black tartar oats, of about forty-two pounds to the bushel, bran mashes with a little linseed, and sweet old meadow hay.

The Irlandais colt went beautifully. The Spanish jockey's small brother, Joselito, usually rode it, while the jockey's self, whose name we were told was Frasco, Frasco Moreno – usually called, he told us, Don Frasco – looked on. He constituted himself a sort of sub-trainer for the colt, allowing none else to attend to its feeding. The small donkey was its invariable stable companion, and had to be led out to exercise with it. The donkey belonged to Joselito. Don Frasco rode many trials on the other horses. He might appear small standing, but on horseback he seemed a large man, so straight did he sit in the saddle. The little boys rode with a fairly short stirrup, but the gitano scorned anything but the traditional seat. He never seemed to move on a horse. Yet he could do what he liked with it.

The Irlandais colt was at last named Romany Baw, or 'gypsy friend' in English, as James Carabine explained to us, and Lady

Clontarf's colours registered, quarter red and gold. When the winter lists came out, we saw the horse quoted at a hundred to one, and later at the call over of the Victoria Club, saw the price offered but not taken. My uncle Valentine made a journey to Dublin, to arrange for Lady Clontarf's commission being placed, putting it in the hands of a Derry man who had become big in the affairs of Tattersall's. What he himself and Sir Arthur Pollexfen and the jockey had on I do not know, but he arranged to place an hundred pounds of mine, and fifty of Ann-Dolly's. As the months went by, the odds crept down gradually to thirty-three to one, stood there for a while and went out to fifty. Meanwhile Sir James became a sensational favourite at fives, and Toison d'Or varied between tens and one hundred to eight. Some news of a great trial of Lord Shire's horse had leaked out which accounted for the ridiculously short price. But no word did or could get out about Lady Clontarf's colt. The two gypsy fighters from Dax patrolled Destiny Bay, and God help any poor tipster or wretched newspaper tout who tried to plumb the mysteries of training. I honestly believe a bar of iron and a bog hole would have been his end.

The most fascinating figure in this crazy world was the gypsy jockey. To see him talk to Sir Arthur Pollexfen was a phenomenon. Sir Arthur would speak in English and the gypsy answer in Spanish, neither knowing a word of the other's language, yet each perfectly understanding the other. I must say that this only referred to how a horse ran, or how Romany Baw was feeding and feeling. As to more complicated problems, Ann-Dolly was called in, to translate his Spanish.

'Ask him,' said Sir Arthur, 'has he ever ridden in France?'

'*Oiga, Frasco*,' and Ann-Dolly would burst into a torrent of gutturals.

'*Si, si, Dona Anna.*'

'Ask him has he got his clearance from the Jockey Club of France?'

'*Seguro. Don Arturo!*' And out of his capacious pocket he extracted the French Jockey Club's 'character'. They made a picture I will never forget, the old horseman ageing so gently, the vivid boyish beauty of Ann-Dolly, and the overpowering dignity and manliness of the jockey. Always, except when he was riding or working at his anvil – for he was our smith too – he wore the dark clothes, which evidently some village tailor of the Pyrenees made for him – the very short coat, the trousers tubed like cigarettes, his stiff shirt with the vast cuffs. He never wore a collar, nor a neckerchief. Always his back was flat as the side of a house.

When he worked at the anvil, with his young ruffian of a brother at the bellows, he sang. He had shakes and grace notes enough to make a thrush quit. Ann-Dolly translated one of his songs for us.

> *No tengo padre ni madre . . .*
> *Que desgraciado soy yo!*
> *Soy como el arbol solo*
> *Que echa frutas y no echa flor . . .*

'He sings he has no father or mother. How out of luck he is! He is like a lonely tree, which bears the fruit and not the flower.'

'God bless my soul, Kerry,' my uncle was shocked. 'The little man is homesick.'

'No, no!' Ann-Dolly protested. 'He is very happy. That is why he sings a sad song.'

One of the reasons of the little man's happiness was the discovery of our national game of handball. He strolled over to the Irish Village and discovered the court behind the Inniskillen Dragoon, that most notable of rural pubs. He was tremendously excited, and getting some gypsy to translate for him, challenged the local champion for the stake of a barrel of porter. He made the local champion look like a carthorse in the Grand National. When it was told to me I couldn't believe it. Ann-Dolly explained to me that the great game of Basque country was *pelota*.

'But don't they play *pelota* with a basket?'

'Real *pelota* is *à mains nues*, "with the hands naked." '

'You mean Irish handball,' I told her.

I regret that the population of Destiny made rather a good thing out of Don Frasco's prowess on the court, going from village to village, and betting on a certain win. The end was a match between Mick Tierney, the Portrush Jarvey and the jockey. The match was billed for the champion of Ulster, and Don Frasco was put down on the card, to explain his lack of English, as Danny Frask, the Glenties Miracle, the Glenties being a district of Donegal where Erse is the native speech. The match was poor, the Portrush Jarvey, after the first game, standing and watching the ball hiss past him with his eyes on his cheek bones. All Donegal seemed to have turned out for the fray. When the contest was over, a big Glenties man pushed his way toward the jockey.

'Dublin and London and New York are prime cities,' he chanted, 'but Glenties is truly magnificent. *Kir do lauv anshin, a railt na hooee,* "put your hand there, Star of the North".'

'*No entiendo, señor,*' said Don Frasco. And with that the fight began.

James Carabine was quick enough to get the jockey out of the court before he was lynched. But Destiny Bay men, gypsies, fishers, citizens of Derry, bookmakers and their clerks and the fighting tribes of Donegal went to it with a vengeance. Indeed, according to experts, nothing like it, for spirit or results, had been seen since or before the Prentice Boys had chased King James (whom God give his deserts!) from Derry Walls. The removal of the stunned and wounded from the courts drew the attention of the police, for the fight was continued in grim silence. But on the entrance of half a dozen peelers commanded by a huge sergeant, Joselito, the jockey's young brother, covered himself with glory. Leaping on the reserved seats, he brought his right hand over hard and true to the sergeant's jaw, and the sergeant was out for half an hour. Joselito was arrested, but the case was laughed out of court. The idea of a minuscule jockey who could ride at ninety pounds knocking out six-foot-three of Royal Irish Constabulary was too much. Nothing was found on him but his bare hands, a packet of cigarettes and thirty sovereigns he had won over the match. But I knew better. I decided to prove him with hard questions.

'Ask him in Romany, James Carabine, what he had wrapped around that horseshoe he threw away.'

'He says: "Tow, Mister Kerry." '

'Get me my riding crop,' I said; 'I'll take him behind the stables.' And the training camp lost its best lightweight jockey for ten days, the saddle suddenly becoming repulsive to him. I believe he slept on his face.

But the one who was really wild about the affair was Ann-Dolly. She came across from Spanish Men's Rest flaming with anger.

'Because a Spanish wins, there is fighting, there is anger. If an Irish wins, there is joy, there is drinking. Oh, shame of sportsmanship!'

'Oh, shut your gab, Ann-Dolly,' I told her. 'They didn't know he was a Spanish, as you call it.'

'What did they think he was if not a Spanish? Tell me. I demand it of you.'

'They thought he was Welsh.'

'Oh, in that case . . . ' said Ann-Dolly, completely mollified. *Ipsa Hibernis hiberniora!*

I wouldn't have you think that all was beer and skittles, as the English say, in training Romany Baw for the Derby. As spring came closer, the face of the old trainer showed signs of strain. The Lincoln Handicap was run and the Grand National passed, and suddenly flat-racing was on us. And now not the Kohinoor was watched more carefully than the Derby horse. We had a spanking trial on a course as nearly approaching the Two Thousand Guineas route as Destiny Downs would allow, and when Romany Baw flew past us, beating Ducks and Drakes who had picked him up at a mile for the uphill dash, and Sir Arthur clicked his watch, I saw his tense face relax.

'He ran well,' said the old man.

'He'll walk it,' said my uncle Valentine.

My uncle Valentine and Jenico and Ann-Dolly were going across to Newmarket Heath for the big race, but the spring of the year is the time that the farmer must stay by his land, and nurse it like a child. All farewells, even for a week, are sad, and I was loath to see the horses go into the races. Romany Baw had a regular summer bloom on him and his companion, the donkey, was corpulent as an alderman. Ducks and Drakes looked rough and backward, but that didn't matter.

'You've got the best-looking horse in the United Kingdom,' I told Sir Arthur.

'Thank you, Kerry,' the old man was pleased. 'And as to Ducks and Drakes, looks aren't everything.'

'Sure, I know that,' I told him.

'I wouldn't be rash,' he told me, 'but I'd have a little on both. That is, if they go to the post fit and well.'

I put in the days as well as I could, getting ready for the Spring Show at Dublin. But my heart and my thoughts were with my people and the horses at Newmarket. I could see my uncle Valentine's deep bow with his hat in his hand as they passed the Roman ditch at Newmarket, giving that squat wall the reverence that racing men have accorded it since races were run there, though why, none know. A letter from Ann-Dolly apprised me that the horses had made a good crossing and that Romany Baw was well – 'and you mustn't think, my dear, that your colt is not as much and more to us than the Derby horse, no, Kerry, not for one moment. Lady Clontarf is here, in her caravan, and oh, Kerry, she looks ill. Only her burning spirit keeps her frail body alive. Jenico and I are going down to Eastbourne to see the little Earl and his brother . . . You will get his letter, cousin, on the morning of the race. . . . '

At noon that day I could stand it no longer, so I had James Carabine put the trotter in the dogcar. 'There are some things I want in Derry,' I told myself, 'and I may as well get them to-day as to-morrow.' And we went spinning toward Derry Walls. Ducks and Drakes' race was the two-thirty. And after lunch I looked at reapers I might be wanting in July until the time of the race. I went along to the club, and had hardly entered it when I saw the boy putting up the telegram on the notice board:

1, *Ducks and Drakes*, an hundred to eight; 2, *Geneva*, four to six; 3, *Ally Sloper*, three to one.

'That's that!' I said. Another telegram gave the betting for the Two Thousand: Threes, *Sir James*; seven to two, *Toison d'Or*; eights, *Ca' Canny, Greek Singer, Germanicus*; tens, six or seven horses; twenty to one any other. No word in the betting of the gypsy horse, and I wondered had anything happened. Surely a horse looking as well as he did must have attracted backers' attention. And as I was worrying the result came in, *Romany Baw*, first; *Sir James*, second, *Toison d'Or*, third.

'Kerry,' somebody called.

'I haven't a minute,' I shouted. Neither I had, for James Carabine was outside, waiting to hear the result. When I told him he said: 'There's a lot due to you, Mister Kerry, in laying out those gallops.' 'Be damned to that!' I said, but I was pleased all the same.

I was on tenterhooks until I got the papers describing the race. Ducks and Drakes' win was dismissed, summarily, as that of an Irish outsider, and the jockey, Flory Cantillon (Frasco could not manage the weight), was credited with a clever win of two lengths. But the account of Romany Baw's race filled me with indignation.

According to it, the winner got away well, but the favourites
weren't hampered at the start and either could have beaten the
Irish trained horse, only that they just didn't. The race was won
by half a length, a head separating second and third, and most of
the account was given to how the favourites chased the lucky
outsider, and in a few more strides would have caught him. There
were a few dirty backhanders given at Romany's jockey, who,
they said, would be more at home in a circus than on a modern
race track. He sat like a rider of a century back, they described it,
more like an exponent of the old manège than a modern jockey,
and even while the others were thundering at his horse's hindquarters he never moved his seat or used his whip. The experts'
judgment of the race was that the Irish colt was forward in a
backward field, and that Romany would be lost on Epsom Downs,
especially with its 'postilion rider'.

But the newspaper criticisms of the jockey and his mount did
not seem to bother my uncle Valentine or the trainer or the jockey's
self. They came back elated; even the round white donkey had a
humorous happy look in his full Latin eye.

'Did he go well?' I asked.

'He trotted it,' said my uncle Valentine.

'But the accounts read, sir,' I protested, 'that the favourites
would have caught him in another couple of strides.'

'Of course they would,' said my uncle Valentine, 'at the pace
he was going,' he added.

'I see,' said I.

'You see nothing,' said my uncle Valentine. 'But if you had seen
the race you might talk. The horse is a picture. It goes so sweetly
that you wouldn't think it was going at all. And as for the gypsy
jockey – '

'The papers say he's antiquated.'

'He's seven pounds better than Flory Cantillon,' said my uncle
Valentine.

I whistled. Cantillon is our best Irish jockey, and his retaining
fees are enormous, and justified. 'They said he was nearly caught
napping – '

'Napping be damned!' exploded my uncle Valentine. 'This Spanish gypsy is the finest judge of pace I ever saw. He knew he had
the race won, and he never bothered.'

'If the horse is as good as that, and you have as high an opinion of the rider, well, sir, I won a hatful over the Newmarket meeting, and as the price hasn't gone below twenties for the Derby, I'm going after the Ring. There's many a bookmaker will wish he'd stuck to his father's old-clothes business.'

'I wouldn't, Kerry,' said my uncle Valentine. 'I'm not sure I wouldn't hedge a bit of what I have on, if I were you.'

I was still with amazement.

'I saw Mifanwy Clontarf,' said my uncle Valentine, 'and only God and herself and myself and now you, know how ill that woman is.'

'But ill or not ill, she won't scratch the horse.'

'She won't,' said my uncle Valentine, and his emphasis on 'she' chilled me to the heart. 'You're forgetting, Kerry,' he said very quietly, 'the Derby Rule.'

Of the Derby itself on Epsom Downs, everybody knows. It is supposed to be the greatest test of a three-year-old in the world, though old William Day used to hold it was easy. The course may have been easy for Lord George Bentinck's famous and unbeaten mare Crucifix, when she won the Oaks in 1840, but most winners over the full course justify their victory in other races. The course starts up a heartbreaking hill, and swinging around the top, comes down again toward Tattenham Corner. If a horse waits to steady itself coming down it is beaten. The famous Fred Archer (whose tortured soul God rest!) used to take Tattenham Corner with one leg over the rails. The straight is uphill. A mile and a half of the trickiest, most heartbreaking ground in the world. Such is Epsom. Its turf has been consecrated by the hoofs of great horses since James I established there a race for the Silver Bell: by Cromwell's great Coffin mare; by the Arabs, Godolphin and Darby; by the great bay, Malton; by the prodigious Eclipse; by Diomed, son of Florizel, who went to America . . .

Over the Derby what sums are wagered no man knows. On it is won the Calcutta Sweepstake, a prize of which makes a man rich for life, and the Stock Exchange sweep and other sweeps innumerable. Someone has ventured the belief that on it annually are five million pounds sterling, and whether he is millions short or millions over none knows. Because betting is illegal.

There are curious customs in regard to it, as this: that when the result is sent over the ticker to clubs, in case of a dead heat, the word 'deat heat' must come first, because within recent years a trusted lawyer, wagering trust funds on a certain horse, was waiting by the tape to read the result, and seeing another horse's name come up, went away forthwith and blew his brains out. Had he been less volatile he would have seen his own fancy's name follow that, with 'dead heat' after it and been to this day rich and respected. So now, for the protection of such, 'dead heat' comes first. A dead heat in the Derby is as rare a thing as there is in the world, but still you can't be too cautious. But the quaintest rule of the Derby is this: that if the nominator of a horse for the Derby Stakes dies, his horse is automatically scratched. There is a legend to the effect that an heir-at-law purposed to kill the owner of an entry, and to run a prime favourite crookedly, and that on hearing this the Stewards of the Jockey Club made the rule. Perhaps it has a more prosaic reason. The Jockey club may have considered that when a man died, in the trouble of fixing his estates, forfeits would not be paid, and that it was best for all concerned to have the entry scratched. How it came about does not matter, it exists. Whether it is good in law is not certain. Racing folk will quarrel with His Majesty's Lord Justices of Appeal, with the Privy Council, but they will not quarrel with the Jockey Club. Whether it is good in fact is indisputable, for certain owners can tell stories of narrow escapes from racing gangs, in those old days before the Turf was cleaner than the Church, when attempts were made to nobble favourites, when jockeys had not the wings of angels under their silken jackets, when harsh words were spoken about trainers – very, very long ago. There it is, good or bad, the Derby Rule!

As to our bets on the race, they didn't matter. It was just bad luck. But to see the old lady's quarter million of pounds and more go down the pike was a tragedy. We had seen so much of shabby great names that I trembled for young Clontarf and his brother. Armenian and Greek families of doubtful antecedents were always on the lookout for a title for their daughters, and crooked businesses always needed directors of title to catch gulls, so much in the United Kingdom do the poor trust their peers. The boys would not be exactly poor, because the horse, whether or not it ran in the Derby, would be worth a good round sum. If it were as good as my uncle Valentine said, it would win the Leger and the Gold Cup at Ascot. But even with these triumphs it wouldn't be a Derby winner. And the Derby means so much. There are so many

people in England who remember dates by the Derby winners'
names, as 'I was married in *Bend Or's* year', or 'the *Achilles* was
lost in the China seas, let me see when – that was in *Sainfoin's*
year'. Also I wasn't sure that the Spanish gypsy would stay to ride
him at Doncaster, or return for Ascot. I found him one day standing on the cliffs of Destiny and looking long at the sea, and I
knew what that meant. And perhaps Romany Baw would not run
for another jockey as he ran for him.

I could not think that Death could be so cruel as to come
between us and triumph. In Destiny we have a friendliness for the
Change which most folk dread. One of our songs says:

> *When Mother Death in her warm arms shall embrace me,*
> *Low lull me to sleep with sweet Erin-go-bragh –*

We look upon it as a kind friend who comes when one is tired
and twisted with pain, and says: 'Listen, *avourneen*, soon the dawn
will come, and the tide is on the ebb. We must be going.' And
we trust him to take us, by a short road or a long road to a place
of birds and bees, of which even lovely Destiny is but a clumsy
seeming. He could not be such a poor sportsman as to come before
the aged gallant lady had her last gamble. And poor Sir Arthur,
who had come out of his old age in Mayo to win a Derby! It
would break his heart. And the great horse, it would be so hard
on him. Nothing will convince me that a thoroughbred does not
know a great race when he runs one. The streaming competitors,
the crackle of silk, the roar as they come into the straight, and the
sense of the jockey calling on the great heart that the writer of Job
knew so well. 'The glory of his nostril is terrible,' says the greatest
of poets. 'He pauseth in the valley and rejoiceth in his strength:
he goeth on to meet the armed men.' Your intellectual will claim
that the thoroughbred is an artificial brainless animal evolved by
men for their amusement. Your intellectual, here again, is a liar.

Spring came in blue and gold. Blue of sea and fields and trees;
gold of sun and sand and buttercup. Blue of wild hyacinth and
blue bell; gold of primrose and laburnum tree. The old gypsy lady
was with her caravan near Bordeaux, and from the occasional letter
my uncle Valentine got, and from the few words he dropped to
me, she was just holding her own. May drowsed by with the
cheeping of the little life in the hedgerows. The laburnum floated
in a cloud of gold and each day Romany Baw grew stronger.

When his blankets were stripped from him he looked a mass of fighting muscle under a covering of satin, and his eye showed that his heart was fighting too. Old Sir Arthur looked at him a few days before we were to go to England, and he turned to me.

'Kerry,' he said, very quietly.

'Yes, Sir Arthur.'

'All my life I have been breeding and training horses, and it just goes to show,' he told me, 'the goodness of God that he let me handle this great horse before I died.'

The morning before we left my uncle Valentine received a letter which I could see moved him. He swore a little as he does when moved and stroked his vast red beard and looked fiercely at nothing at all.

'Is it bad news, sir?' I asked.

He didn't answer me directly. 'Lady Clontarf is coming to the Derby,' he told me.

Then it was my turn to swear a little. It seemed to me to be but little short of maniacal to risk a Channel crossing and the treacherous English climate in her stage of health. If she should die on the way or on the Downs, then all her planning and our work was for nothing. Why could she not have remained in the soft French air, husbanding her share of life until the event was past!

'She comes of ancient, violent blood,' thundered my uncle Valentine, 'and where should she be but present when her people or her horses go forth to battle?'

'You are right, sir,' I said.

The epithet of 'flaming' which the English apply to their June was in this year of grace well deserved. The rhododendrons were bursting into great fountains of scarlet, and near the swans the cygnets paddled, unbelievably small. The larks fluttered in the air above the Downs, singing so gallantly that when you heard the trill of the nightingale in the thicket giving his noontime song, you felt inclined to say: 'Be damned to that Italian bird; my money's on the wee fellow!' All through Surrey the green walls of spring rose high and thick, and then suddenly coming, as we came, through Leatherhead and topping the hill, in the distance the black colony of the downs showed like a thundercloud. At a quarter mile away, the clamour came to you, like the vibration when great bells have been struck.

The stands and enclosure were packed so thickly that one wondered how movement was possible, how people could enjoy themselves, close as herrings. My uncle Valentine had brought his beautiful harness ponies across from Ireland, 'to encourage English interest in the Irish horse' he explained it, but with his beautifully-cut clothes, his grey high hat, it seemed to me that more people looked at him as we spun along the road than looked at the horses. Behind us sat James Carabine, with his face brown as autumn and the gold rings in his thickened ears. We got out near the paddock and Carabine took the ribbons. My uncle Valentine said quietly to him: 'Find out how things are, James Carabine.' And I knew he was referring to the gypsy lady. Her caravan was somewhere on the Downs guarded by her gypsies, but my uncle had been there the first day of the meeting, and on Monday night, at the National Sporting, some of the gypsies had waited for him coming out and given him news. I asked him how she was, but all his answer was: 'It's in the hands of God.'

Along the track toward the grandstand we made our way. On the railings across the track the bookmakers were proclaiming their market: 'I'll give fives the field. I'll give nine to one bar two. I'll give twenty to one bar five. Outsiders! Fives *Sir James*. Seven to one *Toison d'Or*. Nines *Honey Bee*. Nines *Welsh Melody*. Ten to one the gypsy horse.'

'It runs all right,' said my uncle Valentine, 'up to now.'

'Twenty to one *Maureen Roe*: Twenties *Asclepiades*: Twenty-five *Rifle Ranger*. Here thirty-three to one *Rifle Ranger, Monk of Sussex*, or *Presumptuous* – '

'Gentlemen, I am here to plead with you not to back the favourite. In this small envelope you will find the number of the winner. For the contemptible sum of two shillings or half a dollar, you may amass a fortune. Who gave the winner of last year's Derby?' a tipster was calling. 'Who gave the winner of the Oaks? Who gave the winner of the Stewards' Cup?'

'All right, guv'nor, I'll bite. 'Oo the 'ell did?'

Opposite the grandstand the band of the Salvation Army was blaring the music of 'Work, for the Night is Coming'. Gypsy girls were going around *dukkering* or telling fortunes. 'Ah, gentleman, you've a lucky face. Cross the poor gypsy's hand with silver – '

'You better cut along and see your horse saddle,' said my uncle Valentine. Ducks and Drakes was in the Ranmore Plate and with the penalty he received after Newmarket, Frasco could ride him. As I went toward the paddock I saw the numbers go up, and I saw we were drawn third, which I think is best of all on the tricky Epsom five-furlong dash. I got there in time to see the gypsy swing into the saddle in the green silk jacket and orange cap, and Sir Arthur giving him his orders. 'Keep back of the Fusilier,' he pointed to the horse, 'and then come out. Hit him once if you have to, and no more.'

'*Sí, sí, Don Arturo!*' And he grinned at me.

'Kerry, read this,' said the old trainer, and he gave me a newspaper, 'and tell me before the race,' his voice was trembling a little, 'if there's truth in it.'

I pushed the paper into my pocket and went back to the box where my uncle Valentine and Jenico and Ann-Dolly were. 'What price my horse?' I asked in Tattersall's.

'Sixes, Mister MacFarlane.'

'I'll take six hundred to an hundred twice.' As I moved away there was a rush to back it. It tumbled in five minutes to five to two.

'And I thought I'd get tens,' I said to my uncle Valentine, 'with the Fusilier and Bonny Hortense in the race. I wonder who's been backing it.'

'I have,' said Ann-Dolly. 'I got twelves.'

'You might have the decency to wait until the owner gets on,' I said bitterly. And as I watched the tapes went up. It was a beautiful start. Everything except those on the outside seemed to have a chance as they raced for the rails. I could distinguish the green jacket but vaguely until they came to Tattenham Corner, when I could see Fusilier pull out, and Bonny Hortense follow. But behind Fusilier, racing quietly beside the filly, was the jacket green.

'I wish he'd go up,' I said.

'The favourite wins,' they were shouting. And a woman in the box next us began to clap her hands calling: 'Fusilier's won. Fusilier wins it!'

'You're a damn fool, woman,' said Ann-Dolly, 'Ducks and Drakes has it.' And as she spoke, I could see Frasco hunch forward slightly and dust his mount's neck with his whip. He crept past the hard-pressed Fusilier to win by half a length.

In my joy I nearly forgot the newspaper, and I glanced at it rapidly. My heart sank. 'Gypsy Owner Dying as Horse Runs in Derby,' I read, and reading down it I felt furious. Where the man got his information from I don't know, but he drew a picturesque account of the old gypsy lady on her death bed on the Downs as Romany Baw was waiting in his stall. The account was written the evening before, and 'it is improbable she will last the night', it ended. I gave it to my uncle Valentine, who had been strangely silent over my win.

'What shall I say to Sir Arthur Pollexfen?'

'Say she's ill, but it's all rot she's dying.'

I noticed as I went to the paddock a murmur among the race-goers. The attention of all had been drawn to the gypsy horse by its jockey having won the Ranmore Plate. Everywhere I heard questions being asked as to whether she were dead. Sir James had hardened to fours. And on the heath I heard a woman proffer a sovereign to a bookmaker on Romany Baw, and he said, 'That horse don't run, lady.' I forgot my own little triumph in the tragedy of the scratching of the great horse.

In the paddock Sir Arthur was standing watching the lads leading the horses around. Twenty-seven entries, glossy as silk, muscled like athletes of old Greece, ready to run for the Derby Stakes. The jockeys, with their hard wizened faces, stood talking to trainers and owners, saying nothing about the race, all already having been said, but just putting in the time until the order came to go to the gate. I moved across to the old Irish trainer and the gypsy jockey. Sir Arthur was saying nothing, but his hand trembled as he took a pinch of snuff from his old-fashioned silver horn. The gypsy jockey stood erect, with his overcoat over his silk. It was a heart-rending five minutes standing there beside them, waiting for the message that they were not to go.

My uncle Valentine was standing with a couple of the Stewards. A small race official was explaining something to them. They nodded him away. There was another minute's conversation and my uncle came toward us. The old trainer was fumbling pitifully with his silver snuff horn, trying to find the pocket in which to put it.

'It's queer,' said my uncle Valentine, 'but nobody seems to know where Lady Clontarf is. She's not in her caravan.'

'So – ' questioned the old trainer.

'So you run,' said my uncle Valentine. 'The horse comes under starter's orders. You may have an objection, Arthur, but you run.'

The old man put on youth and grandeur before my eyes. He stood erect. With an eye like an eagle's he looked around the paddock.

'Leg up, boy!' he snapped at Frasco.

'Here, give me your coat.' I helped throw the golden-and-red shirted figure into the saddle. Then the head lad led the horse out.

We moved down the track and into the stand, and the parade began. Lord Shire's great horse, and the French hope Toison d'Or; the brown colt owned by the richest merchant in the world, and the little horse owned by the Leicester butcher, who served in his own shop; the horse owned by the peer of last year's making; and the bay filly owned by the first baroness in England. They went down past the stand, and turning breezed off at a gallop back, to cross the Downs toward the starting gate, and as they went with each went someone's heart. All eyes seemed turned on the gypsy horse, with his rider erect as a Life Guardsman. As Frasco raised his whip to his cap in the direction of our box, I heard in one of the neighbouring boxes a man say: 'but that horse's owner is dead!'

'Is that so, uncle Valentine?' asked Ann-Dolly. There were tears in her eyes. 'Is that true?'

'Nothing is true until you see it yourself,' parried my uncle Valentine. And as she seemed to be about to cry openly – 'Don't you see the horse running?' he said. 'Don't you know the rule?' But his eyes were riveted through his glasses on the starting gate. I could see deep furrows of anxiety on his bronze brow. In the distance, over the crowd's heads, over the bookmakers' banners, over the tents, we could see the dancing horses at the tape, the gay colours of the riders moving here and there in an intricate pattern, the massed hundreds of black figures at the start. Near us, across the rails, some religious zealots let fly little balloons carrying banners reminding us that doom was waiting. Their band broke into a lugubrious hymn, while nasal voices took it up. In the silence of the crowded downs, breathless for the start, the religious demonstration seemed startlingly trivial. The line of horses, formed for the gate, broke, and wheeled. My uncle snapped his fingers in vexation.

'Why can't the fool get them away?'

Then out of a seeming inextricable maze, the line formed suddenly and advanced on the tapes. And the heavy silence exploded into a low roar like growling thunder. Each man shouted: 'They're off – ' The Derby had started.

It seemed like a river of satin, with iridescent foam, pouring, against all nature, uphill. And for one instant you could distinguish nothing. You looked to see if your horse had got away well, had not been kicked or cut into at the start, and as you were disentangling them, the banks of gorse shut them from your view, and when you saw them again they were racing for the turn of the hill. The erect figure of the jockey caught my eye before his colours did.

'He's lying fifth,' I told my uncle Valentine.

'He's running well,' my uncle remarked quietly.

They swung around the top of the hill, appearing above the rails and gorse, like something tremendously artificial, like some theatrical illusion, as of a boat going across the stage. There were three horses grouped together, then a black horse – Esterhazy's fine colt – then Romany Baw, then after that a stretching line of horses. Something came out of the pack at the top of the hill, and passed the gypsy horse and the fourth.

'Toison d'Or is going up,' Jenico told me.

But the gallant French colt's bolt was flown. He fell back, and now one of the leaders dropped back. And Romany was fourth as they started downhill for Tattenham Corner. 'How slow they go!' I thought.

'What a pace!' said Jenico, who had his watch in his hand.

At Tattenham Corner the butcher's lovely little horse was beaten, and a sort of moan came from the rails where the poor people stood. Above the religious band's outrageous nasal tones, the ring began roaring: 'Sir James! Sir James has it. Twenty to one bar Sir James!'

As they came flying up the stretch I could see the favourite going along, like some bird flying low, his jockey hunched like an ape on his withers. Beside him raced an outsider, a French-bred horse owned by Kazoutlian, an Armenian banker. Close to his heels came the gypsy horse on the inside, Frasco sitting as though the horse were standing still. Before him raced the favourite and the rank outsider.

'It's all over,' I said. 'He can't get through. And he can't pull round. Luck of the game!'

And then the rider on the Armenian's horse tried his last effort. He brought his whip high in the air. My uncle Valentine thundered a great oath.

'Look, Kerry!' His fingers gripped my shoulder.

I knew, when I saw the French horse throw his head up, that he was going to swerve at the whip, but I never expected Frasco's mad rush. He seemed to jump the opening, and land the horse past Sir James.

'The favourite's beat!' went up the cry of dismay.

Romany Baw, with Frasco forward on his neck, passed the winning post first by a clear length.

Then a sort of stunned silence fell on the Derby crowd. Nobody knew what would happen. If, as the rumour went around, the owner was dead, then the second automatically won. All eyes were on the horse as the trainer led him into the paddock, followed by second and third. All eyes turned from the horse toward the notice board as the numbers went up: 17, 1, 26. All folk were waiting for the red objection signal. The owner of the second led his horse in, the burly Yorkshire peer. An old gnarled man, with a face like a walnut, Kazoutlian's self, led in the third.

'I say, Kerry,' Jenico called quietly, 'something's up near the paddock.'

I turned and noticed a milling mob down the course on our right. The mounted policeman set off at a trot toward the commotion. Then cheering went into the air like a peal of bells.

Down the course came all the gypsies, all the gypsies in the world, it seemed to me. Big-striding, black men with gold earrings and coloured neckerchiefs, and staves in their hands. And gypsy women, a-jingle with coins, dancing. Their tambourines jangled, as they danced forward in a strange East Indian rhythm. There was a loud order barked by the police officer, and the men stood by to let them pass. And the stolid English police began cheering too. It seemed to me that even the little trees of the Downs were cheering, and in an instant I cheered too.

For behind an escort of mounted gypsies, big foreign men with moustaches, saddleless on their shaggy mounts, came a gypsy cart with its cover down, drawn by four prancing horses. A wild-looking gypsy man was holding the reins. On the cart, for all to see, seated in a great armchair, propped up by cushions, was Lady Clontarf. Her head was laid back on a pillow, and her eyes were closed, as if the strain of appearing had been too much for her. Her little maid was crouched at her feet.

For an instant we saw her, and noticed the aged beauty of her face, noticed the peace like twilight on it. There was an order from a big Roumanian gypsy and the Romany people made a lane. The driver stood up on his perch and manoeuvring his long snakelike whip in the air, made it crack like a musket. The horses broke into a gallop, and the gypsy cart went over the turfed course toward Tattenham Corner, passed it, and went up the hill and disappeared over the Surrey downs. All the world was cheering.

'Come in here,' said my uncle Valentine, and he took me into the cool beauty of our little church of Saint Columba's in Paganry. 'Now what do you think of that?' And he pointed out a brass tablet on the wall.

'In Memory of Mifanwy, Countess of Clontarf and Kincora,' I read. Then came the dates of her birth and death, 'and who is buried after the Romany manner, no man knows where.' And then came the strange text, 'In death she was not divided.'

'But surely,' I objected, 'the quotation is: "In death they were not divided." '

'It may be,' said my uncle Valentine, 'or it may not be. But as the living of Saint Columba's in Paganry is in my gift, surely to God!' he broke out, 'a man can have a text the way he wants it in his own Church.'

This was arguable, but something more serious caught my eye.

'See, sir,' I said, 'the date of her death is wrong. She died on the evening of Derby Day, June the second. And here it is given as June the first.'

'She did not die on the evening of Derby Day. She died on the First.'

'Then,' I said, 'when she rode down the course on her gypsy cart,' and a little chill came over me, 'she was – '

'As a herring, Kerry, as a gutted herring,' my uncle Valentine said.

'Then the rule was really infringed, and the horse should not have won.'

'Wasn't he the best horse there?'

'Undoubtedly, sir, but as to the betting?'

'The bookmakers lost less than they would have lost on the favourite.'

'But the backers of the favourite.'

'The small backer in the silver ring is paid on the first past the post, so they'd have lost, anyway. At any rate, they all should have lost. They backed their opinion as to which was the best horse, and it wasn't.'

'But damn it all, sir! and God forgive me for swearing in this holy place – there's the Derby Rule.'

' "The letter killeth," Kerry,' quoted my uncle gravely, even piously. ' "The letter killeth." '

PULLINSTOWN

Molly Keane

IT was Sir Richard who asked me to stay at Pullinstown for the
Springwell Harriers' point-to-point meeting. That his children
had nothing to do with the invitation was evident from the
very politeness of their greetings – greetings which they concluded
as swiftly as the conventions permitted, leaving me to the conver-
sational mercies of their father. But he, after a question as to how
my journey had prospered with me, and a comment on the rival
unpunctuality of trains and boats, sank his haggard (and once
splendid) shoulders into the back of his chair, and, setting his old-
fashioned steel pince-nez all askew on his nose, devoted himself to
the day's paper in a manner that brooked of no interruptions on
less trivial matters. Since my cousins (in a second and third degree)
made no demands on my attention, I looked about me and maintained what I hoped was a becoming silence.

The hall where we were sitting was lovely. Whoever designed
this old Irish house had certainly a peculiar sense of the satisfying
fitness of curving walls, of ceiling mouldings continuously beautiful, while the graceful proportioning of a distant stairway drew
the eyes down the length of the oval room and upwards to the
light coming in kindly dusty radiance through a great window on
the stairs. Sheraton had made the hooped table on which lay a
medley of hunting-whips, ash-plant switches, gloves, two silver
hunting-horns, and a vast number of dusty letters and unopened
papers. Through the doors of a glass-fronted cupboard (his work
too), I could see reels and lines, glimpses of wool and bright
feathers for fly-tying, with bottles of pink prawns, silver eels' tails
and golden sprats, all lures for the kingly salmon. There were
pictures on the walls, not many, but Raeburn must have painted
that lady in the dress like a luminous white cloud. She looked out

of her picture with foxy eyes very like those of the silent little cousin who was now reading a discarded sheet of her father's newspaper with inherited concentration. The gentleman in the bright blue coat might have been Sir Richard in fancy dress, but he was a Sir Richard who had died fighting for King James at the battle of the Boyne. This they told me afterwards.

Still my cousins, Willow and Dick, sat saying never a word. Sir Richard sniffed a little, deprecatingly, as he read the paper, and Willow, the light slanting over her, appeared absorbed in her sheet. She was like her own name to look at, Willow, pale as a peeled sally wand, hair and all, and green flickering eyes. Her brother Dick was an arrogant and beautiful sixteen. I disliked the pair of them heartily.

A door opened, breaking the spell of quiet, and a wheezing and decrepit old butler came in to arrange a tea-table in the window.

'Is that the evening paper you have, Miss Willow? Excuse me, Did Silver-Tip win in Mallow?'

'He did not. The weight beat him.' Miss Willow did not lift her eyes during her brief reply, nor when she added, 'Run up to the Post Office, James, after your tea, and buy me fifty Gold Flake. Only I have a little job to do for the Sir, I'd go myself.'

'And what about James?' inquired the old butler with restrained acerbity. 'Haven't he one hundred and one little jobs to do for the Sir? God is my witness, Miss Willow, the feet is bet up under me this living minyute, and how I'll last out the length o' dinner in the boots is unknown to me, leave alone to travel the roads after thim nasty trash o' cigarettes. Thim's only poison to you, child, believe you me.'

'It's a pity about poor James.' Willow addressed her brother. 'I suppose the boots wouldn't carry him as far as the river to catch a salmon in the Tinker's stream to-night. Who stole my claret hackles, I wonder?' This last with sudden vicious intensity.

'An' who whipped six pullets' eggs out o' me pantry to go feed her ould racehorse,' James countered nimbly, 'that poor Molly Byrne had gothered for the Sir – '

'If Molly Byrne had as much as six eggs in the day from those hens, she'd run mad from this to Ballybui telling it out the two sides of the road.

'Are you ready for your tea, Sir Richard?' She whirled round suddenly on her father, 'James, show Mr Oliver his room.'

So I was sufficiently one of the family, I reflected, as I followed James's shuffling footsteps up the stairs, to be Mr Oliver – it was rather pleasing. James peered at me, blinking in the afternoon sun that flooded the bedroom to which he led me.

'The maker's name is on the blade,' he announced with dramatic suddenness. 'Ye'r the dead spit and image of the father. God, why wouldn't I know ye out of him? Wasn't he rared on the place along with the Sir? He was, 'faith. Sure meself was hall-boy under ould Dinny Mahon those times. Your poor Da could remember me well – many a good fish I struck the gaff in for him the days I'd cod ould Dinny and slip away down to him on the river. Didn't he send me a silk out of India and red feathers ye couldn't beat to tie in a fiery fly – may Almighty God grant him to see the light o' the glory of heaven – he was a good sort.'

I was glad some one remembered my father. He had told me so much and so often of his early days there with those Irish cousins that I had come to Pullinstown with a feeling of intimacy for the place and for my cousins which the very politeness of their first greeting to me had dispelled as strangely as the silence that followed it. James left me with a restored right to my pleasant intimacies.

My room was a large one. A vast bed with twisted fluted bedposts, ruthlessly cut down, took up most of one wall – the furnishing otherwise was sparse. A cupboard was full of my cousin Willow's summer clothes, while a large, coffin-like receptacle contained what looked like her mother's or grandmother's. There remained a yellow-painted chest of drawers. I opened the top drawer, which was empty, but as it obstinately refused to close again, I could only hope that the other three were empty too.

The view from the two tall windows held me longer even than my struggle with the chest of drawers. I looked down across garden beds, their disorder saved from depression by the army of daffodils that flung gold regiments alike over the beds and through the grass that divided them, out across a park-like field where five young horses and a donkey moved soberly, and a grey shield of water held the quiet evening light, over the best of a fair hunting country to the far secrecy of the mountains. And looking, I envied my father those wild young days of his fox-hunting and fishing, shooting snipe, and skylarking with those Irish cousins here in Westcommon.

They had waited tea for me, I found to my embarrassment, and with an incoherent apology for my delay, I sat down beside Willow. She bestirred herself to be polite.

'The Sir – er – father was telling us you are an artist,' she said, with less interest if with more dislike than she might have displayed had father told her I was a Mormon. 'Well, I would like to be able to paint pictures,' she continued, studiously avoiding the eye of her brother directed meaningly at her from across the table, a jeer in his silence.

'You would, I'm sure,' said he suddenly.

'I would,' his sister flashed round on him. 'I'd paint a picture of you falling off Good-Day over the last fence in Cooladine last week.'

'I did not fall off her – the mare stood on her head and well you know it.'

'And small wonder for her – the way you had the head pulled off her going into every fence. Dick's an awful coward – isn't that right, Sir Richard?'

'I wouldn't mind him being a coward if he wasn't a fool as well.' Sir Richard eyed his heir sternly. 'When did I give you permission to enter the mare in the open race to-morrow?' he demanded.

Dick blushed. 'I was waiting to ask you. May I?'

'You may not. The mare will go in the Ladies' Race, and Willow can ride her.'

'Oh, father – ' Young Dick's blush sank deeper in his skin. 'I did *not* fall off her.' On the point of tears he was.

'I'll ride my own horse in the Ladies' Race or I'll not ride at all.' Willow's small silvery face expressed more acute determinaton than I have often seen. 'If I can't beat those Leinster girls on Romance, I'll not beat them on that rotten brute Good-Day. You know right well she'll run out with me. Dick's the only one can get any good of her, and well you know it, Sir Richard.'

'I'd sooner put an old woman up to ride the mare than that nasty little officer.' Sir Richard tapped the table forbiddingly with a lump of sugar before dropping it into his teacup.

'Well, *I'll* not ride her,' said Willow. She pushed back her chair, lit a cigarette, and walked out into the bright tangled garden. After a minute Dick followed her, and two sour-looking little terriers of indeterminate breed followed him without fuss. He would show them sport, I thought, watching the light swing of his shoulders in the seedy old tweed coat. It was as stern a business to him as to them.

Sir Richard looked out after his retreating family. 'That's a right good boy,' he said, with sudden almost impersonal approval, 'and b'Gad – a terror to ride. Why wouldn't he? He's bred the right way, though I say it myself. But he'll never be as good as Willow. She's a divil.'

Compared to the terror and the devil of his begetting, I felt that I must appear but a poor specimen to my cousin. However, he suffered my interest in an incomplete series of old coaching prints with kindly tolerance, and showed me a Queen Anne chair, a Sèvres cup, and some blue glass bottles with quickening interest. 'I forget about these things,' he complained; 'the children don't care for them, you see; it's all the horses with them. Come out and have a look at the skins – would you care to?'

We followed a greened path round one of the long, grey wings that flanked on each side the square block of the house, and turning the corner came to the high stone archway leading into the stable-yard. In the dusk of the archway young Dick and Willow stood, fair, like two slight swords in that dark place.

'Father,' said they, 'Tom Kenny is here with a horse.'

'Well, I have no time to waste looking at the horses Tom Kenny peddles around the country. What sort is it?'

'Oh, a common brute,' said Willow, with indifferent decision. 'The man only came over to see you about the fox covert in Lyran.'

'Well, if you say it's a common brute, there's some hope of seeing a bit of bone and substance about the horse. If *you* don't like him, he may be worth looking at.' Sir Richard advanced into the yard, and I, following him, caught just the edge of the perfectly colourless wink that passed between his son and daughter. The match of their guile being now well and truly laid to the desired train, they proceeded carelessly on their way. A minute later the two terriers, a guilty pig-bucket look about them, hurried out of the yard in pursuit.

Inside the archway I paused. I love stables and horses and grooms, the cheerful sound of buckets, the heady smell of straw, the orderly fussiness of a saddle-room; always the same and ever different. The mind halts, feeling its way into gear with a new brave set of values at the moment when one sets foot within a stable-yard.

The stables at Pullinstown had been built for a larger stud than lodged there now. More than a few doors were fastened up, but there was still a stir and movement about some of the boxes. A lean old hunter's head looked quietly out across the half-door of his box, hollows of age above his eyes, the stamp of quality and bravery on him unmistakably. Next door the shrill voice of the very young complained against this new unknown discipline – the sweat of the breaking tackle still black on an untrimmed neck. A bright bay three-year-old this was, full of quality, and would be up to fourteen stone before he was done with. Such a set of limbs on him too. Bone there you'd be hard to span. 'That's the sort,' said Sir Richard, nodding at him. 'Ah, if I was twenty years younger I'd give myself a present of that horse. Go back to your stable, I'd say; I'll never sell you. Good-Day and Romance are over there. I sold a couple of horses last week. Now listen – I *hate* to sell a horse that suits the children; but they must go – make room for more – this place is rotten with horses. Well, Tom' – he craned round to a small dark man who appeared quietly from the black mouth of the saddle-room door – 'did you get that furze stubbed out of the hill yet?'

'B'God I did, sir. Now look-at, the torment I got on the hill of Lyran there's no man will believe. I'm destroyed workin' in it. A pairson wouldn't get their health with them old furzy pricks in their body as thick as pins in a bottle. And then to say five pounds is all the hunt should give me for me trouble! I'm a poor man, Sir Richard, and a long backwards family to rare, and a delicate dying brother on the place.'

'Did Doctor Murphy give you a bottle for him?' Sir Richard interrupted the recital. 'I told him he should go see poor Dan last week.'

'Ah, he did, he did, sir. Sure, then the bottle the doctor left played puck with him altogether, though indeed the doctor is a nice quiet man, and he had to busht out crying when he clapped an eye on poor Dan. He was near an hour there with him, going hither and over on his body with a yoke he had stuck in his two ears. Indeed he was very nice, and Dan was greatly improved in himself after he going. Faith, he slapped into the bottle o' medicine, and he'd take a sup now and a sup again till – be the holy, I'll not lie to ye, sir – whatever was in the bottle was going through him in standing leps. I thought he'd die,' Tom Kenny concluded with a pleasant laugh.

'Did he take the dose the doctor ordered?' Sir Richard's long knotted fingers were crossed before him on the handle of his walking stick. His head was bent in grave attention to the tale. What, I wondered, of Tom Kenny's horse? And what, again, of his brother?

'Is it what poor Doctor Murphy told him?' A pitying smile appeared for a moment on Tom Kenny's face. 'Well, I'll always give it in to the doctor, he's dam nice, but sure a child itself'd nearly know what good would one two teaspoons do wandering the inside through of a great big wilderness of a man the like o' poor Danny. Sure he drank down what was in the bottle, o' course, and that was little enough for the money, God knows.'

'Ah, psha!' Impossible to describe the mixture of anger and hopeless tolerance in Sir Richard's exclamation. 'Well' – he lifted his head, stabbing at the ground with the point of his walking-stick – 'I suppose it's to pay funeral expenses you're trying to sell the horse.'

'Now God is my witness, Sir Richard, if I was to get the half o' what this young horse is worth, it'd be more money than poor Danny'll ever see at his funeral or any other time in his life.'

'Ah, have done chatting and pull out the horse till I see what sort he is.' Sir Richard bent to the match in his cupped hands.

Following on this, Tom Kenny retired into a distant loose-box, from which there issued presently sounds of an encouraging nature, in voices so varied as to suggest that a large proportion of the male staff of Pullinstown had assembled in the box.

'Stand over, Willy. Mind out would he split ye!'

'Go on out you, Tom, before him.'

'Sure every horse ye'll see rared a pet is wayward always.'

'Well, now isn't he the make and shape of a horse should have a dash o' speed?'

'Is it them Grefelda horses? Did ye ever see one yet wasn't as slow as a man?'

'Well, he's very pettish, Tom. What way will we entice him?'

'*Hit him a belt o' the stick!*' came with sudden thunder from across the yard where Sir Richard still stood. Whether or not his advice was acted upon, a moment later the Grefelda horse shot like a rocket out of the stable door, his owner hazardously attached to his head by a single rein of a snaffle bridle.

'Woa – boy – woa the little horse.' Tom Kenny led him forward, nagging him to a becoming stance with every circumstance of pompous ownership.

I am a poor enough judge of a horse in the rough, but this one seemed to me to have the right outline. There was here a valuable alliance of quality and substance, and as he was walked away and back to us, a length of stride promising that he should gallop.

'That'll do,' said Sir Richard, after a prolonged, sphinx-like inspection. 'I'm sorry to see he plucks that hock, Tom; only for that he's not a bad sort at all. Turn him around again. Ah, a pity!'

'May God forgive yer honour,' was Tom Kenny's pious retort; 'ye might make a peg-top o' this horse before ye'd see the sign of a string-halt on him. Isn't that right, Pheelan?' He appealed to a small man with a wry neck and a surprising jackdaw blue eye, who had stood by throughout the affair in a deprecating silence, unshaken even by this appeal.

'What height is he? Sixteen hands?' Sir Richard stood in to the horse.

'Sixteen one, as God is my judge,' corrected the owner. 'Well, now,' he compromised, as Sir Richard remained unshaken, 'look – he's within the black o' yer nail of it.'

Even this distance I judged, after a glance at Tom Kenny's outstretched thumb, would leave him no more than a strong sixteen. However that might be, I more than liked the horse, and so I rather suspected did Sir Richard, the more when I saw him shake his head and turn a regretful back to the affair.

'Sir Richard' – Tom Kenny's head shot forward tortoise-like from his coat collar – 'look-at – eighty pounds is my price – eighty pounds in two nutshells.'

'Well, Tom,' Sir Richard smiled benignantly, 'I'm always ready to help a friend, as you know.' He paused, his head bent again in thought. 'Now if I was to ride the horse, and that is to say if I *like* the horse, I wouldn't say I mightn't give you sixty-five pounds for him,' came with sudden generous resolve.

'May God forgive you, sir.' Tom Kenny turned from the impious suggestion with scarcely concealed horror. Tears loomed in his voice as he continued in rapt encomium, 'Don't ye know yerself ye might do the rounds o' the world before ye'd meet a horse the

like o' that! This horse'll sow and he'll plough and he'll sweep the
harvest in off o' the fields for ye. Look at!' (with sudden drama).
'If ye were to bring this horse home with ye to-day, ye mightn't
have a stick o' harvest left standing to-morra night. And he'll be
a divil below a binder.'

'Faith, true for you, Tom Kenny. That one's very lonely for the
plough,' Pheelan of the jackdaw eyes struck in with irresistible
sarcasm. 'Sure, it's for Master Dick to hunt him the Sir'll buy
him.'

Without a change of expression, Tom Kenny tacked into the
wind again. 'Well, ye'd tire three men galloping this horse, and
there's not a ditch in the globe of Ireland where ye'd fall him,'
said he with entire and beautiful conviction.

'Ah, have done. Get up on him, you, Pheelan, and see would
you like him.' Sir Richard spoke with brief decision.

Following on this the prospective purchase was ridden and galloped into a white lather by Pheelan, whose hissed 'Buy him, sir
he's a *topper!*' I overheard as Sir Richard prepared to mount, and
having done so, whacked the now most meek and biddable horse
solemnly round the yard with his walking-stick, before he changed
hands for the sum of sixty-eight pounds, a yearling heifer, and
thirty shillings back for 'luck.'

'And damned expensive, too,' said my cousin as, the deal concluded, we pursued our way onwards to look at the young horses;
'only I *hate* bargaining and talking I'd have bought him twice as
cheap. . . . Isn't that a great view? You should paint that. I would
if I was an artist.'

We had walked up a hilly lane-way, splitting a flock of sheep
driven by a young lad as we went. The river lay low on our right
hand now. Everywhere the gorse shone like sweet gold money,
and primroses spread pale lavish flames. The whole air was full of
a smoky gold light. It lay low against the rose of the ploughed
fields. It was weighted with the scent of the gorse. The young
horses were splendidly bathed in light. They grouped themselves
nobly against the hillside before they swung away from us, with
streaming manes and tails, to crest the hill like a wave, and thunder
away into the evening. Nor, though we stayed there an hour,
could we get near them again. My cousin, at last exasperated, led
me back to the house and dinner.

'Don't change,' he said as we parted; so only his own round

skull-cap of bruised purple velvet lent ceremony to the occasion of my first dinner at Pullinstown. Willow had not changed, and Dick came up from the river just as we sat down, Willow's hair was as pale as wood ashes in the candle-light, and her infrequent, shadowy voice oddly pleasing. Still she did not talk to me, but held stubborn argument with James as to the date on which the salmon we were eating had last swum in the river. Dick talked to her. He had risen a fish twice on a strange local fly called a 'goat's claret.' They both addressed their father as 'Sir Richard' in ceremonious voices, and he talked to me about my father and the fun they had together, James, as he ministered punctiliously to our needs, occasionally supplying the vital point of a half-remembered anecdote or forgotten name.

After dinner we played bridge, the army of cards falling and whispering quietly between us of our black and red skirmishes, adventures and defeats. Sir Richard and I were three shillings down on the rubber when Willow put the old painted packs of cards back in their pale ivory fort and went out with Dick to plait her mare's mane for the race to-morrow.

'Why in God's name did you not do it by daylight, child?' her father complained.

'Because Pheelan locked the stable door on me. He thinks no one but himself can plait up a mane.'

'And he's right too, I dare say.' Sir Richard contemplated his daughter with serene approval.

'I was ashamed of my life the way he had her mane in Coolad-ine.' Willow was sorting reels of thick, linen thread. 'Will you come, Dick?' she said.

'And the reason why I play cards so well' – Dick rose to his feet, sliding my three shillings up and down his trouser pocket – 'is because I can use my brains to think out problems.' He was not boasting, merely voicing his private ruminations.

'Good-night, Sir Richard,' they both said. '*Good*-night,' they said to me with extreme politeness, and went out together.

Soon after this we went up to bed, Sir Richard and I, armed each with shining silver candlestick like an evening star, and I sat for a while smoking a cigarette, leaning out of my window to the hushed bosom of the night. I saw a star caught in the flat water more silver than the moon. A white owl slanted by and was gone, low among the trees, and the sound of a fiddle jigging out some hesitant tune picked sweetly at the stillness.

'Play "The wind that shakes the barley," ' a voice prompted the fiddler. 'That's not it – it's the "Snowy-breasted Pearl" yer in on now.'

'Jig it for me, you.'

'God, I wouldn't be able to jig it. There's the one turn on the whole o' them tunes – 'twouldn't be easy to know them – '

I was sorry when the fiddling ceased, but when there drifted on the air a tale astir with every principle of drama, I forgot even that I was eavesdropping, and strained against the night to hear. . . . 'Well, it was a long, lonely lane and two gates on it; that'll give ye an idea how long it was – ' Followed a period of sibilant murmuring, and then a sudden protest: 'Ah, go on! It's all very well to be talkin' how ye's box this one and box that one – if a fella lepped out on ye, what'd ye do?'

It was at this interesting moment that a window above my own shot open, and the irate voice of James ordered Lizzie Doyle and Mary Josey to their respective beds.

'Begone now!' he commanded, and with Biblical directions told the garden what he thought of a domestic staff that sat all day with their elbows up on the kitchen table drinking tea, and spent the nights trapseing the countryside.

'Oh, Jesus, Mary and Joseph! Isn't that frightful?' I heard amid the scuffle of retreat, and then, as though in submission to the moods of fate: 'Well, the ways o' God are something fierce.' In the succeeding silence I too betook myself to bed.

The morning was unbelievably young when I woke to the faint squawk and flapping of birds on the water below. A heron in a Scotch fir-tree was pencil-etched against the grey sky. In the very early mornings churches and bridges too have the air of nearly forgotten stories; but never did romance so hinge itself to possibility for me as now when, like two sentinels of the morning's quietness, I saw Willow and Dick ride out of the stable arch and walk their horses away from sight into the slowly silvering morning. The breathless picture they made is with me still – both sitting a little carefully, perhaps, with saddles still cold on their horses' backs. And you could hardly have told, but for the square-cut pale hair of one, which of them was Willow and which was Dick.

Bright and unkind the two blood-horses looked in the grey light, and their riders forlorn in the gallantry of the very young passed on to face who knows what horrors of schooling in cold blood at that deathly hour.

At breakfast they were touched with the unimpeachable importance of those who rise up early to accomplish dangerous matters while others are still in bed. I found them less romantic. Willow ate some strange cereal with lavish cream. 'Good for the body,' she said in reply to her father's comment. 'Have some yourself. Will you have some?' she added to me.

There was a patch of mud on the shoulder of Dick's tweed coat, and Sir Richard scolded and grumbled all through the meal at the rottenness of those who face young horses into impossible fences. Dick made neither defence nor answer. Occasionally he stuck a finger between his neck and the spotted handkerchief he wore round it, loosening its folds abstractedly. He ate an apple and one piece of dry toast very slowly, and just before he lit a cigarette he said, 'There's no one can ride that mare, only myself. She's a queer-tempered divil, but when Cherry'd be good' – there was almost a croon in his voice – '*then* I'd give her an apple.' Whereupon he went out of the room, shutting the door behind him, and Willow, who was feeding the dogs, said:

'That was an awful toss he took. I thought he was quinched. Ah – he was only winded. What time do you want to start for the races, father? You should bring the lunch in your car. Dick and I have to go on early to walk the course.'

Clearly I perceived that I was included under the heading lunch as their father's passenger. I saw them leave the house at about eleven, James following them to pack a suitcase, a medly of saddles, a weight cloth, a handful of boot pulleys and jockeys, a mackintosh coat, a cutting-whip and a spare horse-sheet into the crazy brass-bound Ford car which waited pompously beneath the great, granite-pillared porch.

'Good-bye, now.' He fastened the last button of the side curtains as the Ford started on its way with that unearthly hiccup common to its species.

'Mind!' – Willow put her head out of the car – 'see and squeeze the cherry brandy out of the Sir for lunch.'

James returned to the hall at a busy if rather dickey trot. 'Merciful God!' – he halted in horror – 'if they didn't leave the little safety-hat after them.' He surveyed a black silk-covered crash-helmet with dismay. 'Ah, well, it'll only have to follow on with ourselves and the lunch.'

This was my first intimation that James was to be of the party. Had I known the ways of Pullinstown more intimately it would never have occurred to me that any expedition could be undertaken without his presence. But never can I forget my first sight of him an hour later in his race-going attire. He wore a rather steeple-crowned bowler hat, green with age, and a very long box-cloth overcoat with strongly stitched shoulder patches and smartly cut pocket flaps. It was a coat, indeed, that could only have been worn with complete success by the most famous of England's sporting peers. From his breast pocket peeped a pair of minute mother-of-pearl opera glasses (no doubt removed from one of the glass-topped tables in the drawing-room), and round his neck, tied with perfect symmetry, was a white flannel stock, polka dotted with red.

'James has to sit in front with me.' Sir Richard, more than usually haggard and untidy, slid himself crabbedly behind the wheel of the big Bentley, cursing his sciatica in a brief aside. 'He always remembers where the self-starter is. I never can find it. It's a cursed nuisance to me in race traffic. What's that, James?' He pointed to a small fish-basket which James was stowing away in the back.

'There's a change o' feet for Miss Willow, Sir Richard. There's no way ye'll soak the cold only out o' wet boots, and ye couldn't tell but they'd slip the child into a river or a wet ditch, or maybe she'd be lying quinched under the mare in a boggy place. Sure – '

'Ah, get into the car, ye old fool, and stop talking. Maybe it's a coffin you should have brought with you, let alone the boots. Have we all now?'

'We have, Sir Richard.' James laid the crash-helmet on top of the lunch basket and stepped in beside his master.

By what seemed only a series of surprising accidents, Sir Richard fought his noisy way into top gear, and determined to stay in at all costs, took risks with ass carts and other hazards of the twisty roads which appalled me. What, I wondered, would be our progress though the race traffic, if indeed we ever came so near the course? We had left the wide demesne fields of Pullinstown behind us now, and the country on either hand was more enclosed. Banks

I saw, tall single ones, and wondered if they raced over these in Ireland; big stone facers too, solid and kind, plenty of room on them; and an occasional loose-built stone wall – no two consecutive fences quite alike and not a strand of wire to be seen. The going was mostly grass, though here and there a field of plough showed up rawly, white gulls stooping and wheeling above it, dim like sawn-out pearl in the grey soft air; and always the mountains, ringing the country like a precious cup.

'That's a great bog for snipe,' Sir Richard would say. 'That's a right snug bit of covert.' or 'That's the best pool on the river,' pointing to a secret turn of water low under distant woods. 'I killed a thirty-pound salmon there – on a "Mystery," it was. Two hours I had him on before James got a chance to gaff him. Ah, he was a tiger! God! I took a right fall over that fence one time. No, but the high devil with the stones in it. Wasn't his father out that day, James? He was, of course. Tell him I showed you the place King Spider nearly killed me. He'll remember – dear me, I'm forgetting he's dead – poor Harry! Is this the turn now, James? To the right?'

'Wheel left, Sir Richard, wheel left,' James corrected easily; and wheel left we did, but with such surprising velocity that the heavy car skidded and spun about in the road, pointing at last in the direction from which he had come.

'Oh, fie, Sir Richard!' James, quite unmoved, reached out a respectable black-trousered leg towards the self-starter. 'Do you not know the smallest puck in the world is able to do the hell of a job on that steering? If the like o' that should happen us in strong race traffic, we were three dead men.'

The race traffic, of which I had heard a good deal, did not become apparent till we were within the last couple of miles from our destination, when indeed the narrow lane that led up to the car park was congested enough. Old and young, the countryside attended the races. Mothers of infants who could not by any stretching of possibilities be left a day long without sustenance, avoided the difficulty by taking their progeny along with them; and the same held good, I imagined, in the case of those old men who, had they remained at home, would certainly have fallen into the fire or otherwise injured themselves during the absence of the race-goers. Ford cars conveyed parties of eight or more. Pony carts, ass carts, and bicycles did their share, while a fair sprinkling of expensive cars had to regulate their pace by that of the slowest ass cart that preceded them in the queue. A shawled and handsome fury, selling race-cards, jumped on the step of our car during a momentary stoppage of the traffic; her tawny head blazed raggedly in the sunlight.

'Race-card – a shillin' the race-card,' she bawled hideously. She carried a baby on her arm. I saw the outline of its round head beneath the heavy shawl, but, quite unimpeded by its burden, she leaped like a young goat from the step of our car to attack the next in the line.

'Easy, Sir Richard! Mind the cycle now! Stop, sir! They want the five bob for the car now. Wheel west for the gate. Cross out over the furzy bushes. Slip in there now; that's Miss Willow's car.' So piloted by James we came at last to a standstill.

From the top of the little hill where the cars were parked, we could see below us the weighing tent and paddock (a few horses already stood there in their sheets), the bookies establishing themselves in their stand (we were in good time; they had not begun to bet on the first race yet), and at the foot of the hill the railing run in to the finish; while out in the country here and there the eye picked up the lonely flutter of a little white flag.

'Leave Red Flags on the Right and White Flags on the Left,' I read on my race-card below 'Conditions of the Meeting.' And then:

'First Race, 1.30.
Hunt Race: A sweepstake for horses, the property of members of the Springwell Hunt.'

Then the Sporting Farmers' Open Race, and

'Third Race: Open Race – of £30, of which the second receives £5.
1. Major O'Donnel's Wayward Gipsy (black, yellow cap).
2. Mr Devereux's ch. geld, Bright Love.
3. Sir Richard Pulleyn's br. mare Good-Day, aged (blue, black cap).'

Six more runners were down to go for that race, but I turned the card over and read: 'Ladies' Race. Open. For a cup.' And Miss Pulleyn's Romance heading the list.

'Romance'll win it,' Sir Richard prophesied bleakly, 'But there's a lot of good horses against the boy. Have you me glasses, James? Have you me stick? Right. Come on now till we see the horses saddled for this first race. We'll have lunch then, James.'

Down the hill towards the saddling enclosure we went, almost fighting our way between groups of gossiping country women, stalls of oranges and bananas, roulette boards, and exponents of the three-card trick.

'Clancy's horse'll win it, you'll see,' I heard.

'See now – he's like nothin' only a horse ye'd see on paper; he's like a horse was painted.'

'What about Amber Girl?' interpolated a rival's supporter.

'Well, what about her? Now look-at, I seen this horse win a race in Ballyowen. Well, he was four length from the post and four horses in front of him, and the minute Clancy stirred on him he come through the lot to win be two lengths. Clancy made a matter o' ninety pound about it. Ah! he never let him run idle.'

'Well, what about Amber Girl?' reiterated Amber Girl's supporter.

What indeed, I wondered; how would she run against a horse that could accomplish so spectacular a finish after three miles over a country? But I was never to hear. A section of the crowd melting at that moment, we pushed on towards the paddock, and here, lost in joint disapproving contemplation of the six starters waiting to be saddled for their race, we found Willow and Dick. They were as quiet as two fish in a pool, but I felt all the same that very little in that busy ring escaped their devastating attention.

'Is Pheelan here with the horses yet?' Sir Richard asked them.

'He wasn't here five minutes ago. Did you not pass him on the road?' Willow looked worried. 'I hope he didn't go round by Mary Pheelan's pub,' she said to Dick, as they went out of the ring to look for him. And really, for Pheelan's sake, I found myself hoping that he had not. Nor had he. But his subsequent discovery, blamelessly sheltering with the horses behind a gorse-crowned bank of primroses, wrung from Willow a sufficiently stinging reprimand.

Because of the search for Pheelan we missed most of the first race, and I failed to accomplish my nearest ambition, which was to see a bank jumped at really close quarters. Through my glasses I could see the distant horses flip on and off their fences with the deceptive ease that distance lends to the most strenuous effort, and the last fences before the finish were two that did not take a lot of doing. A disappointing race from the spectator's point of view: won in a distance. Three finished.

We ate our lunch after this. That is, Sir Richard and I ate sandwiches, and Willow and Dick watched us with the avid importance of jockeys.

Dick studied the field for his race: 'The only horse I'm afraid of is that Bright Love – that's a Punchestown horse.'

'Ah, it'll fall,' from Willow, easily.

She read bits from the race-card. 'Patrick Byrne's Sissy – that's a great pattern of a cob. Purplish waistcoat and white shirt sleeves. Could he not say he was wearing the top half of his Sunday suit?'

'Doris is going to ride her own mare in the Ladies' Race. You'll have to mind yourself, Willow.'

'I rode against Doris in Duffcarry, father. I had right sport with her. Sure she was nearly crying with fright down at the start. "Go slow into the last fence, girls," I said, "*whatever* you do – that's a murderous brute of a place." I was only teasing them about it, but didn't Doris and Susan pull into a trot very nearly. Ah, that was where I slipped on a bit and they never caught me. A bad fence? – not it – the sort you'd get up in the night to jump.'

'You know, Dick,' she said, 'I hate the way they jump that narrow one – right on the turn.'

'Oh, there's nothing in it.'

We were watching the second race. They did not eat, but sat on their shooting-sticks and drank a thimbleful of black coffee each.

'I'll have a good drink with you after my race, Dick,' Willow said. They dived into their Ford car, throwing out a suitcase and a weight cloth. James followed them down the hillside.

In the ring Willow held Good-Day, while Pheelan fussed and chided about her saddling. She was a little bit of a mare, Good-Day – a bright blood bay, all quality. The single rein of her plain snaffle was turned over her head. She looked to be fairly fit, and I guessed would take some beating. I said so to Sir Richard.

'Ah, a right mare if she was half ridden.' Dick just caught the answer. I saw the tips of his ears go scarlet against the black cap that Willow was tying on his head. The wind blew cold through his jersey. It looked as though it must whistle through his body too, so fine drawn he was and so desperately keen. Pheelan gave him a leg up. As he sat, feeling the length of his stirrups, Good-Day turned her head round, nipping the air funnily.

'She'll be good to-day,' Dick said, 'you'll see,' picking up his rubber-laced rein.

James came sidling up to say behind his hand, 'Master Dick, keep east the fence before the wood – there's a paling gone out of it. Ye may gallop through. Mickey Doyle bid me tell you.'

Dick smiled a little wintry smile and nodded.

They were out of the ring now, Pheelan leading the mare down through the crowd.

'Stop on the hill, father,' said Willow; 'James and I are going down out in the country.'

'Go down, you,' Sir Richard said to me; 'you'd be more use than old James.' I thought he looked distinctly shaky and just a thought grim as he walked slowly back to the car.

James and Willow and I took a short-cut down to the start. We jumped three formidable banks, pulling James after us, before we reached the place of vantage Willow had in her mind's eye.

Now we could see the field lined up for a start below us – eight horses in it – Dick and the little mare seemed so far away from any hope but each other. Willow was straining her eyes on them. A false start, and all to do over again. They were off. Hardly room to steady a horse before the first fence, and Dick did not even try to do so. They were up – they were over. Certainly Good-day wasted no time over her fences. A rough piece of moorland and every one taking a pull. The horses turned away from us to drop into a laneway. Then we saw them over two more fences. Good-Day leading still – a raking chestnut striding along second; then the bay mare Wayward Gipsy and six more all in a bunch. Two horses fell at the fourth fence, a little puff of dust rising from the bank as they hit it. One jockey remounted, and the other lay where he had fallen, his horse galloping on. Willow did not even put her glasses on him. She was aware of nothing but Dick and Good-Day.

'The mare beat Bright Love over her fences,' she said, 'but he'll gallop away from her, James, if he stands up. He jumped that badly. Steady now, Dick, take a pull on her, this is a divil. He's over. Now we lose them. Come on, boys; we'll slip across to this big fence and see them come home.'

Over a field we ran, Willow just beating me, James a very bad third, to take up our stand beside a high, narrow bank with a ditch on the landing side. Not a choice obstacle for a tired horse. And three fences from home they'd be racing too. 'Oh, a filthy spot,' said Willow.

A little knot of country boys gathered round her. 'Eh, Miss Pulleyns, can ye see the horses? Eh, Miss Pulleyns, did they cross out the big ditch yet? Look-at, look-at! Mr Pulleyns is down.'

'Almighty Lord God! Should the horse have fallen with him?' queried an emotional lady friend.

'No, but he fell from the horse beyond the wood.'

'Oh! Oh! Is he hurted?'

'Hurt! He's killed surely. Isn't the head burst!'

Knowing that my glasses could not hope to equal the hawk-like vision of my informants, I said nothing, but focused them on a point beyond the plantation and waited for the horses to appear. When they did, Dick and Good-day were, as I had indeed supposed, still among them – lying third now, with the big chestnut Bright Love in the lead and Wayward Gipsy second, but I thought she was pretty well done with.

'He'll not catch the chestnut now,' Willow said. 'He's let him get too far in front of him. Wait now – this fence takes some doing. THEY'RE DOWN!' she said. 'Ah, Dick wins now. Wayward Gipsy's beat.'

'Come on, Master Dick,' James piped, hopping from foot to foot in his excitement, his opera glasses clapped on the horses. 'More power, Master Dick – he have the mare cot! 'Tis only a ride home now.'

Two more fences and Good-Day was galloping down to the bank where we stood, Wayward Gipsy half a field behind her; Bright Love, remounted, a bad third; and the rest nowhere.

'Steady, Dick, now.' The boy was burning with the effort of his race. The sour little mare had jumped everything right; nothing could go wrong with them now. He may have let her go on at it a bit faster than he need have done (I am no judge of pace in riding over banks). I only know she failed to get right on top, and came off that tall fence end over end in as unpleasant a looking crash as I hope I may never see again. It shakes one.

Young Dick lay hunched quietly where he had fallen, but the mare was up in a flash. It was I who caught her, and James who threw me into the saddle just as Wayward Gipsy jumped the fence beside us.

Never shall I forget the horror of that ride in. How I sat in Dick's five-pound saddle, the flaps wrinkling back from under my knees and the off stirrup gone in the fall, I shall never know – for one who fancies himself not a little over fences I must, across the two first very moderate banks I jumped in Ireland, have presented a sorry enough spectacle. Had there been an inch more left in Wayward Gipsy we were beaten. As it was, the judge just gave it to Good-Day – a short head on the post.

I weighed in all right. I knew I must ride nearly a stone above Dick's weight (a bit of a penalty for the little mare to carry home after such a shattering fall), and as I walked out of the tent I met Willow coming in to weigh out for her race.

'That was pretty quick of you,' she said to me. 'I'd never have got the weight. Oh, Dick's all right – only shaken and badly winded. The Sir's running mad round the place looking for you.'

Dick was saddling Willow's horse when I next saw him, and too busy to spare any time for me. She was late: three other horses had gone down to the start.

'Now, Doris,' Willow called to a pretty girl who looked excited and nervous as a cat as she was put up by a firmly adoring young man, 'all fences on this course to be jumped at a slow pace. I'm very shook indeed, with my only brother nearly quinched before my eyes.'

The girl laughed; she was all nerves, though I dare say a tigress when she got going. 'Stay with me down to the post, Willow. I'll be kicked off for certain.'

'Very dangerous work this, girls!' Willow laughed, pulling up her leathers. 'Now, Dick, I'm right.' She caught my eye as she rode out of the ring and gave me a small friendly nod as I wished her good luck.

'Go down to the old spot,' she said, 'and I *hope* I won't need you as much as Dick did.'

Nor did she. From the same view-point as before, Dick and James and myself watched the flash of Willow's blue shirt as she led round that course at a wicked pace. . . .

'Wait till Sir Richard sees her,' Dick murmured; 'he'll not leave a feather on her body, and the reason is she's making every post a winning post.'

A hot class of horses and the fastest run race of the day. Romance jumped the fence where we stood in perfect style – on and off – clever as a dog, never dwelling an instant, and galloped home to win in a distance.

Dick saw the last lady over without mishap before we turned to follow James back to the hill.

'Look!' said he suddenly, stooping to the ditch to pick up a half-buried stirrup-iron and leather. He turned it over. 'It's me own.' He looked at me, an expression almost of friendliness dawning in his face. 'And you in trousers,' he murmured.

We found Willow at the car, where her father was measuring her out a niggardly drink and expressing his unstinted disapproval of her method of winning a race, while James alternately begged her to put on her coat and eat a sandwich. Failing in both objects, he presented her with a small comb and glass, and bade her tease out her hair, for it was greatly tossed with the race.

'Ah, don't annoy me, James,' Willow finished her drink, stuck her arms into the leather coat he held out for her, clapped a beret on her surprising hair, and said to her father, 'I'll drive Dick and Oliver home. Major Barry wants you to take him. Come on, boys, till we gather up our winnings.'

Later, as the Ford rocked and bumped its way out of the field, and I sat, shaken to the core, in the back seat with a horse-sheet over my knees and one of Willow's gold-flake cigarettes in my mouth, Dick turned round to say –

'And the reason why I think you should stop on for Punchestown is because that's a meeting you should really enjoy.'

'That's right,' Willow agreed.

And, strange as it may seem, I gloried to know the accolade of their acceptance mine.

OCCASIONAL LICENCES

E. Œ. Somerville & Martin Ross

'IT's out of the question,' I said, looking forbiddingly at Mrs Moloney through the spokes of the bicycle that I was pumping up outside the grocer's in Skebawn.

'Well, indeed, Major Yeates,' said Mrs Moloney, advancing excitedly, and placing on the nickel plating a hand that I had good and recent cause to know was warm, 'sure I know well that if th' angel Gabriel came down from heaven for a licence for the races, your honour wouldn't give it to him without a charackther, but as for Michael! Sure, the world knows what Michael is!'

I had been waiting for Philippa for already nearly half-an-hour, and my temper was not at its best.

'Character or no character, Mrs Moloney,' said I with asperity, 'the magistrates have settled to give no occasional licences, and if Michael were as sober as – '

'Is it sober! God help us!' exclaimed Mrs Moloney with an upward rolling of her eye to the Recording Angel; 'I'll tell your honour the truth. I'm his wife, now, fifteen years, and I never seen the sign of dhrink on Michael only once, and that was when he went out o' good-nature helping Timsy Ryan to whitewash his house, and Timsy and himself had a couple o' pots o' porther, and look, he was as little used to it that his head go light, and he walked away out to dhrive in the cows and it no more than eleven o'clock in the day! And the cows, the craytures, as much surprised, goin' hither and over the four corners of the road from him! Faith, ye'd have to laugh. "Michael," says I to him, "ye're dhrunk!" "I am," says he, and the tears rained from his eyes. I turned the cows from him. "Go home" I says, "and lie down on Willy Tom's bed – " '

At this affecting point my wife came out of the grocer's with a large parcel to be strapped to my handlebar, and the history of Mr Moloney's solitary lapse from sobriety got no further than Willy Tom's bed.

'You see,' I said to Philippa, as we bicycled quietly home through the hot June afternoon, 'we've settled we'll give no licences for the sports. Why even young Sheehy, who owns three pubs in Skebawn, came to me and said he hoped the magistrates would be firm about it, as these one-day licences were quite unnecessary, and only led to drunkenness and fighting, and every man on the Bench has joined in promising not to grant any.'

'How nice, dear!' said Philippa absently. 'Do you know Mrs McDonnell can only let me have three dozen cups and saucers; I wonder if that will be enough?'

'Do you mean to say you expect three dozen people?' said I.

'Oh, it's always well to be prepared,' replied my wife evasively.

During the next few days I realised the true inwardness of what it was to be prepared for an entertainment of this kind. Games were not at a high level in my district. Football of a wild, guerilla species, was waged intermittently, blended in some inextricable way with Home Rule and a brass band, and on Sundays gatherings of young men rolled a heavy round stone along the roads, a rudimentary form of sport, whose fascination lay primarily in the fact that it was illegal, and, in lesser degree, in betting on the length of each roll. I had had a period of enthusiasm, during which I thought I was going to be the apostle of cricket in the neighbourhood, but my mission dwindled to single wicket with Peter Cadogan, who was indulgent but bored, and I swiped the ball through the dining-room window, and someone took one of the stumps to poke the laundry fire. Once a year, however, on that festival of the Roman Catholic Church which is familiarly known as 'Pether and Paul's day,' the district was wont to make a spasmodic effort at athletic sports, which were duly patronised by the gentry and promoted by the publicans, and this year the honour of a steward's green rosette was conferred upon me. Philippa's genuis for hospitality here saw its chance, and broke forth into unbridled tea-party in connection with the sports, even involving me in the hire of a tent, the conveyance of chairs and tables, and other large operations.

It chanced that Flurry Knox had on this occasion lent the fields for the sports, with the proviso that horse-races and a tug-of-war were to be added to the usual programme; Flurry's participation in events of this kind seldom failed to be of an inflaming character. As he and I planted larch spars for the high jump, and stuck furze-bushes into hurdles (locally known as 'hurrls'), and skirmished hourly with people who wanted to sell drink on the course, I thought that my next summer leave would singularly coincide with the festival consecrated to St Peter and St Paul. We made a grand-stand of quite four feet high, out of old fish-boxes, which smelt worse and worse as the day wore on, but was, none the less, as sought after by those for whom it was not intended, as is the Royal enclosure at Ascot; we broke gaps in all the fences to allow carriages on to the ground, we armed a gang of the worst black-guards in Skebawn with cart-whips, to keep the course, and felt the organisation could go no farther.

The momentous day of Pether and Paul opened badly, with heavy clouds and every indication of rain, but after a few thunder showers things brightened, and it seemed within the bounds of possibility that the weather might hold up. When I got down to the course on the day of the sports the first thing I saw was a tent of that peculiar filthy grey that usually enshrines the sale of porter, with an array of barrels in a crate beside it; I bore down upon it in all the indignant majesty of the law, and in so doing came upon Flurry Knox, who was engaged in flogging boys off the Grand Stand.

'Sheehy's gone one better than you!' he said, without taking any trouble to conceal the fact that he was amused.

'Sheehy!' I said; 'why, Sheehy was the man who went to every magistrate in the country to ask them to refuse a licence for the sports.'

'Yes, he took some trouble to prevent anyone else having a look in,' replied Flurry; 'he asked every magistrate but one, and that was the one that gave him the licence.'

'You don't mean to say that it was you?' I demanded in high wrath and suspicion, remembering that Sheehy bred horses, and that my friend Mr Knox was a person of infinite resource in the matter of a deal.

'Well, well,' said Flurry, rearranging a disordered fish-box, 'and me that's a churchwarden, and sprained my ankle a month ago with running downstairs at my grandmother's to be in time for prayers! Where's the use of a good character in this country?'

'Not much when you keep it eating its head off for want of exercise,' I retorted; 'but if it wasn't you, who was it?'

'Do you remember old Moriarty out at Castle Ire?'

I remembered him extremely well as one of those representatives of the people with whom a paternal Government had leavened the effete ranks of the Irish magistracy.

'Well,' resumed Flurry, 'that licence was as good as a five-pound note in his pocket.'

I permitted myself a comment on Mr Moriarty suitable to the occasion.

'Oh, that's nothing,' said Flurry easily; 'he told me one day when he was half screwed that his Commission of the Peace was worth a hundred and fifty a year to him in turkeys and whisky, and he was telling the truth for once.'

At this point Flurry's eye wandered, and following its direction I saw Lady Knox's smart 'bus cleaving its way through the throng of country people, lurching over the ups and downs of the field like a ship in a sea. I was too blind to make out the component parts of the white froth that crowned it on top, and seethed forth from it when it had taken up a position near the tent in which Philippa was even now propping the legs of the tea-table, but from the fact that Flurry addressed himself to the door, I argued that Miss Sally had gone inside.

Lady Knox's manner had something more than its usual bleakness. She had brought, as she promised, a large contingent, but from the way that the strangers within her gates melted impalpably and left me to deal with her single-handed, I drew the further deduction that all was not well.

'Did you ever in your life see such a gang of women as I have brought with me?' she began with her wonted directness, as I piloted her to the Grand Stand, and placed her on the stoutest looking of the fish-boxes. 'I have no patience with men who yacht! Bernard Shute has gone off to the Clyde, and I had counted on his being a man at my dance next week. I suppose you'll tell me you're going away too.'

I assured Lady Knox that I would be a man to the best of my ability.

'This is the last dance I shall give,' went on her ladyship, unappeased; 'the men in this country consist of children and cads.'

I admitted that we were a poor lot, 'but,' I said, 'Miss Sally told me – '

'Sally's a fool!' said Lady Knox, with a falcon eye at her daughter, who happened to be talking to her distant kinsman, Mr Flurry of that ilk.

The races had by this time begun with a competition known as the 'Hop, Step, and Lep'; this, judging by the yells, was a highly interesting display, but as it was conducted between two impervious rows of onlookers, the aristocracy on the fish-boxes saw nothing save the occasional purple face of a competitor, starting into view above the wall of backs like a jack-in-the-box. For me, however, the odorous sanctuary of the fish-boxes was not to be. I left it guarded by Slipper with a cart-whip of flail-like dimensions, as disreputable an object as could be seen out of low comedy, with someone's old white cords on his bandy legs, butcher-boots three sizes too big for him, and a black eye. The small boys fled before him; in the glory of his office he would have flailed his own mother off the fish-boxes had occasion served.

I had an afternoon of decidedly mixed enjoyment. My stewardship blossomed forth like Aaron's rod, and added to itself the duties of starter, handicapper, general referee, and chucker-out, besides which I from time to time strove with emissaries who came from Philippa with messages about water and kettles. Flurry and I had to deal single-handed with the foot-races (our brothers in office being otherwise engaged at Mr Sheehy's), a task of many difficulties, chiefest being that the spectators all swept forward at the word 'Go!' and ran the race with the competitors, yelling curses, blessings, and advice upon them, taking short cuts over anything and everybody, and mingling inextricably with the finish. By fervent applications of the whips, the course was to some extent purged for the quarter-mile, and it would, I believe, have been a triumph of handicapping had not an unforeseen disaster overtaken the favourite – old Mrs Knox's bath-chair boy. Whether, as was alleged, his braces had or had not been tampered with by a rival was a matter that the referee had subsequently to deal with in the thick of a free fight; but the painful fact remained that in the course of the first lap what were described as 'his galluses' abruptly severed their connection with the garments for whose safety they were responsible, and the favourite was obliged to seek seclusion in the crowd.

The tug-of-war followed close on the *contretemps*, and had the excellent effect of drawing away, like a blister, the inflammation set up by the grievances of the bath-chair boy. I cannot at this moment remember of how many men each team consisted; my sole aim was to keep the numbers even, and to baffle the volunteers who, in an ecstasy of sympathy, attached themselves to the tail of the rope at moments when their champions weakened. The rival forces dug their heels in and tugged, in an uproar that drew forth the innermost line of customers from Mr Sheehy's porter tent, and even attracted 'the quality' from the haven of the fish-boxes, Slipper, in the capacity of Squire of Dames, pioneering Lady Knox through the crowd with the cart-whip, and with language whose nature was providentially veiled, for the most part, by the din. The tug-of-war continued unabated. One team was getting the worst of it, but hung doggedly on, sinking lower and lower till they gradually sat down; nothing short of the trump of judgment could have conveyed to them that they were breaking rules, and both teams settled down by slow degrees on to their sides, with the rope under them, and their heels still planted in the ground, bringing about complete deadlock. I do not know the record duration for a tug-of-war, but I can certify that the Cullinagh and Knockranny teams lay on the ground at full tension for half-an-hour, like men in apoplectic fits, each man with his respective adherents howling over him, blessing him, and adjuring him to continue.

With my own nauseated eyes I saw a bearded countryman, obviously one of Mr Sheehy's best customers, fling himself on his knees beside one of the combatants, and kiss his crimson and streaming face in a rapture of encouragement. As he shoved unsteadily past me on his return journey to Mr Sheehy's, I heard him informing a friend that 'he cried a handful over Danny Mulloy, when he seen the poor brave boy so shtubborn, and, indeed, he couldn't say why he cried.'

'For good-nature ye'd cry,' suggested the friend.

'Well, just that, I suppose,' returned Danny Mulloy's admirer resignedly; 'indeed, if it was only two cocks ye seen fightin' on the road, yer heart'd take part with one o' them!'

I had begun to realise that I might as well abandon the tug-of-war and occupy myself elsewhere, when my wife's much harassed messenger brought me the portentous tidings that Mrs Yeates wanted me at the tent at once. When I arrived I found the tent literally bulging with Philippa's guests; Lady Knox, seated on a hamper, was taking off her gloves, and loudly announcing her desire for tea, and Philippa, with a flushed face and a crooked hat, breathed into my ear the awful news that both the cream and the milk had been forgotten.

'But Flurry Knox says he can get me some,' she went on; 'he's gone to send people to milk a cow that lives near here. Go out and see if he's coming.'

I went out and found, in the first instance, Mrs Cadogan, who greeted me with the prayer that the divil might roast Julia McCarthy, that legged it away to the races like a wild goose, and left the cream afther her on the servants' hall table. 'Sure, Misther Flurry's gone looking for a cow, and what cow would there be in a backwards place like this? And look at me shtriving to keep the kettle simpering on the fire, and not as much coals undher it as'd redden a pipe!'

'Where's Mr Knox?' I asked.

'Himself and Slipper's galloping the counthry like the deer. I believe it's to the house above they went, sir.'

I followed up a rocky hill to the house above, and there found Flurry and Slipper engaged in the patriarchal task of driving two brace of coupled and spancelled goats into a shed.

'It's the best we can do,' said Flurry briefly; 'there isn't a cow to be found, and the people are all down at the sports. Be d – d to you, Slipper, don't let them go from you!' as the goats charged and doubled like football players.

'But goats' milk!' I said, paralysed by horrible memories of what tea used to taste like at Gib.

'They'll never know it!' said Flurry, cornering a venerable nanny; 'here, hold this divil, and hold her tight!'

I have no time to dwell upon the pastoral scene that followed. Suffice it to say, that at the end of ten minutes of scorching profanity from Slipper, and incessant warfare with the goats, the latter had reluctantly yielded two small jugfulls, and the dairy-maids had exhibited a nerve and skill in their trade that won my lasting respect.

'I knew I could trust *you*, Mr Knox!' said Philippa, with shining eyes, as we presented her with the two foaming beakers. I suppose a man is never a hero to his wife, but if she could have realised the bruises on my legs, I think she would have reserved a blessing for me also.

What was thought of the goats' milk I gathered symptomatically from a certain fixity of expression that accompanied the first sip of the tea, and from observing that comparatively few ventured on second cups. I also noted that after a brief conversation with Flurry, Miss Sally poured hers secretly on to the grass. Lady Knox had throughout the day preserved an aspect so threatening that no change was perceptible in her demeanour. In the throng of hungry guests I did not for some time notice that Mr Knox had withdrawn until something in Miss Sally's eye summoned me to her, and she told me she had a message from him for me.

'Couldn't we come outside?' she said.

Outside the tent, within less than six yards of her mother, Miss Sally confided to me a scheme that made my hair stand on end. Summarised, it amounted to this: That, first, she was in the primary stage of a deal with Sheehy for a four-year-old chestnut colt, for which Sheehy was asking double its value on the assumption that it had no rival in the country; that, secondly, they had just heard it was going to run in the first race; and, thirdly and lastly, that as there was no other horse available, Flurry was going to take old Sultan out of the 'bus and ride him in the race; and that Mrs Yeates had promised to keep mamma safe in the tent, while the race was going on, and 'you know, Major Yeates, it would be delightful to beat Sheehy after his getting the better of you all about the licence!'

With this base appeal to my professional feelings, Miss Knox paused, and looked at me insinuatingly. Her eyes were greeny-grey, and very beguiling.

'Come on,' she said; 'they want you to start th ı!'

Pursued by visions of the just wrath of Lady Knox, I weakly followed Miss Sally to the farther end of the second field, from which point the race was to start. The course was not a serious one: two or three natural banks, a stone wall, and a couple of 'hurrls.' There were but four riders, including Flurry, who was seated composedly on Sultan, smoking a cigarette and talking confidentially to Slipper. Sultan, although something stricken in years and touched in the wind, was a brown horse who in his day had been a hunter of no mean repute; even now he occasionally carried Lady Knox in a sedate and gentlemanly manner, but it struck me that it was trying him rather high to take him from the pole of the 'bus after twelve miles on a hilly road, and hustle him over a country against a four-year-old. My acutest anxiety, however, was to start the race as quickly as possible, and to get back to the tent in time to establish an *alibi*; therefore I repressed my private sentiments, and, tying my handkerchief to a stick, determined that no time should be fashionably frittered away in false starts.

They got away somehow; I believe Sheehy's colt was facing the wrong way at the moment when I dropped the flag, but a friend turned him with a stick, and, with a cordial and timely whack, speeded him on his way on sufficiently level terms, and then somehow, instead of returning to the tent, I found myself with Miss Sally on the top of a tall narrow bank, in a precarious line of other spectators, with whom we toppled and swayed, and, in moments of acuter emotion, held on to each other in unaffected comradeship.

Flurry started well, and from our commanding position we could see him methodically riding at the first fence at a smart hunting canter, closely attended by James Canty's brother on a young black mare, and by an unknown youth on a big white horse. The hope of Sheehy's stable, a leggy chestnut, ridden by a cadet of the house of Sheehy, went away from the friend's stick like a rocket, and had already refused the first bank twice before old Sultan decorously changed feet on it and dropped down into the next field with tranquil precision. The white horse scrambled over it on his stomach, but landed safely, despite the fact that his rider clasped him round the neck during the process; the black mare and the chestnut shouldered one another over at the hole the white horse had left, and the whole party went away in a bunch and jumped the ensuing hurdle without disaster. Flurry continued to ride at the same steady hunting pace, accompanied respectfully by the white horse and by Jerry Canty on the black mare. Sheehy's colt had clearly the legs of the party, and did some showy galloping between the jumps, but as he refused to face the banks without a lead, the end of the first round found the field still a sociable party personally conducted by Mr Knox.

'That's a dam nice horse,' said one of my hangers-on, looking approvingly at Sultan as he passed us at the beginning of the second round, making a good deal of noise but apparently going at his ease; 'you might depind your life on him, and he have the crabbedest jock in the globe of Ireland on him this minute.'

'Canty's mare's very sour,' said another; 'look at her now, baulking the bank! she's as cross as a bag of weasels.'

'Begob, I wouldn't say but she's a little sign lame,' resumed the first; 'she was going light on one leg on the road a while ago.'

'I tell you what it is,' said Miss Sally, very seriously, in my ear, 'that chestnut of Sheehy's is settling down. I'm afraid he'll gallop away from Sultan at the finish, and the wall won't stop him. Flurry can't get another inch out of Sultan. He's riding him well,' she ended in a critical voice, which yet was not quite like her own. Perhaps I should not have noticed it but for the fact that the hand that held my arm was trembling. As for me, I thought of Lady Knox, and trembled too.

There now remained but one bank, the trampled remnant of the furze hurdle, and the stone wall. The pace was beginning to improve, and the other horses drew away from Sultan; they charged the bank at full gallop, the black mare and the chestnut flying it perilously, with a windmill flourish of legs and arms from their riders, the white horse racing up to it with a gallantry that deserted him at the critical moment, with the result that his rider turned a somersault over his head and landed, amidst the roars of the onlookers, sitting on the fence facing his horse's nose. With creditable presence of mind he remained on the bank, towed the horse over, scrambled on to his back again and started afresh. Sultan, thirty yards to the bad, pounded doggedly on, and Flurry's cane and heels remained idle; the old horse, obviously blown, slowed cautiously coming in at the jump. Sally's grip tightened on my arm, and the crowd yelled as Sultan, answering to a hint from the spurs and a touch at his mouth, heaved himself on to the bank. Nothing but sheer riding on Flurry's part got him safe off it, and saved him from the consequences of a bad peck on landing; none the less, he pulled himself together and went away down the hill for the stone wall as stoutly as ever. The high-road skirted the last two fields, and there was a gate in the roadside fence beside the place where the stone wall met it at right angles. I had noticed this gate, because during the first round Slipper had been sitting on it, demonstrating with his usual fervour. Sheehy's colt was leading, with his nose in the air, his rider's hands going like a

circular saw, and his temper, as a bystander remarked, 'up on end';
the black mare, half mad from spurring, was going hard at his
heels, completely out of hand; the white horse was steering steadily
for the wrong side of the flag, and Flurry, by dint of cutting
corners and of saving every yard of ground, was close enough to
keep his antagonists' heads over their shoulders, while their right
arms rose and fell in unceasing flagellation.

'There'll be a smash when they come to the wall! If one falls
they'll all go!' panted Sally. '! – Now! Flurry! Flurry! – '

What had happened was that the chestnut colt had suddenly
perceived that the gate at right angles to the wall was standing
wide open, and, swinging away from the jump, he had bolted
headlong out on to the road, and along it at top speed for his
home. After him fled Canty's black mare, and with her, carried
away by the spirit of stampede, went the white horse.

Flurry stood up in his stirrups and gave a view-halloa as he
cantered down to the wall. Sultan came at it with the send of the
hill behind him, and jumped it with a skill that intensified, if that
were possible, the volume of laughter and yells around us. By
the time the black mare and the white horse had returned and
ignominiously bundled over the wall to finish as best they might,
Flurry was leading Sultan towards us.

'That blackguard, Slipper!' he said, grinning; 'every one'll say I
told him to open the gate! But look here, I'm afraid we're in for
trouble. Sultan's given himself a bad over-reach; you could never
drive him home to-night. And I've just seen Norris lying blind
drunk under a wall!'

Now Norris was Lady Knox's coachman. We stood aghast at
this 'horror on horror's head,' the blood trickled down Sultan's
heel, and the lather lay in flecks on his dripping, heaving sides, in
irrefutable witness to the iniquity of Lady Knox's only daughter.
Then Flurry said:

'Thank the Lord, here's the rain!'

At the moment I admit that I failed to see any cause for gratitude
in this occurrence, but later on I appreciated Flurry's grasp of
circumstances.

That appreciation was. I think, at its highest development about
half an hour afterwards, when I, an unwilling conspirator (a part
with which my acquaintance with Mr Knox had rendered me but

too familiar) unfurled Mrs Cadogan's umbrella over Lady Knox's head, and hurried her through the rain from the tent to the 'bus, keeping it and my own person well between her and the horses. I got her in, with the rest of her bedraggled and exhausted party, and slammed the door.

'Remember, Major Yeates,' she said through the window, 'you are the *only* person here in whom I have any confidence. I don't wish *any* one else to touch the reins!' this with a glance towards Flurry, who was standing near.

'I'm afraid I'm only a moderate whip,' I said.

'My dear man,' replied Lady Knox testily, 'those horses could drive themselves!'

I slunk round to the front of the 'bus. Two horses, carefully rugged, were in it, with the inevitable Slipper at their heads.

'Slipper's going with you,' whispered Flurry, stepping up to me; 'she won't have me at any price. He'll throw the rugs over them when you get to the house, and if you hold the umbrella well over her she'll never see. I'll manage to get Sultan over somehow, when Norris is sober. That will be all right.'

I climbed to the box without answering, my soul being bitter within me, as is the soul of a man who has been persuaded by womankind against his judgment.

'Never again!' I said to myself, picking up the reins; 'let her marry him or Bernard Shute, or both of them if she likes, but I won't be roped into this kind of business again!'

Slipper drew the rugs from the horses, revealing on the near side Lady Knox's majestic carriage horse, and on the off, a thickset brown mare of about fifteen hands.

'What brute is this?' said I to Slipper, as he swarmed up beside me.

'I don't rightly know where Misther Flurry got her,' said Slipper, with one of his hiccoughing crows of laughter; 'give her the whip, Major, and' – here he broke into song:

> '*Howld to the shteel,*
> *Honamaundhiaoul; she'll run off like an eel!*'

'If you don't shut your mouth, said I, with pent-up ferocity, 'I'll chuck you off the 'bus.'

Slipper was but slightly drunk, and, taking this delicate rebuke in good part, he relapsed into silence.

Wherever the brown mare came from, I can certify that it was not out of double harness. Though humble and anxious to oblige, she pulled away from the pole as if it were red hot, and at critical moments had a tendency to sit down. However, we squeezed without misadventure among the donkey carts and between the groups of people, and bumped at length in safety out on to the high-road.

Here I thought it no harm to take Slipper's advice, and I applied the whip to the brown mare, who seemed inclined to turn round. She immediately fell into an uncertain canter that no effort of mine could frustrate; I could only hope that Miss Sally would foster conversation inside the 'bus and create a distraction; but judging from my last view of the party, and of Lady Knox in particular, I thought she was not likely to be successful. Fortunately the rain was heavy and thick, and a rising west wind gave every promise of its continuance. I had little doubt but that I should catch cold, but I took it to my bosom with gratitude as I reflected how it was drumming on the roof of the 'bus and blurring the windows.

We had reached the foot of a hill, about a quarter of a mile from the racecourse; the Castle Knox horse addressed himself to it with dignified determination, but the mare showed a sudden and alarming tendency to jib.

'Belt her, Major!' vociferated Slipper, as she hung back from the pole chain, with the collar half-way up her ewe neck, 'and give it to the horse, too! He'll dhrag her!'

I was in the act of 'belting,' when a squealing whinny struck upon my ear, accompanied by a light pattering gallop on the road behind us; there was an answering roar from the brown mare, a roar, as I realised with a sudden drop of the heart, of outraged maternal feeling, and in another instant a pale, yellow foal sprinted up beside us, with shrill whickerings of joy. Had there at this moment been a boghole handy, I should have turned the 'bus into it without hesitation; as there was no accommodation of the kind, I laid the whip severely into everything I could reach, including the foal. The result was that we topped the hill at a gallop, three abreast, like a Russian troitska; it was like my usual luck that at this identical moment we should meet the police patrol, who saluted respectfully.

'That the divil may blisther Michael Moloney!' ejaculated Slipper, holding on to the rail; 'didn't I give him the foaleen and a halther on him to keep him! I'll howld you a pin 'twas the wife let him go, for she being vexed about the licence! Sure that one's a March foal, an' he'd run from here to Cork!'

There was no sign from my inside passengers, and I held on at a round pace, the mother and child galloping absurdly, the carriage horse pulling hard, but behaving like a gentleman. I wildly revolved plans of how I would make Slipper turn the foal in at the first gate we came to, of what I should say to Lady Knox supposing the worst happened and the foal accompanied us to her hall door, and of how I would have Flurry's blood at the earliest possible opportunity, and here the fateful sound of galloping behind us was again heard.

'It's impossible!' I said to myself; 'she can't have twins!'

The galloping came nearer, and Slipper looked back.

'Murdher alive!' he said in a stage whisper; 'Tom Sheehy's afther us on the butcher's pony!'

'What's that to me?' I said, dragging my team aside to let him pass; 'I suppose he's drunk, like everyone else!'

Then the voice of Tom Sheehy made itself heard.

'Shtop! Shtop thief!' he was bawling; 'give up my mare! How will I get me porther home!'

That was the closest shave I have ever had, and nothing could have saved the position but the torrential nature of the rain and the fact that Lady Knox had on a new bonnet. I explained to her at the door of the 'bus that Sheehy was drunk (which was the one unassailable feature of the case), and had come after his foal, which, with the fatuity of its kind, had escaped from a field and followed us. I did not mention to Lady Knox that when Mr Sheehy retreated, apologetically, dragging the foal after him in a halter belonging to one of her own carriage horses, he had a sovereign of mine in his pocket, and during the narration I avoided Miss Sally's eye as carefully as she avoided mine.

The only comments on the day's events that are worthy of record were that Philippa said to me that she had not been able to understand what the curious taste in the tea had been till Sally told her it was turf-smoke, and that Mrs Cadogan said to Philippa that night that 'the Major was that dhrinched that if he had a shirt between his skin and himself he could have wrung it,' and that Lady Knox said to a mutual friend that though Major Yeates had been extremely kind and obliging, he was an uncommonly bad whip.

THE GOOD THING

Colin Davy

'CREPELLO, a good thing!' exclaimed the small, wizened-faced man at the end of the bar. 'There ain't no such thing these days.' He spat accurately.

The spotty young man whose discourse had been thus interrupted turned a glance of disdain at the stranger. But something in the latter's appearance suggested more intimate association with racing stables than that gleaned from the pink, midday leaflet protruding from the youth's own pocket. So he tempered his sneer, and enquired: 'Wasn't two stone in hand good enough in your day, Dad?'

The little old man sucked his teeth. 'No it weren't,' he remarked shortly.

'I suppose in your day they 'oooked one up in the Gold Cup to win the seller at Windsor next day,' he suggested, winking at his mates.

'There were good things to bet on without nothing extravagant of that sort,' said the old man gazing meditatively into his empty glass. 'In those days, when the money was down, there were no ifs nor buts . . . No. Nor no short 'eads neither. They *did* win.'

The landlord winked encouragingly at the group, and tilted the gin bottle generously into the old man's glass. The recipient brightened remarkably, took a deep swig, and began: 'It's more than forty years ago . . . ?'

'Yes, Dad . . . ?'

'I was with Jack Quick wot trained at Puddlecombe near Wantage. He hadn't many patrons 'adn't Quick, and those he had seldom paid their bills. So, the establishment got the name of being a betting stable. That means that the trades-people knew not to come for their bills unless the stable's 'ad a touch. . . . We had a

poor lot of 'osses, mostly selling platers, and one or two which at
four and five years old were still waiting to win a maiden race.
'Owever, Quick by name and quick by nature, the boss usually
had something ready when the bailiffs got too thick on the
ground. . . .

'There were no 'igh-falutin' trade union ideas in those days about
one lad doin' two 'osses. I often did three or four, and in bad
times even five. Nor was there any rule about a fiver a winner.
Usually one was on a good 'iding to nothing. . . . '

The speaker emptied his glass and saw it refilled with wistful
eyes. After a pause, he went on gloomily: 'We 'ad one 'oss – one
that I did – a big grey colt called Monastic Calm. Well named 'e
was. By Glastonbury out of Evening 'ymn. 'E was that calm 'e
was only fit to carry monks to matins. Lord Watercress had paid
nine thousand for 'im as a yearling, and he'd hoped to win the
Derby. Well, by the time 'e was rising five, the closest he'd got
to classic honours was third in a selling race of four runners, and
the winner disqualified. Monastic Calm! That described 'im. 'E
wouldn't walk across the box to see if his manger was full. 'E 'ad
to be fed where he stood out of a bucket, or 'e'd have starved
'isself to death. 'E'd stand for hours with his eyes shut, resting as
many legs as possible with his lower lip hanging down like a sea-
lion's. Can't think why young Watercress didn't sell 'im. He'd 'ave
done well at the head of the Life Guards with a kettle drum on
either side to keep 'im awake. Lord Watercress was young and an
optimist. "All he needs is time," he'd say. His lordship was right.
That's what he did need. Time. About five minutes to the furlong.

'Well, one day I was leaning against the grey 'oss's stable door,
talking to Betty Quick the guv'nor's daughter. She was a nice bit
of goods and no slower than her name implied, when the most
extraordinary thing happened. The 'oss that had been standing like
a bleeding statue ever since I'd called 'im in the morning, suddenly
began to move. Very slowly he came towards us, poked his nose
over the door and sniffed. Then suddenly quick as a monkey, 'e
makes a grab and scuttles back into the far corner of his box.

' "Lawks!" screams Betty. " 'E's took the sausages!"

'Sure enough there was the 'oss with a string of Palethorpes
hanging from his mouth and the queerest look in his eye you ever
did see. There was no Monastic Calm about him. Proper baleful,
that's what he looked. As if 'e challenged us to take even a link

from him. Well, we watched those sausages disappear link by link like paper ribbon out of a conjurer's hat, but backwards on, if you know what I mean.'

The speaker watched his glass refilled with melancholy absorption, and continued: 'That night I noticed a change. When I dressed the 'oss down, he swished 'is tail twice and when I brought his feed he half-turned his head. But seeing no sausages, he dozed off again. But next day, he went so different – almost larkey, 'e was – that I could keep up with the yearlings cantering. Usually, I had to bash him all the way.

'After stables next day, I went to Betty and begged some scraps of meat from the kitchen – not much, but the knuckle end of a 'am, and some pork chops wot 'ad got tainted. He ate 'em bones and all, and when I went to him last thing, he turned right round and whinnied same as any other 'oss does at evening feed. And would you believe me? Next morning he went a fair treat upsides with old Bacchus, wot 'ad once won a forty-pound seller at Beverly!

'At first I thought of keeping this to myself, but the 'oss's improvement was so great and the price of meat so high I just had to tell the guv'nor. You should have seen his face when I told him. But when he'd seen the grey eat three pounds of catsmeat, a leg of lamb wot 'ad been spoiled by the sun, and seen 'im work next morning, he went away werry werry cogitatious.

'Later he takes me on one side and sez: "Nat, lad, we'll keep this to our two selves and 'oo knows, maybe get a nice touch out of this. You feed him 'is meat at nights when all the other lads is gone, and from now on you work the 'oss alone."

' "But 'ow are we to know how much he improves?" I asked.

' "Leave that to me," 'e sez. "I can always fix up a trial with one of me brother's from over at Boreham Down. We'll find out how he improves when the times comes."

'Well, I'd hate to think what it cost the guv' in legs of mutton and sides of beef, but he wasn't one to spare the golden eggs that might 'atch a goose. The best of everything wasn't too good for Monastic Calm after 'e'd clocked 'im over a mile once or twice. Of course I couldn't say what the time was, but I knew how me arms ached and how the wind whistled past, when the old sod got into top gear. It was more like riding the flying Scotsman than an 'oss.

'Well, after about two months we 'ad a secret trial with one of Quick's brother's 'osses. I didn't know what the weights were, but Monastic Calm beat the other quad by twenty lengths, and was never going more than half-speed neither.

'That night, I asked the guv'nor: "When do we run the grey? Ain't it time we got something for the butcher?"

'Mester Quick smiled and said: "We wait for Newmarket, and the butcher can wait too."

' "In a seller?" I sez.

' "Seller me foot," sez he. "He goes in the Cambridgeshire. 'E'll get about seven stone and will be a certainty."

'I suppose I said something about flying too high, but he cuts in quick and very supercilious, "Do you know what the 'oss was that you beat this morning?" he asks. "It was Bachelor. Bachelor, wot was second in the Eclipse! And you gave 'im a stone. Now go and give the grey 'is entrée and joint."

'Well, when I thought it over, I realised what that added up to. *We'd got the fastest horse in the world.* With seven stone in the Cambridgeshire, 'e'd be like a racing car against push-bicycles!

'A week before the race, I was sent off with the 'oss to a farm on the Suffolk side of Newmarket, where we lay low to avoid the touts. My orders were to hack him out in clothing in the afternoons when no one expected a horse to gallop, strip 'im quietly behind The Ditch, give 'im a breezer and off back to the farm before anyone twigged. I always finished the gallop not far from the Cambridgeshire winning post where another lad waited with a second set of clothing and a couple of loin chops for the colt as a sort of encourager. Comin' across the flat, the grey seemed to smell those chops, and . . . well, it were like flying. I often laughed to meself and thought of the crowd when they saw this unknown grey hoss 'undreds of yards in front of the others. I could hear them asking theirselves: "Wot's this perisher out in front?" It would be the sensation of a lifetime.

'The night before the race I went to the subscription rooms with Mr Quick to 'ear them call over the card. The guv'nor 'adn't backed him with a penny till then, and our 'oss was a hundred and fifty to one in some places and two-hundred to one in others. Mr Quick started very quietly in fifties and ponies, but 'e'd been busy, for by the time we came out Monastic Calm had hardened to thirty-threes.

'The guv'nor and I went to a quiet pub nearby to tot up what he stood to win. . . . '

The old man paused, drained his glass, and announced slowly: '*Mr Quick stood to win seventy-five thousand pounds, and I was to 'ave ten per cent.*'

The group in the bar stood in gaping silence. Then a dozen ready hands went out to refill the narrator's glass. But though he sipped his drink with relish, he seemed in no hurry to continue. His glance roved slowly and rather sadly from one to another whiskey advertisement decorating the wall.

As last, one spirit bolder than the rest broke in upon the old man's reverie.

'Did . . . did it win, Sir?' he asked.

The old man nodded. 'Aye. Monastic Calm won. Won by nearly a furlong.'

He drained his glass, reached for his cap, but yet the group knew the tale was not told.

'And the bookies paid up?' asked one youth, mopping his brow.

The old man shook his head. 'No,' he said. 'You see the jockey couldn't weigh in. So the horse was disqualified. It were this way. There was no little lad at the winning post with the loin chops as expected. And the 'oss was hungry. He threw the little lad wot rode 'im, and ate him. . . . ' He looked round gloomily and added: 'Boots and all.'

THE LOSERS

Maurice Gee

DINNER was over at the commercial hotel and the racing people were busy discussing prospects for the final day. The first day's racing had been interesting; some long shots had come home, and a few among the crowd in the lounge were conscious as they talked of fatter, heavier wallets hanging in their inside pockets. Of these the happiest was probably Lewis Betham who had, that day, been given several tips by trainers. The tips had been good ones, but it would not have mattered if they had been bad. The great thing was that trainers had come up and called him by his first name and told him what to back. He thought he had never been so happy, and he told his wife again how the best of these great moments had come about.

'He said to me: "Lew, that horse of mine, Torrid, should run a good one, might be worth a small bet." He's a cunning little rooster, but he's straight as they come, so I just said to him: "Thanks, Arnold" – I call him Arnold – and I gave him a wink. He knew the information wouldn't go any further. See? I didn't have to tell him. And then Jack O'Nell came up and said: "Do you know anything, Arnold?" and he said: "No, this is a tough one, Jack. They all seem to have a show." He's cunning all right. But he is straight, straight as a die. He'd never put you wrong. So I banged a fiver on its nose. Eleven pound it paid, eleven pound.'

Mrs Betham said: 'Yes, dear. Eleven pounds eleven and six.' She sipped her coffee and watched the people in the lounger. She was bored. Lew hadn't introduced her to anyone and she wished she could go out to the pictures, anywhere to get away from the ceaseless jabber of horse names. None of them meant anything to her. She realised how far apart she and Lew had grown. If someone

came up and murmured Torrid in her ear she would just stare at
him in amazement. But this whispering of names was the only
meaning Lew seemed to demand from life these days. He had
always dreamed of owning a horse and she had not opposed him.
She had discovered too late he was entering a world with values
of its own, a world with aristocracy and commoners, brahmans
and untouchables. He, new brahman, was determined to observe
all its proprieties. And of course he would receive its rewards.

Lew's horse, Bronze Idol, a two-year-old, was having its third
start in the Juvenile Handicap tomorrow. It would be one of the
favourites after running a fifth and a third. Lew was sure the horse
would win and his trainer had told him to have a solid bet. He
was tasting his triumph already. He excused himself and went into
the house-bar to talk to Arnold. He wanted now to give a tip in
return for the one he had got. Arnold would know the horse was
going to win, but that was beside the point.

Mrs Betham watched him go, then looked round the lounge.
This place, she thought, was the same as the other racing hotels
she'd been in. There were the same pursy people saying the same
things. There were the same faint smells of lino and hops, vinegar
and disinfectant. And Phar Lap, glossy and immaculate, was on
the wall between lesser Carbine and Kindergarten. The Queen,
richly framed, watched them from another wall, with that faint
unbending smile the poor girl had to wear. How her lips must
ache.

Duties, thought Mrs Betham, we all have duties.

Hers, as a wife, was to accompany Lew on these trips. To wear
the furs he bought her and be sweet and receptive and unexcep-
tional. Surprising what a hard job that was at times. She yawned
and looked for the clock, and found it at length behind her, over
the camouflaged fireplace, over the polished leaves of the palm in
the green-painted barrel. With straight dutiful hands it gave the
time as ten past eight. She yawned again. Too late for the pictures,
too early to go to bed. She prepared her mind for another hour
of boredom.

There were a dozen or so men in the bar but only two women.
Lew recognised one of these immediately: Mrs Benjamin, the
owner, widow of a hotel man. She was sitting at a small table
sipping a drink that appeared to be gin. The hand holding the glass

sparkled with rings. Between sips she talked in a loud voice to her brother, Charlie Becket, who trained her horses. Arnold, wiry, tanned, and deferential, was also at the table.

Arnold saw Lew and jerked his head. Lew went over, noticing Mrs Benjamin's lips form his name to Charlie Becket as he approached. When he had been introduced he sat down.

Mrs Benjamin said: 'You're the Betham who owns that little colt, aren't you? What's the name of that horse, Charlie?'

'Bronze Idol,' said Charlie Becket. 'Should go well tomorrow.'

Lew nodded and narrowed his eyes. 'We've got a starter's chance,' he said.

Arnold said: 'Well-bred colt. You've got the filly in the same race, Mrs Benjamin.'

'Ah, my hobby,' cried Mrs Benjamin. 'I bred that filly myself. If I can make something of her I'm never going to take advice from anyone again.'

'She should go a good race,' said Arnold.

As they talked Lew watched Mrs Benjamin. She was over-powdered, absurdly blue-rinsed; her nose was flat, with square box nostrils, and her eyelids glistened as though coated with vaseline. He'd seen all this before, and refused to see it. This was not what he wanted. He wanted the legend. He remembered some of the stories he'd heard about her. It was said she had a cocktail bar built into the back of her car, and the mark of entry to her select group was to be invited for a drink.

Perhaps, thought Lew, perhaps tomorrow. He found himself wanting to mention the bar.

It was said she carried a wad of notes in her purse for charitable purposes connected with racing. Nobody had ever seen the wad, nobody had seen her pay out, but there were stories of failed trainers mysteriously re-entering business, always after being noticed in conversation with Mrs Benjamin. Lew did not believe these stories, but he felt it was more important for them to exist than for them to be true.

Mrs Benjamin said: 'And Bronze Idol is your first venture, Mr Betham?'

Lew told her of his lifelong ambition to own a horse. He kept his voice casual and tried to suggest that he was one of those who would do well at racing without having to do well. He was trying to make it a paying sport.

Charlie Becket twisted his mouth. He spoke about Bronze Idol and said the horse was very promising. Lew said it was still a bit green; tomorrow's race was in the nature of an 'educational gallop'. He saw Charlie Becket didn't believe him, and was flattered.

Mrs Benjamin interrupted the conversation to ask Charlie if he would like another drink. Lew understood that the question was really a request. Her own glass was empty while Charlie's was still half full. He was about to say: 'Let me, Mrs Benjamin,' and take her glass, when he realised it might be wiser to pretend he hadn't understood. He must not appear over-anxious. And his knowledge of women told him Mrs Benjamin was not of the type that liked to be easily read. Perhaps when she brought her request a little more into the open he might make the offer. . . .

But Charlie gulped his drink and stood up. He had a broad face, a broad white nose, and squinting eyes that looked everything over with cold appraisal – an expression, Lew thought, that should have been saved for the horses. Lew wondered if it was true that at training gallops Charlie always carried two stop-watches, one for other people, showing whatever time he wanted them to see, and one he looked at later on, all by himself. Of course, he thought, watching the eyes, of course it's true. I wish he was training my horse.

Charlie said: 'Don't feel like drinking right now. Come on, I'll take you for that drive.'

Mrs Benjamin had barely opened her mouth to protest when he added shortly: 'It was your idea, you know.'

She said: 'Oh, Charlie, why have you got such a good memory?' but she stood up and smiled at Lew and Arnold and said: 'Excuse us,' Charlie nodded and the pair left the bar. The eyes in the steam-follered fox head on Mrs Benjamin's shoulders glittered back almost sardonically.

Arnold sucked his lips into a tight smile, and nodded in a way that showed he was pleased.

'Charlie must be mad about something,' he said. 'He doesn't often turn on a performance like that in public.'

'So Charlie's the boss,' said Lew softly.

'Always has been. It just suits him to let her play up to things the way she does. All the horses she's got, they might just as well belong to him. Even this filly of hers – that'll only win when he wants it to.'

Lew nodded and tried to look as if he understood. It was a shock to have Mrs Benjamin, the legendary figure, cut down to this size. But he experienced also a thrill of pleasure that he was one of the few who knew how things really were. It meant he was accepted. He was one of those Charlie Becket didn't pretend to.

'Good thing too,' Arnold was saying. 'Most of these women get too big for their boots if they start doing well. And hard. My God, that one, she's sweet as pie on the surface but you scratch that and see what you find. She's got one idea, and that's money – grab hold of it, stack it away, that's how her mind works. Don't you believe these yarns about her giving any of it away. If there's one thing you can be sure of it's nothing gets out of that little black purse of hers once she's got it in.'

Lew nodded and said: 'I knew they were just yarns, of course.'

'There's been some fine women in the racing game,' said Arnold. 'But most of 'em go wrong somehow. Look' – he jerked his head – 'you take Connie Reynolds over there.'

Lew looked to a corner of the room where a young blonde woman with a heavy figure was arguing with a group of men.

'You've heard about Connie?'

Lew shook his head reluctantly.

'Christ, man, she's been banged by every jock from North Cape to the Bluff. And now, believe it or not, she's got herself engaged to Stanley John Edward Philpott. You've heard of him?'

'I've heard the name,' lied Lew.

'Stanley John Edward Philpott,' said Arnold, and he swept a hand, palm down, between them. For a moment Lew wondered what racing sign this was, then understood it was a personal one of Arnold's, meaning the man was no good.

'I could tell you a few stories about him. Could tell you some about Connie too.' Arnold smiled, and the smile deepened, and Lew leaned forward, breathing softly, waiting for the stories, feeling fulfilled and very, very happy.

At half past eight Connie Reynolds left the men in the house-bar corner and went into the lounge. She left abruptly after one of them had made an insinuating remark about her engagement. He said it wasn't fair to the rest of them to take herself out of circulation. As she went towards the door she felt she was behaving as

she'd always wanted to behave. She was simply walking out on
them. She glanced at the ring on her finger: pride and anger were
two of the luxuries she could now afford. And the freedom of not
having to please made her for a moment see Stan in the role of
champion and liberator, riding to slay the dragon and unchain the
maiden. But this image, the unreal figures springing on her from
the white delicately haunted innocence she had left long ago, forced
her into a hurried retreat, and, 'Maiden?' she said, shrugging and
giggling, 'that's a laugh.' And Stan as a knight on a white charger,
poor battered old Stanley, who had strength only to assert now
and then that one day he'd get his own back on all the bloody
poohbahs, just you wait and see if he didn't? No, nothing had
really changed, except that she was walking out on them, that and
the fact that she didn't care if she had drunk too much whiskey.
She didn't have to care any more.

Mrs Betham saw Connie come through the door and say something to herself and giggle.

The poor girl's drunk, she thought, and she looked round for
the dark tubby little man who'd been with her at dinner. There
weren't many people in the lounge. Most had gone out or into
the bar. She remembered that the man had gone upstairs with
friends some time ago, and she half rose and beckoned the girl.

'If you're looking for your husband,' said Mrs Betham, 'he's
gone upstairs.'

Connie stopped in front of her. 'He isn't my husband,' she said,
'he's my boy friend.'

'Fiancé,' she corrected. She sat down in a chair facing Mrs
Betham. She saw the woman smiling at her and thought she looked
kind.

'Do you believe in love?' asked Connie.

Mrs Betham could not decide whether the girl was serious. She
was a little drunk, obviously, but drunk people often talked of
things they managed to keep hidden at other times, the things that
really troubled them.

'You know, a man and a woman, to have an' to hold, an' all
that?'

'Yes, I do,' said Mrs Betham.

'Well, I was hoping you'd say no, 'cause I don't. An' I don't
think it's passed me by 'cause I've had my eyes wide open all the
time an' I haven't seen anything that looks the least bit like it.'

Mrs Betham thought of several clever things to say, but she didn't say any of them. 'Would you like me to try to find him for you?' she asked.

Connie said: 'No, he'll keep. And you can bet your life he's not worrying about what's happened to me. Still, I'm used to looking after myself. I shouldn't kid myself Stan's going to take over just because I got a ring on my finger.'

'You know, dear,' said Mrs Betham, 'these aren't the sort of things you should be saying to a stranger.'

'You aren't a stranger. You're the wife of the man who owns Bronze Idol. Stan told me. Stan's got a horse in the same race. Royal Return. You heard of Royal Return?'

Mrs Betham shook her head.

'Well, don't ask me if it's got a chance because it isn't forward enough. That's what I have been told to say.'

Mrs Betham laughed. 'And my instructions are to say that I don't know anything at all. Haven't we been well trained?'

Connie said: 'Yeah, but not as well as the horses. My God, I'd love to be groomed, just stroked an' patted an' brushed that way. Any man who treated me like that would have me for life. But I haven't got a chance. I'm just an old work horse, the sort that gets knocked around. The day'll come I'll be sold for lion's meat.'

'My dear, you sound very bitter.'

'You know why I'm getting married?' said Connie. She put a hand on Mrs Betham's knee. 'I'm getting married 'cause I'm tired an' I want a rest. Is that a good enough reason?'

'I'll find your fiancé,' said Mrs Betham. But she couldn't get up while the hand was on her knee.

'I want to know is that a good enough reason.'

Mrs Betham realised the girl was serious.

'Yes, dear,' she said, 'I think that's a very good reason.'

Connie thought for a moment, her mouth open and twisted to one side, eyes gazing at the Queen on the wall.

'And what's the way to be happy, then?' she asked.

'Why . . . to be happy,' said Mrs Betham, but she could find no answer. 'I suppose each one's got to put the other first,' she said lamely.

'No,' said Connie, her eyes bright and questioning, 'I don't mean him, I mean me, the way for me to be happy.'

Mrs Betham knew she should say: My dear, I think you'd better not get married at all, but instead she said, with sudden sharpness: 'You've got to make sure he needs you more than you need him. That's the only way I know.'

She forgot Connie and thought of herself and Lew. After twenty-five years the roles had been reversed. Now she didn't need him any more and so she couldn't be hurt. But over the years he had grown to need her, she was the faithful wife, part of his sense of rightness. Without her his world would crumble. And she thought, so I'm still a prisoner really, just the way I always was. But now it doesn't hurt, and it doesn't mean anything either. It's just one of the things that is.

She turned back to Connie. The girl was almost in tears.

'Well, then,' said Connie, 'it's all wrong. It isn't Stan who needs me it's me who needs him, because I'm tired and I've got to stop, just stop, you see, and be still and let things go past me for a while. And Stan had to have some money to buy the horse, so I gave it to him and he's got to marry me.'

Mrs Betham tried to speak, but the girl said fiercely: 'It doesn't matter if he needs me. That isn't important at all.'

'No, of course, dear,' said Mrs Betham, trying to soothe her. 'As long as you both put each other first. That's the main thing.'

But Connie jumped up and ran from the room. Mrs Betham wondered if she should follow, then decided against it. She couldn't think of any advice to give if she did catch the girl. She could only tell the truth again, as she knew it. She wasn't the sweet fairy-godmother type to heal with a sunny smile.

After a while she took a magazine from the rack under the coffee-table and opened it at random. *Plump Correspondent Puts In Cheery Word For The Not So Slim*, she read.

She smiled wryly.

Not So Slim. Why couldn't that be the most serious affliction? A world made happy by dieting and menthoids.

She put the magazine aside and looked round the room. The glossy horses posed, the slim Queen smiled down, and over the fireplace the clock said that at last it was late enough to go to bed.

She yawned and went up the stairs, thinking about Connie, and the impossibility of ever helping anybody.

Stan Philpott was playing poker in the room of Jeff Milden, an ex-bookie and small-business man who had failed to survive tax investigations and a heavy fine. He now worked in a factory, where several sly gambling ventures had shown disappointingly small returns, a fact he put down to working-class prejudice against an ex-employer. The truth was that, irrespective of class, nobody he had ever known had really liked him. He was aware of this only in a vague uncomprehending way, and tonight he was directing most of his energy to finding other reasons for his guests' preoccupation. He supposed Joe Elliot the trainer was worried about money or his horses, whereas Joe was really worried about having a stable boy who blushed and giggled whenever he was reprimanded and cried when threatened with being sent home. He supposed Stan Philpott was worried about money and Royal Return. In this he was right. The tremendous complex of preparation, bravado, fear, assessment of chance and luck, which had driven Stan frantic for weeks past had reduced itself on the eve of the event to an urgent knowledge of necessity: Royal Return must win tomorrow or he was finished. It was as simple as that. He, Stanley John Edward Philpott, was finished.

Fingering his cards he told himself that if the horse didn't win there was only one way left to get some money, and that was a way he could never take. He tried to read in the hand he held a sign that he should never even have to consider it. The hand was poor; he threw it aside and watched the others bet.

'Can't seem to get one tonight,' he muttered, and Jeff Milden, pulling in winnings with one hand, pushed the cards towards him with the other, saying:

'Come on, Stan. Stop worrying about that donkey of yours. Deal yourself a good one.'

Stan treated this as an invitation to talk. As he shuffled the cards he said: 'You know, it's that bloody thing of Becket's I'm scared of.' So that he might talk about Royal Return he had told the others to back the horse tomorrow, but had suggested enough uncertainty about winning to make sure they wouldn't.

Joe Elliot shook his head and said with an air of sad wisdom: 'Don't hope for too much, Stan.'

'If there's one bastard who could beat me it's Becket. He's got it in for me.' Stan continued to shuffle though Jeff Milden was showing impatience.

'I'm one up on Becket, and I don't reckon he's going to rest till he gets it back on me.'

'Christ, Stan, that happened years ago,' said Jeff. He snapped his fingers for the cards. But Joe was tired of playing. He asked to hear the story.

Stan smiled, recalling his victory, then began with practised brevity: 'Was when I was riding over the sticks. Becket was just beginning to make his way then. He had a pretty good hurdler called Traveller's Joy. I used to ride it in all its starts so I knew when it was right. We waited, see, we got everything just like we wanted it, an' I said to Becket, right, this is it. So he pulls me aside in that sneaky way he's got an' says, I've got twenty on for you. So then it's up to me, and sure enough I kick that thing home. And then do you think I can find Becket? I chased him all over the bloody course. After a while I give up, and I take a tumble to what's happening. I'm getting the bum's rush. And sure enough next time this horse starts there's another jock up. So I get cunning, see. I think out a little scheme to put Mr Becket where he belongs. I know he thinks the horse is going to win again, an' I think so too, so I decide to do something about it. Becket's got some kid up, and that's a mistake he wouldn't make now, so just before the race I go round and make myself known to this kid, an' I say, Listen, kid, I've ridden this horse lots of times an' I know how he likes to be rode, an' I tell this kid he's got to be held in at the jumps. Take him in tight, I say, he's got to be steady, an' the kid thinks I'm being decent an' he says, Gee, thanks, Mr Philpott, or words to that effect. Well, this horse Traveller's Joy is a real jumper, he likes to stretch right out, so at the first fence the kid takes him in on a tight rein and gets jerked clean over the bloody horse's head, an I look round an' see Becket standing there with his face all red an' I spit on the ground an' say, That's for you, bastard, an' he looks at me, an' I reckon he'll be asking that kid some pretty pertinent questions when he gets hold of him.'

'When the kid gets out of hospital,' said Jeff. 'Come on, deal 'em round.'

Joe Elliot said nothing. Stan hadn't enjoyed the story, either. Surprisingly he had lost heart for it as he went along and the climax hadn't been convincing. He said, in a puzzled voice: 'That bloody Becket.'

The telling of the story hadn't changed Becket; he'd stood through it hard and aloof, clothed in success; and Stan saw that the stories a hundred Philpotts could tell wouldn't change a thing about him, wouldn't draw them up or him down in any way that mattered. There was no way to attack him.

Stan thought, It's only the poor bastards who don't like themselves much that you can get at. A man's only piddling in his own boot if he tries with Becket and the rest of them poohbahs.

He was so shaken by this that he wanted to get off alone somewhere so that he could cry out or swear or beat the wall, break something to prove himself real. He stood up and left the room. There even Joe Elliot's silence, the familiarity of a has-been like Milden, were working for Charlie Becket.

He slammed the door behind him and went along the passage. He was angry that his feet made no sound on the carpet, and when he came to his room he slammed that door too.

'Stan?' said a voice from the bed. It was a wet husky voice with a little ridge of panic in it, and for a second Stan didn't recognise it.

'Connie,' he said, and turned on the light.

She was lying on the bed fully clothed except for her shoes. One shoe was on the floor, the other balanced on the edge of the coverlet. This was so typical of her, of what he called her sloppiness, the way she let her money, her time, even her feelings dribble away, the way she dressed and undressed, and spoke and ate, that he broke into a rage. Becket, grey-suited and binoculared, seemed to stand beside him reproaching him with this blowzy fifth-hand woman. He entered a grey dizzing whirl made up of all he had never won and never achieved, a past of loss and failure, of small grimy winnings, a past of cheap beds and dirty sheets and bad food, of cards, smoky rooms, overflowing ashtrays, of women you could only want when you were drunk, of scabby horses, pulled horses, falls, broken bones, stewards' committees and lies, a past of borrowing and forgetting to pay back, of bludging and cheating and doping, a past of asserting your worth and greeting your winnings with a bull's roar so that you could believe in them, a past of noise and dirt and slipping lower and lower until a frayed collar and a three-day growth and a fifth-hand woman were part of you you weren't even conscious of. All these ran out in words he had never known he could use and broke against the hard withdrawn figure of Becket and made the woman on the bed curl and shrink and turn sobbing into the blankets until she was just tangled yellow hair and a shaking back. And these, the hair and back, were all Stan saw as he freed himself at length from the grey clinging fragments of his past.

He went slowly to the bed.

'Connie?'

He sat down and put a hand on her shoulder.

'Connie, I'm sorry. I didn't mean it.'

He sat stroking her shoulder. In a few moments she was quiet.

He turned out the light and lay down with her. His feet knocked her balancing shoe to the floor. She gave a small start that brought her body more firmly against his. After a while she said: 'Stan?'

'Yes, Connie?'

She turned suddenly and they lay close together, holding each other.

'Tell me it's going to be all right.'

'It'll be all right. Don't worry about it.'

'Can we get married soon, Stan?'

'Don't you worry. We'll get married. Stanley's got it all figured out.'

It was the first time, he realised, that he'd ever been with her and talked quietly, held her like this and not wanted her. He felt her going to sleep, and soon he heard her gentle snoring; and this sound, that she always refused to believe she made, brought him even closer to her, made him realise how helpless she was.

Yes, he thought, yes, it'll be all right. As long as the horse wins. It'll be all right. He stroked her hair as she slept, then carefully drew away and found his coat and laid it over her softly so that she wouldn't wake.

II

Charlie Becket walked from the saddling paddock to the jockeys' room. By the time he was there he had the instructions clear in his mind. The filly looked good, but she wasn't quite ready yet – and there was too much money on her. A poor race, a run home in the ruck, would lengthen her price for the next start. He'd get good money off her, but not today.

He beckoned the jockey and spoke to him in the corridor. The little man nodded thoughtfully then went back into the room to smoke. The instructions were simple. He'd ridden work on the horse and knew her well. She always went wide at the turn. He wasn't to check her; let her dive out, pretend to fight her, make her look green. It was a simple job – if you were a good jockey, a top jockey. He smiled and drew deeply on the cigarette and thought about how much he'd tell Becket to get on the big race for him. There was a sure win there.

Charlie went back to the stand and smiled as he climbed the steps. Betty was looking at him anxiously, like a grandmother fox in her furs. She was waiting to be told what to bet. She must bet on her dear little filly. Twenty quid he'd tell her. It would teach her a lesson to lose.

He took the money and went to the tote. Bronze Idol was surprisingly long. A tenner each way would net him sixty. And a little bit on Philpott's horse. There was sly work going on there. He placed the bets and went to stand beside the judge's box. He liked to be alone. A quarter hour without Betty twitching at his sleeve was something to be valued.

At the saddling paddock Stan had Royal Return ready. The horse seemed jaded and was slightly shin-sore. He shouldn't even be in work with the tracks so hard, but Stan told himself not to worry. He aimed his habitual punch of affection at the horse's ribs and murmured: 'It's over to you, you goori.' Royal Return responded by ambling in a circle. Stan placed his mouth beside its ear and pretended to whisper. The smell of the dope had gone. He grinned as though at his clowning and led the horse past Connie on the fence and into the birdcage. Everything was as right as he could make it. It was over to Lady Luck now. And as he walked Royal Return round and round and saw the white silks of the jockeys moving in the corridor he began to sweat. This formal part of the business had always made him nervous. He felt shabby on the green lawn, and was made to realise how much he had lost, how much he had to win back, and he tried not to think of the things he still had to lose. It was over to Lady Luck – she owed him for a lifetime of losses.

Connie had come to the birdcage fence and was watching the horses circle. Presently the first jockeys came out and mounted, and she wondered how they managed to look so serious. Perhaps just getting into those colours and looking neat and clean made the difference. One of the first things she'd learned about men was that they were horribly vain. But knowing things like that didn't seem to help women – or rather, not her sort of woman. She'd read stories about the siren type who could charm men to them and play them like harps, and she'd tried to be the siren type herself but it hadn't worked. It had failed so badly that now it was all she could do to hold even Stan who, as far as she knew, had never been wanted by another woman, anyway. He looked rather grimy out there among the glossy horses and bright little jockeys. He didn't compare very well with all those steward and owners and trainers under the members stand verandah, with Mr Betham for instance. Betham was rather red-faced, but very handsome in his suit and Stetson and fancy shoes, very prosperous and distinguished looking. She'd tried to catch men like that and once or twice had actually thought she'd succeeded. But she couldn't hold them and soon she discovered that they'd caught her. They'd tossed her back like an eel from a slimy creek.

She wondered what it was that made the difference. Was it clothes, or money, or just not having to worry about so much? She looked from Betham to Stan. Perhaps somehow all three of those put together. But Stan at least was real, you knew where the real part of him began and where it ended. That was something you'd probably never find out about Betham.

She watched as Stan talked to his jockey and helped him mount. Then Stan went off somewhere and the horse was on its own. Everything was naked and simple now. The future was that horse out there and a little Maori jockey in red and white silk. This was somehow a point, an end, the top of a hill or something like that, but there was no way of seeing how you'd got to it and no way of going back. You couldn't even see how you'd started on the way. Perhaps it had begun back there at school. You liked some things and you didn't like others. You did a hundred thousand little things and you didn't do the hundred thousand others you might have done. Then some time later you understood that you'd really been making a great big simple choice. What was her choice? Slut, racecourse bag. Once she'd thought she might be a model. But all the little things she'd done had made her a slut. She'd wanted so much to enjoy herself.

There should be some way of letting people know what they were doing. It was all so serious. Every little thing done was so serious.

A voice beside her said: 'They're really rather beautiful, aren't they?'

She turned and saw Mrs Betham there. Mrs Betham nodded admiringly at the horses.

'Yes,' said Connie.

Watching the horses in the birdcage was the only thing Mrs Betham enjoyed at the races. They were so clean and so polished looking, so sleek and yet so powerful. They seemed to dominate the men, and she wondered how the jockeys ever found courage to climb on their backs. Most of the jockeys were only boys. Yet they sat there so unconcernedly – some of them even chewed gum. There was a Maori boy on number eleven who looked like a trained chimpanzee, but the jockey on her husband's horse was quite old and looked rather tired. She felt sorry for him and wondered how on earth he'd survive if the horse fell over. He looked consumptive; the purple and orange colours didn't suit him at all.

'Which one is yours dear?' she asked Connie.

Connie pointed to the one with the Maori on and Mrs Betham said: 'He looks rather nice.' But the horse that had really taken her fancy was a little black one. It moved daintily, prancing sideways, then going backwards with tiny mincing steps. She was annoyed that the effect was spoiled by the dull moon-faced jockey sitting hunched on its back. The horse was definitely superior. She would have liked to turn it loose in the hills and see it gallop away along the skyline.

Odalisque, she read, *bl. f. Owner Mrs E. Benjamin. Trainer C. F. Becket.* She was pleased it was a filly (smiled that she hadn't noticed) and that a woman owned it, and she made a mental note to look up odalisque in the dictionary when she got home.

The first horses went out for their preliminaries and a bell began to ring over at the totalisator. The horses came back down the track, some galloping, others just cantering. Mrs Betham thought again there was something really graceful and exciting about it all. The worms in the apple were the people. There were queues of them still stretched out at the totalisator scrabbling away at their money.

Connie said she was going round to the hill and Mrs Betham asked if she could come too. Lew would want to be with the trainer for this race. They went round the back of the stand, past the refreshment tents and the smelly bar where men were gulping down their last drinks. Mrs Betham saw the man who was Connie's fiancé come out and hurry into the crowd wiping his mouth. Before she could point him out he had disappeared in front of taller people. She realized then how short he was; and he seemed some shades darker too, but perhaps that was due to his old-fashioned navy-blue suit.

The stream of people moved on and they moved with it until they found a place halfway down the hill. The horses were at the five furlong start when they arrived. The race would soon begin.

'I hope one of us wins,' said Mrs Betham. She was finding it embarrassing to be with Connie. She couldn't get the girl to talk. She decided that if there were things on her mind it would be kinder to keep quiet. She tried to concentrate on the horses, but couldn't pick any of them out, and she knew she'd have to listen to the course announcer to find out what happened. And she'd have to listen carefully. It was one of those short races that was over almost as soon as it started.

'Don't you wish you had binoculars?' she remarked wistfully, thinking of Lew's expensive pair. There was no reply, and she turned, rather annoyed now, and saw that Connie was staring away down an alley in the crowd. At the end of it was the man in the navy suit, her fiancé. Mrs Betham could see that their eyes were meeting.

'Your finacé,' she said. 'Why doesn't he come up?'

The man seemed to be trying to say something, though he was too far away for them to hear; he smiled, with a small twist of his mouth, and lifted his fingers in a V sign, Churchill's way, rather pathetically she thought. Then he moved to one side so they couldn't see him any more.

'He should have come up,' said Mrs Betham.

Connie began to stare at the horses again. Her face seemed thinner and more bony. 'Get them started,' she said. She moved a few steps away.

Mrs Betham shrugged and told herself not to be angry. Connie was perhaps not so ungracious as she seemed – the race must mean a lot to her. For that reason she hoped Royal Return would win, if Lew's horse didn't.

No, she thought, no, I hope it beats Lew's horse. They probably need the money more than we do.

The announcer's voice blared into her thoughts. 'The field is lining up for the start of the Juvenile Handicap.' He mentioned the horses that were giving trouble. One of them was Royal Return. But soon they were all in line and she saw the heave of brown and heard the crowd rumble as they started. She still couldn't pick out any of the horses.

'Bronze Idol has made a good beginning and so has Odalisque.' Then there was a list of names with Royal Return in the middle. She wondered how the announcer picked them out. She couldn't see any horse clearly. They were all melted together, and their legs flickering under the rail made them look like a centipede.

'As they come round past the three furlong peg it's Bronze Idol a length clear of Samba with Odalisque next on the rails on the inside of Conformist. A length back to Song and Dance getting a trail, a length to Sir Bonny.'

The next time he went through them she counted and found that Royal Return was eighth. Bronze Idol was still a length clear of the field. Lew would be getting excited.

At the turn it was the same except that she was pleased to hear Royal Return had ranged up on the outside of Conformist. Then the horses came into the straight and they seemed to explode. They spread out right across it. She thought this was normal, but the announcer was excited and said Odalisque had run wide and had carried out two or three others and Bronze Idol was holding on a length clear of Samba. She didn't hear Royal Return's name. But she was excited herself now. She could see Bronze Idol looking really beautiful, heaving along with his head out straight and his tail flowing and his body slippery with sunlight as the muscles moved; the little consumptive jockey was crouched very low on his back, not using the whip. They were past too quickly for her. She would have loved to see them going on like that for ever.

Above the roar of the crowd the announcer said Bronze Idol was winning as he liked. She was pleased for Lew's sake, and, she admitted, a little bit for her own too. It had been very exciting.

Then she remembered Royal Return. It hadn't been mentioned after the corner. The girl would be disappointed.

She looked round to find her. But Connie hadn't waited for the finish. She had seen Royal Return go out at the straight entrance, and had turned and gone back through the crowd. She had broken past the red paralysed faces of people staring stupidly away at something they didn't know was already over.

III

Mrs Benjamin wanted to stay the night at the Commercial Hotel but Charlie Becket insisted on going home. Finally, after he had threatened to leave her behind, she agreed, and a few minutes before nine o'clock they left town and set off along the Auckland highway. It was a fine night, mild and cloudless. The stars were very bright.

They drove for some time in silence, then Mrs Benjamin began to complain about the meeting. There hadn't been anyone interesting there. All her friends were dying or losing interest.

'Common thing with old people,' said Charlie, hoping to quiet her.

But she seized on the statement and began to worry it with persistent whining energy and he knew she was working to the complaint that nobody cared about her any more. He broke abruptly into her talk, saying: 'That filly isn't right yet. You've been making me push her too fast.'

She grasped this subject eagerly. 'Oh, Charlie, I know she'll be all right. I've never seen a horse I liked better.'

'She over-reaches,' said Charlie. 'Cut herself one day, you see.'

'But I can't afford to lose twenty pounds on her,' she continued. 'Why did you tell me she was going to win?'

'Because I thought she was,' said Charlie. 'It's not my fault if the jockey can't ride her. I'll get someone different next time.' He smiled, remembering how perfectly Armstrong had let her go on the corner. A good jockey, a good man to have, even if he was expensive.

Mrs Benjamin sighed.

'She looked as if she was going to go down, pushing those big horses right out. She's so tiny.'

Charlie said: 'Yeah, funny thing happened about that too.'

He told her how after the race, when he'd been talking to Betham, Philpott had come up and accused him of sabotaging Royal Return.

'I told him I'd hardly do that when I had a few quid on it

myself, and that seemed to make him worse. I've never seen anyone sweat so much or look so mad. He'd have stuck a knife into me if he'd had one. He's got a kink I reckon. He'll end up in the nuthouse.'

'What happened?' said Mrs Benjamin.

'He followed me all over the course until I had to tell him to clear out or I'd call a cop.'

'What did he do?'

'He cleared out. They're all the same these broken-down jocks. Yellow. No guts. That's why they don't last.'

'But he was a good jockey once.'

'Plenty of good jockeys. They're a dime a dozen. Plenty of good horses too. What I'm interested in is good prices.'

'Sometimes you're just too hard, Charlie.'

Charlie said: 'We're not here to make friends.' It was his favourite saying and it never failed to please him. He drove on smiling, and Mrs Benjamin lay back stiffly in her corner and tried to sleep.

After a time she said wearily: 'It was a boring meeting. I didn't meet anyone I liked.'

Charlie grunted.

A little later she said: 'That Betham man is rather nice.'

'Got a good horse,' said Charlie.

'It's a pity his wife's such a mousy thing.'

'Anyway,' she said, 'I took him out for a drink.'

'You drink too much,' said Charlie.

They wound down a long hill. The lights ran off down gullies and over creeks and paddocks. Charlie fought the car, making it squeal in a way that pleased him.

They came to a level section of road. It ran for a mile without a curve and then went sharply left. Just round the corner the headlamps picked out two cars and a group of people standing at the back of a horse-float. The tail of the float was down and men were clustered in its mouth, white and yellow in a glare of light.

Charlie drove past slowly.

'Horse is probably down,' he said.

Then, as Mrs Benjamin said: 'Let's stop, Charlie,' he saw that the float was coupled to a big pre-war Oldsmobile.

'Philpott,' he said. He increased speed.

'But, Charlie, I want to see what's happened.'

Charlie didn't answer. He changed into top gear. Soon the speedometer reached sixty again.

'There are plenty of people there to help. Joe Elliot was there.
He'll know what to do.'

'Charlie, why can't you do what I want to, just for once?'

But again Charlie didn't answer. A hundred yards ahead the
lights had picked up the figure of a woman walking at the side of
the road. She was going their way but she didn't look round as
they approached or make any signal. The car sped past.

'It's Connie. Connie Reynolds. Stop, Charlie.' Mrs Benjamin
was peering back.

'Charlie, *stop*.'

'Charl*ie-ie*.'

'I don't feel like it,' he said. The speedometer kept level at sixty.

For a while Mrs Benjamin sulked in her corner. She didn't see
why she couldn't know what was happening. Then she grew
morbid. She was old – she wondered how many more pleasures
she was to be allowed. Perhaps she couldn't afford to lose this
one.

Charlie said: 'For God's sake don't start the waterworks.'

Mrs Benjamin had not been going to cry but she allowed herself
two or three tears and held her handkerchief to her eyes. Then she
rearranged herself fussily in her seat, grumbled a little about its
hardness, and watched the road in an effort to stay awake. Her
frequent desire to sleep had worried her lately. But this time she
found reason for it in the motion of the car. She closed her eyes
and let her mouth loosen comfortably. Her body sagged a little
and she felt a settling lurch in her bowels. Her hands turned in
her lap until the palms faced upwards.

She slept, as heavily as a child, and soon Charlie Becket put out
a hand and tipped her against the door. He did not want her falling
over him as he drove.

Connie had not found Stan until two races after the Juvenile Handicap. She knew at once he'd been drinking, but believed him when
he said he wouldn't drink any more. He was determined to win
back everything and he asked for money. She gave him the few
pounds she had, keeping only enough for petrol to get home on.
The hotel bills could be paid by cheque and though the cheque
would bounce that was a worry for another day. Now the only

thing that mattered was to keep Stan from doing anything crazy. He went off and she sat down shakily on a seat. She had never seen him looking so bad. His face was always blue-bristled by mid-afternoon, but now the skin under the bristles seemed more yellow than white, and his eyes were blood-shot, the lids scraped looking and salty. She wanted desperately to help him; and she wondered what was wrong with her, as a woman, that the only way she could help was by giving him money.

After the sixth race he came to her again. He had won a little, enough to bet more solidly with. But after the seventh race he did not come. That would mean he had lost. She went to sit in the car. From there she heard the announcer describe the last race. A horse called Manalive won. She had never heard Stan speak of it, and it paid only a few pounds.

Most of the traffic had gone by the time he came. He told her he'd won twenty pounds on a place bet in the eighth. They drove out of the course without picking up the float. He said there was a card game he wanted to get to. His voice was rough and urgent, and impersonal, not directed at her.

'But, Stan,' cried Connie, 'you can't win enough on a card game.' She didn't know what she meant by enough, but the word frightened her, it seemed so full of things that might happen, it uncovered years that might go any way at all.

'I can win something,' said Stan savagely. 'I can win enough so I won't have to . . . ' He too used the word and then didn't finish the sentence: she was more frightened; it was almost as if she had to open a door knowing there might be something terrible behind it. She wanted to put everything farther off.

'Stan, don't let's talk about it. Just drive.'

The card game was in a shabby house down by the harbour. She could see the sad battered hulk of a scow sunk lower than the wharf it was moored to, and over beyond a spit of land three sleek launches in front of a white-sand beach. It seemed they were only lazing, it seemed they could fly away out of the harbour at any moment they chose.

She waited two hours without any tea. The launches slowly faded into the dusk. Then Stan came.

He had lost.

He made her go to a restaurant and went to get the horse. He was gone for a long time. When he came back she tried to buy him some food but he said he wasn't hungry. He wanted to get on the road.

They were some miles out of town when she remembered their bags at the Hotel. He said quickly: 'We can't go back for them now.'

She argued. They were hardly out of town. It would take only a minute.

'We can't go back.' He shouted, and behind the anger in his voice there was despair, a drawing out of the 'can't' so that she knew he had done something that was frightening him.

'Stan, you haven't . . . ?' But he began again before she could finish the question.

'What are you talking about? What do you mean, haven't? I just say we're too far out of town and you start thinking all sorts of things.'

She knew then he had done something back there. For a moment she even wondered if anyone was chasing them, and she looked at the petrol gauge. But the gauge showed the tank was almost full. That, in its simplicity, shocked her terribly, and she said under her breath: Stan, what's happened, what's happened? Stan never bought petrol. It was one of the things he always had to be reminded of. Yet today, after that race, he had remembered.

Now as they drove on she grew more aware of the float, and she thought, That's the trouble, that's what causes all the trouble, we're tied to these horses and we can't get away. We're like servants or slaves.

Why couldn't Stan get another job? Why did he have to do things they had to run away from? Why couldn't he go out to work every day, to an ordinary job, like other men? Everything was so complicated. Why couldn't it be simple, as clean and white as that beach and those launches?

The float dragged heavily, lifting the front of the car in a way that gave her almost a feeling of lightheadedness. In this slight dizziness she knew she must speak of the marriage. She must have that chance, the chance for something different even if she couldn't make it just the quiet and rest she wanted.

She said, hesitating: 'Stan, do you – remember last night?'

He broke out again.

'I said I'd marry you, didn't I? What more do you want me to say? I won't break my promise. That's one of the things I don't do.'

'Stan, why can't you – I mean, you could sell the horse, and then get a job.'

'Sell the horse,' he said, and now he spoke softly, as though not thinking of what he was saying.

'He ran a good race today. He was going well until the turn and that wasn't his fault. Somebody would buy him.'

'He's a mongrel,' said Stan. 'He was so full of dope he could hardly breathe. Without it he wouldn't have got to the barrier.'

His hands were light on the wheel so he could feel it move and jump. The float was swaying as they wound down a long hill.

Connie began to speak again, but she stopped when she realised he wasn't taking any notice. He seemed to be listening. And then, from the way he was driving, she saw he was aware of the float.

'Is something wrong, Stan?'

'What do you mean, wrong?'

He turned on her irritably.

'Back there, in the float.'

'What could be wrong? God damn it you say some stupid things.'

The car sagged heavily into the road at the foot of the hill and she heard a faint whinnying scream from the horse, and then a scraping sound that lasted only a second. She looked at Stan quickly.

'Excitable – excitable horse. Doesn't like bumps,' Stan jerked out, and he tried to smile at her.

They came to a straight level stretch of road and he began to drive faster. His hands were white on the wheel. He was sweating, and the float was rattling louder than it ever had before.

'Stan, have you done something to the horse? Is he down?'

Then Stan seemed to go crazy. He began to sway the car over the road; the float lurched and dragged, and the horse screamed again.

'Mongrel, bloody mongrel,' he groaned. He ran the car halfway over the broken edge of the road. It bucked and jolted along; stones rattled against the mudguards and thumped on the chassis and on the bottom of the float.

'Mongrel,' he shouted.

Connie was screaming at him and tearing at his arms, almost

running the car off the road. Then she turned from him and opened her door. Grass and bracken whipped on the metal. She looked back but could see only the yellow half-lit face of the float, so close it seemed to overhang and threaten.

'Stan, for God's sake stop.'

There was no sound from the horse.

'Stan,' she screamed. She tugged at his arm again and the car jumped to the middle of the road. The open door beat once, like a broken wing.

'Stan.' She fell against him. She was crying, uselessly beating his shoulder with her fist.

At last they came to a corner and he slowed to take it. He said, the first word coming on the rush of a long-held breath: 'All right, we'll stop, but nothing's wrong. Excitable, that's all. Just might have got himself down.'

She had time only to half realise the weakness of his pretence before the car stopped and she was out and back at the float. He followed slowly.

The horse was moaning.

'Christ,' said Stan, but his voice was flat. He pulled her away from the locks and lowered the ramp.

Royal Return was down. At first she could not make out how he was lying. Then she saw that his chest was on the floor and his body was twisted left and right from it, the hind quarters turned one way and raised so she could see a leg that dug spasmodically at the straw (like a chicken's, she thought, and the unnatural likeness struck a sort of terror into her), head and neck turned the other, the neck forced by the wall to an erectness that had dug a great pit in the horse's shoulders. One eye was towards her, but not seeing – it was held in a desperate steadiness just above agony.

'Get the torch,' said Stan.

'Oh God.' Connie moved away from him. 'God. Stan. You *did* it.'

'Get the torch,' he repeated dully.

She stopped at the roadside grass. 'You *did* it.'

'Connie, I . . . '

'You *did*, Stan.'

'Connie, it was for you. Don't you see?'

She turned abruptly at that and stumbled down the road.

'Connie, don't go away.'

She made no answer.

'Connie.'

Soon she was out of sight.

After a while Stan went to the car himself and got the torch. He went down on his knees and looked underneath the float; and stood up immediately, leaving the torch on the ground. He moved to the roadside and sat down in grass with his feet in a gutter. Soon he began to retch. He didn't notice that another car had stopped and other people were climbing into the float, but he heard the horse scream, and he felt himself travelling back with terrible urgency to times and places where there had not been even the smallest beginnings of things like this. He was riding back to salute the judge after his first win, a tiny apprentice in gold and green on a chestnut colt with a white blaze. It was a sunny day and people were clapping.

But then Joe Elliot and another man pulled him to his feet and started asking questions. All he could answer, with his face in his hands, was: 'I'm sick, I'm sick.'

They threw him back into the grass.

The Bethams left the hotel shortly after Mrs Benjamin and Charlie Becket. Mrs Betham wondered if Lew had taken so long over his last drink in order to drive back to Auckland behind them. His pleasures, it seemed, were becoming increasingly simple; but in spite of that she had to admit they seemed to satisfy him as nothing had done before – as she herself had never done: he spoke of Bronze Idol with an enthusiasm he had never displayed for her. In thinking this she was frightened. She did not want her memories attacked, she did not want them involved in this business at all. The present must not be allowed to war on the past. That must be kept intact. She wondered then what this past really was. Just a few short years after all – the slump years, when they had lived on porridge and rice and turnips in a tin shed that filled with smoke from a fire that couldn't warm it. How could those be the happy years? And yet she thought of them as a sort of Golden Age. Lew and she had been together in a way that could never be broken, not letting the outside touch them at all. Or was it, she wondered, just that memory ran the good things together, creating a closeness that had never really existed? It had all happened so long ago. Yet in spite of her doubts those years would continue to live.

It was a sort of Golden Age, she thought, and now's the depression, when we've got everything we want.

She began to study Lew. He was concentrating on his driving, trying to catch Charlie Becket.

Perhaps the immortals are equipped with faster cars, she thought. Or perhaps their cars have wings and can fly while ours remain earthbound. Her amusement was brief. She seemed suddenly to be driving with someone she knew only slightly. The face was familiar, but the intentness was created by an ambition she could never understand.

Lew seemed to sense her mood. 'What are you so quiet about?' he said.

She could tell by his voice he expected her to complain about something.

I should, she thought, but it wouldn't do any good.

'Nothing,' she said.

'Haven't you enjoyed yourself?'

'Yes,' she said.

'Well, what is it then? You don't seem very excited. Don't you realise some people own dozens of horses before they get a winner?'

'Yes, dear. And you've done it first time. That's very clever of you.'

The sarcasm had come in spite of her. She had now to listen to a lecture about her lack of wifely enthusiasm, her inability to enjoy herself as other women did.

'I don't understand you,' he finished. 'I do everything I can to make you happy.'

She had many answers to that but he had heard them all and not been impressed. So she sat watching the dark bush, trying to see into it, imagining some primitive settlement deep in there, a place where life was simple and people had time to know and like each other. But the headlamps never rested on anything for long. Her mind couldn't settle. Lew was driving too fast. There was a car going down the hill ahead of them, disappearing round a new corner every time they caught sight of it. He was trying to get closer to see if it was Charlie Becket's.

On the flat at the foot of the hill they saw it wasn't and Lew seemed to lose heart. He drove more slowly.

'I think I'll stop and have a whiskey,' he said.

Just then they went round a corner and saw what looked to be an accident. Two cars were pulled up behind a horse-float and a third was in front of it. There were some men at the mouth of the float and two inside. They couldn't see the horse.

Lew went past slowly and pulled in at the front of the line. He told Mrs Betham to wait where she was and went back to the float. He was gone for perhaps five minutes.

Mrs Betham would have liked to see what was happening, but she thought if the horse was sick or hurt she'd only be in the way. Besides, she hated to seem curious. But she did notice two rather strange things: this was horse business and Charlie Becket hadn't stopped, and back beside the float a man was sitting in the grass. He was very still. At first she thought he was a small tree or a clump of bracken. Then the shape became clearer. he was bent forward with his arms across his knees, his face in the arms. Nobody was taking any notice of him, although the way he was sitting made him appear lonely and in need of comfort. She felt she should go along and see if there was anything she could do.

When Lew came back she said: 'Who's that man sitting in the grass?'

'Philpott,' he said. It was not so much an answer to her question as something he was saying to himself. Then he swore, using a word he'd never used in front of her before.

'What's happened, Lew?' she asked nervously.

Lew was pouring himself a whiskey. When he'd drunk it he looked at her and said: 'He's just butchered his horse.'

'Butchered it. You mean he's killed it?'

He shook his head and she saw his eyes fill with tears. 'It's not dead yet,' he said. 'They've gone to get a gun to shoot it.'

She couldn't understand, but she listened as Lew told her what had happened. Philpott had loosened the boards at the front of the float so the horse's legs had broken through when the car hit a bump.

'They must have been trailing along the road for miles. They're almost torn off. Just hanging in tatters. You can see bits of bone.'

Lew poured himself another drink. His hands were shaking and whiskey slopped on his trousers.

Mrs Betham was saying to herself: But that's awful, how could he, how could a person do a thing like that? – but she couldn't say it aloud. Nothing was adequate as she pictured the tattered legs and the pieces of bone.

'But, Lew . . . ' she said.

'He did it for the insurance,' said Lew. 'You knew horses were insured, didn't you?'

'There are people who could do a thing like that for money!'she said.

'For money.' Lew threw the bottle into the glove-box.

'I hope he gets ten years,' he said. 'If I was the judge I'd order a flogging.'

'What about the girl?' said Mrs Betham. 'Was she in it?'

'His girl? Connie Reynolds? No, she wasn't there. How do you know her?'

'I saw her on the racecourse today,' said Mrs Betham.

Lew grunted. His mind was still on the horse. Mrs Betham, too, was unable to keep her mind from returning to the horrible picture he had painted. She had had a moment's relief when she heard that Connie wasn't involved, but then she turned and looked again at the figure in the grass. It was motionless, in a hunched cowering attitude.

It's too late for him to be sorry, she thought. And her loathing increased. But strangely it changed so that it was not so much for him as for what had been done. He seemed now to exist outside the act. The act was unimaginable, but he was there, part of the horror he had brought into existence, the only part of it she could really see.

She knew that soon she would feel sorry for him, and she told herself it wasn't right to have that much pity. It was dangerous to forgive too much. There must be things that could never be forgiven, and surely this . . .

The tattered legs and pieces of bone . . .

No, that could never be forgiven.

Lew had started the car and they were moving again. He drove without talking, and she was glad, though she expected him to break out at any minute. Her mind was calmer now, and she was trying to convince herself a person couldn't do a thing like that for money. There must be other reasons.

No, she thought, it's not just the money. That's too simple. It's everything money means. You can't blame a person for failing to survive that. And yet you can't forgive. Here I am trying to forgive.

But as she thought of the horse with its legs torn off, and the man sitting on the grass, both seemed equally terrible mutilations, the one as pitiable as the other.

'There's his girl now,' said Lew. He didn't slow down and they flashed by almost before Mrs Betham saw her.

'Stop, Lew. We'll pick her up.'

'After what happened back there?' said Lew.

But she argued with him and made him stop and back up to the girl. He was angry, but knew she was determined to have her way. He'd showed his disapproval by not looking round or speaking as Connie got into the back seat.

Then, as he drove on and heard his wife explaining that they knew what had happened and heard the girl break into long scratching sobs, he was seized with an almost physical revulsion. He felt he wanted to be sick. The girl and the crying, and Philpott and the horse, were a sort of disease; he felt unclean having her in the car. There must be ways of avoiding things like this, ways of getting about so that you never saw them.

God, why can't things be perfect, he thought.

He heard the girl say: 'I don't know what to do. I don't know.'

'Then wait,' said his wife. 'Just don't do anything. You'll find out what's right.'

A little later Connie said: 'I want to go back, but I *can't*.'

'Just wait,' said the wife. 'Don't think of anything.'

He recognised her 'soothing' voice. It made him jealous when she used it for anyone but him, and he stabbed savagely with his foot to dip for an oncoming car.

The girl said, still crying: 'This is the first time probably he's ever really needed me – and I can't go.'

'Shh,' said Mrs Betham.

But Connie had not been talking to her, and hadn't listened. In a few moments she stopped crying.

'He said he did it for me,' she whispered. She gave a little moan.

'Shh. Don't think,' said Mrs Betham.

'So really – really . . . ' She stopped and seemed to talk to herself, and almost cry again.

'So really – it's as much my fault as his.'

'No. Don't even begin to think that,' said Mrs Betham. She

tried to take Connie's hand but the back of the seat made it awkward for her and Connie made no move to help. So she rested her arm along the seat-back with her fingers brushing the sleeve of Lew's coat, and smiled kindly at the girl, wishing there was something she could give her, something she could do: the dead paws of the fur, dangling over her arm, were no more useless than she was.

Later, when they thought she was sleeping, Connie leaned forward and said 'Stop, please I want to get out.'

Lew stopped quickly. His wife leaned back and put a hand on Connie's arm. 'What are you going to do?'

'I don't know,' said Connie.

She opened the door, got out clumsily, closed it, and came to Mrs Betham's window to say something. Lew couldn't hear for the noise of the engine, and didn't want to hear. He thought her face was yellow and ugly; he wanted to get away.

The car began to move again; Mrs Betham said nothing. She watched until the girl was lost in the darkness. Then she leaned against her door with her cheek against the cold window.

Lew let a little time pass. He said: 'You want to save the Good Samaritan act for somebody worth while. I could tell you stories about that girl.'

'I don't want to hear,' said Mrs Betham.

He shrugged and drove on. He was happy now that Connie was gone.

Soon he saw a tail-light shining in the darkness ahead, and he increased speed, wondering if at last he had caught up with Charlie Becket.

THE ORACLE

A. B. (Banjo) Paterson

No tram ever goes to Randwick races without him; he is always fat, hairy, and assertive; he is generally one of a party, and takes the centre of the stage all the time – collects and hands over the fares, adjusts the change, chaffs the conductor, crushes the thin, apologetic stranger next him into a pulp, and talks to the whole compartment as if they had asked for his opinion.

He knows all the trainers and owners, or takes care to give the impression that he does. He slowly and pompously hauls out his race-book, and one of his satellites opens the ball by saying, in a deferential way,

'What do you like for the 'urdles, Charley?'

The Oracle looks at the book and breathes heavily; no one else ventures to speak.

'Well,' he says, at last, 'of course there's only one in it – if he's wanted. But that's it – will they spin him? I don't think they will. They's only a lot o'cuddies, any 'ow.'

No one likes to expose his own ignorance by asking which horse he refers to as the 'only one in it'; and the Oracle goes on to deal out some more wisdom in a loud voice.

'Billy K – told me' (he probably hardly knows Billy K – by sight) 'Billy K – told me that that bay 'orse ran the best mile-an'-a-half ever done on Randwick yesterday; but I don't give him a chance, for all that; that's the worst of these trainers. They don't know when their horses are well – half of 'em.'

Then a voice comes from behind him. It is that of the thin man, who is crushed out of sight by the bulk of the Oracle.

'I think,' says the thin man, 'that that horse of Flannery's ought to run well in the Handicap.'

The Oracle can't stand this sort of thing at all. He gives a snort, wheels half-round and looks at the speaker. Then he turns back to the compartment full of people, and says, 'No ope.'

The thin man makes a last effort. 'Well, they backed him last night, anyhow.'

'Who backed im?' says the Oracle.

'In Tattersall's,' says the thin man.

'I'm sure,' says the Oracle; and the thin man collapses.

On arrival at the course, the Oracle is in great form. Attended by his string of satellites, he plods from stall to stall staring at the horses. Their names are printed in big letters on the stalls, but the Oracle doesn't let that stop his display of knowledge.

"Ere's Blue Fire,' he says, stopping at that animal's stall, and swinging his race-book. 'Good old Blue Fire!' he goes on loudly, as a little court collects. 'Jimmy B – ' (mentioning a popular jockey) 'told me he couldn't have lost on Saturday week if he had only been ridden different. I had a good stake on him, too, that day. Lor', the races that has been chucked away on this horse. They will not ride him right.'

A trainer who is standing by, civilly interposes. 'This isn't Blue Fire,' he says. 'Blue Fire's out walking about. This is a two-year-old filly that's in the stall – '

'Well, I can see that, can't I,' says the Oracle, crushingly. 'You don't suppose I thought Blue Fire was a mare, did you?' and he moves off hurriedly.

'Now, look here, you chaps,' he says to his followers at last. 'You wait here. I want to go and see a few of the talent, and it don't do to have a crowd with you. There's Jimmy M – over there now' (pointing to a leading trainer). 'I'll get hold of him in a minute. He couldn't tell me anything with so many about. Just you wait here.'

He crushes into a crowd that has gathered round the favourite's stall, and overhears one hard-faced racing man say to another, 'What do you like?' to which the other answers, 'Well, either this or Royal Scot. I think I'll put a bit on Royal Scot.' This is enough for the Oracle. He doesn't know either of the men from Adam, or either of the horses from the great original pachyderm, but the information will do to go on with. He rejoins his followers, and looks very mysterious.

'Well, did you hear anything?' they say.

The Oracle talks low and confidentially.

'The crowd that have got the favourite tell me they're not afraid of anything but Royal Scot,' he says. 'I think we'd better put a bit on both.'

'What did the Royal Scot crowd say?' asks an admirer deferentially.

'Oh, they're going to try and win. I saw the stable commissioner, and he told me they were going to put a hundred on him. Of course, you needn't say I told you, 'cause I promised him I wouldn't tell.' And the satellites beam with admiration of the Oracle, and think what a privilege it is to go to the races with such a knowing man.

They contribute their mites to the general fund, some putting in a pound, others half a sovereign, and the Oracle takes it into the ring to invest, half on the favourite and half on Royal Scot. He finds that the favourite is at two to one, and Royal Scot at threes, eight to one being offered against anything else. As he ploughs through the ring, a Whisperer (one of those broken-down followers of the turf who get their living in various mysterious ways, but partly by giving 'tips' to backers) pulls his sleeve.

'What are you backing?' he says.

'Favourite and Royal Scot,' says the Oracle.

'Put a pound on Bendemeer,' says the tipster. 'It's a certainty. Meet me here if it comes off, and I'll tell you something for the next race. Don't miss it now. Get on quick!'

The Oracle is humble enough before the hanger-on of the turf. A bookmaker roars 'ten to one Bendemeer;' he suddenly fishes out a sovereign of his own – and he hasn't money to spare, for all his knowingness – and puts it on Bendemeer. His friends' money he puts on the favourite and Royal Scot as arranged. Then they all go round to watch the race.

The horses are at the post; a distant cluster of crowded animals with little dots of colour on their backs. Green, blue, yellow, purple, French grey, and old gold, they change about in a bewildering manner, and though the Oracle has a cheap pair of glasses, he can't make out where Bendemeer has got to. Royal Scot and the favourite he has lost interest in, and secretly hopes that they will be left at the post or break their necks; but he does not confide his sentiment to his companions.

They're off! The long line of colours across the track becomes a shapeless clump and then draws out into a long string. 'What's that in front?' yells someone at the rails. 'Oh, that thing of Hart's,' says someone else. But the Oracle hears them not; he is looking in the mass of colour for a purple cap and grey jacket, with black armbands. He cannot see it anywhere, and the confused and confusing mass swings round the turn into the straight.

Then there is a babel of voices, and suddenly a shout of 'Bendemeer! Bendemeer!' and the Oracle, without knowing which is Bendemeer, takes up the cry feverishly. 'Bendemeer! Bendemeer!' he yells, waggling his glasses about, trying to see where the animal is.

'Where's Royal Scot, Charley? Where's Royal Scot?' screams one of his friends, in agony. ''Ow's he doin'?'

'No 'ope!' says the Oracle, with fiendish glee. 'Bendemeer! Bendemeer!'

The horses are at the Leger stand now, whips are out, and three horses seem to be nearly abreast; in fact, to the Oracle there seem to be a dozen nearly abreast. Then a big chestnut sticks his head in front of the others, and a small man at the Oracle's side emits a deafening series of yells right by the Oracle's ear:

'Go on, Jimmy! Rub it into him! Belt him! It's a cake-walk! A cake-walk!' The big chestnut, in a dogged sort of way, seems to stick his body clear of his opponents, and passes the post a winner by a length. The Oracle doesn't know what has won, but fumbles with his book. The number on the saddle-cloth catches his eye – No. 7; he looks hurriedly down the page. No. 7 – Royal Scot. Second is No. 24 – Bendemeer. Favourite nowhere.

Hardly has he realized it, before his friends are cheering and clapping him on the back. 'By George, Charley, it takes you to pick 'em,' 'Come and 'ave a wet!' 'You 'ad a quid on, didn't you, Charley?' The Oracle feels very sick at having missed the winner, but he dies game. 'Yes, rather; I had a quid on,' he says. 'And,' (here he nerves himself to smile) 'I had a saver on the second, too.'

His comrades gasp with astonishment. 'D'you hear that, eh? Charley backed first and second. That's pickin' 'em if you like.' They have a wet, and pour fulsome adulation on the Oracle when he collects their money.

After the Oracle has collected the winnings for his friends he meets the Whisperer again.

'It didn't win?' he says to the Whisperer in inquiring tones.

'Didn't win,' says the Whisperer, who has determined to brazen the matter out. 'How could he win? Did you see the way he was ridden? That horse was stiffened just after I seen you, and he never tried a yard. Did you see the way he was pulled and hauled about at the turn? It'd make a man sick. What was the stipendiary stewards doing, I wonder?'

This fills the Oracle with a new idea. All that he remembers of the race at the turn was a jumble of colours, a kaleidoscope of horses and riders hanging on to the horses' necks. But it wouldn't do to admit that he didn't see everything, and didn't know everything; so he plunges in boldly.

'O' course I saw it,' he says. 'And a blind man could see it. They ought to rub him out.'

'Course they ought,' says the Whisperer. 'But, look here, put two quid on Tell-tale; you'll get it all back!'

The Oracle does put on 'two quid', and doesn't get it all back. Neither does he see any more of this race than he did of the last one – in fact, he cheers wildly when the wrong horse is coming in. But when the public begin to hoot he hoots as loudly as anybody – louder if anything; and all the way home in the tram he lays down the law about stiff running, and wants to know what the stipendiaries are doing.

If you go into any barber's shop, you could hear him at it, and he flourishes in suburban railway carriages; but he has a tremendous local reputation, having picked first and second in the Handicap, and it would be a bold man who would venture to question the Oracle's knowledge of racing and all matters relating to it.